PENGUIN BOOKS

CITY OF SMOKE AND BRIMSTONE

Kayla is the author of the House of Devils series – *City of Gods and Monsters*, *City of Souls and Sinners*, *City of Lies and Legends* and *City of Smoke and Brimstone*. She is also the author of the upper-YA romantasy novel, *Dreams of Ice and Iron*. She started writing *City of Gods and Monsters* when she was in high school, so the characters and the world they live in are very close to her heart. When she isn't writing, she enjoys traveling, spending time in nature, and binge-watching her favorite television shows with her husband.

BOOKS BY KAYLA EDWARDS:

Dreams of Ice and Iron

The House of Devils series

City of Gods and Monsters
City of Souls and Sinners
City of Lies and Legends
City of Smoke and Brimstone

CITY OF SMOKE AND BRIMSTONE

HOUSE OF DEVILS
BOOK FOUR

KAYLA EDWARDS

PENGUIN BOOKS

PENGUIN BOOKS

UK | USA | Canada | Ireland | Australia
India | New Zealand | South Africa

Penguin Books is part of the Penguin Random House group of companies
whose addresses can be found at global.penguinrandomhouse.com

Penguin Random House UK,
One Embassy Gardens, 8 Viaduct Gardens, London SW11 7BW

penguin.co.uk

First self-published by Kayla Edwards 2025
This edition published by Penguin Books 2025
005

Map illustrations © Virginia Allyn
Proofread by Christina Routhier
Printed and bound in Great Britain by Clays Ltd, Elcograf S.p.A.

The authorized representative in the EEA is Penguin Random House Ireland,
Morrison Chambers, 32 Nassau Street, Dublin D02 YH68

A CIP catalogue record for this book is available from the British Library

ISBN: 978-1-405-98886-5

Penguin Random House is committed to a sustainable future
for our business, our readers and our planet. This book is made from
Forest Stewardship Council® certified paper.

For the Dariens and the Romans—those who shelter others when the rain gets heavy.

Remember to look after yourself, too.

BLOOD ROSE

SILVER TORCH

ACU

TO ANGELTHENE NATIONAL FOREST

GRIFFIN PARK

VAMPIRE TERRITORY

BLUE LILY

HAMMER ORCHID

CORPSE FLOWER

ANGELTHENE ACADEMY

UPPER WEST GLEN

FLEET HQ

HOSPITAL

BLACK ALDER

LAMBS-QUARTERS

BRIGHT PENTHOUSE

CITY PARK

AGATHA'S

ARTHUR'S HOUSE

DATE PALM

MIRACLE PLAZA

VICTORIA AMAZONICA

CONTROL TOWER

HELL'S GATE

VIPER'S DEN

OCEANA

FINANCIAL DISTRICT

ERASMUS'S HOUSE

MORDRED & PENELOPE'S

WHISKING WITCH

AVENUE OF THE SCARLET STAR

BONE FIELD

MEDEA'S

ROOK & REDDING'S

ARTS DISTRICT

LOWER WEST GLEN

FLOWER DISTRICT

HOODED SKULLCAP

CHALK DOOR

JEWELRY DISTRICT

H.I.M.

HISTORIC CORE

CAIN'S HOUSE

THE PIT

STONE'S END

MEATPACKING DISTRICT

PUERTA DE LA MUERTA

CRYSTAL TEETH ROAD

SABRINE'S HOUSE

NARROW HILLS

HOUSE OF SOULS

WHITE GARDEN

TO THE HOUSE ON THE PIER

OLDTOWN DISTRICT

AIRPORT

ANGELTHENE CEMETERY

BONEFISH MARKET

CASA BREWERY

TRANQUIL SHORE

FORBIDDEN BEACH

WELCOME TO

WE HOPE YOU

DARKSLAYING CIRCLES OF ANGELTHENE

THE SEVEN DEVILS

Marked with a horned letter S in the gothic script of an ancient world, they answer to Darien Cassel, Head of Hell's Gate

---

THE REAPERS

Marked with the cloaked and masked god of death, they answer to Malakai Delaney, Head of the House of Souls and Right Hand of Darien Cassel

---

THE HUNTSMEN

Marked with a Hellhound, they answer to Lionel Savage, Head of the Hunting Grounds and former Right Hand of Randal Slade

---

THE ANGELS OF DEATH

Marked with overlapping wings in white ink, they answer to Dominic Valencia, Head of Death's Landing

---

THE WARGS

Marked with a crescent moon in luminescent ink, they answer to Channary Graves, Head of the House on the Pier

---

THE VIPERS

Marked with an animated striking serpent, they answer to Jude Monson,
Head of the Den of Vipers

————

*All Darkslaying circles in Angelthene answer to Darien Cassel, Head of all
circles in the city. No one outside of these six circles may operate on Angelthene
soil. To do so is punishable by death.*

DARKSLAYING CIRCLES OF YVESWICH

THE SHADOWMASTERS

Marked with the bleeding black skull of Obitus, god of death and the dying, they answer to Roman 'Shadows' Devlin, Head of the Hollow and the House of Black

In some parts of Terra, they are better known as 'Wraiths'

THE SELKIES

Marked with the teardrop of Caligo, goddess of water, mercy, and rebirth, they answer to Athene Cousens, Head of the Riptide and the House of Blue

---

THE WYVERNS

Marked with the flame of Ignis, goddess of fire and the Seven Circles, they answer to Cerise Brinton, Head of the Dunes and the House of Red

In some parts of Terra, they are better known as 'Flameweavers'

THE JACKALS

Marked with the eye of Tempus the Liar, outcast of the Terran pantheon and god of time, they answer to Griffin Brand, Head of the Labyrinth and the House of Sage

---

THE SYLPHEN

Marked with the white feather of Vita, goddess of the sky and flight, they answer to Raina Cruso, Head of the Eyrie and the House of Violet

---

All Darkslaying circles in Yveswich answer to Donovan Slade, Head of all circles in the city. No one outside of these five circles may operate on Yveswich soil. To do so is punishable by death.

For a full list of characters, flip to the back of the book

This book contains subject matter that might be difficult for some readers, including intense violence, violence against children, brutal injuries, graphic language, discussion of domestic violence, substance use disorder, drug dependence and symptoms of withdrawal, death, gore, suicidal ideation, and psychological torture. This book also contains explicit sexual content. Please read with caution and prepare to return to the streets of Angelthene and Yveswich...

PROLOGUE
SIX MONTHS AGO

A ngelthene was always quiet at night, but here in the sequestered district of Ebonfield, the thick silence felt especially eerie.

Fog curled around the car, making it difficult to see, and although the sprawling city was baking in the heat of a long, dry summer, the temperature in these parts took a sudden plunge, the shift a warning to all who wandered too close to the Crossroads. *Turn back,* it seemed to advise, *while you still have a chance.*

Cyra Sophronia held her breath, her wide eyes scanning her surroundings for any sign of movement as Erasmus steered the car through the fog.

It was the sky that drew her focus. Rather, what flew through it.

Firebirds. No bigger than the average crow, they lit up the starless expanse with shimmers of gold and ruby, their radiant plumage impossible to miss, even through dense fog. The birds' most active time was the end of the growing season, the period during which they gathered tinder to build their funeral pyres. Once built, they would brood their glasslike eggs in the nest of wood and spices for a fortnight, then set the nest ablaze with rapid flaps of their wings, cremating themselves in a show of flames and combustion. This sacrifice was necessary for the hatching of their chicks—a cycle of life and death that was tragic, yes, and yet strangely beautiful, in its own way.

Cyra's throat tightened to the point of pain, her heart pulling downward as if fastened to an anchor she dragged behind her.

The Firebirds were so like the phoenix. And the phoenix would always remind her of her many, *many* mistakes.

The tires thumped about as the car rolled down the dusty, uneven road. Peeking through the fog up ahead was a second road—one that intersected with this one to form an X. As that second road loomed, Cyra concentrated on steadying her breathing, her perspiring hands squeezing and twisting her seatbelt into a tube.

All at once, the fog cleared, and the field on the other side of the barbed wire fence spread before them, the gold of the waist-high grass reduced to a gray blur under the velvet cover of night.

Erasmus stopped the car just shy of the intersection.

They sat awhile in the quiet. Minutes passed, and during this time neither of them dared to even move.

Cyra was about to risk breaking the silence when a brittle voice beat her to it with a whisper of her name—her old one.

"*Helia.*"

Her head snapped toward Erasmus, the rasp of that ancient and terrible voice slashing deep into her bones, like a knife freshly sharpened on a whetstone. "Did you hear that?"

"Hear what?" He glanced about, the round lenses of his glasses reflecting the cool glow of the dashboard.

Cyra's mouth dried out. "It must've been the wind."

As if her words were a summoning, a supernatural draft crept through the vents, the clammy tongues of otherworldly spirits pebbling the skin on Cyra's nape.

Once upon a time, she had been a part of the spirit realm, roaming the mist-veiled land of the dead as goddess of neither here nor there, her every step jingling with the ring of keys that could open any door, any latch. But centuries had passed since then, and those long centuries had changed her, molding her into something new. Ground that was once familiar was now foreign; beings she once considered friends were now strangers. She no longer belonged, nor was she welcome, on the other side of the curtain.

We're here to talk, she reminded herself, *not trade.* Surely no harm would come from talking.

Right?

Erasmus must have sensed her distress, because he said softly, "All we'll do is talk." He shut off the car, the sudden absence of the engine's purr causing the silence to swell like a too-full balloon. "There's n-nothing to be afraid of, my love." Despite the reassurance, the smile he gave her wobbled. "Ready?"

Cyra drew a breath, the scent of magic—warm sugar and smoke—coating her tongue, and said on the exhale, "Ready."

Erasmus cracked open his door. Cyra followed suit, her fingers trembling on the handle.

The moment she was out, the wind picked up, blowing her hair upward like a flame. Tree branches creaked and cracked like frail bones, and fallen leaves and palm fronds swooshed by in gusts of unseasonably cool air. The sounds were oddly amplified, as if boxed in by walls no one could see.

They walked, side by side, across the field—to the old, crumbling fountain squatting in the center of it. Thousands of fountains just like this one were scattered throughout Terra, but only one was home to the granter of wishes the world called *The Widow*.

A rusted pail sat on the fountain's edge, a hungry mouth begging for a meal.

The sight of the pail brought Erasmus to a sudden stop, his throat jouncing with a swallow.

He hated this part. Cyra didn't particularly enjoy it either, but it had to be done.

So she retrieved the switchblade from her pocket. "It'll be over quickly," she promised, the reassurance blown away by another gale that howled through her ears. She couldn't promise that he'd feel no pain, but she could promise that the pain wouldn't last.

She dragged the sharp edge of the knife across her palm, a hiss of discomfort catching in her throat as her skin split open. After wiping the blade clean on her pants, she cupped the back of Erasmus's hand and carefully cut an identical line across his palm. Where his skin was weathered and wrinkled, hers was smooth and ageless, its only imperfection the single scar that ran from the heel of her hand to the base of her pinky. Human and hellseher blood welled in the moonlight, the smell drawing the attention of the predators skulking in the dark gaps between the trees.

They held their fists above the pail and squeezed, blood dripping, then tossed in the coins they brought as payment. The pieces of silver clanged when they struck the bottom, but the pail itself made no sound when dropped into the fountain. Not even a splash.

"Ready?" Erasmus asked again, taking her good hand into his.

She nodded, the wound already clotting. "Ready."

They stepped up onto the stone rim...and waited, as if ringing a doorbell.

Two heartbeats passed before a fresh blanket of fog folded over them like a sheet. For a moment, nothing existed except the sound of their breathing and an endless canvas of white.

And then they arrived, the fog dropping to the floor like spilled milk, leaving them standing in a dark room, the walls of which were curved.

Crossing made them feel nauseous, so they took a moment to compose themselves before stepping off the edge of the fountain. Muck splashed beneath their shoes.

The spider had wedged herself into an alcove on the other side of the room, her gargantuan body supported by a hammock of webs that sagged under her weight. Wispy shadows clung to her like affectionate pets to their master, briefly tricking Cyra's eyes into seeing more than eight legs.

"Well, isn't this a delightful surprise?" the Widow remarked, her curious voice bubbling through the room. "I cannot say I expected to see the Sophronias anytime soon. How very delightful, indeed."

"We come for advice," Cyra began, tripping over her words. She was out of practice. Nineteen years—that was how long had passed since she had last sought out a creature of the Crossroads. Nineteen years since her last bargain.

Nineteen years since her greatest creation...and her biggest mistake.

The spider made a hungry, smacking sound. "And what have you brought me in exchange?" The webs of her resting place were studded with cocooned insects, their dead bodies sparkling like berries crusted with frost.

Cyra shared a glance with Erasmus. "Well, we—" She cleared her throat, the sound carrying. "We don't..."

Foolish—they were foolish for coming here. The Nameless were chronically bored, chronically starving creatures with endless time at their disposal. Time to feast—to torture the poor souls they deemed unworthy.

Quite plainly, this was suicide.

But the Widow did the unexpected. The exhale she let out was one of... of understanding, Cyra thought. "You do not have anything left to trade."

"We realize this isn't customary," Erasmus said tightly.

The spider chuckled. "Not at all. But I suppose I can spare you a listen."

"Our daughter is being hunted," Cyra confessed, the words turning her stomach. The running, the hiding, the many sacrifices they'd made—were all their efforts for nothing? "We come to you seeking advice on how to help her."

"Liliana Sophronia." The Widow spoke their daughter's name as if it were a bird she'd held captive for quite some time, and was desperate to set it free. The name given to a mortal baby with a rainbow aura, who'd watched quietly—no tears, no fussing—as she was lifted from a pool of impossibly deep water, her skin scented with the delicate fragrance of violets.

Cyra swallowed the lump in her throat. "Yes," she whispered.

It was the reason they had come back to Angelthene. The minute they'd received word of the bounty on their daughter's head, they had vowed to find a way to make her safe again. No matter how steep the price.

The Widow added, "She goes by 'Loren Calla' now."

Cyra turned the name over in her mind, committing it to memory.

Loren Calla—the name her new parents had given her.

The name her new, *better* parents had given her. Had they raised her properly? Given her a full and happy life?

Did they love her?

"Will you show her to us?" Cyra blurted, regret piercing a hole in her heart. Not just regret, but guilt too—so much guilt, she knew it would hold her prisoner forever, even after death.

As the creature considered the request, she kept her gaze fastened on Cyra, reading her like a book. Cyra dropped her own under the scrutiny, studying the muddy water at her feet as the spider judged her for her sins, seeing far beyond what lay on the surface. The monster wearing a hellseher's skin. That was all she was now: a monster.

"Your heart is heavy," the spider observed.

Cyra lifted her head; it, too, was heavy. "It is."

"You've made many mistakes."

"I have." A sob cracked the confession apart.

A peculiar silence. Then the Widow whispered, "But you're sorry."

Tears slipped down Cyra's cold face. "I've never been more sorry in all my life." But being sorry, she'd learned, did not fix anything.

Erasmus came closer, taking her hand in comfort.

"You've been alive for a very long time," the spider said. "Everyone makes mistakes, even those who have lived a fraction of your years."

Cyra knew the Widow was right. And maybe this was a truth she desperately needed to hear, after spending many years beating herself up for her missteps and oversights. But she would never forgive herself for her many blunders—that, she refused.

The Widow seemed to already know this, because she said then, her words coasting on a saddened sigh, "Look into the fountain."

Cyra's heart swelled with hope as she and Erasmus stepped up to the fountain's gaping mouth. The water inside was no longer murky, but sprinkled with stars and motes of light. A miniature galaxy.

As they stood there, the churning water stilled, turning glass-smooth. The stars winked out, and fat drops of liquid dribbled from the ceiling, casting new ripples across the surface. Slowly, the face of a young woman took shape in the water, and Cyra had to concentrate on breathing as she beheld her adult daughter for the very first time.

Her hair was honey-blonde, her skin fair, her eyes a vivid blue. A smattering of freckles dotted her nose, her smile bright and carefree. Cyra watched, enraptured, her shaking hands moving to grip the fountain's rough edge, as the girl tipped her head back and laughed. She was lounging on the dock of a sunlit beach with two friends—two witches, one a redhead, the other a brunette.

Cyra swallowed. "When?" she asked the Widow.

"Two weeks ago."

Her throat tightened with emotion, but she managed to say, the words strangled, "And where is she now?"

"Sleeping. Safe."

Cyra couldn't tear her eyes off her daughter as Lily and her friends jumped to their feet. They raced each other to the end of the dock and jumped, laughing and shrieking, into the ocean.

"She's beautiful," Cyra whispered. Erasmus came closer, wrapping an arm around her. Tears sparkled on his cheeks. "Erasmus, isn't she beautiful?" She extended a hand toward the water—reaching for Lily, who'd resurfaced in the ocean, laughing as she pushed her wet hair back.

A flood of black engulfed the image, and Cyra's stomach sank with disappointment as Lily disappeared, leaving Cyra's own reflection—the face that hadn't changed in a hideously long time—staring back at her in the gloom.

"Your daughter is being hunted," the Widow said, reiterating Cyra's confession in a metallic tone. "Many a person looks for her."

"Bounty hunters?" Cyra asked. They had no idea *who*, exactly, was hunting Lily—only that many people were.

"Some."

"We have to stop them." Cyra stepped around the fountain, pressing her hands together in supplication. "How do we stop them? Please. *Please*, if you can help us, just tell us what to do. I'll give anything—"

"My dear, you must hire someone stronger," the spider said.

Cyra blinked. *Hire someone stronger...* It wasn't a stupid suggestion; in fact, it was...clever. What better way to deal with an opponent than to hire someone who could beat them at their own job? Someone who could find Lily and...well, Cyra wasn't certain what would happen after.

"Are you saying," Cyra began, her brows knitting together, "we should hire someone to act as her...*bodyguard?*"

"Precisely."

Her shoulders sank. A moment ago, she'd considered the Widow a genius. But now...now, she wasn't so sure.

Still, she wet her chapped lips and asked the spider, "Who do you recommend?"

"Only the best," she said plainly. "Only the strongest, most capable person in all of Angelthene would be fit to protect your daughter."

Cyra mulled it over. The strongest people were Darkslayers. But that couldn't be the answer here, because Darkslayers didn't protect—they hunted and they killed. In what world would a slayer be willingly saddled with a human girl—

"Darien Cassel," the Widow said. But—

"No." Erasmus's rebuke—shaky with fear—clapped against the walls. "Ab-absolutely not!"

The Widow stirred, rock clacking. Mist coiled around her legs like agitated snakes. "Do you take issue with my advice, Erasmus?"

Cyra's lungs tightened with terror. She looked toward the fountain— their only way out. Gauged how many steps it'd take them to get there— how long they'd have to wait for the magic to spirit them away.

When Erasmus spoke again, he did so carefully. "I beg your p-pardon, Araneae, but yes, I do take great issue. I mean, let's be reasonable here—" A nervous chuckle. "This man you speak of is *Darien Cassel*. The m-most ruthless Darkslayer in the entire city!"

"In the state."

Erasmus glared, throwing caution to the wind. "Pardon me?"

"I was simply correcting you." The Widow blinked her many shining eyes. "He is the most ruthless Darkslayer in the city, yes, as well as the state."

Erasmus threw his hands in the air. "Unbelievable! We're wasting our time—"

"Darling," Cyra tried.

But Erasmus wasn't listening. "This must b-be a joke. Allow me to make sure I understand what you're saying. You expect us to hire the most d-dangerous Darkslayer in the city—a man who's killed hundreds, maybe even thousands of people, someone who kills because he *enjoys* it—and trust that he will—*poof*—" He flourished his hands. "—miraculously choose to *protect* our daughter?"

The Widow blinked. "Yes."

Erasmus pushed, *"Randal Slade's son?"*

"Yes."

"What are the odds?" he demanded. "A thousand to one?"

"Perhaps."

Erasmus shook his head in disbelief and started to pace, water sloshing around his shoes.

"You came to me seeking advice, Erasmus, and I have given you exactly that. You don't have to do as I say, but I am not in the habit of changing my answers simply because someone does not agree with me."

Cyra and Erasmus had been gone for a long time, it was true, but there wasn't a soul alive who hadn't heard of Darien Cassel. Son of Randal Slade... Fearless leader of the Seven Devils... A spawn of evil—spat out of the deepest pits of hell. He'd broken Darkslayer records, having slaughtered more people and monsters at the age of twenty-three than most of his kind killed in a hundred. No mercy, no regret—just coldblooded killing. Merely the thought of him was enough to tempt Cyra to find Lily herself and take her far away from here. Surely there had to be *someplace* where no one would find her—

But she knew that was foolish. After all, she herself had spent decades in hiding; if anyone understood how difficult it was to remain hidden, it was Cyra. Only a near-impossible trade had allowed her and Erasmus to start over with new lives, new identities, new auras... If a Darkslayer as gifted as Darien Cassel wanted to locate someone badly enough, there was no place in the world where a person could hide—no land, sea, or sky where he couldn't find you.

"A word of caution," said the spider, her echoing words stilling Erasmus's restless feet. "Place your daughter's life in the hands of anyone other than Darien Cassel, and she will be butchered."

Cyra's skin prickled with chills. "How could you say that?"

"I merely speak the truth," the Widow said. "I see a thousand different futures for your daughter; trust me when I say they are all ugly. Shall I list the outcomes? Tortured. Beaten. Raped—"

"Stop," Cyra whispered, her voice weak with fright.

"All ugly...except for one." The future that involved Darien Cassel.

But how could that be? When Cyra had gazed upon her daughter in the fountain, she had seen a ray of sunshine. A beauty. A bright and bubbly personality who simply didn't fit, didn't *belong* in the underworld. Was it possible that the man she'd heard such vile things about could fall for Lily? Protect her? *Love* her, even?... Cyra could not imagine it.

"Let's go." Erasmus stepped forward, winding an arm around Cyra's shoulders. "We're d-done here."

Cyra shrugged him off and approached the spider.

"Cyra," he hissed, his heart pounding through the Crossroads.

She ignored him, turning her focus to the infernal being squatting in the bluish light. "Tortured, beaten, raped...," Cyra croaked. "Darien Cassel will do none of these things?" She was asking too many questions, her time nearly spent, but she *had* to know.

"Nothing is set in stone, my dear—they call it *free will* for a reason. But believe me when I say he is your best option. With Darien Cassel's protection, your daughter may stand a chance. May yet survive...in a world of people who will soon want her dead." Her words brought a fresh wave of goosebumps to Cyra's skin.

Erasmus hurried forward, taking Cyra by the arm. "Let's g-go."

"Thank you, Araneae, for your time," Cyra said as Erasmus pulled her toward the fountain. Their time was up; they couldn't linger—not without payment.

'Helia.' The Widow's voice floated through Cyra's mind—audible only to her now.

She turned.

'To forgive is to set yourself free. Tormenting yourself over your past mistakes will not fix them. What you choose to do with your future is far more important. If you truly love your daughter, I implore you to heed my advice—heed my warning, and find Darien Cassel.'

The pit in Cyra's stomach widened. *'But he's a monster.'*

'I don't deny that. But he may be one of the only monsters capable of changing. Should he choose to protect your daughter, there will be nothing he wouldn't do for her. You must find him. He is her best and only chance.'

The fog thickened before Cyra could reply. It carried them away—back to Angelthene. When it finally cleared, they stood in the grass of Ebonfield, the faint sounds of cars and sparse nightlife trickling through distant streets.

Cyra crossed her arms, her skin tingling with chills. "What should we do?"

Erasmus lifted his hands in defeat. "It's y-your decision. Say the words, and we'll do it."

Butchered, the Widow had said.

Tortured.

Beaten.

Raped.

Could Cyra live with herself if she chose to ignore the creature's warnings? If Lily ended up dying because Cyra was too afraid to trust the one man the Widow claimed would protect her? The Nameless were incapable of lying, their knowledge of the world and its occupants deeper than the deepest ocean. Vaster than outer space. If the Widow said they could trust Darien Cassel, not only did she mean it, but it was also the gods' honest truth.

Erasmus awaited her answer.

Place their trust in the leader of the Seven Devils...or sentence their daughter to death.

Take a chance...or risk losing everything.

"We trust the Widow," Cyra decided, the winds of change gusting around her. "And we hire Darien Cassel."

PART ONE

THE SLAUGHTERHOUSE

EMERGENCY ALERT: EXTREME

ISSUED BY THE YVESWICH MAGICAL PROTECTIONS UNIT: POWER OUTAGE

IN EFFECT FOR THIS AREA UNTIL FURTHER NOTICE

At 6:03 a.m, the Yveswich Magical Protections unit issued a RED warning for a power outage of supernatural origin that may be deadly to those caught without shelter. The cause of the outage is not clear and is currently under investigation.

If you are in the area, seek immediate shelter. It is unsafe to drive in these conditions. Fleet responding. Await further instructions and follow advice from emergency services and local authorities.

I

SOUTH FINANCIAL DISTRICT
YVESWICH, STATE OF KER

L oren Calla met death when she was only a child. As a human living in a world of monsters and godlike immortal beings, her mortality was simply *there* all the time—as constant as her shadow.

At the age of five, Taega and Roark had sat her down and explained to her the unfortunate truth about her life. *You're different,* they'd said. While others stopped aging, she would continue to grow old, forever careening toward the end of a too-short existence. As the years passed, the pain of this harsh reality had dulled from the sharp pang of a fresh cut to the periodic ache of a bruise. Eventually, she'd even come to accept it. Death was simply a part of her life, and nothing would ever change that fact. Yet despite how many years she'd spent preparing for her end, being told she had less than ten months to live was a surprise she hadn't seen coming.

As unsettling as it was to know there was a strong chance she wouldn't make it to her twenty-first birthday, her biggest concern lay not in her own heart ceasing to beat, but Darien Cassel's. The man who'd tied his fate to hers. The incredibly selfless leader of the Seven Devils, who was somewhere out there right now, in this dark city, hopefully, *hopefully* still breathing.

She clung tightly to her faith that she would see Darien again—tighter than she clung to Malakai Delaney's hand—as she navigated predator-infested streets. Her strange magic allowed her to see with vision similar to a hellseher's, but even so, maneuvering the ruins of the city was difficult. The buckled roads, the shattered sidewalks, the dust choking the air... It was endless. And they were a long way from home.

As she walked with Malakai, she tried to keep her feet from shifting too loudly in the rubble, while the Reaper used his magic to mask their human and hellseher scents. Monsters lurked on every road, hunting for prey. Most of these breeds were unable to see in the dark—a blessing that had kept her and Malakai alive this long, though Loren shuddered at the thought of what might happen if they ran into one that could.

"Any idea where we are?" Malakai asked, speaking quietly.

She scanned her surroundings, her all-white eyes gritty from exhaustion and burning from the smoke. The buildings in this area were aglow with rows of colorful symbols, though most were weak and flickering, the spell systems hanging on by a thread.

"There's a mall over there—to your right," she said, using her Sight to read the magic flickering weakly through the sign. The patchy words just *barely* managed to spell out *Starling Shopping Center* in sky blue and cherry red. She still wasn't used to seeing the things she hadn't been able to see before. The colors burned to look at, as if she were staring directly at the sun, and sometimes they all bled together into a muddy mess. "Starling Shopping Center." She blinked to ease the stinging in her eyes. "Can you see the sign?"

Malakai's frustration was tangible, his hand tightening slightly around hers. "Where am I looking, exactly?"

"Umm...one o'clock?"

A beat of silence. And then: "Fucking barely."

They kept walking, moving more carefully as they passed the mall—past a pack of monsters chowing down on something near the entrance. Loren didn't want to know what—or who—they were eating.

Although her powers had kept the Well replica from razing all of Yveswich to the ground, she had failed to save the city in its entirety. The destruction had snuck through the apertures—of which there were many—carving Yveswich apart like a snowflake. While some streets and neighborhoods had been completely pulverized, others had stayed mostly intact, save for perhaps a shattered window or a few overturned cars. It had no rhyme or reason. But then again, not much in her life made sense these days.

Instead of trying to understand her magic, her past, and her life in general, she focused on her goal: get back to Roman Devlin's house and find the others.

Find *Darien*.

"You're thinking about that asshole again, aren't you?" Malakai's question was nearly drowned out by a guttural growl from somewhere behind them—one monster scuffling with another for control over a food source.

She sighed, the exhale wobbling from the cold. Her fingers were so numb, they felt permanently frozen to Malakai's hand. "I'm always thinking about him. And he's not an asshole."

"He is, actually. He's just not an asshole to *you.*"

Rock clacked as Malakai suddenly tripped, stumbling blindly. With her hand in his, Loren stumbled too, her arm jerking about as he nearly took them both down.

"Fuck, man," he grumbled, regaining his balance. "I can't wait till I can see again."

Neither could Loren. It wasn't that she was bothered by his tendency to trip on the many obstacles strewn about the streets, but if they were attacked right now—something they'd managed to avoid thus far—Malakai would be just as likely to shoot her in the head as he would a monster. He couldn't see the many creatures slinking through the dark, could just *barely* see the faint colors on the buildings that still had partial protection. It was strange; Loren was the farthest thing from a hellseher, and yet she could somehow see better than anyone. *How* was simply another of the maddening questions the universe had tossed her way these last approximately six months.

She tried not to consider what this might mean for the others. How they could ever find their way back to safety if they couldn't see. Couldn't protect themselves.

If they were even alive.

She banished the horrible thought from her head. They were alive—she wouldn't settle for anything less.

"How do you feel about the whole *you-die-he-dies* thing, anyway?"

"Pissed," she admitted, a shiver shaking through her. She shut her eyes, remembering the look on Darien's handsome face when she'd told him that she hated him. "Hurt. Betrayed." Hurt and betrayed—exactly how he, too, must have felt in that moment. He had certainly looked hurt and betrayed.

Malakai merely grunted. Such noises seemed to be a frequent response for him. But she wasn't complaining; she would take his grunting over his smart and oftentimes crude comments any day, though she'd spent enough time with him to notice that he took it slightly easier on her with his jests than he did the others.

Slightly.

"You know," the Reaper began a few moments later. Loren braced herself for another of his famous jabs. "I never imagined anyone could hate your prick boyfriend more than I do...but I think his sister might actually beat me this time." He wheezed a long, drawn-out chuckle that hopefully no predators would hear.

Loren wouldn't be surprised if Malakai was right. To say Ivy had been upset upon learning of her brother's trade was an understatement, though they'd all had to leave Roman's so hastily that not many words had been exchanged.

Apart from the words Loren had said to Darien, and Darien to her.

'How could you?' she'd demanded of him.

'I hate you for doing that,' she'd blurted.

And: *'I don't want to talk to you right now, I don't want to see you.'*

'I hate you'. That one bothered her the most.

She may be angry still, may feel deeply hurt and betrayed by his decision to part with his life, but she wished she'd handled the situation differently.

"So, what happened, anyway?" Malakai asked. "Your dog died, Cassel went to the Widow to get it back, and he what, tied his life to yours?"

She wiped her nose on her sleeve. Another nosebleed, if the rusty taste on her tongue was any indication. "Basically, yeah."

"FYI, a dog doesn't cost that much. Not when a hellseher can live forever if they're in perfect health. Your dog would've lived, what—nine, ten years?"

She looked at him in question—at least, she tried to, but he might as well have been invisible. "What are you saying?"

"I'm saying he parted with more by choice."

She nibbled on her chapped lip, her teeth chattering so hard they nearly pierced the skin. "So, the Widow could've given Singer back for...like...a decade of his?"

An upward tug on her arm suggested Malakai had shrugged. "Maybe two decades, maybe three. Depends. Immortal years are worth triple or more what yours are—no offense."

"None taken," she muttered.

"I'm not an expert on this shit, though, so don't go quoting me. All I'm saying is I guaran-fucking-tee a dog didn't cost him his entire immortal life. Just doesn't make sense."

They walked for a few minutes in silence, rock shifting underfoot, the soles of their boots slipping every now and again on sheets of smooth ice.

When she got back, she decided, she would get the story from Darien in full. No leaving anything out—she wanted to know every detail. And maybe she would still be angry with him, maybe she would still feel like he'd betrayed her, but at least she would know the truth.

For a city with a population so large, it was horrifyingly quiet. Whenever Loren wasn't thinking about Darien and the others, which was seldom, her mind was plagued with the question of how many people had died—how many might still die, given the sheer number of predators prowling every block, starving for flesh.

Monsters aside, time was running out in other ways, thanks to the spirit dimension blending with their own, slowly siphoning the life out of everything it touched. The darkness of the Void reminded her of quicksand. It wasn't natural, but like quicksand it had a peculiar way of making you feel like you were sinking or being pulled on. Sucked into a vortex of freezing-cold night.

The temperature was good for one thing, though—it made it *slightly* easier to bear the pain of her wounds. Her back had been blistered by the blast, her hair clinging to the clotted blood. The white armor she wore—a sleek, magically enhanced bodysuit that fit her like a glove from neck to toes —had sustained so much damage, the protective barrier that made it special no longer worked. She could feel everything now, even something as minor as the press of the rocks under her feet. One bullet or bite in a vital area, and she'd be done for.

"Okay, so...Starling." The direction of Malakai's gruff voice suggested he was staring blindly over his shoulder. "Where is that, anyway? Where *are* we?"

She hummed. "I remember driving through this area after Darien brought me to the Avenue of the Waning Moon." The afternoon they'd spent together at the bakery, stuffing themselves with those delicious cinnamon buns, was only yesterday, but it felt like a hundred years had passed since then. He'd asked her if she wanted kids one day—had talked about the future as if she had one to look forward to. As if she weren't mortal, and he an immortal hellseher who should never have fallen in love with a human.

As if they hadn't been doomed right from the start. Since the moment they'd met, they'd been thwarted with bad luck. Everything that could go wrong in their lives had indeed gone wrong. But they'd fought it—had fought hard for each other. For love. But in the end, death always won— even when pitted against the force that could move mountains.

Love.

"The Avenue of the Waning what-the-fuck?"

"Waning Moon," she repeated, breathing deeply to soothe the sudden ache in her chest. It felt like a bullet had sliced into her heart.

How badly she wanted a future with Darien couldn't be expressed in words. She wanted it—wanted *him*—more than she wanted anything in the world. Wanted to live with him and love him forever.

"It's a tourist area like the Avenue of the Scarlet Star," she forced out, swallowing her emotions. Hammering them down the way Darien had hammered his own down for twenty-four years. How he did it so expertly, she had no idea. "I think we're close to there."

"Which puts us how far away from Roman's?"

She did the math in her head. "A while," she admitted.

"Okay, Miss Vague, what's 'a while' mean?"

The air far above their heads began to pulse. A rapid thumping sound ricocheted through the area, starting from one end of the street and carrying onto the other. *Thump, thump, thump, thump, thump...*

"What is that?" Loren wondered aloud. It was by habit that she craned her neck to see, but there was nothing around, below, or above them that wasn't suffocated with shadow. Not even her Sight picked up on what was making that sound.

"Helicopters," Malakai said. Of course—it seemed obvious now.

The rotary wings chopped apart the air like blades, the currents pulsing heavily in her ears, but from way down here they couldn't feel any wind.

"Don't get your hopes up." Malakai sighed. "If we can't see them, they can't see us, either. They won't be coming down far enough to do us any good." He tugged on her hand, urging her along. "Hurry it up, Blondie. I'm tired of this shit."

They walked a bit quicker now, still taking care not to trip, both eager to get out of here. Whoever was in those helicopters might not be able to help them, but maybe there were other poor souls who they could locate. People they could save. Maybe some of those people would be her family. Her friends.

Darien. Her fragile, lovesick heart tacked his name to the end of every thought that crossed her mind.

Please be alive, she begged.

During the long trek, she'd had plenty of time to think. About bargains. About life and death. About everything Darien had given her in six months, everything he'd sacrificed. And she asked herself what she would give—what she would sacrifice—for him.

Anything.

Everything.

Warm tears that glowed with pastel light slipped down her icy cheeks, and she blotted them dry with the back of her gloved hand.

Please, please be alive.

2

UNDERGROUND
YVESWICH, STATE OF KER

'*I hate you.*'

For Darien Cassel, being told by the woman he loved that she hated him was worse than being shot or stabbed. Since the moment the bomb went off, those three words had circled him like hungry vultures, yapping a cruel and tuneless song.

'*I hate you, I hate you, I hate you.*'

He was disgusted with himself for walking out on her. For leaving while she was upset. He'd sped away from Roman's house stupidly believing he'd get the chance to fix the hurt he'd caused her, and now he'd consider himself lucky if he ever saw her again.

He'd fucked up. Badly. Hate was the least he deserved.

'*I don't have time right now,*' he'd told her, in a tone so sharp, he was ashamed to have used it on her. '*We can talk about this when I get back.*'

That was the problem with time: everyone always thought they had more of it.

What a fucking joke this had turned out to be. He and Roman had been trapped down here in these tunnels, blind and running out of air, for gods knew how long. Hours, definitely, though he'd lost track of exactly how many. One minute, one *second* was too long, but *hours?*

He had to get out of here. For Loren. For his family—who, apart from Roman, Darien hadn't seen since a storm of darkness had blasted through the city, swallowing everything like a black hole.

Cell reception was down. No light—not even the tactical lights on their guns—could penetrate the gloom. Tracking did sweet fuck all when everyone's auras were untraceable.

Useless. He'd never felt so useless.

'I hate you.' He'd use the memory like a weapon—would cut himself with it a little more each time, until he found the strength to get the hell out of here, Loren safe in his arms again. Even if she *did* hate him, even if she wanted nothing to do with him, even if she wanted to break up with him, for the gods' sake...he refused to rest until he knew she was safe.

He lifted the sword of adamant with his good hand and studied the reflection in the blade. The once black material had transformed into a mirror shortly after the explosion, its mysterious power allowing him to see through the darkness that blinded the naked eye. If he looked over his shoulder, he saw nothing but thick, choking darkness. But if he looked into the blade, he could see everything, clearer than crystal, in its reflection. Every last detail, right down to the pebbles on the ground. He hadn't a clue how, but it wasn't the first time the sword had changed itself in a time of need.

A miracle, that's what it was. A *miracle*—and the sole reason he and Roman had managed to make it more than three feet without tripping, staggering into walls, or falling prey to the beasts hunting in their vicinity.

'I hate you.' The vultures were circling again, and with them came another unwelcome reminder.

Ten months. Loren Calla, the sweetest, most beautiful woman who'd ever walked into the ashes of his life, would die sometime in the next roughly ten months. Darien had known for a while, but had buried it down, deep in the graveyard of the rest of the shit he suppressed, for as long as he could stand it. Now that the cat was out of the bag, it was all he could think about.

Ten. *Fucking*. Months.

Fuck if he was going to just *let* her die. He still had time, however short —a chance to save her before that bullshit prophecy came to fruition.

He drew a deep breath, the cold air of the Void sawing apart his lungs like jagged shards of glass as he walked with Roman through the tunnels, forever looking into the blade to help him navigate.

After the explosion, the temperature had plunged below freezing, puddles crackling as they iced over in the dark. Shortly after the cold had arrived, the monsters had as well, slinking out of the Dead Realm and into the living. Now, they were everywhere—horrid creatures of every shape, size, and breed.

Darien watched one in the sword—a thickly muscled canine with milky eyes, its form rippling with lightless green flames—as it crept by, entirely unaware of them thanks to the coat of magic Roman kept in place, masking their scents and sounds. It was a handy trick, but Darien knew Roman couldn't keep it up forever. They were both faint with exhaustion, their limbs stiff and slow-moving in the cold.

And it was getting harder to breathe by the minute.

Darien studied his cousin's grimy, scratched-up face in the sword's reflection. He mirrored Darien's steps, each inhale shallow and quivering.

"You all right?" Darien whispered, ice breaking under his boot as he took another backward step. That was the sword's one flaw: Needing to use the reflection to see meant they had to travel backward. If they wanted to walk forward, they first had to make damn sure they wouldn't bump into anything before trying, which would be plain stupid while surrounded by this many ravenous beasts.

"Been better," Roman admitted, matching Darien's volume. "I feel like I can't breathe." He rubbed at the chest of his battle-suit, another inhale shaking through him. "I need a paper bag or something."

"It's not you, it's the Void—it can't support life," Darien explained. "And it's only going to get worse, so we need to hurry."

At first, he'd believed the lack of oxygen was the fault of the debris choking the ventilation passages, and while that was true to an extent, Spirit Terra was a place of death. And death was spreading, seeping into Yveswich like a poisonous gas, poised to kill everything it touched.

Darien figured they were getting close to where he'd slew the Basilisk. They'd decided to head to the cavern the moment the blade had modified itself, giving them a way to see in the gloom. Climbing out of the same chamber they'd rappelled down would take a long time, and might very well be impossible given its extreme height. But right now it was their only option.

On they walked, maneuvering around rubble and stalagmites. Bandit stayed alert in Darien's shadow, Sayagul doing the same in Roman's. The Familiars had been very quiet since the bomb went off, but Darien suspected they were speaking to each other in private.

As if sensing his curiosity, Bandit said down the Spirit Bond, '*I hate to admit it, but...I'm worried about her.*' A whimper drifted down the bond. '*Do you think...do you think she's okay?*'

Darien drew a deep breath, cold air needling his throat. Merely the thought of her not being okay caused him unbearable agony. But he told the dog, who waited for an answer on pins and needles, *'I'm sure she's fine.'* He took a moment to appreciate his own lie. *'And I'm sure she's far away by now.'*

Bandit accepted the lie without argument, which was for the best. Darien didn't have the heart to tell the dog what he really thought.

Because he didn't want to admit it to himself, either—that there was no chance in hell they'd still be alive if Loren hadn't done something to tip the odds of survival in their favor. He and Roman were far too close to the Well replica to have lived through the blast. Not only should they have died—instantly—but the tunnels also should've collapsed. *Instantly.*

She had stayed in Yveswich—Darien could feel it. Had stayed long enough to suffer that awful blast. Which could only mean one thing.

Malakai had broken his promise. He'd given Darien his word that he would get Loren out of the city, and if he hadn't followed through...

Darien's blood heated to a rolling boil, but he clung to the hope—the chance, however slim—that the Reaper had at least been smart enough to get her out of here *after.*

If she hadn't made it out of the city, if she was stuck somewhere in this blinding darkness, if she had suffered so much as a scratch...

Darien would lose his goddamn mind. No amount of fighting or killing would quell the rage he'd feel if he discovered she was hurt.

Stagnant air, thick with rot and blood, wafted down the tunnel.

"What is that?" Roman whispered.

They closed the short distance to the arched doorway that led to the Basilisk's habitat and pressed their backs up against the wall. The vast room echoed with the crunch of bone and the slurp of something wet.

Darien steeled himself, hoping like mad that he wouldn't see the bodies of Jack and Tanner in there, who'd vanished during the explosion...and angled the blade so he could see into the cavern.

Sitting on their haunches in a lake of black blood were pale, skeletal bodies, all of them huddled around a mass of scales.

Monsters. Fucking *hundreds* of monsters, packed inside the room like sardines, leaving little space between here and the door on the other side. They were feasting on the corpse of the Basilisk—sharp teeth grinding against bone, scaled tongues lapping up blood.

"What now?" Roman whispered.

He tipped the blade from side to side, assessing the room and the many different beasts gorging on the Nameless creature. "We go around."

Easier said than done. As they crossed the cavern, it was impossible to avoid bumping their legs into monsters, some turning toward them with eyes a milky blue. Most resembled canines, though closer to the Basilisk were the more humanoid breeds with wings, spiked spines, or horns, a few with bodies like arachnids or bats.

Something nudged his leg. Angling the sword downward, he saw a demon—vaguely canine in appearance—frantically sniffing his thigh. Its teeth were permanently bared, no lips to cover them, its hairless skin oozing with something black and bubbly.

He jabbed Roman in the side with an elbow. *"Shield,"* he hissed.

"I *am.*" But Roman had been shielding for a long time, and Darien sensed that his hold was slipping.

So he snapped a shield of his own up—for now. Roman had suggested he be the one to shield so Darien could reserve his magic in case of an emergency. But shielding for hours was more than even Darkslayers could handle.

Finally, they made it out of the Basilisk's chamber and into the empty tunnel beyond. And they continued to walk. The ground was sloping upward now, so they had to exert more strength to crest it. Soon, they were both out of breath.

Darien used the blade to look up the tunnel—

And stopped with a curse on his lips.

"What's wrong?" Roman asked.

"Look." He passed the sword to Roman.

The chamber they'd rappelled down was drowning in rubble. The whole skyscraper had likely been demolished, slabs of concrete, cristala, metal—you name it—crammed inside.

So much for their escape plan. Sure, it would've taken them a hell of a long time to climb out, but they didn't exactly have options. And there were elevated walkways every few hundred feet for maintenance workers, where they could have rested, making the ascent a little easier.

Now?... Simply put, they were screwed.

Roman was still using the sword to see, but he wasn't looking at the chamber.

"What are you looking at?" Darien asked him.

Roman gave him back the sword. "To your right," he instructed.

Darien turned the blade—

And saw tunnels that hadn't been there before. New openings in the walls—gaping holes and narrow gashes that appeared to have been ripped open by the blast. But no indication as to where they might lead.

Roman caught his eye in the reflection and shrugged. "What other choice do we have?"

None. There was zero choice here, except which of those tunnels they would walk. He looked one more time, weighing their options.

He gestured with the sword to the one that led east. "Let's take this one."

Darien entered the tunnel first, the opening too narrow for both of them. Once they were in, it widened slightly, though not quite enough for two people, forcing them to walk single file.

"Backward or forward?" Darien asked.

Roman thought about it. "Forward. I've had enough of walking backward. I'm getting dizzy."

Darien looked at the tunnel one more time. It was pretty straight—they could probably go for a while before needing to turn.

He tightened his grip on the sword, keeping it in hand in case they needed it. Without it, they were well and truly fucked. "Let's do this."

They started walking, bits of stone crunching under their feet. The ground softened as they ventured deeper, mud sucking on their boots.

"You good?" he asked Roman, his bass voice echoing.

"Fine," Roman mumbled. "Just...thinking."

"About what?"

"Everything." He inhaled, the sound scraping across the walls like sharp talons. "You ever reach a point in your life where you feel like you totally fucked everything up, and there's no going back?"

"All the time," Darien said, Loren's pretty face flashing into his mind. He sighed, missing her so goddamn much it felt like someone had punched their way to his heart and ripped it—raw and bloody and still beating—out. "All the damn time, man. In case you haven't noticed, I'm not very good at this whole *life* thing. Mistakes, though...I've always been good at those. My life is one big train wreck. So yeah, I've definitely reached the point where I feel like I fucked everything up. I feel like that right now."

"You've done better than me, in a lot of ways. Least you don't have your psycho dad to deal with anymore." A beat of silence, and then Roman confessed, "I'm worried Paxton's dead."

Darien's scalp prickled. "He's not."

"How do you know?" Roman challenged. "We don't—*that's* the problem. I promised to keep him safe, and what'd I do? I *left* him. I left my little brother all alone. And now I'm stuck in these gods-forsaken tunnels..." The grinding of his teeth was audible. "Meanwhile I have no clue where he even *is*—"

"You didn't know what was going to happen. None of us did."

"Doesn't matter. I still screwed up. I made a mistake, and I'm not going to even try to pretend that I didn't. He's probably scared. Probably wondering where the hell his brother is. If he's dead, I'll have no one to blame but myself—"

"I need you to listen to me," Darien said, lifting the sword so he could see Roman in its reflection. He looked haggard, dried Venom and blood streaking his cheeks, his eyes wild with rage. With self-loathing. Darien had been in his shoes many times; he wouldn't stand by and let Roman spiral like this. "We're alive right now when we shouldn't be," he began. "So I need you to trust that Paxton is alive, too. You're going to see him again—I promise you that." He clapped Roman on the shoulder. "The best thing you can do for Pax right now is stay strong and get out of these tunnels. All right?"

His next inhale trembled. "Gods, I hope you're right. About him being alive, I mean."

"I am. I can feel it."

A pause. And then Roman said, "I don't suppose you can feel if Shay's alive, too?" He huffed, disappointed with himself all over again. "Another of my many screw-ups."

Darien considered how he should answer. He could tell Roman another lie, if only to make him feel better. But he didn't want to—not when it wouldn't solve anything, and not when promising Pax was okay was enough of a risk. So he settled on, "One step at a time. Let's get above ground, and we'll go from there. Good?"

Roman gave a rigid nod. "Yeah. Good."

They walked on, the tunnel soon stinking of iron. The ground was still squelching—muddy in feel, but with ridges that felt like roots, making it a little easier to find purchase.

"I gotta say," Roman began a few minutes later, "I never really took you for the romantic type."

He smirked, grateful for the distraction. This was the most they'd talked in hours. "No?"

"No." The smile in Roman's voice was audible. "But it kind of suits you. *She* suits you."

Darien's own smile widened. "Thanks."

"I've been dying to know what made my cousin—the famous *Darien Cassel*—"

"Famous? I don't know about that."

"—decide to protect this girl. She give good head or something?"

Darien chuckled. "Fuck off." He paused. "She does give good head though, yeah." Fuck, did she ever. She'd only gone down on him once, but it was the most unforgettable experience of his life.

Roman let out a husky laugh that bounced down the tunnel. "What was it then, if not the life-changing head?"

Darien thought about it, but there weren't enough words to describe all the good Loren had brought into his life.

"Everything," he said on a heavy exhale. "That's the short answer."

"What's the long one?" Roman murmured, every trace of humor gone as he waited intently for his answer.

"She just...dropped into my life one day like an angel. I took one look at her, and I was obsessed. *Completely* obsessed." As he spoke, he almost forgot Roman was there. He could feel his heart peeling open like a flower, baring the thoughts and emotions he'd kept locked behind bars for so long. "The more time I spent with her, the more addicted I got. She taught me how to feel things again—taught me how to...how to love. She saw past the ugly parts of me, and..." He drew a shaky breath and said on the exhale, "I don't know what she found there, but she hasn't run yet. So there must be something she likes." Darien didn't bother adding that his mother being human had a lot to do with it; that was a wound he didn't feel like opening right now.

Roman was quiet for a while. Darien thought he was maybe done with this conversation, but then he said, "The head, probably."

Darien shoved him in the shoulder. "Get out of here."

Roman staggered, laughing. "You sure it wasn't you who put the hit on her? Gave yourself an excuse to track her down, take her home, feel her up a little? Get between those legs?"

He smirked. "Yeah, right." But his humor was soon fading. "Her price would've been higher if it were me." No price was high enough for her.

"How did she not run away screaming from your crazy ass?"

"She did—initially. Then she came back. Invited me out to lunch."

"No way."

"It's the truth. She was completely honest with me too, right from the start. Didn't lie when I asked her questions. She didn't even make up a fake name." His mind flashed between the dark tunnel and that fateful day on the sunlit Avenue of the Scarlet Star. How beautiful she'd looked. Scared, yeah—of him. But still so damn beautiful. "She didn't trust me at first," he went on. "I had to work on her for a bit. But she came around."

"Hm," Roman said. "Interesting."

"Yeah, very. It's been a journey." That was a wild understatement.

"Jokes aside...I'm happy for you."

"Thanks."

Roman abruptly stopped, staring over his shoulder.

Darien's smile melted. His scalp prickled with a warning. "What—"

"The walls," Roman hissed. "The walls—look at the walls!"

Darien lifted the sword—

And saw in its reflection that this tunnel wasn't made of rock or adamant—not anymore. Somewhere along the way, it had turned inky and ropelike, the walls dripping with slime—

Roman stumbled back and slammed into Darien. "Holy shit, do you see that? It's moving."

Darien tried to take a step, but his feet were stuck. Vines were wrapping around his boots, pulling down on them. Constricting.

He pried his feet free and stomped on another vine.

Another reached for him, trying to snake around his throat. He ducked right on time—

The tunnel rumbled, as if from an earthquake. Quickly, he used the blade to look behind him.

The tunnel was caving in.

"Run," he bit out. He grabbed Roman by the shoulder, pushing him down the tunnel. If either of them was getting out of here, it was Roman. *"RUN!"*

They bolted—fast as they could go. The tunnel began to shrink, the vines piling up, reaching for their throats.

Darien pointed the sword upward, the blade carving the ceiling apart. Vines dropped to the ground and curled up in pain. More screaming rattled the tunnel, but the shrinking slowed. Receded before picking up again.

"I'm not gonna die like this!" Roman shouted.

"No, you're *not!* So keep moving, goddammit!" Darien shoved him faster as they tore down the tunnel, unable to see a damn thing, forever in danger of tripping or running into a wall they couldn't see. *"Faster!"*

Another thirty feet, and he heard the roar of white noise. He followed the sound, using it to guide him. Smelled something fresh.

Water. That was a waterfall he was hearing. Water he was smelling.

They rounded a sudden bend, smacking into the curve of the tunnel with surprised shouts. They rebounded off the shifting wall, ripping their fingers and feet free of the grasp of the vines, and kept running.

Fresh air kissed his face. With renewed energy, he sprinted toward it, right on Roman's heels—

And finally, they were out.

He blinked in disbelief as he thumped to a slower pace—as the darkness abruptly lightened, turning from pitch black to dark gray.

"Holy shit," Darien breathed, squeezing his eyes open and shut. He could see.

He could finally *see*.

Roman let out a sob that echoed, his legs visibly shaking in relief.

They'd made it. They were still far from the surface—from safety. But they'd made it this far. That had to count for something.

But fuck, was he ready to drop. His lungs were begging for oxygen, his mouth metallic from all the running. He allowed himself a minute to catch his breath, bending to brace his hands on his shaking knees. Roman did the same beside him, his legs still wobbling, too. They both needed the break. They'd been on the move for hours. Without rest. Without food or drink.

And they had no Venom left.

Roman gave him a little smile, strands of dark, sweat-damp hair hanging in his face. "Close one, hey?"

"Close one," Darien agreed, still panting. Still exhausted as hell. He rallied his strength—his will—and shoved off his knees.

They were in a cavern that was even bigger than the Basilisk's habitat. In the center of the space, tumbling down out of nowhere, was a giant waterfall, the rapids emptying into a deep pit.

Darien stepped up to the edge, tipping his head back to glimpse the top of the roaring falls.

The overspray was refreshing. He shut his eyes, beads of water pattering against his tired, filthy face like rain. The sound reminded him of the ambient videos his mom used to put on to help him fall asleep. Rain and ocean waves were her favorite. His, too.

He opened his eyes to the scuff of Roman's boots as he walked over to join him.

"Think that's coming from Spirit Terra?" Roman asked. He squinted up at the raging torrent, his pulse still thrumming in his neck.

Darien swiped the water off his face. "I'd bet money on it. Which means *that*—"He pointed at the pit looming near the toes of his boots. "—

could lead there too." If they fell in there, who knew where they'd end up. Somewhere in the Void, probably. Which would suck.

They skirted the pit so they could see past the wide waterfall—to the other side of the cavern. There was another tunnel over there—just one—but it was stuffed with shadows from the Void.

"That doesn't look inviting," Roman said, his mouth quirking with dark humor.

"No, it doesn't," Darien agreed. "But we're fresh out of options."

"Dark, foreboding tunnel...," Roman mused, weighing option one on his left hand, "or Spirit Terra." He weighed option two on his right.

Darien pursed his lips in thought. "Is it bad if I want to say neither?"

Roman was about to reply when claws scraped against stone.

"Shit," Roman muttered as they whipped around. "We've got company."

Monsters were pouring out of the tunnel in droves. While some crawled on the walls and ceiling, others stalked forward on all fours—snapping at the air in a show of claim.

Darien lifted the sword with a steady hand. He took up a defensive stance, one foot behind the other, Roman guarding his back.

"Any ideas?" his cousin asked him.

If they ran, they would be chased. But if they fought... They were outnumbered. And they were already surrounded—backed against the pit with nowhere to go.

Like it or not, they would have to fight their way out of this.

Flecks of half-frozen water pelted their backs, dense clouds of vapor fogging the area.

"Focus on the ones on your side," Darien instructed, his words nearly swallowed up by the crashing of the falls. He tried to rally his magic, but all he got was a cooling ember. If he ran out of power, he'd have to use the sword—not ideal, given the state of his right hand. Still, he said, "I'll handle the ones on mine."

"Copy."

The air stirred with a warning, and Darien readied to meet it.

A blur to his left.

Another to Roman's right.

And with a blink that turned his eyes black, Darien let his own monster off the leash.

3

NORTH FINANCIAL DISTRICT
YVESWICH, STATE OF KER

Maximus Reacher awoke to the sound of screaming.

He opened his eyes to a blur of darkness and firelight. He lay sprawled across the ground, his blood-soaked cheek stuck to rock. Where he was, he didn't know. A tunnel, maybe. Or a cave. It was too smoky to tell. But if there was one thing he knew for certain, it was that he should be dead.

He should be dead.

The screams were coming from a female hellseher. She knelt close by, her body all fire, her glowing hands digging through piles of rubble.

The names she was calling out were...strange. They weren't names, he realized—at least, not common ones. They were colors.

"Magenta!" she wailed. "Gold! VIOLET! SAAAAAAGE! Answer me!"

The shouting continued. Magenta. Gold. Violet. Sage.

Max tried to sit up, but he couldn't move. Couldn't feel his body. He could hardly even twitch his fingertips. An otherworldly darkness oozed through the area, spreading like an infection. It felt...alive. Unconquerable, even by firelight.

Passed out on the ground beside him, on stone hot to the touch, was a witch with red hair. A pair of magnificent white wings were fanned out at her sides, more than half of the feathers singed to a crisp.

The witch was bleeding—drip, drip, drip. Max watched the hypnotic drip of blood from her dainty, freckled nose, his eyelids opening and closing with heavy blinks. Drip, drip, drip.

Blink, blink, blink.

Shit, that was Dallas. Dallas was hurt.

He peeled his face off the stone, his pulse lurching into a sprint that sent bolts of pain shooting through his chest, as if Obitus himself still had his deathly claws in his heart. Wringing out what was left of his lifeblood.

The fiery one was still screaming. Screaming and sobbing, flames and sparks bursting from her body with each heart-wrenching cry.

That was Maya he was looking at. Maya 'MJ' Reacher, burning from head to toes, just like in Max's terrible nightmares. Only now, she was alive. And those flames? They were a part of her. Controlled by her.

All of the Elementals were dead. Crushed by rubble or incinerated by the blast, no suits to save them. All except Maya, who Max had hurled himself at with a hellseher's speed, pulling Dallas along with him. He'd shielded them both with his body, his suit taking the brunt of the explosion.

Every Elemental, except Maya—dead.

And the pink one, he realized. By some miracle, the one with the hot-pink braid had made it, too—injured but still breathing.

"Magenta," Maya croaked. She dug the Elemental out of the rubble, where the rest of their friends lay in crushed pieces. She hooked her arms under Magenta's shoulders and tugged her across the ground. Sat down and cradled her head in her lap. "Stay with me," she was saying, her tone frantic. Pleading. "Magenta, stay with me." Magenta was young—fourteen, at most. A child still.

With a grunt of pain, he pushed himself onto his hands and knees, a thick line of blood streaming out of his mouth like paint. His vision shimmered, the ground beneath him going in and out of focus.

It cost him the last of his strength, but he got to his feet. Swayed—

"Max!" Maya shouted. Her voice echoed, over and over again. She eased Magenta's head onto the ground, preparing to stand. "MAX!"

The ground tipped. Maya shot to her feet just as Max fell—

"MAX," Dallas said, shaking his shoulder.

Max blinked the memory away.

They were out of the tunnels—walking the streets of Yveswich. It had taken them hours of blind stumbling, but they'd finally made it out of the dark shroud that was swallowing the metropolis like a monster's mouth.

This section of the city seemed to have not been hit as badly by the

Void, the street dark but still visible. How, Max had no clue. The sky was pitch black, the sun nowhere to be found, but if Max was calculating correctly, it had to be nearly midday.

Just ahead limped Maya and Magenta, conversing in Ilevyn. The pink Elemental's arm was slung across MJ's shoulders, her skin marbled with bruises. In the time in which their group had staggered through the streets, those two hadn't said a word to anyone but each other.

Max was still trying to decide how to feel about that.

"You okay?" Dallas asked, stepping into Max's vision. For a moment, he saw two of her, then three, her head haloed by a streetlight. He was still deaf in one ear, the other ringing. He wondered if the damage was permanent.

"I'm fine," he said, his voice sounding lopsided. "Just trying to figure out where we are." And how long he'd been out of it for.

Up ahead, the streets were packed with people. Cops, paramedics, firefighters, and ordinary citizens were everywhere, many of the latter injured and hysterical with fear. LED street-lamps lined the roads, white pooling across asphalt, and red and blue light bars flashed atop dozens of ambulances, fire trucks, and police cruisers. The lights were behaving...strangely. As if they were covered by a thick haze of fog or smoke, and constantly in danger of guttering out like flames.

"Look there," Dallas said, pointing out a street sign. "North Financial District. That's not far from Roman's house, right?" She turned to him with eyes bright with hope, her copper ponytail catching on a warped wing.

He sighed. "I don't know, Dal." There were many things he didn't know anymore—things he wasn't sure he even *wanted* to know. Such as where his family and friends were—which of them were alive...and which were dead. He didn't think he could stomach it—seeing them if they were... gone. Nothing left of them but corpses. Burying the people he loved was something he hoped he never had to do. He'd rather *they* bury *him*.

"It's going to be okay, Max," Dallas said. But her voice cracked when she said his name, her chin shaking. "It *has* to be."

He cupped her face with a filthy hand. "It will," he told her. Because it was what she needed to hear, even if it ended up not being true.

Max prayed that it would be—prayed to every deity of the Terran pantheon. If the others were dead... If he was the only survivor...

Gods, he couldn't do it—*life*. He couldn't live without them, couldn't imagine a world without the other Devils.

As they limped down the crowded street, Max must've scanned nearly a hundred faces. People did the same to him, as they, too, searched for loved ones. Some sat on curbs, sipping hot chocolate or tea from paper cups, thermal blankets wrapped around them. Others had their vitals checked in ambulances, while the less fortunate were wheeled away on stretchers.

There were people from all walks of life here—vampires, werewolves, veneficae, humans, hellsehers. There was no division on a day like this. Today, they were just people, all of them in need. Funny how the walls came down when it felt like the world was ending.

Still no sign of anyone they knew. Max couldn't decide if that was a good thing.

His ears started shrieking again. Blood rushed through his head, weighing it down. Roaring like a great flood of water.

Something wet dribbled down his lips. His chin. He cursed, pressing a fist over his nostrils to stop the bleeding.

Dallas reached out to steady him. "You okay?"

"Yeah, just another nosebleed." He tipped his head back, blood trickling down his throat. "Maya!" he called. She was about a dozen paces away now, but she turned. "Hold up, I need a sec."

"We can sit and rest for a bit," Dallas offered.

He shook his head. "We have to find the others." He wiped his nose on a clean part of his sleeve—the waffle shirt peeking through the rips in his black armor. "I'm fine—bleeding's already stopped."

Dallas suddenly turned. "Did you hear that?"

"Hear what?" He scanned the crowds. "I'm still deaf in one ear."

But then he heard it, too. It was faint, but... It was a voice—calling his name. Not one voice, but several.

Three.

He pushed back down the street, his heart jumping up his throat.

Was he hallucinating?

No—no, he wasn't, because he heard it again, and he knew in his heart that it was real.

"Max!"

He staggered forward, not believing his eyes.

A tall, black-haired female was heading this way. An even taller male kept pace beside her, his short hair dark. Their eyes were an identical shade of almost-grey blue. The third in their trio was platinum blonde, her figure statuesque, her narrow face worthy of runways.

His family. Not all of it, no—but part of the whole.

"Max?" called the dark-haired female. That was Ivy—it really *was* her, shouting his name. She grinned upon confirming it was him, moving faster now through the crowds. Tears sparkled on her face, visible even from way over here. *"Max!"*

His heart stumbled. Pounded all throughout his body. "Ivy?"

"Max!" This voice was male. The voice of a friend—a brother not by blood but history.

"Travis!" Max pushed himself faster, still dizzy but not wanting to slow down, *needing* to get to them. The ground seemed to rise and fall as if it were breathing, creating the illusion of running on ocean waves.

"Max!"

Max was full-on sprinting now, sobs tearing apart his lungs. People dodged him as he ran like a madman. *"Travis! LACEY!"*

Ivy was the first to reach him.

He collided with her, crushing her to him as violent sobs wracked his aching body. He spun her around, weeping into her hair, the weight of not knowing, of wondering all these long hours if they were alive, finally lifting off his shoulders, leaving him weak with relief. They were talking over each other, Ivy sobbing too, and then Lace and Travis were there with them, throwing their arms around them. Squeezing tight.

For a minute, Max's world paused, and it was just *them*—the people he loved, clinging to each other in the flashing lights of a ruined city.

"Oh gods," Travis was saying, his voice a crackle of emotion. "Gods, we thought you were dead! We thought you were *dead*, Max—"

"Same," Max said, pulling Travis close. Pulling them *all* close. "I'm never letting go of you idiots."

"What happened to you guys?" Ivy sobbed. Fresh tears fell from her eyes, clearing tracks in her dirty cheeks. She rubbed them dry with the back of a hand, smearing filth. "Are you okay?" She sniffled. "You're bleeding."

"I'm fine—it's just a nosebleed."

Lace cut in, "Where were you? We've been looking for you for hours."

"We were underground when the explosion happened," Max replied. "We took a tunnel that brought us out—just south." He pointed. "We ended up here." He scanned the street they'd turned into an emergency medical site. "We got lucky."

Dallas had come over to join them, but she was looking beyond—for Loren, no doubt.

"Dallas," Ivy called softly. "Are you okay?"

Dallas hid the disappointment on her face like a pro; she'd always been good at that. "Like Max said," she began, forcing a smile, "we got lucky. My wings are fried, though." She peeked over her shoulder—at the burnt feathers, the wires and framing exposed—and sighed. "What about you?"

"Where are the others?" Max added.

"We were at the tar pits when it happened," Ivy said. "We were driving back to Roman's, but we decided to come here first to try and find you guys." Driving—that meant Darien's truck had survived.

"Kylar and Asp are with Jewels," Travis said, indicating to an ambulance parked by a streetlight. He then pointed at a different ambulance a short distance away. "Jack's there."

Max blinked. "Wait—*Jack's* here?"

"Has anyone had any contact with Darien?" Lace asked.

"I was about to ask *you* the same thing," Max said. "How did Jack get here? What about Tanner? Roman?" He braced himself for bad news, his stomach dropping through his feet. "Where are they?"

They glanced amongst each other. Max's heart beat faster, pounding in his temples, his back breaking out in a cold, prickly sweat.

With reluctance, Lace said, "We haven't heard from them."

"What did Jack say?" Max demanded.

A pause. Then Travis said, "Paramedics found him in Ardesia. In some neighborhood *past* Roman's house. Like, way the fuck *east.*"

Max gaped. How the hell had Jack wound up way over there? He didn't know Yveswich very well, but...Roman's house was pretty damn far away from Caliginous on Silverway. He knew that much.

"He's still out of it," Lace added. "He isn't talking much." She slid her phone out of a slot in her weapons belt and clicked the button on the side. The screen came on, the soft glow illuminating the striking planes of her face. "Phones are still fucked." She sighed. "I haven't been able to get a bar since this happened. No messages have come through since the emergency broadcast."

"Is that...?" Ivy began, trailing off, her eyes fixating on something behind Max.

Max turned.

Maya and Magenta lingered just down the street. While Maya blended in with a more natural look, Magenta's pink eyes, pink freckles, and pink hair stuck out like a sore thumb.

"I found Maya," Max confirmed. "Right when the bomb went off—go figure." He tried to smile, but it felt more like a grimace, his teeth caked with blood and grit.

"Does she remember you?" Ivy whispered.

Max sighed through his nose. "To tell you the truth, we haven't talked much. She's quieter than I remember." More like closed off, unavailable—and not seeming to want to change that.

Time—she just needed time or something. Max could handle that.

"Can't really blame her, though," Dallas said, shrugging. "Pretty much all her friends died in the tunnels."

Lace's eyes flared. "No way. The Elementals?"

"The pink one's the only survivor," Max said. "Magenta's her name—fake name, whatever. She hasn't said a word to me. Three others were with them—they all died." He scanned the parked ambulances, countless people bustling around. "Where'd you say Jacky was?"

"Over here," Ivy said. "Follow me."

She led the way, weaving around citizens and stepping out of the paths of medical professionals wheeling stretchers. Past the ambulance where Kylar Lavin and Aspen Van Halen waited for Jewels. The purple-haired Reaper was receiving a shot in the arm—likely her near-useless medication for the Tricking.

Jewels gave Travis a little smile as their group passed. She looked like she might throw up, her skin waxy and dotted with sweat, but aside from that and a few bruises, she appeared to be okay.

"How's he doing?" Ivy asked the venefican paramedic tending to Jack. Jack sat on the back step of the ambulance, doors open.

"He has a concussion," the warlock said, zipping his emergency kit shut. He wore the Star of Life on his uniform, along with five symbols that represented each of the species he was qualified to provide care for—an eye for hellsehers, a stave for veneficae, a blood droplet for vampires, a sickle moon for werewolves, and an hourglass for humans. Not very nice, the last one. "He's having trouble remembering what happened between now and about six hours ago. Hellseher healing should speed his recovery time along, but we still recommend plenty of rest, cold compresses, lots of water—the usual."

"I was told you found him in Ardesia?" Max asked.

A nod. "That's correct."

"Was he alone?"

"As far as we could tell."

"No dead bodies?" Max pressed.

The paramedic weighed his response. "A lot of people have died tonight. Even more are injured. If anyone was with him, I wasn't made aware." Kit in hand, he tried to pass.

Max stepped in his way. "Wait—please. I know you're busy, but—did you see anyone else with one of these?" He gestured to the tattoo below the ear that was ringing again. It was suddenly hard to hear his own voice, his ear plugged as if with water.

The warlock's silver-ringed eyes flicked to the horned mark of the Seven Devils. "No."

"You're sure?"

"I'm positive."

"What about Shadowmasters?" Travis intervened. You'd have to be living under a rock to not know the Darkslaying symbols of your hometown, but Travis still described, "A skull on the cheekbone."

"I'm sorry," the man said. "I haven't seen any other Darkslayers tonight."

Max stared blankly at the paramedic, not knowing what he was waiting for—a different outcome, maybe. Some reassurance that Darien and the others were okay. Alive. *Safe.*

The warlock's face softened with compassion. "Feel free to ask around," he said gently. "Maybe someone else has seen your friends."

Max felt like he was outside of his body, but he managed to say, "Thank you." He gazed at the ambulance, his vision fuzzing over.

The warlock nodded in farewell. "Take care." He took his leave.

Max drew a deep breath, forcing himself to keep a level head. No bodies was a good thing.

Hopefully.

"Hey, Jack," Max said.

"Hey." The word was a gruff mumble. He looked dazed. His brow was cut, a ring of bruises around it. A layer of salve that smelled strongly of herbs shone on the wound. Thanks to his hellseher genetics, the bruises were already fading to green and yellow.

"How you feeling?"

"Like ass." He grimaced. "My mouth tastes like it, too." He reached for the mini plastic water bottle by his left knee, missing once. He twisted the cap off and swigged, water dribbling down his chin.

"Listen, Jack," Max began, stepping closer. "I know you've got a concussion and all, but do you have any idea where Darien is? Tanner? Roman? No one's heard from them. I'm starting to get worried."

Jack frowned. "You heard the guy—I can't remember shit." He took another swig, swishing the water around in his mouth before swallowing.

Lace pressed, "What's the last thing you remember?"

"Guys," Ivy warned. "Take it easy."

But Jack said, "Darien killed the Basilisk." He squinted up at them, using the near-empty water bottle to shield his eyes against flashing lights.

Max felt a jolt of surprise. "I'm sorry—Darien did *what?*"

Travis whispered, "We might have to fact check that one."

Jack merely stared into space, uncharacteristically serious. Whenever Jack didn't smile, he looked like a complete stranger.

Ivy squeezed her husband's shoulder in encouragement. "Let's give him some time." Her tone, although pleasant, said it all: case closed. "This has been one crazy night." She turned to stare at the busy street, her face lined with stress. "Or day—kind of hard to tell." She frowned at the chaos going on around them, the city still dark as if it were midnight.

"It's almost noon," Lace said. Well, that answered Max's next question.

Ivy suddenly paled, her heart speeding up. "Shit." She whipped back around. "Shit, shit, *shit.*"

"What?" Travis murmured.

Max began to turn, wondering what had spooked Ivy so badly—

Ivy stopped him with a hand gripping his arm. *"Don't turn around."*

"What's going on?"

"Shadowmasters," she hissed. "Right behind us."

Max caught the eye of Kylar just down the way—near that other ambulance, his face hidden under a blanket he was using as a hood. His eyes were bolted wide; he'd clearly spotted the Shadowmasters, too.

Ivy shifted, putting herself directly in front of Jack—using her body to block him from view. "Nobody move," she whispered.

The voices of several Shadowmasters came into hearing range as they greeted each other on the busy road.

"Any sign of them?" Male. Brusque. Vaguely familiar.

"No." Another male—a voice Max didn't recognize.

"You checked the house?" This question came from a female. Also familiar.

"That's the first place we went. No one was there but some old dude. Pax's aura has completely disappeared."

"Maybe he's dead," said a deeper voice, his words coated with sick hope.

Max became aware of the sound of Travis's heart—thumping with pure rage. His aura had sharpened; Max knew that if he could've seen it, it would have been a deep scarlet-black with stark edges.

Max placed a hand on Trav's shoulder—a gesture intended not only to comfort, but to also warn. Restrain. If Travis let his aura get out of control, there was a chance the Shadowmasters would pick up on it. Even with the Avertera talisman glimmering in the hollow of his throat—glimmering around *all* of their throats—the risk was too great. The Shadowmasters might not be able to *see* their auras, but that didn't mean they couldn't feel them, couldn't detect shifts in emotion if they were strong enough to set off warning bells.

And rage tended to ring a very loud bell.

"Let's split up again," said the first male. "You guys check his school, we'll try the theater. No one rests until we find Paxton. Clear?"

"Clear."

"Meet us at the House of Black in two hours."

They'd checked the house—*Roman's* house. They had to mean Roman's. The very place where Paxton *should* be. There was a chance he'd escaped, maybe—left town with Loren, Malakai, and the others...

But the Shadowmasters had said that no one was at the house except *'some old dude'*. Arthur, no doubt. And if Arthur was still here, there was no way the others had left him behind—a defenseless man in his seventies, who'd done countless favors for them, left to die in a destroyed city. No chance. So—

If they hadn't escaped... If they were still in Yveswich...

Then where the hell *were* they? And what did that mean for Arthur and the others?

"Those assholes are looking for my little brother," Travis said, his voice as lethal as the glare he threw over his shoulder at the departing Shadowmasters. Blaine and Larina Barlowe were among them—the voices Max had recognized from the night Don and his people intruded on Roman's property, dragging him off to the House of Black.

"We have to find him," Max said, his pulse shifting into a determined drumbeat. "Before they do."

4

UNDERGROUND
YVESWICH, STATE OF KER

Even without the aid of Venom, his fatigued body ready to collapse, Darien's dark power was a force to be reckoned with.

Lethal waves of his magic smashed like battering rams into the hordes of beasts trapping him and Roman against the pit. Heads were blasted off in sprays of blood. Bodies were launched into walls at lightning speed, necks and spines snapping on impact.

But it still wasn't enough, because the monsters...

They just kept coming.

A winged creature dropped down on them from above.

"Watch out!" Roman shouted.

Darien stabbed the sword straight up, skewering the monster through the throat in midair. It slid all the way down to the hilt, smearing the blade with bubbling black blood.

With a battle cry, he flung the corpse off, hurtling it into two more demons. He barely had time to recover before a second monster was dive-bombing for his throat.

He ducked and angled his wrist, blade tilted upward. The beast sawed its own belly open on the sword as it leapt clear over his head. It fell into the pit with a keening yowl, claws scrabbling against rock on its way down.

Another dropped on Roman's side, but the thing was swiftly pulled apart by a whirlwind of the Shadowmaster's magic. Wings were torn to shreds, joints ripping out of sockets with wet *pops*.

Two more attacked in unison. Darien gutted the one while Roman reached with blinding speed for the knife at his thigh. He flicked his wrist back and threw.

The blade pierced its forehead—no stone in this one. It slammed into the ground and slid in a smear of blood, Roman dodging it as it tumbled by.

Roman was about to say something when he suddenly fell, as if a rug had been pulled out from under his feet. He landed on his back with a *bang* —missing the pit by mere inches.

"What the fuck!" He kicked his left foot, his ankle ensnared with one of those vines from the tunnel. More vines were lashing out, snatching monsters by the leg or wing and dragging them, screaming, into the tunnel. *"Cut it!"* Roman thundered. *"Quick—cut it off!"*

Darien swung the sword—

It struck rock, sparking, as Roman was sucked into the throng of monsters at blinding speed.

Darien's blood went cold. *"Roman!"* He made to run after him—

Something heavy smacked into his side. The sword slipped out of his hand as sharp teeth clamped onto his forearm, sinking in deep.

He shouted out in pain, his vision going starry as blood gushed out of the wound. The wolflike beast hung on like the jaws of a bear trap— mauling the skin and muscle. He whipped the creature back and forth, working his free hand between its jaws to pry them open—to no avail.

"Get off!" Darien kicked it in the chest. Once. Twice. A third time —*harder.*

It let go with a yelp and plummeted into the pit, its chilling keen echoing long after its body had been swallowed by clouds of mist.

He doubled over, panting through his teeth, his arm cradled against his chest. More blood dribbled to the stone, the wound burning as if it were being eaten by acid.

Focus. He had to focus, had to find Roman. There was no time to waste on bleeding.

His ears were roaring, his head featherlight as he stumbled over to the blade. Forced himself to pick it up, to straighten, but—

Pain stabbed through his arm like a branding iron. He choked out a grunt of agony, his heart pounding so hard he thought he might throw up.

Shit. *Shit.* This was bad—

Suddenly, everything felt far away. Fuzzy. A distant, untouchable dream.

He staggered to one side, the roaring in his ears shifting into a piercing, buzzing scream. The dozens of bloodthirsty creatures packed inside the cavern shimmered. Blurred together into shapeless smears.

He shook his head—once, twice.

Demons that looked like Ignis's wild dogs advanced on him, their maws dripping saliva.

He swung the sword, nearly falling over from the momentum. Staggered like he was drunk.

'Bandit,' Darien tried. His inner voice echoed—again and again.

No response, but...Darien could sense him—a smoky flame taking the vague shape of a dog. He lay in the shadows of Darien's mind, too drained to come out, to speak.

Another two monsters launched themselves at him in a blur of mottled flesh, their eyes feverish with hunger.

Darien punched the sword through their guts, then bisected another, and it crumpled in twitching halves at his boots. Several fled from his wrath, making a beeline for the farthest tunnel with their tails between their legs.

He whipped around, scanning the area. His vision was still warped and muzzy, his ears whirring.

Roman. He had to get to Roman.

But where the hell was he?

"Fuck."

On clumsy feet, he trudged through the cavern—through the thick of the flesh-hungry monsters. He could barely see through the mental haze, but he didn't let this stop him. He chopped his way through, hacking apart anything that moved. Duck, stab, slash. He was soaked in gore, his hair dripping with water and sour-smelling blood. There were teeth everywhere —teeth and claws and leathery wings and eyes straight out of hell.

"Romaaaaaaan!" he called, every breath a labored pant. Blood trickled down his arm and dripped off his fingers, leaving a trail of red everywhere he went. *"ROMAN!—"*

"Darien!"

Relief hit him with the force of a truck. "Oh thank gods." He spun in circles, searching for Roman with fierce blinks, his star-flecked vision pulsing to the rapid thumping of his heart. *"Where are you?"*

"Over here!"

Darien plowed on, moving clumsily through the carnage. Following the sound of Roman's voice—

There. There was Roman, crouching on the ground a few feet away. He was surrounded by barking beasts that paced restlessly from side to side, his only means of protection a flickering barrier of shadow as he fought to wrest his foot free from the vine.

"Darien, get this thing off me—I don't have a knife!—"

The vine suddenly whipped upward, pulling Roman into the air. The movement was so swift it caused him to fall backward, the back of his head smacking against the ground.

Darien dove, grabbing onto Roman's outstretched hand with his broken one. "Hold on!" he gritted out. "Hold on, I got you—"

"Don't you dare let go!"

"I'm not fucking letting go!"

But the vine wasn't letting go either, and to Darien's horror, his boots began to slide across the ground as it pulled and *pulled* on Roman. His hand burned, his arm still leaking blood.

The creatures pushed closer, barking and snapping.

"Stay back!" The air whistled as Darien cut it apart with his sword. To Roman, he shouted, *"Shoot it!"* He pulled as hard as he could, gaining two meters, the vine stretching taut as Roman wrestled a handgun from his weapons belt. "You have to shoot it—I can't reach it from here!"

An inhuman scream shook the cavern. It was so loud, it vibrated Darien's eardrums, making him holler in pain.

Roman screamed too, nearly letting go. All around them, monsters yawped and hissed, pawing at their ears and bowing their heads to the ground in agony.

Darien's eyes watered, his attention snapping to the tunnel.

Writhing vines framed the entrance like thick worms, a few lashing out to grab more prey. Inside the tunnel, monsters cried as they were devoured —as whatever that *thing* was crushed their bones into powder. As it *ate* them.

His boots skidded with another yank, the immense force behind the action causing his upper body to snap forward. *"Shoot it, Roman!"* He pulled, gaining a meter back, then dug his heels in with a grunt as he was again tugged back the other way. *"Shoot it!"*

The air was cleaved by another deafening roar. Darien tucked his head against a shoulder, jaw clenching tight as the sound shot like a missile into his ears. Worse was the red-hot pain blistering through his hand, the bones threatening to splinter in all the places that were still healing.

He could barely breathe, barely think, but he managed to bellow, *"Shoot the fucking thing!"*

"I'M TRYING!" Roman roared as he took aim. His face was flushed from hanging upside down, his body constantly wobbling in midair like an elastic band.

He fired the first shot from his handgun, missing by millimeters.

A demon that looked like a wolf dove for Darien's throat.

He swept the blade up. Unable to balance himself properly, he carved its arm off instead of its head, pulpy blood showering his face.

Roman fired a second round. Missed *again*.

"Come on, man—I thought you were a good shot!"

"I AM!"

He pulled the trigger again. The bullet hit the side of the vine, its insides wriggling like maggots.

The cavern shook with another howl, shards of rock clacking down and bursting into dust. One struck Darien between the brows, splitting his skin open. Blood trickled between his eyes, streaming down the bridge of his nose, his lips. Monsters yelped as they, too, were struck with bits of rock. A few fled the scene, while others were so disoriented they banged into each other and tumbled into the pit.

The vine began to thrash. Back and forth, back and forth, dragging them from side to side. Darien squeezed Roman's hand as tightly as he could, biting back the pain as he was whipped about like a rag doll, boots thumping and sliding. More vines reared up and dove for him, but the moment he swung the sword they screamed and cowered away from it, as if afraid.

"Hold on!" Darien shouted, his grip slippery with blood. The few remaining monsters chomped at the air, leaping for Roman's sides. "Hold on, don't let go—"

Brutal claws caught Roman in the hip. The Shadowmaster barked a profanity.

Darien kicked the thing in the skull, sending it sprawling with a yelp.

His hold on Roman began to slip, the pain in his hand getting worse—

"Fuck—my *hand, Roman!"* His vision went white. His boots slid another meter as the vine gave up thrashing, pulling again toward the tunnel.

Darien feared he was going to let go. He was going to let go, and if he did, he'd lose Roman forever.

"My hand!"

"I know, I know! *Just hold on—"*

He was going to faint. Throw up. Stop breathing.

Roman kept firing, shots popping through the cavern.

A bullet hit stone—bursting a chunk into dust.

Another sliced through a monster's neck, ripping through an artery with a squirt of blood.

"Let," Roman spat, firing another shot, "*the fuck,*" another, "*GO!*"

One shot—he had *one* round left.

Roman squeezed the trigger—*POP.* Darien held his breath as the bullet sped out of the muzzle in a silver blur.

It sliced into the vine, spraying brown sticky liquid.

Another mind-rattling scream.

Darien let out a mighty roar of his own, of triumph and rage, pulling as hard as he could—

The vine let go, retreating toward the tunnel with an eldritch screech.

Roman fell—crashing right into Darien.

Their limbs tangled as they were launched backward, Darien taking an elbow to the jaw, feet tripping over creatures that hissed and scattered.

He felt the heel of his boot teeter on an edge. But he didn't have time to shout out a warning before gravity was sucking him backward.

He took Roman down with him as he fell. Into open air—

Straight into the pit.

5

THE IN-BETWEEN

Darien braced himself for impact, but it never came.

Instead, he and Roman were airborne—caught in a vortex of wind and water, lightning flashing without pause.

Darien tried to reach for Roman, but he couldn't control his limbs. He couldn't feel his body, his face. Couldn't even *scream*.

A rush of shadow came out of nowhere, and suddenly everything went dark. Quiet. A womb full of nothing.

This is it, Darien thought, preparing for the worst. All he could hear, all he could feel, was his heartbeat. Nothing else existed.

But then—

In the space of one dizzying second, he was launched back to life, a flood of freezing liquid crashing around him as he came to at the base of a waterfall, banging his knees against mossy rocks.

He staggered away from the cascade with a ragged inhale. Roman appeared a moment later, spitting up a mouthful of water as he half-crawled, half-walked away from the tiered falls, the pond shallow enough to stand in.

Darien's head whirled as he tried to make sense of where they were—of what the hell just happened.

The first conclusion he drew was that this wasn't Spirit Terra. He could still breathe, still see... If they'd traveled to the Void, not only would they have stopped breathing instantly, but they also wouldn't have been able to see. That was promising.

"Roman," Darien panted as his cousin sloshed up to his side. The black sword slipped from Darien's hand, dropping into the pool with a *plash*. He braced his hands on his knees, coughing so hard his chest burned, his eyes flooding with tears that dripped off his cheeks. "You alright?" This pond they were in was manmade—dug into the ground by landscapers, the small waterfall behind them also manmade.

"I think...," Roman gritted out, clutching his gut, "I'm going to be sick." He barely got the last word out before he was scrambling up the muddy bank and throwing up the meager contents of his stomach.

Darien stood there awhile in the water. Bleeding and shaking from the cold. He wasn't as dizzy as before, his stomach settling, but his arm still hurt like a son of a bitch.

"You going to live?" he called to Roman, his breaths puffing in the air. He bent to pick up the sword and briefly dipped his other hand in too, the bitter temperature numbing the pain.

Roman coughed and spat. Once. Twice. "We'll see," he panted. His face was pallid, his eyes red from hours of trying to see in the dark. He shoved off his knees, tipping his head back to look at the sky. Murmured, "Holy shit," and walked out onto a paved road.

Darien splashed up the bank and followed him in sopping boots, suit dripping.

They stood side by side, taking in their surroundings in disbelief.

Holy shit was right.

Yveswich was under siege. The Void was devouring the city in a colossal wave of thick, pitch black shadow. It ballooned up toward the darkened sky and just kept going, spreading in every direction. Thunder rumbled and cracked, and way off in the distance, in other parts of the city, helicopters flew. Looking for survivors, no doubt.

Although the sky was entirely dark, that massive cloud slowly suffocating everything it touched, this place where they stood...it was lighter here. Not daylight, but half-light, like the sky just before dawn.

They were in a residential area. A treed street with a dog park and perfectly constructed waterfalls.

Now that they were above ground, Darien felt hope swell in his chest. Out here, they stood a greater chance at finding the others. Out here, he felt like he actually had a shot at getting out of this city and back to the woman he loved.

I'm coming, baby, Darien thought, wishing Loren—wherever she was—could hear him. *I'm coming. Hold on.*

Darien swept the icy beads off his numb face. "What does that say?" He gestured to a street sign with a throbbing, shaking hand.

Roman squinted. "Larkin Street." His brow creased, gold eyes meeting Darien's. "We're in East Montgomery. South of the Control Tower."

Darien didn't doubt his cousin—not when Roman knew the city as well as Darien knew Angelthene. But—

"That makes no sense," he said.

He turned to look at the waterfall rushing at their backs, his face smoothing in shock. "No way," he whispered.

Roman's brow furrowed. "What?"

"Tamika...she was right."

"Who's Tamika?"

"The waterfalls...," he murmured, gesturing for Roman to hold on as he thought it through—as he pieced the puzzle together. As he remembered Tamika's words as if she'd said them just yesterday.

'Back in old times, people used to visit the Crossroads to speak to loved ones who had passed away. They would go on the shortest night of the year, when the divide between our world and the spirit realm is rumored to be at its thinnest. If a Crossroads wasn't handy, a person could seek out a weak spot by going to a place of heavy darkness, or perhaps an area where elements meet with constant movement, such as waterfalls.'

Waterfalls. Places of constant movement.

Holy shit.

Darien had believed the waterfall in the cavern would take them to Spirit Terra, but—

But maybe they didn't *just* lead to the spirit realm. Maybe...maybe, now that the Veil was falling, they led to other places, too. A glitch in the fabric of the universe.

His eyes snapped to Roman's confused face. "The waterfalls," he said again. "They're *portals.*"

6

BLACKSTONE ALLEY
ANGELTHENE, STATE OF WITHEREDGE

Sabrine Van Arsdell crept across the living room, taking care not to wake the man dozing in the recliner. The bottoms of his socks were blackened with filth, his weather-beaten face peppered with stubble. Scattered around the chair were empty beer cans, cigarette packets, and oily takeout bags that had probably been there for days. Weeks, even.

He was Claude Van Arsdell, and he was her father. A drunk, a layabout, an abuser...and the reason Sabrine never bothered to come home anymore.

Home. Is that what this place was? She glanced around, her stomach twisting into knots at the sight of this stinking pigsty she'd finally managed to escape last fall. This was still her legal residence, but she had no plans to return here again, unless it was to collect her mail. Hopefully *that* would be changing too, once she packed up the last of her belongings—which, if all went according to plan, would be happening right now.

As she tiptoed across the living room, feet sinking in the soiled carpet, her sharp wolf hearing picked up on the voices drifting quietly through the television speakers. The news channel was on. All morning, the anchors had been covering what they knew of the incident in Yveswich, which wasn't much. A power and spell outage, they were calling it. An outage so bad it was record-breaking, shutting down every power and magic grid in the city—no spells, no alarm systems, and no lights, an equation that always equaled disaster.

Sabrine had a feeling it was worse than an outage. In the hours that had passed since the first report, she had tried calling her friends who were in

Yveswich, but no one had answered. Not Dallas, not Max, not Loren. For all she knew, the latter might still be in a coma, but she had phoned her anyway, just in case. She had even tried Darien, but her only response was a beeping line. No power, no service—just like the news channels said.

But there were two big things about the reports that didn't sit right with her.

Thing number one: The first, unedited video clips—the clips that had shown multiple cameras in Yveswich being swallowed by a blast of darkness —were no longer being aired, as if someone had ordered them taken down.

Thing number two: The reporters were claiming that every power grid in Ker's capital had gone out. If that were even remotely true, the cameras should have stopped working the moment that strange, sinister cloud of darkness hit. Instead, they had remained on, broadcasting the most disturbing, spine-chilling sounds Sabrine had ever heard.

Someone was trying to cover up the truth. And there was only one person in Terra who had the kind of power and influence to do it quickly.

The imperator. The man who'd run off to Yveswich with the blueprints for the replica of the Arcanum Well. The man who'd relentlessly made their lives a living hell for over half a year.

With most of her friends in Yveswich, there weren't many people left in Angelthene who Sabrine could talk to. People she could trust. But there *was* one person...someone well versed in Spirit Terra and Yveswich's dark history. Someone Sabrine planned on visiting within the hour.

But—one step at a time. *Literally.*

She hurried into her bedroom, leaving the door slightly ajar.

The tiny space hadn't changed since she'd last seen it, though it was messier than before—that was a given. Dresser drawers had been thrown open, closet doors had been ripped off their hinges, and clothes had been strewn across her bed among the contents of her lone jewelry box.

Her father had been in here. Hunting for spare change to fuel his alcohol dependency or help pay the rent. Most months, he barely scrimped by, and now that he no longer had access to the shallow pockets of his only child, Sabrine knew that his life had taken a turn for the worse.

She fought the urge to tidy up the mess and instead got to work, shaking open the tote she'd tucked into her book bag. She moved quickly, filling the bag with photo albums, her favorite vintage books, old school assignments she was still proud of, and memorabilia from her childhood. Anything that held sentimental value to her, she took it, keeping an ear on her father's incessant snoring.

Once the bag was full, she secured the strap to her shoulder and picked through the wreckage on tip-toes.

Glass crunched under her sneaker. She paused, bending to pick up the framed photograph of her, Dallas, and Loren, the picture taken by Taega when they were kids. It was summertime, and they were smiling brightly at the camera, Angelthene's old lighthouse standing stately in the background. Loren was in the middle—the very heart of their friendship. Her hair was saturated with ocean water, that same solar amulet hanging from her neck.

Now that Sabrine knew the necklace had contained a wish that would save them all from death a decade later, she found herself viewing the simple piece of jewelry in a different light. It was strange to think that something so important—something they'd played with when they were children, as if it had no greater value than a plastic toy—had been around Loren's neck all these years, waiting in patient secrecy for her to unlock the wish inside it.

Heart aching with memories gone by, Sabrine flipped the frame over and popped it open. She removed the picture and tucked it into her bag, being careful not to mar it with creases or fingerprints.

"Hell are you doing here?" came a grating voice.

Sabrine's head snapped up, her heart skipping like a stone on water.

Claude pushed into the room, his reedy form staggering into the dresser so hard it rocked. "Thought I told you not to come back here." He scanned the space with bleary eyes, his breath reeking of alcohol and stale cigarettes "You stealing from me? Are you stealing from me, bitch?"

Sabrine's mouth dried out, her palms prickling with sweat. Suddenly, it didn't matter that she was an adult. A werewolf capable of shredding him apart. She was the little girl in the picture again, who spent her days in fear of walking the wrong way, talking the wrong way, *living* the wrong way. Nothing had ever been good enough for him, and nothing ever would be.

Claude moved toward her. "Stealing from your old man?" His graying brows flicked up. "That's low, Sabrine. Real low." He reached for her. "Give me that bag," he rasped.

Not today. This wasn't her life anymore.

With a battle cry, she pushed past him, shoving him into the dresser. He shouted out in anger, the dresser tipping onto its side with a *crash*.

Sabrine bolted toward the kitchen, her bags thumping against her hip.

Glass smashed and wood snapped as her father burst out of the bedroom and raced after her, screaming his lungs out. If he kept up with the hollering, Logan would surely come in here and maul him to death—exactly why she'd instructed the alpha to wait outside and let her deal with her deadbeat dad on her own. She could handle this—she *wanted* to handle this.

Her sneakers squealed as her feet hit the kitchen tile, her speed sending her straight into the counter. Her hip took the brunt of the collision with a bone-deep bruise, the dishes in the cupboards rattling. Claude's footsteps shook the house, his nearness charging the air with a warning.

Sabrine grabbed a knife from the wooden block and spun around, pressing the tip against her father's jugular.

He slid to a stop, rocking back on his heels.

Slowly, he lifted his chin, looking down his nose at her.

Sabrine nudged the tip of the knife against his stubbled throat. "Put your hands on me, you *filth*, and see what happens," she snarled, adding a second hand to the knife to steady it.

He stared at her, stupefied, finally seeing her clearly for the first time.

But then he laughed—a low, wheezing sound. "I was just playing, Sab." His fake smile sank into a sour grimace. "You know that."

The corners of Sabrine's lips twitched upward, and she felt something sharp scrape against the bottom one. "I wasn't," she crooned.

She felt it, then—the Shift. Her body temperature cranked up, her eyes glowing like two small suns. The shaking in her hands…it was not from fear at all, but restraint.

Her wolf wanted to play.

Claude's gaze flicked between her eyes and teeth, her canines elongating into wicked, pearly white points.

"What the hell is this?" His question was hollowed out with surprise. Hollowed out—just like the rest of him. "What's happened to you?"

She sidled toward the door, her bag scraping against the cupboards. "Don't follow me," she instructed. "After today, I never want to see you again, do you understand me? I have no need for you in my life, and if you try to get in touch with me—" She let her teeth show, just a little, and gestured to the knife in her hands. "I've got forty-two of these in my mouth now." Her wolf teeth—all forty-two of them—continued to lengthen, her gums stinging as the extra teeth pierced through and claimed their spots.

Claude merely gaped as Sabrine backed toward the screen door. His daughter was not the same anymore—in more ways than one.

With a backward kick, she opened the door and eased over the threshold, letting it slam shut behind her. She crouched down, her father barely visible through the mesh, and set the knife on the porch.

Then she hurried down the steps and into the street, not looking back —not once.

Logan Sands was waiting for her in his truck, the exhaust stinking up the neighborhood with an old fuel called *diesel*. Sabrine got inside, her skin still flaming hot, and dumped her bags at her feet.

"I take it that didn't go well," Logan said. His long, dark hair blew softly in the breeze coming in through his cracked-open window.

"It went as well as I expected," Sabrine said, barely able to speak as her jaw slowly reset, her teeth shifting back into place.

Logan's brow creased. "Do you want to talk about it?"

"Honestly, I just want to get away from here." She buckled up, her dusky razor-sharp nails scraping the seatbelt. Her cuticles stung, but at least they weren't bleeding this time. A small improvement. "If you'd do us the honors."

Logan put the truck in drive and pulled out onto the narrow street, weaving around trash bins, yard sale tables, and other random junk.

It had taken Sabrine a long time to get used to her new wolf side, and even after several months she still wasn't *quite* there.

There were some days, however, when being a werewolf simply felt *right*. People treated her with far more respect than they had when she was a half-breed—she still hated that horrible slur—and she knew, if she ever ran into danger, her wolf side would gladly handle the things her old self wouldn't have been able to. Werewolves, being strong, fast, and at times unpredictable, were some of the most feared people in Terra. Behind hellsehers, of course. They were in a league of their own.

As they drove north, toward the Victoria Amazonica District, the threat of the Shift began to subside.

She exhaled slowly, the last of her teeth sliding back into their rightful places.

"Better?" Logan asked, rolling up his window. Spring might've arrived in Angelthene, but some days were still cool enough to need a light jacket.

"I don't think I'll be shredding one of your seats today."

He gave her a wistful smile. "I appreciate that."

She grabbed her cell phone out of her book bag.

"Anything?" Logan asked her as she pressed the button on the side.

Sabrine crossed her fingers—

But no messages filled the screen aside from the automated ones from campus. The silence was unsettling. When you had Dallas Bright for a friend, your phone never knew a moment's peace. Sabrine missed her. Loren, too.

"Still nothing." She sighed. "Can we listen to the news?" She put her phone away and flicked on the radio.

The host was covering the incident in Yveswich, but it was the same information they'd been recycling all morning—nothing Sabrine hadn't already heard a dozen times. A city-wide power outage, panicking citizens, the Magical Protections Unit working tirelessly to rectify the issue... She grew frustrated by the idle chatter and shut it off as Logan took the exit that led into the Seven Devils' neighborhood.

Sabrine still couldn't get over how beautiful it was in these parts. While Angelthene had more than its fair share of dangerous and ugly districts, there were also plenty of safe and aesthetically pleasing ones, and Victoria Amazonica fell firmly into the latter two categories. Add a house of Dark-slayers to the mix, and it was probably one of the safest places in the city.

Tamika Isley lived several blocks from Hell's Gate. They'd only visited her residence once, so it took them a few wrong turns before they finally found the right house.

The driveway was long, the house that sat at the end of it so large, it was practically a resort or a small castle—maybe *slightly* smaller than Hell's Gate, Sabrine decided. Hell's Gate was the most impressive house Sabrine had ever set foot in—no contest, not even this one. The Devils had great taste.

Gravel crunched under the tires as Logan pulled over by the gates. Sabrine hopped out, leaving the door open behind her, and rang the buzzer.

A balmy wind drifted through the district, spurring wind chimes into making music. Sabrine's wolf hearing picked up on the chattering of magpies and the scratching of squirrel feet on palm trees.

She rang the buzzer again. Tamika's car was outside, and light glowed in several windows, despite that it was daytime and bright enough outside not to need the extra light.

'Maybe she's in the shower,' said Pebble. The crow flapped out of Sabrine's shadow and alighted on her shoulder, talons curling in the slippery material of her jacket.

"She has a butler, though," Sabrine said, poking the button for a third time. "Maybe it's broken."

'If it is, can we take the button home?' Pebble tipped her head, ogling the button—shiny and red, her favorite color—with one eye at a time.

Sabrine waited another minute before heading back to the truck, the shadows of flying birds darting across the pavement.

"Not home?" Logan asked as she hopped in.

"No one's answering, but that's her car." She pointed.

"Maybe some friends picked her up."

She shut the door. "What about Harold?"

Logan's brow puckered. "Who?"

"Her butler." She chewed her lip. "I think that's his name."

"Butlers have to run errands sometimes, Sab." He eyed her while she stared at the quiet mansion in thought. It was too far away to hear anything, and she saw no movement in the windows. "Try again, if you want," he offered. "Or we can wait and see if anyone comes home."

She buckled up. "No, let's get going. Maybe we'll come back later."

"You sure?"

"Yeah. Let's take a drive by Darien's, though." This would be their third time checking on Hell's Gate since the last of the Devils left town. While wolves lacked the Sight that would show them the otherwise invisible spell systems, what they didn't lack was a sense of smell that would tell them if any lurkers had come by.

They pulled out onto the peaceful, palm-lined street. Not a minute later, the red-brick mansion came into view, the house quiet and empty.

Logan pulled over parallel to the gates.

"Be right back," Sabrine said. She got out and shut the door, the muffled voices filling the truck as Logan flicked the radio back on.

Sabrine switched from her witch senses to canine, as if tuning in to a different radio station. She didn't need to shift to get the job done, but she did need to summon her wolf in spirit to filter through scents.

She began by walking along one side of the gate. Nostrils flared, she sorted through the many different smells, being very thorough. Fresh-cut grass, mellow jasmine, dry earth... Spring blossoms, mulch, week-old paint from the neighbor's house, candle smoke...

Her hair blew back as the wind changed directions. It smelled like...

Blood.

A tremor ran up her spine, her skin quivering.

A short distance away, closer to the neighbor's house than Hell's Gate, a brunette witch lay unconscious in the grass, a tangle of bloody hair obscuring her face.

Sabrine paled. *"Logan!"* She lurched into action, gravel crunching under her sprinting feet. "Call an ambulance! *We need an ambulance!*" She threw herself to her knees beside Tamika in the cool grass.

Logan was there in a flash, phone pressed against his ear. "What happened?"

"I don't know—I just found her like this!"

"Yeah, we need an ambulance," Logan was saying into his phone, his voice tight with urgency.

Tamika's pulse was faint—a mere flutter against Sabrine's fingertips.

"Venefica," Logan said, answering the dispatcher's questions.

"Location?" The voice was muted. Miles away as Sabrine begged Tamika to keep breathing. "Keep breathing, Tamika, keep breathing."

"Victoria Amazonica District." Logan searched frantically for the address, finding the numbers by the gate. "775237."

"What's the emergency?"

Sabrine's head spun at the sight of Tamika's shirt—wet with blood. "Oh gods. Oh gods, Logan, she's been stabbed—"

"Sir?" the dispatcher prompted.

Logan managed to spit out, "There's been an attempted homicide."

7

NORTH FINANCIAL DISTRICT
YVESWICH, STATE OF KER

"I can't believe I let you talk me into this!" Loren hissed.

She stood beside Malakai on the sidewalk as he directed his stream into the darkness. He'd insisted she wait right beside him for her own safety while he relieved himself. But now that this was actually happening, she had never regretted anything more. The fact that she couldn't see him was a small blessing, but as for the sound of his pee splashing on pavement...

That was a sound that would haunt her for the rest of her life.

The Reaper gave a theatrical sigh of satisfaction. "Ahhhhhhhhh." A beat of silence passed. And then: "Want to help me shake it?" he offered, a big grin evident in his tone.

Loren rolled her eyes. "Say *one* more inappropriate thing to me, Malakai, and so help me, I will leave you here by yourself and see how you fare then."

He wheezed a chuckle. "'See how you fare then'," he mimicked in a squeaky voice. "I hate to break it to you, Blondie, but hanging out with Darien has given you *major* tiny dog syndrome."

She arched a brow. "Tiny dog syndrome?"

"It's where a small dog develops this attitude where it thinks it can beat the snot out of anything bigger than it—"

"I know what it means!"

"Watch the tone, Tiny Dog—your Rottweiler's not here to bite for you." His zipper hissed through the quiet, his elbow bumping her arm as he slid his ring back on. He was lucky the magic in the bodysuit still worked enough not to have to manually strip it off.

"Alright then, Eyeglasses," Malakai said, adding yet another nickname to his endless list as he fumbled for her hand in the dark, "lead this old dog home."

"I think I prefer 'Blondie'," Loren muttered, lacing her numb fingers with his. She blinked the white into her eyes and started walking.

They'd made it north of the Avenue of the Waning Moon. The streets were calmer up here—less monsters—but they still hadn't run into any people. Not living ones, anyway. Loren had a feeling there were plenty of dead ones, but unless they were actively being eaten by monsters with detectable auras, their bodies were invisible in the dark.

"Where are we now?" Malakai asked. "Which district?"

She scanned the block, searching for a sign bright enough to read. On the corner of an approaching intersection, there was a business called *North Financial Corner Store*. According to the sign, it was one of those rare places that offered diesel and gasoline as alternative forms of fuel. Not many models took liquid fuel anymore; engines, like most things in Terra, had been modified to run on power from the anima mundi, though most were still equipped to take diesel or gasoline in the event of an emergency.

"I think we're in the North Financial District," she said, her eyes flicking with longing over the sign advertising slushies, pizza by the slice, fried chicken, and fries. Her stomach gurgled. What she wouldn't give for a slice of cheese pizza, or some of that crispy, piping hot chicken. Better yet, make it both, and add the fries. Plus a slushie. And maybe a chocolate bar or ten.

"Finally," Malakai said. *"Now* we're getting somewhere."

As they covered more ground, the spells on the buildings grew brighter and more crisp, and Loren felt a glimmer of hope upon hearing more helicopters flying nearby.

"You hear that?" Malakai asked, his tone optimistic.

"Yeah." She nodded, nearly weeping with joy. "Helicopters."

"Not just helicopters, Blondie. *Cars.*"

She strained to hear them, but the chopping of rotary blades drowned most everything else out. Was that a siren she was hearing? An ambulance, maybe? Or a fire truck.

Her heart picked up speed, and so did she, rubble clacking under her jogging feet. If those were cars Malakai was hearing, then the visibility over there was good enough to drive in without crashing. Maybe Darien was nearby. Maybe they'd run into each other on the street. Or maybe he'd made it back to Roman's house, and was waiting for her there. Maybe she'd get to see him again, touch him again, tell him how sorry she was and that she didn't hate him. She loved him, she loved him, she loved him...

Just before the explosion, when she'd poured her magic into the tower, she'd felt it expanding like a soap bubble over the city—weaker in some spots than others. She'd pushed it north, forcing it to stretch across the areas where her friends and family were located at the time.

She prayed her efforts had worked. Prayed that Roman's house, the tar pits, and Caliginous on Silverway—and the tunnels that ran underneath— were still standing.

"Am I crazy," Malakai began, "or are the security spells getting brighter?"

"They're getting brighter," she confirmed, her mortal lungs making her pant harder than the Reaper.

"Wait—hold up." He stopped, jerking her arm backward. "Look at me."

"What?" she demanded.

A pause, and then Malakai said, "Holy shit."

"What?" Gods, she just wanted to get going!

A shadowy finger reached for her face—

And poked her right in the eye.

"Ouch!" She pressed her fingertips against her closed eyelid. *"Malakai!"* she seethed. As if she needed any more injuries!

He grinned, his teeth suddenly visible. His silhouette—she could see it now. Vaguely. "I can see you!" he exclaimed.

"You poked me in the eye, you jerk!"

"I can fucking *see!* Life is good! Life is *great!* Praise Tempus, that lying motherfucker—"

"You poked me in the eyeball with your germy penis hand!" Where was an eye-wash station when she needed one?

"Let's go." He snatched her by the arm and plowed on, practically dragging her, the street now dark gray instead of pitch black.

Buildings, fire hydrants, street signs, benches, bus stops—they were all becoming visible as they hurried farther north. The road was completely smooth too, as if the explosion hadn't even grazed it.

The sirens got louder, and soon she could hear the cars, the honking of horns.

Soon, she could see working lights—streetlights glowing just beyond a gray veil. The darkness lightened with every step, until, eventually, the worst of it was behind her—a massive wall of billowing black clouds, stretching up and up and *up*.

Loren pulled her arm free of Malakai's grasp and turned, walking backward, her jaw falling slack at the sight of all those Void shadows. "Oh my gods," she breathed.

It was the most terrifying thing she'd ever seen. And to think she had been stuck in there for hours, her barely-reliable Sight the only reason she and Malakai had made it out alive...

Other people were still in there. Trapped and utterly blind. She would save them all if she were able—would run back in there and guide as many as possible to safety, if she knew it wouldn't kill her. But she'd already worn herself thin, and without access to the Caliginous Chamber, she had no way of replenishing her magic.

Loren stared into the rippling blackness, her mouth bone-dry.

She had gone surfing only once in her life. About an hour into her lessons, a colossal wave had formed, knocking her off her board and sucking her beneath the ocean. The current had tossed her about until she couldn't tell up from down. She had feared she might never find the surface. Thought she might die under there in the quiet, crushing blue.

This moment reminded her of that day. Only this was far, far worse.

The mass was groaning and creaking like an old house. Like a monster waking up and stretching its limbs after a long slumber.

Loren was not ashamed to admit that she was scared. Horribly scared.

How were they ever going to fix this?

A pair of fingers snapped in front of her face. "Terra to Blondie," Malakai said, snapping again. "Come in, Blondie."

She blinked, backing away from the inky wall. "Sorry, what?"

"Let's get moving." His hair was tangled and covered in dust, his eyes bloodshot. "Unless you'd rather walk your ass back in there, then be my guest. But I'm outta here."

She shook her head—of course she didn't want to go back in there—and looked out at the northern districts of the city, the buildings glowing with lights. With a deep and hopeful breath, she set off, following Malakai as he maneuvered the streets.

Combat and transport vehicles clogged the roads and sidewalks, and thousands of people had sought shelter inside buildings. She had never seen so many fire trucks, ambulances, cop cars, and armored vehicles in a single place. There were even Fleet soldiers stationed on roofs, a few flying between buildings; she wondered if Roark was here.

About fifteen minutes later, they made it to a grid of streets lined with more ambulances and fire trucks, as well as frame tents. Members of search-and-rescue and the police force had set up tables, where they provided citizens with bottled water, snacks, and other supplies.

"Thirsty?" Malakai asked. "'Cause I am." He led the way to a table, waving for her to stand in front of him in line so he could watch her back.

There were so many people here. So much activity, Loren found it overwhelming. As she waited in line, she scanned as many faces as she could, looking for Darien, Ivy, Dallas, Max, Tanner, Travis...

Darien, whispered her lovesick heart. *Darien, Darien, Darien...* His name was etched into every beat. Tattooed on her heart in ink that would never come off.

Deep in her shadow, where he lay curled up in an anxious ball, Singer whimpered. Loren sensed that the dog missed Darien, too.

"Next," called a sharp female voice.

Malakai nudged Loren between the shoulder blades. Pain seared through her back, but she ignored it and stepped up to the table. "Water, please," she said, not really sure how this worked.

That seemed to be good enough for the venefican woman working the table. She handed Loren two bottles of water. "Any snacks?" she asked, already reaching for a box of trail mix and pretzels.

"Yes, please." The medical tattoo on her forearm was getting warmer; she would have to eat right away.

Someone in the crowd bumped into Malakai, who stood just behind Loren—hard enough to make him stagger forward.

The Reaper whipped around, ready to fight whoever had slammed into him. Loren steeled herself for the inevitable drama that came with provoking Malakai, but—

Malakai paused. *"Devlin?"* he exclaimed.

Devlin? Loren's heart ballooned with hope, her breaths quickening. *Travis* Devlin? Or—

"Malakai?" exclaimed a familiar voice. Travis. It was *Travis* Devlin, not Roman.

The venefican volunteer thrust two pouches each of trail mix and pretzels in Loren's face. "Here you go."

Loren took them. "Thank you."

The surprise the Reaper felt upon running into the Devlin Devil, who was weaving his way toward them through the crowd, turned into fury.

"This is *bullshit!*" Malakai spat through bared teeth. "Half the city gets destroyed, and somehow *you're* still not fucking *dead?*"

Travis's eyes went black. "Fuck you, Malakai!"

"Fuck YOU!"

They lunged for each other's throats, the crowd around the table forming a circle. People scrambled to get out of the way, a few screaming for the police.

Loren stepped around a thrashing Malakai, nearly taking an elbow to the nose. "Travis?"

Both men froze, Travis's eyes locking on Loren. Those eyes widened, the black fading out of them. "No way," he breathed. He shoved Malakai aside and pulled her into a bruising hug, their chests trapping the cold water bottles between them, the snacks crushing into crumbs. "You're here!"

Loren tensed up. "Ow ow ow!" Gods, her back felt like it was on fire! The blisters stung, a few opening up and weeping blood.

"Sorry," Travis mumbled. He pulled away, hands up.

"It's okay," she said, though she winced again. "It's just my back."

His hands shot to his head, forming fists in his short hair, eyes wide. "Holy shit, you're alive. You're alive!" He pointed at her, his face transforming with a revelation. "You're not supposed to be here!"

"I know—"

"Neither of you are supposed to be here! *She's* not supposed to be here," Travis said, still pointing as Malakai glowered from a couple of feet away. Travis laughed in triumph, the sound slightly higher—hysterical—from delayed shock. "You're about to be in such deep shit, Delaney."

"Shut your mouth, Devlin," Malakai warned.

"I can't wait for Darien to rip you a new asshole—"

"Loren!" floated a musical female voice.

Gentle hands spun her around.

She came face to face with Ivy, who grinned, tears sparkling in her eyes.

"You're all right!" Ivy gasped. She pulled her into a hug, handling her more carefully than Travis had.

But Loren was tired of being careful. She threw her arms around Ivy's neck, not giving a crap about the pain or the snacks she was crushing in her grip as she held Ivy tight, sobbing into her hair. "I'm okay. *You're* okay. You're alive! I'm so happy to see you!"

"Me too, girl," Ivy said, her voice thick with tears. "Me too."

More voices called Loren's name. She opened her damp eyes to see Dallas sprinting over, Lace and Aspen walking behind her.

Loren let go of Ivy—just in time to intercept Dallas, the witch's body slamming into her own with such enthusiasm, they both nearly fell down.

"Gods, my own family's going to kill me!" Loren joked as her sister squeezed the life out of her, rocking her from side to side.

"Thank gods I'm not an only child!" Dallas said, her grip crushing. "I've been looking for you for hours! I knew you didn't leave—I just *knew* it." She pulled back and settled her hands on Loren's shoulders. "Are you okay?"

"I'm fine, Dal."

Dallas's copper brows flicked up. "You're fine?" she echoed, the silver rings around her pupils glinting like mirrors. "You're *fine?* You look like you got steamrolled!"

"Me? What about *you?* Your wings are all ruined!"

"Calla?" called a deep, male voice. It was Max—Max was here now, too.

"Max—hi!" She scanned their group, naming everyone in her head.

Travis, Malakai, Max, Dallas, Ivy, Lace, Aspen . . .

"Where's Darien?" Loren squeezed out, breathless. No Roman, no Tanner, no Jack...and no Darien.

No one said anything. A few shared heavy glances, but not one person spoke up.

Loren's expression—the brief joy she had felt upon reuniting with them all—sank. "Darien...?" She could scarcely speak, that's how little breath was in her lungs. "Where is he? Is he...is he okay?" Her voice cracked. "Tell me he's okay. Someone please tell me he's okay—"

Max cleared his throat. "We haven't heard from him—*yet*. But Jack showed up—he's okay, but he has a concussion." He pointed somewhere, still talking, but Loren couldn't focus on anything apart from her thoughts of Darien, her chest physically hurting as if someone had punched her in the breastbone.

Gods. Oh *gods,* she was going to be sick—

She blinked the blur out of her vision. "Can we call him?" she asked, interrupting Max. She didn't have her phone, but maybe—

"Phones aren't working," Lace said, her perfect lips twisting into a frown. She indicated to the cell in her hand. "I've been trying all day."

"Day?" Loren echoed. "What time is it?"

"Almost one," Lace said.

A hand came down on Loren's shoulder, and she turned to see Shadow-master Kylar Lavin joining the group. There was a small smile on his face, but Loren could tell that it wasn't sincere. A lot was bothering him, and she was afraid to know exactly what.

"Hey," Kylar said, nodding at her in greeting. "Glad to see you're okay."

"You, too," Loren choked out, blood rushing in her ears.

"Group's almost complete," Kylar observed, scanning everyone's faces the way Loren had, his eyes tightening slightly upon—Loren assumed—not finding Roman here.

"Wait," Ivy said, frantically glancing around. "Kylar, where's my husband?" Her eyes narrowed. "You were supposed to be watching him!"

"Relax, he's taking a piss," Kylar said.

"Where are the restrooms, anyway?" Max asked. "I have to piss like a race horse."

"There aren't really any," Kylar said. "Jack whipped it out in front of some half-lives over there, and they all scattered like flies." He glanced at Loren, as if suddenly remembering she was there, and mumbled an apology for the slur.

Lace snickered. "That sounds like Jack, alright." Her gray eyes landed on her friend Aspen, who stood across from Malakai. Both Reapers had their arms crossed, their mouths opening and closing, as if they wanted to say something to each other but didn't know how. "Are you guys going to say hi to each other, or just stare in awkward silence?" Lace's question earned a few quiet chuckles from others in the group.

"I already said hi," Malakai mumbled.

Max said, "Doesn't count if you say it in your head."

"All of you can go pound sand," Malakai snapped, though he added in a softer tone, "Hi, Aspen."

Her lips twitched with a smile. "Hi, Malakai."

"Glad to see you're, like, you know—alive." He drew a sharp breath, as if it had pained him to say that, and gave his attention to the group. "All right, where's my sister? If she's dead, Devlin, I'm gonna break your scrawny neck—"

"She's right there, you dick!" Travis snapped, pointing.

Indeed, there was Jewels, making her way through the crowd with Jack

Steele. Loren fought the urge to sprint to Jack—to demand to know where he had last seen Darien. There was a big cut in his brow, the skin bruised.

Malakai stalked through the group, pushing past a glaring Travis, and went to greet his sister with open arms—

She wound her arm back and slapped her brother in the face. *Clap!*

Loren's brows flew up.

"What the hell was *that* for?" Malakai growled.

"For not getting *her*," Jewels said, jabbing a long black nail at Loren, who blinked in surprise, "out of the damn city!"

"You wouldn't even be here if we hadn't stuck around!" Malakai fumed, his hands curling into fists. "You'd be fried like a fucking fish stick!"

"Hold up," Ivy said, pinning Loren with an accusatory glare. "Did you do something?"

Loren shrugged one shoulder, well aware that she was about to get an earful. Likely from several mouths. "Just the same thing I did during the Blood Moon," she said quietly as everyone stared at her.

Ivy flicked her brows up. "Just the same thing you did during the Blood Moon?" she repeated, her tone coated in disapproval. "That's the *same thing* that put you in a coma!"

Great, now everyone was mad at her. And Loren realized that Ivy had more reason than anyone to be upset with her. If—*when*—Loren died, Ivy wouldn't have a brother anymore. Her time was already limited, and she'd put herself—and Darien—at greater risk by using her magic.

"Cut her some slack," Malakai drawled. "She's the reason all of these people," he gestured to the busy streets around them with a sweep of his arm, "are still here. The reason why *you're* here. If we left, there's a chance you guys might not've made it, even with those suits."

Ivy was still staring at Loren—nostrils flared, arms crossed, her mouth a thin line. Loren had never seen Ivy look so angry. Apart from last night, when she had found out about Darien's bargain.

"I'm sorry," Loren mouthed, unable to find her voice.

"Tell that to my brother," Ivy said, her pupils expanding as if she were fighting the Sight, "if you ever see him again." Her words, although spoken in her usual careful tone, sliced into her like a knife, and Loren didn't know what to say, how to react.

Loren had thought only of *them* when she'd gone to the tower. All she had wanted was to save them. And although she'd done exactly that, she somehow felt like she had made the wrong decision.

"It's okay, Lor," Dallas whispered. "*I'm* glad you did it." Well, that made *one* person who was glad. But Loren couldn't peel her eyes off the pavement.

"Pass me that water, Blondie?" Malakai's question was miles away. When she didn't respond, he thumped over and took one of the bottles out of her tense hand.

"We need to get going," Max said. "Some of Don's Shadowmasters came through here a little while ago. They're looking for Pax. We need to find him before they do."

Malakai paused his guzzling. "Did they see you?" He swiped the water droplets off his beard.

"Don't think so."

Travis added, "But we heard them say they already went to Roman's house. So who knows what the hell that means for Arthur."

"If they hurt him," Lace began, her tone sharp, "I'm going to personally blow their brains out."

"Umm, sorry to interrupt," Aspen said, craning her neck to see into the distance, "but is Maya supposed to be leaving?"

Heads turned. Loren wasn't sure what Maya Reacher looked like, but she spotted a flash of pink hair among the crowd. A second girl walked beside the pink-haired one, the two of them heading east.

"What the hell," Max muttered. "MAYA!—"

CRACK. A clap of thunder shook the city. People screamed, some running to take cover. Loren threw her arms out to balance herself, Dallas grabbing onto her hand as the ground vibrated so hard she couldn't think.

The Void groaned and stretched, the shadows writhing like living things as they spread farther. Higher.

Jewels fell, Malakai shouting out in alarm as the side of her head smacked against the asphalt, the skin of her temple splitting open like a peach.

Travis screamed for Jewels, his voice barely audible over the deafening noise as he and Malakai dropped to their knees beside her.

Thunder cracked again, the city shook one more time, and fractures began to form in the ground—glowing like molten lava.

Loren was vaguely aware of Dallas hanging onto her. She didn't know how it'd happened, when she'd fallen, but she was on the ground, Dallas crouching beside her.

Jewels was screaming, hands clamped over her ears. She was having a seizure, her body jerking about.

Malakai and Travis were screaming too, both men calling her name—

desperate to help her, and not knowing how. Her eyes were black, and there were thin, dark lines appearing around them.

Suddenly, she fell still. Quiet. Her heart—

It had stopped.

"HEY—WE NEED HELP!" Malakai roared as Travis shot to his feet and sprinted toward the paramedics. *"WE NEED HELP OVER HERE! SOMEONE HELP US!"*

8

NORTHEAST MONTGOMERY
YVESWICH, STATE OF KER

Roman Devlin's every limb had turned sluggish, the cold having wormed so deep into his bones he feared they might snap like the icicles dripping off eaves and overpasses. He and Darien hadn't talked in awhile, both of them too tired and frozen to use their words.

The one and only plus right now was that they could see, though everything looked somber and hazy, as if a giant paintbrush had swept a wash of water-color gray across the city. It was better than being underground, though, with nothing to see by but the sword.

Darien walked beside him, the sword now sheathed down his back, the blade black again instead of glowing reflective glass. This area was quiet, the monsters seeming to gravitate toward the masses of Void shadows, as if confined to the darkness by unbreakable chains. Their keening yawps, clicks, and howls created a monstrous symphony that bounced through the streets.

Shortly after the waterfall had spat them out and they'd begun their trek north, Darien had started displaying signs of fatigue. But Roman knew his cousin would deny it—help, rest—til the bitter end. The one thing about Darien was he always pushed himself to his limits, even at the expense of his own well-being. *Especially* at the expense of his own well-being, which was precisely the last thing Roman needed right now.

"You okay?" Roman murmured.

"Fine."

Roman allowed a minute to pass before he slowed, playing up a limp, and said, "I think I might need to stop for a rest."

Darien looked Roman over, the exhaustion vanishing from his eyes as he checked for injury. "You all right?"

"I could use a breather. And some water." *You could use a breather,* Roman amended mentally, *and some water.* "My feet are killing me." At least that last part wasn't a lie. While his toes were numb, everything else was throbbing like hell.

"'Kay," Darien choked out, wincing again from the pain in his hand. His arm, too, where a beast had sunk its teeth into him in that cavern. Darien gestured ahead with an upward tip of his chin and said, "Let's try one of these houses."

The houses in these parts were nice—likely protected by strong spells on a normal day. But this was no normal day, and those expensive, intricate spell systems that would've deemed this neighborhood one of the safest in Yveswich had been stripped off. There was nothing protecting these homes anymore, apart from simple locks and latches.

Which made it incredibly easy to kick open the front door on the house of their choosing and stroll inside. Pieces of metal flung and tinkled across the floor as the locks were snapped apart.

Despite the copious windows, the interior was even darker than the yard—hard to see, even for a hellseher. It wasn't any warmer in here either, the city so damn cold, their wet hair had frozen into stiff, sparkling strands.

Roman flipped a switch by habit, but no light came on.

Darien's boots pounded on the hardwood floor as he made his way to the fridge and swung the door open. The appliance rattled from the force behind the action, a magnet falling off and rolling toward the living room.

Roman joined Darien in the kitchen and leaned against the island as his cousin rummaged through the contents of the unlit fridge.

"Would be nice if we found some leftover steak in there, hey?" Roman said, his mouth salivating at the thought. He couldn't recall the last time he'd eaten. Yesterday, probably.

"Half the shit in here's frozen," Darien noted as he dug something out from the back of the fridge. "Catch." He tossed Roman a plastic bottle of spring water—partially frozen, a chunk of ice bobbing inside.

They twisted the caps off and drank, Darien finishing his faster than Roman. The water made hollow gurgling sounds as it hit their empty stomachs.

Panting, Darien leaned back against the counter and slid to the floor, cradling his bad hand in his lap. He seemed constantly conflicted as to which to give more attention to—his hand or his still-bleeding arm.

Roman wiped the water off his mouth with the back of his wrist and sat down across from Darien. "Good call?"

"I'll never take water for granted again," Darien said, indicating to the empty bottle in his hand. More—he clearly needed more.

Roman said, "Are there any more?"

"Yeah, they've got a whole flat."

Roman pushed to his feet before Darien had a chance to do it first and grabbed four more waters, passing two to Darien, along with a granola bar he found in the pantry. Roman grabbed one for himself and sat back down. They ate the bars in one bite, hardly chewing.

"How much further do you figure?" Darien asked, crumpling the granola bar wrapper in his fist.

Roman thought about it. "An hour, maybe." They were shooting for the hospital. If the explosion had missed the building, and there were survivors inside, there may be a chance they could get some help. Maybe someone who'd be willing to give them a lift farther north. It was asking for a lot, considering they still hadn't run into any people...but they had to pass the hospital anyway, so it was worth a try.

"If no one's at the hospital," Darien began, pushing his frozen hair out of his face, "we'll try hot-wiring a car. See how far we can make it."

Roman nodded. "Sounds good to me."

How far they made it would depend on how quickly they ran into that wall of darkness, or a road too wrecked to drive on. By the looks of things, nearly the whole middle part of Yveswich was smothered by the Void, which would be impossible to drive in without crashing.

They sat for a few minutes in the quiet. Yveswich was too still. Too... empty. The only activity they had encountered during their walk here was a random *boom*—like thunder—followed by a rapid shaking that felt like an earthquake. The Void was spreading, the rip in dimensions peeling open wider, more shadows—and monsters—trickling out.

Roman shut his eyes, wishing he could sleep, even for a minute. But he had to keep going. For Pax—wherever he was. He *had* to keep going.

Boots scuffed as Darien got to his feet.

Roman forced his eyes open.

"You good?" Darien asked, chucking his garbage into the bin.

"Are you?" Roman countered.

"I'll live." He offered him a hand up, but Roman ignored it and got to his feet on his own. "You suck at lying, by the way," Darien added. When Roman's brow furrowed, he explained, "You didn't need to stop for a rest."

"No," Roman confirmed. "But you did."

Darien made for the front door. "Let's get moving."

They left the house and continued walking. The city shook periodically, though the tremors were on a smaller scale. Nothing that could knock you on your ass like the first one. Roman spotted a fair number of monsters during their route, but most kept their distance, sticking to the walls of dense shadow in other neighborhoods and districts.

They were passing under a street sign pointing them toward Yveswich General Hospital when they heard someone screaming.

Darien froze, his head whipping to the side.

The sound got louder. It was a woman, whose voice resembled—

"IVY!" Darien shouted.

Before Roman could stop him, Darien took off like a bat out of hell.

"Darien!" Roman bolted after him.

The screaming continued, and gods was it awful. It sounded like someone was being tortured. Burned alive. Darien was far away now, his shouts for Ivy bouncing faintly through the deserted streets.

"ROMAN!" the voice screamed. *"ROMAAAAAAAN! HELP! ROMAN!"* But it didn't sound like Ivy—not to Roman. It never had.

To Roman, it sounded like Helen. His mother.

But his mother was dead.

Roman pushed himself faster. *"Darien! DARIEN—SLOW DOWN!"*

'Something doesn't feel right,' Sayagul said down the Spirit Bond, the dragon speaking for the first time in hours. She was groggy, barely able to slur her words thanks to the exhaustion gnawing on Roman's bones.

'I know,' Roman said. He skidded around a corner, his leg shooting out to the side as he fell on loose gravel, landing hard on his shoulder. He grunted. Shoved to his feet, stones digging into his palms. "DARIEN, WAIT UP!"

'Do you think it's a Crossroads?' Sayagul asked.

'Shit, I hope not.' He leapt over a stretch of frozen water on the road, boots shattering the thin ice along the outer edge. *'We have to find him—'*

'There,' the dragon said, indicating with a shadowy wisp.

Roman turned a corner, ducking around a stop sign, and thumped to a halt in front of a row of big, pretty houses, each painted a different shade of pastel—sky-blue, lemon drop, blush, mint-green, and lavender.

It was the sidewalk in front of the lavender house where Roman found

Darien. The yard was encased with a white picket fence, the gate of which was shut. The wind howled like a hungry wolf, its strong gales ripping white and purple flower petals off rose and lilac bushes.

The screaming had stopped. Aside from the wind, the street was dead silent, no one—person or monster—in sight.

Roman approached his cousin on quiet feet. "Darien?"

Darien didn't turn. He just stood there, staring at the house. Then he said, so quietly Roman could hardly hear him, "It was Ivy."

He broke his stillness as if he'd snapped out of a trance and paced the sidewalk like an animal in a pen, eyes glued to the house, his breath forming ghosts in the air. The driveway was lined with more white roses and purple lilacs, what remained of their petals frozen into segments of brittle glass.

"It was Ivy," Darien said again, talking mostly to himself. "She was here —I heard her."

"Darien." Roman spoke with caution, his teeth chattering so violently he could hardly talk at all. "Are you sure it was h—"

"It was Ivy!" he exploded, whirling to face him. His nostrils were flared, the veins in his neck bulging. "I think I know the sound of my own goddamn sister's voice—"

The screaming started again. The sound was coming from inside the house. And this time, there was no doubt about it—it was Helen Devlin.

But that wasn't who Darien was hearing.

"Ivy!" Darien jumped the fence and bolted, across the frosted yard that crunched under his boots. Up the freshly painted steps, heading straight for the door—

The door that was suddenly wide open, welcoming him in.

"Shit." Roman leapt the fence and barreled across the yard, up the steps—

Darien turned, blocking him with an arm that smacked against his chest, sending Roman back a foot. "Wait out here."

"You kidding?" Roman snapped, all too aware of how much noise they were making. They might as well be ringing the goddamn dinner bell. "There's no way we're splitting up—"

"Roman—" Darien paused, breathing heavily, his lips tinted blue from the cold. Bit out, "Something's not right."

"Yeah, no shit." At least he was finally noticing that. Delirious—they were both delirious with fatigue. With worry. And this here—this scream-ing... It could be a trap. A monster luring them into its den.

'He can't go in there,' Sayagul whispered. *'Don't let him go in—'*

"Wait here," Darien said firmly. He turned—

"Darien, I don't like this!" Roman hissed. The open door of the house observed their argument as if it were entertained, the inside eerily dark. "What if it's a Crossroads?"

"It's not. This street is brand new."

"We can't know that for sure! What if Spirit Terra's doing something shady? What if something bad happens to you while you're in there? *Then* what?" he challenged.

"It won't," Darien said—again in that firm tone that left no room for argument.

"Say it does," Roman insisted. "Then I'm supposed to tell your sister that you died because you fell for some stupid trap? I'm supposed to tell Loren that? Who's going to look after her if you're gone, Darien? *Who?*"

"I'll be *fine*," Darien gritted out, though Roman's question—mostly the last one, no doubt—stalled him. "Besides, you've got people to look after, too. A little brother to go home to. Which is why I want you to wait out here—wait out here, and keep watch while I make sure that's not my fucking sister being tortured in there." He pointed at the house—at the open door waiting for guests. A chill prickled across Roman's nape. He could sense when he was being watched, and he sensed it now.

Something was watching them.

Roman pushed, heart thundering, "Darien, I heard *Helen*. My mom. *You* heard Ivy." He jabbed a finger in his face.

A few seconds passed as Darien thought it through. Roman held his breath, begging the gods that Darien wouldn't insist on finding out who—or what—was responsible for all the screaming. Roman understood why his cousin was so concerned about Ivy; they had no way of knowing where their family was, if they were safe. Alive. For all they knew, Ivy really *was* in there.

But Roman stood by his opinion that those screams didn't belong to Ivy. He was certain he would've fallen for it, too—would've reacted the same way as Darien—had the screams sounded like Pax instead of his late mother.

As he waited for Darien's decision, his heart pounded so hard he swore he might throw up again. The screaming had stopped, the street quiet. *Too* quiet.

Then Darien said, "Stand guard."

Roman cursed, the blood leaching from his face.

Darien added, "And stay out of sight."

He vanished through the open door of the purple house before Roman could reply.

Roman glanced around, trying to put a finger on exactly where they were. There were no cars on this street, no people—not even bodies. It must be a new subdivision, everything newly built—uninhabitable for a Crossroads creature.

But stranger things had happened.

Roman paced the porch, palms sweating inside his ripped gloves.

He decided he'd give Darien two minutes. Once those two minutes were up, he was following him in there. That was final.

'I don't like this,' Sayagul whimpered.

'Two minutes,' Roman said, his heart still racing, palms slick. *'That's all he's getting.'*

Roman counted to one and a half before he said screw it and made for the door—

Only to discover that it was shut and locked, and he knew Darien had done neither of those things.

Roman's stomach dropped through his feet.

When he peered through the window by the door, he saw that the house was empty. No furniture.

And as for Darien—

He was nowhere to be seen.

9

THE PURPLE HOUSE
YVESWICH, STATE OF KER

The moment Darien set foot in the purple house, he wondered if Roman was right. Maybe this *was* a Crossroads. Maybe he'd wandered into some ancient beast's lair. The air had the same feel —as if a gate had swung open with enough force to cause a sharp breeze. It even smelled like magic in here.

But the devil was in the details, and these details didn't add up. Crossroads were always located someplace old, someplace with a long and complicated history. And yet he couldn't shake the feeling that he'd gone someplace...*other*.

His boots thumped as he crossed the foyer... The empty living room... The kitchen.... Everything in here smelled new—new paint, new floors, new carpet on the upper levels.

He turned in place, listening for Ivy... But the house was so silent, he swore he could hear his own blood coursing through his veins.

And then the screaming began again. He couldn't pinpoint where it was coming from. It seemed to be all around him, echoing from hidden spaces above, below, and beyond what his eyes could see.

It was Ivy—he was sure of it. Only this time, she sounded...young. And this time, she wasn't calling *his* name.

She was calling for their mother.

"Mom, *Mom!* Somebody help—my mom— *Please! She's hurt, we need a doctor!—*"

"Ivy?" Darien called. His voice clapped through the house. His blood cooled, the hairs on his arms rising under his bodysuit. *"Ivy?"*

Heart pounding, he hurried down the hallway, toward the sound of his sister's voice. His magic—what remained of it—threaded between his fingers like shadowy serpents.

He'd made it halfway down the hall when suddenly, the house vanished into smoke. And then that smoke began to change, morphing into a different setting.

Darien stumbled a step, blinking in disbelief as a street slowly took shape.

It was nighttime. Location: an apartment building in Angelthene.

This was his old home—the building where the Slade family once lived.

Utterly confused, he watched as a cab rolled to a stop out front of the apartment building.

And then his stomach dipped, his heart breaking in two, as he realized—

This was the past. Somehow, he'd walked into the past.

To the very worst day of his fucking life.

The passenger's-side door of the cab swung open, and a human woman stepped out into the balmy, late-summer air.

So many years had passed since he'd seen her, Darien had forgotten how much she resembled Ivy. The tilt of her eyes, her kind smile...Ivy. Though her hair—reddish-brown and gently waving to the middle of her back—was all her own. A feature that had skipped her two children in the gene pool.

Darien's eyes fogged with moisture as he watched his mother enter the apartment building, handbag in hand, her long coat fluttering behind her.

"Mom?" he called.

But the mocking echo of his voice was his only response.

He squeezed his eyes shut, willing this to go away. He didn't want to see anymore, didn't want to witness her die again—

Not real, he told himself. *This isn't real.*

The leisurely pounding of boots had him opening his eyes.

In the short time that his eyes were shut, the street had melted away. He was back in the present—back in the purple house. But the view outside the windows was pitch-black, suggesting that he was still trapped someplace *else.*

Slowly, he turned around...

In the center of the living room stood his uncle Donovan Slade. His two-headed wolf Familiar melted out of his shadow and stalked up to his side, eyes glowing in the dark like four sun-struck rubies.

Darien lifted his chin, his good hand curling into a fist at his side.

Donovan's lips formed an evil smile. "Hello, Darien."

10

NORTH FINANCIAL DISTRICT
YVESWICH, STATE OF KER

I n the back of an ambulance that raced through the streets of Yveswich, Loren tried to stay calm as two paramedics worked over Jewels.

The Reaper had gone into cardiac arrest. Already, her skin was sickly pale, her lips tinged with blue. The paramedics had loaded her into the ambulance so quickly, Loren might've missed it had she blinked, their efficiency worthy of applause. But the tension choking the air told her that regardless of speed, there was still a chance they were too late.

Malakai stood statue-still in the farthest corner from Loren, his eyes shining with emotion at the sight of his sister lying motionless on that stretcher.

Ivy was in here, too—the third and final person granted permission to ride in the back of the ambulance. Ivy had declared that until they found Darien, she would go everywhere Loren went—no doubt to keep Loren from putting more than just her own life in danger.

Loren sat beside Ivy on the squad bench, both hands gripping the edge, as the ambulance was jarred about by potholes and debris.

"Clear." Another press of the paddles sent Jewels's body arcing against the stretcher, but still no heartbeat was detected.

Through the windows in the doors of the ambulance, Loren watched as a once-beautiful city—now hardly more than a wasteland, a slaughterhouse—passed by in half-lit blurs. Bodies were strewn about the streets, some half-eaten, others mangled or burned to a crisp by the explosion.

A nightmare. This was all one big, horrible nightmare.

Just when she had finally made progress—finally made it out of the blinding darkness and reunited with the others—she was being forced to backtrack. She couldn't help but dwell on each rotation of the tires, each mile taking her farther away from Roman's. Away from all the places where she believed she might've reconnected with Darien.

Please be alive, she begged, mouthing the words as the ambulance wove through the streets, more butchered lumps flitting by. She shut her eyes, tears burning behind her lids, and pictured Darien's handsome face in her mind—his rare smile, the dimple in his cheek. *Please, please be alive. I need you.*

She wished she could hear his voice again, telling her that everything was going to be okay. That he was with her, and he would protect her.

But her only reply was the howling of the monsters outside.

The paramedics—a male hellseher and a female witch—were speaking in code. Still fighting death. Malakai had resorted to crouching, his head bowed between his knees, his shaking hands fisting his hair.

Four minutes. Jewels had already been dead for four minutes.

'That was me,' Darien had said to Loren in Roman's training room, when she had called him out on his decision to lie to her, and he'd responded by confessing his feelings for her before the rest of her lost memories had found their way back. *'That's what I was doing, when you said you were drowning? When you said I helped you breathe again? That was me, resuscitating you. I did all of that for* you, *Loren. Because I love you, sweetheart.'* Gods, did he ever.

He'd gone through hell and back with her. *For* her. Had witnessed her heart stop more than once. Had brought her back to life—more than once. Through it all, he had never given up on her. Not even considered it.

How lucky she was to have someone who cared so much.

How lucky she was to be loved by him.

As the paramedics worked on reviving the Reaper, Loren's vision tripled, and she had the sense that she was peering down a narrow tunnel. Watching all of this happening from someplace else—somewhere outside of her body. Nothing in here felt real. Not even Ivy, who sat close enough to touch.

Her heart began to race. Her skin began to tingle and sweat. The next thing she knew, the paramedics were declaring a steady pulse, but by the time the words left the witch's lips, and the ambulance was jostled extra hard by something on the road, Loren lost her balance and toppled off the bench.

"Loren!" Ivy screamed. She dropped to her knees beside her as Loren tried and failed to sit up. "Loren, what's happening? *What's happening?"*

She tried to reply, but she couldn't speak. Couldn't think coherently. A little voice in her memory told her she was going into hypoglycaemic shock —a drop in blood sugar to levels below normal. She recalled going through this when she was a child, but many years had passed since then, and during that time she had forgotten how it felt, what to do. The tunnel kept getting longer and darker, until she could scarcely see—

"Can someone help?" Ivy shrieked. "Please—she has a blood sugar condition! She needs help! *Please."*

The murmur of a male voice—asking Ivy questions.

"I don't know—I don't know what it's called!" Ivy stammered. "Yes, she has a tattoo. On her arm—her forearm. *That* one—yes."

Fingers circled Loren's arm, pulling it straight. A man knelt before her, his face a blur. She thought she must've said something—a name, maybe— because the man suddenly looked up at her.

"Can you hear me?" His question was a never-ending echo. "Miss, can you hear me?" It was the paramedic, scanning her medical tattoo through the rips in her bodysuit with a handheld device. Red light passed across her forearm, and her tattoo—the snake wrapped around a rod—responded by brightening to a blinding shade of white. Just below the base of the rod, rows of numbers and symbols that contained Loren's medical history appeared in her skin like computer code, glowing brighter than the rest of the tattoo.

"Please." Ivy was sobbing. Hysterical. "She can't die!"

Darien can't die, Loren amended mentally, knowing Ivy felt the same way—knew Ivy was really begging the paramedic to save her *brother's* life.

Something sharp bit into her arm. Loren flinched and tried to pull away, but the paramedic held firm.

"This is a glucagon injection," a voice explained to Ivy as Loren's heavy eyelids rose and fell. "It will cause her liver to release stored sugar into her blood. It's what we give to patients who are unable to eat or drink anything."

More voices. Movement in the ambulance. More faces peered at her, but she couldn't see any of them. They were all blurs.

"Keep breathing, Loren," Ivy was saying. Icy cold fingers grazed her cheek with a comforting touch. "You have to keep breathing—"

'I'm coming, baby,' said a deep, rich voice, sounding close and far all at once. Her heart ached for the person the voice belonged to, and a soft, strangled sound—a sob—floated off her lips. *'I'm coming. Hold on.'*

That voice—whether reality or a dream—was the last thing she heard before her eyelids fell shut.

II

THE PURPLE HOUSE
YVESWICH, STATE OF KER

"It was you." Darien's every thought short circuited as he faced Donovan in the empty living room while Skǫll, Don's wolf Familiar, prepared to square off against Bandit. The two snarled at each other, bodies lowered and hackles raised. *"You're doing this."*

Darien had figured it out the minute he saw that sick smile on his uncle's face. Somewhere between here and the waterfall, he'd lost his Avertera talisman, which must've allowed Donovan to track him, bait him. But as for *how* Don was doing this—how he'd forced him to walk into a memory...the sound of his sister screaming...that was a mystery he hadn't figured out yet.

"That's right," Donovan confirmed, his casual tone so at odds with his evil stare. "I thought Roman would be the first to run into my trap, but it turns out it's *you* who's the bigger idiot. Though I must say..." He began to circle Darien, a predator rounding up prey, shadows swirling about his thumping boots. Darien refused to blink, forever turning in place so he faced his uncle head-on. First rule in fighting was never turn your back on your opponent. "I like it better this way," Don said. "How else would I get the chance to spend some quality time with my favorite nephew?"

"What do you want from me?" Darien demanded.

"I want to see if the rumors are true."

"What rumors?"

"All of them," he said plainly. "You've made quite a name for yourself, Darien. Head of the Seven Devils... Undefeated champion in every fighting ring you've walked into... Some even say you're the best fighter on the west coast. That's quite the claim, wouldn't you agree?" His smile widened as he came to a standstill, hands hanging loosely at his sides. How many times had Roman been struck by those hands? How many times had Paxton flinched away from them? Don concluded, "I'd like to test that theory."

"You baited me here for a fist fight?"

Don's cruel grin fell, black eyes glinting in the dark. "You murdered my brother, Darien."

Darien's lungs emptied as if he'd been punched in the gut.

"That's right," Don gritted out. "I know it was you. I've known this whole time. Do you have any idea how long I've been waiting for this moment? How patient I've been? If I'm being honest, it's been torture—knowing you were only a few hours away, taking over as Head of Angelthene's Houses, while my brother greeted the afterlife." His shadows stirred, his face suffused with hatred. "*Torture.*" The last word was a bark that Skǫll echoed with one of his own.

"Why wait?" Darien challenged, stalling. "You could've come to Angelthene."

"See, as hard as it's been, I believe the longer you wait for something, the greater the reward. The more you appreciate the moment when you finally achieve your goal." There was something odd about the way he said it, as if he were referring to something else. "And the look on your face..." A cold chuckle punctured the walls. "Did you really think I had no idea it was you? Your dad's men talk, Darien. Just because he's no longer around doesn't mean they don't talk to me. Just because he's gone doesn't mean they accept you. They hate you, actually."

"I'm flattered."

Don tightened his fists, thumbs dragging across the scarred peaks of his knuckles. "Is there anything else you'd like to say to me before we settle this? Anything *smart?*"

"I'm not sorry, if that's what you want to hear."

Don blew a humorless laugh through his nose, his mouth twitching as if he wanted to bite. "But it wasn't really *you* who killed Randal...," Don mused, canting his head to one side. "Was it?"

Darien didn't respond.

Don started pacing again. "Randal's men say it was a monster—a dark and ancient being that feeds off fear. See, that story makes much more sense to me. I mean, let's be honest." Another laugh ricocheted through the room, like shots fired from a gun. "As if *you* could have ever defeated Randal."

Silence spread like a chasm.

Don spoke the truth—not once had Darien believed that he could've killed his dad. At least not in hand-to-hand combat—not back then. Which was precisely the reason why he'd never even tried. Had he believed he'd stood a chance at putting an end to all that suffering, he would've acted. Anything to spare Ivy and the other Devils from Randal's constant bullshit.

But Darien had changed—*grown*—since Randal's death. If given the opportunity to redo it, he knew he could kill him—easily. But killing the uncle who stood across from him?... That was another challenge entirely.

Roman's warning—the one he'd uttered on their way to Caliginous on Silverway last night—blared through Darien's memory like a civil defense siren: *'Darien, if you try to kill him, you will lose.'*

"So, what do you say?" Don faced him, hands pushing up the long sleeves of his shirt. Skǫll's growling grew to a near roar, the wolf awaiting his master's signal with bated breath. "How about showing your uncle if you're as good at fighting as everyone says you are?"

Darien was always itching for a fight, but tonight, he found his mouth drying up from the invitation. He was all too aware of his throbbing hand —the still-mending fractures that had been agitated from holding onto Roman in that cavern.

Apart from that, he felt the ghosts of his past breathing down the back of his neck. He may not be a child anymore, but in that moment, as his uncle beckoned him forward, he felt thirteen again—felt all the same emotions as the last time this same man had beaten him black and blue. Those were the days before Darien had learned how to fight properly— how to throw a punch that broke bone instead of just bruised.

As he and his uncle stared each other down, he knew that if he managed to walk out of this house tonight, it wouldn't be due to victory. It would be because Donovan—for whatever reason—allowed him to leave.

But the look on Donovan's face told Darien he had zero intention of letting him go anywhere.

"Come on, nephew." Don curled his fingers in invitation. "Don't be shy. I'll even let you draw first blood—how's that sound?"

Darien squeezed his left hand into a fist, the other throbbing in tandem with his heartbeat. "I'm not fighting you."

"Too scared?" Don's obsidian eyes snagged on Darien's right hand—

the pulses of neon red that indicated injury. "My, oh my..." He tutted, a smile tugging on his mouth. "What *ever* did you do to your hand?"

"We're not doing this." Darien stalked toward the door. "I'll take you up on your offer another time."

But Don stepped in his way and shoved him backward.

The assault sparked Darien's temper like flint, his blood heating to a rolling boil. "Don't touch me," he warned through clenched teeth.

"Better you than Ivy."

"Keep my sister's name out of your mouth." He made to move around him again—

Another shove—harder this time. Hard enough to make him stagger.

Darien charged him head-on. *"I said don't fucking touch me."*

Don came forward to meet him—stealing his move. "Or what?" They were inches apart—eye to eye. "Don't be a pussy, Darien—show me how the infamous leader of the Seven Devils fights."

"With a broken hand? How fair of you."

"Hit me."

"No."

"Hit me," he said again.

"No."

"Do it, Darien," Don pressed, stepping closer—crowding him. "If you don't, I'll bring Roman in here and see how you feel when I beat his face into a pulp—"

Darien punched him in the nose with his left hand.

Bone snapped. Don stumbled backward.

Bandit and Skoll broke out into a clamorous fight, tumbling across the floor in a blur of darkness and bared teeth.

Don straightened, reset his twisted nose—*crunch*.

Then laughed like the psycho he was, thick blood oozing down his lips and chin. "There he is!" He advanced on him with a grin. "I was wondering when you'd finally show up." He swung—

Darien blocked the hit with his elbow, and he didn't hesitate this time as he threw a straight punch—

Don dodged the swing, fist swiping up.

Knuckles slammed into Darien's chin, the force rattling his jaw and pinching his tongue between his teeth. Blood flooded his mouth, but he shook off the pain. Ducked and swung again—

Donovan dipped to the side, throwing another punch of his own.

Darien evaded his fist in the knick of time, the puff of air on his cheek indicating how close he'd come to being hit. He acted quickly, landing two hits to the side of the head, a sharp kick to the gut—

He blinked in disbelief as Don laughed.

As if this were a *joke*.

The hits continued from both sides. No room to breathe.

"I hadn't seen your sister in a while," Don said between swings, blood dribbling down his chin. Darien blocked what he could of Don's attacks with his forearms and elbows, but his uncle still managed to sneak through, every blow he landed bone-rattling. His form was good—too good. "She's a pretty thing, isn't she?"

Darien spat a gob of blood-tinged saliva on the floor. "We're talking now?"

"One of my men is interested in her. Obsessed, actually." He threw another right hook—

Darien blocked it, the muscle in his forearm bunching in pain from the bruising hit.

The beast forever hunkering in his soul stood up and began to pace, agitated by the turn in conversation—by every hit that stoked the embers of his rage.

Don went on, "Once I'm done with her, I think I'll let him have his fill."

The beast paced faster, chewing on Darien's skin from the inside.

"She can be his little whore until he grows tired of her. Your sister was always good at that, wasn't she? Being a whore—"

The beast broke off its leash. Shadow magic blasted out of Darien like a fired cannon, launching Donovan clear across the room.

He hit the wall and rebounded off it, landing on his feet in a crouch—

Then rose in one fluid motion.

No longer was he smiling.

"I said *fists*," Don snapped, prowling forward like a lion. Wisps of black ballooned out of his shadow, shivering as they expanded... expanded...*expanded*. Crawling up the walls like billowing smoke. "Looks like I'm not the only one who doesn't play fair. Let's compare, shall we?"

Don lifted his hand, and before Darien could so much as *think* of blocking the attack, a blast of magic barrelled across the room—

It slammed into him.

And he went flying backward.

He smashed through the upper row of cupboards in the kitchen and toppled to the floor, his body banging against the counter on his way down.

Slivers of wood and chunks of plaster rained upon him, dust sprinkling his hair.

Don was there before Darien could stand, one hand grabbing him by the hair, right at the roots, while his other fist collided with his face. *Bang. Bang. Bang.* Each hit whipped his head to the side as if it were a punching bag.

Far from finished, Don grabbed him by the shoulders and pulled him to his feet, flinging him around to face him.

"Let's go, nephew." He beckoned. "Give me a real challenge."

Bloody and battered, Darien stalked forward and swung.

Missed.

Blocked.

Swung again—

His knuckles barked as they split Don's brow open. Any other opponent would've been rendered unconscious—but this was Donovan, and Darien was shit with his left hand.

Don's returning hit was lightning-quick—a blow to the side of the temple that caused his ears to ring, the vision in his left eye going white.

The dog and the wolf kept fighting—and it wasn't Bandit who was winning. The snarling was endless, punctuated with yelps that quickened Darien's already-rapid pulse.

Don made another move. Darien dodged one hit, but a second quickly followed—another jarring thwack to the same temple, the force behind the blow turning his brain to liquid.

He staggered backward. Nearly fell. He couldn't see straight, could hardly see at all, and his arm was bleeding again.

"Is that all you got?" Don's question echoed three times.

Darien took a chance and swung, but he didn't land the hit.

Don struck him in the gut. The ribs. Something cracked, and he barked a profanity, nearly buckling as pain seared like a blowtorch across his side. He had zero time to recover before knuckles were biting into his upper lip, his nose. His eye.

He teetered, falling to one knee. He tried to push back up, but Donovan kicked him in the face—

He collapsed, nearly losing consciousness. Head whirling, he tried to sit up.

A knee dug into his chest, pushing him back until he was lying flat on the floor.

"Make them stop," Darien gritted out, referring to the Familiars.

"Why should I listen to you?" Don hissed, grinding his knee in deep.

Darien tried to push him off, but he had no strength left. "This is between you and me."

"Would you be saying that if it were Skǫll who was losing?"

Don's fist connected with his cheek—once, twice, each hit whipping his head to the side.

Another skull-rattling punch, and his surroundings went out of focus, his head swimming. All sound, apart from the ringing in his ears, ceased.

And the very last spark of his magic guttered out.

"Best fighter on the west coast." Don's sneer was muffled. "You're *nothing*, Darien. No better than a nobody."

Darien pushed, but Don wouldn't yield. "Get off," he choked out, his mouth full of blood.

"There's one last thing I want to do."

A snap of Don's fingers, and the Familiars stopped fighting.

Bandit crumpled to the floor with a whimper, his eyelids drooping shut.

A flourish of Don's hand, as if he were waving a stave, and the house began to change, carrying them back to the past.

To the night when his mother died.

There she was again—stepping out of the cab and walking into the building, her coat fluttering behind her.

The knee on his chest—shifting up to press on his throat—was the only reminder that this wasn't real. This night had long since passed, his mother gone. Buried in a place with no sunlight, no warmth.

It haunted him, that truth. It was a ghost that had haunted him since the day he lost her.

"Beautiful," Don said, as if he had a right to say that. A right to *look* at her. "Just *beautiful*. Your father was a lucky man."

"Get. *Off.*"

"I'd like you to see something first. It'll just take a minute." The scene sped up, a movie stuck in fast forward.

It slowed to a normal pace, and Darien felt like he might throw up as another vehicle—a van—sputtered to a stop in front of the building, and the younger versions of himself and Ivy got out through the sliding door, fountain drinks and crumpled bags of popcorn in hand. They were gushing about the movie they had seen at the cinema, their two friends who were still in the van sharing in their excitement. After about a minute, they said their good- byes, and the van drove away.

He knew what would happen next—knew how badly it would hurt him if he saw it again. But he found that he couldn't look away, so he watched through a mist of tears as the first woman he'd ever loved died a brutal death.

A scream ripped through the night, followed by a streak of color as something plummeted off the roof of the building—

And hit the ground with a sharp *bang,* the sound like a firecracker.

The two teens gasped and stumbled backward.

Ivy was the first to recover from her shock. The first to react. She lurched forward on unsteady legs, a shattered sob floating off her lips.

Several beats of silence passed.

And then they started screaming.

Blunt force trauma, the doctor had told him, when he'd booked an appointment two years after her death, demanding the doctor describe how she'd died in detail—thinking, in vain, that it might give him closure.

It had not.

Somewhere nearby, in the present, a whimpering Bandit dragged himself across the floor. But even as the dog attempted to comfort him, Darien couldn't tear his focus off the scene.

Seeing his mother die once in real-time was bad enough. This second time—watching it from an outsider's perspective—was torture.

He couldn't breathe. And for one horrible moment, as tears rolled down his face, he found that he didn't want to be alive.

Don shook his head, tsking, as a younger, sobbing Darien clung to Elsie's body. Ivy wept on her knees nearby, burying her damp face in her arms, screaming, "Mom, *Mom!* Somebody help —my mom—*please! She's hurt, we need a doctor!—*"

"Awful, isn't it?" Don's knee crushed his windpipe. "Absolutely awful."

Darien pushed against his uncle's hold. "Get the fuck off me," he gasped.

Don grabbed him by the wrist, the memory vanishing the minute the back of his bad hand banged against the floor. Shadows curled up from the ground, winding around Darien's wrists and ankles.

One tendril snaked higher—wrapping around his bad hand with an icy cold touch.

A bolt of fear zipped up Darien's spine. "What the hell are you doing?"

He thrashed, but the shadows had him pinned. Trapped.

"A little bit of payback," Don whispered.

Shadows threaded between his fingers, slowly pulling his bones in the wrong directions. He twisted and bucked, but he couldn't get away.

"I'm going to be honest with you," Don drawled. He leaned in close, as if they were indulging in a secret. "The only reason I'm keeping you alive right now is because I want to see the look on your face when I fuck up Travis. You thought you could protect him?" He grabbed him by the chin, forcing him to make eye contact. "Hmm? You thought you could keep him safe?"

"Don't," Darien bit out. "You go anywhere near him, I'll kill you—"

"Oh, I will—I've got a lot planned for your cousin." The shadows squeezed tighter, the still-healing spots in his hand screaming in agony. "As for you..." The shadows cut in deeper, joints cracking.

Oh fuck, oh fuck—

Quiet as a whisper, Don said, "You're going to watch."

Something in his hand cracked. His vision went white.

And he fucking *screamed.*

His ears rattled and rang. The world went fuzzy. Distant.

Beyond the white haze of his vision, beyond the excruciating pain in his hand, Darien became aware of Don laughing. Don, pushing himself to his feet, making a point to apply all his weight to Darien's hand—

Darien screamed louder.

"Your dad was right." Don's words were muffled—miles away. "You *are* a pussy."

Darien turned onto his side—

And with a sudden retch he vomited all over the floor.

The ringing got louder. The pain got worse. The house spun—

"I look forward to seeing you again soon." The threat echoed, then faded, drowned out by the thumping of his pulse in his ears.

Thump-thump.

Thump-thump.

Thump-thump.

Sometime later, the floor shook with rapid footsteps.

"Darien?" called a male voice. A pause. And then: "Holy gods—" The footsteps started again—faster this time. *"DARIEN!"*

Darien rolled onto his back. He tried to look up, but his vision tripled, and he saw three of Roman spinning like a top. Around and around and around, a dozen times, before he passed out.

12

INTENSIVE CARE UNIT
YVESWICH, STATE OF KER

The bleach the hospital staff had cleaned the floors with was so strong it scalded Loren's nose and throat, the hard lemon candy dissolving on her tongue rendered tasteless by the fumes.

Eyes shut, she tried her best to relax after everything that happened in the ambulance. But her focus was soon disrupted by the rattling of a button being repeatedly poked by a finger.

With a sigh, she opened her eyes to the glaring light of the ICU waiting room on the third floor of the hospital.

Everyone was here now—crowded together in the cramped space. Ivy, Jack, Lace, Aspen, Travis, Max, Dallas, Kylar, and Malakai. It was a good thing Darien's spacious truck had been taken to the tar pits, or they would've been forced to split up again. The only two who were missing—apart from the obvious subtractions—were Maya and her pink-haired friend. They'd slipped away during the commotion, a turn of events that was clearly bothering Max, if the brooding look on his face where he sat across from Loren was any indication. Conflicted—that was the best way to describe how he looked. How *everyone* looked.

Loren wasn't surprised to discover it was Malakai who was pushing that button on the vending machine, his dusty, tangled hair gleaming in the fluorescents like a tarnished penny. That the lights worked at all was a miracle, though they flickered often, earning concerned glances from staff and patients alike. The furnace, too, was working overtime, the near constant stream of air occasionally turning cold.

Malakai paused his assault on the button and glared at the machine as if it offended him.

Loren tucked her knees up and snuggled deeper into her hard chair, stuffing her icy cold hands between her thighs to warm them. She was about to shut her eyes again, hoping Malakai was finished with his distracting pastime, when he suddenly returned to pressing a different button. Vigorously.

"Excuse me, sir!" called a female voice, Malakai's finger moving so quickly it was practically vibrating. *"Sir!"*

Malakai stopped and pivoted on a heel to face the nurse's station.

"You know you have to put money in first, right?" said the middle-aged witch, corded phone cradled against her shoulder. Landlines, being an older form of communication that had its own backup energy supply, weren't affected by short-term power or magic outages. Only the staff had access to the phones, but even if they were allowed to use them, no call would go through to cell phones. Cellular radio systems were still down all across the city, and by the looks of things, that wouldn't be changing any time soon.

"You got keys to unlock it?" Malakai gritted out. "I don't have any change."

The nurse merely raised her brows, said, "Not my problem," and returned to her call.

Malakai scowled at the machine. "Bitch," he muttered. His blood-shot narrowed eyes flicked to Loren. "You got any change, Blondie?"

Loren arched a brow. "You're asking the poorest person in the room?" Her voice crackled from exhaustion.

"I'm poorer than you," Dallas said, plucking a singed feather from her deformed left wing, one leg folded beneath her. "Unemployed student life." The last word was garbled by a yawn.

"Here." Ivy got up and crossed the space, boots clicking. She rummaged around in a pocket in the thigh of her full-body suit, the material such a deep burgundy it was almost black, and handed Malakai two coins. "Is this enough?" she asked him.

The Reaper merely grumbled and pushed the coins into the slot in the machine.

"You remembered to bring cash?" Kylar asked from where he leaned against a wall by an abandoned mop and bucket. Loren wrinkled her nose, the sight of the cleaning equipment a reminder as to why her airways were burning. While strong chemicals tended not to bother immortals, they wreaked havoc on the human body.

"I always try to come prepared," Ivy said. She returned to her seat beside her nodding-off husband—returned to monitoring Loren as if she were watching television. She crossed her legs, fingers tapping against her knee to the tune of a melody that only she could hear.

Those were the first words Ivy had said since Loren regained consciousness inside the ambulance and the paramedics helped her inside, where the nurses had taken over her care and given her a bottle of cranberry juice and a package of hard candies. Like most other people in the hospital, Ivy looked as though these last few hours had aged her. The whites of her eyes were inflamed, her face scratched and streaked with dirt. Loren wasn't eager to look in a mirror anytime soon; she could only imagine the mess she'd see staring back at her.

Malakai plunked into a free chair with such force it was a miracle the legs didn't snap. "I'm starving," he declared. He ripped open his bag of chips with a *pop*. "And mad." He crammed at *least* four chips into his mouth and crunched, crumbs sprinkling his beard. The smell of the salty, baked chips made Loren's stomach growl.

"So are we," Travis snapped. He was leaning against the edge of the desk, arms crossed. When he'd arrived at the hospital, a fight had nearly broken out between him and Malakai. The men had only calmed down when the nurses had threatened to kick them out, an outcome that would've resulted in neither of them seeing Jewels. Travis added with a grumble, "Quit bitching."

Malakai glared, but he was too invested in his chips—and too aware of the threat he'd received earlier—to budge from his chair.

Aspen gave him a look that seemed to say, *You're making progress.*

He merely flashed her a lazy thumbs up and finished off his chips, tipping his head back and dumping the remnants into his mouth.

The room fell into a welcome moment of quiet. Those who spoke did so in subdued voices, their murmurs the only sound for several minutes, apart from the occasional droning of landlines and the swishing of scrubs as staff members bustled by.

Loren had just dozed off, her body begging for rest, when a voice woke her back up. Malakai again—no surprise there.

"Anything you three would like to share with the class?" the Reaper drawled, eyeing Kylar, Lace, and Aspen, who were deep in conversation.

"We're talking about Pax and Gene," Kylar said. Travis, who was slumped against the desk looking miserable, perked up at the mention of his younger brother.

Lace added, "We think we should split up. Some of us can wait here while the rest of us go to Roman's and make sure Arthur and the others are okay."

Malakai pretended to clean out his ear with his pinky finger. "I'm sorry, what? *Split up?* You're out of your damn mind, Lacey."

"You got a better idea?" she fired back. "Because as far as we know, there's an old man and two kids who are probably very afraid right now, given all this shit that's going on. Not all of us have to be here. We'll cover more ground if we split up."

"She's right," Max mumbled. That was all he had to say about the matter, his mind undoubtedly still occupied with thoughts of Maya.

"Okay, and then what?" Malakai challenged, still not convinced. He leaned forward in his seat, planting his elbows on his knees. "Say your group makes it to Roman's house." He pointed at Lacey. "Say Crazy Slade is there. Then you guys either a) get killed, worst case scenario. Or b) you need us to stage a rescue mission. There's strength in numbers, and I'm not convinced splitting up is the right thing to do right now."

"I think Travis and Kylar should be the ones to decide," Ivy chimed in. "Pax and Eugene are *their* brothers."

Kylar's gray eyes zeroed in on Travis, who looked a little more awake but no less distraught now that the topic had returned to his little brother. "What do you think?" Kylar asked him.

Travis thought it through. "I think we should wait," he said, though the decision looked like it pained him. "As much as I want to find Pax, I think Malakai has a point." Several pairs of eyebrows hit the ceiling, Malakai's included. Jack let out a soft chuckle at Malakai's baffled reaction. Travis went on, "We only have Darien's truck, so whoever stays here will be stuck if the other group doesn't come back." Looking like he hated the idea of that, he added, echoing Malakai, "Worst case scenario."

Malakai turned toward the rest of the group with still-raised brows, looking like someone had just told him they had discovered a cure for the Tricking.

"Space is a little tight, even with Darien's truck," Aspen said. "Whoever stays behind could always try and catch a lift from someone."

The debate fell into a lull as multiple minds considered every pro and con.

Travis was the one who broke the silence. "The Shadowmasters already paid a visit to Roman's," he began. "According to what we heard, the only person at the house was Arthur. That makes me think—*hope*—that Dom and Blue were able to hide the boys. Maybe they're not lost at all. Maybe they were just being hidden."

The room once again settled into silent contemplation. As the minutes wore on, the group seemed to come to the same conclusion.

They were stuck here—for now, at least. And until they could get a better plan in place, it was better to stick together.

"Is there a Malakai Delaney here?" called a female voice.

Everyone sat up, their focus going to the doctor who'd entered the space.

Malakai's face paled a shade as he got to his feet.

"Your sister is stable," the doctor said. The room let out a collective sigh of relief. "You may see her now, if you're ready."

Malakai gestured for Loren to go with him. "Let's go, Tiny Dog."

"She can stay with us if she wants," Aspen said. "There are enough of us here."

"Yeah, but I made a deal—a stupid deal, but still. She goes where I go." He waved again, chucking his crumpled-up chip bag into a garbage can as he edged around the desk. "Let's go."

Loren unfurled her legs, her bones howling in defiance, and stood, Ivy following.

The last to trail behind them was Travis.

The doctor began leading the way, but paused mid-turn, the silver of her swinging stethoscope winking like a star. "Immediate family only."

"That's these two," Malakai lied smoothly, gesturing between Loren and Ivy. Of Travis, he said, "Not him—he's not family."

Travis stiffened.

Jack wheezed a laugh. "What a dick."

"Very well," the doctor sighed, though it was obvious that she didn't believe him.

"That's what you get for telling me to quit bitching," Malakai said, not deigning to even *look* at Travis.

Travis didn't argue, nor follow as the three of them tread on the heels of the doctor.

Loren tossed an apologetic glance over her shoulder, but Travis's fuming, black-eyed stare was too fixated on the back of Malakai's head to notice her.

They were halfway there when Travis's self control broke. "Fuck you, Malakai!" The *clang* of a chair being kicked onto its side was the last thing Loren heard before they turned the corner into Jewels's room.

13

EMERGENCY DEPARTMENT
YVESWICH, STATE OF KER

The hospital was fucking chaos. Functioning, yeah—lights on, equipment beeping, heat blasting through the vents. But *chaos*.

Darien followed Roman into the ER, the area so crowded the sliding glass doors barely shut behind them. The line-up—if you could even call it that—of people leading to the triage desk was so long, he figured it would take at least an hour before they reached the front, and gods knew how long after that before a Healer would be available to see him.

"Fuck this shit," Darien muttered, his bruised face aching, mouth still tasting of blood. "I'll get Arthur to deal with it—"

"Darien, your hand is a *mess*," Roman hissed. Well aware of the people surrounding them, who would sure-as-shit take notice of the Devil and the Shadowmaster in their vicinity sooner than later, he added in a quieter volume, "And so is your face."

Darien snickered—then grimaced, the act of forcing a smile causing his battered cheeks and jaw to scream in agony. "Thanks."

"We're not leaving here until you at least get *that*—" He pointed at the mangled hand Darien cradled against his stomach. "—fixed."

Darien swore under his breath, but he didn't budge from his spot in line. Not even when the doors squealed open behind them, cold air blasting his back, and more people squeezed in, crowding him and Roman against those who stood in front of them.

Fuck, this really was shit. This night—day, whatever—was shit, and now they had to waste time standing here like tinned sardines.

But his hand *was* fucked... Roman wasn't wrong about that.

Running into that house was a stupid mistake, and he'd almost paid for it with his life. When he'd woken up on the floor to a panicking Roman shaking him into reality, he had barely been able to stand, but he'd somehow dredged up enough will to walk the short distance here. He still wasn't entirely sure *how*. His hand was in such excruciating, searing pain, it was a miracle he was even coherent. The cold air had numbed it somewhat, making it a bit more manageable, but now that he was inside and warming up, he knew it would only get worse. It already was.

As they waited, Darien scanned the hundreds of people in the area, searching for anyone they knew.

Searching for a head of blonde hair, eyes the shade of a tropical ocean, and the prettiest face he had ever seen.

But she wasn't here, and he wasn't sure how to feel about that. He hoped it meant she was out of the line of fire and on her way back to Angelthene, but he refused to relax until he knew with absolute certainty that she was safe.

About thirty minutes—better than an hour, but still too long—went by before they made it to the triage desk.

"Last name," the venefican receptionist demanded, fingers poised on her keyboard.

"Cassel," Darien replied, keeping his voice down. But his efforts made no difference—people were already staring. They'd been staring and whispering this whole time, turning this experience into an even bigger pile of horse shit.

Thanks, Don, Darien thought. He and Roman hadn't said much about what transpired in that house, but Roman knew that his dad was involved —knew that his dad was the one who'd broken Darien's hand. As for all those other details... The glimpse into the past, to the night Elsie had, according to the police, jumped to her death...

He wasn't looking forward to reliving those details when it came time to finally explain them.

"Spell it for me," the woman said.

"C-A-S-S-E-L."

"First name?"

"Darien. With an E."

"Address?"

He gave a fake one—the same one he'd rattled off the last time he was here.

"What brings you in today?"

Darien lifted his hand in response—swollen, bruised, and throbbing like mad. "Broken hand."

"We don't have an estimated wait time." Keys clacked as she recited the same speech she'd likely given all these other people, most of them human or half. "More urgent cases may be taken back before you. Stay in the area, and we'll call your name when a doctor is ready to see you."

"More urgent cases?" Roman echoed with a scoff. "This man's hand is fucked!"

"I understand that." She sounded bored to tears, and she looked it, too. "You'll have to wait your turn like everyone else."

Roman wore the expression of a rabid dog, but he reined in his temper with a deep, calming inhale. "Can you tell me if a hellseher named Shayla Cousens has been admitted today?"

"I'm not able to tell you anything about the other patients. Step aside, please. We'll be with you shortly."

Roman's pupils flared as he fought the Sight. "Half of the city's destroyed, everyone's in hysterics trying to find the people we care about, and you won't tell us jack shit?"

"Protocol," she said simply, to which Roman ground his teeth. "A person's information is private, and if given out can be detrimental in the wrong hands. I would expect someone like yourselves to already know that." She gave a pointed look at the tattoo below Roman's eye, the black skull of Obitus barely visible through the dirt and blood caked on his face. "We ask for your patience and understanding, or you will be forced to vacate the premises."

Now, Darien was the one grinding his teeth. Livid, he shook his head, wishing he were well enough to punch something. The black-eyed glare he threw over his shoulder sent the closest people backing up, whispering in fear. Knowing it was pointless to make more of a scene, he pushed off the desk and took his leave.

"Next!" the woman squawked.

Darien cursed, shaking his head again as he and Roman claimed a spot by the wall, near a bulletin board littered with colorful flyers. "How often do you think she's repeated that garbage tonight?"

"If she's dead, it's my fault," Roman blurted. Flyers crinkled as he slumped against the board.

"If who's dead?"

"Shay." He toed at a scuff mark on the floor. "I could've told her what was going on with the Well, but I didn't. I *chose* not to. I acted like an asshole and told her to go away. And when Arthur tried to give me that ring —the one he made for Shay..." He swallowed. "I was stupid, and I didn't take it." He shut his eyes and pinched the bridge of his nose between his thumb and forefinger.

No, he hadn't taken the ring—Ivy had. But Darien didn't bother reminding him; he knew exactly what Roman would say in response: what good had it done? And it was true—who the hell knew where Shay was when the replica exploded? She could be anywhere by now—could be buried under rubble or ripped into a million tiny pieces by the blast.

Darien leaned against the wall, hand above his heart, and scanned the room for a second time while Roman idly plucked the phone number tabs off a pest-and-monster-removal poster. The sliding doors were stuck open, so many people in need of medical attention that the line went all the way outside, lights flashing and sirens wailing without pause. By the looks of the feathered wings he glimpsed through the windows, there were Fleet soldiers in the area.

"You think if I ask her if Paxton's been here, she'll have to tell me because we're family?" Roman's lethal gaze was fixed on the triage desk.

"I think if you ask her about Paxton, she'll tell you to go fuck yourself."

Roman's chuckle was unamused.

Darien locked eyes with a brunette Healer standing near the desk. The ER was too noisy to hear what she was saying to the receptionist, but it wasn't long before both of the women were glancing his way.

The receptionist handed the Healer a clipboard, but hung onto her end for a moment, as if she couldn't decide what to do, before finally letting go with a steely glance thrown at Darien.

The Healer walked over, scrubs swishing as she thumbed through the papers. "You punched someone, didn't you?" She flattened the top paper back down and rested the clipboard against her hip.

"How'd you guess?"

Roman glanced between them. "You guys know each other?"

"She fixed my hand," Darien said. "Can you help me out, or what?"

She sighed through her nose. "I'm breaking a lot of rules by letting you skip the line, but..." She glanced over her shoulder. "Come with me."

They trailed her as she navigated the sea of people. Down a hallway, around a corner, all the way to an elevator near another waiting area—a human-only zone, the air tainted with the pungent smell of bleach and blood. The elevator doors opened with a *ding*, and they got on. Taking the elevators was a huge risk when the city's power was on the brink of collapse, but with the way Darien was feeling right now, there was nothing and no one that could stop him from getting to Loren. He'd tear the whole world and all its elevators apart to find her.

"I couldn't help but notice your phones are working," Darien said as the doors slid shut, the lift lurching upward. "Exactly how much of the city's power is out?"

"Almost all. And it's just the landlines that are working, so unless whoever you're trying to reach is old-school, you're not going to have any luck." She glanced side-long at him. "Sorry."

"Can't say I'm surprised."

"The lady at the desk said you aren't allowed to tell us anything about the other patients," Roman ventured.

"Right—protocol."

"Yeah, that's what she said," he muttered.

"Who are you looking for?"

Roman perked up at the invitation to say more. "Her legal name is Shayla Cousens. Works for the Riptide. Strawberry blonde hair, green eyes, waterdrop tattoo." He skimmed the ink below his eye with a knuckle.

She shook her head. "Sorry, no. Aside from you two, I haven't seen any other Darkslayers. But I've only been working emerg, and even if I tried checking the records, I don't think they would tell us much. A lot—and I mean *a lot* of people have come in today in conditions too critical to provide identification." She sighed. "If the city manages to survive this, we're going to have a hell of a time sorting everything out."

The lift juddered to a stop on the third floor ICU. The doors hissed open, the floor of the hallway beyond freshly polished with bleach.

"Any chance you could have a look anyway?" Roman asked as they exited the lift.

They carried on down the hallway, past rooms filled with murmuring voices and beeping machines.

Finally, she said, "I'll see what I can do."

The room they were shooting for was about a five-minute walk from the elevator. They filed inside, and Darien took a seat in the lone chair by the door while the Healer retrieved the mat she would need to channel magic from the anima mundi. She spread it across the floor by his feet and knelt upon it.

It took longer than last time to mend the fractured bones in Darien's hand. As for the pain, it was a thousand times worse. More excruciating than the countless other injuries—bullets, bites, stabbings—he'd sustained during his years as a Darkslayer.

He bit his tongue, sweat trickling down his spine. By the time she made it to the worst of the fractures, his teeth had pierced through the side of his tongue, and he could taste and smell nothing but his own blood.

His memory of Loren's face was the only thing that kept his heart beating, the only thing that kept him from passing out. He had to do this—be strong—for her. If he couldn't use his dominant hand, how the fuck was he supposed to protect her properly?

"All done." The Healer's voice was muffled by the ringing in his ears.

With a deep breath, he opened his eyes, unaware that he'd shut them.

"You can't take this off, can you?" She tugged on the thick, leathery sleeve of his bodysuit—the glove he couldn't strip off. She'd taken advantage of the many rips in the material, needing skin contact for the healing shades of her aura to exit her body and flow into his.

He shook his head. Roman was watching from his spot near the examination table, looking white as a sheet. Having recently witnessed the brutal nature of Roman's everyday life, Darien understood perfectly well why shit like this disturbed him so deeply.

"Would you like me to do anything for your face?" she asked, eyeing the bruises and cuts courtesy of Don.

"Don't worry about it," he managed to say. His hellseher healing would take care of that. "Thanks for letting me cut the line."

"You're welcome." The Healer stood and picked up the mat. "I'll give you a new compression glove to take home with you. Make sure you wear it twenty-four seven." She rolled up the mat. "And don't punch anyone this time."

"Copy." He took another deep breath, his hand on fire. "You got any painkillers?"

"I can grab you some from the nurse's station." She eyed the beads of sweat prickling across his brow. "Think you can manage a bit of a walk, or would you rather wait here?"

"I'm fine." He didn't come this far just to rot in a hospital room. If he didn't keep moving, he'd feel like he was giving up.

The look on her face suggested she was surprised and more than a little impressed, but she masked it quickly. "Right this way."

14

INTENSIVE CARE UNIT
YVESWICH, STATE OF KER

"I don't know what happened," Jewels croaked. She was propped up in bed, looking more washed out than ever in that hospital gown, her pale fingers toying with the vinyl identification band on her wrist.

The rhythmic beeping of the equipment scattered throughout the shared space reminded Loren of her many visits to Angelthene General. She had been poked and prodded by more doctors than she could count, each and every one finding more questions than they did explanations for her long, baffling medical history. But her memory of the poking and the prodding wasn't the only reason this place unsettled her.

Not long ago, she had been lying in a bed like this one, trapped in a coma with no hope of waking up. And just the other day, she'd found out that Darien had slept with her every night—he'd said so himself. Had stayed with her so she wouldn't be alone, guarding her body while her soul drifted through the spirit realm.

With a deep breath that barely soothed the ever-growing ache in her chest, she focused on the female Reaper's quiet voice as she recounted her final moments before her heart stopped.

"I've had seizures before, but...never that intense," Jewels whispered. "It hurt so bad, it felt like my spine was going to snap in half."

She let go of her wristband and scratched absently at a fleck of dried blood beneath her right eye—a spot the nurses had missed when they'd washed her face.

Malakai was pallid. He sat in the lone chair beside her bed, his throat working with a swallow.

"It felt like that really bad Surge I had when I was thirteen—remember that?" she said to her brother. When Malakai managed a nod, Jewels added, "Only this was worse... A thousand times worse. A thousand times more painful."

Malakai opened his mouth to speak, but no words came out. Loren had never seen him so upset. So speechless.

"The most important thing is you're alive," Ivy offered gently. She stood near the cubicle curtain, arms crossed. Malakai—shockingly—gave her a grateful look. "You're going to be okay."

Jewels looked like she had a lot more she wanted to get off her chest, but instead she sighed and settled with a simple: "Yeah." She swept her poker-straight hair—an icy shade of lavender—over one shoulder, exposing the fruit bat Familiar cradled in the crook of her neck, and stroked the fuzz between the animal's pointed ears. The bat was very cute —soft white in color, with pale purple eyes that looked as drowsy as the Reaper's.

"You scared the shit out of me," Malakai confessed, his voice gruff with emotion. He reached across the space to grasp Jewels's forearm, thumb stroking. "Thought I might lose you." He cleared his throat.

Jewels fought a smile. "Don't feel like being an only child yet?"

"Not yet. Annoy me for another few years, then ask me again."

The smile she was attempting to stifle broadened, but the expression didn't reach her eyes. "Where are the others?"

"In the waiting area," Ivy said.

"Everyone?"

"Everyone," she confirmed. "Travis tried to come in and see you, but Malakai wouldn't let him."

Malakai winced, now looking anything but grateful for Ivy's presence. "Thanks a lot," he muttered, glaring over his shoulder.

"Are you *serious?*" Jewels hissed, spearing her brother with black eyes.

"Don't get mad at me—he was pissing me off!"

"*Everyone* pisses you off! And don't even try to deny it."

He huffed out his irritation, crossed his arms, and slumped against the backrest of his chair.

"When are you going to grow up?" Jewels demanded, still scowling.

"The minute you stop having shit taste in men."

"Oh really?" Her tone dripped with a warning.

Ivy said, "Travis is a way better choice than a lot of the men out there. I can vouch for him—I've known him since we were in diapers."

"Thank you," Jewels said vehemently.

"There's not much competition in the way of good men, that's why," Malakai grumbled.

Jewels rolled her eyes. "Oh, for gods' sake! What has poor Travis ever done to you?"

"He asked my baby sister out on a date, that's what."

"I'm not a baby." She added, "You, on the other hand..."

The bat cuddling her neck was giving Malakai a heavy dose of side-eye. Until today, Loren had never seen Jewels's Familiar, and the only other white one she'd seen in person—apart from Singer in the spirit realm—was Shay's seal pup. They tended to feel more comfortable staying in their person's shadow, likely due to always being gawked at. White Familiars were so rare, they accounted for less than three percent of Familiars worldwide.

"Whatever you're thinking, Critter, don't try it...," Malakai warned, glaring down the bat whose response was a sassy snort of disapproval, her eyes narrowing into slits. "This doesn't concern you."

Critter merely shut her eyes and yawned, tiny teeth glinting like shards of pearl in the bright light.

Jewels sighed, then offered Loren an apologetic smile. "Sibling squabbles. Do you and Dallas fight?"

"Not as much anymore, but we used to pull each other's hair a lot." *A lot* was an understatement. Her relationship with Dallas consisted of just as many rocky moments as it did smooth, but their bond felt stronger than ever now.

"I've pulled Malakai's before," Jewels declared, a devious glint in her eyes. "Remember that, big bro?" He merely grunted.

"Dal has a bald spot back here," Loren said, indicating to her own head —the area right above her nape—with a graze of her fingertips, "where her hair never grew back."

Ivy snickered. "Ouch."

"It's true—ask her to show it to you sometime." Dallas was weirdly proud of it, as if it were a scar she'd earned in battle.

This time, when Jewels laughed, her smile reached her eyes.

But it was soon fading as she gave her brother a contemplative look.

He bristled. "What?"

"You already know what. Go get Travis!"

"Fuck no!"

"*Fuck yes,* Malakai."

"*No.*"

"Yes!" she said again. "You're going to stop with this ridiculous attitude right this instant. I refuse to let you bully my friend."

"Friend?" he gritted out.

"Yes. Travis is my friend, whether you like it or not." Was Loren imagining the hint of pink in her powdery cheeks?

Malakai grumbled, but—surprisingly—got to his feet. "As long as that's all he is."

"Friend or more than friend, I get to see who I want to see." She pointed at the door. "Now. Go. Get. Him."

He was still grumbling as he ripped the curtain aside and stomped into the hallway. "Let's go, Tiny Dog!" To Travis he shouted, "Devlin, get your ass in here before I change my mind."

Jewels's ash-blonde brows hit her hairline. "Tiny Dog?"

"Tell me about it," Loren said with a sigh. "It's worse than *Blondie.*"

"*Tiny Dog's* kind of cute, actually." She and Ivy laughed at her expense.

"Would *you* like it if he called you that?" Okay, maybe it was a *little* cute... More annoying than cute, but she had to admit it wasn't bad coming from someone like Malakai, who seemed more likely to choose *dork, goober,* or something too offensive for most people to say out loud.

Jewels grimaced. "Hell no. If he called me that, I'd hang him by his balls."

Malakai shouted from the hallway, "I'd like to see you try, Tiny Dog!" Darn, a hellseher's hearing sure was good.

Quieter, Jewels vowed, "I *will* hang him by his balls."

Ivy fought a smile. "We'll give you and Travis some privacy."

Loren followed Ivy as she ducked around the curtain. "I'm glad you're okay," Loren said.

"Thanks. Take care of yourself, hey?" Her probing stare said everything her lips didn't: We need you.

Malakai whistled sharply, as if calling a dog who'd wandered off.

"She will," Ivy said, her tone rigid with warning.

"Between your brother and Ivy, I think I've got protection duty covered," Loren said with a sigh. She could hear him mimicking her out in the hallway.

Jewels grinned. "He's fun, isn't he?"

"If you equate fun with irritating, then yeah, he's pretty fun." She gave a little wave. "See you later."

"See you."

On her way out, she squeezed past Travis, who looked more nervous than angry as he stepped into Jewels's room.

"Good luck," she said quietly. He whispered a thanks.

Loren drifted down the hall, her tired eyes scanning the colorful wayfinding signs secured to the ceiling. She suddenly had to pee so badly, it felt like her bladder was going to burst. It was a miracle she'd lasted this long without peeing her pants.

She made a beeline through the waiting room, following the signs— past the others who were crowded around talking. But she barely made it three feet before Malakai was shouting in protest.

"Hey, hey, hey!" he hollered. "Where do you think you're going?"

The others paused their conversations to stare.

"I have to go pee!" she hissed, mortified when staff and patients turned to look. She might as well shout it into the PA system! "I'll be back in like five minutes." There was no way she was letting him go with her while she did her business—she had to draw the line *somewhere*.

"I'll go with her," Ivy said, squeezing between Malakai and Kylar. "I doubt she wants your grumbling ass listening outside of her stall."

"You did just fine standing next to me while I pissed," Malakai challenged.

Jack, who was slumped so low in his chair he was practically sliding onto the floor, chuckled. "You forced her to stand next to you while you took a piss?" He adjusted the ice pack he pressed against his head.

"Yes, and it won't be happening again," she declared.

She hurried away, Malakai shouting after her—something inappropriate, probably. But she was too distracted by the ache in her bladder to care. She turned the corner—

And slammed into a solid chest so hard that she bounced backward.

She was about to mumble an apology when her gaze pulled upward— slowly, as if drawn by some unseen force. And suddenly—

She forgot how to talk. How to think. How to *breathe*.

Because Darien Cassel stood before her, looking anything but happy.

15

INTENSIVE CARE UNIT
YVESWICH, STATE OF KER

L oren let out a soft, strangled sound. A sob.

Behind her, the others murmured, those who were sitting rising to their feet.

But Loren paid them no mind while she stared up at Darien, too stunned to speak.

Her face crumpled as the weight of these long, horrible hours crashed down upon her all at once, snapping the tenuous leash she'd kept on her emotions until now.

She started crying in earnest, only half-aware that something wasn't right as she covered her face with her hands and let herself shatter.

The relief she felt from seeing Darien alive and safe was enough to make her knees shake, her mortal body that had managed to carry her all this way finally ready to give out.

"Loren." Darien spoke her name the same way he would a deep and heartfelt prayer. The sound of his voice—so rich and deep and *real*, so very real—only made her cry harder.

"I thought you were dead," she sobbed into her palms, barely able to speak, barely able to breathe, every ragged inhale sawing through her. "I thought you were dead—I was so scared, Darien! I was so scared for you." She hadn't realized how bad it was—how desperately she'd needed to see him again. To know that the man who'd sacrificed so much for her was not only alive but okay. As okay as he could be in this shattered life they shared.

Strong but careful hands circled her wrists.

Loren opened her eyes, looking up at Darien through a mist of tears, as he gently pulled her hands away from her face.

The others came closer, forming a half-circle around them, voicing question after question after question. But while they'd found their voices, Loren had suddenly lost hers.

No words would ever be good enough to express herself to the man she loved. She had so much to say and no idea where to begin. But now that the initial shock of seeing him here was taking its leave, she confirmed that something was indeed wrong. Darien still looked very unhappy—she could see it in the set of his jaw. In the crease that had taken form between his bold brows. In the way his pupils seemed larger than normal, as if he were trying not to lose himself to a Surge.

And when Malakai's voice floated above the din, the Reaper engaging with Roman in conversation, Darien's features transformed with pure rage, his own restraints snapping like brittle glass.

He was upon Malakai faster than Loren could blink.

He grabbed the Reaper by the throat—whipping him around and pinning him to the wall with such brutal force Loren felt it in her own bones.

Shouting filled the ICU. The others tried, to no avail, to intervene.

Shadows poured into the area, spreading like smoke. Several people backed up, calling out in alarm. Loren's heart jumped as the power threatened to fail, the lights strobing.

She sucked in a deep breath and lurched into motion. Knowing she had to stop this before there'd be no going back, she hurried across the space, heart thumping wildly in her ears, and squeezed through the group, getting closer to Darien than the others were willing.

"We had a deal!" Darien bellowed. The veins in his temples and neck were bulging, his face red with rage. "You promised me that you would get her the fuck out of here!"

"Let. Me. *Go,"* Malakai snarled, his eyes shining obsidian pits.

But Darien only tightened his grip. "Do you have any idea how bad that could've been? *What we could have lost?"* His voice was a deafening roar. "What *I* could have lost?" He pushed the Reaper higher up the wall with an arm to the throat.

The lights went out. Patients screamed from their rooms, crying out for help as the entire ward was blackened by Darien's magic.

Loren's eyes widened as Malakai's feet lifted right off the ground.

"*SHE COULD'VE FUCKING DIED!*" Darien's voice ripped through the room.

"Darien," Loren began. More shadows were amassing. Suffocating every last wisp of precious light. Even the dim emergency bulb that had come on by the desk was threatening to shut off. Her heart was beating so hard, she could scarcely hear herself talk, *think*. "Please—"

"Give me one good reason why I shouldn't rip your throat out," Darien snarled. For all the training the Reaper had, that was true fear shining in his eyes.

"Darien, I need you to look at me," Loren tried.

He didn't—but she swore she saw his head tilt toward her by a millimeter.

She took that as a sign to keep going.

"I need you to *look at me,*" she said again, firmer now, knowing that if he was going to respond to any command it would be the one *she* gave him, "and see that I am okay."

A shift in the atmosphere—subtle, but a shift nonetheless. As if he were finally hearing her.

"Look at me," she said again. This time, her voice did not waver.

She counted the seconds it took for the furious Devil to look at her.

One.

Two.

Three.

He obeyed, his head slowly turning toward her—jaw clenched, nostrils flared, eyes so black he looked more monster than man. He was beautifully terrifying. The most beautiful and terrifying thing she'd ever seen.

Three seconds—okay, that was seriously impressive.

"I'm fine," she said, her voice hardly a flutter.

He stared at her for a beat, as if waking from a dream. No—a nightmare.

And then: "I wanted you safe." His statement was gruff with defeat. Broken with regret. The pain lining his face, as if he were being tortured, nearly buckled her knees.

"So keep me safe," she pleaded softly. "I'm here now. I survived and I'm fine. I'm fine—see?" She gestured to herself, her heart thrumming so fast it felt like a hummingbird was caged inside her chest. The hospital was so dark it felt dangerous, and yet there was a part of her—a foolish part, maybe—that told her she didn't have to be afraid. Because these shadows...they were Darien's. These shadows *were* Darien. And she knew he would never hurt her. *Ever.* "So get your shadows under control," she said, her words cracking again from her own emotions—from the unbearable anguish on Darien's face, "and keep me safe."

Tense silence once again filled the area, interrupted only by the droning of unanswered phone calls. The receptionists were watching from behind the desk. One was halfway out of her seat, phone in hand.

It was that same brave soul who called, "Do you got it figured out, or do I need to call security?"

"They're fine," Ivy said, though her tone was frayed, and she looked as frazzled as Loren felt. Her gaze bounced between her brother and the Reaper he was still pinning against the wall. "Aren't you, Darien?"

Darien didn't respond. Didn't let go. Didn't tear his eyes off Loren—not for one second, not for one *millionth* of a second.

"Malakai," Aspen whispered, her tone reproachful and taut with fear.

"I'm not doing anything—it's Darien!" he spat. "It's *always* Darien."

Jack said, "Except for when it's you." He chuckled, but his humor was short-lived.

Loren's attention jumped back to Darien. He was still staring at her, still breathing so heavily it was as if he'd run clear across the city to get to her. Knowing him, it was something he'd do.

"You're fine?" he bit out, his deep voice husky with concern. If her nerves weren't so fried, she might have melted beneath that voice. And that *stare.* The way he was looking at her...gods, she couldn't describe it.

"I'm fine," she said softly. To her surprise, a few of the lights flickered back on to a lower setting. She wrapped her shaking fingers around his forearm, the muscles hard as rock, and tugged gently. "Let go, Darien. Let go. Please."

Her touch melted the tension right out of him, his clenched hands slowly opening, as if made of ice that was thawing under sunlight.

He released Malakai without so much as looking at him. The Reaper's boots thumped as they hit the ground, and he shoved his way through the group with a scowl on his face—going *around* her and Darien instead of between.

Jewels—Malakai was choosing not to fight because of Jewels.

This could have been so much worse, had they fought each other at full power and without restraint. Loren wouldn't have been surprised if they'd demolished the entire hospital.

As the seconds wore on and Darien cooled off, the shadows retreated.

The lights flickered awake, the machines that were scattered throughout the wing beeping as they came back on all at once.

Several moments of quiet passed before the others deemed it safe to start talking. And although Loren heard everything they said, she kept her focus on Darien, who watched her too, as if he couldn't believe his eyes. Loren couldn't believe hers either, and she found that she didn't want to blink in case he disappeared. When she looked at him, everything just felt right. He looked and felt like home.

"Darien?" Travis's shocked question bounced down the hallway as he came out of Jewels's room. He must have decided to stay with her while the power was out, in case she needed him. A brief pause, and then he squeezed out, walking faster now, "Roman? Holy shit, you guys are alive."

"What's going on here?" Roman demanded, as if their location and what it could mean suddenly dawned on him. He looked Travis over, checking for injury. "Did someone get hurt?" His face and full-body armor were as filthy as Darien's. Where had all that blood come from?

Loren swallowed a surge of nausea. It was probably better if she didn't know.

"My sister," Malakai responded, crossing his arms and leaning against the wall by the vending machine. "She went into cardiac arrest."

Roman's eyes flared. "Shit, really? She okay?"

"She is now," Travis said. "She was dead for four minutes. That power outage scared the hell outta me."

Jack indicated to Darien with a jab of his thumb.

Travis cocked his head, not getting the memo.

"Is Tanner not with you guys?" Lace asked, still clutching the cell phone she hadn't let go of in hours.

"We lost him," Roman replied, the words leaden with guilt. He zeroed his focus in on Jack, who stood with Kylar near the back of the group, ice pack melting in his clenched hand. "Same with you. When and how the fuck did *you* get here? And why isn't Atlas with you?"

"He has a concussion," Ivy said. "He can't remember anything that happened during the explosion."

"Paramedics found him up in Ardesia," Max chimed in, still looking burdened by his disappearing sister.

"Ardesia?" Roman echoed. His brows lowered, throwing his golden brown eyes into darkness. "You can't remember how you got there?"

"Not really. But I remember you killing the Basilisk," Jack said, speaking to Darien now, whose gaze was still glued to Loren. The black had left his eyes, but without it he looked...tortured. As if the sight of her here, in a city on the verge of complete collapse, physically pained him.

"*What?*" snapped several mouths, multiple heads whipping around to look at Darien.

Loren was still so distracted by the simple fact that he was here, she barely registered the others' outbursts. She shot Dallas a bewildered glance, her mind backpedaling.

Basilisk?

Jack's expression shifted with uncertainty. "That really happened, didn't it?" he asked Darien.

But Darien didn't answer, his attention wholly on Loren. "Turn around," he instructed. "Let me look at you."

"I'm fine," she said quietly, well aware that everyone was listening, watching. Everyone who'd left Roman's house last night was here now—all except Tanner and Shay.

"Turn," Darien gritted out. "*Around.*"

She crossed her arms, refusing to be a spectacle. "No."

A muscle twitched in his jaw. "Yes." He fought the edge in his tone as he added, "Please."

She stared at him in challenge, but he didn't back down.

So she relented, desperate to get this over with. She began to spin in a circle, arms held out as if modelling an outfit for him, entirely forgetting about her back until—

Darien inhaled sharply through his teeth. "What the fuck happened to your back?"

Oops. She should have argued for longer.

"I'm fine," she said quickly. She tried to turn back around—

But Darien was already there, carefully pushing her hair over one shoulder. She bit back a cry as the strands that were glued to the butchered flesh threatened to rip her scabs right off.

He hissed again, rubbing his stubbled chin. "Fuck me, baby."

"I said I'm fine—it barely hurts anymore."

'*You're not fine,*' Bandit grumbled from Darien's shadow, the dog allowing his words to be heard by everyone. Loren's face warmed from all the attention. So much for not being a spectacle. '*She is not fine. She needs a Healer.*'

Before Loren had a chance to argue, Darien said, "Wait here."

She fully turned back around, desperate to hide her destroyed upper back from prying eyes, and watched as Darien crossed the space to the desk.

He spoke quietly to the receptionist, who, like everyone else in the area—family, friends, strangers—*also* watched her.

Gods.

"I'm very sorry, but you'll simply have to wait," the woman told him. "There's nothing I can do."

He pushed off the desk and came back this way, looking just as pissed as when he'd pinned Malakai against the wall. His eyes weren't black, though—that was a small improvement.

"Come with me," Darien said to Loren, gesturing for her to follow him. To the others he said, "We'll be back in a bit. Roman can fill you in."

Roman's brows bumped up. "I can?" he asked, looking like he had no idea where to begin and felt a little irritated that he was being volunteered.

Jack stifled a laugh.

"Try," Darien encouraged. "And in the meantime, keep an eye out for Don." Merely the mention of that name was enough to churn Loren's stomach.

But she kept her focus on Darien—her anchor in this endless storm—and followed him down the hall.

16

YVESWICH GENERAL HOSPITAL
YVESWICH, STATE OF KER

"Lock the door behind you," Darien said.

Loren stood beside him by the closed restroom door. It was a farther walk than she'd thought it would be—across from a health-care supply room on the boundary between the Intensive Care Unit and one of numerous general wards. She again wondered how she had lasted this long without peeing in her battle-suit. She could only imagine how uncomfortable that would be.

She flattened her hand on the door, preparing to push it open. "It's not a single person restroom, though." A minute ago, he'd gone inside to scope it out for threats while she waited in the doorway, and had given her an exasperated look when she'd asked him what she should do if a monster slithered out of the toilet. It wasn't a stupid question. According to reports she'd seen on the news, it had happened enough times to be a valid concern.

"Doesn't matter," he said. "Lock the door, please."

"But you'll be right outside—"

"Lock. *The door.*"

She blinked. "When did you become so bossy?" But she knew the answer to that. If Darien Cassel had been anything short of bossy from the day he'd learned how to speak, then he wasn't Darien Cassel at all.

His eyes softened enough to make her heart do the same. She could be angry with him all she wanted for keeping secrets from her, but that didn't change the fact that she was hopelessly in love with this man.

"Lock the door, please, sweetheart." The endearment—said in that low, sexy voice of his—sent a curl of heat through her tummy.

"And what if you need to get in and save me? This is my last question, I promise."

One corner of his mouth twitched with a whisper of a smile, but to her disappointment his dimple didn't make an appearance. "Then I'll break the door down," he vowed.

Of course he would.

The hinges squeaked as she pushed the door open. She let it bang shut behind her, then waited a moment—just to irk him—before turning the deadbolt.

When she came back out a few minutes later, he was standing in the exact same spot—right in front of the door, his muscled arms crossed over his broad chest, looking for all the world like a bouncer ready to throw any threat through the wall. Gods, was he a menace.

"Better?" he asked her.

She nodded. "Better."

He uncrossed his arms, the action drawing her attention to the item he clutched in his hand.

"Is that a key card?"

He motioned toward the healthcare supply room, the locked door marked with a sign strictly prohibiting public access.

Loren winced, realizing what the key card was for. "Here I thought the restroom thing was bad," she began in a hushed voice as they crossed the hall, "and now we're about to break into a medical supply room with a key card you somehow managed to steal during the three minutes—three minutes, Darien!—it took me to go pee?"

"Tell me something, sweetheart." His voice was a low purr that made her aching toes curl in her boots. "What about me strikes you as someone who abides by the law?"

"Not a darn thing," she admitted, blinking up at him the way she knew he liked. Indeed, his eyes tightened, pupils flaring—just a bit. But it took a lot to unravel Darien Cassel, so *just a bit* she considered a major success. "But I'm a goody two shoes, and I'm not afraid to admit it." Safe, ordinary, and orderly—that was how she'd always preferred her life.

Until she'd met Darien Cassel and discovered what chaos tasted like, and gods did she love this man's chaos.

"Good." He swiped the card. The security system beeped, the red light turning green. "You should own everything that you are." He pushed the door open, holding it for her as she walked in. Darien followed closely behind her, his presence so electric she felt her skin prickle as if the air were charged with a thunderstorm.

The lights buzzed awake in rows as the sensors picked up on their presence. The place was cold and sterile, most of the furnishing made of metal. It was a good thing a simple key card was the only layer of security they had to get through; without Tanner Atlas and his impressive hacking skills, they would've been in a pickle.

Darien sauntered through the room as if he owned it. "Have a seat." His bass voice echoed. When he saw her glancing around in search of a chair that didn't exist, he clarified, "On the table."

She planted her palms on the surface—cold even through her gloves— and hopped up as Darien began sifting through drawers and cupboards, grabbing everything he needed. Being a Darkslayer came with enough risks and guaranteed injuries that knowing your medicines wasn't a *maybe*, it was a *must*.

Recent events seemed to be shoving her dangerously close to hysterics, because she nearly busted out laughing when he put on a pair of blue nitrile gloves over the ones she knew he couldn't remove. His hands were so big, they barely fit, making this even more funny.

He must have sensed her amusement, because he looked over his shoulder at her. "It's the best I can do," he said, the second glove snapping against his wrist. At least one of them maintained enough sanity to have cleanliness on the mind. That bodysuit of his was mucked up with so much dirt and gore, she shuddered at the thought of what she'd see crawling under a microscope.

She swung her feet and glanced around the room as he prepared everything, feeling safer than she had all day, simply from being in the same vicinity as him. The effect he had on her was pure magic.

A strong arm wrapped around her waist from behind, sliding her backward so she was closer to the other edge of the table—closer to him for easier access.

"This is going to sting," he warned as he worked on parting her tangled hair into two sections that draped over her shoulders. The strands tugged on the blisters and scabs, opening a few of them up.

She flattened her hands against the tabletop, bracing for more pain. Now that she was this far back, there was nothing to hold onto—nothing to squeeze. "Are there any painkillers in here?" She'd be surprised if there wasn't; by the looks of the neatly stocked shelves and cupboards, this place was loaded.

"Shit, that reminds me," he muttered, still working on the matted strands. Every movement was exceptionally careful, especially for someone as dangerous as him. "I was on my way to the nurse's station when this absolutely beautiful blonde decided to bump into me and jumbled my thoughts." Her face turned flaming hot. "She distracted me so badly, I completely forgot what I was doing."

She cleared her throat. "She sounds pretty great."

Darien drew in a hiss through his teeth. "Fuck me, Loren, did your suit melt off or something?" Indeed, her back was exposed from shoulder blades to waist. At least it hadn't burned down far enough that she was walking around with a bare ass.

"Why were you going to the nurse's station?" she asked him.

It took him a moment to respond, as if he were realizing he'd already said too much. Metal clinked as he began opening tubes and bottles and setting out tools. Liquid glugged, and it took all her strength not to cry out as he touched something wet to her back and began cleaning her wounds. Finally he admitted, "Painkillers."

Her brow furrowed. "Painkillers? Who for? Yourself?" She turned her head to the side, trying to peer at his expression, but it was pointless—she couldn't see him from this position. "Darien, did you hurt yourself?" Was that the reason he and Roman were here? When he still didn't answer, she tried to turn around and look at him—

"Face forward, please," he said, stilling her with a gentle hand gripping her waist, his fingers wrapping around her left side. Her stomach did a backflip—but swiftly dropped through her feet when he confessed, "I broke my hand again."

Panic burned through her body like acid. Only then did she realize that he was mostly using his left hand. Even when he'd pinned Malakai against the wall, it wasn't his right hand he'd used.

"How did you break it?" she persisted, clinging to the feel of the heat lingering on her side from his touch. Even with two pairs of gloves and her bodysuit separating his skin from hers, it'd felt amazing to be touched by him.

Darien hesitated for a beat before saying, "I used it too much."

"You used it too much," she repeated with a quiet scoff. She swallowed the dryness in her mouth, his lie forcing her to forget how happy she was to see him and instead remember how hurt she'd felt last night, when they'd gotten into that argument. When she'd discovered the horrible truth he'd kept from her. "I'm going to have trouble trusting you again if you keep lying, Darien. You already didn't tell me about your bargain—"

"I got into a fight with Donovan, and he broke it."

Loren felt like someone had kicked her in the chest. "Donovan?" she spluttered. "He... He broke your hand?" The bruises she'd noticed on Darien's face... Gods, *Don* had done that to him—

The ripping of gauze and tape was the only sound for several long seconds, apart from the frantic drumming of her heartbeat.

"I didn't want to tell you because I know he frightens you," Darien said. "And because *I'm* the fighter—I'm supposed to be able to protect you." Of course he would find a way to shift blame onto himself. A beat of silence as he carefully spread a thin layer of antibiotic ointment across the blistered flesh, his touch soothing. "And I don't know if I'd be able to protect you from him, if he ever decided to target you." He flattened the first strip of gauze across her back, followed by several more. They clung to her like garments with static cling, and he taped them down on unbroken skin. "But I'd die trying."

Several moments of silence went by as he finished tending to her.

"I don't want you to lie to me anymore," she whispered into the quiet room, her scalp prickling from the courage it took her to say it.

She didn't need to be a hellseher to sense the sudden tension rolling off him.

"I don't lie to you," Darien said.

But you did, she thought.

Instead she whispered, "Withholding the truth when it's something that important is just as bad." She hated how her words trembled on their way out.

As much as she trusted Darien, a part of her was afraid there was more he was keeping from her. Maybe not anything that could hurt her, but something that could hurt him—another truth as bad as his bargain.

"So we're back to this?" Darien said, his voice hard. He taped the last piece of gauze down and began cleaning up.

"Well, we didn't technically get the chance to finish," she said breathlessly. She peered over her shoulder at him as he moved about, putting things back in their rightful places. "You stomped out." She knew she had played her own role in how their fight had ended—a role she wasn't proud of—but Darien could have done a better job of handling himself, too. "I meant what I said, Darien. You've practically killed yourself—" Her voice cracked on the last word, her eyes stinging.

She dropped her gaze to her lap.

Get yourself under control.

"I understand why you're upset," Darien said. Out of the corner of her eye, she saw him dumping his gloves and the blood-stained gauze into the trash bin. He turned to face her, hands hanging loosely at his sides. "But you could use a lesson on self-love too, Loren."

She lifted her head and looked at him, her vision swimming.

Looking as tortured as he had in the waiting room, Darien explained, "You never take your medication when you should. You go for way too long without eating. And you use your magic when you know full well that it could kill you." His chest rose and fell with labored breaths. "Am I missing anything? Even if I am, I think I just listed enough evidence to convince anyone that you need to start caring more about yourself, too. You even tried to hide your back from me. I refuse to stand by while you destroy yourself, Loren—"

"Do *not* talk to me about destroying myself, Darien Cassel, not when you're the king of self-destruction!" Her words snagged on a sob. "The fighting, the killing when you don't have to, the self-hatred, the *drugs.*" The last one made him flinch. "Yeah," she said, her voice cracking again, "don't think I don't know about that. Ivy told me you're addicted to Venom."

His left hand curled into a fist. "I'm going to get off it—"

"Don't make it be for me this time," she blurted, hating herself when she saw him wince again. But she stayed on her course of action and whispered, "Make it be for you."

Speechless, he stared at her, his mouth a firm line.

She stared back, willing the tears not to fall.

"Nice little homecoming we've got going on, hey?" he said with a pained scoff. "We've barely been together for thirty minutes, I'm about to have a Surge, and look at you—you're already crying."

She looked away from him, staring down at her filthy boots. Not because she was intimidated, but because she couldn't bear to see the hurt on his face any longer.

She needed to do better for herself—Darien wasn't wrong about that. But more importantly, *he* had to do better for himself.

She tried not to regret where this conversation had gone—not when she knew that all of this needed to be said. Darien was on a collision course with two versions of himself—the man he was and the person he wanted so badly to be. Those two men were so different it was like forcing two magnets together when all they wanted was to repel each other. He was trying so hard to do better for her, and she loved him for it. Gods, did she ever. But he needed to stop trying to change solely for her—he had to do it for himself, too.

Because if—*when*—the Widow's prediction eventually came true, and she died before the age of twenty-one, Darien would need to move on from her. And she wouldn't rest until she knew he could do it without destroying himself out of the grief and guilt he'd surely feel if he failed to save her. So what if his life was tied to hers? She still had time to undo the bargain—time to push him out of the path of the bullet he'd fired from his own gun. Weeks, maybe. Months, hopefully. No matter how long or short, she would use the last of her time wisely and do everything she could to fix what he'd done.

"Are you ready to get out of here?" Darien's question was gruff, and when she lifted her head to look at him she saw that his eyes were a solid black that gleamed like pools of ink under the lights.

Another Surge. And with that newly broken hand of his, he couldn't even use fighting as an outlet. Not that it was an option right now, given everything that was going on.

She slid off the table.

"Hey," he called after her as her feet hit the floor.

She looked his way. Even with the black eyes, and even with the tension of their argument still crackling between them, he managed to speak softly to her.

"Be mad if you want to be mad," he said. "Hate me if you want to hate me. But with all this fuckery going on outside—" He pointed at the door—at the city crumbling beyond these walls. "I want you with me at all times. Even if we're not talking, you go where I go. Understand?"

She nodded, hating that this was where they were at now. "I understand."

17

INTENSIVE CARE UNIT
YVESWICH, STATE OF KER

"Then the waterfall took us south," Roman said. "To a neighborhood in East Montgomery."

Travis Devlin sat across from his brother in the ICU waiting room, listening intently as Roman explained the hellish obstacles he and Darien had been forced to navigate on their way here. The sword that had helped them see in the dark, the vines that had tried to strangle them in the tunnels, the droves of monsters they'd killed, the pit they'd fallen into.

"Darien thinks Spirit Terra colliding with our world is causing the falls to turn into portals." Roman looked like he was having trouble believing what his own mouth was saying. "He said something about the Veil being thinner near places of constant movement, I don't fucking know." He waved a gloved hand in frustration, then cupped his forehead, massaging his temples. "It's hard to explain this shit when I can hardly understand it."

"You're doing fine," Ivy offered.

"I recall Tamika mentioning this," Lace piped up, addressing the Devils in the room. "She said it has something to do with the elements, remember guys?" Travis, Max, and Jack grunted their agreements, though Jack looked like he didn't *really* remember and was only pretending to. "By the sounds of what you're telling us, Roman, Darien's probably right."

Roman drew a deep breath that snagged on its way through. He lifted his head and clasped his hands between his knees, looking aged.

"What happened after that?" Travis murmured.

His brother didn't even look at him—he hardly had this whole damn time. Travis could admit he had a lot to learn when it came to reading people without the Sight, but he was no idiot—he knew precisely why Roman was being pissy with him. The main reason was this: Travis, the middle brother, was stuck here with him, in a city that was quickly imploding—the same city Roman had gone through hell to help him escape only a few years prior, giving him a fresh start and a life of freedom he so badly wanted for himself.

Little did Roman know he'd soon be even more pissed when they finally reached the topic of Paxton. How they were going to tackle *that* issue was still up for debate—and they didn't have the luxury of waiting to address it for much longer. Not when Paxton needed them.

"Then...," Roman began, "we started walking. We almost made it here when we heard you screaming," he said to Ivy.

Ivy's forehead creased, heads turning to look at her.

"At least...we thought it was you. Turns out it was some sort of illusion —like what Shay can do. One my dad was casting."

Ivy held up a finger. "Wait—hold up. What sort of illusion?"

"Sounds more like a hypnotist monster to me," Jack muttered, flopping his melted ice pack between his hands.

"I was gonna say," Kylar said, looking thoroughly confused.

Roman pressed on. "Darien hasn't explained all of it to me, but he swore he heard you screaming, Ivy. So we followed the sound, and it led us to this brand new house in a new subdivision. The atmosphere felt like a Crossroads, so I tried to tell him not to go in. But it was like he was in a trance or something—he wouldn't listen to me. He insisted on making sure you were okay, so he went in, and when I tried to follow him a few minutes later, he was gone. I ended up running up and down the street looking for him, thinking maybe he'd left, and when I made it back to the house I noticed that something about it was different. It was just a feeling, mostly. And when I went inside, I found Darien passed out on the floor, the whole place wrecked, his hand broken to shit. He said my dad lured him into that house and forced him to fight." The horror on his face caused sweat to prickle down Travis's spine. "My dad pinned him down and re-broke his hand."

Travis's jaw dropped.

Everyone sat there, stunned. Even Malakai, who usually had so much trouble shutting the fuck up, had nothing smart to say.

Darien being pinned? *Darien* losing in a fight? It was unheard of.

Roman's throat bobbed. He rubbed the stubble on his chin, looking like he'd seen a ghost. "I still need to ask him what exactly happened but I didn't want to do it until he got his hand looked at. So I convinced him to come here. A Healer fixed him up—" He suddenly bolted upright in his chair. "Oh shit, that reminds me." He glanced around.

"What?" Max asked, following his line of sight to the desk.

"We came here with Darien's Healer—she's the reason we ran into you guys. We were heading to this station so she could give us some painkillers and check the patient records for Shay."

"Shay?" several mouths echoed. Now that Roman was mentioning it, Travis thought he remembered seeing a startled brunette slipping past their group while Darien nearly killed Malakai.

Too bad he hadn't finished the job.

"Yeah," Roman said. "I wanted her to see if Shay's been here for any injuries—" He stopped talking, his features sinking into a frown. "Why's everyone looking at me like that?"

"Shay followed us to the tar pits," Ivy began. "She wanted to help us get into the tunnels, and when we were attacked by some hounds, she..." She cleared her throat, fingers tapping anxiously against her knee.

Roman squeezed the armrests of his chair. "Don't say it."

Ivy's next words came out in a rush. "We got separated from her."

"Is she dead?" Roman's question sounded strangled.

"We don't know for certain," Aspen said, speaking cautiously. "We tried looking for her after the explosion, but we couldn't find her."

Roman slumped against the back of his seat, hands lying loosely on the armrests. "If you've got anything else bad to say, get it over with. I'm not sure I can handle much more."

It was Kylar's turn to take the mic. "Some of Don's Shadowmasters went to your house."

Roman let out a cold, mocking laugh, Kylar's statement pushing him toward the edge. "Great. How do you know this?"

"We heard them talking," Max said. "They're after Pax."

Kylar jumped back in. "They said no one was at the house but Arthur."

"What the hell is that supposed to mean?" Roman forced out, looking like he was having trouble breathing.

"We're hoping," Lace began, leaning down to rub the muscles in her calves, "it means Dominic and Blue were able to hide the kids." Travis had been praying for *hours* that they were able to hide them.

If they weren't... If Paxton was gone...

"And if they weren't?" Roman gritted out.

Kylar said, "Then we're assuming it means they got lost."

"How the hell would they get lost?" Roman demanded. He worked to keep his voice down, well aware that the desk was only a few feet away. They'd covered the area in spells to muffle their voices but not silence them entirely, everyone far too exhausted for that level of magic. "They were in my house," Roman persisted, in denial. "They were safe at home—"

"They could've got scared and ran," Ivy offered gently.

"Especially if they attacked Arthur," Jack said. "That would be traumatizing for anyone, but especially two twelve-year-old kids." His wife nodded.

"Or they believed they could help," Max said.

"Help?" Roman echoed. "Explain."

"They're kids. Maybe they decided they wanted to be heroes and ran off to save the day."

Roman sucked in a breath and clawed his fingers down his face, pulling his lower lids down. "This," he began, "is the worst night of my life."

Everyone murmured in agreement.

"It's day, technically," Lace said, checking the time on her phone. "No matter what, we need to think of a plan. We can't just keep sitting here. We need to make sure Arthur's alive and the kids didn't run away."

Roman suddenly stood up, pausing their conversation. He went to the desk and spoke quietly to the receptionist, and when he came back he had a bottle of painkillers in hand. He sat back down, shook two pills into his gloved palm, then tossed them back dry.

"Anything?" Ivy asked him.

Roman shook his head, flexing his throat muscles as the last pill shimmied down. "No Shay. Anyone else want any?" He offered up the pill bottle.

"I will," Dallas said. He tossed it to her.

"I'm staying here," Malakai said. "I'm not leaving my sister. I still think it's asinine to split up, but you guys do you. Make sure the old guy's fine and put a leash on those kids."

"I'll stay with Malakai," Aspen said. "I think if we're going to split up, we shouldn't spread our groups too thin. Anyone else want to stay behind with us?"

Their conversation came to another standstill as they picked up on the footfall of two pairs of boots, one with a much heavier gait than the other.

Darien and Loren came around the corner, looking miles worse than when they'd left. Travis would be willing to bet they'd circled back to last night's argument, and whatever words they'd exchanged had prompted the

black shining in Darien's eyes. He shadowed Loren like a bodyguard—
protecting her back while his lethal gaze picked apart everything in front of
her in search of threats. As for Loren, she looked dejected and plain tired,
but regardless of what she was feeling it wasn't strong enough to make her
step away from Darien.

Roman rose. "We should go. Paxton's missing, and from what these
guys are telling me, he's got Shadowmasters on his tail."

"We don't know for sure if he's missing," Max clarified for Darien and
Loren's benefit. "We're hoping Dominic and Blue are hiding him and his
friend someplace safe."

"Hope isn't good enough for me," Roman snapped. "As far as I'm
concerned, until I see Paxton standing in front of me with my own two
eyes, he's missing and he needs our help."

"Your truck survived," Lace said to Darien. "It was easy enough to get
here, so we shouldn't have any problem driving to Roman's."

"Who's all coming?" Darien asked.

"So far, everyone except Malakai and Aspen," Kylar replied.

"And me," Travis said, lifting a finger.

Malakai loosed a cold laugh, silver eyeteeth winking. "Oh fuck no."

"Try telling that to Jewels," Travis rebuked. "And I bet she'll finally
disown your controlling ass." Why did the one girl he liked—*really* liked—
have to have a massive asshole for a brother? Lucky him.

Malakai scoffed. "In your dreams, Devlin. I'm her *family*. Only idiots
choose fuckboys over family, and unfortunately for you, Jewels isn't an
idiot."

"Can we please stop?" Ivy groaned, rubbing her temples in a circular
motion. "Either you're both staying here so I don't have to listen to you
anymore, or you're separating so you stop arguing."

"One vote for separating!" Malakai shouted, shooting a hand into
the air.

Travis crossed his arms. "I'm staying here," he declared. "So get used to
it, Delaney."

Ivy slapped her thighs and stood, offering her concussed husband a
hand up. "Alright, that settles it. You're both staying here, and the rest of us
are going to Roman's."

"I hate this," Malakai muttered.

"We need to find Atlas," Darien said, still looming behind Loren. If she
moved, he moved. If something got her attention, he looked at it too, as if
ready to kill whatever *it* was. Travis pitied any poor soul who even *glanced*

at her. "We'll go to Roman's house, figure out what happened with the kids, then take it from there. How soon can they release Jewels?"

"Haven't asked," Malakai replied, his tone still edged with irritation from their run-in.

"You guys can't stay here for long. We all know what's *really* going on out there," Darien said, lowering his voice as he tipped his head toward the windows. Outside, the sky was pitch black, the navigation lights on flying helicopters hardly more than pinpricks in a black shroud. While everyone in their group knew the truth about Spirit Terra and the Well, the rest of the city was in the dark. No pun intended. "If we aren't out of Yveswich by the time that darkness spreads to the other districts, we'll be fucked."

As if the darkness had ears, the lights flickered. One hallway plunged into shadow. Chairs creaked as the people working at the desk shifted, murmuring to each other in fearful tones.

Travis stood up, angling his body toward Jewels's room. Ready to bolt if another outage happened.

"You're really not coming?" Roman asked him as the lights returned to normal.

Travis dragged his gaze to his brother, steeling himself for a full-blown argument. "Is that okay?" He hated that he still felt like he had to ask for Roman's permission to do things.

Roman narrowed his eyes. "You're asking if it's okay that you don't help us look for your kid brother, who's probably scared as hell right now?"

Guilt settled heavily in his stomach like a rock. "Way to make me feel like shit, Rome."

"We'll have more than enough people to look for the kids," Kylar interjected. "I think Aspen's right about not spreading ourselves too thin. And besides, Travis is one of the only people who's willing to stay with Malakai."

"*Jewels,*" Travis corrected. "I'm staying for Jewels."

"Fuck all you sons of bitches," Malakai snapped. He got up and stalked for Jewels's room. "I'm outta here. Try not to die."

"As soon as we locate Pax, we're leaving. All of us," Darien said to Travis. "I don't care if you have to wheel Jewels out of here on a stretcher— you're not staying in Yveswich."

"I didn't plan on it," Travis said, trying not to get his back up as more instructions were fired his way. He was used to getting orders from Darien —it was part of being a Darkslayer who answered to the Head of the House. But having Roman still treat him the same way he did Pax, even after all this time...it was an adjustment. He persisted, "I only want to make sure she has enough people with her in case something bad happens." He could feel Roman's stare burning a hole in his face, but Travis didn't meet his gaze.

"Roman filled you all in?" Darien asked, scanning the group.

"For the most part, but we have a lot of questions," Lace replied, grabbing the sword she'd leaned against the leg of her chair. It was the one Ivy had been carrying. Max had the second, and Darien had the third—and last.

"You can ask me on the way," Darien said. When he addressed Travis next, his tone was stern, his face so grave he looked carved from stone. "If your dad shows up, you are not to engage with him. You are to run. Run as fast as you can and don't slow down until you get away from him and make it someplace safe. Do I make myself clear?" The tension, the fear in the air at Darien's mention of Don, was palpable.

The thought of going head to head with the father he hadn't seen in years tied Travis's gut into knots, but he managed to give Darien a stiff nod.

"Good, that's all settled, then," Darien said, though the severity on his face remained. He tipped his head toward the hallway at his back. "Let's roll out."

Those who were leaving stood, gathered their weapons, and began making their way down the hall, Aspen walking the opposite way after saying a quick goodbye to Lacey.

Roman was the only person who stayed put. Staring Travis down as if he'd spat in his face.

"Are we really going to argue right now?" Travis kept his voice low.

Roman stepped closer. Held up a finger between them. "You stay in this hospital and you don't leave until we get back. With Dad on a rampage to find Pax, he'll be all over you too if he finds out you're back in town." *Rampage* didn't even begin to sum up the lengths Don was likely going to in order to find Pax. And Travis had to admit it made him nervous that *Darien* couldn't even handle Don. The fact that he'd shattered his hand... leaving him passed out on the ground...

Don could have killed him. But, for whatever reason, he hadn't.

Travis swallowed the lump in his throat. "I'll be fine."

Roman lowered his hand, his eyes burning like black fire. "You better be."

18

THE COFFEE CORNER
YVESWICH, STATE OF KER

"Get whatever you want," Darien said from behind her as Loren scanned the selection of premade sandwiches and wraps in the glass-paneled display case. With the massive Devil looming at her back, she wouldn't be surprised if she wasn't visible from behind at all.

The Coffee Corner was on the ground floor of the hospital. Upon seeing her serpent tattoo glowing red through the rips in her suit, Darien had insisted on stopping for food before heading out. But it was so chaotic down here, Loren found it difficult to focus enough to read the tiny labels listing the ingredients on each item.

"Did you read the sign?" a female voice squawked over the din.

Loren looked up to see the employee—half-wolf—peeking over the display case with sunset-colored eyes, her tied-back hair in a net.

"What sign?" Darien asked.

She grabbed the sign on the counter—the one that said CASH ONLY—and spun it around so they could see it better. "Cell service is still down, so our machines aren't working. We can only accept cash."

He cursed, scanning the crowds behind him.

Ivy was already there. "Here." She handed him a twenty.

"I'll pay you back," he said, snapping the folded bill open. She didn't even acknowledge him before walking away, still as upset with him as she was with Loren. "What do you want?" he asked Loren.

"A turkey and cheese panini, please," she said to the worker. "And two chocolate chip cookies."

The wolf grabbed the panini from the case and bagged the cookies with tongs. "Anything to drink?"

"A cola, please." She needed as much sugar and caffeine as she could get, or she just might drop dead before they made it to Roman's.

"Anything for yourself?" she asked Darien as she grabbed a bottle of cola from the cooler.

"Same thing my woman's having," he replied, not bothering to look at the selection. The way he said *my woman* made Loren blush, and it took everything in her power not to look at his face.

Darien paid, and the employee slid their items across the counter.

"Are you okay if we eat in the truck?" Darien said as they navigated the crowds. People moved when they saw the Devil coming.

"Yeah, that's fine." It was more than fine—she was eager to get out of here. To get someplace safe and sleep for fourteen hours.

The others were waiting for them by the sliding glass doors. They walked through those doors the minute Darien prompted them to do so, Ivy waiting just long enough to take what Darien was carrying. Loren followed her through the doors, Darien on her heels—

And sucked in a gasp as a bitter wind slapped her in the face, freezing her to the bone. Flakes of snow floated through the parking lot, looking more like clumps of ash beneath the pitch black sky.

It had gotten even darker while they were inside.

"It's a zoo out here," Roman said, breath fogging before him. It absolutely was.

There were people and vehicles everywhere, blocking each other from getting out of or into the huge parking lot. Cops and Fleet soldiers were fighting to achieve order, some directing traffic, others assisting injured or panicking civilians.

Dallas was standing on her tiptoes, craning her neck to see around the crowds. Loren had no idea what she was peering so intently at—

Until a pair of magnificent white wings, broad shoulders, and a head of windswept copper hair caught her attention.

"Dad?" Dallas blurted. When the man standing several meters away didn't turn, too busy speaking with another Fleet soldier, she took a step forward. Froze before she could get too close, her gloved hands balling into fists. *"Dad!"* Gods, she was so brave for shouting at him while he was busy working. That was the number one rule you didn't break in the Bright household.

Roark turned around.

Loren had spent almost her whole life—apart from when Roark traveled for work—under the same roof as this man, so she knew what to expect from him in almost any scenario. But tonight, she could say with absolute certainty that this was the first time she had ever seen Roark so utterly blindsided.

He stood there, taking in their group as if he couldn't make sense of what he was seeing.

When his amber eyes settled upon Loren, her stomach tumbled under the attention—attention he rarely gave to either of his daughters.

"Loren?" His question sounded as shocked as his face looked.

"Hi," she said, the word a shaky whisper. She wasn't sure why she was reacting this way—Roark had never opened up to her enough for either of them to show much emotion to the other. But that raw look on his face...it rendered her speechless. Made her feel things she had never felt around him before. And made her wonder if she had ever truly understood or seen him for who he really was.

Of course she hadn't. Of course she hadn't, because he had never shown her. The Roark she knew was the Red Baron—that was all. The hard-ass General of the Fleet Army. Father only by title—never by action.

Dallas came up to Loren's left. "What are you doing here?" she asked him, snowflakes settling in her burnished copper hair.

His features shifted into the neutral mask he usually wore. "It's my job, Dallas. It's what I do." There was the Roark they all knew.

His eyes flashed to Darien. When he spoke, his tone was slightly gravelly. "It worked." A question—not a statement like he was making it sound.

Darien stepped up behind Loren. When his arms came around her from behind, wrapping around her like a hug, she realized she was shivering. "It worked," he said hoarsely, his hands rubbing her upper arms to warm them.

Since their argument in the healthcare supply room, they had barely talked or made eye contact. But while they were both upset with each other, arguably equally, Darien wasn't letting this stop him from caring for her. She suddenly felt much warmer, and she knew his chiseled body pressing against hers was only partly responsible for that.

Three soldiers came up to Roark in need of instruction, giving them the chance to figure out their own plan of action.

"Where did you park?" Darien asked the group, angling both himself and Loren toward the others. It was so cold, she might as well be standing here naked. Her suit was doing nothing to warm her.

"Lot B," Max responded. "It isn't far."

"Someone should grab the truck and pull it around while the rest of us wait here," Darien said, his deep voice a rumble against Loren's back. "I want to have a word with Roark, soon as he has a minute."

As if he heard them, the Red Baron gestured for Darien to join him nearby.

Darien let go of her, his hand brushing against her lower back. She took the gesture—the wordless request—for what it was and crossed the short space to Roark, Darien forever shadowing her, while the others stayed put. Listening, Loren would bet.

"I'd wager that you know more about what happened here last night than I do," Roark began, speaking quietly.

"Well replica," Darien said. "The imperator set a trap for us by taking someone we know hostage, and we walked right into it. He was keeping the replica in the tunnels below Caliginous on Silverway."

Roark's eyes darted to Loren, the silver rings around his pupils glinting as he arrived at the same conclusion Darien was about to voice.

"He planted the replica there so when Loren was using the Reverse Chamber the channels funneled her magic down the chamber and into the bomb." Darien added with disgust, "Fucking clever, I gotta hand it to him." So *that* was how the bastard had done it.

Roark lifted his chin, a muscle working in his jaw. "And where is the imperator now?"

"You want my best guess? Far enough away that there was no chance he'd be hit by the blast, but he'll most likely be coming back sooner than later to search for the real Well."

Loren said quietly, "I told him it was in the Void. I lied to protect its real location, but I swear I didn't know anything bad was going to happen, I didn't know he was going to blow up the city and hurt all these people—" The last word got caught as her throat shut.

Darien pressed his hand against her lower back in comfort. She leaned into his touch and breathed in deeply, focusing on touch, sight, sound, smell.

Roark sucked in a sharp breath of his own. "Darien, listen to me. You have until noon tomorrow to get out of the city. *Noon*—and not a second later. The minute I give the order, a new forcefield will go up, and no one will be allowed in or *out* of Yveswich."

Loren's heart tripped a beat, the others who were eavesdropping behind them communicating in frantic whispers.

"Quarantine?" Max asked, his question rising above the panic.

The others quieted down. Waiting for Roark's reply.

Roark kept his focus on Darien. "Tell only who you must," he said. "Take only what you need. If you are not out of the city by noon tomorrow, you will be trapped here, and there is nothing I or anyone else will be able to do to help you."

Loren felt woozy as his words sank in. "They're going to leave all these people behind to die?" The last of the survivors—children and the elderly among them. Walled in like cattle in a city of wolves.

Roark spared her a glance—just one. Loren swore she saw...*something* there. Compassion, perhaps. But it was gone so quickly, she wondered if she imagined it.

"A stronger forcefield is our best attempt at containing the spread," he explained to Darien, lowering his voice as people walked by. "It won't hold —not for long. But we have no other choice. Until we come up with a proper solution, containing it—slowing it—for as long as possible is our best course of action."

Loren's head spun like a carousel, the others speaking over each other, forming plans and raising concerns.

What about Tanner? What if we can't find Paxton and Eugene? What if Shay is somewhere out there, alive and in need of help?

What if we run out of time?

"You need to get out as quickly as you can—do you understand me?" Roark pressed, speaking to them both now. Loren felt a jolt of surprise when the next breath he drew trembled. "Get. *Out.*"

PART TWO
THE CAGE

19

SOMEWHERE IN YVESWICH
STATE OF KER

S hay Cousens awoke to the clinking of glass and the rattling of tires on a cobbled road.

She cracked open her eyes, but it took her several blinks to see through her mental haze. Last she remembered, she was in the tunnels by the tar pits, blinded by the bright flash of an earth-shattering explosion. Glimpses of what happened after were all that remained—not enough to piece together the full picture. And now she was here, in a moving vehicle. Which meant...

She didn't know what it meant. But she did know this: She was lucky to be alive. Battered, yes—but alive. Her head felt like it might blow up, and the ribs in her left side were burning—fractured, she'd be willing to bet.

Groaning softly in pain, she tried to roll onto her back, but she was so disoriented she couldn't tell up from down. The hard surface she was lying upon was cold and grooved and—

A truck. This was a pickup truck with an enclosed canopy. And the lights pulsing through the windows?... Those were streetlights.

The fact that someone had her tossed back here, instead of onto a proper seat... *Huge* red flag. Surely if this was a rescue attempt, they wouldn't be treating her like cargo, would they?

She lifted her pounding head.

There were crates back here. Crates and—

Holy hell, she wasn't alone. Passed out nearby was a man, but her vision was still so blurry—had she been drugged?—that she had to catalogue his appearance in stages and bleary blinks.

Short brown hair. A full-body suit, like the one Shay wore, except his was black instead of dark blue. The magically enhanced material was filthy, ivory skin peeking through the rips. Below his ear, partially obscured by crusts of red that gleamed in the pulses of light, was a tattoo—the letter S in an old-style script, one horn at the beginning and another at the end.

Oh shit, it was Tanner Atlas. Passed out—and bleeding.

Shay pushed herself up onto her elbows, craning her neck to peer through the back window of the cab. Two men were in there, but it was hard to see much of them through the condensation on the glass.

The one in the driver's seat leaned forward to butt out a cigarette in the ash tray, the act of doing so exposing the ink below his eye—

The sight of the tiny black flame of Ignis sent Shay's stomach plummeting out her ass.

"Shit," she mouthed. She ducked down before he could spot her, heart thundering through her whole body.

Shit.

Shit. Shit. SHIT!

She should have felt grateful that she had been rescued from those monster-infested tunnels. Happy, even. And she would've been—grateful, happy—were it anyone else behind that wheel.

But these men were Wyverns—skin-changing Darkslayers who worked for Cerise Brinton and the House of Red. And the last thing a Wyvern would ever do was help a Selkie in need.

Or a Devil. Definitely not a Devil.

Knowing that what these men planned on doing to her and Tanner would be nothing short of terrible, she crawled across the truck bed. Latched onto Atlas's shoulder and shook him.

"Tanner," she hissed. A pothole jostled the truck, crates knocking together. The air was thick with the pungent odor of gasoline and other flammable liquids. *"Tanner.* Tanner, wake up." She shook him again. *"Wake up."*

Muffled voices drifted from the cab. Shay's heart tripped into a swifter beat as the driver suddenly reduced speed.

Oh gods, oh *gods,* they were going to pull over, weren't they?

She shook Tanner harder. "Wake up, Tanner—please. *Please.* Come on, Tanner—*come on!"* She lightly slapped his cheek. *"Wake up, wake up, wake up!"*

A soft mumble. A low groan.

Tanner's brow twitched as he came to, rolling onto his side.

Oh thank gods—

But the relief she felt was short-lived, the blood draining from her head as the truck screeched to a sudden halt in the middle of a road.

Tanner blinked. "Wh—"

Shay clamped a hand over his mouth.

He stared up at her, gray eyes brimming with questions. But there was zero time to explain.

She pressed her index finger against her lips. "Shh."

The truck doors creaked open, then slammed shut.

Shay let go of Tanner and lay down beside him. "Don't move," she mouthed. Maybe they wouldn't come back here, maybe they were stopping for another reason...but it was better to be cautious.

She shut her eyes tight, praying Tanner had done the same—praying they would survive whatever came next.

The tailgate dropped open with a metallic *bang*.

Another *slam* as someone leapt up into the truck bed, shaking the vehicle with a heavy stride. Her closed lids darkened as a figure loomed over her, blocking the limited light where he crouched under the truck canopy.

A boot nudged Shay in the ribs, and it cost her all her strength not to cry out in pain.

Yup, at least two of those ribs were broken. But she held still, keeping her face serene, and her body limp.

"Hey cunt," said a rough male voice.

Oh shit, it was Austin Prescott. Shay had run into this douche bag at a night club not long ago. He was shit-faced and in the mood for fish, as he'd so smoothly told her, trying to grope her between the legs. He hadn't responded well when she'd rammed the heel of her hand into his nose, fracturing it, and when he'd taken his own swing at her, two bouncers and three onlookers had intervened, throwing him out. It went without saying that she did *not* like him.

Another poke of his stupid boot. "You alive?" She wanted to cut his balls off when he nudged her cheek with the filthy toe, tilting her face up.

A kick to her side, and holy gods she could have *died* from the agony. But she kept it together, not reacting.

Through the fringe of her lashes, she watched as Austin turned his attention toward Tanner, his hand—covered in burn scars from his initiation into the House of Red—grabbing Atlas's hair by the roots, wrenching his head up and twisting his neck around so he could peer at his face. Tanner stayed limp as a doll, eyes closed. He was very convincing.

More doors opened and slammed shut. As if this could get any worse, another vehicle had arrived, gravel crunching under two new pairs of approaching feet.

"They awake yet?" called a female voice. Sybil Brinton—Cerise's eldest daughter.

"We want to have some fun," whined a second woman. Eilidh— Cerise's other daughter, younger than her terrifying older sister by two years. But while her sister was stronger in combat, Eilidh's unhinged mind and insatiable thirst for bloodshed made her an equal threat.

Boots scraped as Austin shuffled out of the truck. The tailgate shuddered as he hopped off, wet gravel crunching under his boots. "No," he replied. "But they will be in a minute."

Shay's eyes flew open as a rough hand seized her by the ankle. With blinding speed he yanked her out of the truck—

She hit the ground screaming, the pain that exploded across her ribcage upon impact unbearable.

"Lying bitch," Austin growled over her wheezing gasps as Shay curled over herself, her vision starry. He spat. "I knew you were faking it." The other three Wyverns laughed, circling her like a pack of wolves as Austin dragged her—barely breathing through the blinding pain—several feet down the rain-drenched cobbled road, mud soaking her suit.

"Let me go," Shay choked out, clutching her side, the back of her head thumping against the cobbles. Gods, she was going to throw up or pass out —or both.

He stopped dragging her, but he didn't drop her foot.

The others crowded closer. The second male in the group—Brock Pierson—was even bigger than Austin, with blue-black hair instead of caramel. These four were some of the most ruthless in all of Yveswich— second only to Donovan Slade and his Shadowmasters. Which made Shay and Tanner not just outnumbered and overpowered, but—

Fucked. They were simply fucked.

"Let you go?" Sybil let out a cold chuckle, her pupils narrowing into vertical slits as black as her blunt bob. "Oh, honey, there's no chance of that." She kissed the tips of her fingers and blew—

Flames streamed out of her hand, taking the shape of a dragon, jaws opening to devour. Shay gawked as the dragon moved, its serpentine body wending through the chill air, wrapping all the way around the area where they were parked. It dropped to the ground, where it transformed into a wall of impenetrable fire seven feet tall, leaving no space to run.

They were trapped. She and Tanner were trapped.

Eilidh tipped her head back with a cackle. She was Sybil's opposite, hair white and eyes pale instead of dark. "Fish outta waterrrrrr," she sang as Shay flinched away from the flames that roared ever higher. Shay's skin was sweating from the stifling heat, her ankle still ensnared in Austin's bruising grip. They could burn her right here, in this pocket of heat, if they felt so inclined, while the rest of the city froze.

"Let go of me!" Shay growled, kicking her feet. But Austin did no such thing.

Eilidh gave a venomous smile, her reptilian pupils razor-thin. "Let's see if you burn, little fishy." A snap of her fingers, and a flame of her own appeared on the pad of her thumb, as if she'd struck a lighter—

"Hold on," Brock said, stepping up to Austin's side. He drew his gun from a concealed holster in the front waistband of his jeans. Aimed between Shay's eyes. Clicked the safety off. "We need her to talk first."

"She'll talk if I burn her!" Eilidh argued through gritted teeth. Her tongue was forked, fire dancing in her eyes.

"Hey!" shouted a male voice. *Oh no.* Shay's stomach sank, her eyes briefly shutting in defeat.

No. No, no, no—*not Tanner! No!*

"Hey!" Tanner barked again. "Leave her alone!"

Austin dropped her foot. Shay twisted around on the rain-damp cobbles to see Tanner hopping out of the back of the truck.

"Tanner Atlas." Austin's grin was cold and mocking. "What a surprise. Looking at you makes me feel like I'm looking at a celebrity."

"I'm flattered. I can't say I know who you are."

"Austin Prescott." Austin said his own name as if they should fall to their knees and worship him.

"Never heard of you," Tanner said—just to piss him off, Shay knew.

Austin's jaw flexed.

"What do you want from us?" Tanner demanded, hands hanging open at his sides. He had no weapons—nothing that would give them even the slightest upper hand here. The Wyverns had taken everything they had, even the blades tucked into the ribbing of their bodysuits. Shay could feel their absence as if she were missing limbs.

"We want you to tell us where Paxton is," Brock replied. He pointed his gun at Tanner, teasing the trigger. "And then we're gonna kill you."

"Paxton?" Tanner said. "You're looking for Paxton Slade? Why?"

Eilidh hissed, eyes wild like a hunting cat, "None of your goddamn business, Devil!"

But Austin said, in that hateful I-know-more-than-you tone, "Don's offering a promotion to the first House who finds his kid. And the Wyverns deserve that promotion more than anyone." He stared down at Shay. "Say goodbye to second place, Cousens."

"You say that as if I actually give a shit," she squeezed out, her ribs still burning hotter than the fire crackling around them and the truck. What happened to her mother and the cesspool that was the Riptide was of zero concern to her. She hoped Donovan killed them all.

"Tell us where he is and we'll make your deaths quick," Sybil said.

"How would I know?" Tanner challenged. "I've been drugged and unconscious—"

So they *had* drugged them.

"You know what I'd *really* like you to tell us?" Sybil interrupted. Shay tensed when she saw that her pupils were slitted again, her heart glowing orange in her chest—visible through her pasty skin. The wyvern-scale ring on her finger was the reason the Wyverns were so indestructible. If only they could get that ring... "What a good-for-nothing Devil is doing in our city," Sybil concluded, her teeth sharpening.

"I have friends here," Tanner replied. "Am I not allowed to visit them?"

"Darkslayer law states that any slayer from another territory must report their arrival to the city's Head," Sybil rebuked. Her loopy little sister sniggered, enjoying this far too much. "Is there a reason you didn't want to tell Don that you were coming? A reason you were sleuthing around?"

Tanner kept his mouth shut.

"Secrets," Eilidh hissed. "He's keeping secrets, and I want them, Sybil, I want them!" She curled her snow-white fingers in the air before her, as if to say *give them to me,* her nails black and claw-like.

"Well?" Sybil snapped.

Still, Tanner did not reply.

Sybil lifted her chin, peering down her nose at him with fiery eyes. "Kill them."

Shay's gut dropped.

"On your knees, Atlas," Austin ordered, opening the chamber of his handgun.

But Tanner stayed standing. "No," he said firmly, his throat bobbing. Even from here, Shay could see his pulse racing in his neck.

"He *said,*" Sybil drawled, raising her index finger. "On. Your. *Knees.*" A downward point of her finger, and Tanner dropped like a puppet on strings, knees slamming into the stones so hard he grunted.

Shay's hands flew to the back of her head as Brock grabbed a fistful of her hair. She swallowed a cry of pain as he dragged her several feet, whipping her around like a rag doll until she was kneeling beside Tanner. The cobbles dug into her kneecaps, her scalp burning as badly as her ribs.

"Hands behind your heads," Brock instructed.

Shay obeyed, trembling in the half-frozen rain that was now falling in sheets, plastering her hair to her head. Farther out, it was snowing, the heart of the city suffocating beneath the weight of a massive black cloud that looked like smoke.

Gods above. Was that the Void?

Beside her, Tanner did the same, hands shaking as he interlocked them behind his head.

"Last chance," Austin warned. Bullets clinked as he loaded the last of them into his gun and closed the chamber. "Tell us where Paxton is, and we'll make this quick."

"I already told you." Apart from the tremors in his hands, Tanner was so rigid, he was practically made of stone. "I. Don't. Know."

"Pity. I think I'll shoot off your ear first. Or maybe hers." Austin nudged the barrel into the back of Shay's skull.

She bristled. "Let us go, you fucking assholes!" she spat.

He tsked. "That's quite the mouth." He grabbed her around the back of her neck, fingers digging in. Then bent down, leaning in close, his hot breath grazing the shell of her ear. "I would've enjoyed fucking it that night at the club."

Shay spat at his feet.

He slapped her hard enough that her head whipped to the side.

"Hey, don't touch her!" Tanner snapped.

Austin shoved him in the back of the head. "Eyes forward, Atlas."

Eilidh giggled. "You sure we can't play for longer, Austin? I'm having fun."

"The city's being evacuated. We gotta go. So lucky for you two," he rammed the barrel of the gun into the back of Tanner's skull, causing him to rock forward on his knees. "We can't take our time."

A hollow click as he took the safety off.

"It's truly an honor that I, of all people, get to blow out that brain of yours, Atlas." Tanner's pounding heartbeat was audible, his shallow breaths clouding in the air before him. "That brilliant, *brilliant* brain. I bet Lucent Enterprises would pay good money to study you. Maybe this won't be such a waste after all."

Shay peeked at Tanner, her breaths shaking through her. His hands were interlocked behind his head, the index finger of his right hand twitching toward his left wrist. Pointing at something.

As if it had a mind of its own, the fish skeleton on her wrist—a conduit tat—began to glow.

Illusion. He was asking her to use illusion—the rare magic that wouldn't hold long enough for them to slip away.

But illusion wasn't the only power slumbering inside her.

Could she do it? Could she find the strength to control her uncontrollable gift just enough to survive this? She didn't know. But she had to trust herself.

"Say bye, Atlas," Austin crooned, finger teasing the trigger.

Now. She had to do this *now*.

"I'm so sorry, Shay," Tanner whispered hoarsely, as if any of this was his fault.

Her heart pounded, death so close she could practically taste it.

No. This wasn't happening. They weren't dying—not today.

No.

She squeezed her eyes shut and breathed, her whole body tingling as she summoned her magic—

And scared the shit out of Atlas as she bellowed a battle cry and lit those assholes up with lightning instead.

20

YVESWICH GENERAL HOSPITAL
YVESWICH, STATE OF KER

"*Noon?*" Lace seethed.

Darien stood across from Roark out front of the hospital, the others murmuring behind them, all of them processing the massive fucking bomb he'd just dropped—and calculating how many hours were left before the Fleet army would seal off the city, trapping all who failed to make it out in time behind an impenetrable forcefield. The kind that incinerated anything—living or dead—that tried to get through it.

Lace added, "That's less than seventeen hours from now!"

Less than seventeen hours was a goddamn joke. There were millions of people in Yveswich. *Millions.* Evacuation efforts had already begun, but Darien knew the public was being told so little that a lot of them would choose to stay in their homes. Choose *death*—without even fucking realizing it.

"How much do your people know about this?" he demanded of Roark. To the others, he said over his shoulder, "Someone go and get the truck. We need to leave—now."

Max and Dallas departed immediately.

Loren stood nearby, right where Darien could see her—and jump in front of a bullet for her if need be. She was shaking like a little leaf in the cold, her lips wobbling. It took all his self control not to wrap his arms around her again, not sure if that was what she wanted.

But fuck, did *he* want it. He wanted to touch her so badly it physically hurt him to resist. He still couldn't believe she was here with him—still couldn't believe he'd somehow managed not to lose her during all this insanity.

In one way, at least. He may not have lost her physically, but this stupid rift between them... They might as well be on other planets for how close he felt to her.

Thirty minutes. Thirty fucking *minutes* was all he'd had with her before last night's argument had come back to bite him in the ass. And now they were barely talking, barely looking at each other—

"They know it's the Veil," Roark replied. Darien tore his focus off Loren—off that perfect mouth he wanted so badly to kiss—with difficulty. "We have a unit that specializes in the research of inter-dimensional threats, so they know their history when it comes to the Veil and Spirit Terra. They don't know what or who caused it, they don't know about the Well or the replica. And I can assure you, they know nothing of your involvement, or Loren's—"

"Wait—are you talking about the *real* thing?" Lace interrupted. Quieter, she hissed, *"How?* Literally *how?"* She ventured two steps closer, arms crossed to keep out the bone-deep chill. "I don't understand. What happened to you being spelled?"

"I should be back in Angelthene in a few days," Roark announced, completely dodging her question. He turned his attention back to Darien, whose own mind spun at a hundred miles an hour.

How *was* he talking about the real Well? When the other Devils had made it to Yveswich after surviving an assassination attempt in Angelthene, they'd filled Darien in on what they'd learned, divulging how Roark and the other members of the Phoenix Head Society had been spelled into silence for many years. What had changed so quickly?

Unless it was all a fucking *lie*.

"Noon tomorrow," Roark repeated, as Darien stared him down—wishing he wasn't so impossible to read. "Don't forget."

The truck pulled up alongside the curb—barely managing to squeeze between other vehicles, impatient drivers blaring their horns. It had survived the blast, just like Lace said, though it was banged up, the windshield and back window cracked. At least it was drivable.

"I want to thank you," Darien said to Roark, who paused in the midst of turning away. Darien may not trust him fully, but that didn't erase the fact that Roark had set him onto the path that had saved Loren's life. He owed him a thanks—and he'd been meaning to give him one for a while. "For telling me about the chamber," Darien clarified. "If you hadn't..." He glanced at Loren, who toed at a pebble on the sidewalk, her cheeks flushed from the biting wind that blew flurries into her hair. Darien swallowed. "You're the reason she's alive."

Roark took a moment to respond, his attention flicking between Darien and the mortal daughter he'd adopted—revealing nothing, as per usual. "No, I believe that would be you."

He walked away, leaving Darien staring after him, his mind still spinning.

Loren made to follow Roark, her lips parting, as if she wanted to call after him. But she stayed put, and soon her father was swallowed up by the crowds.

Darien stepped up behind her. "Let's go." He brushed his fingers across the small of her back—stealing a touch he needed like a drug. She shivered —from the cold or the contact, he couldn't tell. "Get in the truck, please."

The others were crowding around it. Max jumped out of the driver's seat while Kylar opened the tailgate at the back. With only five seats—six if you counted the middle seat in the front that he rarely used—three of them would have to ride in the truck bed.

"Someone needs to run back inside and tell Travis what's going on," Darien declared as he and Loren joined the group. "If shit goes sideways and we can't make it back here, they need to know they have until noon tomorrow to get out."

"I'll go," Roman said. "I want to make sure Travis actually listens this time." He was already moving toward the doors—

"Hey," Darien called, stopping him before he could leave. "If you see my Healer, give her a heads up. It's the least I can do for her." Not just for mending his hand, but for letting him cut the line—and for taking him to the third floor ICU, where he'd run into Loren. Coincidence and pure dumb luck had caused their paths to cross, and besides the fact that his hand hurt like a motherfucker—even with extra-strength painkillers coursing through his system—he was glad it'd happened.

Roman nodded once and hurried inside.

"Your Healer?" Loren asked, her teeth chattering so hard the words were broken up.

"She let me cut the line," Darien explained, surprised that she was even talking to him, looking at him. "If she hadn't, I'd probably still be in there." With a tip of his head, he gestured to the ER—still crowded, the line-up out the door, all of those people having no clue what was about to hit them.

"Oh." She stared at the ground, rubbing her arms with the hands that also clutched her food and drink. The pout she wore put him on instant high alert.

Darien dipped his head, trying to catch her attention, but she wouldn't look him in the eyes. "Wait...," he mused, frowning. "You're not bothered by her—are you?"

Those eyes of hers—dark as the ocean at dusk in this lighting—flicked up to meet his. "No," she said quickly. "Of course not. I think it's good that you're looking out for someone who did you a favor. It's kind of you."

He studied that beautiful face—the jealousy she was horribly failing to mask. The jealousy he knew she was fighting—a knee-jerk reaction she'd shown toward any female in his life since they'd met. "But you wish it wasn't a *she.*" If only she knew he'd spent most of that first appointment discussing engagement rings with that same Healer.

And if only she knew that when he'd buried himself in her beautiful body later that same night, on the floor of Roman's training room, all he'd been able to think about, as she'd moaned and whimpered beneath him, was how badly he wanted to marry her. How badly he wanted to make her his in every way possible. Make her a Cassel.

"No," she breathed. But her cheeks burned a brighter pink, and Darien knew it wasn't from the cold.

A muscle twitched in his jaw. He ground his teeth so hard they ached, his blood simmering in his veins.

After everything he'd gone through for her—after everything they'd gone through *together*—she *still* felt insecure. Her jealousy was adorable, yeah, it always had been to him—but she never had anything to worry about, not when it came to his feelings for her. And it pissed him the hell off that she refused to realize that—and refused to realize how utterly perfect she was. As if any other woman stood a fucking *chance.*

Darien breathed in, cold crackling in his lungs.

Fine. *Fine*—if she needed more convincing, he'd give it to her.

As if tying his life to hers wasn't enough.

"Loren, if you had even the slightest idea how much I feel for you...," he trailed off, jaw flexing. He stared out at the snow falling in the parking lot. Took another slow, deep breath before looking back at her. "It's only ever been you," he confessed. He heard her pulse skip, and when she dropped her focus to the snow sparkling on the pavement, all he wanted was to grab her by the chin and kiss the doubt right out of her. "And it always will be," he concluded, the promise husky.

Whether you want me or not.

"Until I'm gone." She said the words so quietly, he barely heard her.

"Is *that* what you're really worried about? Who I would be with after you're gone?"

She shrugged, toeing another pebble.

"Hey. Look at me."

She peeked up at him.

"There is no *after*. Understand? Even if my life wasn't tied to yours, there would be no one after you. If you think for one second that I would be able to move on after everything we've been through together—" He sucked in a breath and pushed his hair out of his face. "Then I guess I need to do a better job of showing you just how insanely in love with you I am. Don't I? Because I am, Loren—insanely in love with you. Whether you hate me or not, whether you want to be with me or not, and whether you refuse to believe me or not. And I will spend the rest of my life—*our* life—showing you just how much I care."

"Did you trade the Widow more years than you needed to?"

Darien turned very still, the breath in his lungs freezing to ice.

Loren lifted her chin, staring up at him with eyes harder than glass, her mouth a tight line. "Did you?"

He managed to exhale. "Loren—"

"*Did* you?"

"Can we talk about this later?" he snapped. "Let me get you someplace safe before you get all worked up. And *then* you can rip into me all you want."

He watched the blood drain from her face, her next words shaky whispers. "Oh my gods. You did."

Roman jogged through the doors then, slowing as he neared their group. "We ready?"

Darien nodded, his blood still hot. Loren's face was so ghostly pale he was worried she might faint. "Let's go," he said—in a tone as soft as he could manage. Which was pretty fucking sharp right now.

She pushed past him, knocking her shoulder into his arm. Regardless that she clearly wanted to get away from him, he stayed right behind her as they rounded the truck, heading for the open driver's door.

He stepped onto the running board and propped one knee on the seat so he could flip up the center console, and then climbed back out.

"Get in the middle, please," he said, motioning to Loren, who was silently fuming, while Roman took the passenger's seat. Jack, Ivy, and Kylar took the three seats in the back. Max, Lace, and Dallas would ride in the bed.

"This is going to take forever, Darien," Max groaned as he climbed onto the tailgate, turning to offer Dallas a hand up. He pointed at the parking lot with his other as the witch clasped his hand. *"Look."*

He didn't have to—he knew it was utter mayhem.

But he had an idea.

He scanned the area, looking for white wings and copper hair—and spotted the person he was searching for standing near an ambulance.

"Hey Roark!" he called.

Roark turned.

Darien motioned, and Roark began walking this way.

When he was halfway here, Darien gestured to the madhouse of a parking lot. "Think you can help us get out of this cluster-fuck?"

Roark shifted his focus to Loren, who peeked around the open door, one foot on the running board, then to his other daughter climbing into the truck bed. "Give me two minutes."

It took him less than that before his soldiers were clearing a path—one that would lead them through the exit and onto the highway. That highway was packed with evacuating cars, but it was better than being caged in this chaotic lot any longer.

"Here, give me those," Darien said, taking Loren's soda and panini out of her hands so she could get in easier.

"I can carry them—" she tried.

"So can I." The last thing he needed was her falling. "Catch," he said to Roman, throwing one item at a time, and then faced Loren.

"I know you're upset right now," he said quietly, noting the splotches of pink in her cheeks and the telltale shine in her eyes. "But you need to keep it together and focus on staying alive. If not for yourself, then for me. Now step up."

She was about to do as he'd asked when the spitting of rapid-fire gunshots made everyone pause.

Several blocks away, soldiers were in the thick of combat, the bright flashes of fired bullets bouncing down the streets.

Monsters shrieked and roared. People—soldiers among them—screamed as claws and teeth ripped into them.

CRACK.

Darien grabbed onto the open truck door with one hand, his other arm wrapping tightly around Loren's waist as the city shook, the ground vibrating beneath his boots.

With Loren clutching his arm, he tipped his head back, peering at the sky as the interdimensional portal that stretched from below ground to the heavens ripped open right before their eyes. The area visibly darkened as more shadows billowed out of the Void, winged creatures moving through the mass as they left the land of the dead and entered the living. Their haunting cries could curdle blood.

The streetlights went out—not just flicking off, but *shattering* with sprays of glass. More people screamed as the windows glowing in apartment buildings flickered and went dark, those that were closer to the ground smashing out.

Roark may have told them they had until noon tomorrow to get out, but they'd be lucky if they survived for that long.

"We have to go!" Roman thundered.

"Step up, please," Darien said, gesturing for Loren to get in.

She stepped up—

CRACKKKKKK.

The city shook again—harder than before.

Loren's boot slipped on the wet running board, and she thumped against the rattling truck, falling backward—

Darien dove, catching her.

But he wasn't fast enough—not with the city still shaking with the force of a high-magnitude earthquake.

Not fast enough to stop her limp body from bowing over his arms as he caught her, the back of her head smacking against the ground.

The others were shouting—jumping out of the truck to help.

But Darien couldn't focus on anything apart from Loren's face—eerily peaceful, a line of blood trickling out of each nostril. And her heart—

She wasn't breathing.

21

AITHNE
YVESWICH, STATE OF KER

A spear of lightning slammed into the cobbled road, illuminating the area with a crackling blue glow.

Screams and primal, gut-wrenching cries sliced through the charged air like newly honed blades.

Shay scrambled backward, crab walking on her hands and feet, as pale lightning skittered across the rain-drenched ground. The bolts dispersed in all directions, missing her and Tanner by inches.

The wall of fire confining them to the immediate area had fallen, not one flame left. Because Sybil—

Sybil was on the ground. Unconscious, no pulse. A screaming Eilidh had thrown herself to her knees beside her, her face a twisted mask of rage and terror as Austin began chest compressions on the black-haired Wyvern, whose heart had been electric shocked into cardiac arrest.

"—now," said a male voice.

Shay's head swam—from panic and confusion and debilitating dread as she tried to make sense of who was talking, what he was saying, where he even *was*—

"Shay." Male hands gripped her shoulders, shaking her.

Shay looked up—

It was Tanner—bending over her, his eyes wild with panic.

"We need to go," he said. *"Now.* Right now—come on, *let's go!"*

Shay twisted around, planting her hands on the ground to push herself up—

Not the ground. That wasn't the ground she was touching, it was a *body—*

She recoiled, falling backward as nausea surged through her gut.

Holy Star, her lightning had scorched Brock Pierson from head to navel, his shirt rucked up so she could see his midsection. Every inch of visible skin was covered in bright red scars that were shaped like ferns, his face utterly mangled. And the *smell—*

Good gods, she had roasted him. Cooked his organs inside his body.

"Let's go!" Tanner pulled her to her feet just as Eilidh started screaming bloody murder at them, her hair wet and sticking to her enraged face. Her sister was still unconscious, her body not responding to the breaths Austin was blowing into her mouth, his hands pumping her chest.

"I'm going to kill you!" Eilidh bawled.

Oh shit.

Shay bolted just as Eilidh lurched to her feet and tore after them—a starved predator bounding after her prey.

Shay's heart was beating so fast she thought it might burst as she ran and ran for the truck, arms pumping, damp air scraping down her throat. She was almost at the driver's door when she heard the wet slap of Eilidh's swift boots, the moon-haired Wyvern right on her tail.

No. No, this couldn't be happening, not when they'd made it this far!

"STAY BACK!" Shay roared, whirling around mid-run, her hand lashing out as if to push Eilidh—

Instead, more veins of lightning slammed into the road with bone-rattling force, their glows blinding. Shay's ears rang as she lost her balance, staggering without sight. Her skin was buzzing, her mind short circuiting as if she'd grabbed onto a high voltage electric fence.

The wash of white light began to fade, and the world reappeared in pieces as her eyes adjusted.

There were the trees, the road, the truck.

And there was Eilidh, lifting herself up from where she'd taken cover on the ground. She bared her dragon's teeth at Shay, smoke jetting out of her nostrils. With a feral scream, she ran toward Shay head-on—

BOOM.

A crash of rolling thunder shook the earth even harder than the lightning, the shock waves sending Eilidh falling flat on her face in the mud.

Shay tripped over her own boots and slammed into the truck, grabbing onto the side mirror for balance.

All around them, the trees lining the road went up in flames as more lightning struck their highest points.

"Get in!" Tanner bellowed from the other side of the truck. "SHAY— GET IN!"

Shay fumbled for the handle, electricity prickling across her palms, up her neck, across her scalp, making her limbs twitch and jerk without pause.

By the grace of the gods, she managed to whip the driver's door open and hurl herself onto the cold leather seat, door thumping shut.

"You sure you're well enough to drive?" Tanner panted. He hit a button below his window, and the locks snapped down. The keys were still in the ignition, nullifying the protection spells that would've incinerated them upon break-in.

More lightning struck with a deafening *clap,* felling a tree.

It hit the road behind them, sparks flying, burning branches scratching across the back of the truck like giant infernal claws.

Shay turned the key in the ignition, engine snarling awake as magic flowed through it.

Fists banged on her window.

"You bitch!" Eilidh roared, yanking on the handle. She struck again, glass cracking under her fist. *"Open this door, you fucking bitch—"*

Not likely.

Shay smiled like a maniac, lightning weaving through her teeth. "Go to hell."

And then she threw the gear into drive and stepped on it.

22

YVESWICH GENERAL HOSPITAL
YVESWICH, STATE OF KER

Not again.

Not fucking *again*.

The others launched into action, tearing the truck apart in search of syringes—the serum that could restart Loren's heart—as Darien began chest compressions, ignoring the pure agony in his broken hand.

"Where are they?" Ivy shrieked.

"I don't know—*JUST KEEP LOOKING!"* Max roared.

Bullets cracked out of guns in rapid succession—closer now, as demons began an onslaught on the parking lot. Metal crunched, and glass buckled and shattered as they leapt across parked and moving cars, their blood-curdling roars and warbling hunting calls ripping through the streets. Cops and Fleet soldiers moved forward in droves, weapons raised, as unarmed civilians ran for cover. Those who had wings took up their positions in the sky, bullets spitting from above.

A snarl rumbled from nearby.

Darien blew a breath into Loren's mouth. Risked a glance up—

A monster was bounding this way—teeth gnashing, claws tearing up the frozen ground.

"Roman!" he bellowed.

Lightning-fast, Roman slid across the roof of the truck and dropped to the ground before Darien—right on time to blow out the beast's brains as it lunged with outstretched claws. Its scream died on the wind, its body tumbling across the pavement in a spray of blood and snow.

Another creature barreled toward Roman's left, but it was felled by Kylar, who punched a knife through its skull.

A third dove for Roman's throat, and he parried the attack with a shield of shadow. Magic hummed as the demon banged into it and ricocheted into the open driver's door, causing it to rock on its hinges. It hit the ground, bucking and scrambling to its feet.

Roman shot it in the head. *BANG*. Brains misted the pavement.

"They aren't in here!" Ivy screamed. *"DALLAS—your dad!"*

Dallas was already running—screaming for her dad's help. The only person who might have more.

Loren's heart wouldn't respond—not without the serum. He was running out of time—

Darien's own heart gave a painful *thump-thump*.

His upper body shot forward as if he had been stabbed in the back, a choked grunt of pain floating off his lips. But Darien kept fighting—fighting for Loren's life, even as his own threatened to end.

"Come on, baby." *Pump, pump, pump,* went his hands, her limp body jerking under his forceful palms, the blood from her nose streaming down the curve of her cheeks, toward her ears. "You're not doing this. *You're not doing this!*"

Another tight *thump* of his heart—sharper, this one. A stab in the chest instead of the back.

He gritted his teeth, shoulders curling forward, and willed his heart to keep beating, and for hers to *start, god-DAMMIT!*

"Come on, Loren!" he begged, his breaths clouding in the air before him, the others guarding the truck, round upon round of ammo emptying from the firearms they'd grabbed from under the back seats. Beasts were blown to bits, gore and body parts smacking into the truck, the pavement painted black and red. *"Come on!"*

His vision fogged over, and he began to see colors and lights. Stars and planets. Galaxies and memories, as if time were moving backward—

"Look at you, my sweet Daredevil," crooned a gentle female voice. He saw the woman's face in his mind as if he were looking up at her from somewhere down below. Long hair the shade of autumn leaves in golden sunlight. Her beautiful smile as she cooed at her baby, so full of life and hope—both of them, so vibrant and hopeful for their bright future. A future that had been beaten to shit and left in smouldering ruins by the hands of one vile, hateful man. *"Look at you—crawling already."* She held out her arms to him, scooping him up off the floor. Lifting him above her head, and then lowering him to rub her

nose against his. He giggled, the sound bubbly. Happy. His tiny hands reached for her, fingers grasping at the air. "You're special, my son. My special boy."

Darien shook his head to clear it, more sharp pangs radiating through his chest. His heart. His lungs were *burning*—

"Come on, baby," he begged, sweat dripping off his forehead, his hair. Loren's skin was pallid and waxy, her lips turning blue. "Come on, baby, *come on.*"

"Darien—*Darien here!*" someone shouted.

He paused long enough to grab what Dallas shoved in front of his face —a syringe. He bit the cap off, spat it out, and punched the needle into Loren's heart, dispensing the full vial of serum with one hard push of his thumb.

"Look at you, my handsome baby boy. Momma loves you so much—"

"Not yet, Mom," he bit out around a breathy, broken sob as he retracted the needle and resumed chest compressions. Loren's heart glowed a pale blue beneath her skin. "I *need* to save her." He pumped harder, hating how lifeless Loren looked as she lay there on the ground, her eyes shut. So different from the bubbly girl he loved.

Fuck, he couldn't take this anymore.

"I love you." His statement was for both women as tears splashed down his cheeks, his infant self giggling in his mind as the mother he'd lost bobbed him up and down. A sob ripped out of him. "I know you hate me right now, I know you're upset with me, but I love you so much, baby. *Please*—"

With every blink of his eyes, with every desperate pump of his hands, he flashed between life and death. Between here and the unknown—the now and the after. He saw things he couldn't explain—things that filled him with fear and awe and surprise and hope and a strange sense of longing. Things that made him wonder if it really wasn't so bad on the other side.

He kept breathing into Loren's mouth, kept pumping that beautiful heart for her, as guns were shot above and around them, his family and friends guarding his back while the city was lit up with a heavy artillery blitz.

"I love you," he said again on a husky whisper, galaxies and long-dead memories spinning by with every blink. "Come back to me. Come on, sweetheart, come back to me. You can hate me all you want—I don't care, but I need you. I need you with me. *Please.*"

The last word echoed as his surroundings turned into shapeless streaks. Sound ceased. Explosives were going off, but he couldn't hear anything, could barely see. His heart was working overtime—beating too fast and too hard, the blood rushing in his head, his ears.

"Stay with me, Loren—stay with me." He heard his own voice as if it belonged to someone else—someone far away. Below the place where he was drifting. "Stay with me. I'm not giving up on you, do you hear me? I'm not giving up on *us.*"

He blew another breath into her mouth. Pumped her heart—

One more time.

Two more times.

His vision narrowed to a tunnel of galaxies and memories passing by at the speed of light—

Three.

Loren jolted awake with a ragged inhale, his name a frightened cry on her lips.

And Darien broke down in tears, right there beside her, as the galaxies faded, returning him to the here, the now.

Life.

He wound his arms around her, scooping her into his lap and holding her tight and sobbing uncontrollably into her hair.

"I heard you," she gasped, hugging him back. Gods, it felt so good to be touched by her, held by her. "I could hear you, Darien." She clung to him as if she were drowning. "I followed the sound of your voice." Her words were shredded apart by gasping, shaking sobs. "I followed you home—I followed your voice. Thank you—"

"I'll never give up on you," he vowed, pulling her back just far enough to look at her face, cupping her cheek with a hand. He rubbed the tears off her skin with his thumb, smearing blood. "No matter how many times you try to die, I'm not letting you go, sweetheart. Ever."

He gave her brow a hard kiss, and then rested his forehead against hers as more missiles struck home, the city a bloody war zone behind shut eyes.

But as life was blown to bits all around him, all he felt, all he saw—

It was all her. Just *her.*

23

AITHNE
YVESWICH, STATE OF KER

Shay stared blankly at the dark road before her. Her heart was beating out of her chest, her white-knuckled hands squeezing the steering wheel.

That was a close call. *Way* too close.

She drove in silence for several minutes, determined to get the hell out of Aithne—a secluded Red Zone in East Yveswich. A place where only Wyverns and the foolish who didn't know any better wandered.

Try as she may, she couldn't slow her heart. Couldn't relax her hands. Not even when they finally left Aithne and entered neutral territory. She still felt like a live wire—ready to burn through anything in her path. Ready to burn through herself, even.

It wasn't a good feeling. She felt...unpredictable. Unstable. A force of nature that could not be contained.

"Why don't we pull over for a minute?" Tanner's voice, though gentle, startled her out of her deep pocket of concentration, and she felt more electric currents skitter between her palms and the steering wheel, causing her hands to vibrate. She'd almost forgotten Tanner was here.

"And do what?" Shay's question crackled with exhaustion. "They could be behind us." Her attention flicked to the reflection in the rear-view. The winding, forested road was mercifully empty.

For now.

"They don't have a vehicle."

Shay frowned. "What about Sybil's car?"

"You hit it with your lightning."

She blinked. "I hit a *car?*"

"I don't know why you're surprised. You also fried that one Wyvern like an egg."

The laugh that bubbled out of her suggested she was dangerously close to dissolving into hysterics. "Okay, so they may not have a car, but they do have wings." All it would take was for those three jerks—two, if Sybil stayed dead—to shift and take their search efforts to the skies, and they'd be found in no time. Found and likely torched like the trees before they could say *Wyvern.*

"Shay, you're swerving," Tanner said, his tone fraught. "We managed to survive all that insanity back there, and I hate to say this but I'm already questioning my safety again."

Shay squeezed the wheel, thumbs dragging across the leather. "If we stop, they could find us. They can fly, Tanner." Not for long, though, she knew—just like the bracelets that gave members of the Riptide the gift to breathe underwater, the magic in the Wyverns' rings had its limits. They couldn't stay airborne forever. But her knowledge of this hardly lessened her concern.

"Let's stop over there, then," Tanner suggested, indicating to a heavily treed side street up ahead. The gnarled boughs of the ancient oaks arched above the road, creating the perfect shelter. "They won't be able to see us there if they're looking from above." Gods, she hoped he was right.

She pulled onto the side road and put the truck in park. For several minutes, they sat in the dark, catching their breath. Processing everything that just happened. The lightning that had slammed into the road... Eilidh's nightmarish face as she'd vowed to kill them... The smell of burning flesh—

Shay's stomach surged. She pressed a hand to her lips, hurled herself out the door and onto the muddy bank—

And threw up. Violently. Tanner stayed silent in the truck, no sound in the area but Shay's retching and the singing of unbothered crickets.

Her hands were shaking on her bent knees, her face colorless. Half-frozen rain soaked the ground she'd vomited on, washing the mess away, her sopping hair hanging limply in her face. She spat a few times to get rid of the gross taste in her mouth, wiped the sweat off her clammy forehead, then got back in the truck.

Once the door was shut, Tanner waited a few more moments before speaking. "We should figure out a game plan."

"I'm not going to Roman's," Shay said, dragging her sleeve across her mouth. Ugh, she needed water. And tooth paste. And a bath. "With Don looking for Pax, we can assume he's already been there, and he might have his men guarding the place in case Paxton shows up."

Or Roman. Her stomach dropped at the thought of him walking through his own front door, only to be massacred in cold blood by his father's henchmen.

Tanner chewed on his split lower lip. "We should try tracking the others, then."

"How did you end up here?" Shay asked him, all the questions she hadn't had the chance to even think about flooding her mind.

"I was in the tunnels when the explosion happened. I was with Darien, Roman, and Jack at the time." He paused to breathe. Swallow. His face was pale like Shay's, his skin dotted with sweat. "I got separated from them. I can't remember how I got from there to that truck."

"Were they alive?" Shay's throat tightened, the last word barely squeezing past the rigid muscles. "Was Roman...?"

Tanner stared out the windshield, his own throat shifting. "Last I saw, yeah. They were all alive." His chest rose with a deep breath, and when he turned to face her he was composed. "Let's try tracking them."

She nodded. "Okay." After how much magic she'd spent summoning her lightning, she didn't know if her eyes were even capable of turning black right now.

Still, she rested her head back against the seat and shut them—resisting the urge to give in to her body's need to rest and simply fall asleep. "Who do you want to track?" she rasped, automatically picturing Roman's face—his stupid, unfairly attractive face—in her mind.

She swallowed the lump in her throat. *He doesn't want you, stupid.*

'You're getting out of here, Shay,' he'd told her last night. *'You're getting out of Yveswich and you're following your dream, which is. Not. Me. End of story.'*

And: *'This is a fling. It's a crush. And a mistake.'*

Mistake. He'd called what had happened between them a *mistake.*

"I'll try Darien's group," Tanner decided. That meant he'd be looking for Darien, Jack...and Roman. "You try Ivy's."

Ivy was a part of the group that had gone to the tar pits—the group Shay had gifted a head start when they were attacked by Hounds. If Shay made it out of there alive, then maybe...maybe they had, too.

Beneath closed lids, her pupils ballooned with the Sight, eyes flicking about as she focused on her memory of what everyone looked like. She decided to start with Ivy—Shay really liked her. She knew her kind face the best.

But barely two minutes passed before she felt her pupils shrink to their regular size, and her mental image of the glowing grids that made up Yveswich's districts blurred as if the lens she was looking through was out of focus. If she couldn't even see the streets, which was the first step to tracking someone, she would never be able to pinpoint a target.

A growl rose in her throat. "Gods, I can't focus!" She banged her fists against the steering wheel.

Tanner flicked open the glove box and sifted through the junk inside, his face limned with dingy orange light.

"What are you doing?"

"These are Wyverns. There's got to be drugs in here." Sure enough, he pulled out a bag of Stygian salts packed tightly into a brick, the plastic secured by clear packing tape.

"I don't usually take any drugs," Shay said.

"Neither do I." He ripped open the plastic so hard he dumped a quarter of the salt on his seat. He brushed off the pile that had fallen between his thighs, the crystals hissing as they hit the floor. "But I need help or I won't be able to do this." So would Shay. Unless you were the Head of a Darkslayer House, someone who had a ton of experience tracking people, it was hard for hellsehers to do so without the aid of a drug.

Salt crunched as his hand delved into the bag, fisting as many tiny pieces as he could hold. He dumped them onto the console that separated their seats and spread them out in a thin layer. "I think this is enough," he murmured to himself. "Darien does this all the time, but I've never really— Never mind. We should hurry."

He found a hollowed out pen and a cut straw in the glove box. When he held each out to her in offer, she grimaced at both but chose the pen.

They bowed their heads and plugged a nostril, snorting the crystals off the worn leather. Shay tried not to think about how dirty this truck and pen were—or how badly the drug made her nasal passages burn. How people did this kind of shit for fun was beyond her.

"I don't think I can handle anymore, my brain's buzzing," Shay slurred, massaging the bridge of her nose. She felt congested, and she sounded like it, too. She'd probably snorted the equivalent of half a line, and she was already high as a kite. How did other Darkslayers do this?

But the pain in her ribs was...gone. It was gone. She could draw a full breath without wincing. She wondered how long it would last.

"Me neither," Tanner said, wiggling his nose like a rabbit in effort not to sneeze. He dusted off his hands, sat back in his seat, and shut his eyes. "Let's see if this works."

They were silent for several minutes as they focused. The drug made Shay feel buoyant, as if she were floating out of her body. Drifting toward the stars. Her soul seemed to settle back into its vessel at precisely the same moment the glowing grids that made up Yveswich's city blocks reappeared, sharper now, in her mind like a map.

She pictured Ivy's face as if it were a browsing window she was pulling up on her internal computer. The map in her head spun around, then began moving in a blur, pulling toward her target.

As abruptly at it started moving, it spun like a compass needle disrupted by a magnetic field, and then hit a wall, the glowing roads in her mind going dark and colorless.

Hidden, then. Wherever Ivy was, her aura was hidden, whether it was by talisman, Nacht Essentia, or a spell-protected building or vehicle.

Or she was dead. But Shay refused to view that as an option.

She tried Travis next. Then Kylar. Lace. Jewels. And finally, Aspen.

No dice.

Shay chewed her lip. Thinking... And decided to try someone else.

She knew without a doubt that Paxton was hidden—if not, Don would've already found him, easy peasy. So she pictured the face of his friend instead. Eugene Lavin—Kylar's little brother.

Her eyes flickered faster behind her lids, streets and coordinates floating through her brain like computer code—

Eugene's location dropped like a pin on her inner map.

She opened her eyes. Tanner was watching her, waiting for her to finish. "Any luck?" she asked him.

"No Darien, no Jack, and no Roman," Tanner said.

Shay's heart sank.

"I think they were wearing talismans last night, though," he added—for his own benefit and hers. "What about you? Anything?"

"I can't find Ivy or the others, but I found Eugene." She shifted the truck into drive, foot hovering on the brake. "He's not far from here, and I'd bet you anything he's with Paxton." And with Eugene's aura suddenly visible, Don would be hot on his trail.

"Wait—" He blinked. "We're not going to find them... Are we?"

"I think we should. Maybe, if we find them, we'll find the others. Besides, with Donovan looking for Paxton, he and Eugene might need our help. Or maybe they're lost or something." *Or maybe Roman really is with him,* her heart added.

She told it to shut the hell up.

"Or maybe Donovan already found him?" Tanner suggested, looking worried. "He'll be all over Eugene once he realizes his aura's visible—he'll think the same thing we are: that Eugene will lead him straight to Paxton. I thought the goal was to *avoid* Don, not throw ourselves at him."

It was. It one hundred percent was, but—

She thought it through. Maybe it made her crazy, but— "I'll take my chances—"

The city shook with a *clap* that resembled thunder. The keys rattled in the ignition, the steering wheel juddering against Shay's palms. She flattened the brake pedal under her foot as the truck began to roll forward.

"Was that you?" Tanner whispered.

Shay shook her head and turned in her seat, looking west.

The Void was spreading. In the distance, helicopters flew, weaving around tall buildings. Rapid flashes of light that indicated gunfire illuminated the streets. Winged nightmares had taken flight, a flock of five heading straight for the helicopters, airborne Fleet soldiers among them.

The civil defense sirens began their haunting call—late. They were late, but Shay knew, now that someone had made the decision to sound the alarm, the sirens would not stop.

"Please tell me that's not where Eugene is," Tanner murmured.

Shay merely cranked the wheel and stepped on the accelerator, heading straight into the heart of Yveswich.

24

YVESWICH GENERAL HOSPITAL
YVESWICH, STATE OF KER

Loren couldn't stop shaking as Darien held her. She was curled up in his lap, his strong arms wrapped around her waist, his heart thumping steadily against her cheek.

How many more times could her mortal heart fail before it finally decided it had endured enough?

She had drifted *elsewhere* again, only this was a different experience than the last. This time, she'd had no tangible form—no legs to run with, no mouth to scream with, and no dog running by her side down a flowered path. She was utterly alone, disembodied in a black space that roared with white noise, and it was only the sound of Darien's voice that had brought her back. A bridge of colorful light she had managed to cross. The darkness had parted like eyes opening, bringing her back to life. Back to *him*—her heart. Her *home*.

She was very aware that she was clinging to him like a sloth to a tree branch—a very strong tree branch—but she didn't want to go back there. Didn't want to let go of him—

"Did I hurt you?" Darien's voice was gruff.

"I don't think so," she said around chattering teeth. Gods, the ground was so cold, but he was so, *so* warm.

"Your chest—"

"I'm fine."

"You're shaking, baby," Darien's deep voice rumbled from his chest into hers, his hands rubbing her back—being mindful of the bandages.

"I just need a minute," she rasped, holding onto him for dear life. Gods, she couldn't seem to stay angry with him for long. Not when it felt this good to be held by him. *Just one more minute*, her body begged, while her broken heart still wept over his sacrifice, *demanding* distance from him. "Just one more minute," she whispered. Darien stayed put, seeming content to hold her forever.

But another male voice said, "You need to get out of here."

She looked up to see Roark standing with the rest of the group. The gunfire had died down, most of the threats handled, the parking lot bathed in blood. Loren knew the calm wouldn't last. Shots were still being fired, but they were too far away to be considered an immediate danger.

"There will be more of that happening soon," Roark added, turning his head to look at the soldiers regrouping nearby.

Darien slid one arm under Loren's legs, shifting her lower half, his other arm supporting her back. "I'm going to pick you up—hold onto me." To the others he said, "Get in—we're leaving."

She held on tight as he stood, lifting her off the ground, and when he set her on the truck seat she had to practically pry her fingers off him, her pinky snagging on the neckline of his battle-suit. Her head spun like a top, but luckily she stayed conscious, her lungs and heart functioning normally. Doors banged shut as the others got in, and Loren slid to the middle spot.

Darien spoke with Roark outside for a few moments, and then got in behind her, Roark closing his door for him.

Loren blinked. Roark just...*closed his door for him.* Was this real life, or was she still drifting someplace else?

Darien lowered his window. "Thank you." When the glass was down all the way, and he offered Roark his left hand in thanks, Loren realized how agonizing it must've been when he was pumping her heart. She hoped she hadn't caused him any damage.

Roark stepped forward and shook his hand, the gesture causing Loren to gape again. He was shaking Darien's hand. Someone he surely considered lower than him. Rabble.

When he let go, he handed Darien a small black travel case with a zip closure and attached wristband. "Three more," he said. "This is all I have, so I recommend making it back to Angelthene as soon as you can. What's happening here..." His amber eyes swept across the city. "It isn't good for anyone, but especially not her." Loren's skin prickled from the severity of his tone. "If you don't put some distance between her and the portal, it's likely that her heart will continue to have problems."

Darien set the case on the seat between him. "I think I have a few spares in my car, but are you able to get us more?"

"When I get back later this week. I'll speak with you then." He nodded in farewell and stepped back.

"Bye," Loren said quietly as Darien shut his window. Hi and bye—some of the only words she had ever exchanged with him.

Roark locked eyes with her as the tinted glass rose, but he didn't acknowledge that he'd heard the farewell.

She watched him disappear as Darien drove out of the lot under the direction of Fleet soldiers, and when she twisted around in her seat to stare out the back, she saw Dallas doing the same in the truck bed. The witch sat with Max and Lace, guns across their laps.

"Drink, please," Darien said, offering her the soda she hadn't had the chance to open yet.

She took it from him and twisted the cap off, bubbles fizzing. She drank half, the carbonation burning her chest and welling her eyes with moisture. Her heart was racing so fast she felt sick, but at least it was beating. She put the cap back on and laid the bottle down on the seat between her and Roman. She was so close to Darien, she might as well be sitting in his lap, her thigh pressing against his.

Sitting in the middle seat put her right in front of the rear-view mirror, and when she saw her reflection in the glass she cringed. Gods, she looked like a total mess. Blood, dirt, tangled hair, and eyes that desperately needed rest.

"Is that my blood on your face?" she asked Darien, peeking at the fresh streaks on his cheeks and nose. Hardly an inch of his skin was clean. They all needed to have a shower.

He wiped at his face, and then looked at his open hand. Then in the rear-view. "We'll clean up when we get to Roman's."

She frowned. "I'm sorry."

He glanced down at her. "For what?"

"For getting blood on you."

"Don't be ridiculous, please." He tucked a strand of hair behind her ear.

"I can't wait to eat something," Jack groaned as they maneuvered the streets, tires thumping on concrete that had buckled from seismic waves. "My stomach's devouring itself."

Loren leaned forward, the sudden movement causing Darien to stiffen and reach toward her, and grabbed the panini off the dash. "You can have some of my sandwich, if you want." She twisted in her seat—

"No, he can't," Darien said firmly. "You're eating that whole thing. Every last bite. And you're doing it now."

"I don't need the whole thing, though. Jack's hungry."

"He'll be fine," Roman muttered. His elbow was propped against his door, head resting against his knuckles. "He can handle it. He doesn't have a blood sugar problem like you do."

"Here." Darien tossed his own panini over his shoulder, hitting Jack in the knee with it. "You can have mine."

"Aren't you hungry?" Jack asked him as he picked it up off the floor.

"I'll be fine till we get to Roman's."

"Darien, you need to eat, too," Ivy scolded.

"I will. But your husband has a fucked-up head, so he should be the one eating right now."

"His head's always fucked up," Roman mumbled, still staring blankly out his window.

Jack laughed around a mouthful of bread and turkey. "He isn't wrong. Maybe this concussion will tighten a few screws."

Loren opened her sandwich, plastic wrap crinkling, and took a bite. After how long she'd gone without eating, this dry sandwich tasted like a gourmet meal.

"Do you want a bite?" She offered the sandwich to Darien.

"I want you to eat all of that."

"You're being self-destructive," she chided gently.

"*You're* being self-destructive," he countered.

"No, I'm sharing. Sharing is caring."

He smirked, but took a bite.

"We need to think of a plan," Kylar said. "Preferably before we get to Roman's and get shot at by Don's men, if any are there."

Roman, still gazing out his window with a dead stare, said, "We'll get the Familiars to have a look before we go in." To Darien he added, "Park by one of the neighbour's houses."

Darien nodded. "Settled."

The rest of the drive was quiet and tense as everyone mentally prepared themselves for what—and who—they might find at Roman's house.

Loren ate the panini and cookies. She drank her whole pop as well, all too aware of the burning of her magical tattoos.

Both of them were burning—the serpent-entwined rod on her forearm...and the Caliginous on Silverway tattoo on the inside of her wrist.

There was no chamber for her to use anymore—no place to recharge her magic. She was already beginning to feel the weight of what she'd learned last night—the Widow's warning that she would not live past the age of twenty-one. Less than ten months remained until her birthday, but right now it didn't feel like she had months left.

It felt like she had hours.

It felt like she had *minutes.*

MAX KEPT his hand on his gun, finger poised on the trigger, as they drove through the wrecked streets of Yveswich.

The fight out front of the hospital was the most present he'd felt in hours—since Maya had disappeared into the crowds without saying goodbye. Now, he could feel himself sinking back down, below the crashing waves of his own thoughts. Thoughts of the sister he'd only just found and had already lost again.

"Max." Freckled fingers snapped in front of his face. "Terra to Maximus."

He blinked, his eyes refocusing to see a redhead and a platinum blonde staring at him in concern.

He cleared his throat. "You say something?"

A loaded pause.

"Are you okay?" Lace asked him.

"Honestly? No, not really. Maya pissed off without even telling me she was leaving, I have zero clue where she is, I still can't hear properly in one ear, if we're not out of here by noon tomorrow we're all dead meat, Don's probably waiting at Roman's house to flay us all alive, and at any point between now and then a missile could hit this truck and blast us sky-high."

They were quiet for several minutes as the truck thumped about on the uneven terrain. Darien was driving it as if he were drunk, but it was necessary given the many cracks and potholes in the road. They were one popped tire away from being stranded.

All these bad probable outcomes and he couldn't decide which was the most preferable. Probably the missile.

"So, what do you want to do about Maya?" Dallas voiced her question with caution.

Max ran a hand through his dusty, sweat-damp hair, making it stand on end. "I don't know. She left—which tells me she doesn't care about me anymore." He glared at a demolished building.

"You don't know that for sure," Lace offered.

"*I* still care about *her*, though," he said. Darien started driving faster as they reached a smoother stretch of road. Max watched their surroundings flit by—the bodies, the debris, the blood. "And I'm not sure I have the strength to leave without finding her and telling her what's going on," he admitted.

If he didn't, she'd be trapped here. And the sister he thought he'd lost would *truly* be lost. For real this time. There would be no surviving this city once it was given over fully to the Void. Those shadows didn't just blind—they killed. It was only a matter of time before all the oxygen was gone, and this space became unliveable.

"I hate to be the person who tells you what to do," Lace began. "But I highly doubt Darien is going to want you to split up from the rest of us, Max. Not with everything going on."

"He'd leave if it were Ivy," Max argued, hating that he knew Lace was right.

"Probably," she confirmed, speaking carefully. "But Darien's not in the right headspace for an argument. If you get into one with him right now, I don't think you'll win."

Max cursed under his breath, but he didn't bother arguing with Lace—not when he might have to do exactly that with his boss instead.

He would wait until they made it to Roman's. Wait until they figured out what was going on with Arthur and the others. After that, he'd make his decision.

He only hoped that whatever road he took would be the *right* one.

25

ARDESIA
YVESWICH, STATE OF KER

Roman had spent the whole ride here trying not to puke all over Darien's truck. And now that they were parked down the street from his house—the house his dad's men might be watching at that very minute—he once again fought to keep the contents of his stomach down.

The road was quiet and still. By the looks of the empty driveways and unlit houses, most of his neighbors had already evacuated.

Thanks to Loren's shield of magic, the district had been spared in its entirety. Even the streetlights still worked, their foggy halos reflecting in the dark tarmac that glistened with half-frozen rain. But just because the power worked didn't mean it was safe. Demons were prowling along the perimeters of spell-protected yards and skulking in bushes near the mouths of driveways. Lying in wait.

For all Roman knew, his father—the predator he was—could be doing the very same.

No one in the truck made a sound as they waited for Bandit and Grim to report back. Sayagul had wanted to go with them, but it was too risky. She was far too easy to recognize.

'I could've simply stayed up high,' she argued now, though she sounded drained. Just like Roman. *'An aerial view is always helpful.'*

'Next time,' he told her. The rain picked up, ice pellets peppering the windshield so hard they triggered the wipers to move at a faster setting.

Despite his words, Roman hoped there wouldn't be a next time. Not for something like this.

A few more minutes went by before two pairs of glowing crimson eyes appeared down the road, flitting between parked cars, trees, and mailboxes. Even with the streetlights providing a low level of illumination, the area was so dark Roman could hardly see the misty black bodies of the mountain lion and the Doberman as they approached on soundless paws.

Darien cracked open his door, frigid air seeping in. Bandit jumped up into his lap, while Grim padded to the tailgate to report what they'd learned to Max's group. Max, Lace, and Dallas were hunkered down low in the truck bed to avoid being noticed by any prying eyes.

Bandit walked across Darien's thighs and parked his butt in Loren's lap.

"Hey," Darien scolded, his door thumping shut. "Did she tell you that you're allowed to sit on her?"

Bandit turned his head to look Loren in the eyes, his nose nearly bumping against her cheek. *'Excuse me, may I sit on you?'*

She smiled and stroked the dog's cropped ears. "Yes, Bandit, you may sit on me."

Kylar leaned forward in his seat. "Did you guys see anything?"

'No one on the street or in the yard,' Bandit replied, nose twitching. *'The blinds are closed, so we couldn't see in the windows.'*

Roman cursed. "They could be in there. Waiting to open fire the minute we walk through the front door." He rubbed the stubble on his face, feeling like he'd aged three centuries after this whirlwind of a night—and day. Every hour that went by was an hour wasted *not* looking for Pax, *not* looking for Shay, *not* looking for Tanner, *not* getting the hell out of the city.

"If you'd rather a few of us go inside first, while you wait in here, I'm fine with that," Darien offered. "It might be better if we don't all go in at once. In case shit does go sideways."

"We're stronger as a unit, though," Jack argued.

Roman sighed. "Yeah, but does it even make a difference if Don is in there?"

"He can't be that strong, can he?" Jack wondered.

Multiple people turned to stare at him in disbelief, including Roman, who said, "Were you not listening when I told you what he did to Darien's hand? *Darien's* hand, Jack!"

"Yeah, but he's never faced all of us together."

"We're starving and drained," Kylar said. *"All of us together* isn't going to make much of a difference. If we're forced to fight, and Don's involved, we'll lose."

The truck descended into silence again as everyone thought it through. Loren stroked her hand down Bandit's glossy back, her eyes on Darien, who stared at the rain dribbling down the glass.

And then he put the truck in drive.

Roman sat up straight, heart hammering. "What's the plan?"

"The only plan there is: go in and see what the fuck happened—and fight if we're forced to."

He pulled out into the street, and Roman focused on steadying his breathing as they approached the house he'd once seen as a sanctuary—a home. Now, it simply scared the hell out of him.

He wasn't scared for himself—no. Very little of his fear was wasted on his own safety. He was scared for Paxton.

And scared of what sort of *gifts* Donovan might've left for them during his visit. The kind of horrific gifts that involved body parts and blood.

———

THE FRONT DOOR creaked as Darien pushed it open.

Roman followed on his cousin's heels, the others coming in behind him, his heart beating so fast his head was practically floating.

The feeling grew when he saw the shards of glass glittering on the floor in the lamplit foyer.

And blood. There was *blood* all over the floor. Human and hellseher—

Pax. Oh gods, he could smell *Pax's blood*—

He staggered across the room with tunnel vision, every breath a hollow rasp, and braced a shaking hand against the wall.

Darien said something. Reached for him, as if to catch him if he fell, his left hand clasping Loren's right.

"Roman." Darien spoke quietly—muffling his voice with spells, Roman knew, in case any threats were hiding in the house. Roman could barely understand him over his panting breaths, his roaring blood. The shimmering room was going in and out of focus.

"I can't breathe," he choked out. Neither could Sayagul, the dragon panicking in his shadow—

'Paxton,' she cried. *'Roman, no—please! Not our Paxton, I can't—'*

"In here," called a calm male voice. Who it belonged to filled Roman's heart with hope.

Arthur. It was Arthur—

"Roman," Darien said again, as the others stepped around them, heading down the hallway with raised weapons. "Paxton needs—"

"That's his blood." The statement was a hoarse whisper. In his shadow, Sayagul wept harder, calling out Paxton's name in a small, petrified voice.

"Let's speak with Arthur before we make assumptions," Darien said.

Arthur called from the living room, "Paxton is alive, Roman."

And just like that, the weight lifted off Roman's lungs. "Oh, thank gods," he breathed, his legs threatening to fold.

'Oh, Paxton!' Sayagul cried, her voice tinged with hope. *'Oh, Pax, my sweet boy, you're all right.'*

"Do you need to sit down?" Darien asked him. Loren watched Roman with concern. Empathy.

He shook his head. "No. No—I'm good. I'm fine." He pulled himself together and walked with them down the hall, occasionally bracing a hand against the walls and furniture for balance.

Just ahead, the others were waiting for them. Together, they walked the last of the distance to the living room, glass tinkling and crunching under their boots. There were so many bloody footprints on the floor—big among the small.

Had Pax cut himself on all this glass? Or had someone hurt him?

Arthur was sitting in an armchair, pressing ice wrapped in a blood-stained rag against his eye.

"Arthur," Lace said on a choked whisper.

Ivy came up to her left, her face leaching of color. "Gods above, Arthur. What did they do to you?"

Darien slowed the moment he saw Arthur's battered face. "What the hell happened?" His question clapped through the room. The power suddenly rolling off him... It was lethal. The kind of earth-shattering strength they would have so desperately needed if Don were here.

Arthur kept his answer simple: "Donovan."

"Where are the kids?" Roman asked him.

"Gone."

"Gone?" Roman echoed. Sayagul started crying again. The house—his destroyed home—shimmered. "I thought you said—"

"When Donovan and his men showed up, I told Dominic and Blue to take the children someplace safe," Arthur began. "They came back when they heard gunshots." As he spoke, Roman scanned the room—the bullet holes in the walls. There were so many of them, and so close together, there was no question they had come from a machine gun. Fired likely to cause fear. Arthur continued, "They left the kids where they were hiding, thinking they'd be safer there than here, but by the time they made sure I was alive and went back for them, they were gone."

"Where are they now?" Max asked. "Dominic and Blue, I mean."

Arthur shifted the ice to the split in his lip. "They're still out looking for them." He looked up at Roman, his one eye swollen shut.

The dread coursing through Roman had shifted into something violent. Something untameable. The kind of emotion that made him see red.

Or black.

"For the record, Roman," Arthur said, "I don't believe your father's men got their hands on them. I think something else went wrong during Dominic and Blue's absence, and they ran."

Roman was so mad, he was trembling. So much for the relief he'd felt a moment ago. "Or they got killed by something else!" he snapped, unable to stop the words before they came lashing out. He kicked a piece of broken furniture out of the way, sending it smashing into the wall. "The blood," he gritted out, whirling to face Arthur with flared nostrils, a Surge so close he was seeing the hazy outline of Arthur's multi-hued aura. "Where'd it come from?"

"Your father's men didn't knock, they broke in during a brief power outage. They came in through every door. Paxton must have cut himself on the glass while he was trying to find a way out. Dominic flew the kids away—"

"Were they seen?" Roman interrupted.

He shook his head. "I don't believe so."

"What about Blue—you said she went, too?" Lace asked.

"She made it out herself and followed Dominic on foot."

Darien said, "Was Paxton wearing a talisman?"

"I gave him mine," Arthur replied. "Eugene, however, is not wearing one." He tossed an apologetic glance at Kylar, who looked too stunned to speak, his gray eyes flicking about the wreckage. "Not to my knowledge, anyway."

Roman couldn't decide if that was a good thing or not. On the one hand, it meant they could try tracking Gene and find him and Paxton that way. But on the other, Donovan could be using the exact same strategy and get to the kids first.

"I'm sorry," Arthur choked out, his lower lip trembling. "I was only trying to do what was best for them."

"You don't have anything to apologize for," Max said.

"Don and his men are the ones who should apologize," Jack chimed in. "Beating up an old man." He shook his head in disgust. "Bunch of pigs."

"Oh, Arthur," Ivy whispered, noting the shine in Arthur's eyes. She walked across the room, stepping carefully through the wreckage, and sat down on the rolled arm of Arthur's chair. She took the ice out of his wrinkled hand and held it against his face for him, giving him a much needed break from doing it himself.

"Which one of them did it?" Darien demanded. "Which one of them put their hands on you?"

"I don't know all of their names," Arthur replied, wincing as Ivy touched the ice to a tender spot. "And it doesn't matter who, Darien. They're all vile."

"It'll matter when I line them up and shoot them in order of importance."

Kylar, who'd spent these past few minutes looking like he was trying not to faint, managed to find his voice. "Did Dom and Blue say where they were hiding the kids?"

"I asked them not to tell me," Arthur replied. "I didn't want anyone to be able to torture it out of me."

"You're too smart for your own good," Darien said. He eyed the puffy skin on Arthur's cheekbone. "Literally."

"I'm old, Darien," he mumbled, wincing as Ivy adjusted the ice pack. "Those kids have their whole lives ahead of them. If anyone's going to die, I'd rather it be me."

"Where's Itzel?" Roman asked, scanning the kitchen behind him. If his Hob was gone, too—

But Arthur said, "In the snack cupboard. I told her to hide, and she listened."

Roman's brows shot up his forehead.

"I know," Arthur said, reading his reaction. "I was surprised as well."

Ivy said, "How'd they get past Itzel's spells?"

"She's young, she's still learning," Kylar responded. "We use regular spell systems on the house."

"Has Tanner been here?" Lace asked Arthur.

"Tanner?" He peered up at her, squinting in the light. "No. Why would Tanner be here? I thought he went with you."

"He did," Darien confirmed. "We lost him during the blast."

Loren suddenly moved to the end of the couch that didn't have debris all over it, extracting her hand from Darien's grip as she went, and sat down.

The Devil was already shadowing her. "What's going on?"

"Nothing, I just need to sit." But she was short of breath, and everyone could hear it.

Darien's next question was for Arthur. "Is everything in the house still working properly?"

"As far as I'm aware."

He was already turning toward Loren. "I think you should try recharging before we leave."

"We don't really have time for me to take a swim right now," Loren breathed, rubbing her chest. Her heart.

Darien noticed, of course. And he looked so livid at the abrupt turn in her health that Roman was surprised when he didn't punch anything.

Ivy said, "Take a shower and use the sauna." She shifted her focus to Darien. "Water and heat. And on the way out she can walk barefoot in the grass." Her steel-blue eyes flicked to Loren. "Sound good?"

She nodded. "Yeah. Sounds good to me."

Darien didn't look convinced that it would be enough, but he was already reaching for her hands and helping her up. "Come on. Let's see if we can get that suit off."

26

ROMAN'S HOUSE
YVESWICH, STATE OF KER

Loren stood with Darien in one of Roman's bathrooms, the steam from the running shower fogging up the mirror. Her back was facing him, his hands carefully shimmying her suit down just far enough for her to get the rest off by herself. The magic in the ring wasn't working anymore, so they had to remove it manually.

Gods, the melted material was so stiff it felt like it was glued onto her body. Without the magical enhancements that made them so indestructible, the suits were utterly useless. To make matters worse, this model didn't even have a zipper down the front like the last one.

"I might have to cut this thing off you," Darien growled.

She looked sidelong at him in the mirror, but the glass was too foggy to see much of him apart from a blurry, black-clad figure towering over her like a dark guardian angel. The longer he struggled, the more she wondered if it was because his right hand was bothering him.

She should be doing this herself. He already did too much for her.

He exhaled through his nose, his breath ruffling her hair. "You bruise like a little peach." He brushed his thumb across a spot on her right shoulder. His touch—even through his glove—sent a shiver of pleasure and longing down her spine. "I'm going to have to take better care of you." As if he wasn't already doing a stellar job of that.

"You didn't give me these bruises, Darien."

"Doesn't mean I like to see them," he said, gently tugging one sleeve at a time down her arms.

As soon as they hit her elbows, she stepped away from him.

"Baby, I'm not finished—"

"I can take it from here," she said, clutching the front of her suit to her breasts as she turned around to face him. "You need time to get cleaned up, too." Neither of them had discussed that they'd be taking separate showers —it was a decision that sort of just...happened. A silent assumption they'd both made the minute they had walked up the stairs. And Loren didn't know how to feel about it. The close moment they'd shared outside of the hospital, when they'd clung to each other on the cold ground, was gone, and now...now, they were back to this.

He simply stared at her, conflicted. And the awkward way that he was holding his hand...yep, it was definitely bothering him.

"I'll be fine, Darien. I'm sure the serum is still in my system, so you can take a few minutes to yourself." The gods knew he needed it—a break from having to watch her like a hawk. When he refused to budge, she added softly, "Go."

But he still wouldn't move. "You'll make sure to come and get me if something feels off?"

"Yes."

He scanned her from head to toes, as if searching for injuries he might have missed. Of course there were none—nothing escaped this man. "Promise me," he said.

"I promise."

He nodded once. And then he moved toward the door, his eyes still fixed on her. "Take off your talisman, please." He left, shutting the door behind him.

Only after he was gone did she realize he might have been stalling to give her an opportunity to invite him to shower with her. But it was too late now, and even if she wanted him in here, it was true that he deserved time to himself. If he stayed in here with her, there was no way he would allow himself to relax.

Not that there was even the slightest chance he'd be doing that on his own, either. There was no winning right now.

She yanked her suit down to her thighs with difficulty, and then sat down on the edge of the soaker tub to do the rest, taking off the scraps of clothes underneath—ripped, burnt, and filthy—too. Everything would need to be thrown out. She unclasped her talisman, placed it on the counter by the sink, and then stepped into the shower.

Her skin was so grimy and raw, the soap and hot water literally stung.

She scrubbed every inch of her body and washed her hair twice, being careful not to overly disturb the bandages on her back. Darien had told her they'd be fine while she showered, and the tape he'd used to adhere them wouldn't come off that easily, but she'd rather not risk it.

When she got out, she wrapped herself in a towel and brushed her teeth, beyond happy to finally feel clean again.

Her hair dripped down her back as she crept across the hallway and into her bedroom. The salt lamp was glowing on the nightstand—she had a feeling Darien had turned it on. She heard a few of the others speaking downstairs, along with the running of water in multiple bathrooms.

She put on a pair of faded jeans and a white t-shirt. As soon as she had her socks on, she grabbed her hairbrush and fought through the knots before sectioning her hair down the middle and styling it into two braids. The cold weather would be extra brutal with wet hair, but she didn't feel like wasting time with a blow dryer. Besides, she would still have to go in the sauna at some point, which should help it dry faster.

As she grabbed her bag and began packing her folded clothes, a misty silhouette crept out of her shadow on lethargic paws.

"Hi, Singer!" she exclaimed with a whisper, the dog peering up at her with pouty eyes. "I've missed you, buddy." He wagged his tail. The fact that he was awake was a good sign. Familiars were usually absent and unresponsive when their people felt weak or sick.

She packed the last of her belongings and zipped up the pockets before kneeling to give Singer some attention. He accepted every scratch with contented panting, his tail swishing across the floor.

"Alright, buddy, let's go downstairs," she told him. He stayed by her side the whole walk there.

She found the others—everyone except Dallas, who was still showering, her destroyed wings likely hindering her speed—deep in discussion at the kitchen table, all of them cleaned up and dressed in normal clothes.

Loren wasn't surprised to find that Darien had beaten her here. He was squeaky clean and dressed in black jeans and a black t-shirt, his damp hair slicked back. He already had his combat boots on, one foot braced on a chair he'd pulled out from the table, an elbow resting on his propped-up knee. When those steel-blue eyes of his flicked up to meet hers, a strand of inky hair hanging in his face, she pulled her gaze away from him, not wanting to distract him from what was evidently an important conversation.

"As much as you don't want to admit it, Darien," Ivy was saying, "you can't be multiple places at once. You need to get Loren—" She abruptly glanced at her, noticing her quiet entry, and finished, "Out of the city and back home."

"They shouldn't go by themselves," Lace said. "We should make sure we're split into strong enough groups, in case anything happens."

Jack chimed in. "But one Darien equals like ten of us."

"I want you to go with Darien," Ivy said to her husband.

He straightened in his chair as if Ivy had tased him. *"What?* No chance!" He shook his head, slicing his hands through the air. "There's *no chance* I'm leaving you, Ivy—"

"Yes, Jack," she said firmly. "You are. You're still feeling dizzy—"

"I'm fine right now."

"You're going with Darien, and so are Lace and Arthur."

Lace blinked, taken aback. "Ivy—"

"You just said we should make sure we all have strong enough groups," Ivy responded evenly. "I think you should go with Darien, and Max and I will stay behind and look for Tanner. Besides, Travis is still here, too—we'll make sure he comes with us when we leave."

"I'm not going, Ivy," Jack said. "Not without you. You can forget it."

Frustrated, she turned to Darien for backup. "Darien?"

A beat of silence as he decided. And then he said to Jack, "You're coming with me."

Jack swore. He thumped his elbows onto the table and rubbed his eyes, muttering, "I don't like this."

Darien said, "You guys need a plan. The city's huge—you need to narrow down your search and figure out where to start."

Roman leaned forward in his seat and grabbed a plastic bag of Stygian salts from the fruit bowl. "I'll track Gene."

"Has anyone tried tracking Tanner?" Darien asked as Roman dumped out a small pile of salt and used the edge of a credit card to divide it into rails.

"I did," Lace replied. "I couldn't see him."

"I tried, too," Max said. "I got nothing."

Roman snorted the rails through a rolled-up banknote and sat back, eyes shut, strands of his still-wet hair dripping down his face.

Loren's eyes clashed with Darien's. He took his foot off his chair and angled it toward her. "Have a seat, Loren."

"I'm fine."

"Sit down, please."

She walked to the other side of the table, Singer on her heels, and when she sat down, Darien leaned his arms on the back of the chair.

Kylar said, "I say we start with the kids. Tackle one problem at a time."

"You have less than fourteen hours," Lace pointed out. "I'm not sure one problem at a time is wise."

"I'm going to have to side with Kylar on this," Darien said. "If you guys split up, you're putting yourselves at a disadvantage. The kids are the priority right now—"

"What about Atlas?" Lace demanded, looking wounded.

"They'll look for Atlas," he replied in an even tone. "If you don't find the kids, Donovan will, and we'll likely never see them again, so right now they are the number one priority. Tanner is smart—he'll find a way to either get to us or expose his aura so we can get to him."

"Unless he's in grave danger himself, and exposing it would put him at a greater risk," Arthur called from where he still sat in the living room.

"Regardless," Darien said, well aware that each and every one of his Devils was staring at him—desperate to find Tanner, "you can't find Tanner right now. No matter how hard you try, you will not find him unless he exposes his aura. So here's your plan: stay in one group, at least to begin with, find Paxton and Eugene, and the minute you have an inkling of where Tanner is, you go, you find him, and you bring him home. You utilize every last minute you have, and you do not give up until you find him. Understand?"

The room filled with murmured agreements, some of them doubtful, others determined.

"I got a read on Gene," Roman said. The declaration was flat and distant, his eyes still shut. "Pen," he requested, turning his right hand that was resting on the table palm up.

Ivy placed a pad of paper before him and slid a pen into his waiting hand.

Roman blindly scratched numbers into the notepad, his eyes flickering behind closed lids. Loren watched, fascinated. She'd always wondered how tracking worked. Hellsehers had more than one way to pinpoint someone's location, and the most difficult but reliable method was by using very precise coordinates.

Lace came up behind him, phone in hand, a map of Yveswich on the screen. Her nails clicked as she typed the coordinates into the search bar.

The others crowded around. Loren stayed in her seat, Darien still standing behind her, his fingers toying with the end of her left braid.

Lace showed her screen to Roman. "Archie's?" She glanced down at him.

Roman shared a look with Kylar, their eyes solid black as they said in unison, "The fucking arcade."

27

THE THEATER DISTRICT
YVESWICH, STATE OF KER

By the time Shay rolled the truck to a stop in the Theater District, the city had descended deeper into chaos. The sky had darkened. More helicopters flew about. Fleet soldiers moved among them, urging civilians to evacuate.

This cobblestone road they were on made Shay feel like she'd stepped through a time portal. Shops that sold records, comic books, video games, and various collectible items lined either side of it, and right in the heart of it all, next to a rundown cinema that only aired dated films, was an arcade called *Archie's*.

"I gotta admit," Tanner said, his eyes wide with fascination. He looked like a kid in a candy store. "This is so totally my jam."

"And Pax and Gene's, too, if I'm tracking them properly." But the road was as quiet as it was dark, and when several minutes went by with no sign of them she began to doubt herself. Had she made a mistake?

"Maybe they're inside?" Tanner guessed.

"How would they have gotten in, though?" she challenged. "Everything's spell-protected." A wash of colorful runes shimmered over every building, from foundation to roof. Even the streetlights still worked.

When she had tracked Eugene, she'd used two methods to find him: coordinates and street view. Street view had given her a glimpse of the sign above the door to Archie's, which had led to their decision to come here, but coordinates were...tricky. Coordinates were far more precise than street view—accurate enough to zero in on a single tree or a person. But she rarely used that method—and *definitely* could use more practice at it. A *lot* more practice. In other words, Archie's was nothing but an approximate guess. Pax and Gene could be anywhere on the block—or beyond by now.

Shay was about to ask Tanner to pass her the Stygian salt so she could try tracking them again, when suddenly he spoke.

"I just saw something." He leaned forward in his seat, his eyes jet black.

Then he opened his door.

"Hold up—are we sure we want to go out there?" She didn't feel great about that decision, not when the *something* Tanner claimed to have seen could simply be a hungry predator.

"There are kids over there." That was all she needed to hear.

She opened her door, a cold wind that threatened to slam it shut slashing across her face and whipping her hair back. If Paxton and Eugene had been out in this weather for hours, they'd be lucky if they still had all their toes.

They walked together down the deserted road, periodically crouching behind parked cars in case Don or his men were in the area.

The kids Tanner had spotted were in an alley several blocks away from Archie's. There weren't two of them, though—there were five.

And three of the five were picking on the smaller two.

"Get off me!" Eugene's panicky voice bounced down the alley as the biggest kid in the group wrestled him to the ground, a knife to his throat. They hit the cobblestones, knife clattering across the ground.

Another boy was holding onto Paxton—pinning him to the brick wall by his neck and spitting threats in his face. The third also had a knife, and he was using it to scare Paxton into not fighting back.

The sight of children brandishing weapons like that... Shay felt sick.

She was about to fry those little shits with lightning when Tanner yanked on the back of her suit, dragging her down behind a car.

"What are you doing?" she hissed. "We need to help them!"

Tanner merely said, "Look."

Two big men were heading this way.

"Oh shit," Shay whispered.

It was Trey and Simon—two of Don's men. These assholes had beaten the shit out of Roman at the House of Black the night Shay found him strung up in chains. The same assholes who had a tendency to grab onto Paxton by his arms with a too-tight grip.

Shay knew there was a strong chance this would happen tonight. With Eugene's aura sparkling on the map like a colorful dessert laid out on a silver platter, it was only a matter of time before Don noticed and sent his men to collect. And that time had already arrived.

In the alley, the kids continued to fight. Shay's heart pitched about like a boat on waves at the sheer panic, the *distress* in poor Paxton's voice.

Gods, it made her furious. Where were these brats' parents? Shouldn't they have evacuated by now?

The kid pinning Eugene down pulled his fist back and punched him in the jaw. *Thwack*. Eugene cried out in pain.

Paxton wrested himself free from the other two, abandoning his jacket in his efforts to get away. When the kid who'd pinned him whipped his jacket aside and lunged, Paxton struck—

He punched the bully in the nose so hard, the kid crashed to the ground.

Shay gave a quiet laugh of delight. That was a good swing.

But Trey and Simon were there now. The moment the bullies saw the men rounding the corner, they scattered like flies off shit.

Shay's short-lived smile faded

"If you've got any lightning left," Tanner whispered, "now would be a good time to use it."

Eugene had scrambled to his feet, he and Paxton cowering away from the advancing men. Trey and Simon were speaking too quietly for Shay to hear what they were saying over the roaring wind that burned her eyes, but she knew the words were as heartless as they were.

She tried to summon her magic, but she was drained. So drained that her conduit tattoo *still* wasn't glowing at full strength, even after the lengthy drive here. Frying anyone was out of the question.

Had her immense output of magic tonight broken something within her?

She pushed to her feet and started heading the other way—back the way they'd come. "Let's go."

Tanner got up and raced after. "What's the plan?"

I don't know, she thought. It was true—she had zero clue how to deal with those monsters of men, especially not when she and Tanner were both at a disadvantage when it came to fighting. They were Darkslayers, yes, but they both held the kind of positions that rarely included them in combat. Tanner was no Darien or Roman, and Shay was no Lace or Ivy. No matter how badly she wanted to be like them, she simply wasn't built for what they did.

Still, no matter what, she refused to abandon those children.

"We're going to follow them," she declared. She picked up speed, running back to the truck as fast as her legs could take her.

28

ROMAN'S HOUSE
YVESWICH, STATE OF KER

The plan was in motion.

Those who would be going after Paxton and Eugene were ready to leave, Devils and Shadowmasters exchanging one last goodbye near the front door. As for Loren, her group would be heading out the moment Darien was convinced that the shades of her aura were saturated enough to keep her stable for the long drive home.

She walked across the messy living room, sticking to the path Darien had cleared through the wreckage for her so she wouldn't cut up her feet, toward the hallway that would take her to the pool. She wouldn't be going for a swim, but she'd agreed to a session in the sauna. Warmth, she needed. No doubt about that. The city was getting colder by the minute, sleet thrumming on the roof and windows.

Darien shadowed her every step with pounding boots, the air between them as electric as ever.

Loren briefly hesitated when she saw Ivy coming around the corner just ahead. In her hand she carried a small suitcase. The moment Ivy saw them, she averted her gaze and picked up her speed.

As she drew near, Loren stepped out of her path, refusing to wonder which of them Ivy was avoiding the most.

Darien stopped his sister with a hand to the arm. "Ivy."

It took her a moment to look him in the eyes, and when she did her face was blank. "What, Darien?"

"I think your plan is great," he began quietly. "You've always made a fantastic leader, and I'm really proud of you for that. But I would *really* like for you to switch places with Lace and come with us back to Angelthene."

Her dark brows flicked up. "Oh?" Her tone was cold. Mocking.

Darien looked utterly confused by her reaction. "Why's that so surprising?"

She cleared her throat, clasping the handles of her bag before her with both hands. "What's surprising, Darien," she began calmly. Too calmly. "Is how you've always placed such high value in everyone else's life but not your own."

Loren winced on Darien's behalf.

As for Darien, his expression shifted into an unreadable mask as his sister stared up at him with harsh eyes.

Ivy drew in a sharp breath through her nose, and for the first time in Loren's life she saw her fighting the black of the Sight, her pupils nearly swallowing the steel blue of her irises. "Get out of here, Darien." The words slightly wobbled, as if she were holding back tears. "We can manage without you for once." When her eyes flicked to Loren, there was no warmth in them. "Take care of yourself." An order—not a request.

Ivy walked away.

Darien stared after her. Loren may not be able to read auras, but she felt his pain. And it cut sharper than a knife.

But he buried it quickly, just like he buried all his emotions. It was an art he'd perfected a very long time ago. He scrubbed his good hand down his face, and then gestured toward the hallway they'd barely set foot in. "Let's go."

They had just started walking again when Max called from the living room, "Darien, can I talk to you for a minute?"

Loren slowed again—

But Darien nudged her forward with a gentle hand on the small of her back. "Not now, I need to get her in the sauna," he said over his shoulder.

Boots pounded and glass crunched as Max followed behind them. "I know, it'll just take a minute, though—"

"I don't have a minute right now, Max, and neither do you. We can talk after, if I'm still around."

Max came to an abrupt standstill. Loren didn't have a chance to brace herself before his next words lashed out like cracked whips. "Would it kill you to care about something else for like two *fucking* seconds?"

Darien froze.

Loren did, too, her heart stumbling two beats.

Slowly, too slowly for the reaction to not be considered a threat, Darien turned around, black swallowing his eyes, and said through his teeth, "Pardon me?"

Oh no.

Oh no—not again.

Loren edged around him, stepping slightly in front of him to try and make him look at her. "Darien, please don't start a fight—"

"I'm not, but he can watch his tone," Darien said, that hostile glare fastened on Max.

Loren's heart tripped into a sprint as Darien stalked up to Max—getting so close, there was barely a foot of space between them.

"Let me get something straight with you," Darien began. His lethally soft tone sent a prickle of goosebumps up Loren's arms. "I care about everything going on. I care very much, but I will *never* stop caring about her, not even for *two fucking seconds.*" Loren held her breath when he pointed a finger behind him—at *her*. Gods, where was a hole to crawl into when she needed one? The last thing she wanted was to come between Darien and his family, and that was exactly what was happening. First Ivy, and now Max? In the span of *minutes?* Darien continued, "She's the reason we're all alive right now, and if we lose her, we're *fucked*. Understand?"

"I know that," Max began, fighting to keep his composure. "I know, Darien, just—" He held up his hands. "Listen. Can you forget what I said—"

"Alright, I'm forgetting. Let's start again," Darien prompted sharply.

"I want to look for Maya," Max blurted.

Loren couldn't see Darien's face from this angle, but she knew him well enough to tell that he was taken aback and likely blinking in surprise. "You what?" The question was flat—another threat that had her stomach turning somersaults.

Max's explanation came rushing out. "I found her last night—right before the replica exploded. She survived, and so did her friend Magenta—Magenta's an Elemental, too. They were with us right up until Jewels went into cardiac arrest, and then she left—"

"She *left?*" he scoffed. "That's nice of her. Did she tell you where she was going?"

"No," Max admitted. His shoulders sank.

"Okay," Darien began, but Loren could tell from the way he said it that none of this was okay. "I want to make sure I'm understanding you correctly. Your sister ditched you without telling you where she was going

—without even saying *goodbye,* is that right?" Max said nothing, but his jaw clenched, and his hands curled into fists. "And you want to go looking for her," Darien concluded, his every word saturated with disbelief.

Max's response was defensive. "I'm sure you'd do the same for Ivy."

"And I'm sure Ivy wouldn't leave me like that," Darien fired back.

"I'm her brother!" Max fumed. His own eyes were onyx now. He took a step closer to Darien, getting right up in his face. Loren's pulse hammered faster. "I owe it to her to at least warn her about what's going on—"

"You're a Devil," Darien countered. "You owe your loyalty to the people who've been by your side for years, not the one who fucked off."

Darien abruptly turned and came back her way. "Let's go," he said, his hand warming her back. She stayed put, though. Because Max wasn't letting this go, and she could already see that this wouldn't end well.

"This is bullshit, Darien!" His words clapped through the house, his boots doing the same as he pursued Darien. "I'm going after her, whether I have your permission or not."

Darien whipped back around so quickly, the two friends nearly smacked into each other. Loren got out of the way, barely managing to squeeze between Darien's back and the wall, his shirt brushing against her cheek. The men had their backs to opposite walls now, both of them so close and so big they almost didn't fit in the narrow hallway.

"If you leave," Darien gritted out, his nostrils flaring, "consider yourself out."

"Why?" Max flung his arms wide. "Because I want to save my sister? Because I won't be able to live with myself if she suffocates in here—"

"Because you're choosing someone who doesn't give a shit about you over the people who do!"

Loren let out a gasp as Max pushed Darien in the chest so hard his back hit the wall.

For a moment, Darien stared at his friend—utterly stunned.

Max stared too, as if he couldn't believe what he just did.

"Darien," Loren tried—

"Put your fucking hands on me again—" He didn't get his warning out before he was pushing Max in return—pinning him to the opposite wall so hard it rattled, his forearm ramming into Max's throat.

"Alright, guys—time out!" Lace exclaimed. She ditched her suitcase on the couch and hurried over, Jack and Ivy tailing her. "Let's take a moment to calm down—"

"It's fine if he wants to go, Darien," Ivy said, her voice an octave higher from stress. "He can look for Maya while I find Tanner. But we need to *go.*" Despite her offer, she sounded far more uncertain than she had in the kitchen, and for a moment Max looked like he hated himself for asking to separate from her.

"You're not looking for Tanner by yourself," Darien said without so much as glancing at his sister. "I won't stand for that."

"She'll be with us," Roman said, stepping into vision in the living room. "The minute we find the kids, we'll all go looking for Tanner."

"What about *you,* huh?" Max spat his question in Darien's face.

"What *about* me?" he growled.

"You're fucking off to Angelthene instead of looking for Tanner—"

"Don't you fucking give me that!" he barked. "You know *exactly* why I have to leave!"

"Let it go, Max," Jack warned. He came closer, his eyes blackening as he prepared to intervene. "I hate to say it, but Darien has a point—Maya left. You don't owe her anything."

"You don't get it! You don't have any siblings—"

"Watch it," Darien warned.

"It's okay, I can take it," Jack said. "Think it through, Max. You don't want to be excommunicated, do you?"

"I won't be," Max said, breathing heavily. "He wouldn't do that to me." He looked at Darien for confirmation. For reassurance. His words were slightly strangled by Darien's forearm squishing his throat. "Because we're not just a Darkslayer House, we're a family. Even if we are fighting, and even if we hate each other's guts right now, we're still a family. Right, Darien?"

Loren held her breath.

She took a step toward them, but thought better of it and stayed where she was, her fingers fidgeting with her charm bracelet.

Darien lowered his arm from Max's throat. "If you leave," he said, his voice low and lethal. Amended, "If you leave your *family*...at a time when they need you most...you're out, Max. It's your choice."

He walked away before Max could reply—passing Loren, who was too shocked to move.

Judging from the look on Max's face, even if Darien had given him the chance to reply, he wouldn't have known what to say.

29

ROMAN'S HOUSE
YVESWICH, STATE OF KER

Loren sat on the wooden bench in the sauna, bouncing her knees up and down. She watched the sand dribble through the small hourglass that was mounted to the wall, desperate for the ten minutes Darien had insisted she spend in here to end. She hadn't bothered with a bathing suit and had stripped and wrapped herself in a towel instead—anything to speed this whole situation up and get them on the road home sooner.

Through the pane of frosted glass in the door, she watched Darien and Roman's silhouettes as they conversed. Roman was leaving, and there was no telling when they would see each other again.

She hated this. Hated that it had come down to Darien choosing between her and Tanner; between her and Paxton; between her and his family. Especially when she only had months left to live, and after that, these people were all Darien would have.

And he chose *her*. The guilt was so excruciating it felt like her skin was being gnawed on by millions of sharp teeth.

At the three-minute mark, the two cousins embraced. And then Roman left, leaving Darien by himself. Seven more minutes, and she'd be on her way back to Angelthene.

The last few grains of sand were trickling toward the bottom when Darien rapped a knuckle against the door, his timing impeccable.

She got up, the floor hot beneath her bare feet as she crossed the small room and opened the heavy door. Cool air that smelled of chlorine coasted across her face.

The house already felt so much quieter—emptier—compared to before.

Darien scanned her with the Sight.

"How do I look?" she asked him.

His attention lingered on her lips a moment before he said, "Beautiful."

She would have blushed, if her face wasn't already scarlet from the heat. "I meant my aura."

He held out the talisman she'd given him for safekeeping, the clasp open, one end in each of his tattooed hands. She stepped forward and turned around so he could put it on for her.

"Red and orange are looking a little better," he replied, the necklace passing across her vision as he brought it down over her head. "But your other colors are dim. I think we'll skip Ivy's suggestion to have you walk barefoot outside. It's too cold for that. It'll only set you back, and you need the heat right now more than anything."

"Has everyone left?"

"For the most part."

She tried to swallow, but her throat felt like it had closed. "What about Dallas?"

He did up the clasp, his scarred knuckles skimming the back of her neck, and then he fixed her braids, draping them evenly over her shoulders. "You can say goodbye before we leave."

"The *one* time I decide to take a long shower, and you go and get yourself *excommunicated?*" Dallas hissed.

"You're always taking long showers," Max replied, mud splashing under his boots as he stomped down Roman's front steps. He threw on the hood of the sweatshirt he wore under his jacket, his hair already soaked with sleet. "And I didn't get excommunicated."

"That's not what I heard the others saying!" She rushed after him, muck splattering her sneakers and jeans. "Max, this is serious."

Maybe it looked like it from an outsider's perspective, but Max had been a part of Darien's life for a long time. And although they'd never had an argument quite like this, they had locked horns more times than Max could count. They'd even gotten into it physically on numerous occasions, beating the shit out of each other until their faces were black and blue. Darien would forgive him for this.

Hopefully.

He walked through the closest garage door, all of them open to the night, and found the others—Ivy, Roman, and Kylar—piling into one of Roman's cars. A modern muscle machine with sparkling black paint.

"Take whatever you want." Roman's offer echoed in the cavernous space as he swung open the driver's door. "Keys are on that wall." He pointed.

Max scanned the pristine selection of vehicles and bikes. "I'll follow you guys to Archie's."

"Go find Maya, Max," Ivy said, leaning out of the passenger's-side door. Kylar was already in the back—she'd had to move the seat forward for him to get in. "I promise I'm fine with it. You'll just have to answer to my brother when you get back home."

Max walked over to the wall Roman had indicated to and scanned the labels on the keys hanging from hooks. Roman sure was organized.

He picked one and hit the button to unlock the doors. "I'll help you find the kids, and then I'll figure out what I'm doing from there," he said, answering Ivy, who still watched him through her open door.

Roman fired up the engine. Its sexy growl filled the garage, the candle-smoke scent of magic flavoring the air.

Ivy shut her door.

"Wait, Max," Dallas called as she followed him to the vehicle he'd selected. "What about Loren?"

"What about her? She's leaving soon, too."

"Yeah, but I haven't said goodbye." Despite her words, she was already walking to the passenger's side.

"You can go with her if you want, Dal." He opened his door. "Unlike Darien, I won't try and stop you."

"Don't you think you're being a little hard on him?"

"Whose side are you on?" Max fired the question before he could stop it.

Dallas's lopsided wings drooped. "I don't want to pick sides. I've come to care about all of you guys, even when you're all treating each other like a bunch of stupid jerks."

He braced his hand on his open door, his expression softening as he gazed at her from across the roof of the car. These past few weeks, Dallas had become so much easier for him to read. And right now, she looked so torn, he was tempted to leave her behind so she wouldn't be forced to choose between him and her adoptive sister. After the argument he'd just had with Darien, one of his very best friends, he knew too well how it felt to have to choose.

Roman backed out of the garage, sleet pounding the roof of his car like bullets.

"Dallas, I swear to the gods I won't be upset if you decide to go with Loren. I'll see you back in Angelthene, and everything will be the exact same as it is now."

She took a moment to think about it as Roman turned the car around in the driveway.

"I want to come with you," she decided.

His brows bumped up. "You're sure?"

Her chest rose with a slow breath, her attention briefly flicking to the door that led into the house. She faced him again, and nodded once.

"We need to leave now, then. Roman's not waiting for us." He ducked inside and started the car.

Dallas hesitated for a moment longer before getting in, reclining her seat to accommodate her wings.

Max backed out of the garage and followed Roman to Archie's Arcade.

DALLAS WAS ALREADY GONE.

No one was here anymore except Arthur, Jack, and Lace. They were currently in separate areas of the house, probably doing their final rounds to make sure they weren't forgetting to pack anything.

Loren tried not to feel hurt by Dallas's decision to leave without saying goodbye. Time was not on their side, and she figured Dallas had been forced to decide quickly—and she had chosen Max. Loren didn't hate her for it—not at all. Not when she knew she would have chosen Darien, if the roles were reversed. They used to be attached at the hip, but ever since they'd fallen in love with the most unlikely men, their relationship had changed. They weren't bad changes, though. Somehow, Loren felt closer to Dallas now than ever before.

She flicked off the salt lamp on the nightstand. The room was completely dark now, apart from the hallway light slanting in through the open door. She put her jacket on, grabbed her travel bag off the bed, and checked one more time to make sure her few belongings were indeed packed.

And then she stepped out the door for what would probably be the very last time.

Darien was right there waiting for her. He had his black leather jacket on, a duffel and backpack slung over his shoulder. A rebellious strand of hair hung in his face, the end of it nearly reaching the tip of his nose. The urge to smooth it back—to take any excuse to touch him—was so strong, she had to curl her free hand into a fist.

"Ready?" he asked her.

She nodded, and he motioned for her to walk in front of him.

"I'm beginning to think you just want to look at my butt," she said as she squeezed by, getting so close she swore the air crackled with sinful energy.

Sure enough, when she peeked over her shoulder she saw his gaze pulling upward, confirming her suspicions that while her butt may not be the whole reason he was guarding her back, he was indeed enjoying his view.

"My eyes are up here, Darien."

His pupils flared, nearly eclipsing the steel-blue of his irises. "Even when we're fighting, your ass is mine."

She gulped, blush spreading through her cheeks. "Except for when I say it's not."

Darien's mouth settled into a firm line, and that potent gaze of his rapidly darkened—not with the Sight, but with claim. As if he were daring anyone to take what was his.

He broadened his strides, getting so close he almost bumped right into her. She swallowed a squeak as he warned, "Keep walking." His deep voice made her shiver, his breath warming the hair on the top of her head as he bent down. She was already moving faster, her body one big chill as he added with a husky whisper, "Or I'll spank your ass so hard, you won't be able to walk for a week." He straightened to full height, still matching her step for step.

The thought of being spanked by those hands of his liquefied her core. She knew he could sense it—her arousal. Even through the talisman's protection, she couldn't hide her feelings from him, not when they were this close.

And even when their world was crumbling around them, her body still went completely crazy over him. Gods, she was so pathetically obsessed with this man. She was going to have a hell of a time putting distance between them. She already was.

The others were waiting downstairs—jackets and shoes on, suitcases at their feet. Jack was staring out the window by the door looking miserable, Lace looked conflicted and stressed, and Arthur...Arthur looked like he needed a very long nap and a fresh ice pack. Loren felt bad for him—he was far too old for this much excitement.

"Who's driving?" Darien asked, taking two sets of keys out of his pocket. He looked like he already knew the answer, though, and was likely asking simply to be polite. With Jack still recovering from his concussion, and Arthur looking like he was one step from the grave, the answer was obvious.

Lace came forward. "I am."

"You can take the truck," Darien said, keys jingling as he tossed them into her outstretched hand. "Follow us and stay close."

30

EAST YVESWICH INDUSTRIAL PARK

YVESWICH, STATE OF KER

S hay watched from a distance as Simon and Trey herded the kids into a seedy warehouse. In order to see them from this distance, she had to use her Sight. While Paxton's aura was hidden by a talisman, Eugene's was visible, his colors so prismatic, especially when compared to Simon and Trey's.

Her blood was surging—not just with adrenaline, but also with the line of Stygian salt she'd sniffed a minute ago to help her focus and curb the splitting pain returning to her ribcage. If she stood a chance at getting those kids out alive, she would need all the help she could get.

Suddenly, Tanner leaned forward in his seat and peered up at the sky. "Do you feel that?"

She did. It was a subtle shift in energy—undetectable by mortals. It skittered across her bones and made her arm hairs stand on end.

Before she could ask him what, exactly, it was, he said with unmistakable awe, "The cell towers are working." He frantically patted his bodysuit, his eyes bright with hope that was quickly crushed. "Oh no." He sank in his seat.

"What?"

"I think those assholes took my phone." Of course they had—he was Tanner Atlas. He could do a lot more with a phone than most people. He quickly searched the truck—the glovebox, the dash, the space under his seat, the storage pockets in his door. Shay did the same on her side, and when they both came up empty, he cursed. Nothing about tonight was easy.

"If the cell towers are working, I bet you they're already messaging Donovan," Shay said.

If Donovan got his hands on the kids, there was no way of knowing where he'd take them after that. The city was being evacuated, so it was only logical to expect that Donovan would be leaving soon, too, until it was safe to return to his empire of shit. He just needed his kid first.

Shay unbuckled her seatbelt. "Wait here and keep watch. I'll go see if I can find a way in."

"I think I should come with you."

"I'll be okay."

"Are you *sure?* Look, Shay, I don't doubt that you can handle yourself after that lightning show you put on. But these men are *insane.* And three times your size, in case you didn't notice."

Yeah, they were. Insane and practically three times her size. But at least she could use illusion to slip away if need be. It was easier to conceal one person than it was two, so it would be better if Tanner stayed here.

"I won't go inside," she said. It wasn't a promise, though. Depending on what she witnessed, she could end up inside so quickly. "I just want to get a look at what they're doing and who's in there." Hopefully Donovan wasn't already inside, and the reason Trey and Simon had come here was to meet up with him. If he was...gods, she didn't know what she'd do. She opened the door, her body instantly tensing as biting air gusted into the truck. "I'll leave the keys here. If I'm not back in fifteen minutes, drive away without me."

Tanner looked utterly horrified by the idea of her not coming back, but he didn't argue as she stepped out into the street.

31

THE WAREHOUSE
YVESWICH, STATE OF KER

In a warehouse deep in an industrial park in eastern Yveswich, two twelve-year-old boys sat on the ground. Their eyes were downcast, their arms wrapped tightly around their knees.

Paxton Slade couldn't stop shivering, though the cause had more to do with fear than it did the cold and the wet.

Simon sat in a hard chair in the heart of the warehouse that was so crowded with junk, the building was practically a maze. His elbows were resting on his knees, his thumb flicking a metal lighter open and shut.

Trey was here, too—leaning against a wall nearby with unnatural stillness. Both men watched Paxton, the occasional glance spared for Eugene sitting next to him on the icy concrete.

"Your dad will be here soon," Simon said to Paxton. A pause, the lighter clinking open and shut. *Clink... Clink... Clink...* He checked his watch. "In about...half an hour." *Clink... Clink... Clink...* "He's really upset with you, you know. Do you have anything you'd like to say?" A pause. "No?"

Paxton shook his head.

"Sorry, perhaps?"

He shook his head again.

"Why did you run?"

"Because we don't like any of you!" Paxton said sharply.

"Hey," Trey warned.

Simon held up a hand. "That's okay." *Clink, clink, clink,* went that lighter.

All of a sudden, the power went out, plunging the building into darkness.

An earthquake began, shaking so hard Trey lost his balance and staggered.

In the sudden darkness, Paxton and Eugene seized their chance.

They shot to their feet and bolted.

SHAY LAY flat on her belly outside the warehouse, peering through the glass of a window that gave her a not-so-great view of the inside.

Even with the benefit of being a hellseher, it'd been hard to eavesdrop from this far away, but she'd gleaned enough about the situation to understand that Paxton and Eugene had gotten away from Simon and Trey. But the warehouse was so crowded, it was practically a maze, and the kids couldn't find their way out. They were hiding somewhere in there, and Shay had to get to them. *Before* Simon and Trey found them.

And, even more importantly, before Donovan got here.

Now that the power was out, it was so quiet, she could hear the howling of hundreds of beasts and the chopping of rotary blades as helicopters flew over the city.

Shay twisted around, dropped down onto her ass, and scootched closer to the window. With a deep breath, she kicked the glass out, hoping Trey and Simon wouldn't hear. It tinkled to the floor inside the building in shards and slivers.

With a deep breath, she gripped the top of the window frame and launched herself feet-first into the warehouse.

ON LIGHT FEET, Shay crept through the cluttered warehouse, scanning her surroundings for any sign of Eugene's aura.

She cleared her corners the way Anna had taught her, spheres of lightning forever crackling in her palms. She owed her ability to control it to the salts coursing through her blood—without their help, she'd be screwed.

There was a narrow passage up ahead that was lined on either side with stacked boxes and portable wood pallets.

With agile steps, she squished through, her black eyes sweeping about.

She could see other areas of the warehouse through the gaps between the stacked boxes and pallets—but there was still no sign of Paxton and Gene.

A piercing scream sliced through the building.

She moved faster, following that scream—

Trey had found Eugene and was backing him into a corner. A fox trapping a rabbit. "Found you," Trey drawled. Eugene was so focused on the Shadowmaster approaching him that he didn't see Shay as she hurried up behind Trey—

She was about to slap her lightning-charged palm against the back of the bastard's neck when he whipped around.

His hand lashed out, pushing her so hard he might as well have hurled a brick at her chest. She flew back into a stack of pallets with a startled cry and hit the concrete floor with a bone-jarring *slap*.

A rough hand fisted her hair, wrenching her head so far back her neck muscles *screamed*. "Well, if it isn't Shayla Cousens," Trey drawled with a wicked smile, his black eyes shining in the dark. "Don's had his eye on you for a while. You're that little whore Roman's fuckin'. Aren't you?" He pulled harder, moisture leaking from the outer corners of her eyes.

"I don't know what you're talking about," she said through clenched teeth, hating—absolutely *hating*—how this prick said Roman's name. It made her want to wash his mouth out with soap.

"I can smell him on you," he hissed. He came in close, his nose skimming the shell of her ear. Her heart pounded out of her chest. "I think I'll take you to the House of Black. Show that whore cunt of yours how a real man fucks." His teeth grazed her ear lobe. "How does that sound?"

Shay hawked and spat in his face.

"You bitch!" He let go of her hair and backhanded her across the cheek so hard her lips bled.

Shay sucked in a breath and surged up from the floor, her open palm swinging for his cheek.

He ducked to the side, causing her hand to flatten against his throat instead. Fine by her. Either worked; she merely needed contact.

Trey jerked about, as if he were being tased.

And then he fell face-first onto the ground, thwacking his head against the concrete. The moment he broke contact, the electric currents flowing through Shay faded, leaving her wholly fatigued—drained, just like a battery—but otherwise safe from harm.

Trey lay there on the floor, still twitching uncontrollably. He stared up at her with ferocious hatred, lightning zigzagging from the soles of his feet to the crown of his head.

Shay drew a breath, choking down the nausea swelling in her gut, and walked over to Trey. A smile of triumph spread across her face as his bladder loosened, a wet stain darkening the front of his jeans.

"Hilarious," she crooned, breathless. "One of Donovan's best men, and all it took was the baby seal of the Riptide and a little bit of lightning to make him piss himself." She wiped the blood off her lips with her sleeve. "Also, Trey, I think my *whore cunt* will pass on your offer, thanks."

He kept jerking about—a fish twitching on land. "Watch," he gritted out through clenched teeth, every wobbling word splintered by an electrical current, "your. Back. *Cunt.*"

Yeah, she would really need to do that from now on.

"Have a nice nap." She waggled her fingers—

And then stomped on his face, knocking him out cold.

She rushed over to Eugene, who stood in the corner. His hands were flattened over his ears, eyes shut tight.

She grabbed him by the shoulders and shook him. "Eugene!"

He cowered backward, banging into a wooden board that was leaned up against the wall, and screamed, eyes still shut. "AHHHHH! Help me, HELP—"

"Eugene!" She grabbed onto him again, shaking harder. "It's me!"

He forced open his eyes. Blinked up at her. "Wh-what?"

"Where's Paxton?" He kept staring at her, utterly bewildered. She shook him again, his glasses nearly bouncing off his face. "Where. Is. *Paxton?"*

"I don't know, I lost him!" he blubbered.

She cursed and straightened, her eyes turning black as she used her Sight to look for Simon, spotting him on the far side of the building.

"Let's go." She took Eugene by the hand and ran.

Deeper into the warehouse.

PAXTON COULD SCARCELY BREATHE.

He tore through the warehouse as fast as he could, searching for a way out. Running from Simon—

Simon, who pursued him with unhurried steps, taking each corner slowly, leisurely. Paxton had gotten separated from Eugene in their haste, and now they were both lost.

Paxton flew around a corner and ducked behind a stack of crates, his breaths sawing apart his lungs, limbs wobbling like jelly.

A whimper threatened to come out, but he clamped a hand over his mouth to stifle the sound. He slid backward on his knees on the cold ground, searching frantically for a better place to hide.

There was none.

Thump, thump, thump, went Simon's boots. He walked slowly. Dragging this out. Trying to scare him, he knew.

The thumping of his footfall paused.

Paxton peered between the crates. Simon was *right there,* so close he'd surely spot him within seconds, and then he'd be trapped again, no way back to his brother.

Heart racing, he got to his feet and backed up, searching for a way out, but not finding one. No windows, no space between the clutter that was big enough to squish through.

Dead end. He'd run into a dead end.

"Paaaaxtonnnn," Simon called.

Paxton squeezed his eyes shut, praying for his brother to find him.

"Ohhhhhh Paaaaaxtoooonnnnn..." His voice sharpened into a hateful sneer. "Where are youuuuu?"

"Turn around," said a deep, male voice.

Paxton's eyes flew open. Panting, he spied between the crates—right on time to see Simon whipping around.

And a tattooed hand lashing out—grabbing Simon by the throat.

His brother. The Wolf of the Hollow.

Going in for the kill.

32

SOUTH YVESWICH CITY LIMITS
YVESWICH, STATE OF KER

The city was disintegrating into complete *fucking* mayhem.

Darien rolled the car to a stop behind the longest line of multi-lane bumper to bumper traffic he'd ever seen. Thousands upon *thousands* of people were scrambling to evacuate via every exit and major highway, some of those people driven by such blind panic they'd abandoned their vehicles and fled on foot.

"I'm sure this won't take long," Loren offered quietly as Darien squeezed the steering wheel with his good hand, leather groaning beneath his twisting grip. She was a sweetheart for trying to calm him down, but any amount of time was too long when her tattoos indicated that her health was rapidly deteriorating.

She had tried to hide their red glows of warning when he'd brought her down to the sauna in Roman's house. When she'd come out of the change room, she had tucked her forearm against her side, partially concealing it in the folds of her white towel. But her attempt to keep him from noticing had failed. Nothing escaped him—especially when it came to her.

They were running out of time, and the last thing he wanted was to have to perform CPR on her again. It was too damaging, and he was lucky as hell that her ribs hadn't cracked from the force he'd had to use while compressing her chest. He figured the magic serum had something to do with that, but he didn't want to chance it again.

And now, to make matters worse, he was being forced to sit here.

Traffic was at a total standstill. The cars way, *way* up ahead, at the very front of the six-lane highway, were just...idling. Judging from the crowds of people who'd resorted to getting out of their vehicles to confront the authorities, they hadn't budged for some time.

Darien leaned forward and summoned his Sight with one firm blink, his vision shifting to a canvas of black with neon silhouettes. He scanned the auras of MPU workers, cops, firefighters, Fleet soldiers, and other military personnel. Fire trucks, squad cars, and army tanks formed blockades across every lane.

Something compelled him to scan the forcefield itself—the green runes that ran in columns that bubbled above the city.

Except they weren't green—not anymore. They were red.

The blood drained from his head, and so did the Sight from his eyes, the air from his lungs.

No.

No.

The forcefield—

They'd already *fucking* put it up.

33

THE WAREHOUSE
YVESWICH, STATE OF KER

Roman had never hungered for someone's blood as strongly as he hungered for Simon's tonight. This moment was a long time coming, and he didn't intend on wasting it with an easy death—not after everything this man had done to him. To Pax. Roman would bleed him dry like a butcher bled a pig. He would not make it quick.

"Hello, Simon." Roman's greeting was quiet and deadly. With a steady hand, his grip crushing, he picked Simon up by the throat, lifting him so high his feet dangled above the ground. Roman used his magic as a shield, stopping Simon from effectively fighting back. "You look surprised to see me."

A person's body was like a tomato—very easy to squish. And the throat, Roman had learned early in life, was one of the best places to target in a fight. You couldn't build muscles to protect yourself there, so all a person had to do was catch you unawares. A throat punch or non-fatal strangulation served very well in combat.

Roman summoned his magic in full with one firm blink, black engulfing his eyes.

Shadows seeped out of him, ballooning into an inky cloud, just like the darkness swallowing the city. Roman directed a few wisps of it upward, snaking the shadows around Simon's neck. With a featherlight touch, they tickled the back of Roman's hand, as if to say, *Let go. We got this.*

So Roman did, using his powers instead of his muscle to lift Simon into the air.

"I've been waiting a very long time to kill you," Roman said, every word spoken in a deliberately unhurried way. "A very, *very* long time."

He loosened the shadows that were crushing Simon's windpipe—just enough to allow for a response.

"You won't," Simon squeezed out, his heartbeat thumping beneath the skin of his neck. "You lack the guts."

"What I've lacked is opportunity," Roman countered. It was true—Simon and Trey had been very strategic over the years, taking precautions to ensure they were never caught anywhere alone with Roman. They'd hidden behind Don many, many times. But not tonight.

Not anymore.

"But tonight...," he continued, pinning Simon with a cold, black stare. "Tonight feels like the perfect time. Don't you agree?"

"You won't," he said again, though his eyes shone with doubt. "Your dad—"

"My dad isn't here," Roman snarled. "And by the time he arrives, I'll be long gone. As for you...you'll be dead, Simon."

Roman circled him, watching him hang there like a fox caught in a snare. Tonight, Roman was the bigger, more powerful predator. One that had paced inside his cage long enough.

Simon squirmed, his booted feet kicking in the open air like a fussy child in need of a nap. How rewarding it was to finally watch this man— this bully—get what he deserved. "Fuck you," he spat.

With a flourish of his right hand, Roman lifted him higher—till the top of his head nearly brushed the ceiling.

Roman squeezed the hand he still held aloft into a fist.

The shadows around Simon's neck obeyed his command—and tightened, just like his fist, slowly digging into Simon's flesh like wires. Crushing his neck, like a snake squeezing the life out of its prey.

Simon's face turned a bright red that quickly deepened into a dark shade of purple. His eyes bugged out of his head, the blood vessels bright and threatening to burst. His tongue poked out of his mouth like a thick worm.

"Asphyxiation has always been a favorite of mine," Roman said, again tightening his fist, his knuckles cracking. "There's just something so... rewarding about it."

The shadows dug in deeper.

Roman gave a little smile, his eyes black as pits. "Have a nice time in hell, Simon. You won't know a moment's peace where you're going."

He whipped his hand in a downward motion—

And ripped Simon's head off.

Roman exhaled deeply, the tension in his muscles melting away.

He set his shadows free, releasing Simon's body. It struck the floor with a *thud,* his head doing the same. He swore he could almost hear Ignis cackling as she welcomed another irredeemable soul to her realm of torture.

Not a moment's peace, indeed.

One down. One more to go—

Reality hit him like a slap to the face, the blood draining from his head so quickly he felt woozy.

Pax.

Roman spun around. "Pax?" he panted. The black was already out of his eyes, his act instantly forgotten. Paxton was out of sight—crouching behind the crates, his heart thrumming so fast Roman could hear it from here. Roman took a tentative step toward him. "Pax, it's okay, buddy—it's just me. It's Roman."

Paxton didn't move.

"You can come out now," Roman tried again. "You can come out, Pax —you're safe. I've got you."

Paxton—wide-eyed and pale—stepped out from behind the crates on wobbling legs.

And coming around the corner a short distance away, her arms wrapped protectively around Eugene, was someone Roman feared he'd never see again.

Something inside his chest cracked, and so did his voice as he whispered her name. "Shay."

34

SOUTH YVESWICH CITY LIMITS
YVESWICH, STATE OF KER

"Darien?" Loren whispered. Her voice was small, her pulse way too weak for his liking.

Darien's, on the other hand, pounded with rage.

He threw open his door, pausing to grab his heavier black jacket from the back seat. "Put this on, please." He passed it to her, and she took it with a grasp as weak as her pulse. "Come with me."

He stepped out, slamming the rain-slick door. Loren got out on her side, his jacket big enough to easily fit over her own. He met her behind the car and took her cold, delicate hand—drowning in the sleeve—into his, leading her to the driver's side of the truck idling behind them.

Lace lowered her tinted window. "What's going on?"

"I'm about to find out. Keys are in the ignition," he said to Jack, who was listening in from the passenger's seat. He and Lace both had black eyes, which told Darien they suspected the same thing as him and had taken it upon themselves to scan the forcefield. "If traffic starts moving, take my car and drive until you find us."

He was gone before they could reply, guiding Loren between lanes of traffic. It was a long and cold walk; Darien worried Loren might not be strong enough to make it in her condition. She managed surprisingly well, though, the exercise raising her body temperature, just enough to take the edge off his concern.

As they drew closer to the cars idling at the front of every lane, Loren squinted to see through the downpour, her mortal eyes finally making out the crowds of people gathered around the battalion of military personnel, police officers, and YMPU agents blocking the exit, their vehicles staggered every few hundred feet.

She stepped closer to Darien, her pulse quickening. "What's happening, Darien?" Police lights oscillated in patterns across the drenched road, limning her soft features and the braided strands of her hair with blue and red.

He tightened his hold on her hand, tugging her forward so she was right in front of him as they reached the crowds of people obstructing the highway. Darien guided her from behind, weaving between the bodies of witches, warlocks, humans, half-breeds, vampires, and werewolves. A few of the latter were fighting to keep their emotions in check, twitches and tremors rippling through muscles that were rigid and overheating.

Everyone was on the edge of hysteria, which made walking among them all the more dangerous—though Darien could admit they had every right to feel frustrated. Their concerns and complaints were falling on deaf ears, the authorities providing zero explanation as to why they were being barred from leaving the city. The only help the authorities were offering came in the form of empty promises and verbal threats, guns and staves out to discourage rioting.

Darien scanned the crowds, spotting a familiar face speaking with other officers of the MPU near the first blockade .

He pushed forward, still keeping Loren in front of him—guarding her from all sides. He got as close as possible to the authorities while staying far enough back to avoid being shot, and snarled in the stunned face of warlock Finn Solace, *"What the fuck is going on?"* He jabbed a finger at the forcefield, waves of vermilion washing across the highway by the sign that said *Now Leaving Yveswich*. "That's not supposed to be up until noon tomorrow!"

Finn gaped, evidently shocked to see him here. But he recovered quickly, cleared his throat, and said, "Change of plans."

"Says who?"

"We're doing our job. We're following orders—"

"Fuck your orders. Who told you to do this?"

A vampire cop stepped forward, his milk-white hand drifting toward the gun strapped to his hip. "Back up, please—"

Darien didn't give him the time of day. "I have it on good authority that this forcefield is *not* supposed to be up until Roark fucking Bright gives the word!" He amplified his voice so every officer, agent, and soldier in the immediate area could hear him.

"Sir, we're going to have to ask you to step back—"

"Take it down," Darien growled at Finn.

Finn's throat bobbed. "We can't do that."

"Take," Darien repeated through clenched teeth, his eyes shifting into inky pools, "It. *Down.*"

Finn's attention flicked to Loren. She was tucked against Darien, her back flush to his front. Her pale fingers were grasping his left arm that was crossed over her chest—over her heart.

Solace swallowed again, rain sliding down his face. "It's not that simple," he said in a hoarse whisper.

Darien's nostrils flared, his blood *boiling.* "So you're just going to trap everyone in here? Leave them to die like pigs in a slaughterhouse and sneak out the minute the government gives you the okay? Where's your conscience, Finn? Did you leave it in the same place as your common sense?"

Finn's ears reddened. "This is my *job,*" he hissed.

"Slaughtering people? No, Finn, that's *my* job. You're supposed to be a shining example of a hero, but right now you just look pathetic," he spat. "You don't deserve to wear that badge. Who's in charge here?"

"I am," said a harsh male voice.

Darien whipped around.

A warlock with a shaven head was sauntering over, hands in his coat pockets.

Fuck.

Bandit let out a low growl in Darien's shadow.

This was the same detective who'd arrested him and Jack when the hotel called *The Blood Queen* blew up. He was glaring at Darien with hateful eyes, his cruel features accentuated by the shadows beneath his sodden hood. His throat was slashed with a pink scar from the chains of the handcuffs Darien had strangled him with in the interrogation room.

As if the prick knew exactly what Darien was thinking, his upper lip curled with a sneer. "Now back the fuck up or you'll be leaving here in cuffs!" he snapped. He gave Loren a once-over and added, *"Without* your lady."

Darien saw red, his palms itching with the need to slice this prick's lips and eyelids off. Loren's heart raced under Darien's hold, her fingers tightening around his sleeve.

"Your threats don't scare me," Darien said. "Keep hiding behind that badge like a pussy like you did at the precinct."

"Keep running your mouth and see where it gets you," the detective countered. "Stir up trouble, you get arrested. It's that simple, Cassel."

"Where's Roark?" Darien fired his question at Finn, beads of rain flying off his lips.

"Not here."

Darien dug his phone out of his pocket. The cell towers had started working not long ago—they'd better *still* be working. "What's your dad's number, sweetheart?" he demanded. He tried to soften his tone, but it came out sharper than a newly honed blade.

Finn tried to say something, but Darien tuned him out, focusing on nothing but the numbers Loren recited, her sweet voice the only one he was interested in hearing.

"This forcefield is coming down," Darien snarled, his statement directed at everyone in earshot as the line began to ring. The bald detective's glare burned a hole in his face as Darien added, "Right the *fuck* now."

35

THE WAREHOUSE
YVESWICH, STATE OF KER

Looking at Roman made Shay's heart hurt.

For one agonizing moment she found herself wishing she'd never come here. She had been so focused on saving the boys, she had thought of nothing else, least of all herself.

So it hadn't dawned on her how her heart might feel the moment she set her sights on this Shadowmaster again.

Bad—that was how this felt. How her heart felt. It felt really, *really* bad.

The more she thought about it, though, the more she realized how selfish she was being. She could never regret her decision to help Paxton and Eugene. They were innocent children, and merely the fact that they had men as horrible as Simon and Trey in their lives should be a chargeable offense.

Maybe what she *really* regretted was ever getting involved with Roman in the first place. If she had kept her hands to herself—*literally*—instead of letting him touch her in that motel room, she wouldn't be feeling this way right now. Like someone had punched their hand into her chest and ripped out her still-beating heart.

Roman, Pax, and Sayagul were locked in a tight embrace, their eyes shut. Roman's hand cupped the back of Paxton's head, his fingers curling in the boy's mop of hair, while the small dragon perched on Pax's shoulder. Her wings were draped around him, her head nuzzling his neck. The low vibratory sound coming from her chest was almost a...purr. Could dragons purr?

All the same, it was the sweetest thing Shay had seen in a long time. And even though she wasn't a part of it, she felt whole.

Well, apart from that gaping bullet wound in her chest.

She drew a deep breath to ease the ache, but all it did was make it worse, as if clusters of barbed wire were puncturing her lungs.

Was she a fool for having feelings this intense for a man she had met only a short time ago? Or was Roman just *that* easy to love?

It was definitely the latter, she decided. This boy and dragon clinging to him like he was their raft in a stormy sea were proof of that.

Roman's eyes—a rich blend of amber and chestnut flecked with gold—opened, locking on hers. "You're alive." His husky voice skittered across her every bone, resurfacing memories of words whispered to her in that motel room. The loving ones—and the sinful ones.

She cleared her throat. "So are you."

"Oh man, Pax!" Eugene squealed, leaping and pumping a fist in the air. "You should've seen it! She *roasted* Trey like a hotdog!"

Paxton's eyes lit up with awe. "Really?" He gazed up at her like she was a superhero from his favorite comic book, the reaction so wholesome and genuine that for a moment she really felt like one.

"Do you have a built-in taser or something?" Eugene asked her, his lisp extra thick.

"I have lightning powers."

"Sick!" the boys exclaimed.

Paxton grinned and tipped his head back to look at Roman. "That's even cooler than what you can do!"

"Watch it," Roman warned, though a smile flirted with his lips, deepening the scar by the one corner. Shay had to try really damn hard not to stare at that smile for too long. The mouth she'd had the pleasure of kissing. "You killed Trey?" he asked her.

"No, but I made him piss himself," she replied.

Roman's brows flicked up.

"He's passed out somewhere over there." She pointed. Unless he'd already woken up and fled, which would align with the kind of luck they'd been having.

Roman mussed up Pax's hair. "You sure you're okay, kid? Look at your face." He gently skimmed the tip of Paxton's scraped nose with a knuckle.

"I'm fine."

Sayagul squawked out her disagreement. *'He needs bandages,'* she said. *'And a bath.'* She blew a puff of smoke through her nose.

Paxton laughed. "Do I stink?" He lifted his arm—

"Eugene?" called a husky voice—choked with concern. Kylar Lavin was hurrying down the narrow passage between the boxes and pallets. He stumbled when he saw them—saw his brother.

And then he picked up speed, sweeping Eugene into a hug that lifted the kid's sneakered feet off the ground. "Holy shit, termite—you're alive!" He set him down and rubbed his knuckles vigorously across the top of Eugene's head, making the kid growl and push his hand away.

"Dad's supposed to be here any minute," Paxton said, his short-lived joy already fading. "Simon called him."

"Shit, we gotta go, then," Roman said. "Let's go—get moving." He beckoned the kids into motion. Sayagul disappeared into Roman's shadow with sparkling wingbeats. "Where's your jacket?"

"I lost it," Pax said.

"Here—wear mine." Roman stripped his off, leaving him in a grey long-sleeve shirt with a short row of buttons in the center of the neckline, the trim fit drawing attention to his sculpted body. The man was a work of art.

Shay cursed him for taking that damn jacket off.

Paxton shrugged it on, his beanpole physique drowning in the fabric.

Together, they navigated the warehouse. On the way, the kids filled them in on what happened. How they had ended up at Archie's Arcade.

When Donovan and his men had raided Roman's house, Dominic and Blue escaped with the kids. They'd made the decision to hide in a park down the road, and when they heard gunshots Dominic and Blue had left the kids at the park and gone back to check on Arthur.

"And then this monster started chasing us," Paxton said. Every word was breathless with adrenaline and excitement. "So we ran, and we hid in this random guy's truck—"

"And then the truck started moving," Eugene chimed in, "and we got too scared to jump out until we got to the school. There were other students there. The teachers were planning an evacuation, so we thought we'd be safe—"

"But then Blaine and Larina showed up," Paxton interrupted, desperately clawing for his brother's attention. "So we ran to Archie's before they could see us, but Zac, Ty, and Brendon followed us and we got into a fight—"

"And Pax punched Zac right in the face!" Eugene exclaimed.

Paxton scowled. "Hey, I wanted to tell him!"

But Eugene was too excited to reel his emotions in. "Awe man, you guys should've seen it! Zac was like *bam*—" He punched the air. "But Pax was like *BAM*—"

The building shook.

Light bulbs popped in sprays of glass.

The boys cried out in alarm. Everyone covered their heads.

The intensity grew to an unholy magnitude, making it difficult to stay standing, to *think*. Shay half-crouched half-fell to the ground and seized hold of a stretch of chainlink that was leaned up against stacks of pallets, the others doing the same. There was nothing to hide under, so the older brothers were shielding the younger ones with their bodies as dust fell and debris and boxes clattered around them.

The shaking subsided as suddenly as it had begun.

The power was out—not just on the block anymore, but district-wide.

"What the hell was that?" Shay panted.

As if this couldn't get any worse, they heard the spitting of gunfire, the roaring of monsters, and the rhythmic pulsing of helicopter blades.

Roman's wide eyes snapped to hers, terror stark on his face. The gunshots outside...the voices, the *shouts* Shay was just now picking up on...

He and Kylar had not come here alone. There were others outside, and by the sound of the madness going on just beyond these walls, they had run into trouble.

Tanner.

Ivy—if she was out there.

Bile burned Shay's throat.

They all pushed to their feet and ran like hell for the way out.

36

SOUTH YVESWICH CITY LIMITS
YVESWICH, STATE OF KER

Loren was having difficulty breathing, and this time she suspected that it had more to do with the rapidly declining state of Yveswich than it did her own health.

She clung to Darien's steady arm as the city quaked. The tremors weren't as bad over here, but the heart of Yveswich and everyone trapped there would surely suffer their might.

Darien's family—*her* family. Her friends.

They were all still in there.

She watched in horror as the black mass pouring out of the Void grew and *grew*, claiming yet more districts with its blinding grasp. It wouldn't be long before it would swallow the rest of the city, turning every last survivor into sightless and vulnerable prey. Lights flashed at intervals as missiles were fired into the gloom, exposing hundreds of roaring beasts invading under the cover of darkness. Clawing their way out of Spirit Terra and into the land of the living. Of flesh and blood. To feast. To triumph.

Death would prevail. Unless they could find a way to stop it, death would be the world's new ruler, and life—balance—would be no more.

The shaking subsided. The piercing screams of the crowd on the highway died off in the wind.

Darien returned his focus to his phone, hitting CALL on the number that had already gone to voicemail twice.

Come on, Dad, she thought. She squeezed her tired eyes shut, her fingers grasping the rain-slick worn leather of Darien's sleeve. *We need you. Please.*

I *need you.* She'd always been too proud to admit it, but there were many times growing up when she really could have used her father. Either one, it didn't matter which. And she really needed him now—*this* father. The only person in the city who might be capable of getting them out of here alive.

The warlock with the shaven head—Detective Glen Campbell was the name she had spotted on the identification badge sewn into the chest of his jacket—smirked. "The forcefield's coming down right now, is it?" he taunted over the pounding rain. He shook his head and sauntered away, though he stayed close enough to keep a hostile watch on them.

Phone to his ear, Darien stared out at the ruins of the city, his saturated hair dripping rainwater down his face. His strong arm was wrapped protectively around her, his eyes black as sin.

"Bright here." The sound of that brusk voice drifting through the phone speakers sent a wave of relief through Loren's body, so strong her knees shook.

Oh thank gods.

"It's me," Darien replied. A loaded silence followed the greeting, indicating that Roark was shocked to hear from him. Before he could press for more information, Darien continued, "We have a problem. I'm on the I-5, and your men won't let me through." He shot a black look over his shoulder. Loren turned, peeking under his arm to see Glen pacing, frowning deeply at them. She had no idea what that guy's problem was, but she really didn't like him. Darien went on, "I've got one of your daughters with me, and the other's still in the city. If you can't convince your men to take this forcefield down, neither of your girls will make it out of here alive."

There was a fraught silence. "They've assembled the forcefield already?" Roark's question—hollowed out with surprise—crackled through the speakers. Loren prayed reception wouldn't be lost.

"Yeah, and I'm staring down the longest line of fucking traffic I've ever seen. They're not letting anyone through. People are going insane—I won't be surprised if you start having riots on your hands. Can you help us out, or what?"

Another crackle. Loren strained to hear him. "Loren's with you?"

Darien's eyes—blue again—roved over her rain-speckled face. "She hasn't left my side." It was such a simple statement—pure fact—but it warmed her chill body by several degrees.

"Give me five," Roark said. "I'll call you back." He ended the call.

Three minutes ticked by before a commotion rippled among the authorities. Arguments ensued. Officers looked their way, Glen included.

Loren crossed her fingers.

She trusted that this would work. Trusted that Roark, out of anyone, could accomplish the impossible. He wasn't a good father, not by any means, but there was one thing he was very good at, and that was his job. Nothing about earning his title had been easy, and with the kind of authority he now had...

At the five minute mark, the forcefield came down with a tangible shift in energy. Even as a mortal, Loren could easily feel it while standing this close. It blew the loose strands of her damp hair back and sent a curl of nausea through her gut. She swayed, as if she were standing in a boat on a choppy sea. Darien's hold on her waist kept her steady. Her anchor in this endless storm.

"Let's go," he said softly. He turned, shooting one last glare over his shoulder at that hateful detective. "Looks like it's down," he called.

Glen did not reply.

They walked together down the highway, through crowds of people who were also heading back to their vehicles. With Darien shielding her, his heavily muscled body every bit a weapon as his guns and blades, she was not jostled by a single person. Not even once.

A little over five minutes later, Darien's phone started buzzing. He took it out, not missing a step, his free arm still wrapped protectively around her. Loren strained to hear both ends of the conversation as he answered.

"Cassel."

"I can buy you three hours," Roark said.

This time, Darien *did* miss a step. "Three hours?" he echoed. Loren had wondered if she'd heard Roark correctly, but Darien's spoken confirmation had her stomach exiting her body. Darien's arm tightened around her, as if he sensed her distress and was shielding her from the bad news. "What happened to noon tomorrow?"

"I'm not the only one calling the shots. Three is the best I can do, and I've already been told that I'm pushing it. Get Loren out, and wherever the others are, you need to tell them to get out, too."

Three hours. *Gods.*

But—

"We've ran into a few...complications that have led to a shift in orders," Roark went on. The rain picked up again, making it hard to hear, see.

Loren squinted, her eyelashes soaked. "I can't speak of them over the phone, but you need to get everyone you care about out. Starting with Loren." This was the most he'd said her name in...gods, *years*. "Can you do that?"

They were almost at the car. Traffic was beginning to move, the first of the vehicles making it through the forcefield that was passable again as cops, fire fighters, and military personnel rushed to dismantle the barricades. When Loren saw the forcefield's greenish tint shimmering in the corner of her eye, she vowed never to take that shade for granted again.

"Where are you getting your orders?" Darien demanded.

A pause. And then Roark said, "The imperator."

37

INTENSIVE CARE UNIT
YVESWICH, STATE OF KER

J ewels was asleep.

Apart from her rhythmic breathing and the ticking of a clock in the hallway, the room was quiet. Peaceful.

At least it would've been—quiet and peaceful—were it not for the putrid stain that was Malakai. The idiot was glaring Travis down as if he'd punted Creature across the room like a Flightball. Every breath he drew was so heavy it was practically a snort. A bull preparing to charge.

Travis's gloved hands curled into fists. "Are you ever going to stop with your crazy possessive *bullshit* attitude?" he snapped, failing to keep his voice down. Aspen was asleep, too. She was curled up in her seat like a cat, cheek resting in the crook of the elbow she'd folded on the arm of her chair. She looked really uncomfortable, but that chair was the only choice she had, unless she'd rather lie on the gross floor.

Malakai hadn't blinked in so long, his eyes were veiny. "You first."

"I'm not possessive!" Travis hissed.

"If that were even remotely true, you would've left with the others instead of staying here. You chose my sister, who you barely even know, over your own family." He arched a brow. "Desperate much?"

It was more than a low blow. It was a kick to the nuts. A hard one.

Travis hadn't stopped thinking about the others since they'd left. Especially Roman. Malakai was right—he *had* chosen Jewels, a Reaper he barely knew, over his own family. His brothers. His Devils. Darien, Lacey, Ivy, Jack, Maximus, Tanner... The guilt was eating at him.

Had he done the right thing? It wasn't that he doubted his feelings for Jewels, but he doubted how she felt about him. Definitely. They'd only had one real date, and he wasn't even sure she liked him all that much. Maybe he *was* desperate.

Maybe he just really needed to get laid.

He settled deeper into his chair with a sigh, stretched his legs out, and crossed his arms, the change in position wafting the tang of his own sweat across his face.

He wrinkled his nose. Fuck, he smelled nasty. He was long overdue for a shower—and some rest.

Delaney continued to watch him as if this were some sort of staring contest and drugs were the prize. Travis didn't partake in it, though—he stared at Jewels instead. He was already pissing Malakai off by merely existing, so he might as well live life to the fullest and do whatever the hell he wanted. And right now, what he wanted was to look at Jewels.

She seemed to be improving, but maybe that was just his optimism speaking. Her skin was still sickly, her body drowning in that hospital gown. She looked so frail for a hellseher. Like Loren, sort of.

Yeah, come to think of it, she really wasn't looking much better.

"Do you always creepily stare at girls while they sleep?" Malakai demanded, the question hissed through clenched teeth.

"Do you always terrorize every guy your sister hangs out with?"

"Just the ones who try to date her."

Lucky him.

The clock ticked. Outside, the city was rocked by more gunfire, more explosions. Helicopters flew so close to the building, the windows shuddered.

The portal was growing. They had until noon tomorrow—or was it today, now, technically?—to get out, which meant they would have to travel while Jewels was at risk of suffering complications. Being a hellseher meant she'd recover from this quicker than if she were mortal or half, but being ill with the Tricking put her at a huge disadvantage.

She was too young to be plagued with this horrible disease. The Tricking didn't usually target people in their early twenties. Usually thirties, forties... And usually people who abused their magic. People like Randal. Which, from what Travis had seen, Jewels didn't do. He didn't think he'd ever even seen her track anyone.

"If your dad shows up," Malakai began, "I'm leaving with Jewels and Aspen and I'm locking you in here with him."

Travis stiffened. "That's an asshole thing to say," he growled, thoroughly disturbed by the idea of that happening. Donovan still had no clue his runaway son was back in Yveswich, and Travis wanted to keep it that way. If he found out he was here…

He shivered.

Malakai shrugged. "I'm an asshole," he stated. "What'd you expect?"

"That really is an asshole thing to say, Malakai," chimed a female voice. Jewels was awake—and glaring at her brother. "Travis's dad is an awful piece of shit. We wouldn't like it if someone said they'd lock us up with Cathal, would we?"

"Who's Cathal?" Travis asked.

She slowly slid her attention his way, the ice gradually thawing from her expression. "Our stepdad."

"How are you feeling?" Malakai asked her.

"About the same as before. If you guys would stop arguing for longer than five minutes, maybe I could get some rest," she quipped.

Malakai grumbled and cracked three of his knuckles.

Jewels looked toward the dark windows. "And maybe if the city would shut up…" She sighed and rubbed her eyes, her IV lines tugging across the sheet. "What time is it?" she asked around a yawn.

Travis took out his phone—

And saw an incoming call from Darien. The volume was on silent—he would've totally missed it if he hadn't looked.

"Oh, holy shit," he breathed. "The cell towers are working." He lifted the phone to his ear. "Hello?"

"Change of plans," Darien said, his voice loaded with urgency.

Travis sat up straight. He knew that tone.

"You have exactly two hours and fifty-four minutes to get out."

Travis tightened his grip on the phone. Jewels and Malakai were listening in, murmuring to each other. Aspen stirred awake, and when she opened her mouth to speak, Malakai lifted a finger to his lips.

"Are you still at the hospital?" Darien asked.

"Yeah."

"All right, I need you to listen. I'm on the I-5. When I got here, they already had the forcefield up. We almost didn't make it out, but I got a hold of Roark and he told them to take it down. The imperator's dictating his every move—less than three hours, and after that the city will be in full military quarantine. Nobody will be allowed out. That means you."

Sweat prickled across Travis's back. "Who's all with you?" he managed to ask, his lungs shrinking. "Where are the others—"

"I tried calling Ivy, but she's not answering." Horns beeped in the background. If he wasn't with Ivy, then who all was he with? Just Loren? "I'm going to try her again, and then I'll call you back. Two hours and fifty-two minutes, Travis. I need to get Loren back to Angelthene, and you need to get your ass up and get out of there. *Now.* It's not a request, it's an order. Do I make myself clear?"

Travis tried to speak, but only a croak came out.

"Travis," Darien snapped. "I don't have enough time to get back in there and help you, and even if I did they're not letting anyone in. I need to know that I can trust you to do this."

Travis nodded, forgetting—like an idiot—that Darien couldn't see him. "Yeah," he rasped. He cleared his throat. "Yeah, I can do it. You can trust me."

"I hope you're on your feet. Time's ticking."

He planted them firmly on the floor and gripped the arm rest of his chair for support. "What about Roman, is he with you?"

"Roman can handle himself." That was true.

Still, Travis's heart pounded so hard he could scarcely think. "Did you call him yet? Is he—"

"Travis, you need to focus on *yourself*. You and I both know what Roman would want you to do, so you need to buckle down and fucking *do* it." Yeah, Travis knew what he'd want all right, but that didn't mean he had to like it. He also didn't like how Roman obviously *wasn't* with Darien. Which meant he was still somewhere in the city. Looking for Paxton, probably. Darien continued, "I'll call him again, but you need to evacuate— right now. I'm telling you not as your friend, not as your cousin, but as your boss. Get the fuck out, Trav—now."

The others were already moving, Aspen detaching the IV lines in Jewels's arms and hands.

"Travis," Darien snapped again, his sharp tone shooting like a bullet into his eardrum. The phone speakers crackled as vehicles whooshed by. Where the hell was he? The I-5, he'd said. Was he standing at the side of the highway?

"Yeah, I hear you, Darien—I'm moving." Travis stood.

"Be fast."

He hung up.

"I can carry you," Malakai was saying to Jewels, his arms held out to catch her as she eased out of bed.

"Just let me walk," she insisted, shooing him away. "I'll tell you if I need help." She paused, glancing at her bare feet. "I don't have any clothes." Shit —that was right. The paramedics had cut her suit off.

"We'll find you something to wear on the way out," Aspen assured her, rolling her food tray aside. "Most hospitals have get-well shops, but if that fails, there's always the Lost and Found."

"Whatever works," Malakai said, ripping the curtain aside. "Let's go, Bean. Fast as you can, or I'm throwing you over my shoulder."

They left the shared room, where two other patients lay sleeping in blissful ignorance, and made their way down the hall.

It was eerily quiet. The lights were dimmed, not one person in the waiting room where they'd all gathered yesterday. More patients and staff must have evacuated.

As they passed the nurse's station, Travis saw that it, too, was deserted. A phone had been bumped off its receiver and lay on the desk.

A chair had been knocked on its side.

Someone had dropped a mug of coffee on the floor and left it there.

Tension rippled among their group. Hands eased toward guns.

Had these people left so hastily that they'd knocked all this shit over? Or had something else happened? It seemed unlikely, given how they hadn't heard any noise, but—

Travis drew a pistol and kept walking.

Malakai was first to reach the corner.

A wet, fetid odor slapped Travis in the face. Ugh, that *smell*—

As they rounded the corner, Malakai froze.

Everyone froze.

"What the hell?" Malakai breathed.

There was blood all over the walls. Blood and claw marks.

People lay dead in every room and hallway. Throats were slashed. Bellies were ripped open, innards smeared across the floor.

The lights flickered.

The power shut off, darkness falling like a quilt.

Deep in the hospital, something roared.

38

EAST YVESWICH INDUSTRIAL PARK

All hell had broken loose outside.

Roman kept Paxton close as he stalked out of the warehouse and straight into a bloody war zone.

Clumps of snow and ashes fell from a charcoal sky. Buildings were burning, flames casting the ravaged street in flickering relief.

But the fire's glow was still no match for the Void. The otherworldly darkness just kept growing, blotting out their world bit by bit, structure by structure. A parasite feeding off light. Off life itself.

The others were engaged in combat, dead monsters lying in gory lumps all around them. Bullets flashed in the ever-darkening street, and several blocks over, soaring above and between buildings, he spotted Fleet soldiers and attack helicopters. Members of various armed forces were going up against droves of winged demons with bullets, crossbows, and magically enhanced blades. Bellowed commands and the spitting of rapid-fire gunshots rang through the night. Those monsters—some of them belonging to breeds Roman had never seen before—had one thing in common.

The stones embedded in their foreheads. Pulsing with dark magic that rendered them practically indestructible. The bullets, the blades, the bolts fired out of crossbows—those soldiers might as well be brandishing sticks and stones for what good they were doing.

This was not a war they could win. This city, his home—

It was already lost.

A demon barrelled toward them from the black sky.

Roman felled it with a net gun of magic, shadow snapping its leathery wings shut.

It crashed to the pavement and tumbled straight into the path of Max's obsidian blade.

He punched the sword through its skull, then planted his boot on the back of its jagged spine and wrenched the blade free.

That was the last of the immediate threats. Which gave them approximately five seconds to talk before they needed to fucking *go*.

"Shay!" Ivy exclaimed. She sprinted across the blood-slick lot and caught Shay in a spinning embrace Roman found himself envying.

It had been hard as hell to keep his hands to himself, not just when he'd seen his thief coming around the corner, alive and well and as breathtaking as ever, but when the earthquake happened, too. When she'd grabbed onto the chainlink and dropped to the ground, he'd wanted nothing more than to shield her. Keep her safe, like he had Pax.

The relief he'd felt when he first saw her was short-lived. Entirely forgotten the moment he recalled the threats that his trash excuse for a father had made on her life.

'If you step out of line again,' Don had said, his cruel words echoing now in Roman's memory, *'she will be raped bloody by several of my men.'*

Roman would die—break his own heart—before he let that happen.

"How many vehicles do we got?" Roman asked as everyone—panting and sweating—formed a group. "How'd you get here?" he asked Tanner, who Roman was just noticing. Apart from some dried blood and bruises, he was fine. Darien would be happy to hear it.

"Beats me," the hacker replied, breathless. He tucked a pistol into his weapons belt—empty apart from that single firearm. "I woke up in the back of that truck with Shay." He pointed down the road, at a black truck with a canopy.

"Long story short," Shay said, "that truck belongs to Wyverns. They were looking for Pax, and they thought we might know where to find him. Apparently Don has every Darkslayer House out looking for him."

"Wyverns?" Kylar repeated. He cursed. "How'd you get away?"

Shay waggled her fingers in answer, pale violet lightning crackling at the tips.

Kylar's head whipped in Roman's direction, his eyes so wide the whites showed. "Lightning *and* illusion?"

"She's got a built-in taser!" Eugene boasted, bouncing on the balls of his feet.

Roman shrugged in response to a still-gaping Kylar. "She's incredible." The statement slipped out before he could stop it, and he didn't miss the way Shay's body tensed in response.

Eugene was still bouncing. "She cooked Trey like a wiener!"

"Trey got away," Max said to Roman, his unfortunate news causing Eugene to cease his jumping and stomp his foot. "He booked it out of the building the minute we pulled up."

"Back to the plan," Roman interrupted. The addition of that truck gave them a total of three vehicles. There were nine people here altogether, which meant... He tallied up the seats. It gave them more than enough room. "We need to evacuate," he said, his next words for the benefit of Shayla and Tanner. "We ran into the Red Baron at the hospital. They're putting up a new forcefield at noon tomorrow, and once it's up no one will be allowed through."

"Dare's already gone," Kylar chimed in. "Loren's body is reacting funny to the portal, so he's taking her back to Angelthene."

"Lace, Art, and Jack left, too," Ivy added.

Tanner blinked. "Wait a sec—they're already locking everything down? What about all the people? There must be millions—"

"They aren't waiting," Max said. "And I need to find Maya and warn her, or I won't be able to live with myself."

"Hold on," Ivy shouted above the din, explosives going off several blocks over. She had her phone out, her face suffused by the glow of her phone screen. "Hold on—everybody quiet, Darien's calling me." She answered the call, plugging her free ear with a finger as yet more explosives went off. "Hello? *Darien?* I can barely hear you!"

The group fell silent as she spoke, the city shaking all around them.

"If you're going looking for Maya, I'd do it now," Roman shouted over the noise, addressing Max. An abrupt cease in fire gave them a moment of false calm, allowing Ivy to hear better. "People are already panicking. I bet the highways are jammed—"

The ground trembled as something landed just behind him.

He whirled, hand drifting toward his gun—

It was Dominic, black wings spread. In his arms, he carried Blue.

He set her on her feet. "We've been looking everywhere for you guys," the Angel said, breathless. The blood smeared across their faces and battle-suits suggested they'd encountered more than one obstacle along the way. "What the hell happened?"

Roman said, "Long story."

"Guys," Ivy interrupted, her voice high with stress.

Another missile hit several blocks away, the noise causing Pax to stumble and clap his hands over his ears. Roman steadied him, then laid his hands on top of Pax's, giving him a better buffer against the noise.

"That was Darien!" Ivy shouted. "He said they already put the force-field up, but Roark was able to get it taken down." The panic in her eyes, the pallid shade of her skin... Roman saw it coming a second before she spoke. "We have less than three hours to evacuate."

Terror washed through the group.

"Three hours?" Kylar and Dominic repeated. Another missile hit.

"He wants us out now," Ivy said, looking dazed. "Darien and Roark—they want us out."

"What do we do about Travis?" Dallas asked. "He's still at the hospital."

Fucking *Travis*—making everything worse by coming back here, by being stupid enough to stay at the hospital. What *were* they going to do about him?

What was *Roman* going to do about him?

He ground his teeth.

"Darien said he already called him," Ivy replied. She looked like she was trying not to puke, and Roman felt like he might hurl his guts up, too. One brother found, another already lost. "I'm setting a timer." Her hand went to her watch. "You guys should do the same—make sure you don't lose track of how much time we have left."

Max was the only one who did as she suggested, the others either not wearing watches or frozen in place as they processed the warning.

Three fucking hours.

Less than three. Roman knew this city like the back of his hand, had driven these streets so many times he could do it blindfolded.

Less than three hours, when combined with mass hysteria and bumper to bumper traffic...

The odds weren't good. Not good at all. They were shit.

Roman still had to get Paxton back home, grab some of his stuff, and get out. He didn't have time to run around Ignis's half acre wrangling everyone up.

But he wouldn't be able to live with himself if something happened to Travis.

He shook back his shirtsleeve and set his own timer. Ivy came over and helped him adjust it so it was as accurate as possible, almost down to the second.

"I'm leaving," Max announced. "Dal, if you want to go with them, feel free. I'd rather you get out, anyway. But I need to find Maya. How many seats are in that truck?"

"Three," Shay responded.

"I'll take it, then." He underhanded his car keys to Kylar. "You guys need the extra room." The cars didn't have much extra room, but they did have back seats.

"Max, wait!" Ivy called. But Max was already moving, Dallas rushing after him with a backward glance.

Paxton tugged on Roman's sleeve. "Roman," he whimpered.

"Not now, bud," Roman gritted out. Fuck, Travis—Roman was so irritated, his blood was boiling. What the hell was he supposed to do now? *Leave* him here? Trust that he could get out without his help?

"Roman." This time, Pax's voice was a broken sob, his hand tugging on Roman's wrist. He was staring at something, his eyes wide as saucers.

Two vehicles, both familiar, pulled to a stop down the road.

Roman's soul left his body.

'No!' Sayagul cried from his shadow, fear splintering her voice. *'Roman, no! Don't let him take him! He can't have Pax! He can't—'*

"Oh fuck no," Kylar whispered, pulling Eugene close. The others gathered around, weapons drawn, Max and Dallas retreating back this way.

They were too late.

They'd taken too long.

Roman took Paxton by the arm, guiding the kid behind him as Donovan fucking Slade stepped out of the first car, five Shadowmasters with him.

39

YVESWICH GENERAL HOSPITAL
YVESWICH, STATE OF KER

Travis ripped a gray sweatsuit off the rack and passed the hanger that was marked with an M to Jewels. "Here, I found one. Hurry."

They were in the hospital gift shop on the ground floor, surrounded by racks and shelves stuffed with *Get Well* and *New Baby* items. With the power out, they'd had to take the stairs, and from there they'd broken into this store by smashing the window. Most of the stuff this place sold was not helpful in this particular situation—cards, stuffed animals, balloons, candy, snacks, magazines, jewelry. But there was one clothing rack in the back with sweatshirts and matching sweatpants, which made their lives a bit easier.

Jewels hurried into the single change room and ripped the curtain shut while Malakai kept watch by the door. Aspen had sprinted to the Lost and Found and was now darting back this way. In her hand she clutched a pair of basic white running shoes.

This area of the hospital had been evacuated and shut down, dead people everywhere. They had been lucky enough not to run into whatever the hell had killed them on their way down. If it was one of those things from Spirit Terra, they'd be fucked. Especially with Malakai being sober for the first time in his life, no Venom on hand.

While he waited for Jewels, Travis stuffed his pockets with snacks, ripped open a granola bar, and shoved the whole thing into his mouth. The taste of the chocolate chips and oats made his stomach rumble. He was starving.

When Jewels came out, Aspen helped her get the shoes on. "What size are these?" Jewels asked, stuffing her bare feet in them.

"Six and a half. It was all they had."

"Six and half?" she hissed. "I'm going to get blisters from hell!" She wiggled her feet into the tattered shoes, forcing them to stretch. The baggy sweatshirt she wore had the phrase *I survived Yveswich and all I got was this lousy sweatshirt* printed across the chest.

Fitting, given all this insanity.

"Let's go, people!" Malakai hollered, waving them toward the smashed window, fallen mannequins and popped balloons lying in the glass. "Shit's going down outside, and we've got piss-all for time!"

"Come on, you stupid thing," Jewels muttered to the shoe. She used her finger to coax her left heel in and tied it up, Aspen already finished with the laces on the right.

And then they were running—well, almost. Jewels was still breathless, her body weak, so their running was more like jogging. At a mortal's speed. Which was torture. They jumped out the smashed window, hurried down the hallway, through a side door—

Straight into the pure chaos that was the parking lot.

"Shit!" Malakai growled, ripping a hand through his tangled hair, evidently thinking the same thing that just dawned on Travis. "The brilliant Darien didn't think about how we don't have a fucking car!"

"Don't blame Darien, you didn't think of it either, you fucking dumbass!" Travis snapped, sleet pelting his face. The parking lot was solid ice, all the snow and rain from earlier having already frozen.

As if Darien could hear them talking, Travis's phone rang.

He swiped to answer. The moment the din surrounding the hospital drifted through the speakers on Darien's end, he spoke. "You're trapped, aren't you?"

"How'd you know?" Travis asked, his tone tight with stress.

"Lucky guess," Darien said flatly. He added, "I'm tracking you."

Travis's hand shot to his throat, fingers groping the bare skin. The Avertera talisman Roman had given him—he had a shit-ton of them that he'd hoarded over the years and had divided up between everyone in their group yesterday—was already gone.

"Yeah, you're going to have to watch your back," Darien said, as if he'd seen where his hand had drifted. "Don't want your psycho dad to find you. How are the streets looking? Crowded?"

"Another lucky guess."

"Alright, I want you to get out by boat." Before Travis could ask questions, Darien explained, "It'll take you too long to get through traffic, and that's if you can even manage to catch a lift. If you can get to the water, you'll have a straight shot to the forcefield."

"Darien says we should get out by boat," he told the others, shouting above the noise. To Darien he said, "Where are you?"

"I'm parked on the I-5. I can see Yveswich from here. The roads are nuts—you'll never make it to an exit on time, and the military has blocked the eastern highways. North, South, or the water are your only options. You'll have to trust me on this."

"I'm not sure we can make it to the water, either, though," he panted. The hospital was in the heart of Yveswich. Every open highway exit was farther in distance than the ocean, but not by a whole hell of a lot.

But Darien was right about the traffic—the whole city was gridlocked, especially the main roads and exits. They'd have a better chance if they fled on foot than they would fighting through this congestion. Once they made it to the water, there'd be nothing to stop them but the water itself.

And what lived in it.

"You need to try," Darien said. "And you need to start moving. Right now."

Travis cursed, but wasted no time launching into motion. The others kept pace with him as he ran, sleet blinding him.

"Can you call Roman for me?" Travis panted, boots clapping on the pavement, the dark and frozen world bouncing with every step. "Tell him I'm sorry—"

"You can tell him yourself," Darien interrupted brusquely. "Just get out, Travis. Don't make us bury you." He ended the call.

Fuck, Darien was harsh sometimes, but his words succeeded at one thing: they made him run faster. Jewels was now on Malakai's back, unable to move fast enough while still recovering.

They needed to find a way to get to the water. Hotwire a vehicle, maybe. The districts closest to the coast were the least likely to be jammed, most of the people flooding the major highways and downtown core. They could run the whole way, yeah—a hellseher's speed and resilience would allow for that—but it would be hard, given how tired they were.

A little over two hours remained. If they couldn't make this happen, they'd be stuck here.

And Travis might never see his family—the brothers he'd all but abandoned—again.

40

EAST YVESWICH INDUSTRIAL PARK
YVESWICH, STATE OF KER

"Use illusion," Max said to Shay. He could barely breathe, his body tense and overheating from stress as he watched Donovan Slade and his Shadowmasters—Blaine and Larina among them—make their way down the road.

Paxton's mom was here, too. She walked at the head of the group, bundling her coat around her, her face a perfect portrait of a loving mother's concern.

Bait—that was all she was in this scenario. Donovan had brought her as bait. An attempt to lure Paxton into his grasp.

And bait was exactly what *they* needed.

Max would be that bait.

Shay's head turned in Max's direction. She, too, was barely breathing.

"It's the only way we can get Pax out of here," Max explained. Even while standing this close to her, he had to practically shout over the gunfire, the monstrous roaring, the missiles blasting creatures of nightmares out of the sky. "Cast an illusion—make it look like it's Roman and Pax getting in the truck. I'll lead them away."

"Max," Ivy croaked, her eyes shining.

The others peered at him, their faces filled with apprehension.

Tanner opened his mouth to argue. Shut it.

Max loved these people. For them, he would do this.

So he put on a brave face. Swallowed the lump in his throat. "Do it," he urged. "It'll wear off and he'll turn around soon enough, but it'll buy you guys more time to escape."

Donovan was getting closer. Walking leisurely, as if he had all the time in the goddamn world. Knowing full well he could massacre each and every one of them while barely lifting a finger. Cocky bastard.

Paxton's mother was drawing near, her dark hair swirling about her face. She was calling Pax's name, begging him to come to her.

She crouched in the center of the road and opened her arms to him.

Her child did not budge. He stayed behind Roman. Fearing his father more than he trusted his mother.

How horrible it was to watch this unfold. To see the conflict in Paxton's tear-lined eyes. A boy in need of his mother's love, but too afraid of his father to go to her.

"Do it," Max urged, though his stomach roiled. His odds of getting away from someone like Donovan... They weren't good. Still he said, "We're running out of time."

Shay thought about it another moment longer, then nodded once.

"No tricks," Ivy said sternly as Shay shut her eyes. "Not this time."

Shay drew in a long breath through her nose. Blew it out through her mouth. The ground rumbled beneath Max's feet, the air shifting with energy—whose, he didn't know.

Because Donovan was rallying his magic too, his power so strong there were stones and debris floating all around him, as high as he was tall. The darkness closest to him seemed thicker, as if a piece of the Void lived inside him. Begging to be unleashed. Just one whisper of that dreadful power— that was all it would take to end them.

White light glowed through the rips in the arm of Shay's battle-suit— her conduit tattoo.

It was almost time.

Max angled his body. Getting ready to run.

They *all* got ready to run.

"I love you, Max," Ivy said. Though the words themselves were softer than a flower, her tone was stronger than steel. "Try not to die."

"Three...," Shay began.

"I'm not dying today," Max replied, his heart beating out of his chest.

The debris floating around Donovan began to vibrate so hard it blurred.

"Two...," Shay whispered.

Max added, "None of us are." They hadn't come this far just to lose.

"One." Shay opened her shining black eyes. Sucked in a breath and screamed, "NOW!"

None of them were prepared for what happened next.

AN EAR-SPLITTING *CRUNCH* cut through the night.

Wind whipped down the street in violent gusts, stirring up debris and dust as a military-grade helicopter suddenly lost control, rapidly careening to the ground. Two big monsters that looked like bats were latched onto the aircraft, a third ripping its way inside and devouring the screaming soldiers and pilots. One of the men jumped out, breaking his back on the way down.

Roman's eyes widened. "It's going to hit," he breathed.

It was going to hit right where they were standing.

"Holy gods," someone whispered.

"LOOK OUT!" Roman bellowed.

He tackled Paxton and Shay to the ground and threw himself over them—shielding them with his body.

The helicopter crashed to the road and smashed into pieces, the impact bursting what was left of the aircraft into flames.

Blood sprayed.

Objects were hurled through the lot with horrific force, smashing glass and breaking streetlights apart.

In the end, it was only their shields of magic that saved their asses.

And among the commotion, as the helicopter slid across the pavement in a roar of fire and smoke, rotary blades snapping off, they seized their one and only chance.

"Run." Roman's command came out in a hoarse whisper. His next was louder—cracking on its way out as he pushed himself up off the ground, pulling Pax and Shay with him. *"RUN!"*

Everyone bolted.

Donovan and his people, being in the path of the destruction, had been forced to take cover.

It was the first blessing they'd had in hours.

The second was the smoke—thick plumes covering their escape.

"Faster!" Roman ran like hell, crushing Pax's hand in his grip. Clare was shouting Paxton's name—begging him to come to her. Roman refused to lighten up on his grip, knowing exactly how this would end if his father got

his hands on any of them. What was happening in this city—the pandemonium, the monsters, the gunfire, the goddamn *war* itself.

It was nothing compared to Don. What he was capable of doing.

Shay ran with him, Paxton's free hand in hers, the others booking it to their own vehicles. It did not escape him that this might be the last time they ever saw each other.

Roman slid to a dust-choked stop beside the car and ripped open the door. "Get in, get in!"

Pax climbed between the front seats and squished into the back, Shay already in the passenger's seat.

Roman got inside and started the engine. "Shay?" he ground out as he threw it in drive. She knew what he was asking as his eyes flicked to the mirror—to the others.

"I did it," she replied, her words breaking on a sob. "I did it, but I didn't want to do it! He could kill them! Roman, *he could kill them!*"

His heart raced as he looked in the reflection. At Ivy, Tanner, Kylar, and Eugene, who were already peeling away in the other car.

Down the road, Don, his wife, and his Shadowmasters had returned to their own vehicle and were speeding after Max, Dallas, Dominic, and Blue.

It had worked. He'd taken the bait.

Don had taken the bait and was now chasing an illusion.

MAX FLOORED IT, his breath sharp as a knife in his chest.

Donovan was coming after them, his headlights drawing near.

Dallas and Blue were in here with him, Dominic in the truck bed.

The reason? Apart from the lack of space.

The gun he was aiming at Donovan's car.

It was a spur-of-the-moment idea that had flashed into the Angel's mind while they'd sprinted down the road. One they'd had zero time to discuss. Trust was all they could do.

Shay's illusion—the magic that would wear off within seconds if they were unlucky, minutes if they were blessed—kept Don and his men from spotting the Angel of Death as Max steadied the car on a straight stretch of road, giving Dominic a clear shot.

"Come on, Dominic," Max whispered, pushing the truck so fast the magic coursing through the engine hummed. The smell of candle smoke floated through the vents. "Come on."

Max knew the only reason the asshole hadn't already used his power to blast them off the road was because he really believed Paxton was in here. Believed he'd kill his kid if he subjected him to a collision of such sheer magnitude.

"Come on," Max whispered, heart pounding. Dominic was a great shot —Max knew he wouldn't miss. He was not just an Angel of Death, but an ex-Fleet soldier. He could do this.

The headlights brightened. The car was close.

Dominic fired.

The front-left tire on Donovan's car exploded.

He careened out of control, spinning in a complete rotation, the other car with the rest of the Shadowmasters screeching to a halt behind him as Don's car blocked both lanes.

Holy shit.

It worked.

Max cheered, the girls whooping, his first grin of this wretched night breaking like the sun across his face.

Dominic drummed his hand on the truck canopy in victory. "Got him!"

"Hell yes," Max panted. But his smile was soon fading.

Because they were far from safe. Donovan was taken care of—for now. But the city was collapsing, and they were almost out of time.

And he hadn't said a proper goodbye. Ivy, Tanner—he may never see them again. May never get a chance to mend his friendship with Darien.

And he had less than three hours to find Maya and get out of Yveswich, or he'd be as dead as the soldiers and pilots in that helicopter.

41

I-5

STATE OF KER

P arked on the side of the I-5, Loren sat in Darien's car. She had her door open to the night, her sneakered feet bouncing in the frozen dirt.

Gods, it was so cold out here, but she didn't want to shut the door and miss out on anything important. Darien had left the car running, warm air blasting through the vents, her seat heater on high.

And she was still so cold. Even while drowning in his heavy jacket.

Lace stood by the front of the car, the burning tip of the cigarette she pinched between her fingers glowing a vibrant orange as she took a drag. Her worried gaze was fixed on Darien, who paced nearby on the shoulder of the road, phone to his ear. Arthur and Jack were still in the truck, their silhouettes masked by the magic spells and tint.

The others had roughly two hours to make it out of Yveswich, and that was only if the authorities obeyed Roark's command to keep the forcefield down until then. Loren wasn't feeling very optimistic, not after they'd already failed to do so once—and not when she knew that Roark was getting his orders from the imperator himself, who could overrule him at any time.

She stared at the phone cradled in her hands. She'd used Darien's car charger for a few minutes before ripping the connector out, certain that she had changed her mind about using it. But she was already back to feeling undecided, her stomach melting into nausea.

When she checked the screen, she saw that the device had less than a ten percent battery charge and barely one bar of patchy service—just enough to maybe send a few messages, if she so decided.

Vehicles were pouring out of the city, headlights pulsing white. Every lane was full, drivers fighting to move faster as the homes they'd abandoned fell prey to a threat they knew nothing about.

Even out here, a ways beyond the forcefield, the darkness was pressing. But it was also nighttime, so it was hard to tell exactly how far the Void had spread. A thorough study of the damage would have to wait until morning, and by the looks of things they'd be gone by then.

She typed in her passcode, nails clicking on the screen, and pulled up her list of contacts as vehicle after vehicle drove by—quicker now, some moving with enough speed to shake the car.

She scrolled through her contacts. She didn't have many. And before she'd met the Devils and had made more unlikely friends through their tight circle, she'd had even less. So it wasn't hard to find the contact she was looking for. She so seldom messaged him that merely the sight of his name had her nausea tripling in intensity.

It spun completely out of control as she tapped the name *Roark Bright* —never *Dad*—and hit the message icon.

A timid little voice in the back of her head told her she shouldn't be bothering him. Especially when he was working—and *especially* tonight, when he was in the middle of a war zone. That voice had stalked her every waking moment since the day she was born. For twenty years, fear had dictated every step she'd taken in life, no matter how small.

Her *old* life. That was her old life. Not her new. Fear was no longer her god.

So she told that voice to go meet Ignis and typed up her message.

Because she didn't know if she'd get another chance.

Because she was going to die before her twenty-first birthday, and she was determined to greet death with as few regrets as possible.

She would not pretend that Roark was a good father. He wasn't—not even a little. But she could admit there were far worse parents out there than him. He'd taken Loren—a helpless mortal baby—in when surely no one else would have. Had given her a safe place to live for twenty years and —against all odds, in a world that routinely ridiculed and scorned her kind —had secured her an acceptance letter from her dream university.

And he'd pulled through and saved their butts tonight, which called for a thank-you, bare minimum.

Maybe, if they all survived this, things would change. Maybe things could finally be different. Better.

She hit SEND.

LOREN

Thank you for tonight.

It was funny how her heart could pound this hard when the person she was contacting was miles away and probably wouldn't even see the words for many hours. Those four simple words.

She typed her other messages and sent them off before she could over-think them and change her mind.

LOREN

And for everything else too. For opening your home to me all those years ago, when I had nowhere else to go.

I know Dallas is worried about you. She worries about you a lot, she just has trouble showing it.

Stay safe.

The screen blurred. It wasn't until she blinked and felt a drop of mois-ture slide down her cheek that she realized why. She never thought she'd cry over someone like Roark, but... Well, things *had* changed already. Maybe not for him, but for her. In more ways than one.

Boots crunched in the dirt.

She scrubbed the tear away as Darien approached, phone and cigarette in hand. His strong features were carved with shadow, every stunning edge and curve limned with bluish light from his screen. He typed for a minute —mostly with his left hand, the right in a black compression glove—before shutting the screen off and sliding the device into the back pocket of his jeans.

"What's happening?" Lace asked him.

Darien took a drag. "Travis is heading to the harbor," he replied, smoke curling out of his mouth. "Ivy didn't tell me where she was, but they found the kids." He blew out a stream of smoke and turned his gaze to the force-field washing over the sprawling city. It was green again—Loren could just barely see it in her periphery—but it wouldn't stay that way for long.

Darien's eyes found hers—black, until he blinked it away, making them blue again. "How are you feeling?" Before she could reply, his attention dipped to her phone she clutched in her numb fingers. "Did you call someone?"

"I wanted to send a message to my dad," she said, her teeth chattering. "Roark, I mean." She paled as she realized— "Oh gods, was I not supposed to?" She hadn't even thought of the fact that the imperator could hack her phone!

But Darien was entirely calm. Unconcerned. "You can do whatever you want, baby. It's not like I haven't been in contact with the others." He took one last drag before putting his smoke out under the heel of his boot. "I'll get Tanner to clear everything the minute he's out."

Lace's head snapped his way. "Did they find Tanner?" she asked, her gray eyes brightening with hope.

"Yeah, he's with Ivy."

"Oh thank gods," Lace breathed, tipping her head back. She stayed like that for a moment, as if quietly thanking the stars. There weren't many of them out, most of them dim. But they were there.

Darien stepped up to Loren and crouched before her. He studied her face for a moment, undoubtedly noticing any dried tears on her cheeks, as evidenced by the way his eyes tightened, one corner of his mouth tipping down, before asking her, "May I see your tattoos?"

She straightened her arm out, and he grasped her wrist and pushed up both of her jacket sleeves as Lace stubbed out her cigarette and went to check on Jack and Arthur. Or to give them privacy. Maybe both.

The C on the inside of her wrist was pulsing with a bead of white light —not as brightly as before, though. And the serpent-entwined rod on that same forearm was a pale shade of red. Warm, but not burning.

Still not good signs, either of them. But they were small improvements compared to before.

Darien was frowning. He tugged her sleeves back down and looked up at her, his warm fingers still circling her wrist. "When was the last time you took one of your pills?"

"I can't remember," she croaked. Gods, she was so exhausted she could barely keep her eyes open. Hellsehers could go days without sleep while hardly being affected by the loss, but she was suffering. "I didn't take any when I was using the chamber." The Caliginous Chamber was a godsend— and it no longer existed. Was lying in a heap of rubble in the Financial District, according to what Darien had told her. She nibbled on her bottom lip. "Maybe a few days?" she guessed, thinking back to her time after coming out of a coma.

He stood, his fingers trailing off her wrist with noticeable reluctance, the tips of them skimming hers. "I'd like you to take one at the first rest stop, please." The first rest stop—because they didn't have any water in the car, and he knew she couldn't swallow pills dry. She'd likely choke. Which was an avoidable problem they didn't need.

But she wasn't sure her pills would even help at this point—they hadn't really done much in the way of helping her since she'd come out of a coma —and Darien didn't look like he was sure, either. But, just to put his mind at ease, she told him, "Okay."

"Dare?" Lace called. He turned. She was walking back this way, hands buried in her coat pockets. Her cheeks were rosy from the biting cold. "I think we should start heading home. Arthur's not doing so well, and the longer we wait the greater our chances that Jack will snap and make a run for the forcefield."

"He can't get back in, it's one-way only."

"Yeah, but I don't really think he's using logic right now, and I'd rather not watch him get incinerated if we can avoid it."

Darien glanced at the truck. "What's going on with Arthur?"

"He needs sleep. He's old—he can't keep up with us." That made two of them. The two humans in the group—both dead on their feet.

Loren yawned.

Darien gave Lace a nod. "Alright, let's go." When he grabbed the top of Loren's door, she tucked her legs inside so he could shut it. Through the glass, she heard him say to Lace, "I'll wait for a big enough gap in traffic so you can get right behind me. Stay close and call me if anything urgent comes up." He got in.

Reality was finally setting in. They were leaving. They were safe now —somewhat.

Loren watched the city disappear in the mirrors as Darien pulled the car into traffic, Lace following.

They were going home. But it didn't really feel that way when half of the people who made their house a home were still trapped in that city.

42

ROMAN'S HOUSE
YVESWICH, STATE OF KER

"Okay, Itzel, get in," Roman urged. He stood in front of the stainless steel fridge in his kitchen, holding Pax's backpack open like a safety net.

Kylar, Eugene, Ivy, and Tanner were already on their way out of Yveswich. They hadn't come back to the house—hadn't wanted to risk pausing for any length of time. And time was precisely what they were short on, less than two hours remaining until military lockdown. But Roman refused to leave without Itzel.

This Hob just might be the death of him.

She had wedged herself into the narrow space between the top of the fridge and the bottom of the cupboards that were built above the appliance, peering out at him with distrustful hot pink eyes.

"Itzel, *please,*" Roman growled. "Time is *ticking.*" If they ended up not making it out because of this ridiculous, stubborn critter he'd rescued two years ago, who since then had been nothing short of a pain in his ass with her pots and pans and other antics...

He ground his teeth so hard his jaw ached. It would be so like him to get trapped here because of something this absurd, wouldn't it?

The Hob, detecting the edge in his tone, slid farther back, the swirly pink flames on her head dimming.

He growled. *"Itzel—"*

Shay came up beside him, moving so quietly he hadn't even realized she was there, and reached for the freezer door. "Here, get out of the way." She shooed him. "Let the professional handle this."

Roman raised a brow but stepped aside.

Shay opened the door, cool air floating across their faces, and shoved her hand into the ice bin, grabbing a fistful of cubes.

She dumped them into Pax's backpack. The cubes clattered inside among all his textbooks and homework.

"Those'll melt and wreck all his shit," Roman objected.

A black shape launched itself off the fridge in a blur.

Next thing Roman knew, Itzel was in the backpack, the force of her descent causing it to bounce in his hands.

Crunch-crunch. Snap. Munch.

Roman's brows went up. At that speed, the ice wouldn't even have a chance to melt.

Impressive.

Shay gave him a triumphant smile, her green eyes twinkling like emeralds in the kitchen light. "You were saying?" she purred.

Roman zipped up the backpack, his focus wholly and undeniably magnetized to those pretty eyes of hers. He just couldn't look away from them. He almost got his finger caught in the zipper.

Shay was the first to break eye contact. Having her rip her attention off him so abruptly like that...it felt like duct tape being torn off broken skin.

Her expression was impossible to read as she grabbed his jacket off a kitchen chair and passed it to him. "Here."

He took it and draped it over his arm, still failing to look away from her. Fuck, was he pathetic, or what? But to his defense, she wasn't looking away from him, either. Not like before.

He cleared his throat. "You ready?" He swung the strap of Pax's backpack over his shoulder, Itzel still happily chewing away inside.

Shay held her arms out at her sides and frowned down at her torn, bloodied, and filthy battle-suit. "As can be." She crossed her arms, her guarded expression returning. "Once we're out, we can find me something else to wear." Memories of a cherry-print thong and a yellow bathing suit flashed into his mind.

His blood warmed in his veins.

"You can always wear some of my stuff if you want." The husky offer slipped out before he could stop it. He was supposed to be keeping her safe and at arm's length, not letting her wear his clothes, for fuck's sake.

"Hoodies and shirts or whatever," he added, feeling more pathetic with every word spoken.

Yeah, as if seeing this beautiful woman prancing around in his clothes was going to make it any easier to get over her.

"No thanks," she muttered, her eyes rolling upward. The refusal stung, and so did her tone, but they both seemed to have learned their lesson.

Whether or not the lesson stayed learned remained to be seen.

Feet thumped on the stairs.

Pax came around the corner, shrugging on a jacket of his own. The cuts on his face were shining with antibiotic ointment—likely thanks to Shay, who'd gone upstairs with him to help him pack. An adhesive bandage had been taped across the freckled bridge of his nose.

"Ready?" Roman asked him, eyeing the suitcase in the foyer. Comic book print, like almost everything else he owned, apart from the plain backpack he lugged to school every day. Hindsight told Roman he'd opted for plain in effort not to be teased by the bullies he'd never told him about.

"Yup." He gave him two thumbs up.

Roman strode over and took a quick look in the bag. Most of what he'd packed were video games, comic books, and action figurines. He'd even stuffed the board game called *Cryptic Crypts* inside, the box taking up most of the room.

"Where are all your clothes?" Roman asked him.

Pax shuffled over to stand beside him—judging his response while Roman judged what the kid deemed essential.

"I put some socks and underwear in there," he responded defensively. "Oh, and my toothbrush, too." It was in a plastic bag, the bristles sticky with a glob of toothpaste he'd failed to rinse off properly.

Roman sighed and shook his head. Good thing he'd already packed some of Pax's things in his own bag, not trusting him to prioritize what was most important. Like keepsakes and family—minus Don—photos. A toothbrush hardly mattered when there were dozens of charging stations and supermarkets between here and Angelthene, and he was clearly overdue for a new one.

"Do you really need all these games?"

"Do you need the air in your lungs?" Paxton fired back. Roman couldn't help but chuckle.

"Fine," Roman said, still fighting a smile. He zipped the bag shut. "You win."

"Is Travis coming with us?" Paxton's question was quiet. Cautious.

Roman met his troubled gaze. "Travis is evacuating as we speak, bud," he said softly. "We need to go and catch up with him."

Darien had called just before they got here. Travis was making his way to the harbor with the others who'd stayed behind at the hospital. Had he been any closer, Roman would've left to get him. But the hospital was too far. He just had to trust that Travis would make it through the forcefield on time.

But gods, was it hard to trust. Hard to let go of control when he was the eldest brother, the one who'd always protected both of his younger siblings with his life. Literally. He'd do it again now, without question— would lay his life on the line not just for Pax, but for Travis, too. His arrival in Yveswich had thrown a huge wrench in the little slice of inner peace Roman had attained upon getting him away from their asshole dad years ago.

And Travis had completely shattered that peace. Betrayed his trust. And now, if he died...

It will have all been for nothing. Every sacrifice, all those years spent apart...

Wasted.

Pointless.

Shay flicked off the kitchen light, plunging the house into shadow, and grabbed Roman's phone off the island on her way over. "Someone keeps messaging you."

"Who is it?"

She checked the screen. "Willow Adams?"

Shit—Willow. Roman was ashamed to admit he had totally forgotten about her during all this insanity. And now he felt sick with guilt. Time had flown by, his search for Pax and his worry for Travis occupying so much thought space that he hadn't had a second to think of much else. Meanwhile his Third was still somewhere in the city.

He had to warn her. Tell her to get out.

Roman straightened. "What did she say?"

Shay was frowning at the phone. "She said..." Her baffled eyes flicked up to meet Roman's. "She's in your house."

Roman blinked. "What?"

Shay shrugged. "That's what she said."

"Let me see." He beckoned.

She came over and showed him the message.

"Maybe these were sent earlier," Roman mused, taking the phone from her. "And I'm just getting them now," he added. With the cell towers being down for so many hours, it wasn't impossible.

"The time stamp was two minutes ago," Shay pointed out as Roman read the messages for a second, third, fourth time.

> WILLOW
>
> I'm at your house.
>
> Meet me here?

His brows pulled together. "What the fuck?"

He blinked the Sight into place and scanned the top and bottom floors. There was no one here but them.

The sound he heard next was almost imperceptible—a deep, familiar growl of an engine approaching the neighborhood. It could have belonged to any car, but he'd heard this one enough times that he had a full-body reaction to the sound. Muscles locking, chest tightening, heart racing.

He paled, the puzzle pieces sliding into place with a sickening *click*. "Oh gods."

43

WEST FINANCIAL DISTRICT
YVESWICH, STATE OF KER

Max tracked Maya to a construction site in the Financial District. When he'd pulled over for all of five minutes to pinpoint her location, Dallas had raised valid concerns that Maya's aura could be masked by a substance or a talisman. It wasn't, though, which was why he'd made the decision to go after her in the first place. Had her aura been veiled, he would've had zero chance of success. But he'd already read her yesterday, while they were walking the streets. Before she'd up and disappeared without even saying goodbye.

Not only was her aura visible, but it had changed during the years they were apart. She was still Maya 'MJ' Reacher, sure, but...different, somehow. He didn't know how to explain it. It was like there were new threads woven into her very being, whole new layers and facets, which would have made it impossible for him to track her without first seeing and reading the *new* Maya.

All that genetic modification had really done a number on her.

She was here, though. In that partially constructed apartment building straight ahead. He could sense her. He'd concentrated on the tug of the Sight the whole time he drove, determined not to make a mistake. There was no room—no time—for error.

He parked and got out.

The others followed, and together they walked to the entrance.

Apart from one foggy streetlight, the darkness was stifling. The dirt parking lot was covered in a thin layer of snow and ice that crunched under their boots. The weather right now was as crazy as everything else going on —while it rained in one district, it snowed in another. If only Spirit Terra would glitch and decide to send some of that Angelthene late-summer heat.

They walked up the concrete steps and tried the door knob.

Locked.

"Stand back," he told the others.

He kicked the door open with a *bang*—

Blackness greeted them.

Dominic flicked on a flashlight, the beam bouncing through the building.

The coppery tang of blood slammed into them.

"Holy gods." Dominic's husky whisper echoed.

Max staggered through the door frame, his chest tightening as he took in the space bit by bit, the smashed glass and body parts and blood—so much blood—lit up by the darting glow of the flashlight. Red covered the floor and walls—thick puddles and sprays of it.

"Maya?" Max's shout broke out of him. The empty building echoed it back three times.

No answer.

His sharp breaths chewed up his lungs. *"MAYAAAAAA?"*

The body parts on the floor...whoever it was, they had been torn apart so thoroughly, they didn't even look *real*.

As a Darkslayer, Max had seen his fair share of fucked up shit, had killed many of his own victims in brutal ways, but this... This was repulsive. A murder of the most gruesome kind.

It wasn't Maya. It *couldn't* be Maya. He'd tracked her here. Felt her aura the whole way. She *had* to be alive—

He lurched forward, boots splashing in blood he hoped didn't belong to his sister. The others followed, blind apart from the beam of the flashlight.

Dominic crouched before a pool of red, eyes black, and dipped his fingers in. "Still warm," he murmured.

Oh gods. There was a woman's head in the corner—

Click.

Max whirled—

And nearly fell to his knees in relief as he beheld Maya standing in a doorframe, her features veiled in shadow.

The relief quickly faded as his attention dipped to the gun in her trembling hands. The gun she was pointing right at his head.

She stepped into a beam of greyish light slanting in through a window and rasped, "Put your hands in the air."

Max swallowed the ache in his throat. "Maya, it's—"

"Put your fucking hands in the air!" She pointed the gun between everyone in their group. Her eyes began to glow orange. *"All of you—right now! Hands where I can see them!"*

Max did what she wanted, the others copying.

Dominic slowly set down the flashlight—

She gripped the gun tighter. *"Don't move!"*

"I'm just putting this down," Dominic replied, speaking calmly. Slowly, he stood back up and raised his hands. "It's okay. We're here to help."

Maya glanced between them. Her wide-eyed gaze settled on Blue.

Recognition—and a fleeting moment of shock—flitted across her face at the sight of her old friend.

Scarlet's old friend.

"Scarlet," Blue whispered. She gave a shaky smile. "It's me."

But Maya did not lower the gun. "Let me see your eyes," she croaked.

Max's brow creased. "Wh—"

"Let me see your eyes! *All of you!*"

What was she talking about? They were already looking at her—what more did she want?

"Black eyes!" she barked, the order clapping through the cavernous building. "Black fucking eyes—now! Right now!"

"Okay," Max breathed. "Okay, we're doing it. Just help us understand."

But she wasn't hearing him. She was wild-eyed, panting, and shaking.

Max blinked his Sight into place. Blue and Dominic did the same.

Dallas said softly, "I'm a witch, I don't have the Sight."

"Stay where you are," Maya warned. "All of you." She crept across the space, gun trained on them, and snatched up the flashlight.

She backed up to a distance she deemed safe before shining the beam in their faces—one at a time. She even did it to Dallas, checking to see if there were silver rings around her pupils, no doubt.

When the beam bounced to Max, he drew in a hiss, the light stinging his eyes. But he refrained from shifting a hand to block it.

Maya lowered the flashlight. Put the safety on her gun.

Her vivid eyes swept about the area. Passing over the blood and body parts of gods knew who.

Her face crumpled. "We didn't know," she wept.

Max shared a glance with the others

"We thought it wouldn't happen again," Maya said. "It's my fault. *I* did this." Max knew that was guilt speaking. Knew his sister did not do this.

They lowered their hands.

"Maya…," Max whispered. "Who did this?" No response. The person —pieces of them—lying dead on the floor…that could have been her. He swallowed bile. "What happened here?"

"Her name is Aurora," she whispered, the words jagged with emotion. The warm glow of her eyes reflected in the tears streaming down her face, making it look like she was crying fire. She wiped her cheeks with the back of her wrist. Sniffled. Corrected, *"Was."*

So that was who all this blood and body parts belonged to. An Elemental named Aurora.

The Elemental who, Max now recalled, Gold and Blaze—the other Elementals they'd ran into at the Facility—were searching for out in the desert. The girl they'd supposedly got separated from during the breakout.

Maya continued. "Onyx, he—" She sucked in a ragged sob. "He lost it, and…" She clamped a hand over her wobbling mouth. *"I tried to stop him!"*

"Where's Magenta?" Max asked softly. "Is she okay?"

His hearing picked up on a great whirring outside.

He peered out the door—to the snow and dust blowing about.

Maya's head snapped back, her black eyes searching the upper floors.

She backed toward the shadows.

A surprised smile flickered across Dominic's face. "Anyone call for a chopper?"

THEY WALKED out of the building, squinting in gusts of dust-choked wind, to find a military helicopter landing in the lot, air assault soldiers inside.

One hopped out and walked this way, squinting beneath the brim of his forest green combat helmet. "Dallas Bright?" the man shouted. Louder he said, *"Are you Dallas Bright?"*

"Yeah!" Her response was barely audible over the noise. A few feathers ripped free of her wings and spun like snowflakes through the air.

"Your father sent for you! We're getting you out of here."

"Wait," Dallas said, grabbing Max by the hand. "My friends—I'm not leaving without my friends!"

"Then round them up and let's go!"

Max gave Dal's hand a light squeeze. "Be right back," he told her before hurrying back inside.

Just in time to see Maya limping through the building, her arm wrapped around Magenta's waist. Supporting most of her weight, just like yesterday. There was a nasty gash in her thigh, but it was the only visible injury. One she would recover from quickly, thanks to her hellseher healing properties.

He stepped aside to let them through, beyond grateful that she had listened to him when he'd begged her to come with. The moment that helicopter showed up, he'd known exactly why they were here.

But Maya froze when she saw the soldiers.

"It's okay," Max said. He tried to speak softly, but having to shout over all the noise wasn't helping. "We can trust them. They aren't here for you—they're trying to help us. They just want to get us out of the city—that's all. I swear."

She took a step forward. Back.

Max checked his watch. They still had time to get out, but only if they left now.

"Maya," Max urged. Her eyes—glowing like embers again—flashed to his face. "I'm your big brother. I'm Max—remember me?" He smiled and poked himself in the chest. "I won't let anything bad happen to you, okay? I promise."

She stared out at the helicopter. Dallas was already inside with Blue, headset on. Dominic was climbing in, wings tucked in tight.

"We have to go," Max urged. "If we don't get out now, we won't have another chance." When she still didn't move, he took a step toward her.

She stiffened, but didn't back away.

"Maya, I want you to pretend like we're kids again. I want you to pretend like these past few years never happened. And I want you to trust me. I would never ask you to do anything that would end up hurting you. We've both changed, I can admit that. But I haven't changed in that regard. I'm still your brother, and I still want what's best for you."

The edge in her eyes softened.

"Please trust me on this. If they" —He pointed at the air assault soldiers — "Hurt or scare you in any way, I will step in. I swear."

Maya took a deep breath, her glowing eyes dimming, and tightened her hold on Magenta's waist.

Max thanked the gods as he walked with his long-lost sister across the lot, following the soldiers' instructions as they got in the helicopter and strapped themselves in.

He took Dallas's hand into his, lacing their fingers, and held back a sob of relief as the aircraft took flight.

They had made it.

They were going to make it.

44

ROMAN'S HOUSE
YVESWICH, STATE OF KER

A trap.

Donovan had planned on baiting them back here with a trap in the form of a message sent from Willow's phone.

But what Don didn't know was that Roman had made it back to the house before him, so they already knew that Willow was not here. His trick had failed.

The fact that Donovan and his Shadowmasters had Willow's phone was a very bad sign. While she could very well still be alive, a part of Roman deeply believed there was a very slim chance of that.

He blamed himself. If she had been murdered, it was his fault. Don had likely targeted her during his search for Paxton, had probably tortured information out of her. And Roman hadn't even had the decency to spare a single thought for her.

Some friend he was.

They were all in the car now, waiting for the front gates to open.

The moment there was a wide enough gap, Roman slammed his boot down on the accelerator and peeled out of the driveway. He hung a left, leaving his house—dark and quiet and empty for the time being, maybe forever—behind.

Donovan was coming from the right. Roman knew because he could hear the engine. It was getting closer—and fast.

As he ripped down the street, he watched in his rear-view for any sign of those familiar headlights cutting through the dark fog. He blew past evacuated houses at maximum speed. Through the neighborhood he may never see again.

The corner up ahead—he had to make it to that corner before Donovan reached his street. Had to stay out of his father's line of sight and book it to the closest highway exit. Being in Ardesia—a district not far from the I-5—gave them a better chance of making it out during these final minutes, but not by much.

He would need to be fast. Smart.

The tires screeched as he cut the corner—

Still no sign of Donovan.

Neither Shay nor Pax were breathing. Roman wasn't certain he was, either. He squeezed the wheel, driving like a fucking maniac, blowing past monsters and cars and fleeing pedestrians. It was a miracle he didn't hit anything at this speed. His obsession with cars and racing was finally paying off.

He checked the time on his watch—

They were down to their final hour.

Down to *minutes.*

He boosted his speed with a button on the steering wheel, the world a blur.

Fuck, this was exhilarating. At least if he died tonight, he'd be leaving this world with his hunger for adrenaline satiated.

For Paxton and Shay, he would try not to.

He had to stay alive.

Keep them *all* alive.

45

THE SKY
YVESWICH, STATE OF KER

The aerial view of the ruins of Yveswich was eye-opening.

From way up here, in the rainy gloom, there was no mistaking the hard truth.

The city was completely destroyed. Few districts had been fortunate enough to evade the explosion, and those that had would succumb to the Void's dark grasp sooner rather than later. Death was coming for them—for every last district, every last street, every last home. No one and nothing would be left unscathed.

Loren had done everything she could, but in the end she had only managed to save a little over a quarter of the state's capital. Everything else, all the people and homes in the path of the blast... Destroyed. Incinerated.

Gone.

Max's throat pinched shut with emotion as he scanned the wreckage down below. Darkness cut through the once magnificent city in billowing black walls and plumes, forming a shape that reminded him of spider-webbed glass. Where it'd hit was entirely sporadic—there was no pattern, at least not one he could identify. By the looks of things, the Void had quarreled with Loren's power, sneaking in like a thief through every crack and fissure where her protection was weakest.

There were many.

Pillars of smoke, otherworldly smog, and sheets of half-frozen rain plagued the streets that remained visible. It was getting colder and darker by the minute, the air slowly thinning in a peculiar way. Max knew it had nothing to do with how high up they were and everything to do with the Void breathing death into a planet of life.

They had no choice but to take the long route through the city, staying out of the path of military planes and helicopters actively engaged in combat. The darkness that would render the pilots blind was another obstacle they were smart to avoid. They were cutting west, heading out toward the open ocean. From there, they would probably be let out on one of the highways, where they would then need to find a lift to Angelthene.

How they would go about doing that was a problem they could wait to tackle. Right now, all Max wanted was to get out of Yveswich. Get on land. Reunite with the others.

"You okay?" he asked Dallas. The witch was squeezing his hand so hard, it felt numb. "You're not scared of heights, are you?"

He knew that his question succeeded at distracting her when her copper brows flew up. "You're asking someone who has wings?" Her shout filled his headset; evidently she had never ridden in a helicopter before.

He grinned.

She smiled back—a shaky thing, but still a smile.

They were above the harbor now. The docks and boats looked so tiny from way up here.

Max checked his watch. Sixteen minutes remained.

He used his Sight to scan the interlocked columns of glowing green runes that curved skyward, forming the forcefield. They sliced like a blade through the water in the distance, diving all the way down to the ocean floor. Aquatic demons had snuck through the forcefield's protection over the years, some likely tunneling their way in through the sand, and from there had rapidly multiplied and invaded the coastal waters. The same exact thing had happened in Angelthene. There were some breeds down there that were probably so old, they predated the technology that had given them forcefields.

Max had never really been fond of the ocean. Too many unknowns with teeth.

They were passing Athene's island now. The rocky stretch of land owned by the Riptide. He spotted the House of Blue peeking between towering evergreens. Shay's home.

Boats dotted the expanse of gray. Civilians making one last ditch attempt at a watery escape. More helicopters flew about, likely taking other evacuees to safety. Serpents swam through the strong sea, their spiked backs breaking the surface of the white-capped waves.

The helicopter shuddered as a mighty pulse of energy rippled across the ocean. Max's heart jolted, his hairs standing on end.

Suddenly, their surroundings blackened. He couldn't see a thing.

He held his breath, his hand tightening around Dal's.

"Max?" she said quietly, grasping him with both hands now.

"It's okay," he said, lightly squeezing her tense fingers. "It's okay, we'll be fine."

But the helicopter shook again—harder this time. So hard that several people shouted out in alarm. Soldiers readied their weapons as the blackness gradually cleared. They were flying slower now, as if something was hindering their speed.

He shared a loaded glance with Dominic.

Checked his watch.

Nine minutes.

Another shake, a jarring *boom*, and suddenly they were falling.

Max's soul snapped out of his body as the aircraft lost control, careening toward the ocean at rapid speed.

"Max!" Dallas cried.

Screams ripped into his eardrums—

And so did the high-pitched shredding of metal as claws tore into the helicopter.

The glass in the cockpit smashed out.

Blood misted Max's face.

His surroundings spun. He couldn't tell up from down, left from right. Couldn't have jumped even if he wanted to.

"Mayday," a voice chanted. *"Mayday."*

The ocean surged up—

46

THE OCEAN
YVESWICH, STATE OF KER

These low clouds and squalls of driving rain might be the death of them.

Travis clung to the wet handrail with one hand and used the other to hold onto Jewels, fisting the back of her slippery life jacket to keep her steady, as Malakai steered the speedboat they'd stolen from the docks through the choppy sea.

These were predator-infested waters, and they were out here by themselves. No one else was around, the few other boats he'd spotted having already made it out.

Behind him, the city was steadily growing darker.

He squinted, gusts of wind and rain battering his face, the latter so cold they felt like shards of ice. It was already difficult to see through the darkness and eddying fog, and this damn storm was only making it worse. They were practically blind.

Something rumbled.

It was the portal—opening wide. A gluttonous mouth eager to devour.

A swirling blast of supernatural darkness burst forth. It chased the boat—

And swallowed their surroundings.

Travis held his breath, his hand tightening on Jewels's life jacket—

Slowly, the shadow dissipated like mist in sunlight, allowing them to see once more.

He exhaled. The city still had time.

They, however, were running out.

His pulse pounded like a hammer on an anvil.

Jewels had her phone out, the screen barely visible in the choking blackness. Whatever she saw sent her stumbling against Travis's side, her wet hair lashing her panic-stricken face.

Her head snapped up. *"MALAKAI!"* she screamed.

Travis didn't need to look at her screen to understand why she was losing her cool.

They were down to their final minutes.

Aspen's eyes—wild with fright—locked with Travis's.

Every city in all of Terra had a Control Tower—it was where the power came from. The core of every grid. Yveswich's tower was what Travis searched for now, his head swiveling about.

There it was. Standing proudly in the rain-veiled heart of the city, the sleek panels of cristala gleaming like liquid silver. The beam of magic that shot out of the pinnacle of the tower like a laser was beginning to change color, the base shifting from acid-green to bright red. From way out here, it was barely a faint line. To mortal eyes, it would have been completely invisible.

It was times like these when Travis envied them—the mortals. Ignorance was indeed bliss.

Early. The forcefield was being assembled early. Minutes, yeah. But every last second mattered right now.

Red rapidly began to dominate. It climbed the beam, chasing and devouring the vibrant green he was so used to. Shooting straight for the storm-addled sky.

Malakai squinted over his shoulder with black eyes. Judging from the look on his face, the way his eyes widened and his jaw clenched, he saw it, too. He twisted back around and tried going faster, but the engine was at full throttle.

Travis was going to throw up.

Roman was going to kill him.

If he managed to survive this, Roman was going to *kill him.*

"Oh gods, oh gods," Jewels chanted, her head tipping back as she watched the forcefield change color. "Oh gods. This isn't happening, this isn't happening, this isn't— *Malakai! FASTER!*"

"I can't go any FUCKING faster!"

The forcefield shimmered just ahead—still green. But not for long.

The boat skimmed over the waves, saltwater soaking the deck.

Travis sucked in a briny breath and held it. "Come on, come on," he mouthed. The boat dipped and splashed. Dipped and splashed, the navigation lights barely cutting through the gloom. "Come *on.*"

They were almost there.

Too soon, the red light curving over the urban sprawl of Yveswich reached the coast and headed straight for them. It spread across the water like spilled wine, capping the surface waves in blood-red instead of white. Within heartbeats, it had reached their boat, passing over their heads as it formed a new enclosure—an impenetrable cage—above the city. Down it came, heading straight for the sea level horizon.

They had almost made it when Jewels's timer went off.

Travis's stomach fell out of his ass. "No," he exhaled.

The forcefield came down, cutting through the water with such immense power it generated a massive tidal wave that pushed the boat back.

"NOOO!"

Jewels screamed, clinging to the handrail with both hands as the ocean began to rise, gray water threatening to swallow them whole.

Travis's hold slipped.

He slid, taking Jewels down with him as he toppled over the seats and slammed into the back of the boat.

Jewels hit the rail screaming. Flipped over the edge.

"TRAVIS!"

He grabbed her by the arm, grunting in pain as his shoulder nearly dislocated, Jewels's feet just barely missing the propellers.

The tide pushed them back. *Back—*

He barely had time to suck in a breath as the boat was overturned, and they were consumed by the frigid, monster-infested waters of the Ceto Ocean.

47

NORTH YVESWICH CITY LIMITS
YVESWICH, STATE OF KER

T his was suicide.

This was complete fucking *suicide,* but Roman didn't care. He was a speed demon, an adrenaline junkie, and nothing had given him a high this intense in a long time.

It was pure fucking *bliss.*

At least it would've been. Pure bliss. Had he not been racing for his life —literally. For Pax's life, too. Shay's.

He sped down the bare highway on the wrong side of the median strip, pushing the whirring engine as fast as it could go. On the right side, outgoing traffic was at a standstill, cranky drivers beeping their horns. Completely unaware that only minutes remained before their lives would change. Minutes before a new forcefield would cage them in this madhouse. A few were fleeing on foot, making a mad dash for the force-field, as if sensing that something bad was about to happen.

The only plus right now was the lack of obstacles—living and non-living—in Roman's path as he made his swift exit.

This road was the only way out—the only way they stood a chance at getting through the forcefield on time. He'd already blasted several barri-cades apart with his magic, ripping fire trucks and squad cars to burning shreds.

He tilted his wrist, checking his watch.

Sixty seconds remained.

The needle fluttered at maximum speed.

His heart raced just as fast.

Forty seconds.

The steering wheel trembled.

His surroundings were nothing but a blur.

Twenty seconds.

The car was utterly silent, Shay and Pax holding their breath.

Ten seconds.

They were almost there.

One last barricade waited up ahead. The officers manning it scattered like flies off shit.

Eyes black, Roman summoned his powers, his blood crackling with it. He exhaled, unleashing a blast of shadow magic that blew the vehicles apart. Blinked the Sight away in time to avoid crashing.

A new forcefield washed the highway in red. Chased the car.

Three seconds.

Two seconds.

One.

The timer on his watch went off—

They ripped through the forcefield with not a second to spare, the ominous red glow descending so swiftly it nearly grazed the roof of the car.

Roman let out a slow breath. Let up on the accelerator. Twisted in his seat to stare out the back window, his hands relaxing on the wheel.

Holy shit.

They'd made it.

Paxton was grinning.

Roman grinned back.

"Yes!" Shay cheered as Roman twisted back around. "Yes, yes, *yes!*"

"Phew," Paxton panted. He dramatically wiped his forehead and gave Roman another little smile in the rear-view. "Close one, hey?"

Shadow exploded through the city with a deafening *bang*, shockwaves shaking the car. Roman watched in the mirrors as the new forcefield shimmered above Yveswich, runes glowing all different shades of red as the magic contained the darkness—right in the knick of time.

For now.

It billowed against the forcefield like smoke, spreading to the far reaches of the city. Not utterly blinding, by the looks of it—not yet. But soon.

Close one was right. They'd made it.

Barely...but they'd made it.

That was what Roman thought, at least.

Until Paxton started screaming.

Not in fear, but in pain.

Roman whipped around in his seat, his pounding heart jumping up his throat as Paxton wailed. *"Pax?"*

"What's wrong with him?" Shay yelled, unbuckling her seatbelt.

Paxton was thrashing and bucking and writhing, hands clamped over his ears, his mouth open in an infinite, ear-shattering scream that threatened to saw apart the car.

"Pax, *talk to me!*" Roman begged, his attention flashing between his brother and the dark road. "What's happening? Are you hurt? *Talk to me. Talk to me!*" But he only kept screaming.

Roman watched in horror as the blood vessels in Pax's eyes burst, red blooming into the whites.

"MAKE IT STOP!" Paxton screamed, his face turning purple, tears leaking from his eyes. *"MAKE IT STOP!"*

"Pax," Roman choked out. *"Pax—"*

"Stop the car!" Shay shrieked.

Black swallowed Pax's eyes. Dark lines sprouted in the skin around them, extending into his cheeks and above his brows. Growing and stretching like tree roots.

And he kept screaming. Louder.

Louder.

Shay dove between the front seats.

"PAX—"

Power blasted through the car, shattering the windows.

Roman threw his hand up, shielding his eyes as glass exploded in his face, fragments biting into his skin.

The car sped on without direction, as if it had a mind of its own.

Roman slammed his boot down on the brake, but it didn't slow.

He tried again.

Again.

Nothing.

"What the fuck?" he panted.

"Slow down!" Shay cried. She was stuck halfway between the front seats while Paxton screamed his bloody lungs out.

"I'm trying!" He pulled the e-brake, but the car kept going at maximum speed. It was smoking now, clouds of gray blocking his view of the road.

"ROMAN, SLOW DOWN!"

"I CAN'T—" The steering wheel cranked itself to one side. And the vehicle spun off the road.

PART THREE
THE ROADBLOCK

48

⅂-5

STATE OF KER

Paxton wasn't breathing.

Roman was pumping the boy's chest with his hands, his expression so utterly broken, Shay could hardly bear it.

She stood nearby on the side of the highway, wind howling through the dark, while one brother clawed for the other to return to life.

"Come on," Roman whispered. His tone was defeated, agony crumpling his handsome face. "Come *on*, Pax."

He pinched his nose shut. Leaned down to breathe into his mouth.

More chest compressions.

"Shay." Roman's call for help was a ragged sob that ripped out of him through clenched teeth. "He's not waking up." *Pump, pump, pump.* Another two breaths. "Am I doing it wrong?"

Shay stepped forward, practically falling to her knees beside him in the dirt. She acted on instinct, not sure if this would work, but at this point she'd try anything. If there was even the slightest chance that it would wake this precious boy up, she'd try it.

She couldn't let this happen. Couldn't let this man, who'd sacrificed and lost so much, lose his little brother, too.

This was *not* happening. Not on her watch.

So she told him, "Let go, Roman."

Roman let go.

"Back up," she added. Somehow, she managed to keep her own

emotions out of her tone. When he hesitated, she added softly, "I need you to trust me."

He did exactly what she'd asked him to do, sliding backward on his knees in the dirt—just far enough to be considered safe but close enough that he was still right beside his brother.

She shut her eyes and breathed in, summoning her magic. It crackled in her blood, her lungs filling with the fresh, crisp scent of petrichor as the sky reopened with new rain—heaven's tears.

Lightning sparked in her palms. With a slow exhale, she flattened her hands over Pax's chest—

His body arced off the ground.

Still lifeless. Still pale.

"Again," Roman gritted out. There was a note of hope in the command.

Shay drew another deep breath. Exhaled. Flattened her palms over his torso once more as rain drummed all around them.

Another surge of lightning flowed through him. Again, his body arced.

"Now," she told Roman.

He resumed chest compressions. Counted thirty before pinching Pax's nose shut and breathing into his mouth.

They continued like that, Selkie and Shadowmaster alternating between shocks and chest compressions, both of them quietly breaking as Pax remained still. Dead. Sayagul was curled up in an anxious ball between the boy's limp knees, her slitted eyes shining. She was so silent—this whole time, she had been nothing but silent. Already heartbroken. Already grieving.

Roman cried, "I can't handle this—"

"One more time," Shay insisted, even as her heart cracked into two jagged halves. "We're not giving up." Like hell they would ever give up on this boy.

She shocked him again—

And just like that, Pax came back to life.

He let out a gasp, lurching up to a sitting position.

Roman sobbed and gathered the kid into his arms, Sayagul scrambling up to wiggle between them.

"It's okay," Roman was saying, hugging a shocked and gasping Paxton tightly, the dragon squished flat between them but utterly happy to be there. "It's okay, Pax, I got you. You're home."

His heart was beating properly and he was breathing and he was indeed home.

Roman, still holding Pax, turned his head, his eyes meeting Shay's. "Thank you," he mouthed, hugging his brother tightly, his fingers curling in Pax's muddy jacket.

Sayagul echoed her person's thanks with a whisper of her own, the dragon peering up at Shay with eyes filled with gratitude.

Shay had just begun to respond when she felt it—the warning signs of a surge in magic. The same signs she'd spent her whole life running from. Her whole life taking medication to avoid.

With a panicked gasp, she staggered to her feet and hurried off—away from the highway. Away from Roman and Paxton and Sayagul as her body and blood and aura sizzled. Turning her into something wild. An untameable force of nature. Like she was not a woman at all, but a bundle of live wires.

A living storm.

A cry of pain broke out of her. Above their heads, the sky echoed her call—shattering like glass. Pale lightning forked through the bloated clouds, illuminating the stretch of highway in an eerie blue glow. The rain fell ever harder.

And Shay crashed to her knees.

She could scarcely breathe. Her blood felt like it was on fire. Her muscles and even her brain, her skull pulsing as if there were electric currents flowing through the bone, threatening to crack it open like an egg. Lightning wove between her teeth, making her gums bleed and *sting*—

"Shay?" Roman called. He got to his feet—

"I'm fine," she gasped. But she turned top-heavy, tipping forward without warning. She planted her hands on the ground, fingers curling in the soaked dirt. "Stay away. Please, just—" She swallowed bile, the muscles all throughout her body twitching, mud soaking through the knees of her bodysuit. "Please stay away," she rasped. Her nose began to bleed, red dripping off the tip. "I don't want to hurt you. Either of you."

Roman listened. Respected her wishes and stayed put.

Shay remained like that for several minutes. Kneeling in the damp earth that slurped up every last drop of her shed blood. Vehicles sped by on the highway, moving so quickly their passing was like a scream that further fried her nerves. She could sense Roman, Paxton, and Sayagul silently observing her.

Slowly, mercifully, the twitching in her muscles began to subside, and so did the nosebleed. The black that had engulfed her vision faded, pupils shrinking back to their normal size.

Safe. She was safe. Fine.

Well, sort of.

They were stuck on the side of the highway, in the middle of the night, with a boy who'd almost died and a car that was still smoking.

What they were going to do now, she had no clue.

49

THE OCEAN
YVESWICH, STATE OF KER

Travis burst out of the water—coughing, soaked, and freezing.

And thoroughly blindsided by what just happened.

The boat was capsized. Turbulent waves and churning foam crashed all around him, bobbing him up and down, the chaotic force of the currents threatening to rip him away from the boat.

As if the water didn't pose enough of a challenge, it was now black as hell out here. He might as well be wading in ink.

He scanned what he could see of his surroundings, the constant pounding of the waves battering and bruising his body.

The others. Where the hell were the others?

'*Noble,*' Travis gasped. Thunder rumbled in the distance. Noble was a Mastiff dog whose greatest love—apart from sweet potato and shredded cheese—was naps. His arch-nemesis? Conversation. He might hate talking, but he always pulled through for Travis, and tonight was no exception. The dog was already watching from his shadow, alert as could be. '*I need your help,*' Travis said, desperate. '*Help me find the others.*'

'*Aye-aye, Cap,*' Noble confirmed, his voice a bass rumble.

Travis was too afraid to look down. To see what manner of creature might be stalking him in the depths.

Luckily, he didn't need to. And neither did Noble.

One by one, Jewels, Aspen, and Malakai broke through the surface of the ocean with ragged gasps.

"*Great!*" Malakai growled, the word garbled by the water in his mouth.

He spat, then whipped his head about like a temperamental dog, fighting to get his drenched hair out of his face. "Just fucking GREAT! We're trapped now, and I'm going to have to spend my last hours looking at *your* ugly mug!" He punched the water and pointed a finger at Travis. Hissed, "This is your fault."

A low growl slipped between Noble's teeth.

Travis glared. Oh hell no. No way would he sit back and let this bearded buffoon blame him and make this horrible night any worse.

"You're a fucking asshole, Delaney!" he snapped. "How is any of this *bullshit* my fault?"

Lightning flashed. Wind howled, carrying the smell of the sea.

"If you had simply pissed off like you were supposed to, I could have gotten us out on time! But *noooooo*—you just *had* to stay, didn't you, because *Oh Jewels, she needs me, I'm important and my dick needs attention* —"Travis glared as he made his voice squeaky for that part. "—And then it was *your* boss—" He pointed again. "—who had the bright idea that we should get out by boat. And now look what's happened!" He gestured aggressively at the stormy sea.

Travis scoffed. "Oh, so now you're blaming Darien, too?"

"You bet I am. We're in the middle of the goddamn ocean, and if we had taken the motorcycles and blown past all the idiots in their cars like I *suggested,* I bet this wouldn't have happened—"

"GUYS!" Jewels shrieked. "That's *enough!* It's nobody's fault, okay? *Nobody's!* And Malakai—" She rounded on her brother, pausing briefly to cough as a wave splashed her in the face, forcing her to swallow water. "You know for a fact that we *still* wouldn't have made it out on time—"

"Not at my speed," he argued.

"Stop!" Jewels wailed, slapping the water with both fists. "Just *stop it!* We need to focus! We're in the middle of the ocean, the boat's upside down, and—" She paled. Her eyes flared, whites showing around the irises. "Holy shit, something just touched my leg."

Fantastic. Now the hunters were being hunted. It couldn't get any worse than this.

Try as he may, Travis could not muster the courage to use his Sight and scan the waters below. He'd only ever taken jobs on land, the ocean a monster hunting-ground he'd never even stuck a toe into. What lurked down there was none of his business. He'd save those horrors for the Dark-slaying Houses that specialized in slaying aquatic breeds. People like Athene Cousens and the members of the Riptide.

"We need to get back in the boat," Aspen said. She pushed her hair out of her face, her teeth chattering. "We need to figure out a plan, but boat first. We're nothing but fish food out here."

"I can't believe this is happening," Travis muttered.

"Shut up, Devlin, you big old bitcher," Malakai snapped.

"Soon as we get on land," Travis snarled, "I'm coming for your throat." It was his turn to point.

"Guys, seriously, smarten up!" Jewels fumed. "We need to work together, or we could die out h—" Her last word tapered off as her gaze snagged on something behind Malakai.

Travis saw it, too—barely. The spiked backs of not one, not two, but *three* water serpents twining above the surface. It was the eyes—six of them glowing red— that gave away how many there were, the splotches of color barely penetrating the dark water.

Finally, something was coming to end this prick.

End them all, probably. But at least Travis wouldn't have to put up with Malakai anymore. Getting eaten didn't sound as bad as it had a moment ago.

"Oh gods." Jewels paled, her eyes flaring. "Malakai, there are three serpents behind you." She paddled her arms backward. "Oh hell, they're coming this way—"

"I don't *CARE!*" Malakai bellowed, his furious outburst echoing far and wide. His eyes were a gleaming jet-black, his soaked hair flattened to his head. "You want to know *WHY?*" Every word got louder. Angrier. "Because I'm so fucking mad, *no one,* not even the sharks and the silly little sea worms, is going to *FUCK WITH ME RIGHT NOW!*" He whipped his right hand out of the water, fingers curling like claws as he directed his shadowy power to the overturned boat.

The water serpents did not come any closer.

In fact, they turned tail and fled, the curves of their wending backs vanishing into the foggy distance.

The boat flipped right-side up, water spraying.

Malakai twisted around, arm still outstretched, and used his power to lift Jewels into the boat. Then Aspen. He handled both of the women carefully.

He flung Travis.

Travis hit the far side of the boat, nearly tipping right over the edge and falling back into the water. He thumped against the handrail with a grunt, narrowly avoiding banging his teeth on the metal as he grabbed onto it, then pulled himself off the deck and onto a water-slick seat, suit and hair dripping.

Well, he could've done without the aggression, but this was better than being left behind.

Malakai swam up and hauled himself in.

Travis emptied his pockets of soaked snacks. Checked his phone—

He frantically pressed all the buttons, but the screen stayed dark.

The device was wrecked. Completely wrecked.

He hung his head in his hands.

He couldn't even call Roman. Tell him he was sorry.

"Plan?" Aspen panted, dragging herself onto the front passenger seat. Merely voicing that single word seemed to cost her all her strength, her body limp and shaking from the icy cold.

"Shore," was all Malakai said before he restarted the boat and steered it through the waves.

50

Ꞁ-5

STATE OF KER

The hum of the tires on the road lulled Loren to sleep.

How much time had passed, she didn't know. But when she opened her eyes, it was still dark out, so she figured she had been asleep for maybe a few hours, maximum.

She was bundled up in Darien's winter jacket, her seat partially reclined. It was comfortably warm in here, which told her that her condition had improved, if only a little, after getting some rest. But she was still so tired her bones positively *ached,* and a wicked tension headache was setting in. Likely from lack of adequate sleep, hydration, and nutrition.

That and everything else that was wrong with her.

Darien was so lost in thought, he hadn't noticed that she was awake. His face was grave, his features washed with the cool glow of the dashboard. The silver monster's head rings on his left hand caught the bluish light as he steered, the tips of the horns winking like little stars.

She observed him in silence for a few minutes. He grabbed his phone. Checked the screen. Set it down. Then rested an elbow against his door, hand idly rubbing his chin.

Watching him fight for his family as fiercely as he had tonight was incredible. Calling each and every one of them multiple times to aid them in their escape. He'd even called Max, unaware that the friend he'd argued with only hours prior had opted to go with Ivy to find Paxton, Eugene, and Tanner. But while his actions made her extremely proud, she only felt worse about the fact that he'd gotten her out of Yveswich safely and not the others.

He'd tried, yes. Had done everything he could to help them while isolated on the other side of the forcefield. But until they heard from Ivy, Tanner, Roman, Max, Travis, and everyone else... Well, there was no telling if they were okay. If they had made it out on time. And so this guilt she felt for making him choose between her and them would remain.

"Did you hear from the others?" Her question was a crackle—a barely-there whisper. Gods, she was parched. The last thing she'd drunk was that cola after leaving the hospital. A glass of cold water sounded incredible right about now.

Darien's head turned her way, the surprise on his face betraying that he'd really had no clue that she was awake. It was so unlike him to be unaware of his surroundings—of her, especially. The gods knew he deserved a break from being so hyper-fixated on everything going on in the universe, but it was certainly out of character for him.

"Not yet," he replied. "Did you get some rest?"

"A little." She adjusted her seat so she was sitting up straight.

He returned to staring at the road, an elbow propped against his door, his jaw resting against his tattooed knuckles. There was a crease between his brows, the dark half-moons that were etched under his eyes betraying his exhaustion. And—

She frowned. Were those beads of sweat glistening on his forehead and cheeks? It wasn't *that* warm in here, was it?

She cleared her throat. "Are you okay?"

"I'm fine," he said without looking at her. "Just tired." *Just tired* was an understatement, she knew. While she'd managed to catch a couple of hours' worth of shut-eye, he on the other hand hadn't slept in...over forty-eight hours, she would guess. Best case scenario.

She pulled her sleeves—*his* sleeves—over her fingers. "How close is the next town?" She covered her mouth as she yawned.

He stayed frozen in the same tense position, his eyes briefly flashing to the navigation screen. "About an hour."

"Are we stopping?"

"For food," he replied. He still wasn't looking at her. "And to charge the vehicles. Whether we get a hotel will depend on a few things." Availability was one, Loren figured. With all the evacuees pouring out of Yveswich, hotels with vacant rooms would be slim-pickings. How the others felt about stopping was another factor. Hopefully Arthur had managed to get some sleep in the back seat of the truck.

The interstate was busy, but it wasn't as bad as when they'd first left Yveswich. There were more lanes now—six across on both sides of the median strip—which helped put some distance between each vehicle.

It felt strange to be between cities on unprotected land—especially at nighttime. These past few months had brought many dangerous experiences into Loren's life that she had never once dreamed of doing, let alone living to tell of them.

As the hour wore on, Darien began to show signs of not just fatigue, but irritation, too. Every blink was fierce, every movement he made—checking his phone, adjusting the temperature dials, flicking on the turn signal—brusque and impatient. Instead of sitting statue-still like before, he fidgeted a lot and raked his fingers through his hair.

"Do you mind if I smoke?" he blurted. He was already searching the pockets of his jacket.

She shook her head.

He cracked his window open, placed a cigarette between his teeth, and lit up. He smoked it like it was oxygen, burning it right down to the filter, and then promptly lit a second one. As the minutes ticked by and she hardly smelled any tobacco, she squinted, her imperfect vision just barely making out the shimmer of magic surrounding him.

"Can you do me a favor and message Lace?" he asked, blowing a stream of bluish smoke toward his cracked-open window. "Let her know we'll be stopping in Réalta." When she reached for her phone, he told her, "You can use mine. I added your fingerprint."

She grabbed his phone and flattened her thumb over the sensor.

It unlocked. She opened his messages and clicked on *Lace Rivera*.

The urge to scroll up and read the full conversation was *strong*. Embarrassingly strong.

"You can look if you want," Darien said quietly, his focus still on the road.

Loren stiffened. How the heck did he always know what she was thinking, feeling? Even through the magic of the Avertera talisman, he *always* knew.

He added, "I know she bothers you."

She cleared her throat. "Not as much as she used to." It wasn't a lie. The gorgeous Lacey had bothered her a lot in the beginning—she couldn't deny that. But she'd learned to tolerate her. *Like* her, even, to a certain extent. Still, she couldn't help but ask him, "How long did you date her?"

He didn't react. As if he had been waiting months for her to ask him this, regardless that he'd never told her about his romantic history with the platinum blonde Devil. Thanks to rumors and her ability to read female body language, she had figured it out on her own.

That, and Jack might've let it slip once. In one of his signature offhanded remarks.

Darien wet his lips and took another drag, his cheeks hollowing out. Gods, she could stare at his lips forever. "Officially? Bout a year, maybe," he mused, still completely unbothered.

The urge to ask him more questions was strong, but it was none of her business. His past belonged to *him*, and him only. His years before he met her had made him who he was—had brought him to her. Every step, every decision, and yes, every relationship, too, it was all *Darien Cassel*. She couldn't resent him for any of it.

So, instead she asked him, "What should I type?"

"Just say we're stopping in Réalta." He stubbed out the cigarette in the ashtray.

Her cheeks warmed. Gods, he'd already told her that. It showed how easily she was sidetracked by something so trivial.

She typed the message, sent it, and shut off the screen.

"So you're not bothered by my ex, but you're bothered by a random Healer you've never even seen before?" He was watching her now. Talking to him while he'd had his focus on the road was so much easier than this—than having his potent stare fixed wholly on her. It made her feel transparent. Vulnerable. But—

Now that he was looking directly at her, she noticed the size of his pupils. He was fighting a Surge, which could potentially explain why he was sweating like that. She didn't know a lot about Surges, and what she did know was only what she'd observed during her time under the Devils' roof. But she supposed sweating could be a symptom. He sometimes woke up in the night looking exactly like he did now, but worse.

"I'm not bothered by the Healer," she said—a bit defensively. She didn't mean to give him attitude, it sort of just slipped out. He spared one glance for the road as they passed a semi, but otherwise kept his focus on her. As if her answer—everything she said, really—meant the world to him. "I told you, I was bothered by the *after.*"

"And I told you there is no after." What he—they—were going through put an edge in his tone as well. Not a harsh one, no. But she knew Darien well enough to detect it. "You are my present, my future, and my eternity, Loren." The statement made her blood sing and her heart pound irregularly.

How she wished it were true. She didn't doubt that he meant what he'd said—but they had no future together. Nothing beyond her twenty-first birthday. And gods, did that truth cut like a knife.

She drew a deep breath to ease the ache in her chest, her heart threatening to bleed out.

Darien continued. "I tied my life to yours—that should be enough to convince you, don't you think?" He waited for a response, and when she didn't give him one he said, "I don't want you to be bothered by other women. You have enough shit coming at you from all angles, and if there's one thing I can guarantee that you don't need to burden your beautiful mind with, it's other women. I don't want them, Loren, I want *you*. Just you. Forever. Okay?"

She still didn't respond. She just stared out the windshield, fighting desperately to keep her emotions under control.

Darien didn't press her, and she was glad. If he tried, she might slip up and say something she shouldn't say. Start another argument that neither of them would benefit from.

Or spill her secrets to him.

The *after* would never stop bothering her, no matter how many times he reassured her. Because once they were back in Angelthene, and she figured out how to move forward with her plan, she would give him back his *after*. A future she would not be a part of. Darien Cassel would live— that was her one and only goal right now.

"You're not really going to kick Max out, are you?" she asked him.

Darien took a moment to respond. "No." He sighed. "I forgave him the moment he left." Watching him fight with one of his best friends was rough. Loren had gotten into a lot of fights with Dallas over the years, but they'd always found their way back to each other. She was glad to hear that it would be the same for Darien and Max.

A few minutes later, as her thoughts drifted back to their previous topic —Darien's bargain, the lies, her mortality—she blurted, "Is it true?"

A beat of quiet. And then: "Is what true?"

"What I asked you at the hospital. Did you choose to give the Widow more years than you had to?" Her heartbeat accelerated.

Darien hesitated again. Briefly. And then he admitted, "Yes."

Her eyes shuttered, her throat so tight she felt like she was being strangled. It took her a while before she could open her eyes again, and when she did she found that she couldn't look at him.

"What, exactly, did she say to you?" she choked out.

"That you won't live past your twenty-first birthday. And that the hour of your death could arrive sooner if you use your magic." *He* sounded like he was choking, too.

The dark highway blurred, her eyes burning. For several long, tense minutes, they didn't speak.

Darien was the one who broke the quiet. And by that time, he had composed himself so well that his tone was matter-of-fact. "It's done, Loren. I can't take it back, and even if I could, I wouldn't."

No, she thought in agreement. *No, you wouldn't, because you don't care about yourself at all. And it hurts.*

It hurts.

Silence prevailed. Loren focused on breathing, her heart pounding.

"Are you still cold?" Darien's question alerted her to the fact that she was suddenly shivering. Violently. "I'll shut this." He flicked a button on his door, and the glass of the window rose, sealing off the noise of the highway.

"I'm fine," she mumbled. "Besides, you're sweating."

He swiped the back of his hand across his forehead and glanced at the sheen on his skin, as if completely unaware of this fact.

She added, "I don't want you to have to use your magic if you need to smoke again."

"It's no big deal," he muttered. He unbuckled his seatbelt and shrugged out of his jacket.

"You use your magic a lot, though. There are risks, and you're not really caring about them." The Tricking was a threat he had never taken seriously —not since the moment she'd met him. She remembered asking him about it the night he'd tried tracking Sabrine in the dining room at Hell's Gate.

'There's not a lot I'm worried about, Rookie,' he'd told her. She could hear his words as if he'd said them yesterday. Back then, he was nothing to her but a stranger.

Now, he was taking off the jacket she'd worn multiple times and was tossing it into the back seat of the car they'd had sex in. Multiple times.

"I care," he countered gently as he put his seatbelt back on. His steel eyes locked on hers—and tightened a little, as if he sensed where her mind had strayed. It wouldn't surprise her—it was hard to hide anything from him. "I just care about you more. And sweetheart, you've been using your magic as if you're invincible. You know full well what could happen to you, and you're not giving a single shit."

She glared out the windshield. "We're not really getting along, are we?" she whispered, her throat tight for a million different reasons, many of them things she couldn't talk to him about.

"No," he agreed. "But I'll always love you. Even on the days when we're upset with each other." He added, "And even when you don't love me back."

I do love you, she thought. *I always love you. Every second of every day. And I'll never stop—not even when my heart does.*

But she didn't say it.

Her silence upset him—she could tell. He didn't say anything more, but the look in his eyes, his body language, the way he reached for a third cigarette—just *him* in general right now was unsettling.

He was worried that he was losing her. And from the way he kept looking at his phone, checking the screen for new messages or calls he might have missed, never mind that his volume was on full-blast, he was worried that he'd lost his Devils, too.

51

THE OCEAN
YVESWICH, STATE OF KER

Max opened his eyes to a churning sea.

The sky was so black, it was almost impossible to tell the difference between it and the water. Rain fell in silver sheets that stung his skin and pelted the foamy waves like bullets.

His upper half was sprawled across something hard and smooth, his legs submerged in water so cold they were numb.

There was something fluttering against his wrists.

He turned his head and found Dallas bobbing in the current across from him. She was holding onto him by the wrists, water up to her neck as she fought to keep him afloat on a piece of debris, her arms stretched taut across it.

His thoughts were so muddled it took him longer than it should have to realize those were her hands that were shaking. She hadn't noticed that he was awake, too busy scanning their surroundings with stark terror.

Karkharias, water serpents, and Aequorwyrms were only a few of the beasts they had to worry about out here. The worst of the worst were so old, they didn't even have names. And then there were the sharks, the leopard seals... It wasn't that Darkslayers couldn't easily handle the latter—they could. But when you couldn't even *see* the predator that was trying to take a bite out of you, anything could happen. And he was so drained, he couldn't even use his Sight to look, let alone muster the strength to wield a weapon.

"Dallas," he croaked. His throat burned from the high salt content of the water. He felt like he'd swallowed a bucket of it.

Relief washed across her face. "Thank gods," she breathed, her fingers lightly squeezing his wrists. How long had she been keeping him above the water like this? She looked drained.

"What the hell happened?" he asked.

He didn't need to, though. Memories of the crash came back to him as he glanced around at the parts of the destroyed helicopter floating in the ocean. That demon had completely pulverized the aircraft, most of it scattered in charred shreds. There was another large piece of the fuselage nearby, Dominic, Blue, Maya, and Magenta clinging to it.

They'd survived. Against all odds, they'd survived.

The pilots and the soldiers, however, were not so lucky. Helmets and the odd body part peeked above the sloshing waves.

"We crashed," Dallas said, answering the question Max forgot he'd asked. "You should've seen Maya, she burned the hell out of that monster—it was insane." Probably a good thing he was out for that part, then. "We've been trying to think of a plan, but—" Her teeth chattered so hard they cut off her words. "Dominic's wings are waterlogged. I thought maybe he could fly us to shore one by one, but unless he can get them dry, we're kind of screwed."

Getting them dry in this rain was about as likely as winning the lottery. There were no signs of it letting up anytime soon, either.

He studied the others from afar. Maya was lying in the center of the piece of helicopter while everyone else merely hung onto it as if it were a raft. Max wondered if she was hurt, but... No, it wasn't that.

Water and fire did not mix. They were in the middle of the ocean, and that was a genetically modified Fire Elemental he was looking at. She was balancing her weight carefully, looking terrified that her raft might tip or sink. Temporary contact with water must be fine, then. But prolonged would probably kill her.

This talk of Dominic's wings drew Max's attention to the ones that were attached to Dallas's back. They were fried and warped, adding nothing to her existence but some extra weight for her to have to lug around. They were threatening to pull her below water now, her chin barely above the surface.

He shifted his wrists out of her grasp and grabbed onto her arms, pulling her farther up the fuselage. When she glanced at him in question, he explained, "Take a break. I'm fine."

She didn't argue.

Max looked around, but there was nothing to see but violent waves and the mangled remains—twisted metal and broken blades—from the crash. They were a long way from shore. Which reminded him—

He cursed. "We didn't make it out, did we?"

Dallas frowned and shook her head.

So close. They had been *this* close, and they still hadn't made it.

Max tipped his head back and squinted. He may not be strong enough to summon the Sight right now, but hellseher vision was so sharp that he could see the forcefield without it.

The columns of runes—red, now—were curving above the ocean.

His gut churned like the current.

Trapped. They were trapped now, in more ways than one. Adrift in the ocean with no way back to land. Even if they managed to get back, they were stuck in Yveswich. The darkness would continue to spread, and so would death. They had days, maybe, before the oxygen and the last of the power holding this city together would run out.

The Control Tower in Yveswich was an older model than the one in Angelthene. Outdated in the sense that the controls were located somewhere remote—somewhere outside of Yveswich. So removing the forcefield's core—what Loren did on Kalendae—was not an option. And even if it were, the new magic flowing through the tower was deadly. If a bird flew anywhere close to it, the power would burn it to dust. No one would even be able to walk the blocks surrounding the tower, or they would be incinerated.

So, basically, they were fucked. Completely and totally fucked.

"What about Blue?" Max asked. "Her magic—"

"She can't do it in a storm," Dallas said with a sad frown. "The waves are too strong and unpredictable. And besides, it's not safe for Maya."

Max cursed. Controlling something like the ocean was already a huge ask, but trying to quarrel with the might of a storm, too? He hadn't thought of that. They'd probably all drown if she tried. And the debris from the crash would only stay afloat for so long before it sank. So basically, they were screwed. They'd either drown out here, adrift in the sea, or they'd suffocate in the city once the shadow took over. And those were only two of the things that had a high probability of killing them. Monsters were another. There were probably a few water serpents scenting blood in the water right this very minute.

He let go of Dal's left arm, checking his back that felt too light, the ghost of a strap across his chest—

"Fuck me," he muttered.

"What?"

"The sword's gone." It must have fallen off when the helicopter crashed, which meant...

They had no swords of adamant now. Not a single one. Max was the only one in their group who'd had one. Lace and Ivy had the other two— Darien had given his to Ivy before leaving Yveswich, after Ivy had given Lace hers to carry for a while.

He sighed. They'd better hope they wouldn't need it.

He didn't know how much time passed before he heard a hum.

Was that an engine?

He shared a glance with Dallas as the sound drew closer.

A speedboat loomed out of the fog, the navigation lights capping the waves in red, white, and green.

Max's brows rose as he beheld who steered it.

"Well, well, well," drawled Malakai Delaney. Travis, Jewels, and Aspen were with him, their silhouettes materializing in the soup of fog and shadow. "Look what the bird dragged in."

52

I-5

STATE OF KER

S hay sat in the driver's seat of the car as Roman worked under the hood, his hands black with grease and oil.

Paxton was sprawled across the back seat, head resting against his backpack, fingers clicking buttons on his foldable handheld game console. Sayagul and Chance, his puppy Familiar, were curled up with him, the latter sleeping so deeply he was snoring. Loudly.

Shay had assisted Roman to the best of her ability and for as long as she could, but this migraine was brutal. It'd hit her shortly after she'd shocked Pax's heart, demanding she immediately get someplace dark and quiet. While it wasn't very quiet in here thanks to puppy-shaped chainsaw, it *was* dark. For the most part, anyway. Every time a car went by, headlights pulsing through the night, it felt like her brain was going to explode.

Being in here wasn't so bad, though. In here, she couldn't see the muscles in Roman's forearms flexing as he used those skilled hands of his to get this car back on the road. The last thing she needed was to lust over this man—or his masculine, absurdly attractive hands—any more than she already was. He was off-limits. Forbidden. Not hers.

But gods, did she want him to be.

A tinny chime filled the car as Paxton shut off his game console.

"Done already?" she asked him.

"It's just Rushin' Racers—I play it all the time. You can have a turn if you want." He leaned forward and offered her the console between the front seats.

She started to shake her head, but stopped when a fresh wave of pain bloomed through her skull. "No, that's okay, Pax," she croaked. "I'm a little too dizzy right now." She shut her eyes and pinched the space between her brows.

"Are you sick?"

"It's just a headache."

"Is it from your lightning?"

She managed a nod. "I usually take meds for it, but they're at home." She hadn't had the luxury of going to her apartment to pack, so she'd had to leave all her belongings behind. Even her photographs of Anna and Dad. She'd miss those the most.

"Roman has water back here." The sound of ripping plastic was unbearably loud as Paxton, bless his soul, grabbed a water bottle from the case on the floor and passed it to her.

"Thank you." She twisted the cap off and drank half. "How are *you* feeling?" She set the bottle in the cupholder.

"Sleepy," he said around a yawn. "Is your medication a suppressant?"

"It is."

"I take those, too." A thoughtful pause. "My mom gets bad headaches like yours. From her Surges." His mom. Shay had seen her outside of the warehouse before the helicopter crash.

Paxton fell silent, sadness and guilt weighing heavily on his aura.

Shay peeked at him in the corner of her vision. He was staring out the window, the whites of his eyes still splotched with pools of blood from broken vessels. The dark lines on the thin skin beneath were finally fading. What happened there, she and Roman had no idea. And they hadn't had much time to talk about it, either.

She twisted so she could see him better and folded her legs beneath her. It was a little cramped in here for that, but she had to move them—they were tingling. "Those two sure are attached to you," she said softly, eyeing the lightly dozing dragon and the snoring puppy.

Paxton tore his heavy gaze off the window and scratched Chance's floppy ears. "Chance keeps me awake at night sometimes. He snores like a chainsaw, but he's a good boy." He moved onto Sayagul, lightly dragging the pad of his index finger down the back of her long neck. "Sayagul's always been there for me. Like Roman. Ever since she was an egg."

Shay could have sworn she saw the dragon's mouth lift at the corner.

"Your seal pup is pretty cool," Paxton said.

Shay smiled. "Thank you."

"Only one kid in my whole school has a white Familiar. Jake. It's a lamb. It's super cute. I'm glad I have a dog and not a wolf like my dad. Skǫll scares me." He shuddered.

"What does your mom have?" Shay already knew the answer, though. She was only making conversation. Kids always ended up with the same Familiar as one of their parents.

"A dog," Paxton said. "Same kind as Chance." He lovingly flicked the pup's drooping left ear, causing him to snort.

"Try it now?" Roman called.

Shay twisted back around, flattened the brake, and turned the key in the ignition.

The car fired to life.

Pax let out a cheer of victory that startled the sleeping animals awake. Chance jumped to his feet and started to woof.

Roman closed the hood.

Finally.

Shay got out, passing him on her way to the passenger's seat as he gathered his tools.

"You can drive if you want," he offered.

"No, thanks. I'm too dizzy." She made for the passenger's-side door.

"Still bad?" He was peering at her over the roof of the car, looking far too concerned for someone who was supposed to be keeping his distance from her.

Dammit, why couldn't he just go back to being an asshole?

"I don't think it's going away anytime soon."

"There are painkillers in the glovebox," Roman said as they got in. "Help yourself."

Shay did exactly that, squinting in the light that flicked on inside the glovebox. As she rummaged around inside, a small tube caught her eye. She grabbed it and read the label.

"Bubblegum lip balm?" She raised a brow at Roman. "Which poor girl does this belong to?"

"Me," Roman said, deadpan. "I'm the poor girl it belongs to."

Paxton snorted in the back seat.

Shay raised her brows—both of them now—higher. "You use bubblegum lip balm?"

"Yeah. You got a problem with that?"

"No, I just..." She scanned him pointedly—the black combat boots, the chains on his tattered black jeans. "Didn't expect bubblegum flavor. Maybe *roadkill* or *blood-of-your-enemies.*"

Paxton was quietly laughing. At least one of them found her funny. It certainly wasn't the brooding Shadowmaster, whose eye was suddenly twitching.

Roman didn't deign to answer her. Instead, he twisted in his seat to check on Paxton. "How you feeling?"

"Fine."

"Your eyes are looking better," Roman said. He eyed the backpack Paxton was using as a pillow. "Is Itzel still in there?"

"Where else would she be?"

Roman wasn't convinced. "Hey, Itzel," he called. No answer. He frowned. "You alive in there?"

When the Hob hissed at him like a cat, Shay had to try not to choke on the painkillers she was in the midst of swallowing.

"All right, I'll take that as a yes," Roman muttered.

"Do we have a plan?" Shay asked as she set her empty bottle in the cupholder and buckled in.

"Get to Angelthene," he replied. "That's about it." And stay away from Donovan, wherever he was. That was a given.

It would be a long drive. They'd left via the northern exit, which meant they would have to go around Yveswich. It would add another day's time to their journey, but at least the car was working now.

"Why don't you recline and get some rest?" Roman suggested as he pulled into traffic. "I've got this."

Shay didn't argue. Not when her head felt like it was going to explode like the Well.

She reclined and shut her eyes, ignoring the sense of calm that washed over her.

Somewhere along the way, she had gone from not trusting Roman Devlin at all to trusting him completely. And that scared her.

Because unless Donovan and Athene were still trapped in Yveswich, they would be looking for them. Sooner rather than later. Being out of Yveswich didn't mean they were safe. If anything, they were in greater danger now than ever.

Because they were together. A Selkie and a Shadowmaster, on the run.

With Donovan Slade's kid in the back seat.

53

THE OCEAN
YVESWICH, STATE OF KER

If there were ever an award for *World's Biggest Asshole,* Malakai Delaney would win in a landslide.

Travis had never wanted to get away from anyone more than he wanted to get away from this prick. He had been nothing but an ass to everyone on this boat from the minute they'd climbed on, making snarky remarks and imitating in a squeaky voice every chance he got. It was like he was making it his own personal mission to completely and thoroughly sabotage the hours—days, if they were lucky—they had left.

They were getting close to shore, though. That was a small blessing.

Boats lined the docks, the white sails on a few abandoned vessels snapping and blowing in gusts of wind. Travis had spent the whole ride here briefing Max on what'd happened, and now Max was finishing up with his own explanation.

"And that's when you guys found us," Max concluded. He sat beside Travis on the bench seats in the bow, both of them sopping wet and frozen to the bone. "I have to admit, that was probably the first time I've ever felt genuinely happy to see Delaney."

Travis grunted. "He has his uses, but there aren't many." He glared at the long-haired idiot steering the boat. Aspen was the only person who was close to him by will. The two were talking quietly, as if indulging in secrets. Travis wondered what the hell she saw in him. Was he even capable of holding a conversation without saying something rude or offensive? Doubtful.

"He still giving you a hard time for the whole dating his sister thing?" Max asked. They had a sound barrier up, but it was thin. Jewels was sitting on the bench across from them, arms wrapped around her knees. On either side of her sat Dallas and Blue. The three were talking quietly with their own invisible barrier up. Travis couldn't help but wonder what they were saying.

What a shit experience this was for Jewels. It sucked for everyone, yeah, but Jewels had gone straight from cardiac arrest to being thrown from a boat and forced to tread frigid water, all while her brother was terrorizing everyone around her, *including* her. That soaked sweatsuit looked cold as hell, her hair hanging in dripping strings that lashed her face. She sure was pretty, though.

As if she'd heard him thinking that, her green eyes flicked to his.

He looked away. Sucked in a breath of wet, salty air. "I don't think he'll be stopping anytime soon," he replied. He'd thought he and Delaney were turning a new leaf the night they'd drunk together on Roman's roof. Turned out, he was dead wrong for thinking that.

"She worth it?" Max lowered his volume to a near whisper the howling wind threatened to snatch away.

Travis slid his gaze back to Jewels, who quickly tore her eyes off him and turned to stare at the waves. Was this stupid sound barrier working at all? Or was he making a complete ass of himself in front of the girl he liked? His life had already plummeted so far down the shitter, it wouldn't surprise him if the universe decided to embarrass him, too.

"Still figuring that out," he muttered. He dropped his attention to the puddled water and sopping seaweed on the deck. "I don't even know if she likes me that much," he admitted. He picked at the dirt and salt caked on his gloves.

"You've had—what, one date?" Max asked.

"Yup. And it came with an assassination attempt." He snorted a laugh. His love life, as of late, was one big tragedy.

"Give it some time," Max encouraged. Travis refrained from being a dick by not pointing out that time was the one thing none of them had anymore. He at least wanted to get laid before he died. One last hookup. He vowed to make it a good one. Max added, "We're kind of in the same situation, actually. You and I." Travis gave him a quizzical look. Was he having problems with Dallas? Seeing the look on his face, Max said, "Bit different, though." He gestured subtly to where Maya Reacher sat on the deck closest to Malakai and Aspen's seats. Magenta and Dominic were with her. None of them were talking, all of them looking miserable. Apart from Dominic. The Angel always tried to look on the bright side in any situation, no matter how bleak.

'Bright side?' Noble rumbled. *'When he finds the bright side in this catastrophe, pray let me know.'*

"She still not talking to you?" Travis asked.

"Hardly. I'm surprised I even got her to come with us, honestly. If everything that went down with that Onyx guy never happened, she probably would've stayed behind. Not that it matters anymore." Max scowled up at the forcefield. "We're all dead meat. I'm half expecting her to ditch the minute we hit the docks."

"If she does, there's nothing you can do," Travis said. He gazed out at the Control Tower pulsing with energy in the rain-battered heart of Yveswich, and sighed. "I need to find a way to contact Roman."

Max looked sidelong at him. "He'll flip the minute he finds out you're in here."

"Yeah, which is exactly what I don't want." He massaged his throbbing left temple in a circular motion. The thought of Roman, who already carried so much weight on his shoulders, being burdened with this *catastrophe*, as Noble had called it, was...not a good thought. But neither was the idea of never talking to him and Pax again. "But..." He switched to vigorously rubbing his ear. It felt like there was water in it. "I want to tell him I'm sorry, you know?" He cleared his throat, the muscles tight. "For all of it. Not just this." His eyes started to burn. He blamed it on the salt.

"You're talking like you're already dead."

"Feels like it."

"We've still got time," Max said. "We'll figure something out. Besides —" It was his turn to clear his throat, his words coming out strangled. "— Roark's daughter is here. Roark is the one who sent the helicopter. Maybe he can get the authorities to let us out." Despite his words, he looked skeptical. Max had very little faith in Roark—they *all* had very little faith in Roark. Expecting him to achieve the impossible task of lowering the forcefield just so a small group of people—out of *millions*—could get out was...a lot to ask.

Still, Travis said, "Maybe." Because hope was what they both needed right now.

They docked as close to shore as they could get. The marina was crowded, and part of the dock looked like it had recently been destroyed, leaving even less room.

Malakai and Aspen jumped out and fastened the spring lines. The rest of them disembarked once the boat was secure, boots thumping on soggy wood. The coastline was eerily quiet, no other people around. Seagulls scavenged for food, caring about nothing but their next meal. Travis wished he could be like them—stealing fries and shitting on the heads of unsuspecting people. What a life.

"We need to decide on a plan," Max said as everyone gathered around.

"We could go back to Roman's," Dominic suggested, peeling a strand of dark hair out of his eyes. His black wings were so waterlogged, they drooped. "Now that he and Pax are gone, I highly doubt Donovan will have his eye on the place."

"You're right," Dallas agreed. "It's probably one of the safest places there is."

"It's a good idea, but it's a little far," Aspen pointed out.

"Look at us!" Jewels said, flinging her arms—sleeves completely drenched—out at her sides. "We're soaked and freezing. I say we find accommodations somewhere closer so we can dry off and rest up, or we're all going to die of hypothermia."

"I know where I'm going," Malakai shouted from a distance. The idiot was sauntering away.

"Care to share with the rest of us?" Travis barked. Seagulls yeowed, the sound like laughter. Everything seemed to be mocking him, even the damn birds.

Malakai turned, gesturing to the sprawling luxury hotel several miles down the coast. "Waterfront hotel, anyone?" He turned with a sloppy wave and kept walking. "Catch you dipshits later."

Soon, everyone was following him, none of them in the mood to argue. And although Travis hated to admit when Malakai was right, that hotel, with its hundreds of windows glowing with buttery light, was probably their best bet. Food, a hot shower, and a warm bed—that was all Travis wanted right now.

So he kept his mouth shut and walked.

54

RÉALTA
STATE OF KER

At a convenience store attached to a charging station in the city of Réalta, Loren came out of the restroom to find that the line-up she'd had to wait in had grown by a startling number of people.

The little business was packed. Food, beverages, and supplies were flying off the shelves, the frazzled employees behind the counter rushing to ring people through.

A long line-up wasn't the only thing waiting for her as the restroom door banged shut behind her, a witch at the front hurrying forward for her turn.

Her personal bodyguard was waiting for her, too. Right where she'd left him by the restroom door. Though his features—Devils tattoo included—were obscured beneath the hood of the black sweatshirt he wore under his leather jacket, it was easy to tell that this was not a man you should mess with. Which was probably why several people had offered for her to cut ahead of them in line.

She'd felt bad for them. Had fought the urge to tell them that her guard dog wouldn't bite—okay, fine, *might* not bite—unless she let him off the leash. But she hadn't turned down their offer.

Now, Loren kept her mouth shut and her head down to hide her identity as she walked past the line, Darien shadowing her. She could feel the odd curious gaze gliding across her and the Darkslayer looming at her back, but no one dared look for longer than a moment. She squeezed between people in the aisle closest to the windows, Darien mirroring her every step of the way, and pushed through the door that chimed with their departure.

The weather was milder here than in Yveswich. She still needed her jacket, though, and Darien's. Another small plus was that it was dry here—no rain. Soon, they would be back in Angelthene's balmy spring weather.

She was looking forward to it. Seeing Sabrine again was another thing she couldn't wait for. She missed her friend, who she hadn't spoken to since before she had fallen into a coma. They had a lot to catch up on. Sabrine had always been good at listening, and right now Loren had a lot to say.

The truck and the car were parked around the corner of the building. Jack, Lace, and Arthur stood talking near the blinding beams of the headlights. This area was safe, no monsters prowling the parking lot that was shared by the charging station, a supermarket, a blood donor clinic, a clothing store for lycanthropes, and several drive-through restaurants. But staying close to a source of light was a force of habit not easily broken in a world crawling with predators.

Arthur gave them a tired smile as they joined the group. "Got some snacks while you were using the loo," he announced, lifting the plastic bag in his hand.

Darien frowned. "I didn't want you going in there, Art."

The old man blinked. "Why not?"

"Someone could've spotted you."

"*You* went in there," Arthur challenged. "Someone could've spotted *you.*"

"I had to go in there to look out for Loren," Darien said, taking cigarette number four out of the pack—empty now, by the looks of it. "No offense, but I don't want to have to look out for you, too." He lit up, shielding the flame with his hand as a breeze stirred through the lot.

"That won't be necessary. I may be more than three times your age, but I can handle myself."

Lace attested, "He *did* just take a pretty thorough beating. He's tough."

Darien wasn't convinced. "You didn't even hide your face, did you?" he accused. "Where's your hood?" Arthur's jacket was a windbreaker—no hood.

"Enough, Darien," Arthur said, dismissing his concerns with a wave. "No one's going to notice an old man the same way they will a six foot five menace." When he poked Darien in the chest, Loren had to press her lips together to stifle a laugh.

Darien glanced at her, as if requesting backup.

She merely shrugged.

"I stand corrected," Darien said.

"Good. Now go on and pick your snacks." He held the bag open in offer, plastic rustling in the wind. "Everyone gets to pick two."

"Ladies first," Darien said. He waved her forward, smoke from his cigarette curling through the air.

"The pretzels are mine," Arthur declared as Loren selected sour candies and a small bag of cheese puffs.

"What if I wanted the pretzels?" Darien crooned, tossing Loren a wink as he reached into the bag. Gods, it was hard to stay angry at him when he flirted with her like this. They had barely said a word to each other for the last portion of the drive here—after he'd told her that he loved her and she hadn't said it back. The fact that he was talking to her at all after how upset he'd seemed was a surprise.

"Then you, Mr. Moneybags, can buy your own damn pretzels," Arthur said with playful attitude.

Darien chuckled. "You're grumpy."

"Because I somehow got dragged into running with you lot," he clipped as Darien grabbed a cookies-and-cream chocolate bar. Arthur added, "I'm too old for all this hullabaloo."

"Are all the pretzels yours, or just the plain ones?" Darien asked him.

"Just the plain. If you want the yogurt pretzels, go on and take them."

Darien grabbed the twist-tied bag of yogurt-covered pretzels.

"You don't even really like those," Loren accused softly.

"You do." He gave her another wink.

Her stomach filled with butterflies. "You should be choosing the snacks that *you* like," she said.

"I'll do what I want, Loren Calla," he crooned. "Besides, knowing you, you'll finish yours right away and then reach for mine, so I might as well be prepared." The crooked smile he gave her made those darn butterflies flutter faster.

"What do you guys think," he began, addressing the group as a whole. "Should we try a hotel?" The ash end of his cigarette glowed as he put his mouth on it.

Loren tore her eyes off him. Searching for anything—anything at all—to look at *besides* Darien's unfairly attractive mouth. She settled for a pop can that had been flattened by someone's tires.

"I highly, *highly* doubt any rooms will be available," Lace said. Cool air eddied around her, swirling her moon-pale hair.

"Probably not," Darien agreed. "I'm good to keep driving, but it depends on how the rest of you feel. Jacky?"

"I don't care," Jack mumbled. He was leaning against the truck, hands in his pockets. Gazing north—toward Yveswich and the wife he'd left behind.

Loren's heart twinged for him.

Darien took his phone out and checked the screen. Put it away.

Still no messages; she could tell from Darien's expression.

"We've got a long drive, but it's your call," Darien told Lace. "Are you good, or are you going to fall asleep at the wheel?"

She held up her energy drink, stiletto nails tapping the can. "I think I'll be just fine." She swigged, long and deep.

"I need to run back inside before we go," Darien said.

"What for?" Lace asked.

"Smokes." He tapped the ash off the one burning in his left hand. "Need anything?"

"I could use some, actually. I'm almost out. And gum."

Darien's eyes—grayer than blue in this light—found Loren's. "I'd like you to come with me."

She didn't argue. Besides, she was thirsty and needed water to take her medication.

"Jack's really upset," she said as she walked back to the store with Darien.

"He has every right to be." He paused by the trash can, taking one last pull on his cigarette before disposing of it in the ashtray.

"You haven't heard anything?" They were far enough away that Jack probably couldn't hear them, but she whispered just to be safe.

"I'll tell you the minute I have." He held the door for her as she walked in.

They had to stand in line for a while. As they waited, she watched the television mounted above the tills.

The news channel was covering the situation in Yveswich, but what the anchors were telling the public was vague. The names they were giving it were *security breach, power outage,* and *blackout.* A rare occurrence that had prompted government officials to restrict access to the city. Nothing was said about the shadows, the portal, the forcefield, the new breeds of monsters with brute strength... Even the fact that the Fleet had been called to the city was being left out.

Loren turned and looked at Darien. "Are you watching this?" she whispered.

He was. And he looked furious. "They're covering it up."

DARIEN LOOKED at the TV one last time before grabbing his smokes off the counter and heading out.

It didn't surprise him that the authorities were covering up the mess in Yveswich. With the Terran Imperator alive and in full control of the city from somewhere outside of it, he'd be doing everything in his power to stop the severity of the situation from leaking to the public. It would cause panic. Outrage. Bad publicity.

Apart from the backlash he was undoubtedly avoiding, the imperator still believed that the real Arcanum Well was hidden somewhere in the Void. Which meant he'd throw every excuse he could possibly think of at the news reporters before admitting the truth, especially when admitting it risked setting more greedy people like him after the one thing in the universe that he coveted most.

The Magnum Opus. The fountain of miracles and eternal life. The source of every problem they'd barely managed to survive these past six months.

As Darien shadowed Loren back to the car, the others already waiting for them in the truck, he reflected on the drive here.

He hadn't even realized that he was sweating. Not until she'd pointed it out and he'd swiped the back of his hand across his wet—*wet*—forehead. Loren seemed to be under the impression that it was because the car was too warm, but that wasn't it at all.

He was having withdrawals. The sweating, the fidgeting, the mood swings, the threat of the worst Surge of his life pounding its fist against his skull.

Angelthene. He had to get back to Angelthene, where he could deal with this shit in private. If a Surge took control of him and blackened his vision, he wouldn't be able to drive safely. And he refused to even try while Loren was in the car with him. Endangering her life was not an option. Ever.

Before he'd met her, he'd made himself a promise that his days of indulging in recreational drugs were behind him. Using a dangerous drug like Venom had been a last resort, sure—a means of protecting Loren and his family from the thousands of threats coming at them from all angles.

But it didn't erase the fact that he was addicted again, and Venom was one of the hardest drugs to quit.

He watched her get in the car, her hair blowing in a breeze. Once she was safely inside, he shut her door for her.

'Don't make it be for me this time,' she'd told him at the hospital, when he'd said that he would work on getting off Venom. *'Make it be for you.'*

But his chains—all of them, not just the drugs—were heavy. And breaking them, even when his motivation was her, was proving to be the hardest fight of his miserable fucking life.

55

THE WANDERER
ARBOR, STATE OF KER

The last place Shay expected to end up was at another motel with Roman Devlin.

The Wanderer, it was called. Fitting, given how they were both wanderers now. Darkslayers without homes. It was a decrepit old thing, just like Motel 58. The stucco was chipped, the swimming pool unmaintained, the parking lot potholed and littered with debris. But the faded sign said VACANCY, unlike the many others they'd passed during their long and tiring search for a place to sleep. Beggars couldn't be choosers.

"Wait here," Roman said as he pulled the car to a stop by the office. Paxton was fast asleep in the back. "I'll get us a room." He was out of the car, door thumping shut, before Shay could even think of a response.

A room, he'd said. Singular.

She sighed. Hopefully it would have two beds.

While he was gone, her thoughts began to drift. Memories she'd had zero time to think about while scrambling to escape Yveswich were resurfacing, clear as crystal. She wished they wouldn't.

Roman's mouth on hers.

Cigarette smoke shaped like a howling wolf.

The feel of his callused hands squeezing her thighs as he'd carried her on his back beneath a hot desert sun.

Roman's husky voice telling her to beg. Say his name—

The door opened, startling her and chasing the memories away.

Roman was back, key in his tatted hand—the hand she had been fantasizing about a moment ago. The little tag attached to the key had the number nineteen written on it in faded black marker. Another room with the number nine—what a coincidence.

He must have seen where her focus had gone, because he told her, "I made sure there are two beds."

She tried to swallow, but her mouth was as dry as the day he'd carried her through the desert.

"Okay," she managed to say. It was a good thing it was so dark out, so he couldn't see her face turning red.

At least Paxton was with them this time, which meant neither of them could make the colossal mistake of putting their hands on each other again.

Roman paused in the midst of pocketing the key. "Do you want to hold onto it, or do you trust me?" He dangled it in the air between them in offer, silver winking in the outdoor lights streaming in through the windshield.

Did she trust him? Hadn't she just been thinking about that?

It was odd—she trusted Roman with her life, and she trusted him to keep her secrets, too... But she didn't trust him with her heart. And she wasn't so certain she trusted him not to ditch her, either.

Regardless, she told him, "You didn't ditch me at Motel 58." It *was* the truth. "I think I trust you enough not to leave me now."

She could have sworn his eyes tightened, the few gold flecks in his irises dimming, but she didn't know what the reaction meant. *Was* he planning on ditching her? Or was that just her *trust issues,* as Roman liked to call them, speaking?

He watched her for a moment, as if trying to figure her out, before pulling the car into the parking spot in front of the door labeled with the number nineteen. No businesses were open at this hour for her to buy clothes, so Shay planned on sleeping in a bath towel. Sleeping nude wasn't an option, and she couldn't keep wearing this disgusting battle-suit forever. A towel would have to suffice, and hopefully the clothes she wore underneath would be salvageable enough to throw into the motel laundry machine.

If they even *had* one.

Shay got out and carried their bags in while Roman lifted a sleeping Pax out of the car and lay him down on one of the beds. Unsurprisingly, the room was a total shit-hole, but at least they had a place to sleep.

"You probably want to have a shower," Roman whispered as Shay placed the bags on the tiny table and chairs by the window. "Bathroom's all yours. I'm going to try calling the others." He slid his hand into the back pocket of his jeans and took out his cell phone and a pack of smokes. He placed a cigarette between his teeth, eyes fixed on his phone. "I'll be outside if you need me," he added, the words muffled by the cigarette.

Again, he was gone before she could respond.

Shay blinked. He seemed to be making that a habit. It was perfectly reasonable for him to want to get a hold of Travis, but she couldn't help but think he was using any excuse he could think of to carve out some space between them. They hadn't talked much during the long ride here, though truthfully she hadn't really known what to say. They'd both lived through a ton of shit recently and were more than a little exhausted. Maybe tomorrow would be different.

She disappeared into the dingy bathroom and shut the door.

Without the aid of the magic in the ring, the suit was absolute hell to remove. She had to take a knife to a few spots that were warped from the explosion and literally cut her limbs free. Now that she was off the Stygian salts, her cracked ribs were bothering her again, the searing pain making it even harder to get the suit off. She would have to ask Roman for more painkillers.

When she came out of the shower wrapped in a towel and opened the creaky bathroom door, she stepped on something soft.

A folded black band t-shirt lay on the floor. It was one of Roman's

She scanned the quiet room. Pax and the Familiars were the only ones in here, all of them asleep. Roman was still outside smoking, his silhouette barely visible through the crooked blinds on the window.

At some point in time, he'd paused what he was doing and had come inside to find a shirt for her to wear. Had placed it on the floor so she'd find it the minute she came out.

Shay stood there for a moment, shifting her weight, thinking up every possible excuse not to wear Roman's shirt. It was too big; maybe he had few spares and would need this one back; it wasn't her style; it had too many rips; she didn't like the band. The last one was a total lie. In the end, she caved and put it on.

Just as she'd feared, it smelled like him—the cologne and body wash that had become her favorite scent. Gods above, was she weak.

But so was Roman. He knew better than to do this. They *both* knew better. They were playing with fire like a couple of pyromaniacs.

She stared at herself in the bathroom mirror, her body drowning in Roman Devlin's shirt, and sighed.

This was going to make it even harder to get over him.

HE WAS A FUCKING IDIOT, wasn't he? The *biggest* fucking idiot in all of Terra.

Roman stood out front of the motel room, phone in hand, a fresh cigarette in his teeth. Silently kicking himself for giving Shay his shirt.

He could see her through the blinds, but he tried not to look. She'd come out of the bathroom wearing the shirt, the frayed hem skimming her toned thighs—

And drawing his attention straight to her too-perfect ass.

Gods, she looked sexy in his clothes. That ass was hard to look away from, no matter what she was wearing, but especially in his clothes. His sexual past was extensive, the number of women he'd slept with high, thanks not just to his libido, but also his psychotic dad's determination to wreck any relationship he tried to have. But Shayla Cousens had left the kind of impression on him that he was having a hard time shaking.

How his name sounded on her lips when she came. The way she'd swirled her tongue across the head of his cock when she'd gone down on him, her technique so goddamn incredible he'd thought his heart might explode from pleasure. The faces she'd made when he'd had her on her back in the bed at Motel 58 and fucked the hell out of her. The way she wanted it rough. Begged him to fuck her as if she were unbreakable.

Then there was the softer side of Shay, too. The Shay who'd walked willingly into the torture chamber that was the House of Black and unlocked his chains. Taken him back to her place and held him while he slept. Ran her fingers through his hair.

She was exactly his type. And he wasn't allowed to have her.

He lit up and took a drag, smoke curling in front of his vision, and watched as she climbed onto the available bed and got under the covers. She made herself comfortable on the pillows, beating them into submission in a way that almost—*almost*—made him laugh despite everything, before grabbing the television remote.

Yup, he was an idiot.

He shook his head and tore his attention off her before she could notice him gawking like a creep through the blinds.

'*You do look a little creepy,*' Sayagul said from inside the room.

Roman peered through the blinds and found the dragon curled up on the bed between Pax and Chance, one slitted eye peering at him from above Pax's ankle.

'Thanks,' Roman muttered.

She snickered, but her humor abruptly faded as she asked him, *'Have you heard from Travis?'*

'I'm about to try again.' He hit CALL on his screen and lifted the phone to his ear.

The line just kept ringing.

Travis was not picking up. Neither were Kylar, Ivy, Max… He'd tried Tanner as well, before remembering his phone had likely been stolen by the Wyverns.

Nobody was answering.

He ended the call with a slam of his thumb on the red button.

Morning. He would give them till morning. For all he knew, their phone batteries might be dead. Cell service could be spotty. As he stood there, puffing on his cigarette, he thought of a million different excuses for why they weren't answering. Anything was better than the one he feared most.

That they hadn't made it out of Yveswich on time.

56

HELL'S GATE
ANGELTHENE, STATE OF WITHEREDGE

"Sweetheart."

A male was speaking to her. A male with a deep, sexy voice. But gods, she was *so* tired, she just wanted to sleep.

"Sweetheart," the man said again—a little louder this time, but no less gentle. A warm touch skimmed her cheek. "We're home."

Loren's eyelids fluttered open.

The sun was setting, and they were parked in front of Hell's Gate.

She let out a sleepy groan, her eyes shutting again. "How long have I been asleep?" she slurred. She was still wearing Darien's jacket. It was so warm, and she was so comfortable. She didn't want to move. She just wanted rest—

"A few hours," Darien replied. Even while half-asleep, that voice gave her pleasant full-body shivers. "I can carry you in if you want."

"No, that's okay." When she opened her eyes this time, she managed to *keep* them open. She scanned the twilit yard, the driveway, the many windows of the impressive mansion glowing with golden light.

Darien shut off the car and opened his door, the sugary scent of pink jasmine and the earthy fragrance of freshly cut grass sweeping in on a gentle breeze. Loren breathed it in until her lungs were full; it smelled divine.

It smelled like *home*.

"Let's get you inside so you can get some proper rest," he said. It was an offer she couldn't refuse. The drive here was long—about twenty-two hours—and although she'd slept for most of it, she'd woken up frequently from the sound of traffic and the pulsing of streetlights.

She got out and walked with Darien to the house she had feared she might never see again. Up the front steps that were framed with pillars and lion statues, and through the door that was already open.

Reality finally hit as she sucked in another deep breath of air laced with more familiar smells.

Home. They really were home.

The others were already inside. Their murmuring voices were coming from the kitchen.

Loren squinted in the bright light of the chandelier—and paused mid-step as glass crunched under her shoe.

She blinked. Looked down.

Oh.

Her stomach sank as she scanned the foyer.

Hell's Gate looked like a tornado had gone through it. Smashed glass, limen coins, flower petals, and bits of broken wood and metal covered every inch of the floor. There were holes in the walls, framed photographs that had once hung on hooks now lying in pieces.

So much had happened these past few days that Loren, to her shame, had totally forgotten about this very important detail.

Darien set down their bags by the stairs and walked left through the foyer. The living room. The dining room. And finally, into the kitchen.

She trailed behind him, minding where she was placing her feet. Her throat tightened as she watched him quarrel in silence with the reality that his home had been invaded. Trashed. Disrespected.

Jack was digging around in the cupboards under the sink. He found a box of trash bags and ripped one from the roll.

"Pass me one too, please," Arthur requested. Jack handed him the one in his fist and retrieved another, his face grave, as Lace walked by with a broom and dustpan and began to sweep the floor.

Eyes a shining black, Darien used his sixth sense to pick apart the mess with careful attention to detail. Loren knew exactly what he was doing as he stepped up to the stainless steel fridge, his frown deepening, and trailed the tips of his fingers across the top edge.

That was where the little Hob had sat every day. Behind those cereal boxes that were now tipped over. Different types of cereal had been spilled across the floor among shards of glass, shattered dishes, and broken bits of furniture.

Darien was still touching that spot on the fridge when he said quietly, "He hung on here." Loren had the feeling he hadn't meant to say it out loud.

Everyone froze. Jack and Arthur paused cleaning up. Lace's broom stilled mid-sweep.

He dropped his hand, his jaw flexing.

Loren's eyes welled with tears. She tried to see what he saw, but there was nothing there that stood out to mortal eyes. Familiar Spirits did not have fingerprints, so whatever Darien was looking at must be streaks of color. Evidence that an innocent creature had clung to the fridge while some awful person who had no right to touch him had ripped him off, prying his fingers free with force, and stuffed him into a bag.

She hated them for doing this. For taking Mortifer. For wrecking the house that had become her home. For causing that look of unbearable agony on Darien's face. *Hated* them. She had never been the type to wish death on anyone, no matter who they were or what they'd done, but in that moment she wanted nothing more than for whoever had done this to be brought to justice. Even if justice was delivered in the form of a bullet or a blade. In a house of Darkslayers, there was no shortage of those.

From the look in Darien's eyes, his expression no longer pained but fierce with determination, he'd see it done.

"I'll check the rest of the house," he said without looking at anyone. Behind them, the others quietly resumed cleaning. "I want to make sure everything's clear before I'll feel comfortable leaving you by yourself for any length of time." It took Loren a moment to realize that he was talking to her.

"You're leaving?"

"I just meant separate rooms," he clarified.

She blinked, because it still wasn't very clear to her. Did he simply mean separate rooms while they went about their day to day lives, such as when she was upstairs and he was downstairs, or would they be sleeping separately now?

Her throat constricted. She knew what they both needed right now was some personal space, but she hadn't thought this far ahead in detail. To what their lives might look like the minute they made it back home. Things weren't *normal* anymore—but they never really had been, had they? There were harsh realities, old and new, that they had to come to terms with, the biggest being her mortality. She could no longer pretend that she had forever with Darien, and neither could he. Weeks or months if she was lucky. Days if she wasn't.

Darien added quietly, "I know you're tired and probably want to shower." He still wasn't looking at her.

She swallowed the lump in her throat. "I can help, too." But she was drained, and she knew, when his eyes finally slid to hers, that he could see it on her face. Sleep was calling to her—*proper* sleep. Her mortal body could only handle so much. At any point in time, the Widow's prediction could come true, and her heart could permanently stop. She had to survive long enough to make sure Darien's wouldn't, and sleep was exactly the thing her body needed right now.

Darien said, "Let's see how you feel after your shower."

She went with him as he checked the rest of the house. Thoroughly. No corner or closet was forgotten. She saw rooms she had never seen before. Hidden passageways that ran from one fireplace to another; from the laundry room cupboard to the storage room. There weren't many of those, but she never would've guessed they were there.

The house was clear. The majority of the damage had been done to the ground floor, the rooms on the upper levels mostly untouched. A small blessing.

Now, Loren watched from the top of the stairs as Darien crossed the foyer down below, his pounding boots smashing glass into smaller slivers, and returned to the kitchen to help the others.

She made her way to her old room to shower, leaving Darien's free for him if he came back up—and in case he really was serious about staying in separate rooms. Even if he wasn't, he probably wanted to clean up, too. Traveling could make a person feel so dirty, and neither of them had showered since leaving Yveswich.

After unpacking her bag, she hopped in the walk-in shower she hadn't used in months, meticulously scrubbed herself from head to toes, and removed the bandages on her back. The ointment Darien had used on her at the hospital must have been enhanced with venefican magic, most of the wounds already healed with minimal scarring.

It felt strange to be back in her old suite. Ever since her twentieth birthday, she had spent every night, apart from when she was at the academy, in Darien's bed. The first time they'd made love was the last night she had slept in *this* bed. The one with the cream and teal pillows.

She stared at it now, her body wrapped in a fluffy white towel, hair dripping water down her back—and shivered.

This was not where she wanted to be.

Boots pounded in the hall.

Darien appeared in the doorway, one hand gripping the frame, the other squeezing the handle.

He stared at her.

She stared at him.

His mouth opened. Shut. Opened again. "I...am at a complete loss for words right now."

Okay, so she'd misunderstood him. That was her bad—she'd fix it. "I was just having a shower—"

"In *here?*" He looked like she had kicked him in the nuts. "Does that mean you're sleeping in here, too?" His hand—the broken one—gripped the handle tighter. She knew that simple action was causing him a great deal of pain, and yet he seemed to embrace it. Seek it.

His pupils flared. Even from this far away, she could see them swell.

She tightened the towel under her arms. "Darien, I just—"

"Never mind." He pushed off the doorframe and backed into the hall. "Whatever. It's whatever you want, baby. You want to sleep in your old room, that's fine. I'm here if you need me." He stalked off before she could reply.

She stood there, stunned. A couple of minutes later, she heard the shower come on in his bathroom.

She drifted into the hall, debating what to do. Maybe it was psychological, but she was suddenly shivering, the house drafty compared to before.

Singer crept out of her shadow and came to stand at her side.

"He's mad," Loren whispered.

Singer let out a low whine, his ears flattening back.

A dark shape appeared in her periphery.

Bandit was poking his head out of Darien's doorway. *'Of course he's mad!'* the dog whisper-shouted. *'You've kicked us out!'*

She swallowed. Great, now *he* was mad at her, too. "I kicked *myself* out," she corrected.

Bandit chuffed and disappeared into Darien's room—

BANG.

Loren blinked. Did...did Bandit just *slam the door?*

She sighed and slumped against the wall. This wasn't going well.

For a few minutes, she stood there, debating if she should try talking to him, but Darien wasn't in a good headspace. He was upset, not just because of her decision to shower in her old bathroom, she knew, but because of his house, too, and Mortifer being taken. He hadn't even given her a chance to explain herself. The last thing she wanted was to try to talk to him and wind up having a worse argument.

She drifted into her bedroom and left the door open an inch.

This would be one horribly long night. But she needed sleep—desperately. Darien wanted her to start caring more about herself, and her tattoos glowing on her arm confirmed that was exactly what she should do.

She would try this again tomorrow.

THE HOUR he spent beneath the stream of water—scalding hot—cleared his head and made him realize he was being a total fucking asshole.

Darien came out of the bathroom—hair wet, skin damp. He chucked the towel he'd wrapped around his waist onto the bed and grabbed a pair of boxers, gray sweatpants, and a white shirt from the dresser. As soon as he had them on, he was out the door and walking down the hall.

He paused in front of Loren's room—her *old* room. The door wasn't fully shut, the glow from the lamp on her end table slanting through the crack.

She was already asleep.

"Fuck my life," he muttered.

He stood there for a few minutes, debating what to do. There was no way he'd wake her up, not when she was this exhausted, but the last thing he wanted was to sleep in his bed—*their* bed—without her.

So he lay down on the floor.

A few seconds passed before he heard the padding of approaching paws.

Bandit appeared by his head. He peered down at him with crimson eyes, his chops floppy from this angle. *'Are you a dog now?'* He cocked his head.

'Well, I'm in the doghouse, so yeah, I guess.'

Bandit tilted his head again before turning and leaving. Probably to seize the rare opportunity to sprawl across the king-size bed by himself.

'Bye,' Darien called. *'Thanks for the support.'*

But the dog came back a moment later, a pillow in his mouth.

He dropped it on Darien's face before pancaking on the floor beside him, paws kicking him in the side and snagging his shirt.

Darien grabbed the pillow and stuffed it under his head. *'Thanks.'*

'Do you think she'll stay mad at us for long?'

'I hope not.' If she did, he really would get on his knees this time. Crawl. Beg. He had no shame when it came to her.

He turned his head and looked at her closed door. He was so close to it, he'd roll right into it during the night if he wasn't careful.

'Goodnight,' Bandit slurred, already half-asleep.

Darien shut his eyes, hoping tomorrow would be better. *'Night, Bandit.'*

57

THE DUCHESS
YVESWICH, STATE OF KER

Travis woke up slowly. gradually. He had never been a morning person, and although he could remember shit-all about anything, he had the feeling *awake* was the last thing he wanted to be right now.

Voices. He was hearing voices. Male and female.

Was that Dominic? And Dallas?

And Malakai *fucking* Delaney?

Yeah, he'd keep sleeping, thank you very much...

He groaned and rolled onto his stomach, his bare feet catching in starchy sheets that smelled fresh and clean.

"Rise and shine," chimed a pleasant female voice. It was Jewels.

Wait—

Jewels was in his room?

Was he dreaming? Had he died and gone to the Fifth Dimension?

He squinted his eyes open and found her standing beside his bed.

Not really *his* bed, though. It was one of two in a room at the Duchess Hotel, an opulent waterfront building that was so flooded with panicking evacuees, the only room they'd been able to secure—with painstaking difficulty and hours wasted in a chaotic line-up—was this one. A single room with two beds.

It was all coming back to him now. The rock, paper, scissors match he'd won against Malakai and Max that had allowed him to sleep by himself in one of two beds. Jewels and Aspen had taken the other, while everyone else had claimed they were fine sleeping on the floor. Hardly an inch of space had remained by the time everyone got comfortable, and Travis might have stepped on Delaney on his way to the bathroom during the night. It might've been on purpose. Oops.

Now, Jewels was coaxing him awake with the promise of food and new clothes, a bag in one hand, a takeout container of what smelled like hot breakfast in the other. She wore faded jeans and a tight white tee that drew his attention to her pierced nipples. The shirt was another tacky souvenir made for Yveswich tourists—

Oh gods, he was stuck in Yveswich. And if this city didn't kill him, Roman would.

He shut his eyes again. He was in hell. And he was not ready to face this nightmare again.

But Jewels said, "Come on, Travis, wake up." She spoke to him in a far sweeter tone than the one she reserved for Malakai. "You need to eat. I can guard it for only so long before Malakai scarfs it down."

A grunt came from somewhere nearby. A gulping swallow. "Give it here, I already ate all of mine," Malakai said.

Fuck this asshole.

Travis rolled onto his back—

"Okay, whoa! Pause!" Jewels exclaimed. He froze, confused. "Stay there, don't—don't move. Whatever you do, do *not* move." Was there a spider on him, or something?

He squinted up at her, confused, to see that she was shielding her eyes with a hand.

"Umm. Hmm." She threw the bag of clothes on his crotch so suddenly, he flinched. "There. Those are yours. You might want to get dressed," she stammered, her cheeks powder-pink.

Travis lifted his head off the pillow. Peered down the length of the naked upper half of his body...and saw the reason for all the stammering and blushing.

His cock was hard. With no clean clothes to wear, his suit destroyed, he'd gone to bed with nothing on but a white towel wrapped around his waist. Now, it was slipping off, along with the sheets and the duvet. His right leg was fully exposed, the shape of his erection showing through the towel.

He grabbed the bag of clothes and held it there. Groaned and dragged a hand down his face, pulling on his eyelids.

The room was crowded. Everyone was flapping their gums and stuffing their faces and being annoying. He was in hell and he couldn't even relieve any stress by jacking off in private.

"I'll put your food over here," Jewels said. She set down the takeout container on the dresser by the TV, where a bunch of their weapons had been lain out to dry. "Malakai won't touch it."

"Don't make promises for me," Delaney said.

Travis groaned again.

This...sucked. It sucked.

He secured the towel around his waist before standing. Using the bag of clothes as a privacy shield, his cock still pitching a tent, he walked to the bathroom, passing Jewels on the way. She pivoted in place, fighting to look anywhere *but* at him. He shut the bathroom door and locked it.

There was more than just clothes in the bag. Jewels, Aspen, Dallas, and Max had gone for a supply run, grabbing everything from socks and underwear to toothpaste and deodorant. They'd fully stocked up. The clothes were plain—basic t-shirts and long-sleeves, jeans, winter jackets, boots—but they were functional and they fit.

Now that he was dressed, he sat on the end of his messy bed and stuffed his face. He was so hungry, he hardly chewed the eggs, hash browns, sausage, and toast, chasing whole chunks of them with gulps of orange juice. Apparently there were still a lot of volunteers in the city who were helping out—people who worked for the police, the fire department, and the military. Now, if only those same people could get them *out* of here...

He was almost finished when he realized that Jewels was watching him. She was sitting in a chair by the window that overlooked the stormy ocean. It must be daylight in the real world, because it wasn't totally pitch black out there. It was...gray. That was good. And they could still breathe— another thing that was good.

"Thanks," Travis said to her as he popped the last bite of breakfast sausage into his mouth.

She nodded and dipped her focus to the food she was picking at.

Travis frowned. She wasn't still bothered by the whole erection thing, was she? He didn't think it was that big of a deal.

He dropped his plastic fork in the container and placed it beside him on the mattress. "So," he began, addressing the group. Well, *his* part of the group. Maya and that Magenta girl didn't seem interested in listening to or talking to anyone. "What's the plan?"

"None of your concern, that's what," Malakai snipped.

Travis grabbed his fork again. "See this fork?" He held it up. "I'm going to stab your eyes out with it."

Malakai flashed him an unfriendly grin—a baring of teeth, really.

Travis bared his in answer.

Max said, "The military's set up camp three blocks from here. Dallas will be going there to see if she can find her dad. And I'm going with her. Anyone who wants to come with feel free, but anyone who doesn't should stay right here in this room. We can't afford to lose track of each other." He gave his sister an extra long stare that she didn't return.

"Okay, and what if Operation Find Roark fails?" Travis asked.

They didn't have an answer for that.

"I'm hoping it won't," Dallas said. "He's also the highest ranking officer in the Fleet—I can't imagine he'd be anywhere but here right now." She slugged the last of her orange juice.

"He's the best plan we have," Max said. "So until finding him is no longer an option, I'd like to hang onto my little bit of hope for as long as possible, if that's all right with everyone."

"I think we should find a way to get a hold of Darien," Travis said.

"The fuck's Darien going to do?" Malakai scoffed. He was stuffing his face again—Aspen's scraps this time.

"He'd have a better plan than your dumb ass."

He scoffed again. "Sure, because the boat was such a brilliant idea."

"It actually was, and if you hadn't held us up with your bitching about which motorcycles we should steal—"

"Enough!" Jewels exclaimed, flinging her fork down. "It's way too early for this. Maybe you guys and your childish *bullshit* is the reason my heart failed."

"Ouch," Travis muttered at the same time as Malakai.

They glared at each other.

"We *should* find a way to contact the others," Max said. "Even if it's just so we can talk to them one last time." The weight of that reality set in, silencing the crowded room for a long moment.

Malakai was the first to break the quiet. "You guys can go ahead and die, but I'm not. And even if I do, mark my words, my ghost will haunt this stupid city until the end of time."

Dominic said, "While you guys are gone, I think I'll speak with reception and see if they can move us to a bigger room."

"What about going back to Roman's?" Aspen suggested. They had come close to going to Roman's house in Ardesia before they'd managed to secure this room. It had taken so many hours to get their key, Travis was about ready to sleep in the lobby with the other evacuees who'd had that same idea. The place was short-staffed—understandably. The city was collapsing like a house of cards, so there weren't many people outside of healthcare and law enforcement who were willing to volunteer, let alone go to work.

"That's an option," Dominic said, "but in case it doesn't end up happening, I'd rather we get a place with more beds."

Max added, "We shouldn't count on Roman's place being secure until we know for sure that it is. We'd be stupid to stay there if Don still has his eye on it."

Travis's brow furrowed. "You really think my dad's still in the city?"

Max shrugged. "Better to be safe than sorry." Yeah, he was right. If Don was still here... Travis would be in deep shit if he found out his middle son was trapped in the same city as him. He'd probably turn chasing him into some sick game to pass the last of their time, and Travis would rather not play.

Nobody said much else after that. Maya and the pink one still weren't talking—they hadn't this whole time—but the room quieted down for a few minutes as everyone finished eating and prepared to face the day.

Step one: military camp.

Step two: get a bigger room.

Step three: find phones.

It all sounded so easy, but something told Travis it would be the opposite.

58

HELL'S GATE
ANGELTHENE, STATE OF WITHEREDGE

Darien awoke to the pearly light of a clear dawn streaming through the windows.

He was at Hell's Gate. The house was quiet, and he was...on the floor? How the hell had he ended up here?

Memories from the previous night slowly returned to him, and so did his emotions. He preferred being numb.

Eyes shut, he rolled onto his stomach and burrowed deeper into the pillow. He wasn't ready to wake up yet.

Sometime later, he heard footfall descending the stairs from the floor above. Whoever it was paused when they reached the landing.

"What are you doing?"

Darien lifted his head off the pillow.

Lace stood in her pajamas by the staircase. Staring at him in utter bewilderment. When he didn't respond, she raised her brows higher in question.

"Sleeping," he answered. He lay his head on the pillow and shut his eyes against the daylight, sliding an arm up to block it. "What's it look like?"

"Did she kick you out?"

"No," he mumbled into his arm.

"Then what are you doing out here?"

What *was* he doing out here? Being a possessive freak? Hurting his back? Sleeping poorly? All of the above. He settled with: "Guarding."

A pause. And then: "You're insane."

He grunted in agreement. He really was insane. And in love. Insanely in love. With a girl who currently hated his guts. Ah, life was good. "I'm also hungry," he said.

"Is that a hint?"

"Only if you were already planning on cooking."

She hummed. "What do you want?"

"Whatever you're making."

"Beans and liver, then."

He grimaced. "Eww."

Lace gave a quiet, husky laugh. "Bacon, eggs, and toast?"

"That's better."

She laughed again. "I'll start right away."

He tried to drift off again after she left, but now that he remembered why he was on the floor—in the fucking *doghouse,* and not even with the dog anymore, Bandit gone—there was no chance he'd be able to sleep again.

Loren, on the other hand, was still sleeping peacefully, her quiet breathing drifting through the bedroom door. That and her heartbeat created a lullaby he loved to listen to, but right now it didn't help him sleep. It just made his heart hurt even worse.

When he smelled bacon sizzling on the stove, he got up and went downstairs, his stomach growling too loudly to ignore.

Bandit was already in the kitchen, the beggar. Staring up at Lace with his tongue out as she flitted about the room they had managed to return to a liveable state after endless sweeping and tidying.

Lace had gone all out. Pans of fried and scrambled eggs, bacon, and breakfast sausage had been laid out on the stove and counters, along with plates of toast, bagels, and pancakes; bowls of fresh-cut fruit; jars of peanut butter and jam; maple syrup; and tubs of cream cheese. She'd even found a bag of shredded hash browns and had cooked those, too.

"Are you trying to get a raise?" Darien asked her as he made his way to the island. "Because it's working."

"Here." She slid a plate overflowing with food before him. "Arthur's just waking up. He should be down shortly." She poured a glass of orange juice and set it down by his plate.

As if he had been summoned, the old man drifted into the kitchen in a housecoat and slippers, his wrinkled face still battered from his run-in with Shadowmasters. Darien couldn't wait to get a hold of those assholes and settle the score. Unless they were trapped in Yveswich and were dying a slow death in there, in which case good riddance.

"Good morning," Arthur greeted them.

"Morning," they responded in unison.

He headed for the cupboard where they kept the tea. "Can I interest either of you in a cup of tea?"

"I think I need something stronger," Darien said.

"Like whiskey?" Arthur joked as he filled the kettle with water.

"I was thinking coffee, but that might work."

"I just put a pot on," Lace said as she finished dishing up another plate. Darien assumed she was making that plate for herself when she said, "I'll be right back, I'm taking this to Jack." She grabbed a fork and a stack of napkins and left for the stairs.

"Loren's still sleeping, is she?" Arthur asked as he put the kettle on the stove and turned the burner on.

"She was very tired." He took a bite of bacon—and nearly groaned. Damn, that tasted good. He shoved the rest in his mouth and started on a second piece.

"I'm sure she'll be around soon." He grabbed two mugs from the cupboard. "Coffee's finished brewing."

Darien wiped his hands on his napkin and made to stand. "I can get it."

But Arthur was already pouring, so Darien stayed where he was, and soon Arthur was stirring in cream and sugar and placing the mug before him.

"Thank you."

"You're welcome."

A damp nose nudged the hand he had resting on his thigh.

Singer was staring up at him. That the dog was awake was a good sign. Loren's absence was beginning to remind him of her time in a coma, but Singer's presence put him at ease.

He scratched behind the dog's floppy ears. "Hey, buddy," he said quietly as the dog sat down. "Sleep well?"

Singer swished his tail.

"Is your girl still mad at me?"

He merely wagged his tail again, though the action was less energetic than before. What he wouldn't give for this dog to talk.

When Lace came back and slid onto the stool beside him with a plate of food, Darien asked her, "Have you heard from the others?"

"Not yet." She sighed. "I tried calling Ivy, but it went straight to her voicemail. I tried Roman, Max, Tanner, Travis, Kylar, Asp..."

His brow creased. "Nothing from any of them?"

She shook her head and bit into her toast.

"What about tracking them?" Arthur asked.

She swallowed before responding. "I tried. I couldn't see them. You might have to do it," she said to Darien. He would—right away. Depending on where they were, they might be too far for Lace, who had less experience with tracking than Darien, to pick up on.

"Give them time," Arthur said as he claimed the spot beside Lace, considerably less food and no meat on his plate. "Cell service was already terrible when we were there. It might have spread beyond the city. Let's not jump to the worst conclusions just yet." He sipped his tea.

They ate in silence for several minutes while Bandit terrorized Cinder in the living room. Sprawled across the back of the couch in a stream of sunlight, the cat looked down at Bandit with disdain. A fluffy queen on her throne.

When he bounced onto the couch, she hissed and swiped a paw, sending him bounding backward.

'Take a hint, or you're going to get scratched,' Darien warned.

To Lace he said, "How's Jack?"

"Sulking," she replied. "And rightfully so."

He *did* have every right to sulk. Darien felt like a jerk for taking him away from Ivy, but Ivy had wanted him safe. And after everything Darien had done behind his sister's back, he wasn't about to get on her bad side even further by siding with her husband. He owed his loyalty to Ivy first.

The whole time Darien sat at the island, Singer didn't move from his spot by his leg, the dog's head resting against his knee. At least *he* still seemed to like him, even if Loren didn't. He'd prefer the one without fur, but considering a Familiar was closely bonded with their person, he took it as a reassurance that he could still earn Loren's forgiveness.

Turned out, earning her forgiveness would take longer than he thought. Because Loren slept through breakfast, lunch. Hours dragged by, and still she slept.

He didn't disturb her. But he might have said more than one prayer to multiple gods that her inability to wake up didn't mean anything bad.

59

THE WANDERER
ARBOR, STATE OF KER

The beds at the Wanderer were lumpy and uncomfortable, the blankets scratchy. But Shay slept like she had never slept before.

By the time she awoke, it was half past one in the afternoon.

She lifted her head and scanned the dark, quiet room. Outside, the sun was stifled with clouds. Normal clouds whose only threat was a sprinkling of rain.

Paxton was still asleep. Roman wasn't in here, the bathroom empty and unlit.

'He went to find food,' said a quiet female voice.

It took Shay a moment to locate Sayagul. The dragon was cozied up with Paxton, her shining green eyes barely visible beneath the blanket she was tucked under.

"Do they offer a complimentary breakfast here?" Shay whispered.

'No.' Not surprising, given everything else about this place. *'He had to cross the street. He asked me to keep watch.'*

Shay rubbed her gritty eyes. "How did Roman do during the night?" she asked around a yawn. She'd worried about him when they had gone to bed without a lamp on. There was only one light in here, and it was affixed to the ceiling. None of them, not even Roman, had wanted to sleep with it on.

'He slept well,' Sayagul replied. *'Nugget was a huge help.'*

Nugget was a rare Familiar who glowed white in the dark, but the seal pup usually dimmed his light while he slept. Last night, he'd kept himself bright for Roman's benefit, glowing softly beside Shay like a fuzzy moon. He was still there now, looking content to sleep forever.

"I'm glad," Shay whispered.

Sayagul squinted her slitted eyes in a dragon's attempt at a smile before shutting them.

Roman came back a few minutes later with takeout from a restaurant that served all-day breakfast. He walked in, rain sparkling in his wind-swept hair. His charcoal shirt was—obviously—ripped, his black jeans tattered too, chains hanging from pockets.

He hesitated when he saw that she was awake. "Morning." It sounded more like a blunt statement than a greeting. He shut the door.

"Morning," she replied. She said it in the same flat tone—she couldn't help it.

He placed the drink tray and paper bag of takeout on the little table by the window and untied his combat boots. "Hungry?"

"Starving."

He took off his boots and waved her over.

They sat at the table together and ate in complete silence while Pax continued to sleep. Shay expected him to rouse from the tantalizing smell of bacon, but he just kept sleeping. Roman checked on him often, still concerned about what'd happened yesterday. They ended up putting his portion of the food in the mini fridge, where Itzel had taken up temporary residence. The Hob almost gave Roman a heart attack when he opened the fridge and found her in there peering out at him.

"Itzel!" he hissed. She hissed back. *"Move."* She hissed again. "Stop being a menace!" he whisper-shouted. "I need to put this in there."

Hsssssss! Like an angry feline, she swiped a tiny hand at him and backed herself into a corner. A few more seconds of hissing and whisper-shouting, and he managed to slide the container in and shut the door with her still in there, trapped between the container and the back of the fridge. A moment later, Shay heard the container thunk against the door as the Hob pushed it away with another muffled hiss. *Thunk thunk thunk. Hiss hiss hiss.* It sounded like she was punching or kicking it.

Shay fought a smile. "You said you rescued her?"

He stood, dragging a frustrated hand through his hair. "I'm regretting it."

"You might want to check on her previous owner. They might have been the one in need of rescuing."

He sighed. "I would, but I decapitated him."

Shay blinked.

Hours passed, and Paxton still slept. Shay lay down on her bed and watched a tacky vampire soap opera while Roman took a shower, and when he came out she kept her focus glued to the television as he walked shirtless in front of it, nothing but grey sweatpants on.

She snuck a peek at him as he organized the contents of his bags and sifted through the pockets of the jeans he had been wearing before his shower. The scars and tattoos on his back stood out in the silvery light slanting in through the blinds. While his arms and hands were covered in ink, only one side of his back was tattooed, the bare skin on the right side of his spine making the hundreds of raised scars marring his flesh much more noticeable.

He caught her looking when he straightened, cigarette in his teeth.

She looked away in a flash.

He took the cig out of his mouth. "We need to talk." His deep, husky voice skittered across her every bone. It was the first thing he'd said to her in a while, and it didn't exactly sound promising.

Ugh, was someone she wasn't even dating about to break up with her? *Again?* That would be just her luck, wouldn't it?

"About?" she muttered without looking at him. Goddamn him and that perfectly honed body of his. Seeing him half-naked like this only served as a reminder that she'd had him *completely* naked not long ago, the hard lines of his lean muscle pressing against her. They'd breathed each other's air for hours, their bodies moving as one in the pool and on the bed in the motel room. Having sex with Roman for just one night had done the exact opposite of sate her appetite for him. That one taste had her starving—*feral* —for more. To learn what else he could do with those hands and that body.

She had never been fucked by anyone the way Roman Devlin fucked. And a part of her wished she had stayed completely oblivious to his talents. You couldn't miss something if you had never experienced it.

He merely walked out the door, leaving it partially open in a clear invitation.

She sighed. This wouldn't be good. She could feel it.

She got out of bed. It wasn't until she was standing that she remembered she still had to buy clothes. And shoes. She left the room in bare feet, the pavement refreshingly cool and speckled with rain. A chill wind brought a rush of goosebumps to her skin and billowed the shirt that barely covered her ass.

Roman stood by the water-streaked car—smoking, shirtless, and brooding, those gray sweatpants hanging scandalously low on his hips. Gods, he was hot. She couldn't get over him. Someone should come arrest him, because this was criminal.

She crossed her arms, willing her eyes to have some dignity and not dip downward. "What?" she asked him as he pocketed his lighter.

He stared at her for a moment, as if she were a book he was having trouble understanding. Smoke curled toward the sky from the cigarette he held loosely at his side.

"I want you to leave," he said.

Shay blinked and drew back her head. "Excuse me?"

He took a drag, then rolled his shoulders, muscles rippling, and blew a stream of smoke to his left.

The wind gusted it right back in her face, and she waved a hand to clear it. "Care to elaborate—" She coughed. "—Or am I just being booted to the curb like trash?"

"You're not being booted, and you're not trash. But you're not safe with us—"

She rolled her eyes. "Oh fuck off, Roman." His brows went up. "I'm far safer than I was in Yveswich."

"Okay, which leads me to my next point."

"I'm listening."

"You're not in Yveswich anymore, pup. You can leave. Start a new life. This—a fresh start—is what you've always wanted. Right?"

"So?"

"So it's a blessing for you, in a way. Athene has no clue where you are. For all she knows, you could be dead. Take advantage of this and fucking *run.*" He gestured to the road like it was that easy.

"Run," she scoffed. "Yeah, okay. Sure. Are you going to take your own advice?" He merely stared at her with a cold expression she couldn't read. He was the wolf again, the curtain on his stage closed. She no longer had a back-stage pass to see the real side of him—and that hurt. She explained, "You're out now, too. Don's empire of shit is *burning,* Roman. It's *burning.* You can finally get away—"

"I *can't,*" he snapped. "He'll hunt Paxton to the ends of the earth, and I can't have you with me while that's happening."

"So you're doing all this—pushing me away—to keep me safe?" She wasn't flattered—she was pissed. She could handle herself, and Roman deserved to be free as much as she did.

"Don't be dumb, Shay. I'm begging you. Don't forfeit your life for a fling."

She tightened her crossed arms, fingers curling in her shirt—*his* shirt. She would rip the stupid thing off right now if it didn't mean she'd be standing here stark naked. "That's not really what happened between us, and you know it."

He stared at her with dead eyes. There was no spark in them, no emotion, not a single fleck of gold. "It was a fling, pup. A one-night stand. I've had plenty of those—I'd like to think I can recognize them at this point."

Ouch.

He relit the cigarette that had gone out in the wind.

"A three-night stand," she corrected.

He squinted at her, smoke rippling out of his mouth. "What?"

"We had five days alone together, and I think we fucked for three."

He dragged his red-hot stare down her body, watching far too closely as his shirt undulated against her in the wind, the fabric switching between pulling taut and blowing up like a sail. "All right, a three-night stand. I think I've had a few of those, too." Ouch again. Two points for Roman.

She watched him as he smoked. He watched her as she glared. But while she felt like a horribly open book whose back cover was in danger of flashing itself at the whole town if the wind decided to change directions, he was perfectly closed off. The emotionally unavailable Wolf of the Hollow she'd met in the Onyx Skull.

"If you're worried about money, I can help you out," he said.

"I'm not worried about money!" she retorted. But it was a lie. She had no money, and he knew it. Now was literally the worst time for her to start over. All her belongings were still in Yveswich, including the last of the money she had stolen from Roman. Her bank account was monitored by Athene, so instead of depositing the cash she'd received from selling the Hound on the Black Market, she'd had to keep the bills.

Roman stared at her, vexed. "Shay—"

"You're *trying* to be an asshole," she accused. "I can tell. You're weaponizing your words because you're afraid for me, but you don't have to be afraid. I can handle myself—"

"I want you gone."

"And I want you to put on a shirt."

Roman blinked.

"Everyone's staring at you." And by *everyone* she meant the two young women—a wolf and a witch—exiting their car across the street.

Shay wanted to poke their eyeballs out. Pull their hair for staring at... what was he, *her* man? Nope, they were hardly even friends, and they certainly weren't together—but that didn't stop her from wanting to gouge straying eyeballs out for daring to look at the work of art that was Roman Devlin.

'Truth or lie?' Roman had asked her at Motel 58 as he'd spun her around in the water. *'I think I'm falling for you.'*

Truth or lie? She was a *fucking* idiot.

"How about I take that shirt back, then?" he threatened.

"Then I'd be naked," she said without looking at him.

"Exactly." What was he trying to be, funny? Cute? Flirty? She wasn't in the mood. And besides, he'd already wrecked his chance by telling her *We need to talk* and *I want you gone.* She'd take Roman 'Asshole' Devlin any day, thanks. At least that one was easier to hate than Roman 'Loveable' Devlin.

Slightly easier.

When Roman shifted to the right, catching her attention, she realized she was still shooting daggers at the giggling women. They were disappearing into the restaurant, the witch throwing one last glance of appreciation over her shoulder.

Shay balled her hands into fists.

Roman was studying her with narrowed eyes. "Are you jealous?"

She huffed. "Of course not." She inhaled, long and deep, and wiped every last trace of jealousy off her face. "After all, what we had was just a fling, right?" she crooned, batting her lashes. "We don't *really* like each other. Right, Shadows?" She turned on a heel and walked into the motel room.

Just before she shut the door behind her, she could have sworn she heard Roman mutter, "Fuck."

60

SOUTH COASTAL DISTRICT
YVESWICH, STATE OF KER

Roark had been discharged. Pulled from Yveswich and replaced by another commanding officer.

The reality of this was still setting in as Max wove through the crowds of people protesting in the South Coastal District. He was having trouble catching up to Dallas, who'd turned and fled at a near run after receiving the news they'd waited over two hours for. Officers of lower rank had insisted on confirming her identity and speaking to their higher-ups before divulging any information, and so they'd stood there. Waiting. Pissing away time they didn't have, only to receive the news they didn't want.

They were on their own. Roark, for whatever reason, was gone, and they had no way of reaching him. Dallas had asked the authorities to pass along the message that his daughter was trapped here, but whether he really received it—and *when* he received it—was out of their hands.

The coast was one of the only areas in the city that wasn't smothered by night-like darkness. Instead, it was gray here, as if the sky were merely overcast with the threat of a bad storm. While other districts were slowly but steadily being buried under the blinding, monster-infested blackness of the Void, they could still see, breathe. Right now, this was the safest place in the city—until nightfall, anyway. There were no monsters here, and the military had set up camp several blocks from the Duchess.

Max hurried to catch up to Dallas. "What do you think that means?" Max called. It was still raining, the air cold enough to see his breath. "Dallas?" But Dallas didn't turn. He elbowed his way through another group of warlocks and witches and pried apart two wolves, who cussed him out, to get to her. "Dallas, what do you think that means?"

They made it to a stretch of the road that was thinner with people before she stopped and faced him. "I don't know," she admitted, swiping at her face.

Max gaped. Was she crying?

"I don't know," she said again, sniffling. "And I'm torn."

He took a step closer, but he didn't touch her. He knew better than to crowd her when she was upset like this. Dallas was the type of girl who had trouble processing her emotions and liked her space because of it. "It's okay, we'll figure something out. We've still got time—"

She shook her head. "I'm not talking about that. I mean, this whole situation sucks, yeah, but I meant my dad. I'm torn because of him. I've spent most of my life thinking he hated my guts, and then he sent a helicopter for me—" She roughly wiped at her eyes again, pulling the lids toward her temples. "I want to talk to him," she confessed around a pained gasp, "and now I might never get the chance."

It had always been hard for Max to watch Dallas fight for her parents' approval. During the time they had dated, most of what she'd divulged to him about her shitty home life had come in the form of complaints and angry outbursts and a million different reasons why Roark and Taega deserved to be hated. She'd kept most everything else—everything but her anger—locked away. Bottled up.

That was why this was worse. Seeing her struggling—especially so out in the open like this—to understand why her father, who had been nothing but unkind to her for twenty years, had bothered to send a group of soldiers to find her. And now she was trapped here, he was gone, and she may die never knowing why. Never understanding him.

Max didn't understand him, either. The few interactions he'd had with his girlfriend's dad had been nothing short of terrible, and yet Roark had surprised him—all of them—by pulling through in such huge ways. The warning he'd given them about the forcefield, the way he'd ordered it taken down when Darien had called him in distress, the helicopter he'd sent for Dallas.

What the hell was his deal? Why had he seemed to hate his daughters so much, and why was he suddenly changing his tune? The Roark that Max thought he knew wouldn't have warned them, wouldn't have ordered the forcefield taken down when Darien had called—and, as bad as it made him, he probably wouldn't have sent a helicopter for the daughter he'd all but shunned for twenty years, either.

But this wasn't the first time Max had caught a glimpse of another side of Roark. The first time was when Loren was in a coma, and he had gone to the hospital to speak with Darien.

Had seeing Loren in the hospital like that changed him? Made him want to be a better parent? It was the only thing that made sense.

Dallas was staring into the distance. Raindrops rolled down her face, disguising whether she was still crying.

They needed to find a phone. Needed to contact Roark. Darien.

Parts of the city still had power. The lights in this district were working, and he spotted a few people in the crowds using cell phones. Until the power went out, which wouldn't happen in full while the Control Tower was functioning, they still had a chance. If it stopped working...

Well, by then, it'd be too late for them.

"I'm sorry," Max said hoarsely.

Dallas looked up at him, blinking rapidly as a fat raindrop got caught in her eyelashes. "Why?"

"For getting you into this mess."

The harsh expression on her face thawed. "You didn't get me into anything, Max. I'm an adult, I'm capable of making my own decisions. And I chose to stay with you." She crossed her arms, shielding herself against the chill wind gusting down the street, and analyzed the black cloud billowing against the curve of the forcefield. "I don't regret staying," she whispered, so quietly he barely heard her. "If I had gone back to Angelthene and found out you were still trapped in here... *That* is what I would have regretted."

He swallowed. "Dal, if you die in here—"

"Then at least I'll be with you," she said firmly. Her silver-ringed eyes slid back to him. "I've never been afraid of death, Max. Life scares me far more." At that, his brows pulled together, but he didn't have a chance to ask her to explain.

Because he caught sight of Travis and Jewels rushing this way.

Max was about to ask them what was happening when Travis skidded to a stop and panted, "We have a problem."

TRAVIS PEERED through a window of the hotel lobby as police officers and MPU agents moved about the area they had sectioned off with caution tape.

Two dead bodies lay on the floor by the elevators. One was a female witch missing a huge chunk from her throat. The other was a male hellseher, his corpse riddled with bullet holes, black eyes bolted open in death.

The hellseher's mouth was the strangest thing about this. His lips were syrupy with blood that coated his chin and neck and puddled on the floor. The kind of shit you'd only see when a vampire or a werewolf committed murder—or simply fed, he supposed. The more uncivilized way. He might not have been top of his class, but it sure as hell looked like the hellseher had ripped the witch's throat out with his teeth.

Yuck.

"This some weird-ass zombie shit, or what?" Travis murmured. His forehead was pressed against the tinted glass, hand cupped over his eyes to see better.

Max, Dallas, Jewels, and Dominic were here too, all spying through the glass. They weren't the only people who were being nosy. The whole sidewalk in front of the Duchess was crowded, everyone vying for a glimpse of the macabre scene.

"What do you mean?" Jewels asked him.

"You ever watched a zombie show before? That's what this reminds me of." He pointed, accidentally tapping the glass with his finger and causing an officer to look over. "Doesn't it look like he bit her throat out to you?"

"I mean...yeah." Jewels cringed.

The automatic doors they'd shut off to keep the public out opened, an officer pushing them apart manually. "Alright, people, everyone clear out." He waved his hands at the dozens of people peering in the windows, including them. "There's nothing to see here."

"Nothing to see my ass," Travis muttered under his breath. But they stepped back, moving together down the sidewalk.

Dominic said, "I thought this was as bad as it could get, and now we have to watch out for lunatics like that guy." He gestured to the hotel with an upward tip of his unshaven chin. They couldn't go back in yet—not until the cops cleared the scene. Travis wanted to ask reception if he could use a phone, but they were shit out of luck for now.

"What happened?" Max asked the Angel. "Did you see anything?"

"I was standing there minding my own business when I heard screaming and gunfire. He apparently attacked the woman unprovoked. I got us a penthouse suite, by the way." He dug into his jacket pocket and took out a couple of card keys.

Thank gods. Now he shouldn't have to challenge Malakai and Max to a rock, paper, scissors duel again.

"It's like what happened at the hospital," said a female voice.

They turned and found a teenaged venefican girl smoking by the building, one foot propped against the wall at her back. The black liner on her eyes was smudged, her limp brown hair hanging over her shoulder in a messy braid.

"Pardon?" Max asked sharply. AKA: why are you eavesdropping?

"Didn't you guys hear?" She puffed on the cigarette she was too young to have purchased on her own. "Same thing happened at the hospital. A bunch of staff and patients were murdered."

Travis said, "I thought that was a monster." They had been there when it happened. He remembered hearing a roar.

A look of amusement flitted across her gaunt face. "Was it?" She lifted the cigarette to her chapped lips.

Max turned fully to face her. "What all do you know?" he demanded.

She was unfazed by his tone. "I have an aunt who works there as a laundry attendant. She said two of the patients and one member of the staff —all hellsehers—went loopy during one of the power outages and just started attacking. Their eyes went all black and crazy—"

Travis interrupted. "You do realize you're talking to hellsehers right now, right? I'm a hellseher, our eyes always *go black and crazy.*" Who did this chick think she was?

She shrugged. "I'm just telling you what I heard." She puffed on the cigarette that smelled like it was laced with something highly illegal.

The bodies they'd found in the hospital—ripped open as if an animal had attacked them. The blood all over the walls.

A wave of cold dread washed through Travis.

He looked over his shoulder at the hotel entrance. Two ambulances had pulled up along the curb, paramedics unloading stretchers—with police escorts.

Travis's frown deepened. The city was collapsing, and they could spare police escorts for something like this?

Max said, "What exactly do you mean by *black and crazy?* Did they look any different than this?" He blinked the Sight into place.

The witch tapped the ash off her cigarette. "My aunt said they had a fan of black lines around their eyes."

Travis shared a loaded glance with the others.

Black lines...

Like Venom users?

———

Max burst into the hotel room, startling Maya and Magenta, the girls watching television on one of the beds. Malakai and Aspen were lounging on the other.

"What's up?" Malakai drawled, scanning their group with a bored expression.

Blue sat in the chair by the window. Upon seeing the looks on their faces—in particular Dominic's—she unfurled to her feet.

But Max turned his focus on his sister. "I need you to tell me everything that happened with Onyx," he said. "Right. *Now.*"

61

THE DUCHESS
YVESWICH, STATE OF KER

It took Maya a while to explain everything. Max drilled her with questions for over an hour while the others listened intently, all of them sprawled across the beds, the floor, the chairs. They would move up to the penthouse later, once the crime scene in the lobby was cleared.

According to Maya, Onyx was a genetically modified hellseher with shadow powers similar to Darien, Roman, Malakai, and Travis. He could control shadow—bend it to his will. He could even black out an entire room or street if he so desired. He was extremely powerful.

And very dangerous.

Onyx had been transferred to a different facility before the other test subjects had staged the breakout that resulted in Maya coming to Yveswich. What had prompted the transfer was...concerning.

"He lost control," Maya was saying. "One day, he just...snapped. He killed twelve members of the staff and injured at least five others. Killed a few test subjects, too. The orderlies determined him too unstable to stay, so they made the decision to transfer him. They manacled and muzzled him, as if he were a rabid dog. I saw him from the window in my room the day they paraded him by in chains. The look in his eyes when he stared in at me..." She paled. "I've never forgotten it."

Magenta sat quietly beside her, staring at the patterned carpet with glassy eyes. She looked like she might throw up.

"Muzzled?" Travis murmured. "Why the muzzle?" Max knew precisely why he was asking.

"He bit all of the victims," Maya answered. "Mauled them to death—as if he were a bear or a lion."

Travis shared a glance with Max. Then Jewels. The Reaper looked deeply disturbed by what she was being told.

Maya continued. "We never saw or heard from him again, until we made it to Yveswich. He found us at the apartment building we were staying at. Where you found us," she said to Max. "I was nervous about him being around us, but he insisted that he was fixed. That whatever was wrong with him had been...fixed," she said again, as if that explained anything about this mess. "*Cured* might be a better word. Anyway, I worried he was keeping secrets from us, but being alone as we were and having nowhere to go, we chose to trust him." Her throat shifted with a swallow. "It was a mistake."

"You said he killed Aurora," Max prompted. "Did you see it happen?"

Her eyes—glowing like embers—lifted to his. "I wish I hadn't," she whispered hoarsely. A single glowing tear slipped down her cheek. She scrubbed it away.

"I know this is hard," Dallas said gently. Maya looked at her with reluctance. "But can you tell us exactly what happened?"

Max added, "What did he look like? When it happened, I mean."

"A monster." Maya's voice quavered. Her chin did, too. "His eyes were black, like ours, but...there were thin lines in the skin around his eyes." She gestured to her under-eyes, brows, and temples. "We heard Aurora screaming, and we ran to help her. By the time we got to her, she was already dead —" She broke off with a ragged inhale.

Everyone gave her a few minutes to compose herself. Beside her, Magenta wept in silence, her arms hugging her knees.

Max felt a shred of sympathy. She was only a little girl. Only a couple of years older than Paxton. Fourteen, maybe. Too young for all of this.

"Has Onyx ever taken drugs?" Max asked.

Maya blinked another incandescent tear free. "What do you mean?" she sniffed.

"Street drugs. Like Venom, Stygian salts, Black Crystal, Trip, Devil's Chalk, Malice."

"I mean...anything's possible. They had us on all sorts of things at the Facility."

Dominic said, "I highly doubt they had you on street drugs. As bad as those assholes are, killing their test subjects with addiction and overdose doesn't seem like something they'd do." Max had to agree. They would seek to protect their investments, not destroy them.

"What about after?" Max asked Maya. "When he found you here, did you see him using any eye drops? Snorting anything?"

She shook her head. "I don't think so."

Hmm.

Travis piped up. "There's something I'd like to know. When we found Blue, the only language she knew was Ilevyn. So how are you talking to us right now?"

Blue was the one who answered him. "Scarlet—" She paused to correct herself. "Sorry, I mean Maya—"

But Maya said, "Scarlet is fine. You can call me Scarlet." Her eyes swept about the group, making it clear that Scarlet was the name she preferred to be called by.

Max tried not to frown. Dal's eyes—soft with empathy—met his.

"Brainwashing didn't work on every patient," Blue explained. While her accent was still heavy, she was pretty fluent in their tongue, all her lessons with Dominic paying off. "Scarlet managed to hide it from them. It's why she can still remember Maximus."

Max met his sister's blazing eyes.

Maya—Scarlet—cleared her throat. "Aurora is the reason why Magenta has all her memories back. She healed everyone after we escaped the Facility. Our friends who died in the tunnels... She'd healed them, too. Restored everything they had forgotten."

"This Aurora you speak of," Dominic mused. "What kind of magic did she have?"

"Every type," Scarlet replied. "Every elemental power. Every mind power. Everything. She was rainbow. Full spectrum."

Like Loren, Max thought.

"Do you know where Onyx is now?" he asked her.

She shook her head. "He ran off after we found him with Aurora."

Magenta said, "It's l-like he...he came out of a t-trance." Her words were splintered apart by breathy sobs. "Like h-he...realized what he did—" She broke off and sobbed silently into her knees.

Scarlet consoled her and rubbed her back.

"I want you to keep an eye out for him," Max said. "Let us know if he comes around. And stay away from him. Both of you." He shot a firm glance at Magenta.

Her pink eyes slid to his. They were wary, but she nodded.

"Yo, pink one," Malakai said. "What's your magic?"

"White and red." Magenta's response was a crackle.

"Okay, *and?*" Malakai pressed. "What can you do? Give us a party trick, or something. Put on a show."

"She's an Empath," Scarlet replied. "She can discern emotions even when the Sight fails. Even when a person's aura is hidden, she can sense how they are truly feeling from a greater distance than we can."

Aspen said, "So it's not like fire for red and illusion for white?"

A shallow crease between Scarlet's brows was the only indication that she was surprised by their level of knowledge. "Hers is different. She was part of a separate experiment. They wanted to see what abilities they could achieve if they blended different types of magic together in certain quantities. Magenta is not an Elemental, she is an Empath."

Holy shit. This just kept getting more complex. Max wondered what that meant for Loren. Because she was human, she couldn't use her abilities to their full potential without the risk of killing herself.

But...if she ever *could*... If they somehow found a way around it...

She'd be unstoppable. A goddamn powerhouse.

He glanced at the windows. It was getting dark out.

"We should go," he said to Travis as he got to his feet.

Travis stood, and so did Jewels.

"Wait, wait, wait!" Malakai protested. "Where do you think you're going?" he demanded of his sister.

"With Travis," Jewels said, exasperated.

Malakai was shaking his head. "Uh-uh. I don't think so. It's getting dark out there."

"She'll be with us," Dallas said. She struggled to don her jacket while her broken wings were in the way. Max went over and gave her a hand. She muttered a thanks as he draped the slits in the back of the jacket over each wing and fastened the buttons. "She's not a baby," Dallas added. "Quit treating her like one, you're embarrassing her."

"I'm going, Malakai, and that's final," Jewels said firmly. "You and Travis really need to sort your shit out. It's getting old." When her brother opened his mouth to argue, she held up a finger, the nail painted a glossy black. "Do *not* try to argue with me." She snatched her coat off the hook by the door and put it on.

"Fine, *go,*" Malakai snapped. Max was hopeful that he might be staying behind—for *real* this time. But after a moment, he sighed—growled, really —and got to his feet.

Travis seethed, "Oh, so now you're coming?"

Malakai stalked up to him, getting right up in his face. "You got a problem with me, Devlin, say it, and I'll take the liberty of loosening some more teeth for you."

Travis merely shook his head, scowling. "You're not worth my time."

"We'll wait here," Dominic said of himself and Blue. The rest of them —Max, Dallas, Travis, Jewels, Malakai, Aspen—were going, by the looks of things. All except Dom, Blue, Maya—*Scarlet*—and Magenta.

"Let's go, then," Max said, heading for the door. "It's not getting any lighter out there."

He was putting on his boots when a pair of socked female feet appeared before him. He finished tying his laces and straightened.

His sister stood before him, looking torn.

"Where are you going?" she asked him. The question was as stiff as her posture.

"To find a phone. We need to contact our families." He tried not to say the last word bitterly, but it came out knife-sharp.

There was no fire in her eyes anymore—they were simply brown. Like the Maya he remembered. The sister who'd watched movies with him, played sword fights with wooden swords in the back yard, raced each other to the neighborhood park to push each other on the swings...

"You don't want us to come with?" she asked him.

"I'm not going to force you to have a relationship with me, Maya. Scarlet—sorry." He gave a dismissive wave. "If you want to have one, cool. But if you don't, whatever. You can leave if you want, and I won't stop you. I'd just tell you to be careful."

He opened the hotel room door and walked out.

His sister didn't follow. And this time, he found that he didn't care.

It was freeing.

62

ARBOR WALK-IN CLINIC
ARBOR, STATE OF KER

In a tiny sterile examination room in Arbor's walk-in clinic, Roman leaned against the back wall, hands in his pockets, and listened to the clock tick. Pax sat in the lone chair beside him, knee bouncing, his erratic pulse filling the room.

Pax had finally woken up late that afternoon, after sleeping non-stop since making it to the motel. He hadn't used the bathroom that whole time and barely touched the breakfast Itzel had turned into her personal punching bag. The pools of blood in his eyes were mostly gone, the dark lines underneath faded. But he was pale and gaunt and still didn't have much of an appetite, so Roman had decided to bring him here. The clinic was closing in one hour—they'd barely snuck in on time.

Shay was out in the waiting room. Only family members were allowed back. After their argument, Roman had hoped Shay would decide to leave, but so far no luck. She was still here, and any day now Donovan and his men could track them down. *Rape her bloody and slit her throat.*

The mere thought of that made his heart pound with rage.

Bounce, bounce, bounce, went Pax's knee.

Roman placed a hand on his shoulder. The gesture stilled his bobbing knee. "You're going to be fine," Roman said gently as the kid stared up at him in fright. "It's just a check-up."

Pax returned to bouncing his knee, eyes that were wide as saucers fixed on the open door.

A few minutes later, a male doctor—a hellseher—walked in wearing scrubs. "Afternoon, gentlemen," he greeted them with a smile. "I'm Doctor Aimes. You must be Paxton." He gave Pax another friendly smile as he shut the door and took a seat on the stool.

Paxton's nod was as bouncy as his knee.

Aimes scanned the papers on his clipboard. "Are you Donovan?" He glanced up at Roman.

"Roman," he replied. "I'm his brother."

He jotted something down. Roman resisted the urge to rip his pen out of his hand and snap it in half. This was bad enough without the note-taking. "What brings you in today?"

Paxton peeked up at Roman from beneath his mop of hair.

"I'm worried about my brother," Roman responded politely. He wanted answers, reassurance. So he'd swallow his attitude and be civil, even as the doc kept his pen poised. "We're evacuees from Yveswich, and the night before last he went into cardiac arrest. I had to perform CPR. Some of his symptoms were the same as a typical Surge—black eyes, intense feelings of panic. He was fine once I got his heart working again, but he slept for over twenty-four hours without waking up."

There he went with the scribbling again. More evidence that they'd been here. "Has Paxton experienced Surges in the past?"

"Once in a while, but they're never like this. And there was something else I wanted to mention..." He pushed back Paxton's hair so the doctor could see his face better. "Dark lines appeared under his eyes. You can kind of see them still." He traced Pax's left cheekbone with the tip of his index finger.

"Huh," the doctor said, squinting. "Okay." He took more notes before setting the clipboard on the counter and inserting the earpieces of his stethoscope. "I'm going to have a listen to your heart, okay?" he said to Pax as he stood and rolled the stool aside. "And then I'm going to take a look at your eyes. It's super easy—nothing to be afraid of." He gestured to the examination table. "If you could have a seat up here, that'd be great."

Roman ruffled Pax's hair. "Go on. You'll be fine."

When Aimes was finished with listening to Pax's pulse and shining a light in his eyes, he asked Roman a few more questions. "Is Paxton on any suppressants?" He clacked away on the computer in the corner.

Roman shifted his weight. "No." It was a lie. But medical records showed that Pax wasn't on any, and he had to keep it that way. If Donovan found out that Roman had put the kid on them years ago...

"His father doesn't have him on any?"

"Not that I'm aware of." Absolutely not. Don wanted his youngest son's magic to manifest in its strongest form. He'd never weaken him like that. "Why do you ask? Could suppressants cause something like this?"

"It could," he began. "I've seen similar incidents where, over time, a person's magic will swell like a balloon, until eventually it just—" He mimed a balloon popping. "Pops. It can cause an intense panic attack, ruptured blood vessels, and even cardiac arrest, I suppose, if it's bad enough." He returned to typing.

"What would cause it, though? What would set it off?"

"The short answer is too much restraint. Suppressants are only so strong. In some cases, if a patient's magic is too powerful, they'll develop a tolerance for the drug, and their magic will break through that barrier by force. It's why a lot of patients need to up their dosage as they age."

Huh. "So, say he *was* on suppressants," Roman mused. "Would you recommend he get off them, or upped the dosage?"

He hemmed and hawed. "It depends. Certain prescriptions have significant withdrawal symptoms, so that's something to keep in mind. If he has a good support network and *wants* to wean off the drugs, then yeah, I always recommend doing so and learning to control your magic instead. Trying to suppress it isn't always best for people like us. Suppressants work better on, say, veneficae or half-blood folk. Full-blood hellsehers have a high resistance to them, so they're not always the best option."

"Okay," Roman said, thinking. "So you're not concerned? About what happened?" He gestured to where Pax sat on the examination table. Crepe paper crinkled as he swung his legs, sneakered feet thunking together.

"Not overly," Aimes said on an exhale. "Like I said, it sounds like a few incidents I've seen in the past where a person's magic breaks through that shield of suppressants and causes a very intense Surge. I wouldn't dwell on it too much." From the way he was talking, he seemed to have drawn the conclusion that Pax was on suppressants, even if Roman wasn't willing to admit it. This was *the* Donovan Slade's kid—he likely knew that not everything was going to be on record.

"Thanks," Roman said.

The doctor nodded. "Any time." He was gathering his things when Roman remembered something.

"I almost forgot," Roman said. The doctor paused. "Have you ever heard of machinery reacting to a hellseher's magic?"

His forehead crinkled. "Could you elaborate?"

"I was driving when Pax had his...episode. The brakes failed, the windshield shattered, and we went off the road with the car smoking."

This time, when the doctor glanced at Paxton, he looked as though he were viewing him in a different light. Seeing him clearly.

His aura—it felt...off.

Fearful.

Suddenly, his face went cold and stony. "I've never heard of that before," he said tightly. He tucked his clipboard under his arm. "You gentlemen have a great rest of your afternoon."

He swung open the door and left.

Roman blinked. "Okay, that was weird," he muttered.

Paxton hopped off the examination table and came to stand at Roman's side, Chance creeping out of his shadow to join. The pup let out a low whine and cocked his head to one side.

"Yeah," Pax agreed. "Really weird."

SHAY SAT in the waiting room of Arbor Walk-In, the latest gossip magazine open in her lap.

They'd managed to find a decent clothing store not far from the motel. Since she'd had nothing to wear, Roman had gone without her and picked out some clothes. Jeans, hoodies, t-shirts, underwear, socks, sneakers. And thank gods he had. She had worn his shirt for as many hours as her forlorn heart could handle. It was bad enough that she was sleeping in the same room as the man, let alone wearing his clothes that smelled way too much like him.

As she flipped through the magazine, the TV droned in the background. The news was on, volume on low. She wasn't paying attention to the bullshit the reporters were spewing about the incident in Yveswich, but when they switched to another topic, the magazine slipped out of her hands and slid across the floor.

"Paxton Slade," the news reporter had said.

The blood drained from her head as she leaned forward and read the subtitles.

...TWELVE-YEAR-OLD PAXTON SLADE, A MALE HELLSEHER FROM YVESWICH, HAS BEEN REPORTED MISSING AS OF THIS MORNING. PAXTON WAS LAST SEEN WITH HIS BROTHER,

ROMAN DEVLIN, AND FEMALE HELLSEHER SHAYLA
COUSENS, WHO AUTHORITIES CLAIM MIGHT HAVE SOME-
THING TO DO WITH PAXTON'S DISAPPEARANCE...

"Oh. Shit," Shay mouthed as she watched her face appear on the news
—right next to Roman's. They looked like mugshots. Magical renditions
from photographs that had been provided to the authorities.

...POLICE AND THE MAGICAL PROTECTIONS UNIT ARE
INVESTIGATING HIS DISAPPEARANCE AND ARE ASKING
FOR THE PUBLIC'S ASSISTANCE IN LOCATING PAXTON.
ANYONE WITH INFORMATION IS ASKED TO CONTACT THE
YVESWICH DIVISION OF THE MPU. DEVLIN AND COUSENS
ARE DARKSLAYERS AND ARE BELIEVED TO BE ARMED AND
EXTREMELY DANGEROUS. IF SEEN, THEY SHOULD NOT BE
APPROACHED...

"Oh shit," Shay said again.

A chair creaked. The receptionist peeked at her over the desk.

Shay whipped her head the other way—toward the window.

This was the work of Donovan—no doubt about that. Darkslayers did
not report their missing family members—they tracked them down themselves and brutally murdered whoever had dared to take them. The fact that
the psycho had gone so far as to report his son to the police and have
Paxton's face—and hers and *Roman's*—plastered all over the news...

This was bad. Horrible.

Light glinted off the windows of a car pulling into the lot.

"No," Shay whispered.

It was a squad car.

ROMAN CAME out of the examination room and fucking *collided* with
Shay so hard she almost fell.

He grabbed onto her. "What the hell's going on?"

"Police are here," she panted. "I managed to sneak past reception, but
we need to go—out the back door. Now." She pushed him.

Roman bit his tongue against the questions threatening to come out.
Why were the police here? And why did that matter?

They hurried down the hallway. Past the tiny laboratory and the examination rooms where other patients waited to be seen by the two doctors in the building.

The neon sign above the door just ahead said EXIT.

Shay shoved it open, and Roman followed behind her with Paxton in front of him.

"Over here," she breathed. They took shelter behind a dumpster shared by the businesses in this tiny strip mall. She faced them, panting. "Wait. Wait here. We have to wait." She gestured to the tattoo of a fish skeleton on her wrist. It was half-full with white light.

They couldn't make it to the car. Not without being seen.

Because those cops had parked right beside them—Roman had spotted their cruiser through the front window on his way out.

The dumpster thumped and rattled as something in it chowed down on scraps. The sun was setting, a few of the more stupid and desperate breeds of monster creeping out for a twilit meal.

Paxton cowed away from the sound.

"Can you disguise my car?" Roman whispered, tucking Paxton against his side. "Do you have enough magic to do that?"

"I'll try." That meant she'd have to disguise not just the car but all three of them. It was a lot to ask.

They waited, Shay watching her tattoo as if it were a watch and she was checking the time. It only took seconds to refill, but it felt like forever. Roman's heart pounded the whole time, his hand in reach of the gun in the holster strapped to his thigh.

When Shay's tattoo was finally full, she said, "Everyone hold still. Don't say anything." She shut her eyes, nostrils flaring as she summoned her magic.

Roman's heart was sprinting, eyes flicking toward the door they'd exited.

Shay opened her black eyes. "Let's go."

They walked—*walked*, which was torture—around the building and back to the car.

Shay had disguised it so well, Roman would have walked right by it if she hadn't been with him. It was an ugly white mini van, its longer size making it a little hard to find where the real doors were. If he squinted, he could see the real image of the car overlapping with the illusion of the van —something he assumed he was able to see because he was a part of the illusion she'd cast.

They got in, the cops still speaking with reception inside, and drove back to the Wanderer in silence. Nobody spoke until they were parked out front of room number nineteen, and by then the illusion had faded. They were exposed. Vulnerable.

Shay explained everything she'd seen on the news.

Roman cursed. He formed a fist and made to punch the steering wheel when he remembered Pax was in the back seat. He reined in his emotions. Loosened his fist. "It's my dad. It's got to be. Or Clare." His breathing was labored, the black of the Sight blurring the edges of his vision.

"Clare?" Shay questioned.

Paxton said, "That's my mom. She's probably worried about me."

"You can't fall for that, though, bud," Roman said gently. "I know she cares, but you have to promise you won't fall for any sob story." He twisted in his seat to look at Pax. "Promise?"

Paxton nodded. Roman was afraid, though—afraid the kid, who had such a good heart, would break because of his mother.

He'd have to keep a close watch over Paxton's phone. Maybe block Clare's number, in case she tried reaching out to him. For now. For his safety.

"They showed your picture on the news," Shay said. "Mine, too. Do you think Clare would do something like that?"

Roman rubbed his stubbled chin in thought. "Depends. She doesn't like me, she probably thinks I abducted her child. If she wants to find Pax badly enough, she'll try anything, even dragging my name through the mud." He slumped an elbow against his window and dug his fingers into his thick hair, fisting it.

"She seemed pretty desperate at the warehouse," Shay mused, chewing her lower lip. "Maybe it *was* her. I don't know why she would include my picture, though..."

"Because Donovan is involved," he said with disgust. "Whether it was Clare's idea or not, Don would have had to okay it. She'd never go behind his back." Clare was terrified of the man she'd married. Taking such drastic measures as to report to the authorities that her child was missing would get her murdered if he hadn't given her the okay.

"It could be my mom, too," Shay said. "Maybe they're working together."

He chewed the inside of his cheek so hard he tasted blood. "Maybe," he said with a sigh. He ripped the key out of the ignition. "We can't stay here.

One more night, so Pax can rest up, and then we're leaving." He opened his door and stepped out.

I want you gone. Roman almost said it again. Because his dad now had the whole world looking for Pax, and Roman knew that once his dad found them he'd kill his eldest son once and for all. Roman had crossed the line when he'd taken Pax. He would be shown zero mercy. Brutally slaughtered, no question.

And if Shay was still around when that happened, she'd get caught in the crossfire.

63

HELL'S GATE
ANGELTHENE, STATE OF WITHEREDGE

The others still weren't back. And every time Darien tried to contact them, his calls wouldn't go through.

He spent hours pacing the house debating whether to send Jack and Lace out to look for them. But doing that while everyone's auras were invisible would be like searching for a ghost in fog. Ivy and the others could be anywhere by now—could have left via any exit in Yveswich and gone to any town. There was no use in spreading themselves even thinner to look for people they were unlikely to find.

Roman was the only person he managed to get a hold of. He had made it out, and he was with Shay and Paxton in a small town called Arbor. That was a total of three people accounted for, but that still left everyone else's fates up in the fucking air.

Darien spent the day obsessively checking on Loren, who slept as if she were under a spell, and blowing off steam with the exercise equipment in the basement. The punching bag wasn't quite as satisfying when his right hand was broken, but he had to keep busy. If he stopped moving for any length of time, his appetite for hard drugs grew to the point of being unbearable. And so did his worry for his Devils.

He left the house only long enough to pick up a little something for Loren, but apart from that he stayed and paced. Smoked a dozen cigarettes to curb his cravings for something stronger. Push-ups, sit-ups, punching, running, weight training—he did it all.

Evening rolled around, and he came up the stairs to the ground floor after another round of boxing with his lifeless opponent and heard the sound of light footsteps in Loren's room. She was awake, and thank gods for that. But just because she was out of bed didn't mean she'd come down anytime soon. He'd heard her get up one other time today and had gotten his hopes up, but she had gone straight back to sleep.

Still panting with exertion, his shirt clinging to the sweat on his body, he walked up to the third floor landing and stood there for a moment. Listening but trying not to be a creep as she came out of the bathroom—

And went right back to bed, just like he'd suspected. The mattress creaked as she collapsed on top of it, and she let out a soft, sleepy groan before promptly drifting off again.

He frowned. Was she sick? Should he call Doctor Atlas or something? Was she staying in there to avoid him because he'd acted like a complete asshole?

He walked toward her room—

And paused. "Fuck," he muttered, pushing his sweat-damp hair back.

Time. He'd give her a bit more time.

He went up to the fourth floor and rapped his fist against Jack and Ivy's door.

"Come in," Jack mumbled.

Darien opened it and found Jack throwing knives at a target on the wall.

"Hey, Jacky," Darien said, trying his best to sound more upbeat than he felt, even as his brother-in-law refused to look at him. "How you feeling?" He crossed his arms and leaned against the doorjamb.

"Do you want my honest answer?" He snapped his wrist back and threw the knife at the target. The blade found its mark in the tiny space between two other knives, hilt vibrating from the impact. Jack's brown eyes flicked to Darien's for a millisecond. "What do you want?"

"To tell you that I'm sorry," Darien replied as Jack walked to the target and plucked the three blades off.

"Why? It's not your fault," he muttered without looking at him. He looked tired. Aged. A million times different from the Jack they were all used to. "Ivy wanted me gone, and there's nothing we could've said to change her mind." His tone was bitter. He returned to his throwing position on the other side of the spacious bedroom and rolled his shoulders, preparing to throw.

"I'm still sorry," Darien said.

A pause. Jack drew a breath that scraped through him. "I think you owe

Ivy more of an apology than me." He threw—another perfect bull's eye. "If you ever see her again."

Darien frowned. "Don't say shit like that."

"Why not? It's the truth." His eyes finally found Darien's for longer than a second. They were bloodshot, the skin underneath puffy. "She should be back by now. We both know that." He threw a second knife, this one missing the mark—no doubt from the blur of fresh tears Darien had spotted in his eyes.

Jack cursed.

"Depends on which exit they took," Darien offered. "If they went north like Roman, it'll take them longer to get here."

He wiped his nose with a knuckle. "You heard from Roman?"

"He's in Arbor."

He threw the third knife. "Who with?" He walked back to the target to retrieve the blades.

"Pax and Shay."

He palmed all three knives. "Where's Loren? Shouldn't you be watching her or something instead of dicking around with me?" His tone was glacial.

"She's asleep," Darien responded, keeping his own tone polite. "She hasn't come out of her room since we got home."

He grunted and resumed position.

"Besides," Darien added, "I think I can spare a few minutes of my time for my brother."

"In law," Jack added before throwing the first knife.

"Makes no difference to me."

"She sick or something?" Instead of throwing at the target, he lightly tossed the second knife above his head, catching it by the tip.

"I hope not."

"So you won't be dying in two hours?" Another toss and catch.

"Hope not," Darien said again, knowing exactly what he was getting at.

"Ivy's really upset, you know." He aimed at the target and threw the blade so hard the room shook.

Darien felt a pinch in his heart, as if Jack had thrown that knife at him instead of the target. "I know."

Jack sniffed. "She loves you."

Quieter, Darien said, "I know."

Jack threw his last blade. "We all do. So what you did kinda feels like a kick in the balls." He turned then and stared at him, empty hands hanging at his sides. This time it was Darien who felt like he couldn't meet Jack's gaze. He forced himself to anyway, because Jack deserved it. Any time he opened up, he deserved the full attention of whoever he was pouring his heart out to. "You gave me a home, Darien," Jack said. "You gave me a family. You did that for all of us, not just me. Did you not even consider how we'd feel when you decided to end your life?"

"I haven't ended it."

A cold smirk. "You're stuck in a slow motion crash. It's gonna happen before the new year—you said so yourself. We've all been too busy to really discuss it, but this shit stings." He shook his head and chewed his lip. "I know you love her, man, but—" He glared at the target with gleaming eyes. "Do you ever regret it?"

"No," he answered truthfully. "Never." He never regretted anything when it came to Loren. "I only regret the pain it's causing everyone else." That last part was true, too. He could count on one hand the amount of times he'd seen Jack upset like this, and although he knew that most of these emotions stemmed from concern for his wife, the things he was admitting right now...

They weren't lies. Jack didn't lie.

"I don't know what hurts more," Jack began. His words were thick with emotion, his face red. "Watching my wife bawl her eyes out over losing her brother, or coming to terms with the fact that you really don't give a shit about yourself at all. You think you're this horrible person who doesn't deserve to be alive or happy, but Darien, man, we hunt horrible people all the time." He gave a quiet, unamused chuckle, the tears threatening to fall. "You're not one of them." He fiercely wiped at his eyes, smearing moisture across his flushed cheeks, and crossed the room to the target. "If you were, you would've killed me back when I deserved it," he added with a mumble.

Darien straightened. "Jack—"

"I want to be alone." He kept his back facing him, and when he turned to cross the room again he did it with his head down. "Thanks for stopping by. Maybe I'll come down tomorrow."

He resumed throwing. He didn't look Darien's way again.

So Darien left, closing the door softly behind him.

Two hours later, while he sat by himself at the dining room table with nothing but the ticking of the clock for company, the remnants of the salt he'd snorted while trying to track his family scattered across the wood, he heard the sound of tires rolling down the driveway.

He pushed out of his seat and hurried toward the front entrance, boots and heart pounding.

"Lace?" he called into the quiet house. Something about his tone had Lace getting up immediately on one of the upper levels.

Hope filled his heart, but he refused to let it take full control as he swung open the door—

And found one of Roman's vehicles parking out front.

The driver's door opened. A familiar male voice drifted through the twilit yard.

Relief washed through him, so strong his head spun. "Jack!" he bellowed. No response. Shit, he was going to wake up Loren, wasn't he? *"Jack!"* Still no response. He cursed and hollered louder, "JAAAACK!"

Jack opened his door. *"What?"* he called from the fourth floor.

"Get down here."

A low groan. "I'm not in the mood, Darien."

"Get down here, Jacky. Now. That's an order."

Jack cursed. Then he stomped down the stairs, muttering, as Tanner and Kylar stepped out of the car, moving their seats forward for Ivy and Eugene to climb out.

As Jack descended the stairs, the big arched window above the front entrance gave him perfect view of his wife as she grabbed her bag out of the car. The minute he saw her, he almost tripped before going perfectly still. Just for a second.

And then he broke into a run.

He cleared the last of those stairs faster than Darien had ever seen him move. Darien stepped aside just in time as Jack blew past him and out the door like a bullet—

"Ivy!" Her name tore out of Jack on a ragged sob.

Ivy dropped her bag, meeting Jack in a run.

He swept her off her feet and into a spinning hug. Both were sobbing. Ivy was apologizing—telling Jack why she hadn't called, how they hadn't wanted to risk contact, in case Don was still after them. Jack didn't care about the reasons, though—he only cared that he had her back.

Darien's lips lifted—his first real smile in quite some time.

This—Jack's love for Ivy—was exactly what had earned him the title of the seventh Devil. A permanent spot in their family.

Lace appeared beside Darien. "Thank gods," she whispered.

Ivy looked their way as Jack kissed her cheek. The moment her eyes met Darien's, the happiness on her face fell.

Jack looked Darien's way, too. Though the softness he felt for Ivy lingered in his gaze, Darien could recognize when he wasn't wanted, and right now neither of them wanted anything to do with him.

Still, he forced a smile. "Hey," he said. She might not be happy to see him, but he was so relieved that she was back that he didn't give a shit. She could be mad at him all she wanted, as long as she was alive.

"Hi," she whispered tightly, still clinging to Jack. "Nice to see you're still alive." It was a kick in the nuts, but he took it.

"You too."

Darien shifted his attention to Tanner as the hacker approached the front steps, a small smile on his face.

"Atlas," Darien said, welcoming him with a nod.

"Hey."

Darien stepped down to meet him, and when Tanner offered him a hand in greeting, Darien pulled him into an embrace instead. "Welcome home," he said, clapping him on the back.

"Thanks," Atlas said as they broke apart, the word gruff with emotion. "I was starting to think I'd never make it."

"I knew you had it in you."

Kylar and Eugene were walking this way, bags in hand. Eugene was rubbing his left eye, looking like he just woke up from a nap.

"Feels like déja vu," Kylar said with a grin that showed off the fleck of diamond in his eyetooth. "Except *you're* greeting *me* this time." He shook Darien's hand, then waved at Lacey at the top of the steps.

"Hey, Ky," she said with a smile.

"Hey." He gave the blonde an appreciative once over that Darien was certain he didn't mean to do.

"How was the drive?" Darien asked him.

"Hell," Kylar admitted with a heavy exhale. "I could use a drink."

"I'll make you one," Lace offered. She pushed off the doorjamb she was leaning against. "Come on in."

They filed inside, Darien the last to enter. He was just shutting the door behind him when his phone buzzed in his pocket.

He took it out and saw SABRINE VAN ARSDELL flashing across the screen.

Now here was a girl they hadn't heard from in a while. His immediate thought was that something was wrong, but he realized that she had probably seen what was happening in Yveswich on the news and was desperate to know if they were alive.

He swiped and lifted the phone to his ear. "Cassel."

"Umm, *hi?*" Sabrine practically shouted. It was hard to gauge her tone. She sounded startled and...excited? "Are you back, or did you die and that's your ghost I just saw walking into your house?"

His brow creased. "Yeah, we're back. Things have been a little hectic..." He opened the door and looked out.

Sabrine and Logan were standing at the gate, truck idling. Sab jumped in place and waved her free arm above her head, as if he couldn't see her perfectly well from right here.

"Is she alive?" Sabrine panted, still jumping.

"Hold on, I'll buzz you in."

"Don't leave me hanging, Darien!" Her voice was audible not just through the phone, but also from the short distance between them. It was like he was hearing her twice. "I need to know—"

"Yes, she's alive. And don't shout when you come in, she's sleeping."

Sabrine stopped bouncing, her labored breathing rattling the phone speakers. "Coma sleeping or normal sleeping?"

"Normal." And thank fuck for that. He hung up and buzzed the wolves in.

64

SOUTH COASTAL DISTRICT
YVESWICH, STATE OF KER

Citizens of Terra lived by a set of stringent rules designed to keep them alive for as long as possible in a world honed to kill. A survival code, so to speak. That code was tweaked depending on where a person lived and the dangers that were unique to that particular region.

In Yveswich, there were three rules you never, *ever* broke. Not unless you wanted to be chewed up, digested, and shat out by a hungry monster, that is.

1. Keep out of the fog.
2. Don't swim beyond the buoys.
3. Stay away from waterfalls after the sun sets.

The first was, obviously, the most crucial. It was easy enough to avoid waterfalls, and unless you were boating and fell in it was equally as easy to steer clear of the deep end of the ocean. Fog, on the other hand, was a little more random, a little more unpredictable, a little harder to avoid.

So leaving the safety of a spell-protected building at night, when the streets were smothered not just by darkness but also by dense fog, went against the code. But desperate times called for desperate measures. And right now, Travis was desperate to find a phone.

He stayed close to Jewels as they navigated the streets of the South Coastal District, wind that tasted of blood, sulphur, and ocean salt wending between the buildings. There were no pay phones in the hotel, and reception had a strict policy against letting guests use their phones.

And so here they were, forced to walk. In the brutal cold. In the near-blinding dark.

Malakai was heading the group—speed-walking down the icy sidewalk, turning corners sharply, and simply looking beyond pissed to be out here. But what else was new? The guy was deranged, but at least he could annihilate anything that dared to breathe on them. Only for that reason would Travis tolerate him.

The monsters were beginning their evening hunt, their howls slashing apart the night. Some soft-hearted god must be taking mercy on them, because none of these creatures were from the Void. Those they passed were breeds they were familiar with and had hunted their entire Darkslaying lives. Smart enough to recognize when something with bigger teeth came along, these creatures stayed away from their group and stuck to the shadows and alleys, where they ate their fill of rodents and stray cats. In these parts, Darkslayers were the predators with the biggest teeth.

For now. Travis hoped that by the time that changed they'd be back at the hotel—and Darien would be on his way to ask for Roark's help with breaking them the hell out of here.

"What do you think of everything we learned about Onyx?" Jewels asked him as they walked, numb hands bundled in their pockets. The streetlights in this area were still working, though they buzzed and flickered more often than not. Light-starved moths flitted around the fuzzy halos of white.

"I think it's freaky," Travis admitted, his breath puffing in the air like smoke. "And I'm not convinced about the drugs thing," he added. He'd done a lot of thinking since Scarlet and Magenta had told them about Onyx. While Dominic made a decent point that it was unlikely that the test subjects had been given street drugs, they *were* exactly that: test subjects. Who's to say Onyx hadn't been given doses of Venom as a part of the experiment? If the people who ran that facility were desperate enough to enhance the abilities of their lab rats, why would street drugs be out of the equation?

Jewels said, "You still think it's Venom that could be causing it?"

He shrugged. "I don't know. Maybe. That's the only time I've seen anyone with black lines around their ey—" He choked as if he'd swallowed a moth.

Then stumbled to an abrupt halt, boots skidding across an icy patch on the sidewalk.

Jewels stopped and turned to face him, her ashen hair—the purple starting to fade—stirring in a frosty breeze. "Travis? Is something wrong?"

He stared at her beneath a foggy streetlight, his mind spinning like a top.

Venom users were not the only people he'd seen with black lines around their eyes.

He had seen them on Jewels, too. The night she was rushed to the hospital. The night her heart stopped as the city shook, and she'd screamed and had a seizure as the portal peeled open wider.

He stared at her now, searching her pale face for any dark lines.

"Travis...?" she asked. Her question wavered with suspicion.

She stepped away from him, as if *he* were the threat. Her eyes—green, no lines around them, the pupils a normal size—flicked to the rest of the group that was getting farther away, their voices bouncing down the block.

Travis blinked. *Get a hold of yourself and talk to her,* he thought. *You're freaking her out.* "Sorry," he managed to say, "nothing's wrong, I just—" He cleared his throat. "I thought of something, but it's not important."

A beat of silence, her eyes flickering toward the others. "Are you sure?" She still had her body half-turned, as if waiting for the signal to run. Her right hand was grasping something inside her coat pocket, the shape bulging against the fabric.

A gun.

"Yeah, I'm fine," he breathed, forcing a hard chuckle. "Totally fine. Let's go, or we'll lose the others." He waved her onward.

"O...kay." She took just one step before pausing again, reluctant to turn her back on him.

They had that in common.

"I'm fine, I swear," he said. "I won't bite you, I promise."

She smiled at that. Let go of the gun in her pocket and started moving.

"Biting's kind of a turn-on for me, actually," she panted as they jogged side by side, watching their step on patches of black ice. Travis suspected the new flush of pink in her cheeks was from more than just the cold.

She peeked sidelong at him.

"Yeah?" he breathed. "What else are you into?" If only she'd decided to tell him this when he wasn't freaked out by the thought of her potentially turning on him. Ripping his throat out instead of kissing him. This was the first time they'd talked in a remotely sexual way since the day he'd seen the vibrators in her bedroom. He'd wanted to get to know this sexy, mysterious Reaper on a more personal—*very* personal—level for a while. But not like this. Not while something so disturbing was dousing every naughty thought in his head like a bucket of icy water.

She snickered. "Oh, Travis." The way she purred his name almost —*almost*—made him forget all about the Venom, the black eyes, and the idea of being bitten anywhere outside of the bedroom. "I'm not sure we should talk about my kinks while my big brute of a brother is eavesdropping." She playfully bumped her shoulder against his arm.

A nervous laugh slipped out of him, and before he could stop himself he blurted, "Have you ever taken Venom?" The moment the implication was out, he winced.

Understanding washed across her face. "Ohh." Travis prepared for a swift kick to the nuts, but she merely grinned and said, "I get it. You're worried about Malakai, aren't you?"

Uhh...okay—that was better than Jewels believing he didn't trust her.

"It's just something I thought of," he said quickly. "Back there—that's why I was, you know, acting weird." It was a detail—a very big detail—he wasn't willing to brush off as unimportant, not when Darien was addicted to Venom.

And not when they had another Venom addict in their group, and he was currently storming around up ahead.

"I'm about to turn around," Malakai threatened as he marched on, turning yet another corner that yielded no pay phone. "The only cardio I like to do is in the bedroom. This is *way* too much exercise."

Aspen caught up to Malakai, the male Reaper spitting with rage by a deserted intersection, their silhouettes obscured by milky fog.

"There's one right there!" Aspen exclaimed, the echo of her words bouncing as she pointed across the street.

"Finally," Max muttered.

"Thank gods," Dallas breathed. The witch looked relieved.

"I've about had enough of *that one's* shit," Max whispered to Travis, inclining his head toward Delaney.

Travis chuckled.

"I don't think we have to worry about Malakai," Jewels said quietly to Travis as they crossed the road on a green light, the rain-soaked cobbles glinting like emeralds. "He hasn't taken any Venom lately."

"That's good," he forced out. Her words hardly put him at ease, though. If Venom *was* to blame for these bizarre new attacks, there was no telling if someone like Malakai was a threat, regardless of how long ago he'd taken the drug.

And Jewels still hadn't answered his question. *Was* she a Venom user? If she was, that made a total of two people in their group who had the potential to turn on them and rip out their throats.

Two people they could no longer trust.

"Who wants to be the one to call Darien?" Max asked as they crowded around the pay phone on the gloomy street corner. That was right—Max had recently had a falling out with Darien, so he likely didn't want to be the one to call.

"This is all you guys," Malakai grumbled, stepping aside. "I'm not interested in talking to that prick."

"I'll call," Travis said. He squeezed through the group and fished three silver mynet out of his pocket.

"All this for a phone," Malakai growled. "This better be worth it."

Travis plunked the coins into the slot and started dialing. "Calling Darien when you're in trouble is always worth it."

He lifted the phone to his ear. As he waited for the call to connect, he thought of everything he wanted to say—how he should word the message he would ask Darien to pass along to Roman. He owed his older brother an apology, so he'd start there. He'd tell him how much he loved him, too—that was important. Pax, as well. Too much time had passed since he'd told his brothers that he loved them—he'd always had trouble saying it. Now was not the time to hold back.

But—

His brow creased.

The line... It wasn't ringing.

A loud rasping sound sliced through the speakers.

"What the hell?" He yanked the phone away from his head with a wince, his eardrum throbbing as if someone had stabbed a screwdriver into it and twisted.

The sound was so loud, everyone could hear it. They shared glances, confused.

Then it cut out, and a robotic voice came through the speakers. "No service. Please try again." More ear-bleeding static. And then: "No service. Please try again."

The voice cut out, and so did the static. The line started beeping.

Beep. Beep. Beep. Beep. Beep.

Travis felt like he had no strength in his hand as he put the phone on the receiver. His coins were spat out through the slot, one dropping on his boot and rolling down the sidewalk.

Lost and confused, he faced the others, who stared at him with expectance. Denial—that was denial he was looking at. He knew they'd heard everything themselves, but he said, his lungs so small he could hardly breathe, "No service."

A pause. Dallas shared a wary look with Max, her crossed arms tightening.

This was their one shot. Contacting Darien to see if he could find Roark was their only plan, and now...

Now...

Fuck, Travis didn't know.

"Maybe it's just pay phones?" Jewels offered.

The spitting of gunfire drew their attention east.

"What is that?" Aspen murmured, glancing at Malakai.

Frowning, Malakai peered down the street. "Sounds like it's coming from the military base."

65

HELL'S GATE
ANGELTHENE, STATE OF WITHEREDGE

L oren had the feeling that she had been asleep for a very long time.
When she finally opened her eyes, she was greeted by a moonlit room, a snare of sheets and pillows, and the lovely fragrance of fresh flowers.

It took her a moment to remember where she was. How she had ended up here. She was at Hell's Gate. She was home, but this was not where she usually slept.

This was not Darien's room.

On her nightstand stood a beautiful bouquet. White roses, pink and white lilies, snapdragons, and other blooms, all arranged neatly in a slender glass vase. Beside the vase sat a white cardboard box from Whisking Witch, the air around it sparkling with enchantments that kept the treats inside fresh without the need for refrigeration. And—

Her heart stumbled two beats.

There was a folded card beside the box. With a deep breath, she grabbed the card and opened it.

Loren,

    I know you're upset right now, and you have every right to be. I fucked up. I should've thought about how you'd feel about my decision, but I didn't. I was inconsiderate, and for that I

am truly sorry. I never intended to hurt you, sweetheart. I
wouldn't dream of it.

I don't expect you to forgive me right away, or ever. But I'm
begging you not to shut me out. Give me the chance to earn
back your trust. Please. Whatever you want, however long it
takes, I'm willing to work through it together.

All my love,
D.C.

The tears in her eyes blurred Darien's handwriting. One dripped off her
cheek and soaked into the paper, causing his initials to bleed. She set down
the card before she could wreck it and inhaled. Rubbed the moisture from
her eyes.

She was reluctant to get out of bed now. She had been awake for all of
five minutes, and already her heart had been ripped out and violently
stomped on.

And there was still a box she hadn't opened next to the flowers.

With careful hands, she grabbed it, sat up, and balanced it on her knees.
The sparkles bobbing about like teeny fireflies tickled her skin as she flipped
open the lid, well aware that whatever was in here would make it even
harder to keep ignoring him.

Inside were chocolate-dipped strawberries nestled in paper cupcake
liners.

She sighed. Gods, he was *not* making this easy, was he?

Singer pawed the door open and padded into the room with a wagging
tail that sent curls of shadow through the air.

"Hi, Singer," she whispered.

He sat down by her feet, his warm, panting breaths smelling like candle
smoke. Like magic.

She scratched Singer's misty head with one hand and inhaled three juicy
strawberries with the other—she just couldn't resist—before heading to the
bathroom to brush her teeth and splash her face with cold water. She
changed into jeans and a white long-sleeve shirt and fought a brush through
her tangled hair. Walked out into the hall—

And paused when she found a pillow on the floor. Right in front of her
door.

Her brow scrunched.

Why was there a pillow on the floor? And why did the pillowcase—a deep shade of gray—suggest that it had come from Darien's bed?

"Did you bring that here?" she asked Singer. She pointed at the pillow.

The dog stared up at her with big, innocent eyes.

Wait a minute...

Oh gods.

"He did *not* sleep out here." She was in denial. Darien *had* slept out here, and she knew it.

Singer glanced at the pillow and wagged his tail with not much enthusiasm—whatever that was supposed to mean.

She sighed.

Voices were coming from the ground floor. Was that Ivyana she was hearing? Had she made it back?

She hurried down the stairs, Singer bounding after her in a streak of glittering darkness. Across the foyer, around the corner—

The number of people crowded around the dining room table gave her pause. Her socked feet slid across the floor as she came to a sudden stop, her brows shooting up.

"Loren?"

Her head whipped toward the sound of that voice.

She spotted her at the table beside Logan.

"Sabrine?" Loren breathed. She stumbled forward.

"Loren!" Sabrine jumped to her feet and ran to her with a smile, arms opening wide. Loren opened her own right on time—

They collided, her friend squeezing her in a tight embrace that crushed the air out of her lungs.

She didn't care, though. She hugged Sabrine back just as hard, the weight of everything that'd happened these past few weeks threatening to snap her self control.

"Sabrine," Loren breathed, her eyes shutting tight. "I'm so happy to see you! I missed you so much." There was so much she wanted to tell her. So much she couldn't wait to get off her bleeding chest. She needed her friend more than ever, needed a shoulder to cry on, an ear to vent to, and she was so, *so* glad she was here.

"I missed you too, girl! They just told me everything. I can't believe all of this, this is *insane!*" Sabrine pulled back and scanned her with sunset-colored eyes, her hands lightly grasping hers. "Are you okay?"

"I'm fine," Loren said, half-laughing, half-sobbing. *Was* she fine, though? Not really. She was going to die sometime between now and

Kalendae, and so would the man she loved. And that awful truth—him dying—hurt more than her own impending death. "Are *you* okay?"

"I'm fine!" She grinned and squeezed her hands. "I'm totally fine. I've only been obsessively checking my messages every second of every day." She laughed and gave her one more hug, her hands rubbing her back. "I'm so glad you're okay."

"Me too." She sniffed. When they broke apart, Loren gestured to the room full of talking people. "I have all of them to thank."

She was only just noticing *all of them*. Putting names to faces. Jack and Lace were here, but that wasn't all—not anymore. Ivy, Tanner, Kylar, and Eugene had made it out of Yveswich. The latter was sprawled across the couch, completely absorbed by a video game he played on his handheld device. A game show on television had Arthur—the only other person, besides Eugene, who wasn't crowded around the dining room table—fully engrossed.

Darien sat smoking at the head of that table, looking way too appealing in a fitted black shirt and black jeans. The moment she met his potent stare, he seemed to remember what he was doing and reached across the table to put his cigarette out in the ashtray.

As if she hadn't seen him smoking a hundred times by now.

As if it made any difference when it came to her feelings for him.

As if he were capable of doing *anything* that she didn't like.

"Why don't you come sit down?" Sabrine suggested. Her question had Loren breaking Darien's stare. "You look a little faint."

"I'm fine," Loren said, but she didn't argue as her friend took her by the hand and towed her across the space. The dining room windows were open behind Darien, a fresh jasmine-scented breeze drifting through the screen and mixing with the hint of cigarette smoke.

As they joined the others at the table, Darien's attention dipped to Loren's hand—clasped in Sabrine's—before slowly lifting to her face.

She couldn't read his expression. He couldn't be jealous, though, could he? It wasn't like Darien to be jealous of her female friends. But there was something about the gesture that was bothering him. She could tell from the set of his mouth, the crease between his bold brows...

Lace rose from her seat at Darien's left. "You can sit here." She angled the chair toward her and put her own cigarette out in the ashtray.

"That's okay, I can stand," Loren replied.

But Lace had already stepped aside. Loren let go of Sabrine's hand and sat down beside Darien, fully aware that he was keeping watch over her like a hawk. She tried not to meet his stare, instead turning her body toward Sabrine as the wolf claimed the free chair to her left.

"Tattoos, please," Darien said quietly.

She glanced his way, but instead of making eye contact she focused on his necklaces—and pushed up her sleeve so he could see her ink.

Clearly satisfied, he sat back in his seat.

She cleared her throat. "When did you guys get back?" she asked no one in particular. She didn't care who answered, as long as it wasn't Darien. She could still feel him staring.

"Couple of hours ago," Kylar replied. He gave the amber liquid in his glass a swirl and sipped.

Darien said, "You slept for over twenty-four hours."

Her brows flew up, and she made the mistake of looking at him.

Over twenty-four hours? She'd known it was a long time, but...wow. She hadn't expected that.

From the look on Darien's face, neither had he. "I was worried about you," he confessed in a low tone. Steel eyes scanned her face, the hand he had resting on the table sliding an inch closer, as if he wanted to touch her but thought better of it.

"I'm fine," she said quietly. She directed her next questions at the group —anything to stop her from looking at Darien again. From reaching for the hand he was now sliding back, fingers curling into a fist on the wood. "Where's Dallas? Is she back yet?"

"Not yet," Lace answered. "We've been trying to get a hold of them, but we haven't had any luck."

"Roman's in Arbor," Darien said. "He's with Pax and Shay." That was a relief. The fact that Roman had managed to find both of them before the forcefield went up was impressive. He deserved a trophy.

"They told me Roark helped you guys get out of Yveswich," Sabrine said to Loren. "That's...surprising."

"I know, right?"

"Maybe he's finally coming around?" It would be a dream come true. Not just for Loren, but for Dallas as well.

"Yeah, I don't know. Maybe. He seemed different. Like he's changed or something." She tugged her sleeve back down, forgetting that she'd pushed it up. The motion drew Sabrine's attention to the new ink on her palms.

The wolf grabbed her left hand. "You got new tats?" She grabbed the right too, and Loren opened her fingers so she could inspect them.

"They're conduits. They're supposed to help me channel my magic like a stave so I won't drain myself so quickly." Without them, she likely would have died when she'd poured her magic into the Control Tower in Yveswich. Or fallen into another coma.

As if reading her mind, Ivy said, "She won't be doing that again anytime soon." Loren accepted it for the threat that it was.

"Yeah, no kidding," Sabrine breathed, tilting her hands. The metallic ink of the sun and moon caught the dining room light, shimmering like gold and silver dust. "It's time to start taking better care of yourself," she said, letting go of her hands. "You should've seen Dal when you were in a coma—she was a wreck. We all were." Loren didn't doubt that. She also didn't doubt that the person who'd taken it the hardest was sitting right beside her, desperate for her to look at him.

She didn't. "Did they tell you how I've been recharging my magic?"

"Yeah, the saunas and the pool? That's pretty wild."

"It doesn't work the greatest," Ivy cut in. Her tone—sharper than shattered glass—made Loren flinch. "Caliginous Chambers are best for her, but she'll have to be even more careful now, since it's not like we can go back there anytime soon. Right, Loren?"

Sabrine looked between them with a puzzled expression. Clearly, she could sense that something was up.

"Ivy." Darien spoke the warning—or maybe it was more a request to lay off—softly.

His sister immediately pushed to her feet, snatching Jack's empty glass from his grasp, and walked to the kitchen to fix them both a drink.

Loren cleared her throat. "So. Did anything happen here while we were gone?"

Sab took a moment to think about it, still distracted by what just happened. Ivy was setting things down on the counter and shutting cupboard doors so loudly, she managed to distract Tanner from what he was doing on his tablet. Just for a second, but it was still an accomplishment.

Sabrine's face smoothed with shock. "Oh gods," she breathed.

"What?" Lace asked.

Ivy came back, setting Jack's drink before him as she sat down.

"I almost forgot to tell them," Sabrine said to Logan.

"Tell them what?"

"About Tamika," Sabrine responded.

The alpha's eyes widened. "Oh, that's right."

"While you guys were gone, Tamika was stabbed," Sabrine said.

Tanner fumbled his tablet and nearly dropped it.

Loren sucked in a gasp. "Is she going to be okay?"

"I don't know," Sab admitted. "I hope so. She lost a lot of blood, so they put her in a medically induced coma."

"What happened?" Darien demanded. "How'd you hear about this?"

Logan responded, "We were the ones who found her."

"Logan and I were keeping an eye on your house while you were gone," Sabrine explained. "The day the explosion in Yveswich happened, we came here and found her unconscious not far from your driveway."

Darien's brow furrowed.

Tanner said, "Sounds like she was trying to get to our house."

"Mm-hmm...," Darien agreed, his expression severe.

His phone buzzed on the table.

The room grew so silent, you could hear a pin drop. Loren had the feeling she wasn't the only one holding her breath as Darien picked up the phone and checked the caller identification.

The look that crossed his face... Loren wouldn't say he was disappointed—that wasn't the right word. But she knew Darien well enough to tell that it wasn't who he'd hoped it would be.

"It's not them, is it?" Jack asked with a frown.

Darien shook his head. "It's Roman."

66

HELL'S GATE
ANGELTHENE, STATE OF WITHEREDGE

"I just wanted to give you a heads up," Roman was saying, "in case he shows up before I get there."

Darien stood on the back deck, phone in one hand, cigarette in the other, as Roman filled him in on everything that had happened today at the walk-in clinic in Arbor. The shit Shay had seen on the news. The cops that had turned up looking for Pax. He told him everything that happened before, too—Pax's bizarre, Surge-like episode. How Roman's brakes had failed, sending their car spinning off the road, windshield shattering.

And Roman's fear that Donovan was heading straight to Hell's Gate on his mission to find his youngest son.

While Darien listened intently to everything his cousin was saying, his gaze was fixed on the living room window and the beautiful blonde behind the glass.

Loren was deep in conversation with Sabrine. The two sat on the couch, sharing the same blanket. The one Darien had pulled from its spot on the back of the smaller sofa and draped across Loren's lap before coming out here. Ever since the moment she'd walked downstairs, Loren had done everything she could to avoid looking at him, talking to him, acknowledging him in any capacity. Still no mention of the flowers, the strawberries, the note.

Whether Loren liked the card or not, he'd meant every word. He knew he'd screwed up. And while he could admit that she had every right to be upset with him, this—being ignored by her—was torture. Way too many hours had passed since he'd got to touch her outside of protection duty, and the distance was chewing him apart inside. He wanted Loren more than he wanted air, and right now she seemed intent on suffocating him.

He took a long, *long* drag on the cigarette. On the exhale he told Roman, "I don't want you to worry. About anything. That includes Travis. Just get here safely, and we'll figure out where to go from there."

Donovan was a concern, Darien wasn't denying that. The fact that his psycho uncle could be heading to Hell's Gate at that very moment changed things. They'd just made it home, and already the one place in all of Angelthene that was supposed to be safest for Loren and his family was jeopardized.

They would need to leave, preferably tonight.

Roman cursed. "I never should have let him stay at that hospital."

"It's not your fault."

Roman had taken the news—or lack thereof—about Travis poorly, but Darien hadn't expected him to react any differently. Roman was livid at his brother, for a number of reasons. Number one was for choosing to stay behind. Number two was for lack of contact. They had no clue where the hell Travis was, and until he called or made his aura visible, they would be left to wonder if he was alive. If Don had caught up to him—or if he was still trapped in Yveswich.

"Travis is an adult," Darien added. "He made his decision. If the roles were flipped, and it were you who decided to stay behind with Shay, *he* would be pissed at *you.*" He took one last puff before putting the cigarette out in the ashtray they kept on the deck. Tobacco was hardly cutting it right now. He needed something stronger. Something illegal, he didn't care what.

"I'm not taking her with me," Roman declared. "To your house. She's staying here."

"Have you told her that?"

"No. I'll be leaving tonight while she's asleep."

Darien chuckled—he couldn't help it. "Good luck with that."

"What's that supposed to mean?"

"Remember how you tried to get rid of her last time? That girl's stuck on you like gum."

"She can't come with us. I won't be responsible for her dying."

"You can't control everyone, Rome. Sometimes people do dumb shit. Sometimes they get hurt. That doesn't make them your responsibility." Roman was the worst for holding himself responsible for the people he couldn't control. Worse than Darien.

"Okay, but she actually *is* my responsibility," he argued. "Because I fucked around with her. I could have kept my dick in my pants while I helped her look for her sister, and I didn't. Now Don's got her in his crosshairs, and it's my fault. I refuse to let her die because of me."

"It takes two, Roman. She knew exactly who you were and who your dad was when she got involved with you."

A pause, and then Roman swore. "I hate how reasonable you are sometimes."

Darien gave a quiet laugh.

"She's still not coming," he growled.

"That's *your* battle—I'm staying out of it. Just keep me updated on what's going on."

Roman growled another sigh, but said, "Yeah, same for you. I should be there by tomorrow night, I think. Oh, how are your spells?"

"Tanner's working on them as we speak." Literally. He could see Atlas through the kitchen window. Without Mortifer here, Hell's Gate's security was jeopardized. It had been a while since Darien had needed to worry about updating the spell system, so the current one was shit. "We won't be staying here, though. Not after what you just told me. I'll be getting everyone to pack the minute we're done talking."

"Oh? You got a back-up house I'm not aware of?"

"Actually, yeah."

Roman snort-laughed. "Hell's Gate 2.0?"

He chuckled. "Ivy prefers *Heaven's Gate.*" It was a back-up house they'd purchased a few years ago. It was fully furnished and equipped with the same spell system as Hell's Gate, but they'd never been pushed to the point of having to use it.

Why was he not surprised that Donovan would be that first push?

"The Devils at Heaven's Gate," Roman mused. "I like it."

"I'll have to meet you somewhere when you get to the city. It's safer that way."

"No problem. We're wearing talismans, but I need to buy more. You got any?"

"I need to buy more, too." He'd given the very last one to Loren, and the talisman he wore around his own neck was turning brittle, his skin dusted with gold. "Maybe it wouldn't be so hard to find them if *someone* hadn't bought them all." The price had been jacked up so high, Darien might be forced to take some jobs soon just to pay for them all. It was no longer just Loren who needed to wear one—it was everyone.

"Who, me?" Roman asked.

"Yeah, *you*, you fucking hoarder."

"Oh." Roman chuckled. "Well, I need them."

"So do I," Darien said.

"Tough. I gotta go. I'll talk to you soon."

"Don't let your guard down."

"Same to you." He hung up, and Darien had just slid his phone into his back pocket when he picked up on the murmur of voices—frantic with worry—coming from inside the house.

He looked in through the blinds and saw Ivy, Tanner, Kylar, and Logan gathering around the couch.

Around Loren.

Atlas caught Darien's attention through the glass and waved him in.

Darien was already moving. The blinds on the back door rattled as he whipped it open and slammed it shut. "Fuck's going on?"

Everyone cleared a path for him as he pushed through to the couch.

To the girl sitting beside Sabrine. Loren looked up at him, her eyes wide with terror. Her hand was flattened over her chest, her mortal heart beating as rapidly as it had her first night out of a coma.

Her tattoos were flashing.

Both of them.

67

THE WANDERER
ARBOR, STATE OF KER

I tzel would not come out of the fridge.

It was late, and Shay was fast asleep. This was Roman's only chance to get out of here. To save Shay from Donovan and his henchmen by forcing her to go her own way.

And if Itzel didn't smarten up and get in the backpack right this instant, Roman would lose that chance. And Shay would be brutally tortured. Raped. Murdered in cold blood.

He refused to let that happen.

So this damn Hob had to move. *Now.*

"Itzel!" Roman whisper-shouted. He pointed at Pax's backpack—at the main compartment zipped open on the floor in front of the fridge—with a stern finger. "Get in the bag. *Now.*"

A shield of magic shimmered around him, preventing Shay from picking up on the hissing, the whispering, the *spitting*. Yeah, the Hob was *spitting*. Like a distressed cat with her back up. Paxton stood nearby with raised brows, his wide eyes flashing between a slumbering Shay and the absurd scene playing out in front of him in the dark motel room.

This *was* absurd, wasn't it? Itzel was making a complete ass of him.

And his brother looked like he didn't know whether to laugh, take out his phone and start recording, or intervene.

Itzel bared her sharp teeth with another hiss and crammed herself into the back corner. As if there were anywhere to even *go*. She had flattened herself back there so thoroughly, she was practically a pancake.

Roman growled and clawed his fingertips down his face—

"Roman?" Shay croaked.

Fuck.

He froze. So did the Hob.

Sheets stirred. Roman muttered, "Nice going, Itz," and dropped the barrier of silence as Shay sat up in bed.

"What's going on?" She squinted into the dark.

Roman straightened out of his crouch and slapped the fridge door shut. *Hsssssss!* "We're leaving," he declared. He zipped up Pax's backpack. "You can have her." He gestured to the fridge—to the Hob still throwing a temper tantrum inside. *Thump. Thump. Hss. Hss.* "She's your problem now. Let's go, Pax." He swung the strap of Pax's backpack over his shoulder, grabbed his own bags, and made for the door.

Pax followed, dragging his feet.

"You're leaving?" Shay's question was a tired crackle.

Roman opened the door. The harsh light of the bulb mounted outside slanted into the room, the shadows of bugs flitting about.

Head down, lower lip extended, Pax walked out into the cool night.

Roman didn't dare look at Shay—at the hurt he'd no doubt see on her pretty face—as he stepped out, said, "Don't follow us," and closed the door.

Gravel crunched under his boots as he made for the car. He wanted to get this over with—*now*. Before he could do something selfish. Like storm back inside, grab Shay by the chin, and kiss the breath out of her, which he hadn't stopped fantasizing about since he'd laid eyes on her in the warehouse.

He crammed their bags into the back seat, leaving as much room as possible for Paxton. It was late, and Roman had woken him up shortly after ending his call with Darien. He would need to sleep.

'Are you sure about this?' Sayagul asked. Her question was heavy with guilt.

'We've already been through this. Would you rather she be safe or dead?'

The dragon fell silent. A moment later she admitted, *'Safe.'*

'It's settled, then.'

'She's upset.'

'She'll get over it.' The only thing Roman cared about was Shay's life.

No, that was a lie. He cared about *everything* when it came to Shay. It deeply bothered him that she was in that room by herself, slowly waking up and probably confused as hell as to why they were ditching her in the middle of the night. But caring for her would get her killed.

This was better. No matter how much it utterly destroyed him to leave her behind. Abandon her. Roman suspected Shay had been abandoned by someone important in her life in the past—it would explain her trust issues. Which made this all the worse.

"All right, Pax," Roman said on a heavy exhale. "Get in."

The kid was standing by the closed door to room nineteen, squeezing the handle of his comic book-print suitcase with white-knuckled fingers. "No," Pax said, lifting his chin.

Roman sighed. "Pax, come on, don't do this to me. We have to go."

"I don't want to."

Roman stood facing him for a moment. Debating how to approach this. How to make Pax understand.

He closed the distance to his brother and lowered himself into a crouch.

"Listen, Pax," Roman began softly. "I know this sucks. I know you don't want to leave Shay, and neither do I. But we have to."

Paxton's eyes sparkled with tears. "Why?" he croaked. "I like her."

"So do I," Roman whispered. He more than liked her, but that didn't matter. This wasn't about him.

"I feel like..." Pax hesitated. "When Shay's with us, I feel like..." He dropped his voice to a whisper and said, "Like we're a family. A *real* family."

Roman's heart pinched. "Ah, Pax," he said on a sigh.

"Dad ruins everything." His voice cracked. A tear rolled down his freckled cheek, and he angrily wiped it away with a fist.

Roman's heart sank like a ship. "I know," he whispered. "But we're doing this for Shay. To keep her safe. You want to keep Shay safe, don't you, bud?"

Pax didn't answer. The set of his mouth told Roman he was trying very hard not to cry.

Roman pushed to his feet. Gave Pax's shoulder a comforting pat. "Come on. Let's go."

But Pax wasn't finished. "You're not being very nice."

Roman suppressed another sigh. Turned back around.

Pax still hadn't budged. "We're leaving her in the middle of the night when Dad's already looking for her. If he comes here, she'll be all alone."

"He won't," Roman said—but terror threatened to strangle him, and he barely choked it down. "He won't come here." Who was he trying to convince, *himself*? Don was probably on his way right the fuck now.

Going to the clinic was a mistake. Roman had done it for Paxton, to make sure his brother wasn't dying some slow death he wasn't aware of. But he'd messed up. And now, the cops knew they were in Arbor.

They should have left hours ago. He'd bribed the owner of the motel to stay silent in exchange for a fat wad of bills, but they might've been spotted by someone else.

It wouldn't surprise him—the Wanderer was right on the damn highway. It wasn't exactly the best place for a couple of wanted criminals and a missing kid to hide.

"We don't know that!" Pax argued. "And she doesn't even have a car!" The kid made a point. "I think we should let her come with us to Darien's," Paxton persisted. "How would you feel if someone abandoned *me*?"

"Pax." Roman ground his teeth. "It's not the same. Shay's an adult. She's a grown woman. She can handle herself."

"So why are we leaving her behind?" he wailed. "If she can handle herself, then she should be allowed to come with us."

"Pax, I already told you..." The next sigh that came out of him was damn near a growl.

He couldn't believe this, but he found himself hesitating. Which was exactly what he wanted—*needed*—to avoid.

Suddenly, the door to room nineteen opened, and Shay walked out wearing Roman's shirt over her black pajama shorts. She still slept in that shirt every night, as if doing so was good for either of them.

When she saw them standing there, her strawberry blonde brows flicked up. "Oh, you're still here." The statement was flat. Icy.

Roman watched her walk away in bare feet, the tattered hem of his shirt falling past her thighs—the thighs that had been bracketing his hips not long ago.

Too long ago. What he wouldn't give to feel her body beneath his again.

She disappeared around the corner of the building.

Roman stood there with Pax in silence for a few minutes before Shay returned, plastic cup in hand. As if her body wasn't already the hardest temptation he'd ever had to resist in his life, her nipples were firm, the hard tips poking against the soft fabric of his black Legion band tee. It looked better on her than him.

She vanished into the motel room without a backward glance, the door snicking shut behind her.

"Fuck," Roman muttered.

"You liiiiiike her," Paxton accused, smiling. "If you didn't, you wouldn't let her wear your shirt."

"She had no clothes," Roman said.

"Maybe not before, but she does now," Pax countered. A triumphant smile tipped the corners of his lips up. "And you're *still* letting her wear your shirt."

Time ticked. Roman sensed Sayagul puffing up with victory.

"I saaaaw youuuu," Pax said, goading him on, his smile growing so big his dimples showed. "I saw the way you were looking at her!" He waggled his brows. "You don't want to leave."

"Pax," Roman warned. "That's enough."

"You like her! Just admit it already!"

"Stop."

Time ticked again as Pax—*and* Sayagul—tried not to laugh. The more time went by, the less Roman wanted to get in the car.

Which was bad. Really bad.

Paxton cleared his throat. "Sooooo...can we stay? Please?"

Roman remained silent. Weighed the pros and cons.

Stay and risk getting Shay killed? Or leave her by herself and live with the guilt he'd feel for abandoning her? The mystery of not knowing where she was, or if she was okay? Who she was with?

Okay, the last one didn't really matter, but sue him. He was fucking obsessed with her. The thought of another man touching her...

It was enough to make the shadows around the shoddy motel stir.

Paxton said, "Pretty please."

"Don't do that," Roman warned.

But Pax refused to let up. "Pretty, pretty, pretty, pretty pleeeeeease?"

"Pax," he warned again.

Pax started dancing in place, the sight so funny it was Roman who had to try not to laugh this time. "Please, please, please, please, please—"

"Fine!" Roman growled. "You win."

"Yes!" He jumped in celebration, pumping a fist in the air.

"You're a little shit, you know that?"

"I know," he said with a proud smile. "You only tell me every day."

"Get inside." Roman gestured to the room. "Before I change my mind."

Beaming, he pushed the door open, dragging his suitcase behind him.

Roman grabbed the rest of the bags out of the car and followed Paxton inside. Set the bags by the table.

The room was dark—apart from Nugget glowing on the bed. Shay knelt before the fridge, hand-feeding chips of ice to the Hob.

Shay looked over her shoulder at him, her eyes guarded. "Back so soon?"

"Paxton," Roman began as the kid dumped his bag in the middle of the floor—like always—and toed off his shoes, "reminded me that it's not very kind of us to leave you here by yourself."

"Oh, how nice," she said flatly. She handed another piece of ice to Itzel. "At least one of you is considerate." She gave Roman a slow and thorough once-over. "It certainly isn't you."

"I'm trying to keep you *safe*, Shay," Roman snapped. "Tell me how that isn't considerate. My dad's the biggest psycho that's ever walked Terra, and he's hunting me as we speak—"

"He's looking for me, too," she said with the patience of a saint.

Roman ground his teeth so hard they ached. "And if he finds you, he'll torture and kill you. In case that didn't occur to you."

"I'm fully aware, Roman." Ice clattered as she dug around inside the cup and offered another melting piece to Itzel. The Hob happily took it with tiny hands and stuffed it into her mouth. Was that all she'd wanted? *Ice?* Unreal. Quieter, Shay added, "It isn't your job to save me."

Roman whispered hoarsely, "Is it such a crime to try?"

This time, when she looked over her shoulder at him, Roman spotted agony in her eyes. And the tattoo on the inside of her wrist...

It was dark and slowly refilling with soft white light.

His heart pitched downward as he realized...

She'd used illusion to mask her pain. This whole damn time, while she'd acted so cool and collected, pretending she couldn't give a shit if they left...

She was hurting. Roman had hurt her.

"No," Shay said, responding to his question. "You want to leave to save me, and I want to stay to save you."

Roman's heart didn't just drop this time, it damn near *stopped*. For one painful moment, he couldn't breathe.

Eyes downcast, Shay turned her head toward the fridge and handed Itzel another ice chip. "If it's a crime, then we're both guilty."

Roman still couldn't draw a breath. His lungs were on fire, his stomach sick, but he managed to squeeze out, "I'm going for a smoke."

He left before Shay could see the look on his face.

WHERE SHE KNELT on the carpet, Shay handed Itzel the last ice chip melting in the bottom of the cup, and sighed. "That's all of them," she declared.

Behind her, Pax stood watching. Chance crept out of his shadow and cocked his head. The pup was fascinated with the Hob, but the feeling was not mutual. Itzel wanted nothing to do with any of them—unless they had ice.

Roman had a thing or two to learn about Hobs. And women, for that matter.

Shay said, "That was very brave of you, you know. Standing up to your brother like that."

"Thanks," Pax whispered.

She stood and set the cup on top of the fridge.

"Please don't be so hard on him," Pax said. "He likes you, he's just afraid for you. And I mean he *really* likes you. He's brought a lot of girls home, but he's never gone crazy over them like he has with you."

Shay raised her brows. "A lot of girls, huh?" A smile played with her lips as Paxton, slowly realizing what she meant, began to panic.

"Oh, I didn't mean it like" —he sputtered, his face turning red— "I—I'm sorry, I shouldn't have—"

Shay gave a quiet laugh. "Relax, Paxton. I'm just giving you a hard time—"

The door whipped open.

Roman rushed in, white as a ghost.

Shay's smile vanished as he scrambled to shut the door and the blinds, his hands shaking. "Roman?—"

"They've fucking found us," he panted.

68

ANGELTHENE REC CENTER
ANGELTHENE, STATE OF WITHEREDGE

L oren stood with Darien by the front entrance of Angelthene Recreation Center. His muscled arms were wrapped protectively around her from behind, his solid body sheltering her from the night's chill. It was nearly spring, but evenings in Angelthene were still cool enough to need a light jacket—and, in this case, a Darkslayer's arms.

Letting Darien get close to her was something she was having a hard time resisting. Her heart was begging her to thank him for the flowers, the strawberries, the card. *Especially* the card. But...

But she was still upset. About his bargain. About his decision to part with more years than necessary when bringing Singer back. There was so much going on, so much at stake, and while she vowed to do everything she could to fix what Darien had done... Give him back the years he had not needed to trade, if such a thing were even *possible*...

She had to stay alive in the meantime. And she supposed letting the Devil keep her warm wouldn't hurt. Darien was using every excuse he could think of to get close to her, whether it was to check on her tattoos, use his body to shield her from potential threats, or keep her warm, it didn't matter. He seized any opportunity the moment it came up. She was just as guilty, though, because she never refused him.

They were hooked on each other like bees to honey.

Sabrine, Logan, and Tanner were here with them. The latter was in the process of lowering the spells, his face suffused with the cool blue glow of his tablet screen. Back at Hell's Gate, the others were packing their things and preparing for a temporary stay at the other residence that belonged to the Seven Devils. Loren didn't like the idea of being run out of her home, especially so soon. But it was safer this way. Donovan was on the hunt for Paxton, and if he came to Hell's Gate... Well, it was simply better—safer—if none of them were there when he and his Shadowmasters showed up.

Despite the monsters prowling along the perimeter of the parking lot, their silhouettes restlessly darting about in search of a way in, Loren felt perfectly safe with Darien standing behind her.

It was past Witching Hour. Now was the time when Angelthene's people slept in the safety of spell-protected buildings while its monsters came out to hunt. The glare of the flood lights standing sentry around the sprawling recreation center was the only thing holding those bloodthirsty beasts at bay.

When the spells came down, the abrupt absence of magic was so strong, Loren's whole body reacted to it. Her blood purled in her veins, chills cascading from the crown of her head to the balls of her feet.

She swallowed the nausea eddying in her gut. Drew a deep, steadying breath.

She could do this. She had to stay conscious, had to get healthy. Not just for herself but for Darien, too. It was the two of them now.

Literally.

The slayer's strong arms tightened around her, tugging her harder against his chest. Keeping her warm. She clung to his sleeves like she had back in Yveswich, fingers grasping the worn leather. Their bodies were so flush, she could feel the smooth rise and fall of his breathing against her back, and when he bent down just far enough to rest his cheek on the top of her head, she all but melted.

"Almost there, I promise," Tanner said, still clicking.

"Take your time," Darien murmured, the words vibrating through her. Loren felt his nose skim her hair. Heard him inhale.

"One, two, and..." Tanner looked up from his tablet and glanced at the doors with quiet expectance.

Sure enough, the locks clicked open with a *snap*.

The corners of Tanner's lips tipped up. "Three."

Logan pushed the door open. "Impressive," the alpha said, his throaty voice echoing. He held the door, and everyone filed in.

Darien let go of Loren, but stayed close behind as they made their way through the dark building. The place smelled strongly of chloramines and sweat. Compared to the joyful shouting, laughter, and splashing that went on during the day, the silence, while peaceful, felt...eerie. Moonlight trickled through the big windows lining the outer walls, the calm surface of the water in the pools catching its ethereal glow.

"I'll wait right out here," Darien announced when they reached the dressing room, his rich, bass voice booming through the cavernous space. "Call my name if you need anything, and I'll be there before you can blink."

She gave him a nod before following Sabrine to a bench in the dressing room, where the werewolf dug around in the beach bag they were sharing and passed her a fluffy white towel and a two-piece swimsuit the shade of a robin's egg. It was Loren's favorite. Sabrine had borrowed one of Ivy's—a simple black two-piece—for tonight's swim.

Earlier that evening, while Darien made a few phone calls on the back deck at Hell's Gate, Loren had seized the opportunity to open up to Sabrine about the one thing that was bothering her the most.

Darien's bargain. His—and Loren's—impending deaths. The news had hit Sabrine hard, but the shattered look on Loren's face, and the way her voice broke when she told her, had given her strength. Sabrine had pledged that everything would work out—someway, somehow. Instead of questioning her or dissolving into tears, Loren had opted to stay strong and accept her words for what they were: a comforting lie.

"You're quiet," Sabrine remarked as she tied the strings of her bikini top into a bow. It was so dark in here, Loren could scarcely see her face. If her medical tattoos were good for anything, it was the light they gave off, the rhythmic flashes of vermilion allowing her to see well enough to get her own swimsuit on without falling over or banging her legs against the bench. "Is it getting worse?"

Loren tightened the straps of her top. "I think if it gets any worse, my heart will stop," she admitted. Darien had asked her if she wanted to use one of the syringes, but she'd declined. Those were best saved for a true emergency.

Sabrine's mouth twisted into a barely visible frown. "How long do you usually have to swim for?"

"Half an hour, maybe?" She eyed Sabrine as the wolf scooped up their clothes and stuffed them into the beach bag on the bench to keep them all in one place. She looked weary, the skin beneath her angular eyes puffy from lack of rest. "You shouldn't have come," Loren said softly. "You should be sleeping."

"I'm fine," she insisted. But she yawned.

"You have school tomorrow."

"Loren, let me tell you something," Sabrine began. "When Dallas left for Yveswich, I chose not to go, and I regretted it every day." She pulled her sleek black hair up into a neat bun. "The least I can do is sacrifice a few hours of sleep and go for a swim with you." She offered her a spare elastic.

Loren took it and threw her hair up. "I'm wondering if you can help me with something," she whispered, tightening the elastic.

"Oh?" Sabrine asked. "This is about the bargain, isn't it?" Darn it, sometimes Sabrine was too smart.

Loren nodded and stepped closer. "I want to find out if it can be reversed," she said. "His bargain." She gestured to the door—to where she knew Darien was waiting for her. There may not be any hope for her, but... there had to be a way to reverse Darien's agreement with the spider. "He traded the Widow more years than she asked for," Loren explained. "There has to be some way to get those years back."

Sabrine was studying her with empathy. "I'll see what I can find."

"Thank you."

"Ready?"

Loren nodded, and they grabbed their towels off the bench.

Sabrine took her by the hand and led her out of the dressing room, guided by her keen immortal eyesight and the ink flashing on Loren's forearm.

Darien was right where she'd left him, just like he'd promised. Leaning against the wall by the door, his face stern.

He straightened when they came out, his eyes dipping to their joined hands.

It dawned on her, then—why he looked so bothered by the hand thing. Ever since they'd found each other at the hospital in Yveswich, he'd used every excuse to touch her, even while their relationship threatened to unravel at the seams. Seeing someone else holding her hand, even if the gesture was platonic, when he felt like he couldn't do the same was probably torture for him.

Sabrine seemed to notice, because she literally passed Loren's hand to Darien.

He took it without hesitation, though he watched her closely, as if waiting for—and expecting—her to reject him. Rip her hand out of his. The minute his warm, callused fingers wrapped around hers, her stomach flipped upside down. And so did her heart, the darn thing still skipping like a stone.

It skipped even harder when he laced his fingers with hers, his eyes—

more gray than blue in the moonlight—dragging down her body with the kind of scorching hot appreciation that made her toes curl against the floor.

"I like this color on you," he said, gesturing to her swimsuit. His low, husky tone had heat rushing to her skin.

"Thanks."

"I can take your towel," he offered. She passed it to him, and he tipped his chin toward the pool, spurring her into motion.

Hand in hand, they walked to the steps of the pool. It was drafty in here, the floor so icy beneath her feet that she found herself rising up onto her toes. Even while walking like this, the top of her head didn't reach Darien's collarbone. He was menacing—but gods, did she love it. She would never get over this man, would she?

Sabrine jumped off the diving board, the splash of the water clapping through the building.

"You're still upset with me," Darien said quietly. He chucked her towel onto a pool chair.

She didn't deny his accusation, nor did she look at him. She kept her focus on where she was stepping, puddles splashing beneath her feet and Darien's boots.

They were almost at the stairs when he lightly tugged on her hand, spinning her around so she was facing him completely. Her breath caught in her throat as her gaze collided with his. There was no way to escape him this time, nowhere to hide, but she found that her heart didn't even want to. It just wanted *him,* for better or for worse. But her heart was exactly how she'd wound up in this mess in the first place—a mortal tied to an immortal, both doomed. The most dangerous thing she had ever done was fall in love with Darien Cassel, and she was finally paying for it.

"I meant what I wrote in that card," Darien began. The strong column of his throat bobbed. "I fucked up."

"Darien," she whispered, her voice cracking in the dark. "We don't have to talk about this right now."

"I'd like to," he countered. "I'd *really* like to, because I can't stand this, sweetheart—knowing you're upset with me."

She ducked her head—

But he was soon lifting her chin with a knuckle placed gently beneath it. Then he brushed a tendril of golden hair off her cheek and tucked it behind her ear. Heat blossomed everywhere he touched. Lower, too, in her belly. "What can I do?" he asked her. His question was a broken whisper.

"You can't..." She trailed off, because in all honesty she didn't know the answer—and because there was nothing *Darien* could do. Not willingly, at least. The bargain was sealed—he'd said so himself. It was a done deal, and there was no going back.

"Look at me," Darien said softly. It wasn't until he said it that she realized she had dropped her gaze again. He took both of her hands this time, his thumbs brushing across the fine bones in the backs of them. It never ceased to amaze her that someone as dangerous as Darien was capable of being so gentle. "I love you." The statement, said with so much heart, made her blood sing, her pulse skipping for a reason unrelated to her health. "Anything you want, Loren, I'll do it. You want me to get down on my knees, I'll get down on my knees, I don't care that these assholes are watching," he said of Logan and Tanner, who pulled their eyes off them and found somewhere else to look. "I'll do it right here." He began to lower himself to the floor—

She squeezed his hands, stopping him. "Darien. No."

"Then name it. Whatever it is that'll make you forgive me, I'll do it, Loren. I'll even lick the floor at your feet, if you want me to."

"If you lick the floor, I'll be even more mad at you," she said sternly.

"Fine, no floor licking. But I mean it, baby, I'll do anything." He grasped her hands a little tighter, thumbs again grazing the backs of them as he awaited her response. Her forgiveness.

Her eyes burned, and her throat was so tight she could hardly breathe. But she managed to choke out, "I want to go for a swim." *I want to keep myself—and* you—*alive,* she added mentally.

Her response—or lack of one, really—upset him. She could tell. But he said tightly, "That's what you want?"

"Right now," she said evenly, "yes."

A pause. And then he resigned with a stiff nod. "Okay." His pupils were large enough to suggest that he was fighting a Surge, but he managed to keep the black at bay. "Can we talk after?"

Her throat was closing. Gods, the way he was looking at her...

She nodded—just to appease him. The last thing she wanted was to talk about this. Ever.

They completed their walk to the pool steps. She grasped onto the steel handrail with her free hand and dipped her right foot in the water first, the temperature so cold she drew in an echoing gasp through her teeth, her body exploding with chills. Darien didn't let go of her until distance forced him to—until she was too deep in the water for him to keep holding on. The absence of his touch—and the desperate look lingering in his eyes—was so agonizing, Loren almost turned around and got right back out.

The men kept watch as they swam in the dark. But while Tanner and Logan made themselves comfortable on a couple of chairs, Darien stood poolside, utterly transfixed by her. Her tattoos were still glowing beneath the rippling water, but the gaps between flashes were getting longer.

It was working. Even with just blue magic, it was working.

Apart from the pearly moonlight and the glow of Tanner's tablet, her ink was the only source of light in the spacious room. Tanner was working on restoring the spell security systems for both houses, a task that was proving to be more of a challenge than they had anticipated. A Hob's magic was so strong, you hardly needed anything else when you had one of those remarkable critters living under your roof.

Mortifer had spoiled the Devils, and all he'd asked for in return was access to their ice machine. Now, the poor little guy was gone. Missing. Stolen. Discussions on how to go about finding him had arisen at the house and during the drive here, but Hobs were untraceable, even with the Sight. They were similar to the Arcanum Well in that way—the Devils had told her that if they were to try tracking Mortifer, they would feel him all around them. It simply wouldn't work.

And so they were forced to bide their time. Until they found out who had him and where. The security footage from the break-in had revealed several suspects, namely the imperator, Gaven Payne, and Lionel Savage.

By the sounds of things, the Devils would be picking them off one by one. The only challenge was how to find them. Lionel, being Head of the Hunting Grounds, should be easiest to locate, as all Darkslayer Houses knew where to find each other.

But as for Quinton Lucent and the weapons dealer... Finding them wouldn't be so easy.

Angelthene Recreation Center had everything Roman's house had, and more. Three big swimming pools, a hot tub, a sauna, a steam room, two gymnasiums—one for the immortal population and one for mortals—and waterslides. The pool they were in had a diving board, a rope to swing from, and a ring for shooting hoops with inflatable balls.

"What are your plans for tomorrow?" Loren asked Sabrine as the wolf tossed a volleyball above her head. She was desperate to talk about something normal. She didn't care what, as long as it distracted her from everything bad that was going on. From her heart that was still fluttering so fast, each beat was almost painful.

From Darien's stare she could feel everywhere she went—and from the longing to forget why she was angry with him, pull him into the pool with her, and kiss him.

"Besides school," Loren added, remembering what day it was.

"I was thinking of visiting Tamika at the hospital. Maybe bring her some flowers. She's not awake, but I know if it was me in her position, I'd want people to visit me. You can come with, if you want."

Loren slid her focus to Darien.

He was already looking at her. It was hard to see him in the dark, but she swore she saw sweat gleaming on his forehead.

She frowned. What was going on with him? It was *not* warm enough in here to be sweating like that.

"If you want to go, we'll go," he said.

Sabrine said, "You can help me pick out the bouquet. You have a better eye for flowers than I do."

"Sure," Loren said, but she was still distracted by Darien. That was definitely sweat on his face, and he was wiping it off with the heel of his hand. "Darien," she began. "Are you—"

Flashing red and blue lights pulsed through the big windows, causing the water to shimmer like melted candy.

Darien's boots pounded as he walked to the glass, Logan and Tanner getting up and following.

"Shit, did someone call the cops on us?" Tanner's whisper sliced through the air as he joined Darien by the windows.

White light flared, but unlike the blue and red oscillating through the parking lot and streaking through the glass, this light wasn't coming from outside.

It was coming from Loren's solar amulet.

She didn't even have a chance to draw a breath before clammy fingers were wrapping around her ankle, and she was sucked down to the bottom of the pool.

69

THE WANDERER
ARBOR, STATE OF KER

Shay's blood roared as the window shattered. As Paxton screamed.

Roman threw his brother to the floor, using his body to shield the boy from flying glass, as Shay dove across the bed. Her bones barked in pain as she slammed into the table by the window and scrambled for the weapons in Roman's bag.

She pried a handgun from the side pouch. Heart ramming against her ribcage, she slid across the closest bed, back to where Roman and Paxton were hunkered down behind it, and whirled on her knees, aiming the gun at the door—

It flew open with a *bang*, wood splintering as it hit the wall.

Don's men stormed the room, guns glinting in the dark.

"GET DOWN!" Roman bellowed.

He pulled her down and covered her head as the roar of gunfire filled the room. The walls and furniture were blasted with holes, the stench of burnt powder wafting through the air.

As quickly as it had started, the shooting stopped. Shay's ears rang, blood thumping through her head.

She should be dead—she knew that much. They should *all* be dead, or at least injured, too many bullets—*hundreds*—fired too precisely to have missed all three targets. But they weren't dead, and they weren't injured, because—

Because the shadows stirring through the room, wrapping protectively around them like great wings... Those shadows were Roman's.

And they were darkening and swelling like a supercell thunderstorm.

Shay's blood thrummed with a warning. Her skin tingled with chills. Nausea clenched her stomach as she watched Roman slowly rise from the ground beside her, pieces of glass and bullets sliding off his clothes.

As darkness surged around them, as if alive, shadows moving in a cyclone that blew their hair, the blinds, the quilts.

As Roman's lethal power grabbed every assailant by the throat and lifted them into the air, where they dangled like puppets. Guns clattered to the floor. Their faces turned a deep shade of purple, their tracheas crushing like pop cans.

The shadows around their throats constricted—so quickly, Shay would have missed it, had she blinked.

And all at once, Donovan's men were decapitated.

Blood sprayed through the room. Shay flinched, red misting her shocked face. Bodies and heads hit the floor and rolled.

Holy gods.

For one moment, as Roman stood there, panting among the carnage—eyes a glittering onyx, shadows undulating at his back like the dark wings of an avenging angel—Shay realized just how truly dangerous he was.

Seven. Roman had killed *seven* men.

But their fight was far from over—and Roman was not the only Shadowmaster here tonight. Donovan's men could control shadows too, and there were more coming.

They pushed into the room, shouting commands and threats, and soon it was Roman, exhausted from his output of magic, who was lifted into the air and slammed against the wall between the beds so hard it cracked up to the ceiling. The lamp on the nightstand fell, bulb shattering.

Paxton's scream was drowned out as the air fractured with more fired shots.

Shay shoved Paxton behind her. *"Get down and stay behind me!"* She used the bed as a shield and shot overtop of it. Downed several men. Roman fought to break free of the shadows pulling his limbs taut as his father's cronies pushed farther into the room. Sayagul swooped at them with knife-sharp talons and piercing shrieks, the dragon fiercely protecting her boy with her life.

More shots were fired, bullets peppering the mattress.

One hit Shay's gun. The impact bit into her bones, and she cried out in alarm. Took cover.

Shit, her fingers were bleeding.

"*SHAY!*" Roman bellowed. The sheer panic in his voice had her head snapping up—

Sure enough, two men had gotten a hold of Paxton and were dragging him across the room. Sayagul was in distress, the dragon flying after them on frantic wings.

'*Paxton!*' Sayagul cried. '*No! Roman, help! Help! They're taking Paxton!*'

Shay was up and moving before she could think, narrowly escaping the reach of the men in the room. The noise of the bullets had rendered her half-deaf and turned her brain to jelly, but the adrenaline coursing through her veins was stronger than the shock. It pushed her to move faster, react quicker. It was all she needed.

Gun in one hand, lightning twining around the fingers of the other, she downed every fool who dared to lunge at her. The lightning spread—until she was armored from head to toe with forks of untouchable bluish-white lightning. Every bullet she fired hit their mark with squirts of blood and shouts of pain. Bodies dropped like flies.

She was lightning incarnate. A storm in the flesh.

The moment her bare feet hit the pavement in a mad dash for Paxton, thunder growled a warning. Angry clouds converged, their rain-bloated bellies darkening the street.

Her blood burned hot with lightning, her pulse skittering so quickly she swore her heart might explode. But she kept firing, trigger snapping under her finger.

Bang. Bang. Bang.

There were three cars waiting nearby. Paxton was being dragged toward the open back door of the second sedan, the kid kicking and screaming and fighting to break free—to get to her. Back to Roman.

The sky above the motel shattered.

Lightning speared the first car with a deafening *CRASH*. People screamed.

White light engulfed the property, blinding her. Shay hissed and threw up a hand to shield her burning eyes. She stumbled, fighting to stay upright. To see—

"No," she breathed. Where was Paxton? *Where was he?* She couldn't *see* — "No, no, no, no, no, *no.*"

Too slowly, the light faded. Her eyes adjusted. The ringing in her ears was so sharp, she couldn't hear a thing. She whirled, searching—

There was Paxton. Being hauled to his feet by the rough hands of Shadowmasters who had survived the lightning strike.

Shay pushed her shellshocked body into a sprint. The reek of burnt hair and blackened flesh scorched her nostrils as she closed the distance to Paxton with four powerful strides.

A dark shape lunged at her left. Bruising hands grabbed her by the shirt, yanking her back against a torso clad in a bullet-proof vest. She reached behind her, slapping her charged palm against the bastard's face.

Forks of lightning flowed from her fingertips and into his cheek, his eye. Screaming, he let go and collapsed, limbs twitching. Shay was already moving, bolting to Pax, her feet ripping open on stones and glass. She lifted her gun. Pulled the trigger—

A hollow *click*. She was out of bullets.

She skidded to a stop, feet burning across the pavement, and ducked as the Shadowmaster dragging Paxton lashed out—

Too late. He backhanded her across the face, his rings ripping the skin of her cheek open.

Shay fell so hard, she felt the impact in her teeth. Saw stars. Tasted dirt. She couldn't move, couldn't breathe, couldn't *think* as a boot kicked out, slamming into her face. Paxton screamed her name. Blood gushed from her brow, her nose, down the back of her throat.

Another kick to the jaw, and she fell back on the ground. Hard.

Roman tore out of the motel room soaked in fresh blood, his face a mask of veritable rage.

Pax was almost in the car. They were going to take him—

Shay rolled onto her hands and knees, her eyes locking with Paxton's as he was dragged toward that open door—

They were solid black, his eyes. Gleaming like inky pits.

And there were dark lines spreading through the pale skin around them, like the roots of a blighted tree.

Hands seized her shoulders, startling her—

But it was only Roman. He was screaming, but Shay couldn't hear what he was saying, couldn't hear anything at all, as he pulled her to her feet and shoved her into motion.

Not toward Pax, but *away*.

Shay couldn't make sense of why they were running.

Until Paxton opened his mouth—

And *screamed*, the sound so deafening, it was as if a pipe bomb went off in each ear.

Dark power blasted them off their feet. Shockwaves cracked the pavement apart, like glass shattering under the mighty blow of a fist.

They hit the exterior wall of the Wanderer so hard the impact nearly fractured their bones.

With a cry of agony, Shay crumpled to the ground, landing hard on Roman, her every muscle screaming in pain.

She couldn't breathe.

She. Could. Not. *Breathe.* Couldn't *think*. Could barely see or hear beyond the pain searing through every bone, every muscle, every vein.

By the mercy of the gods, she managed to suck in a shallow stream of sweet, sweet air.

Another...

One more, her lungs stretching to full capacity this time.

Ears shrieking, she lifted her pounding head off Roman's hip—

What she beheld made her ill.

"Good gods," she whispered. Bile burned her throat. Gagging, she clenched her roiling gut.

Paxton's magic had laid waste to everything. Brutally massacred every single one of Donovan's men. Gods, what she was looking at...it was so grisly, she could barely make sense of what anything was.

The bodies of their assailants had popped like balloons. The pavement, the cars, the motel, all of it was sprayed with blood, brain matter, and wet bone that had been shattered so finely it was practically dust.

Paxton had killed them. Every last one.

"Shay," Roman choked out. He shifted his leg out from beneath hers, grunting as he sat up.

He gaped at his little brother, who was staggering to his feet by the side of the road. Paxton blinked, baffled, as if waking from a nightmare.

The vehicles had been blown away, as if they weighed no more than fallen leaves. There was nothing left of them but shattered glass, a few bits of metal and plastic, and the shredded black rubber of tires. Even Roman's car had been blasted across the road and now lay on its roof, a halo of shattered glass glittering around it.

Something touched Shay's hand. She startled, but it was only Roman.

"Are you okay?" he asked her. Shay had to read his lips, her ears still screeching too loudly to hear properly. She managed a nod, and he helped her stand. Brushed bits of glass out of her hair. Swiped his thumb across the thick blood caked on the skin between her nose and lips.

"I'm fine," she assured him. Her voice sounded odd. Distant. A stranger's voice.

Her breath caught for a whole different reason as Roman slid both of his hands to the back of her head, gently cupping her neck with a trembling grip. He scanned her face—just for a moment, as if convincing himself that she was okay. Alive.

And then he nodded—to himself, mostly. Confirming that yes, she was indeed okay. He let go of her neck and took her by the hand, lacing his fingers with hers. Together they approached Pax, walking carefully across glass, blood, and gods knew what else.

Roman paused a distance away, as if it were not his brother he was approaching, but a wild animal. "Pax?" he croaked.

Paxton's eyes snapped their way—and widened, as if he were just noticing them. It took him a moment to find his voice.

"I'm sorry." Paxton's apology was hoarse, his chin wobbling. Tears fell from his eyes, clearing tracks through the filth on his face. The dark lines Shay had seen...they were gone, and so was all the black from his eyes. A ragged sob clawed its way through him. "I'm sorry, *I'm so sorry!*" Another noisy, ragged gasp. "I— I— I didn't m—mean to—"

Roman let go of Shay's hand and stumbled forward. He only made it two feet before he crashed to his knees, his arms opening to Pax. "Come here," he choked out on a sob.

Paxton sprinted into Roman's arms.

"It's okay," Roman breathed as Paxton collided with him, still in shock, and fully sagged in his arms, weeping softly. "It's okay, Pax. It's okay. You're okay, I got you. I got you. You didn't do anything wrong—"

"I *killed* them!" Paxton wailed. Shay's heart broke for him. Those horrible men had tried to hurt him first, and yet here he was, crying over hurting them by accident. *"I killed them, I killed them! I'm a monster—"*

"Listen to me," Roman urged softly. *"Listen."* He pulled Paxton back so he could look him in the eyes, his thumbs wiping tears off Paxton's cheeks. "You're not a monster, Pax. You didn't do anything wrong. It was an accident, okay? It was just an accident, Pax. That's all it was."

Roman hugged him again—hard. Paxton cried on his shoulder, his thin arms squeezing his big brother's neck tight, fingers curling in his ripped and blood-stained shirt.

A glow caught Shay's eye. It was a phone—lying on the ground a few feet away.

Shay tiptoed over to it, limping as pebbles and shards of glass dug into her shredded feet. With bleary vision, she peered down at the screen.

The name she saw above the call duration—11:03 and still ticking—caused her stomach to plummet.

"Roman," she croaked.

In the corner of her eye, she saw Roman turn his head.

Shay pointed at the device with a scraped finger.

Roman stood, wincing. He took Paxton by the hand, and together they came over.

For a moment, they stood there, all three of them. Staring at the phone in silence.

With blood-slick, shaking hands, Roman picked up the phone and lifted it to his ear, holding his breath as he listened. The person on the other end did not speak, but from the look on Roman's pale face, he knew his father was there. Knew his father was waiting to see if his son would dare to break the silence first.

So that was exactly what Roman did. "Come after us again," Roman warned in a low, lethal voice, "and you'll be next."

He threw the phone to the ground and crushed it beneath the heel of his boot.

70

ANGELTHENE REC CENTER
ANGELTHENE, STATE OF WITHEREDGE

Darien barely had time to rip his jacket off before he was diving into the pool, water spraying around him like a bomb blast.

Two seconds was all it took him to get in there, and already Loren was almost at the bottom, reaching out her hand for him as the water wraiths dragged her down...

Down...

Down...

The wraiths—aquatic specters that took the form of crones—were made entirely out of water, no heartbeat, blood, or aura, which made it impossible to detect their presence until they were already trying to drown you.

Impossible to kill, too. Magic didn't work on wraiths. You had to physically be strong enough to break free of their hold, and if you weren't, you drowned. It was that simple.

Three wraiths against one human were not good odds.

A dark shape rippled at the bottom of the pool. It was a jagged scar—black, smoky, and pulsing with sinister energy that cracked the pool floor. To simply look at it made Darien feel dizzy. The wraiths were dragging Loren—kicking and thrashing—toward that scar, their liquid fingers wrapped tightly around her ankles like shackles.

Darien swam as fast as he could. A Surge was breathing down the back of his neck, but he managed to keep the black out of his eyes. If he failed, he wouldn't be able to see properly.

He should already be at the bottom. But the farther he swam, the deeper the pool got. His lungs were burning from lack of oxygen, but he kept moving, diving impossibly deep while Loren was dragged and dragged and *dragged* farther away from him.

The water got darker. Deeper. It got harder to hold his breath.

Something shifted. The water pulsed, and the atmosphere seemed to peel open, as if he were entering a Crossroads. The temperature plummeted to subzero, the drop so sudden it was a shock to the heart.

Loren didn't take her eyes off him as she kicked and pushed against the cackling wraiths. She was getting too close to the black mark in the floor. If the wraiths dragged her down one more meter, she'd be gone.

And Darien would lose her.

With a deep, reverberating rumble, the mark split open wider, a mouth poising to devour—

Fuck. *Fuck, fuck, fuck.* Darien kicked harder and swam deeper, forever reaching out his hand.

Come on, baby, come on, baby, he thought. *Fight, Loren! FIGHT!*

As if she'd heard him, she did. She wrested her arms and legs free of the wraiths' watery grip. Booted one in the rawboned face and kicked herself up through the water, fingers splaying as she reached for his hand.

Their fingers touched—

Rainbow light fucking *erupted*.

He shouted in surprise, a burst of bubbles rushing out of his mouth. But he did not let go of Loren's hand, not even as he was forced to shut his eyes, the light too blinding to see through.

The wraiths fled for the shadows with piercing screams garbled by the water, their bodies steaming in the heavenly light.

Darien kept his stinging eyes half-shut as he felt around in the water for Loren. As soon as he got a firm grip on her, he wrapped his arms around her waist, hauling her against his body, and swam up. Together, they kicked for the surface.

As the light faded, he fully opened his eyes and chanced a glance down at the floor of the pool.

The scar was rippling shut, the black seam stitching together with smoke-like wisps. It seemed to be retreating—as if fleeing from the rainbow light. From Loren's magic.

That scar...

It was a fucking *portal*.

And by the grace of the gods, Loren had just closed it.

They burst through the surface with ragged gasps and gulping breaths.

"Are you okay?" His question resounded through the building. "You okay?" he said again. He pulled her harder against his chest with one arm, his other hand brushing strands of wet hair out of her face as she coughed and coughed, the whites of her eyes red from the chlorine.

"I'm fine," she replied, but she was still coughing. Her arms came up to circle his neck. "I'm okay. I'm okay."

"You sure?"

"Yeah. I don't know what happened, though."

"Come on, let's get you out of here and get you dry." With one arm hugging her waist, he used his other to propel them toward the edge of the pool. She clung to his neck, her body violently shaking from the cold. "Your necklace," he said.

She peeked up at him. "What?"

"Your necklace is gone. Your talisman."

Her fingers went to her neck, groping.

"Take mine and put it on, please."

"Right now?"

"Yes."

She reached behind him and unclasped it. It felt like a hug, and he had to fight the urge to lean into her, her cheek so close to his they almost brushed. She put the necklace on, then held onto him, her arms around his neck.

"I'm sorry." Her apology was broken apart by chattering teeth.

"Sorry?" Darien repeated. He repositioned her, sliding her flush with the front of his body so he could see her face better, still kicking toward the edge of the pool. "What are you sorry for?"

Her fingers shook harder against his skin, the stupid water still freezing as hell. "For getting you all wet."

"You can get me wet any time," he said, the tip of his nose nearly skimming hers as they turned their faces toward each other at the same time. He kissed her on the damp cheek while he had his chance, the gesture warming her face with a flush of pink.

Fuck, he loved that.

"You're not very good at the whole *we're mad at each other* thing," she said.

"You're the only one who's mad, sweetheart," he said softly. "I'm just waiting for you to forgive me."

They reached the edge of the pool. Darien helped her get out first, his hands gripping her hips.

Then he pulled himself up, his sopping clothes splashing water everywhere—

And froze as a pair of unfamiliar boots stepped into his vision.

Slowly, he planted both feet flat on the floor and straightened...

And found eight fucking police officers surrounding him. Tanner was in the process of being cuffed. Logan and Sabrine stood near the edge of the group of officers, looking shocked and conflicted as to what they should do, whether they should stand back or try to intervene. Darien's jacket was draped over Sabrine's arm.

The pair of linked rings they were locking around Atlas's wrists...

They were a shining black with glowing, orange-red lines, like hot lava forking through volcanic glass. Even from here, Darien could feel the raw, ancient magic pulsating through those lines.

His eyes briefly shuttered.

Fuck. He knew exactly what those were.

When Tanner's eyes locked with his, they widened with a warning that seemed to say, *Just behave. Don't make a scene.*

Fuck that. Making scenes was his speciality.

So Darien demanded, "What the hell's going on?"

The officers closest to the front parted, revealing a face Darien wanted nothing more than to punch. And punch. And punch.

And keep fucking punching until this prick was dead, his skull nothing but red goo.

It was Detective Glen of the Yveswich MPU. The same prick who'd put the forcefield up early.

"Darien Cassel," Glen barked, spit flying. "You're under arrest!"

"On what fucking charges?" he snarled.

"Hmm, let's see...," Glen began as two officers came up behind Darien, twisting his arms so far back, the pain would've brought any sane man to his knees. Cuffs bit into his wrists with metallic *clicks*.

"Breaking and entering," Glen began in a sharp voice, ticking the charges off on his fingers. "Trespassing; assault and battery; drug possession; possession of property obtained by crime; theft; vandalism; arson; murder; accessory to murder..." He gave him a cruel smile. "There's more. Shall I go on?"

Darien's blood simmered. Bandit growled in his shadow.

A soft gasp had Darien's head snapping to the side, his arms still pinioned behind his back.

His soul left his body. Because Loren—

An officer was cuffing her.

"HEY—*hands off!*" he bellowed, the command ringing through the room.

"Darien," she gasped. "What's happening?"

"HANDS *OFF!*" He thrashed and whipped his head back, shattering an officer's nose with a sharp *crack*. He yowled in pain, while another officer slipped and crashed into the pool with a pathetic scream as Darien roared, *"I SAID HANDS FUCKING OFF!"*

Glen whipped out a handgun—

And pointed it at Loren's head.

Darien stopped fighting. Went rigid. Held his breath.

The room was so silent, so still, the *click* of the safety being removed echoed like a fired shot.

Darien's heart was pounding so hard, he felt like he was having a heart attack. His skin started sweating, as if it were a million degrees in here and he wasn't sopping wet with cold pool water.

"Darien, it's okay, " Loren tried, the words weak and breathy. But it wasn't okay. They were fucking touching her, pointing a gun at her beautiful head, and he couldn't breathe.

He—couldn't—fucking—breathe. He was shaking so hard, the chains of the cuffs were rattling, power straining beneath his skin.

"Stop," he ground out. Glen cocked his head, his finger teasing the trigger. Darien didn't care how weak he sounded when he begged—literally *begged*, "Point it at me instead."

Another beat of silence. No one moved. No one breathed.

Glen thought it through, his narrow eyes flicking with critical evaluation between Darien—a Devil—and the human girl—an angel in the flesh, who kept staring at Darien with a beseeching gaze.

And then he swung his arm Darien's way, stepping so close the muzzle nearly grazed his forehead.

Loren made a little noise in her throat.

Darien saw black as the Sight engulfed his eyes—

"Ah, ah, ah," Glen tsked, shaking his head. "I wouldn't do that if I were you. Unless you want your little girlfriend—" He briefly swung the gun her way again, the gesture boiling Darien's blood. "—to pay for your bad attitude."

Darien didn't move.

And just like that, the black left his eyes.

The corners of Glen's lips curved upward. "That's better," he drawled. "Good dog." Darien shook harder, his lungs burning. "What you're wearing, Darien," Glen continued, his voice saturated with pompous attitude, "is a pair of brynstan cuffs. Otherwise known as—"

"Brimstone," Darien growled.

"Right. And not only does brimstone nullify a person's magic, it will also—"

"Backfire and kill me if I try to use it," Darien concluded coldly.

Glen gave him a deadly smile. "So he does have a brain."

Loren kept her pleading eyes on Darien as the officer standing behind her finished locking her cuffs. Ordinary—not brimstone. "It's okay," she mouthed. "It'll be okay."

But Darien's chest heaved, all those walls he'd spent twenty-four years building and heavily fortifying finally threatening to crumble.

This was not okay. *None* of this was okay.

"You have the right remain silent," the cop was saying to her. "Anything you say can and will be held against you in the court of law—"

"She needs to get changed," Darien growled. "You're not taking her in like that, she'll freeze."

Glen got right up in his face. Close enough to spit on. To bite. Darien would have done it—would've bitten his cheek clean off, if these assholes wouldn't retaliate by bringing harm to Loren. But he refrained—for her. Even as Glen canted his head from side to side, studying him down his bony nose with flagrant disgust.

It seemed to take forever before he prompted the officer, who held onto Loren's cuffs, with a sharp nod.

"It's okay," Loren once again assured him, but her words were strained, and Darien could tell that she was barely breathing. The officer gripped her by the upper arm and led her to the dressing room.

Seeing another man touch her like that...especially when he knew she didn't like it...

It was torture. He felt like someone had stabbed him in the heart and was slowly twisting the blade, his blood splashing to the floor. That was his whole world he was looking at, and he could do nothing but stand there and watch as they paraded her around like she was a fucking criminal.

He refused to take his eyes off his girl as they stopped by the door, the cop unlocking her cuffs. Even after she had disappeared into the dark room with a backward glance, her eyes briefly meeting his before she vanished around the corner, he kept watching, making sure no one went in there or tried to peek. If they did, he'd slaughter them all, no question. Even if the brynstan ended up killing him too, he'd gladly die defending her.

Glen was still watching him with that same perpetual sneer.

Darien didn't spare him one look.

"Hm," Glen scoffed. "Not only does the Devil have a brain, but he seems to have a heart, too," he mused, his tone glacial. That heart he spoke of was pounding with rage, the chains on his cuffs tinkling with restraint. He was squeezing his fists so hard, the muscles and bones in his right hand were burning. "This should be interesting."

Darien shifted his black stare to Glen—just for a moment. The prick was looking at him like he was shit under his shoe.

Darien spat on the floor between them.

Glen frowned down at his shoes. Lifted his gaze to Darien's. "You're going to regret that," he said quietly.

We'll see who regrets anything about this night, you fucking tool.

A couple of minutes later, Loren came out fully dressed, her spring jacket zipped up. She turned around and offered up her hands to the officer. Darien breathed so hard he was panting as the cuffs snapped shut on her delicate wrists.

"Call Ivy," Darien said to the wolves as the officers prodded him forward. *"Call Ivy—now."*

"Yes, *do* call Ivy," Glen drawled, his tone cruel. Mocking. "We'd like to have a chat with her husband, too." He gave Darien a hostile once-over before barking, *"Take them to the station!"*

71

SOUTH COASTAL DISTRICT
YVESWICH, STATE OF KER

A riot had broken out in the South Coastal District.

Several blocks from the Duchess, near the military base, Max kept his hand wrapped firmly around Dal's as they pushed through the massive crowd gathered in the street.

There had to be thousands of people here. Hundreds were being arrested and loaded into squad cars, while countless others looted and vandalized. Vehicles and buildings were being set on fire. People ran for shelter, barricading themselves inside any safe space they could find. Alarms and sirens sliced apart the air with piercing screams as rioters smashed windows and stole anything they could carry. Many stood their ground against cops wearing riot gear, while others ran from the threat of being apprehended, barking K-9 Familiars in pursuit. Silhouettes were chased down alleys, a few climbing fire escapes, while vampires shifted and fled from the scene on leathery wings.

Armed soldiers were stationed around the fenced perimeter of the military base, guns at the ready. Spells coated the base, the threat of incineration the only thing stopping these people from forcing their way through. Military personnel, cops, and MPU agents shouted into megaphones, warning people to get back, keep order, or risk getting shot or locked up.

Travis and Jewels came up behind Max, squeezing their way through droves of screaming and cursing vampires, wolves, veneficae, humans, and the odd hellseher. Even in large crowds like this, there were never many people like them—hellsehers. Their kind made up only a small percentage of the Terran demographic.

Behind Travis and Jewels came Aspen and Malakai, their eyes coal-black. Malakai's power hummed in a dark glow around him as he craned his neck, peering over thousands of heads at the military equipment and armed soldiers in the fortified space.

"Fuck's this all about?" Travis shouted. Jewels stood in front of him on her tiptoes, sheltered by Travis's tall form as people moved all around them, jostling each other.

"I don't know," Max replied, scanning the crowds. "But these people are not happy."

In front of him stood a witch, her back facing him. In her hands she held her cell phone, the camera recording. She was talking loudly for the mic, as if broadcasting the scene—putting the military on blast for trapping them all in here, by the sounds of it.

He tapped her on the shoulder. "Hey!" he shouted. "Hey—excuse me! HEY!" He had to tap her a few times and shout some more before she finally turned around, the rings around her pupils reflecting the light of a burning car across the street as she looked up at him. "Is your phone working?"

"What?" she yelled over the din, cupping a hand over her ear.

"Your phone!" He pointed at the device in her hands. *"Is it working?"*

"Service, you mean? No, that's why we're here—I'm recording so we have evidence! These bastards cut the service!" She stabbed her hand through the cold air, pointing to the military.

The blood drained from his face.

Fuck me. So it wasn't just the pay phones, then.

"Why would they do that?" he asked her.

"They're covering it up!" said the warlock beside her. "They're trying to silence us and stop this shit from leaking to the public! What they're doing is wrong—they should be letting us out! Bunch of bullshit." He turned back around and resumed shouting profanities at the cops and military, spittle flying.

Max felt like he couldn't breathe. This jacket was too warm, these people were too close, and they were trapped.

They were never going to make it out of here, were they? He was never going to see his family or his home again.

Dallas stared up at him, weary and bone-pale. Defeated—she looked utterly defeated. Aged. Exactly how Max felt.

Travis shouted, leaning in close to Max's ear, "How are we supposed to get a hold of Darien now?"

They couldn't. There was no way—not without service.

They were stuck. For real, this time.

And, for whatever reason, the government had made the decision to cut the telecommunications network. To cover up what was really happening here and feed the public some blatant lie.

Gunshots popped through the air. The crowd screamed and took cover. People ran, bowling others over in their mad dash to get away.

Something smacked into Max so hard, he went down. He crashed into the pavement, chin and palms ripping open.

CRACK.

The earth shook so violently, his brain rattled in his skull. The force pinned him to the pavement, people dropping all around him.

Deeper in the city, monsters screeched and roared as missiles struck their targets. Flashes of color and light from the artillery blitz licked across the curves and edges of the groaning mass of shadow, the Void spreading like spilled ink. Like a great and terrible monster eclipsing the city with vast wings.

Ears ringing, head whirling, Max pushed himself onto his hands and knees, wincing as people stepped on his fingers as they ran by.

Dallas. Where the hell was Dallas?

He struggled to get back up, and when he finally did, he staggered and swayed. He could hardly hear anything, his vision tunneling as he whipped his head about, searching for the others. His heart thumped a frantic rhythm in his ears. *Th-thump. Th-thump. Th-thump.* Shoulders slammed into him from the front and back with bruising force, jerking him this way and that.

Shit. *Shit shit shit,* where the hell was everyone? Dallas and Travis. Jewels, Malakai, Aspen... They were all gone!

"Max!" called a faint female voice.

"Dallas?!" he bellowed, panting. He stumbled forward and nearly lost his balance, head gyrating. *"Dallas!"*

"Over here! Max, over here!"

There she was—sprawled across the ground, unable to get up as people shoved by, tripping over her. She ducked and covered her head with her arms as she took a boot to the back of the neck.

"Dallas!"

"Max!" She tried to stand, but her wings hindered her. People were

stepping on them, yanking her back down. She cried out in pain as her wing got caught on someone's foot, and she was dragged backward as the man tripped and smashed into the ground.

Max charged through like a bull. Punched a vampire in the mouth and a half-blood warlock in the jaw to get to her. Others fell under his might—his blind rage—but he didn't give two shits about them. He had to get to Dal. Had to find Travis.

"Dallas!" He grabbed her by the scraped hands, shoving a warlock who stepped on her left wing aside. He pushed another—a vampire this time, the guy's shoe crushing exposed wires on her other wing. "Get the hell off her!" he bellowed, pulling her up. Her wings were bent, worse than before, her cheek and chin scraped, bloody, and flecked with gravel and a dusting of glass. "You all right?" She winced as he brushed the gravel off her face, smearing blood.

Something clattered to the ground nearby.

White smoke erupted. People screamed and scattered.

Max sputtered and coughed, his eyes burning so badly he couldn't keep them open.

"Oh gods," Dallas gasped, choking. *"Max!"*

Another can clattered across the pavement behind them. More smoke choked the air.

He couldn't breathe.

"Max!" Dallas cried. Her fingers found his jacket, grasping tight. "Max, what's happening? I can't see—" *Cough. Cough.* "My eyes—" *Cough.* "I can't open them—"

"Hold on!" He could barely speak, the tear gas forcing him to cough so hard he gagged. His lungs burned as if they were full of acid. People jostled him from all sides, banging into him and Dallas and nearly wrenching them apart. "Hold on, I got you!" Max promised. "I need you to hold onto me, okay? I got you! I'm gonna get us out of here!"

"Max—" *Cough. Cough.* "Wait—wait, I can't breathe—"

"Dallas, look at me." Maybe that was the wrong thing to say, because he could hardly keep his blurry eyes open, tears coursing down his cheeks. He managed to find her face, and gently cupped it. "Dallas, listen to me. You're going to be okay. But I need you to trust me!"

"Okay." The word burst out of her on a ragged gasp. She couldn't keep her eyes open, either, not for longer than a second at a time. Her nose was running, her face bright red.

"Close your eyes and hold onto me!" he said again. "Don't let go—no matter what happens."

He took her by the hand, lacing their fingers tightly, and led her through the riot, squinting his leaking eyes and hacking up a lung the whole way. All around them, sirens wailed, people smacked into them, more guns went off, more cans of tear gas clattered to the pavement. It was madness.

"Where are the others?" Dallas shouted, her free hand fisting the back of his jacket. "We have to find the others—"

The crack of more bullets drowned her out. People ran away screaming, blinded by the tear gas that was fogging up the block.

"We'll find them!" he promised. "Just keep holding onto me. Don't let go."

He stayed true to his promise and got her out. The smoke was finally clearing, and although they were still coughing and gasping, they could breathe again. They could see. There were less people over here, less threats, no cops or military personnel, just a couple of burning cars.

"Hold on," Dallas squeezed out. "Hold on, I need to stop." She let go of his hand and staggered over to the curb, her bent wings throwing her off balance.

She tripped, smacking into a telephone pole. She wrapped her arms around it, steadying herself, and rested her cheek against the wood, her flushed face glistening with tears.

"Dallas?" he rasped.

For a moment, she just stood there, hugging the pole, her leaking eyes fixed on the pavement that was covered with garbage and shattered glass.

And then her face transformed with rage, and she reached over her shoulder and started ripping feathers out of her wings.

Max took a step forward. "Dallas—"

She screamed, the sound ragged and barbaric. "Stupid, *stupid*, *STUPID!* I hate these stupid things, *I hate them, I hate them!* I need to get them removed!"

"You mean fixed?"

"No—*removed!* I don't want them anymore! I thought I wanted to be a soldier for the Fleet, but that was just my stupid parents talking! My whole life has consisted of nothing but decisions *they* wanted me to make. Roark this, and Taega that! Well, what about *Dallas?* What about *me?*" She poked herself in the chest, her eyes wide with rage.

Max stayed where he was, not daring to get any closer.

Space. She needed space.

Panting, she slumped against the telephone pole and slid to the pavement, kicking her legs out before her. "After everything we've lived through," she continued, her voice a quiet rasp that was nearly drowned out by sirens and distant blasts. "The battles, the explosions, the injuries, the *stress...*" She swallowed, chest heaving. She slid her silver-ringed eyes to his. "I don't want anything to do with it anymore," she confessed.

Max's throat bobbed. "Then what do you want, Dal?" he asked gently. "Tell me what *Dallas* wants."

"I want..." She hesitated. Max would bet she had never been asked that —what *she* wanted. "I want...," she began again, sniffling, "to live a quieter life."

"A quieter life," he repeated, nodding. "Okay, quiet sounds good. It sounds great, actually," he added with a small chuckle as more noise jarred the street.

Dallas wiped her face with both hands, then stared down at the dirt on her palms. "I don't know what that would involve yet, but..." She nibbled on her bruised lip. "I don't know, maybe I'll start taking classes for something different. Something *I* want. But— If you were to remove my parents from the equation...who am I, really? They've turned their careers into their personalities—soldiers are all they are. And...and I don't want that. I don't want to be like them." As soon as the words were out, she looked as surprised that she'd said them as Max was to hear them. "I want...something else. Something different."

I want that with you, Max thought. Whatever it was that Dallas wanted, he'd be there to support her. That would be his promise.

"Max!" called a male voice.

Max turned as Dallas got to her feet.

Travis was bolting this way. His face was red, his eyes watering.

"Travis," Max exclaimed, a cough ripping out of him. "What's going on? Where are the others—"

"It's Jewels!" he rasped as he thumped to a stop. "It's Jewels, she's having trouble breathing."

"Is it the gas?"

"No, man—it's the Tricking! She needs her meds. We need to get to the hospital!" He spun the other way—

"Wait—hold up!" He lunged forward and grabbed Travis by the sleeve, whipping him back around. "The *hospital?* Do you have any idea how far that is? How the *hell* are we supposed to get there?"

Travis paused, gazing out at the black cloud ballooning above Yveswich. The hospital was in there.

Travis's face smoothed with an epiphany. "The water," he murmured.

"What?"

Travis wiped the tears off his face. "The water," he said again. "The canals—we can get there if we take the canals."

72

TORRANCE DRUGSTORE
TORRANCE, STATE OF KER

The cloth was soaked with blood.

Shay kept pressure on her fingers as she pushed open the glass door to the one and only drugstore in the community of Torrance, Roman and Paxton following behind her.

After the attack at the motel, and after deeming it unsafe to stay in Arbor for any length of time beyond how long it took to pack their things, they had driven the short distance to the town of Torrance. Roman had used his magic to get the car back on the road, the shattered glass fitted together in the windows like the pieces of a jigsaw puzzle. It wasn't perfect, the glass flawed in spots and the bumpers dented, but at least the car was drivable.

Now, all they had to do was stop the bleeding in her hand.

"Yeah, we're in," Roman was saying into his phone, his husky voice echoing as they walked through the dark store. "No, we should be good now. Yeah. Sure, I'll call you when we're close. You, too. Thanks, Kylar." He hung up and slipped his phone into the back pocket of his blood-stained jeans.

Their footsteps clapped as they walked to the pharmacy at the back of the store, the space faintly lit with a couple of security lights.

Shay took a seat on the prescription pick-up counter while Roman grabbed things off the shelves—gauze, saline solution, medical tape. Paxton wandered to the public blood pressure kiosk machine to play with the inflatable cuff, its whirring soon filling the building. His backpack sat discarded at his feet, Itzel zipped up safely in the main internal compartment. After the shooting in the motel room, the Hob was being a lot more cooperative.

As if sensing Shay's attention, the Hob unzipped the backpack from the inside and poked her head out, her pink eyes glowing in the dark.

Roman noticed her right away. "Itzel!" he barked from across the area, his hands full of medical supplies. "Get back in there."

Itzel ducked back inside and zipped herself in.

As Shay waited for Roman, she shut her eyes, her head pounding. A migraine was the last thing she needed right now, but she had to admit she was in the best place for one, the shelves stocked with every type of painkiller and suppressant on the market. She'd need to remember to grab extras before leaving. And maybe some ice packs and a heating pad.

The sound of Roman dumping items on the counter beside her prompted her to open her eyes. He stood before her, close enough to feel his aura and the welcoming warmth radiating off of him. Close enough that the front of his thighs brushed against her knees.

"How are you feeling?" he asked as he started ripping open packages. "Still got all your fingers?" When she didn't respond, her stomach turning as the reality of what they had just lived through finally set in, he frowned and said, "Bad joke?" He rolled his sleeves up his forearms, the lean muscle flecked with silvery scars that were barely visible through his ink, and gestured for her to let him see her hand. "Let me see."

She carefully placed her hand—still wrapped up tight in a bloody rag—in Roman's. As he unwound the rag, exposing her blood-slick fingers, Shay turned her head the other way.

"How bad is it?" she croaked, her eyes shutting again.

Roman gently turned her hand from side to side. He sighed through his nose, his breath coasting across her cheek. "Well, I count five fingers, so not *that* bad. You're missing a little chunk of your pinky, though."

Her eyes flew open. *"Seriously?"* she seethed.

"Yeah, look—on the side here." He gestured to a tiny indentation in the outer portion of her littlest finger. The flesh was mangled. Raw.

She scowled. "Those bastards."

"It's better than the whole finger." She couldn't argue with that. He finished his prep, and then he started cleaning her wounds.

Gods, it stung. He was gentle, yes, but gentle only went so far when you were missing a piece of your finger. Bastards, indeed. No wonder her hellseher healing hadn't sealed this shut yet. Her ribs were almost better, though.

She cleared her throat. "I guess this is a little better than a ripped shirt, hey?" she teased, swallowing another wave of nausea. Yep, that was definitely a migraine coming on. Joy.

Roman gave her a look that could only be described as disinterest. It wiped Shay's smile right off her face.

Had anything about their time in the desert together fazed this man? Or was she the only one who'd fallen pathetically hard?

As Roman worked, Shay watched his handsome face to distract herself from the agony searing through every bone, every muscle, every *hair*. That was how much pain she was in, even her *hair* hurt. She was still feeling the effects of being whipped like a rag-doll against the exterior wall of the motel by Paxton's magic, a blast of deathly power they were extremely fortunate to have survived.

But gods, was Roman's face ever a distraction—almost too much of one. Being this close to him, even in the dark, she could see every flake of gold in his eyes...the faint silver scars flecking his jaw, nose, and cheeks...all the minuscule details of the black skull of Obitus tattooed on his strong cheekbone...

As she stared, her body warming as she took him in feature by feature, scar by scar, those honeyed eyes suddenly locked on hers.

"You're making me blush, pup." His voice was a low, husky croon that made *her* face redden.

She snort-laughed. "If you call a dead stare *blushing,* then sure, okay." When he shot her a quizzical look, she clarified, "I see zero color on your face, Shadows. Unless you're talking about the blood." Indeed, his face, while emotionless—and did she mention gorgeous beyond belief?—was filthy.

The corner of his mouth pulled up into an involuntary, lopsided smile, the expression deepening the small scar on his cheek.

Shay batted her eyelashes. "Wow, is Roman 'I Hate the World' Devlin actually *smiling?*" she breathed. "Never thought I'd see the day."

Roman was about to reply when his head whipped in Paxton's direction, the humor on his face shifting into patent concern. "Pax!" he called.

Paxton had gotten to his feet and was currently marching with Chance past all the aisles, standing on his tiptoes to scan the signs above each. He paused and looked at Roman over his shoulder. "Yeah?"

"Where you off to?" Now that he was finished cleaning, Roman moved onto the gauze. Shay bit her lip as he began wrapping a clean strip around the pinky and ring fingers of her right hand. Gods, that stung. She needed extra-strength painkillers, stat.

"I'm looking for snacks," Paxton responded, his face a portrait of innocence. "I'm hungry."

"We can find some together when I'm done. I don't want you wandering off, okay?"

"But there's a chip display right there." He pointed at an end-cap closest to the aisle of coolers.

"You can go to the display, but don't go down any aisles. I need to be able to see you."

Paxton gave him a salute before skipping to the potato chip display and scanning all the flavors. "Meatball?" he muttered, wrinkling his nose. "Gross. What are these companies on?" Bags crunched as he made his selection.

Shay slid her attention back to Roman. His dark hair hung in his eyes as he meticulously wrapped and rewrapped her fingers, making sure everything was perfect in typical Roman 'Perfectionist' Devlin fashion.

"What are your thoughts about what happened at the Wanderer?" she whispered.

Roman glanced at Paxton, who was popping open a bag of chips and cramming a handful into his mouth.

"Mmmm!" Pax's voice echoed through the quiet store. "Sour cream and onion's the bomb!" He tossed one into Chance's mouth. The pup promptly spat it back out and gagged so hard, he made Paxton laugh.

"I'm thinking I'll get him on double the suppressants," Roman responded in a hushed tone. He taped the gauze into place. Sighed. "If that happens again..." He trailed off, shaking his head.

He might kill us, Shay finished in her mind with a shudder. It had taken Paxton a while to calm down and return to his bubbly self, and he still wasn't quite there. Hunting for potato chips was a good start, but Shay sensed that the kid was still deeply bothered by what he'd done at the motel and was trying desperately to forget about it by drowning his sorrows in salty snacks.

"Have you ever seen anything like that before?" she asked.

"No." He tossed another glance Pax's way. "And I never want to see him go through that again," he added quietly. "Not at his age, at least." The deep horror that had crossed Paxton's young face upon realizing what he had done... Shay understood exactly why Roman was deciding that doubling his dose of suppressants was the right route to take.

They fell into silence as Roman finished his wrap job. After a moment of checking his work, he released her hand.

"How does that feel?" he asked her.

"Better." She'd have trouble holding a gun for a couple of days, but at least she wasn't gushing blood anymore. "Thanks."

Roman's eyes met hers—briefly. "You're welcome," he mumbled.

Shay tried to slide off the counter—

Her heart jumped when Roman pinned her in place with a big hand wrapping around the front of her thigh. "Hold up, I'm not finished," he said. He removed his hand from her thigh. "I need to— Your face, it's... You've got a bunch of blood on it still."

She cleared her throat. "Right. Sure." The warmth of Roman's grasp lingered on her thigh. She wanted him to grip her there again. Wanted him to touch her like he had outside of the Wanderer, when he'd cupped the back of her neck. When he'd looked at her as if he cared.

As if he might kiss her.

She held still as he wet a fresh rag with saline solution and cleaned her face. The blood that was caked beneath her nose, her brow, her split lip— he missed nothing. The longer he worked, the fiercer his expression became.

"I fucking hate them for touching you," he blurted.

There her heart went with the leaping again. What was the damn thing doing in there, jumping rope? "The feeling's mutual," she replied, eyeing the bruises and cuts all over his handsome face.

Their gazes clashed again.

Roman froze, his hand that held the rag hovering over the corner of her mouth.

For a moment, the world and all its problems melted away, and it was just her and Roman. The small space separating their bodies felt electrically charged, as if a lightning storm were brewing between them.

Shay reached up, every vein in her body a live wire, and wrapped her fingers around the Shadowmaster's tattooed wrist. As she slowly lowered his hand, they didn't look away from each other, Roman's attention flicking between her eyes and her lips. She watched as his throat shifted with a swallow...listened as his heart began to pound harder, the pulse in his strong wrist drumming beneath her fingers—

"Hey, they sell video games here!" Paxton exclaimed. He was jumping in place, hand buried in his bag of chips. "Can I pick a new game? Can I? Can I, can I, can I, *can I can I can I can I?—*"

"On the way out," Roman replied. Paxton whooped in delight.

Shay cleared her throat and slid off the counter—

Big mistake. Her body brushed against Roman's, the contact far too intimate for two slayers who were forbidden to even be *friends.*

"Sorry," she stuttered, sidling around him. He mirrored her by accident, and soon they were performing an awkward two-step dance as they tried to get around each other.

"No, me— I mean, *I'm* sorry," Roman mumbled, backing up.

Shay gave a quiet laugh. "Not much of a smooth talker right now, are you?"

He smirked. "I'm a little fucked up still." He gestured to his head with a rotating finger.

"You and me both."

She was about to wander away, looking for something else—anything other than Roman this time—to distract her, when suddenly he said, "Truth or lie?"

Shay froze, her breath catching in her throat.

"I suck at using words." Another rare smile flirted with his mouth.

No, you don't, Shay thought, remembering the night they'd shared at Motel 58, when he'd driven all the way out there to find her after she'd left Yveswich. All the things he'd said to her by the outdoor pool.

'Give me one night. Just one. A night where it's just us—no one else, no regrets, no thoughts wasted on other people. I promised you five days, Shayla. And I don't break promises.'

As if sensing where her mind had strayed, Roman broke her stare and busied himself with cleaning up. Shay hovered nearby, the fleeting press of his body against hers lingering like a phantom. A cruel reminder of what it had felt like to have him on top of her. Beneath her, too.

"So," Shay began, toeing a line in the floor. "Am I calling a taxi?"

Roman paused, his brow furrowing. "A taxi?" he echoed. "Why would you call a taxi?"

"Well, you kind of made yourself clear that you don't want me tagging along with you." Damn, had that hurt. When she had woken up to find the two of them leaving.

Come to think of it, she owed the Hob a thank-you for kicking up such a fuss. Had Itzel left without a fight, Shay would either be dead right now or locked up somewhere with Donovan Slade.

A beat of awkward silence. And then Roman said, "Oh."

He returned to cleaning up, leaving Shay hanging. He didn't say anything more until he was finished, the counter spotless. No one would ever know they were here. There were security cameras throughout the store, but Kylar was currently masking them at Hell's Gate. *Leave nothing behind*—that was one of the most important rules for a Darkslayer. And three people on the run.

Finally, Roman said, "If Pax hadn't convinced me to stay, there's a strong chance you'd be dead right now. Or worse."

Shay pressed, "So...what does that mean?"

"It means I'm not making decisions for you anymore. If you want to leave, I'm in full support of that decision. And to be honest with you, Shayla, I'd prefer that." His casual use of her full name made parts of her body tingle.

"But...?" she prompted, raising her brows.

"But...if you want to stay..." Those gold-flecked eyes scanned her face. "I can't say I like it. But I'll leave the decision up to you."

She nibbled on her lip, ignoring how Roman's eyes briefly dipped to her mouth.

"I think what happened at the Wanderer tells us that there's strength in numbers," she offered. "That could've been a lot worse if we weren't together."

From the look on Roman's face, he agreed. He clearly didn't like it, but...he agreed.

"Look, Shay...," he began, the words gruff. "I can't thank you enough for what you did back there. If you weren't with us, Pax probably would've..." His jaw flexed, and he looked away.

Been taken, Shay finished for him.

Instead of saying it aloud, she whispered, "Strength in numbers."

His eyes snapped to hers.

"We stick together," she decided, even as Roman's eyes tightened, the warm shade darkening so swiftly there was not a single gold fleck left. "For now," she amended, if only to make him feel better.

Roman inhaled, the sound, although soft, raising goosebumps all over her body. "For survival." He tried to make it sound like a joke, but the words were strained, and his expression stern.

Shay nodded, though. Because it was true. They needed each other, now more than ever, and what happened at that motel was evidence of that. "For survival," she assented.

Nothing more.

Pfft, sure, Shayla, she thought, as her heart gave an outward tug, as if trying to haul her across the space and into the Shadowmaster's arms. Those lean-muscled, ridiculously attractive arms that looked way too good in his stupid ripped shirt... *We'll see how that goes.*

73

THE HOLDING CENTER
ANGELTHENE, STATE OF WITHEREDGE

The sun was rising by the time the cops granted Loren an audience.

This room she was in reminded her of that fateful night six months ago, when Sabrine had been abducted, but this time her hands were cuffed. Today, she was not a witness, but a suspect—for what crimes, she still didn't know.

Multiple pairs of eyes were peering at her from the other side of the observation window to her right. She didn't need to see them to know they were there, their gazes searing the side of her face like glowing-hot branding irons. And, just like the night Sabrine had disappeared, the one-way mirror showed her how rough she looked.

Her face seemed pale, almost gaunt. Dark circles marred her under-eyes, and her hair was draped over the back of her chair in a curtain of waves in dire need of detangling spray and a brush.

She startled as the door buzzed open, and two men stalked in. One was Detective Glen Campbell. The other, she had never seen before. Both were warlocks. Both physically in their forties.

Chairs scraped like nails on a chalkboard as they took their seats across from her. Glen slapped a folder onto the table and made himself comfortable, his silver-ringed eyes drilling holes in her face.

She twisted her fingers in her lap, her heart already skipping beats.

She couldn't lie and say she wasn't concerned about what might happen next, but most of the stress she was feeling was not wasted on herself.

It was spent on thoughts of Darien and Tanner. Surely, whatever she ended up facing here in this room, at this table that was bolted to the floor, would be one hundred times easier than what these detectives planned on doing to the men. While she was a lowly human whose only crime, if she were to ask the two prejudiced males seated across from her, was being born, Darien and Tanner...

Glen had listed some of their crimes while handcuffing them. Crimes of which the Devils were one hundred percent guilty. Darkslayers may be tolerated by most cops and MPU agents, who chose to turn the other cheek in favor of receiving indirect help cleaning up the streets, but that didn't mean they liked each other. And when one bad egg came along in a position of authority... Needless to say, it didn't always end well for any slayers in question.

She drew a calming inhale.

Darien's reaction when she was being arrested at Angelthene Recreation Center was one she would never forget. The way he had completely freaked out and begged—*begged*—when he saw her being apprehended...

Pushing him away was not the answer. Not anymore. While she may never forgive him for tying his life to hers, she was struggling to keep her distance. She loved him far too much to keep doing so.

Wherever he was in this building, whichever room they had him locked up in...let's just say she was surprised he hadn't yet completely demolished the entire holding center to get to her.

Glen licked the pad of his finger and flipped through the pages in the brown folder. Taking his sweet time while the other detective watched her in stony silence, his beefy arms crossed over his large chest. The clock on the white wall ticked and ticked and ticked.

She opened her mouth to say something—

Glen's brusque voice clapped through the room. "You will speak when you are spoken to, and no sooner, Miss Calla." He wasn't even looking at her, too preoccupied with his papers.

She clamped her mouth shut and interlocked her stiff fingers in her lap. If only she had better vision, so she could see what was written in that file.

At least two minutes passed by the time Glen finished with the papers. He raised his head and stared at her, as if daring her to try to speak again.

She didn't.

"Miss Calla," he began. While his volume was a little quieter, his tone was no less harsh. "From my understanding, you suffer from medical issues that you've been undergoing tests for since you were an infant. Is this correct?"

Her mouth dried out. Her eyes flicked to a red light flashing in the upper right-hand corner of the room. The camera was recording.

She swallowed. "Yes."

Glen folded his arms on the table. "Can you explain to me what exactly it is that ails you?"

"The doctors don't know," she responded, reciting the speech she used to give to everyone, back before she'd learned the truth. Back when the Arcanum Well was nothing more than a legend, and she was nothing more than an ordinary human. She spoke smoothly, lying so well she almost believed the lie herself. "They've run tests my whole life, but they've never found a name for it. I have problems with my blood sugar. It can dip without warning, so I need to carry prescription medication and eat or drink if I start to feel faint." Lies were always easier when they were half-true.

Little did these jerks know there was so much more to it than that.

A beat of quiet as Glen scanned the papers. "I see you fell into a coma a few weeks ago. Was this situation related in any way to these health issues you speak of?" Gods, how deeply had they dug? And *why*?

She managed a shallow nod—

The other man said, "We're going to need you to give us a verbal response."

"Yes." Her voice was a crackle.

"What were you doing in Yveswich?" Glen asked her.

Her heart tripped into a faster rhythm, her palms slick with sweat. "I was...taken to Yveswich..." *Half-truths,* she told herself. *Tell them half-truths.* "To receive treatment. To help wake me up." She tugged on her jacket sleeves. "Out of a coma," she added.

"Taken...," Glen repeated. He picked her appearance apart with narrowed eyes. When his attention snagged on her Avertera talisman, Loren squeezed her hands into fists. "By your boyfriend?"

She set her jaw, her heart racing so fast she felt sick. Her knee bounced under the table.

"Darien Cassel *is* your boyfriend," Glen prompted, his eyes once again dipping to her talisman. "Is he not?"

Her lungs were tight, her hands sweaty. She could no longer find her voice.

"I see no reason why this has to be difficult, Miss Calla. You seem like a nice girl." He fanned the edge of the stack of papers with his thumb, as if doing so backed up his statement. "You have no criminal record. Good grades. You attend one of the most prestigious universities in Terra and come from a respected military family. Though I must say, the company you keep is..." His upper lip curled back. "Questionable."

She stiffened. "What's that supposed to mean?"

"You know exactly what it means!" he retorted. "And if you want to see your *boyfriend*—" He practically spat the word, his face turning red with rage. "—ever again, you're going to need to be honest with us."

An icy tremor wobbled through her. "What do you mean if I want to see him again?" Her words were hollow. Brittle, like her mortal bones.

It was the other man who said, "You don't want him to go to jail, do you?"

"Why would he go to jail?" she demanded. "You'd lock him up for taking me to a medical establishment? Since when is that illegal—"

"That *establishment* is currently under investigation," Glen countered sharply. "Street cameras caught your boyfriend and his pals heading into Caliginous on Silverway on the night of the explosion." He thumbed three photographs free of the folder and slid them across the table so she could see them. "Have a look, Miss Calla. Tell me I'm wrong," he dared her.

She leaned forward...

Sure enough, cameras *had* caught Darien, Roman, Jack, and Tanner going in there. Evidence Tanner would certainly have gone on to erase, had the Well replica not exploded and foiled their plans. Whether these men were aware that Max and Dallas had gone in there too, she didn't know. Wherever they were, she hoped they were okay.

Glen was watching her with cold, cold eyes. "You want to tell me what, exactly, they were doing here?" He stabbed one of the photographs with the end of his pen.

"I don't understand," she murmured, shaking her head. "You think they're responsible for the explosion?"

Their silence was all the answer she needed.

"That's a bunch of crap!" she exclaimed. "We were in Yveswich for *me*. For my treatments, that's all, you can ask Doctor Atlas—"

"Doctor Atlas is facing the prospect of losing her job," Glen interrupted. "You want to know why, Miss Calla?" Every word rose in volume, until he was shouting. "For failing to report to her superiors when she made the decision to remove a patient from intensive care. Losing her job, Miss Calla, is the least that could happen. Worst is jail time, along with your boyfriend and his little pals—" He jabbed another photograph with his pen. "—if we find out they had *anything* to do with what's happening in Yveswich."

Loren could scarcely breathe. "I want to speak to a lawyer," she whispered.

"You know what I find odd, Miss Calla?" Glen clipped, completely ignoring her.

Firmer, she repeated, "I want to speak to a lawyer."

"Is why a human like yourself would go for a treatment at a *magical* facility," he snapped.

Loren stopped breathing, the hair on her scalp prickling.

"Either you're all lying," Glen continued, "or you—" He pointed his pen at her. "Are not human." He gave a cold smirk of disbelief. "And I think we all know the answer to that," he concluded around a humorless chuckle.

His smile faded. He stared at her, his eyes hard and unblinking.

Loren stared back, fingernails biting into her perspiring palms.

"So let's try this again," Glen growled. "What were you doing in Yveswich?"

DARIEN SAT PERFECTLY STILL, the black chains of his brynstan cuffs dangling between his muscled thighs. He stared at the wall straight ahead with a black onyx gaze, watching as the varicolored runes of the security spells covering the interrogation room shifted about in rows and columns, like millions of restless bees in a hive.

He didn't even blink as the door buzzed opened, and eight armed officers and two detectives filed in. The officers formed a line in front of the wall he was staring at, guns at the ready, while the two detectives—Glen was one of them—took their seats across from him at the metal table in the center of the room.

Darien continued to stare at that same spot. Not blinking, not moving, hardly breathing. If it weren't for the cuffs rendering him as powerless as a mortal—apart from the Sight they couldn't take away, not even with brynstan—he'd have killed them all. Brutally.

He would've saved Glen for last—a bloody and well-earned dessert after a nine-course meal. Once this was over, and he got out of here, it would be

Loren who decided the fate of this clown. If Glen had made her feel uncomfortable in any way—if he'd even dared to *look* at her wrong—Darien would kill him. Tear him limb from limb. Peel the flesh off his back, his scalp, his face. His eyelids would go, too. And then, for even daring to look at her *at all*, Darien would take his eyes as well. He'd carve them out slowly. Painfully.

His mouth watered.

"You look like shit," Glen spat. "You always sweat like that?"

Slowly, Darien blinked the black away and slid his gaze to Glen's scowling face.

The other detective said, "Must be drugs."

"You on any drugs?" Glen spoke slowly, as if he were too stupid to understand. When Darien didn't deign to reply, Glen smirked and muttered, "Of course you are." He folded his hands on the table, fingers interlocking. "Your girlfriend's quite the darling. Not sure why she's with someone like you."

Darien's chair creaked as he leaned forward and rested his cuffed hands on the table. Every movement he made was slow. Deadly. He laced his fingers. Looked Glen right in the eyes with a dead stare.

"The thing about brynstan cuffs," Darien began in a low and lethal voice. "They still have chains." He snapped those chains taut in illustration, his eyes flicking to the grisly pink scar across Glen's throat.

Sweat—more than just Darien's—permeated the room.

Glen's bobbing throat was the only indication that he was disturbed. "I'd watch what you say," he warned.

"Or what?" Darien challenged. "You'll find there's not a lot that scares me, *Glen.*"

A moment of tense quiet.

And then Glen flipped open the file on the table and slid three photographs into a neat row. "Care to explain what you were doing at Caliginous on Silverway the night of the explosion?"

Darien's attention dipped to the photos—just for a sec. He kept his mouth shut, one edge tipped up with a hint of a cold I-dare-you-to-fuck-with-me smile.

"No?" Glen prompted through clenched teeth. "Then how about this?" He showed him another photo. An aerial view of the destruction of Yveswich. According to the time stamp, it was taken yesterday. By that time, black clouds had already engulfed over half of the city.

"What's your question?" Darien demanded.

"The shadow," said the other detective. "What is it and where's it coming from?"

Darien spared the photo another half-glance. Then his eyes flicked up, clashing with Glen's hostile gaze. "You're asking me as if I fucking put it there."

"Our teams have pinned down the blast location to the maintenance tunnels below Caliginous on Silverway," Glen said. "You and your boys were the last to enter, with no footage showing you—*any* of you—coming back out. Care to explain?"

"What about the imperator, it show him?"

"That's quite the implication, kid," said the detective at Glen's side.

"So is the one you're making about me," Darien fired back.

"Maybe you can explain...," Glen began, beckoning over his shoulder. An officer came forward and handed him a tablet. "What this is," Glen concluded as he clicked the screen on. He balanced the device's bottom edge on the table, holding it there so Darien could see the screen, and pressed the play button.

The video was less than thirty seconds long, but it showed enough.

Enough to make Darien's stomach fucking *drop*. But he masked his expression carefully, revealing nothing. These assholes wouldn't get even a hint of a reaction out of him.

But what he saw, right there on that screen...

The shadows in Yveswich were quarreling with white and rainbow light. *Loren's* light. Loren's magic. Her aura, distributed through the Control Tower and the channels of the anima mundi. It was barely visible, the video footage likely enhanced with expensive technology.

That magic—still coursing through the Control Tower and the last of the buildings that had power—was the only reason Yveswich was still standing. The only reason the last of its citizens could see at all. The only reason Ker's historic capital had not been wiped right off the map.

"Well?" Glen prompted sharply. *"Explain this."* He gestured to the video feeds of the sparkling multicolored shield. That's what it was—a shield. Like the one Loren had created on Kalendae, shielding Angelthene from a terrible fate.

"Tell me what I'm looking at," Darien said.

"Why don't *you* tell *me?*" Glen growled.

Darien snapped. *"I can't, because I've never seen this before!"*

Glen shot out of his chair and slapped his palm on the table so hard it would've startled any sane person.

Darien didn't even flinch.

Glen dipped his head to his level, the veins in his neck bulging as he bared his teeth. "You're going to break," he hissed. "And I'm going to be the one who breaks you."

"Come a little closer and try saying that again," Darien threatened.

Glen stayed standing, his palm flat on the table. "How about your little girlfriend? Hmm?" More sweat beaded on Darien's forehead. "If I drag her little blonde head in here, will you talk then?"

Darien kept his face unreadable. They wanted a reaction, and if he gave them one, Glen might do exactly what he was threatening. Drag Loren in here by her beautiful blonde hair.

If he did, Darien would slaughter all these pricks. He'd have to do it with his bare hands, no magic allowed while the brynstan cuffs were on. They'd likely shoot him. And then Loren would be on her own. Vulnerable.

He couldn't let that happen.

Glen sat back down. "Your sister knows you're here. She says her husband's out of town. He still in Yveswich?"

Darien didn't answer.

Glen's frown deepened. "You're going to talk, you son of a bitch. I don't care if takes all day, all night, all day tomorrow, and all night again." A pause. And then: "What about your cousin?"

"Which fucking cousin?" Darien snapped back.

Glen slammed the tips of two fingers onto the middle photograph, the one that showed a clear view of Roman's side profile.

"This cousin. Roman. Fucking. *Devlin."*

"Never heard of him," Darien quipped.

Glen blew a humorless laugh through his nose. "You think you're funny, don't you?"

"Sometimes, yeah."

"You won't be laughing when I tell you we have a warrant for his arrest," Glen spat. *"Where the hell is he?"*

74

I-5

STATE OF KER

S hay awoke to the car bouncing, the back of her head thwacking against the headrest.

It was morning, and they were flying down the sunlit interstate at a speed way beyond legal.

"Sorry," Roman muttered when he saw that she was awake. "These roads are shit."

Shay sat up, blinking the sleep out of her eyes as she looked for evidence that this road was indeed shit. There was the odd pothole here and there, but it didn't look different than any other in Terra.

She fought a smile. "I think they're meant for people who don't drive as if they're fleeing from the cops," she teased.

The edge of Roman's mouth quirked with humor. "There's no fun in driving slow. Besides, the minute you get behind a wheel like this baby—" He dragged his large, scarred hands along the curve of the wheel. The gesture—so simple, yet so attractive—made Shay gulp. "—the only correct way to drive it is like you stole it."

That she felt hot all over was downright embarrassing. All the man had done was caress his steering wheel, and here she was, sweating like a sinner in Temple.

"Have you always been into cars?" she asked him. Getting to know Roman Devlin better was probably a bad idea, but she had to fill the silence somehow. It was either that or shut her eyes again and pretend to be asleep. That was the less desirable, but smarter choice.

"Since the moment I set foot on a race track," he replied. "My Uncle Dean took me, my mom, and Travis to see a race when I was a kid. The minute I smelled the hot rubber and fuel..." His expression turned wistful, his eyes sparkling. "I was a goner. A changed man." He gave her another of those roguish smiles that made her stomach tighten, her pulse accelerating.

"Your...uncle," she mused. "Your dad's brother, or your mom's?"

"Dad's."

Her brows jumped up. "Wow. A Slade brother who isn't a total psychopath?" Hopefully she wasn't jumping to conclusions, and this story that had started out so wholesome wasn't about to take a bad turn.

But Roman snorted a laugh. "I know—shocking. Apart from their looks, they have zero in common. *Dean the Mean*—that's what Travis and I call him. He's the good apple. The one brother who didn't turn into a complete rage-aholic." The dreamy smile teasing the edge of his mouth... It made Shay smile. "Dean's normal," he went on. "Funny. Kind." That little smile faded into a frown. "Nothing like Don."

"How did *you* end up this way?"

He glanced sidelong at her. "What way?"

"So...*you.*" She gestured to all of him with a wave. *All of him* was damn near perfect. "So different from your dad. You're nothing like that horrible monster, either."

"Oh. Well, thanks." Despite his flat tone, she could tell the compliment meant a lot to him. He cleared his throat. "It was my mom, mostly. Seeing how horribly my dad treated her made me want to be a better man than him. It was hard—watching her live in fear, constantly walking on glass every time my dad came home... I decided from a young age that I didn't want to be anything like him. The example he set...it was terrible. He was always hitting things, always screaming and swearing at us..." A chill pebbled the skin on his arms. He cleared his throat. "When Travis was born, and I watched him grow up, I saw a lot of myself in him. Protecting him and setting a better example became a sort of personality for me."

"Well, I'd say you succeeded," she said. "With Travis." He looked pleased to hear it. "What made your mom decide to marry him, anyway? Did he beg her until she agreed?" She was trying to lighten the mood, but she didn't think it was working. Hopefully he didn't think she was being insensitive.

Roman briefly hesitated. Finally, he said, "A lie. My dad's a manipulative mastermind. Long story short, he put on an act until she was in too deep to turn back. She fell in love with the fake Donovan, and she stayed because she was afraid of the real one." That explained Clare as well, then. Why Paxton's mom hadn't run.

It was easy to judge as an outsider looking in. Everyone always asked, *'Why didn't you run?'* When really, they should be asking, *'Why did he make you feel like you had to?'*

As the conversation stalled, Shay noticed how Roman's expression had darkened, his aura melancholy. Was it wrong of her to have brought up his mother?

Desperate to see the light come back to his eyes, she changed the subject. "What happened to your other car? The white one."

"You mean the one you scuffed up with your shoe?"

She answered his faint smile with a grin. "Yeah, that one."

"Wrecked, probably." He raked his fingers through his hair. "That's the one we took to Silverway." Damn. She liked that car.

"I'm sorry."

"Don't be. I don't get too attached to specific cars. They're replaceable. It's people that aren't." His attention flicked to the rear-view, his hand reaching up to adjust the mirror.

Paxton was fast asleep in the back seat, exhausted after spending hours playing the new action-adventure video game he'd picked out at the drugstore. Chance lay sprawled beside him, his smoky back paw twitching as he dreamed.

"I had him take double while you were asleep," Roman said quietly.

"How'd he feel about that?"

"It was his idea. I didn't want to push him, so I thought I'd give him one and see what happened. But he asked for a second one right away, and I wasn't about to say no."

"It must've really scared him, what happened with your dad's men."

"Yeah." He exhaled heavily. "I've been thinking it's too bad my dad wasn't there. Maybe he'd be blown to bits right now, too." He pondered his own words before shaking his head. "Then again, maybe not," he muttered. "Who knows."

"Did you recognize many of those men?"

"Some. He has a lot of people doing his dirty work—I don't know all their names. Adham was there, though—I think he was the one who hit you." His hand tightened on the wheel, the barbed wire inked on his skin pulling taut across white knuckles. "It's about time he's gone."

"What about Trey?"

"I didn't see him."

"I wish I had killed him at the warehouse." She had been too focused on finding Pax to waste another second on that asshole. She'd thought the effects of her lightning might last longer, but...well, it was good to know it wore off fairly quickly, in case anything like that happened again.

They lapsed into silence. The navigational screen was a bit glitchy now, after the attack that had launched the car down the street, but it looked like they were nearing the state-line. They should arrive in Angelthene late tonight, as long as they didn't encounter any delays.

As the minutes ticked by, Shay got to thinking about other things, most involving Roman and the short time they had spent together. The secrets, buried deep in their souls, that they'd taken a chance on trusting each other with.

The car was so quiet you could cut the silence with a knife when she said abruptly, "It was my dad."

Roman glanced at her, his forehead creasing. "What?"

She drew a deep breath. "You once asked who hurt me," she said on the exhale. "Well, that's the answer. My dad's the reason I have...'*trust issues*'." She curled two fingers in the air. "Why I tend to assume everyone I'm with is going to ditch me. He was the first to do it, and I've never...never really gotten over it, I guess."

It took him a moment to speak. "I thought you said your dad—"

"Died? He did." Her heart twinged. "But he left when I was ten. He said he was going on an important business trip and he'd be back in two weeks. We—Anna and I—kept waiting and waiting and waiting for him to come home..." She swallowed the lump in her throat.

There was empathy in Roman's gaze. "You spoke so fondly of him, I had no idea..."

"My dad was a good man, in a lot of ways. He was a great dad, when he was around. He loved us. But he hated our mother more." She picked at the stitching on her pants. "Can't say I blame him for leaving."

"Did you see him at all after that?"

She shook her head. "Never. I followed his achievements in the paper— he was a scientist for Lucent Enterprises in Laurel. Anna and I found out he was dead when we saw his picture in the obituary. It was the Tricking that got him. Finding a cure was his calling, and he preferred to use himself as a test subject instead of others. He was a little too selfless, always sacrificing himself for the greater good." *Kind of like you,* she thought. "He developed the disease when we were young, and he died before he hit fifty." Most hellsehers met the same end. While they had the ability to live forever, the Tricking was an epidemic that ended many lives far before their time. The longest lifespan recorded in hellseher history was only about a hundred and sixty years.

"Did he ever come close?" Roman asked. "To finding a cure?"

She shook her head. "I don't think anyone has." Lucent Enterprises had boasted for many years that they would be the first to develop a cure for the Tricking. But many generations had passed since then, and they were still no closer to success than they were on day one.

A sign was approaching up ahead, marking the border between Ker and Witheredge soil.

And a little farther down, traffic was at a standstill.

Roman reduced speed, the swift deceleration snapping Shay's seatbelt taut across her chest.

"Construction?" she wondered aloud, tugging on the belt to get it to loosen.

Pax stirred awake. "Are we there yet?" he asked around a big yawn.

Roman rolled the car down the highway at the speed limit. Other cars came up behind and beside them, fencing them in on this side of the median strip. There was nowhere to go, which wouldn't be a problem if this were simply a construction zone. But—

"*Shit,*" Roman hissed, spotting the police officers moving from car to car on foot at the same time Shay spotted them.

Shit was right.

This was a roadblock.

75

THE HOLDING CENTER
ANGELTHENE, STATE OF WITHEREDGE

S ometime later, as Darien sat alone in the thick silence of the interrogation room, the buzzer went off and the door whipped open.

Glen was back with more officers in tow, their hands in easy reach of the firearms and staves strapped to their uniformed bodies. The number of officers and their weapons didn't faze Darien, though. Not at all.

What *did* faze him was the human girl they were herding along in the center of their group, her small form just barely peeking out between their bodies.

Darien shot to his feet, the sudden movement causing the officers to draw their weapons. "What the *fuck* are you doing?" he growled as multiple officers shouted at him to *stay back, don't move, keep your hands where we can see them,* as if he wasn't already cuffed, the idiots.

He didn't acknowledge a single command. And among the many loud and aggressive voices echoing in the tight space, above the roaring of the blood in his head, it was only *her* voice that managed to reach him.

"Darien, it's okay," Loren was saying. "It's okay, just stay c—"

"Let. Her. *Go,*" he snarled.

Glen drew a handgun—

And pointed the fucking thing at Loren's temple.

Darien stopped breathing.

"Not unless you agree to talk," Glen threatened.

There was no air left in his lungs. No air in the world. His heart was pounding, his stomach in knots.

He'd *kill them.* He wanted to *kill them,* every last one of these pricks. Rip that gun out of Glen's hand, break his fingers, and blast his skull open with bullets.

The reason he hesitated? Loren. She was breathing unevenly, her wide, ocean-blue eyes shining with fear as that gun hovered within three inches of her temple. Red light pulsed beneath the thin sleeve of her jacket, her low blood sugar the main cause of her pallid complexion and unsteady posture.

That and the gun this prick was pointing at her.

Darien felt like he was suffocating, but he managed to grit out, "I'm not saying a single thing until you let. Her. *Go.*"

Silence.

He chanced a step forward—

A soft *click* sent Darien's heart hopping up his throat as Glen toggled the safety off.

"Take one more step," Glen warned, "and I'll blow your bitch's blonde brains out."

Darien didn't dare move. Fear was an emotion he seldom felt, but in that moment, as he watched Glen's finger brush across the trigger, Loren's pulse fluttering in her tense neck, he had never been more afraid in all his life.

One bullet. Just one, and her precious life would end.

Glen's lips curved with a cruel smile. "So he *can* be tamed. Ready to talk, Cassel?"

"I don't need my magic to kill you, Glen," Darien said, his tone lethal. "I can do it with my bare hands. I can strangle you with just these chains." He pulled the chains of his cuffs taut, brimstone rattling. "You push me far enough, and I'll make you regret it."

Glen sized him up with a condescending smirk. His finger teased the trigger—

Darien detonated like a bomb. *"IF ANY OF YOU TOUCH HER, I'LL BREAK EACH AND EVERY ONE OF YOUR FUCKING NECKS!"* He whipped his ferocious black gaze about the room. His every breath sawed through him, his head swimming.

Fingers brushed across triggers. Sweat and fear permeated the room like a heavy coat of oil.

A drop of perspiration rolled down Glen's temple. But he didn't lower his gun.

"Let," Darien said again. A deep, animalistic growl rumbled through his chest, the chains on his cuffs rattling with restraint. "Her. Go. *Now.*"

Several officers shared glances. Others whispered to each other in fearful tones. One man backed up, ready to bolt out the door.

In the reflection of the observation window, Darien saw the scene in the corner of his eye, as if he were watching this on a live feed. Saw himself, surrounded by cops and shaking with rage, his expression more monster than man. He hardly recognized himself.

Darien's breathing shifted into a rapid pant, the leash on his magic about to snap. "I'm giving you to the count of seven," he began. "If I make it to one, and you haven't lowered your guns and let my girlfriend walk out of here *safely,* you're all fucking dead."

A deadly silence choked the room.

"Seven," Darien began. "Six—"

"You sure you want to be the one counting?" Glen challenged, looking pointedly at the gun in his hand. He brushed his finger across the trigger, squeezing—

"You sure you want to be the one pointing that gun?" Darien snapped. "I'm in love with this woman, and you're not going to like the animal I'll become if you take her from me."

The silence that fell this time was more suffocating than the previous.

"Five," Darien said, his pupils swallowing his eyes. "Four. Three. Two—"

The door swung open, and three more officers walked in. The one leading the trio was Finn Solace.

"Alright, that's enough!" the warlock barked. "Take the cuffs off—right now. He's coming with me."

But Glen wasn't having any of that. "Nobody move, or you're all *fired!*" he warned, freezing two of his own officers, who'd stepped forward at Finn's command, in place. He engaged the safety on his gun and tucked it away at his hip before rounding on Solace, his face twisted with fury. "Stand down, Detective. This isn't your case."

"It is now," Finn responded coolly.

"Says who? *You?*" He smirked. "This man is a criminal, Detective Solace!" He jabbed a finger at Darien. "He's not going anywhere."

Darien's blood boiled. He lowered his chin, the black of the Sight pooling in his eyes—

"Oh yes, he is," Finn responded evenly.

Another of those condescending smirks. "I'm afraid your word no longer applies here. Move along, Detective, you're embarrassing yourself."

"It's not my word," Finn countered smoothly. "If you've got a problem, Glen, you'll have to take it to the higher ups. Now put the guns away! All of you, guns away." He waved a hand, his silver-ringed eyes—brimming with command—sweeping among the officers. "And for crying out loud, let this poor girl go, before you end up with innocent blood on your hands."

"It wouldn't get that far," Darien warned, turning his deadly gaze on Glen. Over his dead body would they ever harm a hair on Loren's head. He might die trying to protect her, but he'd take all these assholes down with him before he'd ever let them touch her.

Glen continued to argue, a child throwing a temper tantrum. But his words fell on deaf ears as Finn took out his own keys, tired of waiting for someone else to step forward, and crossed the room. Glen followed, shouting in his face.

"Turn around," Finn said.

Darien complied, but kept his head turned, keeping watch over Loren as Finn shimmied the key in and unlocked the cuffs.

The second they were off, he felt his magic expand, like a squished lung that was finally able to draw a full breath.

He turned back around—

And came face to face with Glen.

Now that the cuffs were off, Glen's security blanket stripped from his shoulders, the prick rocked back on his heels...

And immediately shut his trap.

Jaw clenched so tightly his teeth ached, Darien slid his focus to Loren. He didn't blink, his chest heaving, his hands squeezing into fists, as another officer slid a key into her cuffs.

The moment her wrists were bare, Darien was moving, pushing past Glen and stalking across the room. The officers who were in his way wisely stepped aside to let him through, while the few stupid fucks who still had their guns out kept them trained on him, ready to fire.

Darien didn't spare them one glance—his eyes were all for Loren.

And his girl was looking at him too, practically running across the room toward him.

She opened her arms to him at the same time he opened his.

And then they collided, and she was hugging him, her fingers curling in his shirt, and it was the best thing that had happened to him in days.

He held her tight, bowing over her to bury his face in her soft hair and breathe in her scent, feeling her inviting warmth, her body pressing against his.

"You all right?" His question was hoarse. Frayed, just like his heart felt after watching them drag her in here like she wasn't worth the dirt under their shoes.

She nodded against his chest, her heart racing so fast he could feel it fluttering. "Yeah," she whispered. "Yeah, I'm okay. Are *you* okay?" Of course she would be thinking of him, the sweetheart she was. "Gods, Darien, you're shaking."

Fuck, he was, wasn't he? Speechless and still in shock, he clung to her, wrapping one arm around her waist, the other hand—shaking, yeah—coming up to cradle the back of her head. He didn't give a shit that they had an audience—let them watch. Maybe if they saw how much he loved this girl, they wouldn't dare cross him again. Wouldn't ever touch what was his.

"Get them the hell out of here!" Glen roared. Of course it was him who'd interrupt.

Finn opened the door, beckoning for them to follow.

Darien felt Loren tug gently against his hold, silently urging him to loosen his grasp on her.

"Come on," she said softly. "Come on, Darien. Let's go home."

He had to force himself to let go of her. He cupped her face, tipping her head back to look her in the eyes.

Safe. Alive.

He kissed her on the forehead before gently spinning her around to face the door Finn held open. Darien kept her in front of him, guarding her from all sides as they left the interrogation room. The two officers accompanying Finn took up the rear while Glen and his people stayed behind.

As they walked down the hallway, Darien threw a black glare over his shoulder—

And saw Glen stomping out of the room, hands on his hips. He didn't follow, but he watched with a hateful glare.

Darien glowered back. *Prick.*

Up ahead, the door to another interrogation room opened, and Atlas walked out, cuffs off.

"All right?" Darien asked him. His muscles were still rigid, his chest burning as if it were filled with acid.

Tanner fell into stride beside him. "Yeah." Gray eyes flicked between Darien and the beautiful blonde walking in front of him. "You guys?"

"Been better, but we're alive." He flattened his hand against the small of Loren's back, urging her into a quicker walk. "Let's get the hell out of here."

They picked up speed, officers and other staff stepping out of the way as they passed.

Logan and Sabrine were waiting for them by the front desk. Ivy and Lace were here as well, sitting in a couple of chairs by the windows. When they saw them coming, they got to their feet, their surprised murmurs drawing the attention of staff and guests.

The whole building went quiet, unanswered phones droning with incoming calls, as people stared at the two Devils and the lone human with police escorts, the one Devil still touching his hand to the human's lower back.

Sabrine broke the stillness and came forward. "You guys okay?" She handed Darien his jacket, and he put it on.

When he didn't respond, his blood still hot and roaring in his ears, Loren answered her instead. "Yeah," she said, glancing up at Darien. Ocean blue eyes—brimming with concern—scanned his face. "Yeah, I think we're okay."

Darien tried to slow his breathing, but the edges of his vision were fogging with black. Now that the brimstone cuffs were off, he felt like he was going to snap. He was a lit fuse, his skull pounding with a wicked headache.

He needed to hit something. Needed to get in a ring and rip some piece-of-shit lowlife into bloody scraps.

Finn gave them back the rest of their things—phones and the weapons the officers had confiscated at the rec center. When they were ready, he escorted them out.

As they walked through the holding center, Loren slightly ahead of Darien, he collected himself just enough to speak.

"What was that all about?" His question was for Solace, who walked at his side, keys jingling.

"Just trying to do the right thing."

"Right, because that worked so well for you in Yveswich."

Finn bristled. "Look, I know you and I haven't always got along—"

Darien snort-laughed.

"But I'm trying to make things right here. All that shit that's going on in Yveswich..." He shook his head, his chest deflating with a tired sigh. "Let's just say I don't agree with it."

"Who put that asshole in charge?" Darien demanded, gesturing behind him.

"He's a transfer," Finn responded in a hushed tone as they squeezed past two officers in the hallway. "His background's been kept on the downlow, but rumors say he was designated by Lucent."

Darien's head whipped his way. "The imperator?" Why did that not surprise him?

Finn stared straight ahead with a poker face. "You didn't hear it from me."

Darien squeezed his left hand into a fist, more sweat prickling across his back. It wasn't until he pushed his hair out of his face that he realized his hands were still trembling.

Powerless. That was how he'd felt in that room, when he'd watched Loren walk through the door, surrounded by armed men. There had been many times—too many—these past six months where he feared he might lose her, but he'd always felt at least *somewhat* in control of the situation.

But with those brynstan cuffs leashing his magic like that... If Glen had pulled that trigger...

There was nothing he could have done to save her. Not even hellseher speed would have allowed him to get her out of the path of the bullet.

As they walked, he stared at the back of her head, trying to convince himself that she was alive. Safe.

She must have sensed that his attention was on her, because she slowed, peering over her shoulder at him with those gorgeous blue eyes.

Then she reached behind her. It took him longer than it should have to realize that she was reaching for *him*.

He clasped her hand, the feel of her soft skin grounding him.

And for the first time since they were arrested, he managed to draw a full breath. Slowly, he exhaled, the tension melting out of his muscles.

She was alive.

Safe.

Alive. Safe. Alive. Safe. No matter how many times he thought it, it didn't feel true. Didn't feel good enough.

"Are you okay?" she whispered.

He nodded. "Yeah." He used the heel of his other palm to wipe more sweat off his forehead.

"Look, Darien," Finn began. They weren't far from the front entrance now. "If you know anything that might help us with what's going on in Ker—"

"Was this your plan all along?" he whisper-shouted. "Be the good cop who comes in afterward and gets me talking?" It would be so like Finn to do something shitty like that, wouldn't it?

"Not exactly." Finn resigned with a sigh. "Forget what I said—we'll talk another time." He hurried ahead to hold the door.

In your dreams, Darien thought.

He walked out behind Loren, their hands still joined—

And skidded to a halt, his lungs emptying with shock. "No way," he breathed.

Waiting for them in the parking lot, his tall form leaning against the front of a white sports car, was Roark Bright.

Loren's mouth fell open. "Roark?"

76

KER TO WITHEREDGE STATE-LINE

"Pax," Roman began, speaking evenly as two cops approached the car, muffled voices spitting through their radios. His throat felt too narrow, as if a hand were strangling him, his heart thumping so hard his chest burned. "I'm going to need you to stay calm. I'm going to need you to stay calm—and trust me. Can you do that?"

He glanced at Pax in the rear-view. The boy was holding himself ramrod straight, his arms locked around Chance's fuzzy neck.

"Shay?" Roman inquired. He didn't have to say his question out loud —she already knew what he was asking.

"I can't," she responded with a hoarse whisper. "It won't last long enough. And if they see..."

Then the whole world would know, and the wrong people could get a hold of her and exploit her for her rare gift. Roman would never ask that of her—not unless the odds were one hundred percent in their favor.

This roadblock... All these cops... This was all because of *them*, he knew. Whether a roadblock was standard procedure for locating a missing child, or if Donovan himself had specifically arranged for this after learning of their whereabouts last night, Roman had no idea. It made no difference, though.

This was the end.

But he'd do it all over again, if given the chance. Would still choose to take Pax with him when fleeing Yveswich. In no world would he have willingly left Paxton alone with their father. He hadn't done it when he'd turned eighteen, and he still wouldn't do it now, at twenty-seven.

"No matter what happens," he began. One officer was speaking into the small mic clipped onto his vest upon seeing their license plate number, the other heading for the driver's-side door. "It's going to be okay," he concluded, but his throat constricted like a boa.

A knuckle rapped against his window.

Chance barked.

The other officer knocked on Shay's side. "Open up." Wrapped tightly around his hand was a spirit leash, his K-9 Familiar frantically sniffing the car—

The dog reared up and started barking. Spit strung between its jaws and flew through the air, the glowing metal links of its leash snapping taut as it lunged forward, standing on hind legs.

Chance barked in response.

"Roman, what's happening?" Paxton croaked, clutching Chance against his chest. "What do they want with us?" His puppy barked and barked—

"Pax, I need to know that you can keep it together," Roman said firmly, holding Pax's stare in the rear-view mirror.

If Pax lost control... If anyone found out what he was capable of...

How *dangerous* he was... Darien had been arrested at the age of fifteen, when cops had deemed him unstable when they'd witnessed him unraveling beside his mother's corpse.

They would not hesitate to do the same, or worse, to Paxton, if they had even an inkling of what he had done out front of the Wanderer.

He prayed his suppressants would work.

The officer on his side knocked again. "Open up."

"For me," Roman added. "Can you do that?"

It took him a moment, but Paxton dipped his chin into a nod.

Roman took a deep breath...

And flicked the button on the door. The tinted glass lowered, spring air so warm it was suffocating wafting across his sweating face.

The cop was a warlock, the rings around his pupils glinting like quick-silver in the sunlight as he glanced between Roman and Shay—then at Pax in the back seat.

"Roman Devlin?" the cop inquired.

"Yeah," he replied tightly. There was no point in lying. All the evidence this cop needed was right here in this car, staring him—quite literally—in the face.

The cop backed up. "Step out of the car, please."

Shit.

Fuck.

'No,' Sayagul gasped. *'Roman—'*

Roman couldn't feel his body as he opened the door and stepped out onto the road that was packed with traffic. The world looked distant, as if he were peering in on a stranger's life.

He couldn't kill them. Killing cops and MPU agents was the one thing a Darkslayer avoided at all costs. At the end of the day, Darkslayers were criminals, and the quickest way to end a Darkslayer's life was to throw them in jail.

If he killed them, right in front of all these people, he would have to say goodbye to Pax. Forever. He couldn't protect his brothers from behind bars, so he'd do everything in his power to stay *out* of them.

On the other side of the car, another officer was giving Shay the same orders. She stepped out of the vehicle and turned around, slowly flattening her hands on the roof.

"Turn around slowly and put your hands on the roof of the car," said a male voice. It took Roman a second to realize this command was for him.

He obeyed, his eyes locking with Shay's as they were pat down, their weapons and phones confiscated. Cops were directing traffic, making room for other squad cars and—

A prisoner transport van.

His soul left his body.

So much for staying out of jail.

"You are under arrest for the abduction of Paxton Slade," the officer was saying. "You have the right to remain silent. Anything you say can and will be held against you..."

Roman's eyes shuttered. His hearing was muffled, but he managed to comply when the officer requested that he move his hands behind his back. A pair of cuffs bit into his wrists, clicking shut.

The brimstone sucked his magic dry, like a sponge sopping up water. His ears rang, and he felt off-kilter. Weak. *Wrong.* He'd never been cuffed with these before, but he'd heard enough about them to recognize what they were straightaway. Brimstone was rare and very expensive—and only legal when in the hands of law enforcement.

Hands pinioned his arms, hauling him away from the vehicle.

Roman's eyes snagged on Shay as she, too, was dragged away from the car.

"Test them," a voice said.

Another officer approached with what looked like a temperature gun. But instead of raising it to Roman's forehead, he pointed it at his eye instead. Bright light flashed.

He flinched. "What the hell is that?" They were doing the same to Shay.

"Clear," said the first officer.

"Clear here, too," said the other.

"Roman?" called a small, frightened voice.

It was Pax, stumbling out of the car. A different officer tested him with the same device, causing Paxton to flinch away from the bright light.

"All clear," the officer said.

"Roman?" Paxton called again—more frightened this time.

"Pax," Roman choked out. "It's okay." But his heart pounded so hard he could feel it in his feet.

"Time to go, kid," said the officer at Pax's side. In his hand he held Pax's backpack.

"Wait!" Paxton begged. "Wait, what about my brother? Where are you taking him?—"

But the officer snatched his arm. "Let's go." He began dragging him down the road. "You'll be back home with your dad in no time."

Paxton paled. "No! No, no, no, wait—wait, please!" He fought harder, his tone turning frantic. "I don't want my dad, I want my brother!" He lunged, reaching out with his free hand, his other arm snapping taut and yanking him backward as the officer held on with an iron grip. He started sobbing, and so did Sayagul. "Wait! *Please—* You can't do this—"

"It'll be okay," Roman said, speaking to them both—boy and dragon— as another officer joined the one pulling Pax toward the open back door of a sedan. A woman wearing a suit and sunglasses waited beside it. "I'll find you!" Roman called, his ragged promise bouncing down the crowded highway. "I promise, Pax! You hear me? I *promise—*"

"*Let me go!*" Paxton fought with all his might. Pushing and pulling against the officers, tears streaming down his face. *"Let me go! Let him go! He didn't do anything wrong—please! Please. Roman! ROMAN!"*

Sayagul wept. *'Paxton. Oh, Paxton. I can't. I can't do this, Roman—'*

"Pax, it's okay," Roman rasped. "Be strong—"

"I don't want to go!" Paxton screamed, the words raw and shattered like glass. "I don't want to go with you, I want my brother! I want my brother! *I want my brother! I WANT MY BROTHER!*"

Forceful hands loaded Roman into the back of a prisoner transport van —empty apart from the benches on the outer walls. They brought Shay in behind him, the vehicle shuddering as she and the other officer stepped inside. There was no metal partition down the center, nothing separating him from Shay as they were directed to sit on opposite sides.

"ROMAN!" Pax wailed. He was still fighting, his eyes black and crying —no dark veins, thank gods.

"Pax, I need you to be strong!" Roman called as the officers cuffed their hands again—in front of them this time—and fastened the cuffs to the chains attached to the benches. "I need you to be brave, okay? Everything is going to be all right, I promise—"

"I love you!" he sobbed. "Roman, don't leave! Don't leave me! *You can't leave me!*"

Roman's eyes burned. "I'm not leaving you," he vowed, his chest hurting so badly it felt like he had been shot. The officers spoke into their radios and stepped out of the van. "I'll find you, okay? I'll never leave you, Pax, I prom—"

The doors banged shut. A thick layer of magic rippled over the van, sealing them inside. Through the gaps in the window guards, Roman watched, breathing so hard he swore he might pass out, as Paxton continued to fight, screaming his lungs out as he was dragged down the street.

They were taking him away.

They were taking Paxton away, and he may never see him again.

77

THE CANALS
YVESWICH, STATE OF KER

"Rev, rev, rev your boat, aggressively down the canaaaaal," Malakai sang, his grating voice slicing through the fog, like a fork scraping across a plate. "Un-merrily, un-merrily, un-merrily, un-merrily, life is but a nightmaaaaaaaare."

Where he sat with Max in the bow, keeping watch over the silky waters of the canal they were coasting down—rather, *revving* down, making way too much noise for a city swarming with monsters—Travis glared at the back of Malakai's head.

The rest of their group—everyone was here, including those who were at the Duchess during the riot—was stationed along the sides of the vessel, firearms at the ready. All except Jewels, who sat in the front with Malakai and Aspen, and Magenta, who Travis assumed didn't have enough experience firing guns for Scarlet to feel comfortable giving her one.

Jewels was having a hell of time breathing. Apparently acute dyspnea was a symptom she had struggled with since she was diagnosed with the Tricking, but this was by far the worst bout she had ever experienced. Travis wondered if the portal was to blame for her sudden decline, but—

Nah. It didn't make sense. If Spirit Terra were the reason she couldn't breathe, the rest of them would be having trouble, too, including him. He was breathing fine, though, and everyone else seemed to be, too.

Maybe it was her brother. Giving her a heart attack or something.

"Gods, he's annoying," Travis grumbled.

"And a terrible singer," Max replied with a whisper, his black eyes fixed on the water.

Malakai started singing his twisted version of that old nursery rhyme again. Each time he belted out the word *rev* he hit the throttle, jerking the boat forward. "Rev, rev, *rev...*"

Travis was going to be sick.

Dallas clutched her stomach. "He's going to make me puke."

"Delaney!" Max hissed. All around them, fog curled and darkness eddied like thick smoke. There could be just about anything lurking in there. Waiting for an opportunity to pounce and sink its teeth into the sweet, juicy morsels who were stupid enough to be out here in this boat.

Hopefully, they'd go for the idiot steering the boat first.

Malakai paused and glanced over his shoulder. "Huh? What'd you say, Reacher? You got a problem with me?"

"Cut it out!" Max hissed. "You're going to get us eaten."

"You," Malakai corrected, entirely unbothered. "I'm going to get *you* eaten, Reacher. I'll survive—I always do." He returned to his song, and this time he belted the words out louder. "Rev, *rev, REV...*"

Travis ground his teeth. "If we die," he whispered, "it'll be his fault."

"No wonder Jewels is having heart problems," Dominic grumbled.

"That's what I was thinking."

"Heard that," Malakai drawled. "If you guys got a problem with me, you can swim your asses to shore and walk."

Travis rolled his eyes and gripped his gun tighter, scanning the water that looked like a black mirror.

A warning prickled up his spine as the surface suddenly rippled with a serpentine motion.

A barbed tail flicked up, spraying water before vanishing into the depths.

He shifted his index finger across the trigger.

"Did you see that?" Max murmured.

"Sure did." He blinked the Sight into his eyes.

Below the surface of the canal swam an Aequorwyrm, its aura a pulsating mess of acid-green lines and smoky gray splotches, its gaping mouth full of long, needle-thin teeth. Not only was that thing big and strong enough to drag this boat and everyone in it to the bottom of the canal, but its body was armored with impenetrable scales. If they were to shoot it, the bullets would bounce right off like rubber balls. It didn't matter that the boat was covered with security spells; if it managed to drag them under, they'd be done for.

"Blue?" Max called softly over his shoulder.

Feet thumped as she crossed the deck and knelt on the seat between them.

"Aequorwyrm," Max said. "Eleven o'clock."

"I see it," she confirmed, her eyes black. With a deep breath, she thrust her hands out in front of her, fingers curling. Her eyelids slid shut as she inhaled.

On the exhale, her magic generated a strong current that pushed the wyrm backward. It floundered about, as if ensnared in a net. Travis watched, fascinated, as the neon hues of its aura twisted and thrashed, water splashing as the creature banged its ugly, snarling face against the cobalt scales of Blue's magic, struggling to break free.

Visible. Now that the Veil was collapsing, everyone's magic was visible. It was wild to see shades other than black and Loren's rare white.

Once there was enough distance between the boat and the Aequorwyrm, Blue drew another deep breath before opening her arms wide, like a bird about to take flight.

The water in the canal parted, creating a dry path that stretched from one bank to the other. The Aequorwyrm's skeletal face and grinning mouth were starkly visible through the wall of murky water, as if it were a specimen trapped behind glass. As they coasted away, it gave up and turned around, bellowing a roar that rumbled through the waterway as it swam back toward the ocean.

Blue waited a bit, making sure it was really gone before releasing her power. Water lapped as the gap in the canal closed.

"Thanks," Max said, taking his finger off the trigger.

She nodded and returned to her spot on the bench between Dominic and Magenta. The pink Elemental sat close to Scarlet. Her pink topaz eyes flicked about the fog, her teeth worrying her lower lip.

"So," Travis began, "Magenta."

Magenta startled. She was either shocked that he was speaking to her, or afraid of what he was about to ask.

"How does your power work? The Empath thing."

Scarlet answered for her. "It's not much different than what unmodified hellsehers can do," she said.

"No offence, but I was asking her."

Scarlet's mouth became a thin line.

Good—let her hate him. He already hated her for how poorly she was treating Maximus. This was not the Maya they remembered.

"It's like what you can do, but...stronger, I guess," Magenta said, her voice so quiet Travis could hardly hear her. "It can be hard sometimes, to feel everything. It's stronger for people like me. I can't tune it out like normal hellsehers. Sometimes I have trouble telling the difference between someone else's feelings and my own. It can get...confusing."

Dallas said, "That must be hard for you. Especially if you're around somebody who's going through the stages of grief."

"Or rage," Travis said. Another person's rage was bad enough as it was. He had been extremely sensitive to his father's wrath while growing up. Roman had been his sanctuary. His shelter in the storm.

Magenta nodded, still looking startled by all the attention. "Grief is the hardest," she admitted.

"What about Aurora?" Max asked. "You said she was considered *full spectrum*. What does that mean? What exactly could she do?"

Magenta gave the stage to Scarlet with a look of shy expectance. The two had the full attention of everyone on this boat. Even Delaney had shut his trap, his head angled toward them.

Of all the people in Terra, it was likely this Aurora chick who was most similar to Loren. The fact that she was dead didn't help—but if Scarlet knew anything, anything at all that might help them solve this issue with the Veil... Not that they could do anything about it, now that they were trapped, communications cut, but...

"Full spectrum means she had the power of every element and everything in between," Scarlet began. "Water, fire, earth, sky. She could take every Elemental body, too, not just one."

"Elemental body?" Malakai asked. "What's that mean?"

She transformed into her Elemental form in the blink of an eye, becoming a woman made entirely of fire, her hair spiralling upward like a flame.

Max nearly dropped his gun in the canal.

"Wow," Aspen breathed.

Travis whistled. "Impressive. Can you do that, too?" he asked Blue.

Blue nodded, but didn't demonstrate.

Scarlet shifted back, her hair—hair again, not flame—falling to her shoulders. The embers of her eyes were the last to cool. She looked completely ordinary again. With hair a natural reddish brown, instead of something more wild, like pink or blue, you'd never even guess she was modified. "She could summon and control fire, water, and the atmosphere," she concluded.

Aspen said, "What about her earth powers? What could she do with those?"

"Control the flora and the fauna."

Travis shared a loaded glance with Max.

"You mentioned mind powers," Dominic cut in. "What did those entail?"

"She could create illusions." *Like Shay,* Travis thought. "Freeze time. Speak to spirit creatures, such as Hobs. Animate lifeless objects."

Dallas turned toward Max. "Freeze time," Dallas mused. "Loren did that at the carnival. Remember?"

Max nodded.

They lapsed into silence as the boat coasted through the water, all the way to a bridge not far from Yveswich General Hospital.

Malakai moored the boat along the quay, and everyone got out.

This place was quiet compared to the last time Travis was here. But he spotted lights coming from the direction of the hospital, a muddy glow stifled by supernatural darkness that was difficult to see through, even with the Sight.

Shoes scuffed as Jewels came up beside him.

"You okay?" he asked her.

"Fine," she gritted out, but she was hugging her middle, as if she were trying to physically hold herself together.

"Someone should stay behind and guard the boat," Aspen suggested. "If some asshole steals it, we'll be screwed."

No one volunteered.

"Malakai, you stay," Jewels said, the sentence broken apart by labored breaths. "I'll go with Travis—"

"Oh-ho no!" Malakai interrupted. "Not happening, Bean. Nice try."

"Malakai." She paused to catch her breath. "I am *really* not in the mood."

The sight of Jewels flattening a hand over her heart kept him from arguing further, though he muttered under his breath, as if arguing with *himself.* There were so many loose screws in that head, Travis wouldn't be surprised.

"We need to split ourselves up evenly," Jewels continued, breathless, "so I say you stay behind with whoever else wants to stay—" She paused again, panting. "—and I'll go with Travis and a few of the others to get my meds. I know what I'm looking for—it shouldn't take long."

Aspen spoke up, cutting off Malakai's next objection. "Why don't you two—" She gestured between Travis and Jewels with a black-gloved hand. "—go with Max, Dallas, and Dominic, and the rest of us will stay here?"

Five and five.

Travis shrugged. "Fine by me." He could use a break from Delaney.

And some time alone with the *other* Delaney.

"It's settled, then," Max said. "Let's move."

78

I-5
STATE OF KER

The hum of the tires on the road and the tinkling of chains were the only sounds in the prisoner transport van.

Shay sat on the hard bench opposite from Roman. There was nothing separating them, no metal partition down the middle. But he might as well be oceans away for how close she felt to him.

He was bent forward, his elbows propped on his knees, hands cupping his face. He was crying—she could smell the salt of the tears coursing down his cheeks. Since the moment the doors had slammed shut, trapping them in here, they hadn't said one word to each other.

The silence stretched on as the cops drove them back the way they had come. All the progress they had made, all these miles and all this suffering, the fight they'd won at the Wanderer...

Nothing. All of it had amounted to nothing.

Shay breached the silence with a quiet noise in her throat.

But Roman didn't move. The tires continued to hum. The chains of their cuffs that were fastened to the benches continued to rattle.

"Are you okay?" she whispered. It was a stupid question—she knew he wasn't okay. Until he had his little brother back and they were safe from their father, he would never be okay. But she couldn't bear to watch him suffer in silence any longer. She had to talk to him. Had to try.

It took him so long to respond that Shay was beginning to think he wouldn't.

But then he inhaled sharply, his back shuddering as the breath clawed through him. When he finally lifted his head to stare out the back windows, and Shay saw his crumpled, tear-streaked face and his puffy red eyes, she broke, hot moisture pooling in her own.

He did not deserve this.

"No," he confessed. The whisper cracked like thin ice.

"Is there anything that I can do?" Another stupid question. But what was she supposed to say in this situation? No words would fix this. She just wanted him to know that she was here and ready to listen if he wanted to talk.

Roman just kept staring out the window. The pain in his damp eyes, so raw and real...it was so much worse than the dead stare she was used to.

Another few minutes ticked by before Roman whispered, "I'm so sad, Shay."

Her own tears began to fall. One down each cheek. They dripped off her jaw and rolled down her arms, the chains of her cuffs rattling as the van hit a rough patch in the road.

Neither of them said anything more. Roman continued to stare out the windows, watching as the miles between them and Angelthene piled up one tire rotation at a time.

Close. They had been so close to Witheredge. So close to the Devils.

So close to making it.

The van had four police car escorts, two in the front and two in the rear. It was the car at the very back of the line where they were keeping Paxton. Shay could only imagine what was going through the head of that poor, innocent child. How frightened he must be. How alone he must feel.

"I feel like I failed him," Roman croaked. "He's always trusted me to keep him safe, always believed me when I said that things would one day be better for us." His throat bobbed. A tear rolled down his nose and dripped into his lap. "I don't know where I went wrong."

Shay wiped her cheeks dry. "I know it's hard not to blame yourself," she said, the words thick and wobbling. "But this isn't your fault."

"One chance." He lifted an index finger, still staring out the back windows as fresh tears rolled down his face. "This was our one chance." He lowered his hand and formed a fist with both, cuffs clinking together. "And I fucked it up." A pause. "The worst part is that I *know* we would've made it. If we hadn't gone to that clinic..." He shook his head, disappointed with himself. "I know we'd almost be in Angelthene by now."

She couldn't blame him for thinking this way. When life constantly dealt you shit hands, it was hard not to dwell on the maybes and the what-ifs. She and Anna used to talk all the time about life outside of the Riptide. What it would have been like for them, if Dad had taken them with him when he'd divorced their mother and started over in Laurel. But once you were caught in that sticky web of what-ifs, it was difficult to extricate yourself. Too many nights she had laid awake in her bedroom at the House of Blue, thinking the same sort of things Roman was thinking now. What if this, and what if that...

But there were no redos in life. Time marched forward.

Roman scrubbed his face and drew another ragged inhale.

"For what it's worth, Roman," Shay began, "you've done an incredible job with your brother. You're the reason that boy still has his soul."

He picked at the blood and dirt caked under his nails. "Don't know what good it did. If I ever see him again, I'll be looking out at him from behind bars. He still has six years before he's legally allowed to move out, and it takes a lot less than six to break someone." Another tear slipped down his cheek. He knuckled it away. "I'm living proof of that."

Fresh tears pricked Shay's eyes. She shut them.

Who had protected Roman when he was Paxton's age—and younger? His mother? Roman had done everything he could to shelter Paxton and Travis, but...

At one point in time, he had been an only child, just him and his mother against the world. Against Donovan. And when Travis was born, it was still Roman who had taken the brunt of their father's abuse. He'd taken Travis's share, Shay knew. He didn't have to say it. For too many years, he had willingly weathered his father's storm with no promise that the skies would clear. But he hadn't run.

Roman Devlin did not run.

The silence returned—thicker than before, with nothing to fill it but the continuous hum of the tires and the tinkling of their gods-awful chains. Shay didn't know what else to say. There was nothing she could do to make this right, but if there were, no matter what it would cost her, she would do it. Would give anything to bring these two brothers back together. Now that Anna was gone, and she was being forced to navigate the world without her big sister by her side, she knew how much it hurt to lose a sibling. Someone you loved with your whole heart. Someone you trusted completely.

Someone you'd die for.

She didn't know how long they sat there, Shay staring at the floor of the van with blurry vision while Roman gazed through the window guards at the car that held his youngest brother captive. He wasn't crying anymore; instead, that dead stare was back. He looked defeated. Worn down. Hollow.

"I'm sorry I got you into this," Roman said suddenly.

She lifted her eyes and saw that he was watching her. There were no gold flecks in his irises. Zero warmth.

"You didn't get me into anything. I blackmailed you, remember?"

He didn't smile, but she hadn't expected him to. He just slid his attention back to the windows and whispered, "I'm still sorry." He interlocked his fingers between his thighs, rested his head against the wall, and shut his eyes.

Besides the barbed wire and the wisps of shadow, she had never looked closely at the designs tattooed on his fingers. There were two different symbols etched into the skin of each—one between each knuckle—in black ink. Letters from an ancient alphabet. It was hard to read them at this angle, but she thought that five of the runes spelled out a name.

HELEN

A few minutes went by before Shay picked up on the deep growl of multiple engines.

She slid across the smooth bench, her chains pulling taut when she reached her limit, and craned her neck to peer between the gaps in the window guards.

Sunlight glinted off the windshield of a muscle car coming up quickly on the road behind them.

Two more appeared, spreading out behind the first car like unfurling wings.

Her heart broke into a sprint.

Shit.

"Roman," she squeezed out on a shallow breath.

He opened his eyes.

She pointed with cuffed hands. "I think your dad is here."

———

ROMAN WAS a living example that no matter how bad the situation, it could always be worse.

Today was no different.

When the cops had cuffed him and taken Paxton away, he'd truly believed that he had hit rock bottom. But as it turned out, his father had followed him down to torment him some more.

Donovan wasn't waiting for the police to bring his sons to him. He had come to them.

Those three cars sped up, engines growling. One stayed at the back, front bumper aggressively nudging the back of the car Paxton was in, while the other two came up on either side of the prisoner transport van. The cop driving the van didn't slow, but even through the partition separating him from the prisoners in the back, even through the security spells, Roman could feel his aura.

He was panicking—as he should be. Don *hated* cops. It didn't matter that they were bringing his sons to him—he'd repay the favor by slitting their throats and leaving their corpses out to rot in the sun.

Gripped by fear, Roman jumped to his feet and started pulling on the chains of his cuffs.

"Come on," he growled, pulling harder. *Clang. Clang. Clang.* "*Come on.*" Shay did the same on her side. Magic sparked, but this was brynstan. There was no way in hell they were getting out of these.

"What do we do?" Shay panted, dropping her chains. Roman's head was spinning so quickly he felt like it might fall off. "Roman, what the *hell* are we going to do—"

An ear-splitting explosion rocked the road. Tires screeched as the van bounced and swerved.

Shay screamed as they lost their footing and crashed to the hard floor. She landed on top of him, winding him with an elbow to the gut.

Brakes squealed as the driver slid to a stop, the van spinning in one complete rotation that turned Roman's stomach and sent him sliding into Shay so hard he pinned her against the base of the bench.

A blast of fire engulfed the road. The heat was sweltering, even through the spells.

Sweating, Roman staggered to his feet, his cuffs digging into his wrists as the chains snapped taut, and peered through the window guards.

The skeletons of three squad cars were burning.

Three of four. Only Paxton's remained.

And it was Paxton's car that was now idling about a mile back, walled in by two muscle cars that belonged to Shadowmasters.

Chains rattled as Shay came over to stand at his side.

Their hearts raced as they watched and listened.

The front doors of the van opened. Footsteps clapped on the pavement as the two cops fled for the barren land on either side of the interstate.

Shots popped through the air. *Pop. Pop. Pop.*

Bodies hit the ground with dull thuds and muffled cries.

More shots came from behind them—near the car that held Paxton.

Pop. Pop. Pop.

Roman's wide eyes snapped to Shay's face. She wasn't breathing, and neither was he.

Thick smoke from the burning cars had swallowed the road. It veiled the windows and kept them from seeing what was happening outside. Where Paxton was.

Where his father was.

Roman's heart quaked in fear as Donovan's tall, broad-shouldered silhouette materialized in the smoke.

His pulse quickened. Beating dizzyingly fast as he watched that too-familiar silhouette approach the van with that cocky gait he so hated.

This was it. His dad was going to execute him, right here on this road. Force him to kneel on the pavement and shoot him in the back of the head, probably. He'd make Paxton watch as his big brother's blood pooled across the ground.

It would break him. His funny, selfless, kind, and loving little brother... His life would be shattered.

"Roman." Panic choked Shay's voice. She tried to back away, tried looking for a weapon, but there was nothing and nowhere to go.

The doors shuddered with a bang.

Roman backed away, his heart jumping into his mouth.

Shit. *Shit shit shit.*

"Oh gods!" Shay panted, pressing against his side. "What do we do?"

He didn't know. He was going to faint—

The left door swung open. Then the right.

Sunlight flooded the van. Roman instinctively threw a hand up to block it.

He blinked.

Blinked again.

"No way," he breathed. His knees shook—not from fear, but relief.

The man standing before him smiled. A real, *genuine* smile, the skin at the outer corners of his eyes crinkling.

"Hey, kid," the man said, his square jaw, dusted with stubble, working the gum in his mouth. That smile—so similar to Donovan's, yet so...*not*—spread into a big, dimpled grin. "Miss me?"

Roman's legs gave out, and he practically fell onto the bench. *"Uncle Dean?"*

PART FOUR
THE BATTLESHORT

79

HELL'S GATE
ANGELTHENE, STATE OF WITHEREDGE

Loren was so surprised to find Roark waiting for them out front of the holding center that by the time they made it back to Hell's Gate, she still hadn't found her voice.

Never in a million years would she have believed the Red Baron would willingly set foot in a Darkslayer House. And yet here he was, striding into the clean, bright foyer at her side, his head tipping back as he scanned the white walls and the high, vaulted ceilings of the impressive mansion that had become her home. His wings were concealed by a spell, his hands tucked away in the pockets of his expensive suit jacket.

"So," he began, his voice echoing in the big open space as she shut the door behind him. "This is where you've been spending all your time."

Eyes the color of brandy slid her way. As always, she couldn't read them. Roark wasn't just a closed book—he was a locked one.

She cleared her throat, taken aback not just by his shrewd gaze, but by the fact that he was bothering to make small talk with her. "I love it here," she confessed. "Darien has made me feel very at home."

The slayer she spoke of was currently coming down the stairs. He'd gone up the minute they'd arrived—to change his clothes, she realized now. Those were different jeans and a different shirt he was wearing, his hair no longer messy, but smoothed back.

She was so distracted by Darien that at first she didn't notice Roark was watching her closely.

Was it something she'd said?

She clasped her hands before her. "I can show you around, if you'd like."

"No need. I won't be here long." They were the same words he'd said the day he had gone with her and Dallas to Angelthene Academy a few weeks before their classes had begun. The Headmaster had offered to give him a tour of the grounds and the dorm room in the House of Salt where his daughters would be staying. *No need*, he'd said. *I won't be here long.* He never was. He didn't care enough about his girls to bother with seeing things like dorm rooms.

Or the Darkslayer House where his one daughter had been spending most of her time since almost being abducted last fall. No big deal.

She was used to being rejected by him. But she had not expected this particular rejection to sting this much. Maybe it was because this house they were standing in was her home. Her new one. A place that had changed her in so many huge ways that to share it with her father figure—the man she had looked up to her whole life—would have meant a lot to her. She hadn't realized just how much until the offer was out and he hadn't accepted it.

But she managed to hide her disappointment behind a fake smile and told him, "Maybe another time, then."

He weighed her response—studying her face with eyes that always seemed to see too much while giving nothing away.

Darien reached the bottom of the stairs, drawing Roark's attention away from her face. Everyone else, including Arthur, Kylar, Eugene, Sabrine, and Logan, was waiting for them in the dining and living area.

Darien tipped his head toward the sound of their voices. "Shall we?"

Loren walked in first, Darien following closely behind her, like he had every day since they had bumped into each other in the hospital in Yveswich. Guarding her, even in the safety of his own house.

Roark came in behind them, and everyone quieted down.

This was a man who dealt with crowds and uneasy situations all the time, so she knew there was nothing about this that unsettled him. It unsettled her, though. Because she had no idea why he was here, or what he was about to say. Did he have bad news? Good news? Did he know why Dallas wasn't back yet or why she hadn't called?

They hadn't exchanged many words out front of the holding center, hadn't received an explanation for the hell they had been put through in those interrogation rooms. But they all knew it was Roark who'd ordered the cops to release them. The *higher up* Finn Solace had referred to when addressing Detective Glen.

If it weren't for Roark... If what had happened in that room with Detective Glen had lasted *one* second longer...

She shuddered.

Darien pulled out his chair at the head of the dining room table, but instead of taking a seat, he gestured for Loren to sit there instead.

She did. She was still feeling faint from spending so many hours at the holding center without food or rest. Merely the thought of standing fatigued her. Darien stood behind her like a bouncer while Roark drifted toward the free chair at the opposite end of the long table. The others claimed their own seats, a few opting to stand, only eight chairs at the table. Though Arthur and Eugene chose to stay in the living room, their attention was on Roark, Eugene's video game discarded beside him on the couch.

"Have a seat, if you'd like," Darien told Roark. "Make yourself comfortable."

"I'll stand," he replied.

"Suit yourself. You mind if I smoke?" Darien was already reaching for his lighter and packet of cigarettes on the table.

"It's your house." His response was another surprise. Roark hated smoking, but you'd never guess with the casual tone he was using and his expression that was so...at ease. As if he were interacting with people he regularly spent time with.

Darien lit up, the lid on his metal lighter clinking shut. "That shit with the cops stressed me out," he said, the words slightly muffled by the cigarette in his mouth. He tossed the lighter onto the table and took another drag before adding, leaning his arms on the back of Loren's chair, "I didn't expect to see you so soon. They pull all the military out, or just you?"

"Just me."

The way Darien paused suggested that Roark's answer was not what he had expected. Why pull just Roark?

He explained, "When the imperator found out that I challenged his authority and had the forcefield taken down after you called, he put me on a leave of absence."

"For how long?"

"They haven't said. But I won't be returning to Yveswich."

Tanner said, "So does that mean you're no longer being briefed on what's happening there?"

"Correct. I've had a few people report to me without his knowledge, but the imperator doesn't want me involved at the site anymore. And that includes Taega. She was supposed to join me in Yveswich for several more days, but when I was discharged, she was forced to take a leave of absence as well. Have you been watching the news?"

"I've had it on all day," Arthur chimed in. He was sipping tea in his favorite spot in the living room. "They're certainly being selective about what they tell the public, aren't they?"

Roark nodded. "They're doing everything they can to cover it up," he said, addressing everyone now. "The imperator wants as few people as possible knowing the truth, and he is willing to go to great lengths to keep the people of Yveswich quiet. People like us, as well."

"Speaking of people being kept quiet," Lace interjected. "You were talking to us about the Veil when we were in Yveswich. How? We thought you had a silencing spell put on you when you left the Phoenix Head Society."

"I did. It's been lifted—how, I don't know."

"As of when?" Kylar asked.

"The day the portal opened," Roark replied. "When the replica exploded, I was fast asleep at home. I startled awake to the sensation that half of my weight had been stripped away. Like something heavy had been lifted off my chest." He stared down at the engraved table, his eyes fogging over with deep thought. It was almost to himself that he added quietly, "It was the lightest I've felt in years."

Could this be the reason he was acting so...different? Had the spell had that bad of an effect on him? He almost seemed like a totally different man.

Darien said, "You think the explosion somehow cut the spell, or what?" He stepped around Loren's chair to put his smoke out in the ashtray. She could hardly smell it, even as a haze of it hung in the air around her. He was using his magic again.

She tried not to frown.

"That, I don't know," Roark admitted.

"Wouldn't you have to go through one of the Nameless for a spell that complicated, though?" Sabrine asked.

"Usually, yes," Roark replied. "One that lasts that long and covers an entire group of people such as the Phoenix Head Society would require a greater trade." Not like the silencing spell that the imperator had put on her, then. The potion he'd made her drink. This was something far stronger. Something that could not be purchased at a spell-shop.

"What if it was the Basilisk?" Jack asked. He was looking at Darien.

Darien now stood with crossed arms beside Loren's chair instead of behind it, so she saw when he tilted his head in thought.

Roark glanced between Jack and Darien. "I'm not following."

Tanner explained, "Before the replica exploded, we were in the maintenance tunnels below Caliginous on Silverway. We accidentally walked into the Crossroads where the Basilisk lived. Darien was forced to kill it. And I guess Jack thinks that's what broke the spell?" He, as well as several other people, looked Jack's way.

Jack shrugged. "It's just a guess."

Loren cleared her throat. "Basilisk? Isn't that a type of serpent?"

Darien smoothed her tangled hair before resting that hand on the back of her chair. "Yes. A serpent king, they're called."

She twisted in her seat to see his face. "And you killed it?"

He dipped his chin in answer. Ivy whispered something to Lace.

Loren stared blindly at the floor in thought. "That's what I saw," she murmured. "When I was in a coma." She looked across the table at Roark. "I saw you," she whispered. She had seen Erasmus, Cyra, and Roark—*Elix* —while drifting through the past. Had witnessed parts of the conversation they'd had with the giant snake, its massive, scaled body shifting continuously around the perimeter of a dark cavern.

Roark's eyes tightened, his hands that were braced on the back of the chair he refused to sit in tensing. "You...saw me," he repeated. "What do you mean you saw me?"

"When I was in a coma, I went...somewhere else. I saw things that happened in the past. And I saw you—when you were younger and still... human. You were with Erasmus and a woman named Helia. You were speaking with a giant snake." When she paused, the room was so silent you could hear a pin drop. "Was that the Basilisk?"

It took Roark a moment, but he nodded and said, "It was."

Her lips parted in surprise, and she found herself looking up at Darien again. He looked at her as well, as deep in thought as she was.

Everything that had occurred while she was unconscious seemed so much like a dream, she'd half-expected Roark to tell her that she was wrong. Or lie, even, since he had never been willing to help them in the past, but...

It was all true. Everything she had seen while drifting elsewhere... The horrible past her parents had attempted to bury... The past that *this* parent —Roark—had also played a role in...

True. All of it was true. And it made her ill. All those secrets they'd kept, the horrific sacrifices they had made to the Well in exchange for power, status, and immortality... It made her sick to think about. Made her hate her parents for those heinous acts that had resulted in so many innocent deaths.

But—

But maybe it wasn't just Roark who could now speak freely. Maybe the spell that was placed on Erasmus and Cyra—*Helia*—had been broken, too. Maybe they could finally help them right their many wrongs.

"No matter the details of *how* the spell was broken," Roark began, severing Loren's eye contact with Darien, "I'm simply glad that it was. I came here today to warn you." A beat of tense silence pulsed through the room. "The Veil is going to fall." The severity in his tone made Loren's scalp prickle. "It's falling as we speak. Yveswich has days, if we are lucky, before every street will be blackened out and every person trapped there will perish."

Murmurs rippled through the room. Loren's heart skipped a beat, her thoughts drifting to the others, who they still hadn't heard from. Max, Travis, Dallas, Dominic, Malakai... Where were they? Were they okay?

Ivy said, "The cops are trying to blame us for everything that's happening there. That's why Darien, Tanner, and Loren were taken into custody. They saw them on the street cameras and think they had something to do with it. They were looking for Jack, too." She gestured to her husband.

"And Roman," Tanner added. "They tried getting me to tell them where he is. They supposedly have a warrant for his arrest."

Darien said, "They asked me about him, too." To Roark he said, "I spoke to Finn on my way out. He said that prick detective Glen was a transfer selected by the imperator. Is that true?"

"I believe it could be. Like I said, he's doing everything he can to cover up the truth, so sending cops on a wild goose chase and using Glen as an instrument could simply be another part of his plan. He needs someone to blame, and I think it's obvious why he would choose to blame you." To get rid of the Seven Devils and the threat they posed to his plan, as well as the threat that his true intentions could wind up being exposed. It would be his downfall. His plan, while not as sufficient as simply killing the Devils, was smart.

Because they were resilient. And perhaps Quinton was finally learning just *how* resilient they were. *If you can't kill them, lock them up* appeared to be his new motto.

"How much *do* they know?" Kylar asked.

"Next to nothing," he admitted. "The Fleet and the military know more than the cops, as we've dealt with threats from other dimensions in the past. Most of what we've dealt with has been kept confidential. Members of the Fleet undergo extensive training to handle otherworldly threats like what's happening in Yveswich. But even I can admit that they are in over their heads with this one."

"Do you know how to get the Veil back up?" Darien asked him.

"That's partly why I came here to speak with you today. To see if we can work together to solve this. Erasmus and Helia were careful about the information they chose to divulge to the society. They had a lot of secrets, those two. The closer they became, the farther I drifted. Helia was the one who erected the Veil hundreds of thousands, maybe even millions, of years ago. She is the reason our world is completely separate from the spirit realm. While I unfortunately don't have all the answers myself, *they* do. So it's safe to say that if we want to fix this, we need to start by talking to Erasmus."

The room shifted with uncertain glances. Jack snorted a laugh.

Roark looked side-long at him. "Is there something about this that amuses you?"

"Sorry, but—yeah, kinda. We've tried talking to Erasmus in the past," Jack explained. "He's pretty useless."

"Maybe not now," Lace pointed out. "If Roark can speak, I don't see why Erasmus won't be able to. Especially if it *was* the Basilisk's death that broke the spell." Loren knew where she was coming from, but... Something didn't add up.

"But why would they spell themselves?" Sabrine asked, putting Loren's confusion into words. "I mean, it was Erasmus and Helia who put the spell on the Phoenix Head Society, right? To protect their secrets. So why would they be under the same spell? Why do that to themselves?"

"Doesn't make sense," Logan agreed.

"Maybe they were tricked?" Tanner offered.

"The Basilisk was known to do that," Roark said. "The serpent kings are creatures of the Void—the oldest and most cunning. The Basilisk was one of the most powerful creatures in the universe, but not the most trust-worthy. While the Nameless cannot lie, if you miss a detail or a loophole in whatever trade you choose to make, if you don't read the fine print, so to speak... Well..."

"You're fucked, basically," Jack concluded.

Roark nodded. "Basically, yes. Whichever way we choose to go about this, we need to act quickly. If we cannot get the Veil back up..." He didn't finish his sentence.

"How long will the forcefield contain it?" Darien asked.

"We don't know."

"So, we've got days to figure this out," Jack concluded with a hard chuckle, his lips curling with a frown. "Lucky us."

"Days until Yveswich is engulfed, yes, but it will take longer than that for the Veil to fully fall," Roark said. "The Veil extends clear across Terra, so it won't fall overnight. We've got time yet."

"Do you have an estimate?" Darien asked.

"Weeks, maybe. Months. I really don't know. In the meantime, containing it with a forcefield is truly the best course of action. But..."

Loren held her breath. She'd seen that look before.

"I'm afraid the imperator has taken it upon himself to move forward with another plan, which further limits the time that we have. The forcefield, it...it might have helped us for longer, if he hadn't approved a new strategy that was recently proposed by the military."

"And what strategy is that?" Darien pressed.

"Three days from now, at Witching Hour, the military will fire anima mundi missiles into Yveswich in attempt to close the portal."

The floor tilted beneath Loren's feet.

"Missiles," Tanner mused. "But— Won't that just kill everyone who's trapped in there?"

Jack said bitterly, "Doesn't sound like he gives two shits."

"Why missiles?" Darien demanded. "What's the reason? What makes them think this'll work?"

"They are under the impression that the pressurized magic in the missiles could potentially seal the portal," Roark explained. "They've been analyzing video footage from the street cameras, and what they've concluded is that the Control Tower is the reason Yveswich is still standing. The magic the tower is pulling up from the anima mundi is the only thing holding back the darkness of the Void. Without it, the whole city would have been destroyed the minute the bomb went off. No one would have survived, and no street would be untouched by the darkness. It would have been...a very different outcome."

"Yeah, the cops showed me the footage," Darien said. "But here's the problem with their little plan: The magic they're looking at is not *normal* magic."

Roark's forehead creased. "I don't understand."

"That's not magic from the anima mundi," Darien explained. "It's *hers.*" He gestured to Loren.

All eyes fell on her.

Roark's brows went up. He pointed a finger at her. "Yours?"

"I went to the Control Tower before the replica blew up," Loren began. "I poured as much of my magic into the tower as I could. I managed to shield parts of the city, but... There were some areas I couldn't cover. I tried, but...I wasn't strong enough." And because of her, countless people had died.

Because of her, the Veil was falling.

Because of her, the imperator had blown a hole in the fabric of the universe and unleashed the worst dimension of all.

"Is the imperator aware?" Ivy's question was for Roark. "What I mean is, does he know it's Loren's magic and not the tower doing it, or does he believe the same as everyone else?"

"I'm not certain," Roark said. "All the imperator cares about is finding the real Arcanum Well. So, as far as this operation goes...I doubt he's hung up on the details."

"Maybe he wants the city wiped out so he can have a clear shot to get into Spirit Terra?" Lace guessed.

"Sounds like it," Darien agreed. "If he actually believed for one second that these anima mundi missiles would seal the portal, he wouldn't have given the military the okay to do it." No, he certainly wouldn't have. Cutting a doorway into the Veil to get to the Well was his plan all along, and was precisely the reason why he went to Yveswich and planted the replica in the first place. Which answered their question.

He did not believe the same as the military at all. He *knew* the missiles wouldn't do anything other than destroy what was left of Yveswich and kill the last of the survivors. He *wanted* the city destroyed.

The group broke out into conversation.

Loren met Roark's gaze across the table. "Do you know where Dallas is?" she asked him above the din. The others quieted down. "We haven't heard from her since we left Angelthene."

"I sent a helicopter for Dallas," Roark replied. "But I was discharged before the pilots reported back."

Loren's head spun faster. Her breathing thinned.

Darien stepped closer, his fingers smoothing her hair.

"What about Max and Travis?" Ivy asked. She shifted her attention to Darien. Her eyes were wide, her face pallid. "What if they're trapped in there?"

"Try tracking them again," Darien said. "One of you—track them. Right now."

Jack got up and went to the kitchen to get a plastic zip-lock bag of Stygian salts. When he came back, he dumped half on the table and used the dull edge of a kitchen knife to drag some into a line.

"Is there any way you can get the forcefield down?" Darien asked Roark as Jack snorted the salt off the flat part of the blade. "Or even get me back in there?" Loren's heart thumped out an uneven rhythm at the thought of Darien going back in there. Gods, if he left—

But Roark shook his head. "I can't. I'm sorry, but my hands are tied."

Tanner said, "What about programming people out? Is that doable?"

"Not at this point," Roark replied. "The military and others in positions of authority had their auras programmed in before the switch in forcefield. No one else can be added."

Tanner swore.

"They'll be pulling out before the missiles hit," Roark concluded.

"Hidden...," Jack murmured, his eyes shifting beneath his closed lids. His hands were in fists, his left knee bouncing under the table. Through clenched teeth, he said, "I can't see anyone!" Ivy rubbed his shoulders and murmured words of comfort.

Darien faced Roark. "There's no way you can get the forcefield down?" he pressed. "No way at all?"

He was already shaking his head. "Even if I were still on site, it wouldn't have made a difference. The imperator has implemented what we call a *Battleshort,*" he explained. "The forcefield cannot, under any circumstances, be shut off, not even by him."

Oh gods. Loren's heart raced so fast, she felt lightheaded. When Roark's eyes locked with hers, she wondered if he, too, was thinking of her. Dallas.

Was she trapped there? Was that the reason she hadn't called?

Jack opened his eyes and shoved the bag of salt and the knife aside in anger before hanging his head in his hands.

"If these friends of yours really are stuck in Yveswich...," Roark mused. He sighed, his face grave. "I hate to say this, but...I'm afraid they're on their own."

80

THE TRICKING WARD (YGH)
YVESWICH, STATE OF KER

"It's that one there," Jewels said. She sat on the counter in the cold-storage medication room in the Tricking Ward of Yveswich General Hospital, her pale fingers gripping the counter's edge. "You just had your hand over it."

Travis moved his hand back to the left, his fingertips hovering over the small glass vials in the neatly stocked medicine cabinet. There were hundreds of the same identical vial, all labeled with funky names that were impossible to pronounce. How could anyone be expected to say these out loud? If he tried, he'd embarrass himself.

"This one?" He peered over his shoulder at Jewels.

She squinted to see better. "The next one over."

Glass clinked as he grabbed the vial she'd indicated to.

They were on the second floor. They were alone in here, the others standing guard out in the dark hallway. The hospital was deserted—no staff or patients. There was a lot of blood, though. On the floor, the walls. The ceiling, even. Not exactly encouraging.

But neither was Jewels's condition. Not only was her skin ghostly pale and drenched with sweat, but she could barely sit up. When her legs had given out halfway up the stairs, Travis had insisted on carrying her on his back the rest of the way. It was only Dominic, who had been walking behind her when she fell, that had stopped her from tumbling all the way down to the bottom. He'd bent down to stop her mid-roll, and from there Travis had carried her.

"I hope you're not afraid of needles," Jewels said as he joined her at the counter and opened a new syringe.

"I used to be," he admitted. "I got over it, though. I think my obsession with tattoos helped, somewhat." He grabbed the vial. "You're going to have to tell me what to do," he said as he tilted the vial in his hand, the silver cap winking like a fading star. There were no lights on in here besides a couple of dim security bulbs. "I've never used one of these before."

"You stick the needle in through the top." She indicated to the rubber membrane at the top of the vial. "Then you pull up on the piston to fill the syringe."

"How far?"

"This line here." Her fingers brushed against his as she showed him the correct measurement line on the syringe.

Their gazes clashed. They looked away at the same time.

Travis took a breath. "Okay," he said on the exhale. "Let's do this."

He followed her instructions, pushing the needle through the rubber membrane and pulling up on the piston. But by the time he set the vial aside, he realized he didn't know what to do from here. What if he didn't do it right and ended up hurting her or something?

"Uhh…" He laughed, nervous. "Now what?"

Jewels stripped off her jacket and rolled up the sleeve of her tee. "Now you stick it in."

"Pssh. At least take me out to dinner first."

She snickered.

"Sorry. Probably a bad time for jokes."

"It's never a bad time for jokes. Right here's fine." She tapped a spot on her upper arm. "I'd do it myself, but it makes me queasy. It's a little easier when someone else…sticks it in." Her big green eyes danced.

Travis chuckled, that look in her eyes heating his blood with desire. "Okay, let the pro *stick it in,* then." He positioned the needle. "Is this going to hurt?"

"It bites a little, but I'm used to it."

"Good biting, or bad biting?" He winked.

She fought a smile. "You're quite the flirt, aren't you?"

"Guilty as charged." He forced himself to focus, his humor fading. "Tell me when you're ready."

"I've been ready for like five minutes."

"Sorry," he mumbled. "I'm kind of new at this."

"I'm just teasing, Travis. You're doing fine."

He moved as carefully as he could as he eased the needle into her smooth skin and pushed down on the piston. "Is that okay?" he asked her, watching as the medicine in the syringe began to drain.

"That's fine." She was breathing deeply, though, and Travis detected that, no matter how many times she claimed to have done this, she didn't like it. He didn't blame her. Getting stuck with sharp objects wasn't exactly a fun time.

He pushed the piston down until every drop of the translucent medicine was dispensed. Then he drew the needle back out.

"There," he said. "That wasn't so hard." He disposed of the needle in the sharps container. "You want one of those fun colorful bandages they give to the kids? Something sparkly, maybe?"

"A cotton ball and some tape is fine."

He was already heading for the drawers. "Oh, come on. They've got to have something a little more fun in here." He started searching.

Jewels waited as he rummaged through boxes of adhesive bandages.

Plain, plain, plain, plain... He kept searching. There must be at least one box of multicolored ones somewhere in here...

Ah-hah! "Found some," he declared. He showed off the box over his shoulder.

Jewels smiled faintly as he crossed the room. He ripped the box open and dug around inside, flinging bandages across the counter until he found the color he was looking for. Then he peeled the package open and stuck the bandage over the mildly inflamed skin on her arm.

"There." He grinned at the round purple bandage. It had a smiley face on it. He was starting to feel like an idiot when he noticed Jewels smiling back at him. So pretty, that smile. Her eyes. Her heart-shaped face.

"You found purple," she said.

"Your favorite color," he stated proudly. Wait—had she ever really *told* him purple was her favorite? His smile fell. "Right?"

She gave a soft laugh. "Yes."

He studied the sheen of sweat on her face. "You okay?"

"Yeah. I'm feeling better already. That stuff works quickly." She watched him as he finished clearing the counter and chucking the garbage out. "I never asked how *you're* doing."

He kept his back facing her as he grabbed a few extra vials of medication from the cabinet and pocketed them. She would eventually need more, and he doubted anyone would want to come back here. "Is four okay, or should we take more?" He grabbed syringes, too.

"Four's fine. That's like two months' worth." He took a fifth, just in case. "You still haven't answered my question," she said.

He lingered in front of the cabinet, his back facing her. "What question?"

"How are you?"

"Oh. I'm fine," he mumbled. He kept his eyes down as he returned to where she sat.

"Travis," she reproached.

"What?" he asked innocently as he leaned a hip against the counter.

"You're lying."

"No, I'm not."

"Yes, you are."

He didn't say anything. He wasn't fine—he hadn't been since the moment he'd split up from the others in the hospital. The moment he'd watched Roman walk away all pissed. But he didn't want to admit it. He liked this girl, and admitting he wasn't okay seemed...gods, he didn't know. Cowardly, maybe? Wimpy? Bit of both?

But Jewels wasn't letting it go. "Travis," she repeated in that same, reproachful tone.

"Jewels," he countered with the same attitude.

"We're trapped," she began, using her fingers to tick off all the reasons why she believed he wasn't fine. "Aside from Max, you don't have any of your family with you. You miss your brothers—it's obvious. And we have days, if we're lucky, left to live." Softer, she added, "It's okay to be honest."

Travis chewed on his lip as he considered how to respond. "I...have been beating myself up ever since Roman left the hospital," he confessed. He leaned back against the counter and crossed his arms, staring straight ahead at nothing as he let it all out. "I'm mad at myself for not getting out on time. I feel guilty for not going with Roman when he left to look for Paxton. And... And I feel like an awful person for coming back to Yveswich in the first place. Roman gave me a new life, and when I came back here..." His vision fuzzed over as he stared at the floor. "I might as well have spat in his face. It would've been less of an insult."

"Oh, Travis," Jewels whispered.

He had to force himself to lift his gaze to her face.

She was watching him with sympathy. "Why *did* you stay? Was it really just because of...me?"

He looked away and cleared his throat. "I mean... Yeah. Yeah, I guess." He peeked sidelong at her. "Is that bad?"

Her shoulders sank. "Look, Travis... I think you're a really great guy—"

"Oh gods," he said with a hard chuckle. He pushed off the counter and started to pace. "I totally didn't see this coming. I *really* did not see this coming."

"Let me finish. You're not letting me finish."

He turned and faced her. Waited.

"I think you're a really great guy," she began again, "but..."

Yeah, there was always a *but,* wasn't there?

"I'm sick," she concluded.

His brows went up. Okay, he hadn't expected that. He'd expected more of, like, *You're not my type* or *We're too different* or *I decided I don't like you after all. Sorry about that.*

His brow creased. "I already knew that, Jewels."

"I need you to really think that through, though. If we make it out of here..." She sighed and looked to the left, staring at nothing. "I'm never getting better, Travis. There is no cure for what I have. The doctors...when they diagnosed me, I asked for an estimate on how much time I have. I asked for three separate opinions, just to be sure, and each doctor gave me the same answer."

Travis's mouth was so dry, it felt pasty. He crossed his arms again, his fists hidden beneath them. "And what...what did they tell you?"

Her eyelids slid shut, her face twisting with pain. "Two years."

Every coherent thought left his head.

A cruel and mocking silence filled the room.

Two years... That meant she had Stage Two. The second-worst stage.

"I was diagnosed near the end of last year." Which meant she now had *less* than two years. She opened her eyes and slid them his way. "I meant what I said," she began with a hoarse whisper. "You're a really great guy."

When she didn't elaborate, he told her, "Thanks?" Was that the right thing to say? He was ass at talking, wasn't he?

She smiled a little. "I'm not going to lie, my first impression of you was..." The laugh she let out was musical—the kind of sound he would gladly listen to every day. But her eyes were shining with emotion. The sad kind. "Not great," she finished.

He flinched. That...was not what he'd expected to hear. "Ouch?"

"I don't mean it like that," she said quickly. "What I mean is...when I agreed to go out with you, I honestly believed you were the kind of guy who..." Her cheeks reddened. "That we would just..."

He questioned her with an upward flick of his brows. "Just what?" he pressed. "Fuck?" He didn't blame her—he'd volunteered himself at the House of Souls when she'd claimed she wanted some good dick. He'd never really been the dating type, either. Getting laid was all he'd cared about.

She winced. "Maybe?"

He shrugged. "That's okay—I actually thought that, too."

"That was *before,* though," she said. "Before all of this. Before everything that happened in Angelthene with the ice cream and the knives..."

"Ice cream and knives," he repeated with a chuckle. "What a date, hey?"

Her smile was wistful. "I really do like you, Travis. Which is why..." She picked at her nails. "Why I don't think it's fair of me if I let this continue." Ouch again. "Let's say we started, I don't know, catching feelings for each other, or something. *Real* feelings." Was that not what he already had? Real feelings? Was he an idiot for believing that Jewels actually liked him? All this time, was she really just another girl who'd heard the raunchy rumors about him and wanted to hit the sheets with the Devlin Devil? Had *anything* changed, or was he just delusional? "Then what?" she concluded.

He couldn't hide the frown on his face. "Then we...catch feelings?"

"Then you lose me in less than two years."

He blinked. "Oh."

"Do you understand where I'm going with this?"

"Yeah," he admitted. Was this how Darien felt? When he'd found out about Loren? When he'd realized he was in love not just with a mortal, but a sick one? "But you're missing a pretty big piece of the puzzle there, Jewels."

Her sandy brows inched together. "What piece?"

"You don't have two years, you have like two days." The laugh that barked out of him was forced; nothing about this was funny. "And so do I."

Her answering laugh was bubbly and a lot more genuine. "Okay, so... what you're saying is, we should just enjoy ourselves while we can?"

He shrugged. "Yeah, sure—two years, two days, what difference does it make? We're going to die eventually." It was kind of funny, actually— mortals were treated so poorly because of their short lives, but hellsehers hardly lived any longer. They could, yeah, sure, if they abstained from using magic. Most didn't, though, and so they died young.

Jewels stared down at her shoes, her hands gripping the counter's edge.

When he stepped closer, she peeked up at him. "Let's make a deal," he said.

"Okay," she began, her tone cautious. "What sort of deal?"

"No more serious shit. We're already in the worst place in the world. We'll be lucky if we live to see tomorrow. So let's just...be."

"Be," she repeated, her brows rising.

"Let's live," he clarified. "While we still can." He took one step closer and extended a hand. "Deal?"

For a moment, she just stared at his hand. Thinking.

And then she clasped it, the corners of her lips tipping up. "Deal."

SLUMPED on the floor in the hallway by the cold-storage medication room, Max tried not to fall asleep. Dallas was dozing against the wall across from him, while Dominic wandered around muttering nearby.

"Who are you talking to?" Max asked the Angel.

"Sirocco."

Max grunted in response; he was too tired for words.

"Thought I was talking to myself, didn't you?" Dominic asked with an over-the-shoulder smile. His hawk Familiar—Sirocco—cawed a laugh from his shadow.

Max leaned forward and craned his neck to try to see in the doorway of the medication room, but it was impossible from this angle. "What's taking them so long?" he grumbled.

"They'll be around," Dallas said groggily.

Max's wince was apologetic. "Sorry. Didn't mean to wake you."

She stretched her arms out above her head. "I wasn't really sleeping," she said around a yawn, her eyes watering. "Mostly thinking."

"About what?"

Dominic called from down the hallway, "Hey, you guys want anything from the vending machine?"

"Just water," Max said.

"Same," Dallas called. To Max she said, "About what Scarlet and Magenta said in the boat. About Aurora." Right—that shit about all her different powers.

Cast illusions. Freeze time. Speak to spirit creatures. Animate lifeless objects. And all that didn't even include the Elemental powers.

Their conversation took a pause as Dominic smashed the vending machine open. Bottles cascaded out and rolled across the floor. The Angel scooped three up and came over to join them. He handed out the waters and sat down, the dark feathers of his wings hissing as they spread across the floor.

"Thanks," Max said at the same time as Dallas.

"Welcome."

They twisted off the caps and drank. The hospital was so eerily quiet, the glug of the water shifting down their throats sounded loud.

"Do you think Aurora might have been modified at the Facility as an attempt to create a new Skeleton Key?" Dallas asked, breathless from chugging three quarters of the bottle.

Max said, "To use the Well?" He swirled the last of the water in his bottle, forming a cyclone.

"Yeah."

"Could've been."

Dominic said, "If we found a way for Loren to use her powers without it causing her harm, she'd be a powerhouse."

"That was exactly what I was thinking," Max said to the Angel.

Dallas said, "I'm glad Darien got her out of here. If we have any hope of closing that portal and putting an end to all of this, we're going to need Loren."

Max nodded his agreement and finished off his water.

The poor girl had already been through so much. And now the fate of the world quite literally depended upon her.

Footfall drew their attention to the door to the medication room as Jewels and Travis walked out.

"How'd you make out?" Max asked them.

"We didn't, unfortunately," Travis said. Jewels snickered and tried to pinch his neck, but he ducked to the side. When he took note of Max's unamused face, he gave him a serious answer. "We took a few vials, so hopefully we won't need to come back here."

"We won't," Jewels confirmed. "I have enough for two months."

"Two and a half," Travis corrected. "I took another when you weren't looking." Two and a half months—that was optimistic when the city was getting darker every day.

Max heaved himself to his feet, his body tired and aching. "All right. Let's go. I'm about to pass out, and something tells me Delaney's throwing a tempter tantrum." He gave Dallas a hand up, and they began making their way out.

"Hey, Max?" Dallas said quietly as they approached the stairwell. "I wanted to talk to you about something before we get back."

"Yeah? And what's that?"

"Maya."

He couldn't help but scowl at the thought of his sister. How disappointing it was that their reunion had led to...this. To nothing. "Scarlet, you mean."

She grimaced. "Yeah, about that. I just want you to know that it isn't your fault—how she's behaving."

He pushed the door to the stairwell open. "I know." His voice echoed.

"I can tell that you don't want to talk about it," she said. "But do you remember what you said to me at my father's event? *A toxic relationship is a toxic relationship, no matter who it involves?*"

He glanced at her. "I said that?"

"Yes."

A proud smile pulled at his mouth. "Damn. I'm pretty good, aren't I?"

"Max, what I'm trying to tell you is that your sister is toxic. She isn't treating you the way you deserve. And if she doesn't want anything to do with you after we get out of here, that's her loss. And you've done nothing wrong."

The sound of their feet clapping on the stairs was deafening. When they got to the bottom, they pushed through the door and continued walking.

"Okay?" Dallas pressed.

He sighed. "I know. I guess I'm just...disappointed. I expected her to be happy to see me, not..." He shook his head. "Not whatever *this* is."

"It's not your fault," she said again. "Sometimes people change, and she unfortunately changed for the worse." She could say that again.

They left the hospital and continued back to the canal. Being out here was...unsettling. The darkness was almost oily, and Max could have sworn it was harder to breathe in these parts. That could just be his imagination getting the better of him, though.

As expected, Malakai was pacing on the boat, looking pissed. When he spotted them coming, he faced them, hands curling into fists at his sides. He looked like a bull ready to charge.

"*Well?*" he demanded.

Max said, "Travis and Jewels made out."

They both swung their heads around to glare at him. "Max!" they hissed.

"I beg your finest pardon?" Malakai drawled.

Max jerked his thumb at the lovebirds walking beside him. "Ask them."

Travis muttered, "Thanks a lot," and climbed into the boat.

81

HELL'S GATE
ANGELTHENE, STATE OF WITHEREDGE

"Roark?" Loren called. The door to Hell's Gate slammed shut behind her as she jogged down the front steps.

Roark was almost at the driver's door of his car when he turned around, clearly startled that she'd followed him out here.

As she breached the distance between them, she slowed her pace, her fingers fiddling with the long sleeves of her shirt. It was warm out, the yard fragrant with heady jasmine and the earthy tang of freshly mowed grass.

"You should go back inside," Roark said. "It's safer for you in there." While he didn't say it rudely, he didn't sound overly concerned, either. It was more of a...suggestion. Or maybe a way to dodge what she planned on saying to him.

"I will, I just...wanted to thank you," she began. "Not just for everything you said in there—" She gestured to Hell's Gate. "But for everything else, too. What you did for us in Yveswich...I know what it cost you. And I just want you to know that I'm grateful."

The long pause that followed her words was awkward. But Loren didn't regret saying any of it. If he wasn't ready for this kind of relationship with her—open and honest—that was fine. But her days were numbered, and she, for one, refused to die with regrets.

Roark nodded—just once—before turning toward his car.

"Maybe we can talk alone sometime?" Her question froze him in place. "I still have questions. A *lot* of questions," she amended with a forced laugh. "And maybe...maybe I can show you around next time?"

He studied her the same way he had in the foyer, as if she were still talking and he was hearing so much more than she was saying.

Then he nodded again, his expression unchanging. "Of course." He opened the driver's door—

"Do you think Dallas is okay?" she blurted.

When Roark paused again, but made no indication that he was going to reply, she couldn't help but wonder if she was pressing him too hard. It was difficult to move past that mentality—past the Loren who'd tiptoed around this man for so many years. The little girl who'd wanted nothing more than to be loved and seen and accepted by the warlock and the witch who'd raised her.

Behind her, the front door swung open. Darien was already talking as he hurried down the steps. "Those missiles," he said, his boots crunching on gravel. "What are they made of?"

Roark propped an arm on the top of his open door. "The structure is made of cristala, mostly. The warhead is raw magic from the anima mundi."

"Are they hard to make?" He came to stand at Loren's side.

"There's someone in your house who shouldn't have a problem figuring out how."

Darien glanced over his shoulder, clearly deep in thought.

"Look, whatever it is that you're planning on doing," Roark said, "as far as I'm concerned, I don't know anything about it." He held his hands out in a show of innocence. "It's none of my business. You just do what you need to do, and...know that your secrets are safe with me."

Loren interlocked her fingers before her, still waiting for an answer to *her* question.

As if reading her mind, Roark told her, "I'll see if I can figure out if the helicopter made it out and where it landed. But you need to watch out for yourselves in the meantime," he added, speaking to them both now. "If the imperator wants you locked up, he's not going to give up just because of what happened today."

"We won't be staying here," Darien said. "We're leaving within the hour."

"Good. And don't tell me where you're going. Just in case."

Darien agreed with a dip of his chin.

Roark got in the car and shut the door, the window down.

"Roark," Darien called, stepping forward as Roark slid the key into the ignition. "Thanks. For helping us out. Here and in Yveswich."

He nodded. "You're welcome."

"We'll see you tomorrow, then."

Another nod. "Tomorrow." He put his sunglasses on and started the car.

Tomorrow seemed so far away. She had not lied when she'd told Roark that she had a lot of questions, and now that he was finally free to speak about any topic he wanted and seemed willing to help... It was so much harder to wait for those answers. To be patient.

She watched him as he drove away. Through the gates that swung open with his departure. He turned the corner, the car disappearing behind the red brick wall surrounding the property.

Darien's gentle touch brushing across her lower back eased the tension in her muscles, the breath she held slowly releasing.

"Do we really have to leave?" she asked him, still staring unseeingly at the now empty road. She already missed Hell's Gate, and they hadn't even left yet.

"Come on, baby," he said softly, his fingers trailing across the ends of her hair. "Let's go pack."

DARIEN PACED in the foyer as Kylar dug through the contents of his bags that were piled up with the others by the front door.

They were alone in here. Everyone else was rushing around in other rooms, grabbing things last-minute. Loren was drying her hair with her blow dryer upstairs; Darien could hear the shitty old thing screaming bloody murder from way down here. She needed a new one. Ivy had helped them out by packing most of their things while they were at the holding center, giving Loren enough time to shower off the chlorine.

And giving Darien just enough time to take a hit of Venom—if Kylar could find it, that is.

'Are you sure this is a good idea?' Bandit asked from his shadow.

'We both need it. You've been gnawing on Cluckles nonstop.' He said it like it was a bad thing, when really he should be glad. At this rate, there wouldn't even *be* a Cluckles for much longer.

Bandit let out a low growl. *'Heard that.'*

'Kidding,' Darien drawled.

Bandit chuffed. *'If she finds out about this, and you end up sleeping on the floor again, don't try blaming me.'*

'You'll be in the doghouse with me. You can keep me company.'

'Absolutely not. I'll be sleeping in the bed with her.'

'Good luck with that.'

Bandit snort-laughed. *'I look forward to seeing the look on your face when I get to cuddle with her, and you don't.'*

'Cuddle? You don't cuddle anyone. You hog the bed.'

'I'll cuddle her just to piss you off.'

'Again: Good luck.'

"Found it," Kylar declared, rummaging around in an over-stuffed plastic bag of toiletries.

Finally. Darien stopped pacing and held his hand out in request—

But Kylar paused. "No, shit, sorry—these are regular eye drops."

"Fuck me, Kylar," he muttered. He pushed his sweat-damp hair back and returned to pacing.

"I would, but I think that would upset Loren." He flashed Darien a bright smile that he was quick to drop. "Not funny?" He started searching faster.

Darien was ashamed to admit that he could hardly handle this. The withdrawals. He could feel himself fraying at the seams, and if he didn't get some Venom into his system...

"Here," Kylar said, holding out a small black bottle.

Darien took it from him with unsteady hands, twisted the cap off, and dripped two drops into each eye.

The moment they were in, he let out a sigh of relief, so deep and rough it was practically a growl, and braced his hands against the wall by the doors, head bowed and eyes shut. The drug took immediate effect, the difference between now and before staggering.

"Finally," he muttered, breathing in and out...in and out. For the first time all day, he felt his pulse slow, the fire coursing through his veins cooling off until only a few dying embers remained.

Fucking *sublime.*

He could feel Kylar eyeing him. "That bad, hey?"

"I made a mistake," Darien admitted, his head still down. "I should never have started using this shit." He took another deep, deep breath and rolled his stiff shoulders.

"Maybe try weaning off of it instead?"

He nodded and opened his eyes, looking down at his boots. He could see normally, but he knew his eyes were solid black, the surrounding skin etched with faint black lines. The look should hopefully wear off in the next ten, fifteen minutes, leaving him with a satisfying high, but nothing that would give him away to Loren. He didn't want her to see him like this.

Weaning off the drug was exactly what he planned on doing. It was the easier option than flat-out quitting. Easier on his body, easier on his mind. The sweats, the racing thoughts, the inability to sit still... He couldn't be dealing with that right now, not with everything going on. He had to be of sound mind to protect Loren and his family, so reducing his intake of Venom was safer than simply quitting.

Darien stayed where he was for another few minutes, hands on the wall, focusing on the feel of the drug coursing through his system. Kylar zipped his bags shut, others in the house passing through the area. They were almost ready to go, by the sound of things. Logan and Sabrine had left a little while ago, so it was just Loren, Tanner, Jack, Lace, Ivy, Kylar, Eugene, and Arthur here.

"Everything okay?" Lace asked him as she walked by. He still had his eyes shut, head down.

When he didn't answer, Ivy said, "Darien? Is something wrong?"

"Fine," he managed to say. A little louder, he assured them both, "I'm fine. I'm just taking a minute." They returned to whatever they were doing.

He inhaled deeply, one more time, and straightened. As soon as he confirmed that no one was paying attention to him, he indicated to the Venom in his hand and said quietly to Kylar, "You mind if I keep this?"

"It's yours," Kylar said. He looked concerned, though.

"I'm fine," Darien told him.

He didn't look convinced. "If you say so."

Loren was coming down the stairs.

Quickly, he shoved the bottle into his pocket.

'Doghouse,' Bandit warned.

'Shh.'

'Don't say I didn't warn you.'

Darien ignored him and focused on Loren, who was carrying a travel bag and—

The vase of flowers and the enchanted box of chocolate-dipped strawberries he'd bought for her. Her hands were so full, she had to peek around the flowers to see where she was placing her feet.

Darien sprinted up the stairs and took everything but the flowers from her.

"Thanks," she said, steadying the vase as it tipped in her hands. She didn't say anything about his eyes, which likely meant the Venom was fully absorbed.

Good.

'Doghouse, doghouse, doghouse,' Bandit sang quietly.

Darien ignored him. "I can take the flowers, too," he offered.

"No, that's okay. I've got them."

"All right, Miss Stubborn," he crooned. She gave him a saucy smile, her eyes flicking up to meet his. "But I'd better not see you smash that pretty face up on my stairs."

Her eyes danced. "Are you quoting yourself?"

The smile teasing his lips spread. "You remember that?"

She broke eye contact. "How could I forget? It was only the most terrifying day of my life. No big deal." She tried to hide her smile from him, but he could hear it in that beautiful voice of hers. It was better than music, that voice.

"It was the best day of mine," he countered. Their gazes collided, and her cheeks turned rosy, her eyelashes fanning out as she looked down. He gestured for her to walk in front of him. "After you, Miss Calla."

"Setting yourself up for a view, are you?" She started walking, bracing her hand on the rail as she maneuvered each step. Everyone else was waiting in the foyer, ready to go.

"The best view I've ever seen or will see," he said, low enough that only she could hear, his gaze dipping down to the view she'd accused him of setting himself up for. Even through her talisman, he could feel her aura glow with warmth. It was like a hug from the sun.

And gods, was the view incredible. She had the most beautiful ass he'd ever seen. His hand tightened around the box. He had to force himself to loosen his grip before he crushed it and the strawberries inside.

What he wouldn't give to get on top of her right now.

When they got to the bottom of the stairs, Darien slid the box from Whisking Witch onto the glass table and placed Loren's bag on the floor so he could put on his jacket. Loren surrendered the flowers to Ivy just long enough to get her own jacket and shoes on.

"Everyone ready?" he asked the group.

Heads nodded. Several people—Ivy, Tanner, Lace, Jack—were quiet and solemn. Bothered by the idea of being run out of their home, Darien would bet. He didn't like it, either. But he'd do anything to keep these people safe, and leaving Hell's Gate was a small price to pay.

He grabbed Loren's bag, the strawberries, and the last of his own things as Arthur opened the door. Everyone filed out, Eugene so distracted by his video game that he nearly tripped down the front steps.

"Put that away until we get in the car," Kylar grumbled.

Darien stepped over the threshold and got his keys out.

Loren lingered in the foyer, her eyes roving through the open space. But while she studied the home she was being forced to leave, Darien studied her.

Her long hair tumbled over her shoulders in soft, sun-bright waves, a few strands draped across the flowers in her hands. The light of the sunset streaming in through the windows caused the blue of her eyes to shimmer like a tropical ocean. And her freckles... *Gods,* her freckles.

An indescribable ache spread through his chest.

This woman right here was *his* home. His guiding light. As long as he had her, he would never be lost.

"We'll be back," he told her, even as that ache continued to sharpen, and he found himself missing two homes. The one named Hell's Gate—

And the one named Loren Elizabeth Calla. She may be standing right in front of him, but until he earned her forgiveness for his screw-ups, he'd always feel miles away from her.

She drew a deep breath. "I know." She took one last look at everything, as if trying to imprint the image in her memory, before her eyes found his.

"Ready to see your other home?" he asked her.

That earned him a small, pretty smile. "Okay."

He beckoned for her to lead the way. As she walked out the door, her arm brushed against his sleeve. Love-starved, he clung to the feeling, wishing for more. He watched as she walked down the driveway and got in his car.

And then he took one last look of his own at Hell's Gate—empty and quiet—before locking up.

'Do you really believe we'll be back?' Bandit asked him with a low whine.

'Of course I do.' Believing things would one day be better was the only way he could move forward. It was how he'd managed to survive this long.

Keep looking up—that was what his mom always used to say.

And so he would—keep looking up.

He got in the car and left Hell's Gate behind.

———

THE SUN HAD DIPPED below the hills by the time Darien drove the car down the driveway to Heaven's Gate. The others followed closely behind, headlights cutting through the gloom.

Heaven's Gate was a huge, white-stone house in Angelthene's pristine North End, with a black roof, black accents, an in-ground swimming pool, and a guest house. Out front, in the center of the circular driveway, was a statuary fountain of an angel crying colors. Her wings were spread, her face tipped toward the heavens.

His phone buzzed in the cupholder. He grabbed it and read the message.

ROMAN

Gonna be late. Should be there tomorrow instead.

Darien typed a reply with his good hand, his attention flicking between the screen and the dark, quiet house looming at the end of the driveway.

DARIEN

Everything alright?

ROMAN

Had a close call, but we're good now. I'll fill you in tomorrow.

DARIEN

Text when you're close and we'll pick a place to meet up.

ROMAN

Copy.

Still no word from T?

DARIEN

Not yet

ROMAN

Kk

"Who is it?" Loren asked, covering her mouth as she yawned. Her medical tattoo was glowing with soft red light. He'd make sure to fix her something to eat, as soon as he got her settled. Ivy and Arthur had done a grocery run before finding out they were at the holding center, so food wasn't something they had to worry about tonight.

"Roman," he replied. He slid his phone into his pocket.

"Is he okay?"

"He's fine, but he's going to be late. He said he'll be here tomorrow." He didn't like the sounds of this *close call* Roman had mentioned, but as long as he was fine, that was all that mattered.

He parked out front and got out, grabbing all the bags before Loren could get to them. She gave him the eye but didn't argue, settling with carrying the flowers and the box of strawberries. Darien would have taken those too, if he'd had an extra hand—or at least one that wasn't broken.

The muffled closing of car doors and the splashing of the fountain out front were the only sounds in the quiet of the night.

Ivy unlocked the doors and disarmed the spell system.

And then they were in, their voices echoing in the foyer. High ceilings, white walls, a crystal chandelier, more black accents. It'd been about a year since he'd set foot in this house; he'd almost forgotten what it looked like. While Heaven's Gate had more square footage plus a guest house, it shared a similar layout with Hell's Gate, which was why they'd snatched up the new build when it had gone up for sale—to feel like a second home if they were ever forced to vacate their first.

"Make yourselves at home," Darien said. He set down his and Loren's bags by the double staircase, the wood so new it shone like polished gold. "All the bedrooms are furnished. Take your pick. Doesn't matter to me who sleeps where, as long as everyone's happy."

Ivy said, "You guys can choose—Jack and I are fine with whatever. I'm going to start dinner." She headed for the kitchen, flicking lights on along the way. "I hope everyone's okay with tacos."

"I love tacos," Arthur called after her. "If you need anything, Ivy, let me know and I'll be there in a jiffy."

"Just relax, Art," she said, her echoing voice getting farther away. "I've got this."

"Coming through," Jack said, squeezing his way through the group and hurrying after Ivy.

"I'll give them a hand," Lace said. "I don't care which room I get, either, by the way—you guys go ahead and choose, and I'll take whatever's left." She disappeared toward the kitchen that overlooked the backyard, her cat Familiar leaping out of her shadow to follow on soundless paws.

Darien faced Loren and the others who remained. To those who had never been here before, he said, "Come on. I'll show you around."

82

HEAVEN'S GATE
ANGELTHENE, STATE OF WITHEREDGE

"Well, sweetheart? What do you think?"

Where she stood with Darien by the floor-to-ceiling windows in the bedroom of her choosing, Loren parted the curtain and scanned the twilit backyard, the trees and spring blossoms gilded by the warm glow of garden lanterns and string lights. It was beautiful.

So was the room, the color scheme soft and calming. In the center of the tidy space sat a plush, king-size bed, and on the wall straight across from it hung a moody painting of a storm-addled ocean. Just like the rooms at Hell's Gate, there was also an attached bathroom and a spacious walk-in closet big enough to be a bedroom.

Loren let go of the curtain and turned on a heel to face Darien. He was right in front of her, so close the space between them felt electrically charged, as if a magnetic field—one that was getting very, *very* hard to ignore—were drawing them together.

"I love it," she told him. "I think it's a very lovely home."

A charming smile flirted with one corner of his distracting mouth.

"I need a rubber neck to date you," she blurted. He was so tall, she had to tip her head back to see his face. That beautiful, breathtaking face.

He exhaled. "That's a relief," he said.

She blinked. "What's a relief?"

"That we're still dating."

"Oh." Silly Darien. As if she could ever break up with someone as self-less and incredible as him. Someone who'd sacrificed so much for her.

Darien cleared his throat. "Now that we're alone, I'd like to talk, if you'll let me."

"Okay." She already knew what he was going to ask her, though—and she already had her answer. She loved this man far too much to keep snubbing him the way she had these last few days.

But, instead of speaking, Darien drew a deep breath and lowered himself to one knee before her.

Her stomach bottomed out, her heart dipping so swiftly it felt like it fell right out of her body—

"It's not that," he said quickly. "It's— it's not what it looks like. It's— Shit." He chuckled, briefly tipping his face to the ceiling. Despite her erratically pounding heart, and the nerves twisting her stomach into tight knots, she found herself distracted by the sight of his laughing face. That big, dimpled grin that gave her so many butterflies. "I'm getting on *both* knees," he declared, doing exactly that, planting both knees on the hardwood floor. "But if you'd rather I popped the question, I can make that happen, too." He took her hands into his.

The offer stunned her—and so did the easy way in which he said it, as if he'd already thought about proposing to her a dozen times. As if he were testing the waters by mentioning it to her in such a casual way. "I..." Gods, her heart was *racing,* and her stomach was doing backflips and somersaults and all kinds of other acrobatics. The butterflies were still in there, too. It was intense, how he made her feel. *Intense.*

"Forget the question popping," he said gently. "Hear me out instead."

She took several deep, deep breaths. "Okay."

"Relax, baby."

"I'm relaxed," she lied.

"Your heart is racing."

It really was. "You scared me," she confessed.

An emotion she couldn't read flickered across his handsome face. "Does the thought of me getting down on one knee frighten you that much?"

"No," she said—wholeheartedly and without hesitation. "No, it doesn't."

Quite the opposite, actually. It made her happy. Really, *really* happy. The thought of wearing Darien Cassel's ring on her finger... She'd dreamt about it a lot. Ever since the moment she realized she was in love with him and he was, utterly and without question, perfect for her. "You just...caught me off guard," she said. "I panicked."

"All right, note to self: Don't catch her off guard next time." He chuckled, and her heart tumbled at his mention of *next time.* "Can we move onto the real reason I'm on my knees, or are you going to collapse on me?"

"I'm fine," she said. But the words came out breathy and strained.

"Loren," he reproached. His tone was soft, and his eyes even softer. "I need to know that you're not going to faint."

"I won't faint."

He waited a few seconds, just to make sure she really wouldn't faint. As soon as her heart slowed to a normal rhythm, he began to speak.

"I'm sorry, sweetheart." The words were so gruff, so heavy with emotion, her eyes instantly welled up. "I know you're upset. And I know I can't take back what I did. But I need you to understand how sorry I am. I've been beating myself up over it non-stop. I feel like the worst boyfriend in the world. I hate knowing that you're sad and that I'm the person who caused you to feel this way." He paused just long enough to swallow. "After this, once I get up off this floor, if you decide you still want space, you can have it, I'll respect your decision and I won't pressure you anymore, but— I'm not going to lie, I'm going insane over here. You've been right in front of me ever since we ran into each other in Yveswich, and yet I feel like I've lost you. And I'm willing to do anything—*anything*—to get you back."

She dropped her gaze to the floor, a breath shaking through her.

Darien dipped his head to catch her eye. "You're my everything, Loren. I need you to understand that. You're my whole world. I love you more than I can put into words, but I'm trying, baby, I'm trying to express myself properly, but gods, it's hard." He forced a chuckle, and when she looked him in the eyes she saw that they were shining, the dark fringe of his lashes damp. He continued, "No words are good enough to adequately express how I feel for you. I just— I'm begging you to forgive me, sweetheart. Please."

He gave her a moment to decide, his words—the words he believed were inadequate, but were so damn perfect to her ears—hanging in the air between them. He stayed right where he was, gazing up at her from where he knelt on the floor, his hands gently clasping hers.

She tugged on those hands, urging him to stand. "Stand up," she said softly.

He obeyed. Again, she had to tip her head back to look him in the eyes, the rubber neck she'd mentioned sounding more appealing by the minute.

"I already forgave you," she said. "The minute I saw how upset you were at the holding center. When you told those awful men that you'd turn into an animal if they took me from you." Despite the heavy emotions weighing both of them down, a laugh slipped out of her.

He cracked a smile and tipped his head to the side, the action causing a strand of dark hair to sweep across his brow. "That's what made you forgive me? Me, threatening to turn into an animal?" It was his turn to laugh—a smooth, attractive sound that gave her pleasant, full-body shivers.

She shrugged. "I think I forgave you the minute you left Roman's. After you told me about the bargain. I ran out of the house and watched you as you drove away, and I wished...I wished I hadn't been so hard on you."

He brushed his thumbs across her hands, his calluses scraping across her skin. The sensation was so inviting, she found herself wishing he would touch her in other, much more sensitive places. "I guess we both said a lot of things that we didn't mean, hey?" he said, his voice husky. His eyes dipped to her mouth, his stare heating as she licked her lips. "So...you forgive me?" Hope shone in those steel-blue eyes.

She nodded. "Yes. Yes, I forgive you."

He exhaled in a rush, as if he'd been holding his breath for days, the tension visibly leaving his body. "Thank fuck."

She stopped breathing as he took her face into his hands. Gently, he tipped her head back, his thumbs brushing across her cheeks. Her heart began to skip whole beats as he slid those hands to the back of her head, tunneling his fingers into her thick hair...and then slanted his soft mouth over hers.

It was her first time kissing him since before they'd run into each other in Yveswich, and gods, had she missed it. Missed *him*. At first, he kissed her gently, carefully, but gentle wasn't what she wanted, and it wasn't he wanted, either. Soon, they were kissing like their lives depended on it, and she was arching against him, and he was fisting the hair at the back of her head with those big, tattooed hands she wanted to feel everywhere. They were both out of breath, teeth and tongues clashing.

She'd forgotten what this felt like, what he tasted like. She never wanted to forget again.

Mind-blowing—that's what it was like. What *Darien* was like. Mind-blowing.

She wanted him closer closer closer.

The noise he made in his throat—a cross between a growl and a groan

—sent a rush of heat through her body. His kisses turned frantic. Aggressive, almost. He was losing control, but so was she.

By the time they broke apart—too soon—she was so dizzy the room was spinning.

He planted another kiss on her mouth—softer, this one—before resting his forehead against hers. "I've been wanting to do that since you bumped into me in Yveswich," he confessed.

"I know," she said in a cheeky tone that made him smile. But then *her* smile was fading as she remembered something—a different topic she had been meaning to bring up to him, ever since she saw how rough he'd looked at the holding center. The fidgeting, the shaking, the excessive sweating...

She couldn't believe how long it had taken her to figure it out. Looking back now...she should have recognized the signs sooner. And she felt terrible that she hadn't—hadn't been there for him when he needed her.

He noticed her change in expression immediately. "What's the matter, baby?" he asked, pulling back a little to see her face better.

"You're struggling to get off Venom," she began. "Aren't you?"

He winced. "How'd you know?"

"I may not have the Sight, but I've known you for a while now, Darien. There's not a lot you can hide from me."

He looked down—just for a minute—before raising his head and meeting her eyes with a steadying inhale. "I'm ashamed of it," he confessed on the exhale. "And I didn't want to tell you because...because I didn't want to bother you with my problems. You've got enough going on as it is."

She felt a twinge in her heart. "Darien, you and I are a team. If I'm struggling with something, you want me to tell you so you can help me, right?"

He gave a faint nod.

"Well, it goes both ways. I want to know when you're going through something, so I can be there to support you."

For a moment, he just stared at her, as if he were seeing her for the very first time. Then he blurted, "I fucking love you, you know that?"

She couldn't help but smile. "I know. I love you too, Darien. And right now, I'm going to take care of you." She flattened her hand against his solid chest and gently pushed him backward—across the room. Toward the bed. When the backs of his legs hit the mattress, she told him, "Sit."

He listened, and she got down on her knees before him and took off his boots, unlacing them and setting them aside.

When she was finished, she stood, grabbing onto the hem of his shirt.

He lifted his arms so she could tug it over his head, his necklaces softly tinkling with the movement. She dropped his shirt to the floor, then flattened her hand on his chest again—right above his thumping heart—and pushed him back, until he was propped up on the mattress on his elbows.

As she undressed, he watched her, not taking his eyes off her—not for one second.

She took her shirt off first, then her jeans, her heartbeat accelerating with each inch of skin she exposed to him. She unclasped her bra and slipped it off, then shimmied her panties down to her ankles and stepped out of them.

Her mouth dried out as she watched Darien's eyes rove across her naked body, lingering the longest on her breasts and the intimate space between her thighs. Knowing he'd want to read her aura as they did this, she reached behind her head, unclasped the talisman, and placed it on the nightstand.

Wearing nothing at all, she crossed the room and climbed onto the bed to straddle him.

She wanted this man—badly. *So* damn badly, and she was tired of fighting it. So she pushed him back on the bed until he was lying flat on his back, then she bent down, sweeping her hair over one shoulder, and locked her mouth with his.

The kiss was so good, so intimate, they were both groaning into each other's mouths. He flicked his tongue against hers, and as he slipped a hand between her thighs, she felt chills erupt all over her body, his rough fingers going straight to her clit.

A whimper slipped out of her, and Darien swallowed the sound as if it were fine wine. Their kisses turned frantic. Aggressive, teeth clashing and lip biting, that hand of his rubbing her so good her legs were twitching.

When they broke the kiss, he breathed against her mouth, "You like that, baby?" His stare was scorching hot as he watched her squirm above him, her legs flexing around his hips.

"I love it," she gasped. "*I'm* supposed to be taking care of *you*, though."

"You are. Making you feel good makes me feel good." He spanked her ass, then squeezed it. "Look at you," he growled. "You're so perfect, sweetheart. I can't get enough of you."

He slipped two fingers inside of her, pushing them in as deep as they could go, the sudden intrusion making her gasp and rock her hips into his hand, her own fingers fisting the sheets.

"Keep going," she begged, her whole body tightening as he moved those fingers in and out of her, his other hand grabbing at her breasts and ass as if he couldn't get enough of her. When a breathy cry slipped out of her, he surged up off the mattress to kiss her—hard. Devouring every cry, every gasp, every breathy moan as he coaxed her closer to the edge of pleasure

When he broke the kiss, he kept his eyes on her, watching her face as she came undone. "Fuck, you're hot," he breathed, his words coasting across her lips. He nipped the bottom one. "Be a good girl and come on my fingers." He spanked her ass with his free hand while his other moved faster, that thumb of his rubbing so good—

"Oh gods," she gasped, her legs tensing around his waist.

"Fuck, yes, baby—that's it."

"Oh gods," she said again. "Gods, Darien, don't stop—"

He didn't. He kept going and going and going—

Her pleasure crested, and she cried out his name before his other hand came up to fist her hair and he pulled her face down to his, slamming his lips against hers. Every muscle in her body tensed and released as pleasure cascaded over her in a delicious, sensual wave.

And then he was withdrawing his fingers, and she was holding her breath as he undid his jeans with frantic movements, shifting them down just far enough to get his hard cock out. His breaths were shallow and ragged as he rubbed the crown up and down her entrance, teasing himself before relenting with a hissed, *"Fuck."* With his free hand, the other circling the base of his erection, he gripped her firmly by the waist—

And pushed her down onto his cock, all the way to the thick base. Once she was fully seated and stretched by him, they both groaned.

She rolled her hips, making him swear. Her legs shook as she lifted herself up, guided by Darien's hands squeezing her waist, then sank back down.

"Fuck, I love your pussy," he breathed as he eased her down farther—pushing himself in as far as her body would allow. He kissed her on the mouth, the edge of her jaw, the space below her ear.

They started moving—both of them together now. She picked up her pace quickly, desperate not just for her own release, but to watch this gorgeous man come undone.

"I should get angry at other people over you more often," he growled, his tone tight with pleasure—with need—as she rode him. His hands gripped her hips, helping her keep up with the rhythm she'd set.

Pleasure coursed through her in a hot, honey-like wave. A gasp floated off her lips, her eyelids falling shut as it worked its way through her.

"Good girl, Loren," he growled. "Good girl."

She started moving faster, knowing he was close. He thrust his hips up, meeting her stroke for stroke as he pounded deep. So deep it almost hurt, but she could not get enough. She wanted more.

More.

More.

"Little faster, baby," he gritted out. "Little faster. There—there, that's perfect, that's perfect, just like that." He tipped his head back, sweat glistening on his chest, his upper lip. He was lost in a haze of pleasure—lost in *her*. "Fuck. Fuck—that feels so good. Keep going. *Keep going,*" he practically begged, the muscles in his arms and chest tensing and flexing as he neared release, his grunts and groans electrifying her blood.

Several rapid thrusts later, and he pushed down hard on her hips, burying himself right to the hilt with a deep, sexy moan. She gasped, grabbing onto his tense hands as release found him, his body shaking with pleasure beneath her.

"Fuck, baby. *Baby*—" His eyes were so black, she could see her reflection in them. He picked up speed again, wringing himself dry as he bobbed her up and down. The slap of flesh against flesh echoed in the room, the sound gradually fading as their movements slowed, both of them utterly spent.

When they fell still, panting and hearts pounding, they stared at each other for awhile. Then Darien slid a hand across the back of her neck and pulled her down to kiss her deeply.

"I'm so in love with everything about you, Loren," he mumbled against her lips, still catching his breath. One more kiss. Another, both of them gentle. Loving. "My heart has been searching for you my whole life. I'll never hurt you again—I promise." He gulped down another panting breath, cupped her face with both hands, and repeated, "I promise."

"No more fighting," she said, still breathless and shaking.

He kissed her again and said, "No more fighting."

Because her heart had been looking for him, too. And now that she'd found him, she would never let go.

Not even after that heart of hers stopped beating.

———

ABOUT HALF AN HOUR LATER, Loren was lying in bed, fighting to catch her breath. Her heart was having a hard time recovering from the intensity of their joining, the darn thing fluttering like the swift wings of a hummingbird.

She wouldn't tell Darien. Causing him unnecessary stress was the last thing she wanted to do, especially when he already had so much he was dealing with.

He was in the bathroom, light spilling through the partially open door, his shadow occasionally blocking it as he toweled off. She had finished cleaning up before him and was now wrapped up in the soft sheets, her skin damp and smelling of soap. Candlelight flickered across the walls and the tangle of blankets, spurring shadows into a hypnotic dance.

The door opened, and she watched as Darien crossed the room. His muscles rippled with every languorous step, every dip and hollow of his impressive physique supplemented by the candlelight. He was shirtless, his upper body sparkling with droplets of water from the shower they'd taken together. The black jeans he wore drew attention to the V that disappeared beneath his waistband—a sight that always made her heart skip.

"See something you like?" he teased as he approached the bed, one corner of his mouth twitching with a smile.

"Love," she corrected, her face warming. "I see something I love very much."

He sat down on the bed beside her. She rolled onto her side to face him, the sheets ensnaring her waist. When he took one of her hands into both of his, her rose gold charm bracelet tinkling beneath his touch, she felt his fingers trembling.

Her stomach clenched with unease. "You're shaking."

He held out his right hand and looked at it, frowning as if he hadn't even realized. The trembling wasn't obvious, but it was definitely there.

She sat up, taking the sheets with her and keeping them wrapped snug around her body as she faced him.

"Baby, I'm fine," he said softly. "I've dealt with this before—it'll go away."

"Well, you're not dealing with it alone—not anymore," she said gently, taking both of his hands into hers. "We'll swing by Mordred and Penelope's tomorrow. I know of a few things that can help you get back to your old self in no time."

"I'm not sure my old self is any better."

She flicked him in the nose.

He scrunched it in answer, and she scrunched hers back.

The smile he gave her was a real one—the kind that touched his eyes and showed the dimple in his cheek. "The first time you did that to me, I knew I was already a goner," he said.

She tipped her head to the side, her hair that was tangled from all their fun slipping to one shoulder. "Did what?"

"Scrunched that cute little nose." He bopped her on the nose with his index finger. "You ruined me, baby."

Blush spread through her cheeks. When she ducked her head, he tipped her chin up, his thumb brushing across her lower lip and tugging it down. Then he grasped her chin, leaned in, and pressed a featherlight kiss to her lips.

She got greedy quickly—sliding her tongue over the seam of his lips until he opened them to her. His answering groan that filled her mouth had her body tightening with a wave of desire.

When they broke apart, he kept his eyes—darkened with carnal need—on her mouth as he licked his lips. "I cannot get enough of you."

"Likewise," she breathed as she bit her lower lip, coaxing it into her mouth—tasting him on her.

He looked like he wanted to eat her alive.

"What's this from?" She dragged the pad of her index finger across a scar in his side. It wasn't a new scar, but she had been meaning to ask him about them—*all* of them—for a while.

He tipped his head down to see which scar she was referring to, the movement causing a strand of damp, night-dark hair to shift out of place. As she smoothed it back, he said, "A knife." He took hold of the hand that she'd used to smooth his hair and pressed a tender kiss to the inside of her wrist.

"And this?" She slipped her hand free and circled the puckered scar on his right shoulder.

"Bullet."

She dragged her pinky finger over another in silent question. This one looked almost identical to the previous.

"Bullet," he said again. And those weren't even the bullet wounds from when they were attacked outside of Blackbird.

"Gods, how many times have you been shot?"

"I've lost count." He was fighting a smile.

Loren, however, frowned. "It's not funny."

Darien looked like he didn't agree, and she swore he was biting the inside of his cheek to keep from laughing.

"What about this one?" She slid her hand across his left forearm, dragging her thumb across the jagged silver line. It was hardly visible through his ink.

"Barbed wire."

"What about..." Slowly, she moved her hand down toward his waistband, tracing the contours of his muscled stomach. Her heart picked up speed, so swiftly she knew he could hear it.

Indeed, his steel-blue eyes flashed up to meet hers. Desire simmered in his stare, and when his gaze went to the sheets hugging her body, her firm nipples pressing against the soft fabric, she knew they wouldn't be able to keep their hands off each other for much longer. Even if she had a million years with this man, she would never get tired of him.

She cleared her throat. "This one?" she finished, dragging her fingertips along the waistband of his jeans, her thumb catching on his belt buckle as she indicated to the scar peeking out above it.

He answered her by forming a claw with his left hand, the monster's-head rings on two of his fingers winking in the lamplight.

"What breed?"

"A Hound."

She took that hand into hers and ran her thumb across the ridges on his knuckles. "And these?"

"Hitting. Most of them." While his body was a work of art, it was also a story. Each of these scars had a story, and she longed to read them all.

Most of the few scars on her own body had arrived *after* she'd met Darien. The worst of those scars were from shards of glass—the day they'd fallen through a window of a skyscraper together.

"What are you thinking about?" he murmured. He tucked a strand of hair behind her ear, then lovingly skimmed the curve of her jaw with a knuckle.

She started to shake her head—then said, "Just memories."

"What sort of memories?"

She didn't answer him right away. She just looked at him for awhile, admiring how the soft, rosy light from the candles kissed his handsome features. Finally, she told him, "Good memories."

"Darien!" Ivy's voice floated up from downstairs. "Loren! Come on down—dinner's almost ready!"

"Be right there!" Darien shouted back. "You hungry?" he asked Loren.

"A little."

But instead of getting up, he put her on her back and rolled on top of her.

"Darien!" she gasped—not in protest, no. In no world would she ever object to this man putting her on her back.

But she *did* let out a squeak of alarm as he ripped the sheets aside, exposing her naked body to the crisp evening air.

"Yes, Miss Calla?" he breathed against the side of her neck, his hair tickling her skin as he settled heavily between her thighs, pinning her to the mattress with his hips. She didn't feel cold, though—not for long. Not with Darien on top of her, kissing the side of her neck, her jaw, then pulling back just far enough to marvel at her—as if she were a dream he couldn't believe he was living.

He was *her* dream, too.

"How about a quickie, first?" he asked, his words—spoken in a low, husky voice—coasting across her mouth. She didn't miss how, even as he said it, and even as desire was making a clear attempt at pushing him over the edge, he checked on her tattoos. He was trying to be subtle about it, but she noticed.

And now that he knew she could go without eating for a little while longer, he bent and kissed her, parting her lips with his tongue. She brushed her hands across his back and inhaled his shaving cream, his cologne—just *him*. Just Darien Cassel. The most delicious, irresistible smell in the world.

Sometimes it scared her, how intense things were between them.

Sometimes it scared her, how much she loved him.

But she refused to think of that now. Of the future and all its uncertainties, the goodbyes she might one day have to make. Right now, Darien Cassel was hers. And it was the right now that mattered.

Her hands went to his belt buckle, and soon they were joined again, their bodies moving as one as rain began to pelt the windows behind the bed. It was just them, the rain, and their silhouettes that were painted on the walls by candlelight.

And it was perfect.

83

WACKY'S WAFFLES
STATE OF KER

Wacky's Waffles was a diner in the Middle of Nowhere, State of Ker. It was outdated and damn near falling apart. But the food?

To die for.

At a table by the windows that overlooked the twilit highway, Roman slung an arm across the back of the booth and surveyed his uncle sitting across from him. They were alone for the first time since they'd sat down to stuff their faces with waffles, burgers, fries, milkshakes, you name it. Shay and Pax were occupied by the arcade game on the other side of the diner. Dean's men were keeping watch outside; Roman could see their silhouettes moving about in the glow of headlights, their muffled, carefree laughter filtering through the glass.

Dean—who had practically materialized out of thin air to save their asses after not even speaking to Roman in almost a year. Dean—who was currently slurping up the last of his strawberry milkshake, noisily sucking air through a straw as pink as the shake. The pink looked hilarious when paired with his black leather jacket and general fuck-with-me-and-I'll-make-you-regret-it persona, but that was Uncle Dean for you.

Roman felt his brows rise. Slowly. He still couldn't believe this was happening. That he was sitting across from the man he'd idolized his whole life after being arrested by the cops and fully convinced that his world was about to crash and burn.

Dean released the straw and gave a theatrical, contented sigh, a big grin on his face, before pushing the glass aside and lacing his fingers on the table. "So," he said, still grinning, his combat boots thumping beneath the table to the beat of the old song blasting from the jukebox.

"So," Roman repeated. He lifted the hand he had resting on the back of the booth in a what-are-we-supposed-to-talk-about-now gesture.

"So," Dean repeated, that smile broadening. "You look like you've got a million questions for me, and I'm the man with the answers, so go on and hit me, kid." He snatched a fry off Paxton's plate and stuffed it into his mouth.

"Okay. Um." He lifted his hand in question again, thinking. Where to begin? He settled with: "How'd you find us?"

The moment Uncle Dean opened the doors to the prisoner transport van, Roman had been too shocked to say much, apart from his name. And the relief he'd felt the moment a sobbing Paxton had sprinted down the road and collided with him was so intense, he hadn't spared one thought for how everything had played out. He hadn't given a shit. The only thing that had mattered was that he had his little brother back and they weren't dying today. But now that he'd had time to cool down and think, he had questions. Lots of them.

"Tuned into the cop radio," Dean replied. He dunked a second fry in ketchup. "Not that hard." He winked and stuffed the fry into his mouth.

"You were obviously close by, though. How'd you get over here so fast?" Dean lived in Tyrmouth, a city that was closer to Angelthene than it was Yveswich. Driving from Tyrmouth to Yveswich would take...about three days, he'd estimate. Maybe four. But Dean always drove like a lunatic on a race track with a death wish, so it was probably more like two and a half.

"I *was* close by," Dean confirmed. "Soon as I heard what was happening in Yveswich, with the power outage or whatever the hell's going on there, I packed up and left. And then the missing-child alert went out for Paxton, and the minute I saw that, I knew something serious was going on and I had to find you before your psycho dad got to you first. So I followed allllllll those little clues—" He walked two fingers across the table. "—And voila." He flourished his hands. "Now you're here, enjoying some waffles and a milkshake with your favorite uncle. Easy peasy, right?" He dusted the salt off his fingers and took the liberty of polishing off Pax's chocolate milkshake.

"Easy peasy," Roman repeated with a murmur, still in disbelief.

On a more serious note, Dean added, "I've been waiting for this day for a long time, Rome. I knew it would come, I just didn't know when."

Roman dragged his tongue stud across the roof of his mouth. "Huh."

"What *is* going on in Yveswich, anyway? I hear they've locked the city down." He ate another fry.

Roman sucked in a breath and said on the exhale, "Um. Yeah, I don't really know. They're trying to contain some sort of...threat." Dean's brow creased. "From another dimension, or something—I don't know. They're not saying much." It felt weird to withhold the truth from Dean when Roman trusted him with his life, but...this wasn't about him. It was about Loren.

"Hm. Okay, well— First of all, let's get the pleasantries out of the way. I'm glad you're okay. Nice to see ya." His eyes danced.

Roman smirked. "You, too."

"So, you just heard my side of the story. What's yours? Minus the power outage shit."

What the hell *was* his story? What could he get away with telling this man?

"Long," he settled with. "My story's long."

"I've got time." When Roman kept his mouth shut, Dean suggested, "Why don't you start with how you managed to get away from your dad? How'd that all go down? Tell your old uncle a story."

"Okay." Roman chewed on his lower lip. Crossed his arms. "The night we were being evacuated, I got separated from Pax. Trey and Simon got a hold of him and his friend Eugene—"

"That Kylar's brother?" Dean asked.

"Yeah. They took them to a warehouse to wait for my dad. The kids managed to get away from them, but they got lost in the warehouse. I got there before my dad did. Killed Simon—"

"You killed Simon?" His dark brows rose. While his resemblance to Don was uncanny, Dean had shorter, gray-flecked hair, bolder features— more weathered, too, with pronounced smile lines—and a five o'clock shadow that never seemed to go away.

Roman nodded.

Dean's impressed smile spread. "Good for you."

"Thanks. Anyway, with the city being evacuated, there was no way—" He gestured behind him, to his little brother, Pax's contagious laughter bubbling through the diner. "—No way I was separating from him. And no way I was going to give in and have us go with our dad, either." Gods, what a nightmare that would've been. What little freedom they had would've been gone. "So, I took him and we just...ran." Looking back now, it was a good thing they were in such a hurry, or he might not have had the guts to do it.

"Good for you," Dean said again wholeheartedly. "I'm proud of you. Not just for getting away from Don, but for everything else, too. You've done a great job with him." He gestured to Pax. "And Travis."

He sighed. "Yeah, *that's* a problem that I still need to solve..." He thumped his elbows onto the table and rubbed his temples with his fingertips.

"What do you mean? What problem?"

"Travis. I don't know where the hell he is." As soon as he'd gotten his belongings back from the cop car, he'd checked his phone, but Travis still hadn't called or messaged. And every time he'd tried tracking him—and Max, Jewels, Malakai, Aspen—he got nothing. "He was in Yveswich when the explosion happened. I split up from him and...I don't know where he is now." If he was still stuck in there... If he'd died—

"Wait—rewind. *Travis* was in *Yveswich?*"

Roman sighed deeply through his nose and pushed his plate aside so he could fold his arms on the table. "It's a long story."

"So? Tell it. I told you, Rome, I got nothing but time."

"It's...not really my story to tell."

He frowned, confused. "What does that mean?"

"It means..." He looked over his shoulder, then out the window—at Dean's men. There were four of them—four Death Dealers from Tyrmouth, all deadly. All strangers. Dean personally vetted each of his Death Dealers, selecting only people that he trusted with his life, but... Not his story. He had no right to tell it. So, he said quietly, "It means it isn't safe. To talk about. Not here, anyway."

"Okay," Dean said, eyeing him with concern and curiosity. "Well, what's your plan now? Where you headed?"

"I *was* on my way to Darien's when that shit with the cops happened. I told him I'd be at his house by tonight, but..." He glanced out the window —at the last of the sunlight slipping below the horizon. "Doesn't look like that's happening anymore."

"So we'll go tomorrow."

He blinked. "We?"

"Yeah, *we,*" Dean said, as if it should be obvious. "You really think I came all this way just to say goodbye and fuck off? I'm here to help."

"And what happens if my dad shows up?"

"Then we've had a good life." He reached for more cold fries.

Roman smirked. "Thanks for being optimistic."

He sighed. "Roman, I've told you this a million times. If you worry about something that hasn't happened yet, all you're doing is living it twice. Let's get through tonight, we'll get you to Darien's, and we'll go from there. 'Kay?"

Roman looked over his shoulder—at Paxton first, then Shay. Then he turned back around, scratching at the back of his neck, thinking.

Dean was studying him. Likely seeing right through him. He tended to do that. Sure enough, he said quietly, "She's quite the looker, hey?"

"Tell me about it," he grumbled. "I can't stop *looking* at her."

"She Athene's girl?"

He nodded. "Her youngest. Shayla Cousens."

"How'd you get tangled up with her?"

Roman raised his brows, wondering how he should go about explaining *that* one. "Another long story."

"So give me the short version. Come on," he said with a smile, beckoning with a curling of his inked fingers. "I feel like I'm fishing here and you're doing everything you can not to bite. You not trust me anymore, or something? What changed?"

"Of course I trust you." There weren't many people who Roman trusted, but Dean was the one person, apart from Travis, Pax, and Kylar, who he'd always trusted. *Completely* and without question. Dean had never broken that trust, never betrayed him in any way, shape, or form. If Dean could be summed up in one word it would be *trustworthy*. "Okay, short version is...she blackmailed me into helping her look for her sister, Anna. Anna was missing, Shay convinced me to go with her to try to find her, Dad found out, and..."

"And now he's got her in his crosshairs," Dean concluded.

Roman nodded. "And I feel like it's my fault. I told her she can come with us to Darien's, but..." He sighed. "I think, after that, we should go our separate ways." The thought of saying goodbye to Shay again made him want to peel his own skin off with a knife, but... Safe. He wanted her safe. Not tortured. Not raped.

And sure as hell not dead.

"And what does *she* say about that?" Dean asked, pointing to Shay with a floppy fry.

"I haven't talked to her yet. Last night, I told her the decision is up to her, but..." When he looked over his shoulder, his gaze slammed into Shay's. She immediately tore those pretty green eyes off him and found something else to look at. Which wound up being the ceiling. Roman turned back around. "The longer she sticks around, the worse it'll be."

"You got feelings for this one?"

He sighed. "Too many." Way too many.

"Don't let her go, then—that's my advice. If she's *The One,* you fight for her. No matter what—no matter your dad and his stupid fucking rules. You understand me?"

"You say that like you speak from experience."

"I do. Trust me—I know how it feels to fuck up and let *The One* get away." He ate the last fry off Pax's plate. Every dish was now empty, nothing but crumbs and melted whipped cream left. Dean was a bottomless pit—he was always eating. Burgers and milkshakes were his favorite.

"Who was she?" Roman asked, curious. "*The One* you speak of?" He smirked. Dean had never talked about his romantic life before, beyond flings.

He waved the hand that was marked with the symbol of his Darkslayer House—a pair of fiery bat wings with tips that curved inward like horns, worn by Death Dealers on the skin between their thumb and index finger—in dismissal. "It was before your time."

Roman was about to prod when the waitress came by. "Can I get these out of the way for you?" she asked.

"That'd be wonderful," Dean said, flashing his famous charming smile that won all the ladies over. Sure enough, the woman blushed. "We'll take the bill, too, darling, soon as you got a sec."

"Sure," she said, fighting a smile as she tucked a loose strand of hair behind an ear. She stacked the plates and set the cutlery on top. "I'll be right back with that." She swished her hips as she walked away.

As soon as she was gone, Roman chuckled under his breath and said, "Still the ladies' man, hey?"

"Always." He winked.

'He can never resist,' grumbled a voice from Dean's shadow. It was deep and rumbling, like thunder. Roman felt Sayagul perk up; she had always looked up to Brutus. *'It gets tiring.'*

Roman chuckled. "Hey, Brutus. Long time no talk." *Or see,* he thought. Brutus was almost always sleeping, the lazy spirit. "How's it going?"

Brutus let out a smoky, deep-bellied sigh that vibrated the floor beneath Roman's boots. *'Peachy, Roman. Just peachy...'* Brutus barely got the last word out before he fell back asleep.

Sayagul sniggered. *'Nice to see you, too, Big Brute.'*

Brutus's distant, growly snoring faded away.

When the waitress came back, Dean covered the bill—with cash—and she bid them a good night. And a backward glance for Dean, of course.

Roman shook his head, amused. Always the ladies' man, was right. He yawned, his eyes watering. Gods, he was tired.

Dean said, "You ready to sleep with both eyes shut tonight?"

"Fuck, yeah, finally. That'd be nice. You think there are any motels around here?"

"There's one. Blue Gables. It's about ten miles that way." He pointed.

"Fine by me."

They got up and began making their way out. Shay spotted them coming and turned to face them as Paxton finished his round on the arcade game. It was that jumping frog one that Tanner was addicted to.

"Ready to go?" she asked, her eyes darting between nephew and uncle. The bruises on her face were finally fading.

Good. Roman hated seeing this beautiful woman marked up like that. If the men who'd touched her hadn't been ripped to pulp courtesy of his little brother, Roman would have hunted them to the ends of the earth, until each and every one of them had paid for their mistake in blood. No one else would touch Shayla Cousens—he'd make sure of it.

"There's a motel not far from here called Blue Gables," Roman told her, his blood thrumming as he watched her attention dip to his mouth, as if hearing his words wasn't enough, she wanted to *see* them, too.

Fuck, he wanted this woman so badly, it was insane. Every part of his soul, his aura, his body *begged* for her. Shay was the perfect woman for him. He forced himself to get a grip and added, "We thought we'd crash there for the night."

Those vivid green eyes he always had trouble looking away from scanned his face, as if searching for some hidden meaning. "Okay. Sure." Her expression was aggravatingly unreadable, and so was her tone. Bland, almost.

Roman frowned, his eyes dipping downward—

Just in time to see Shay clasping her wrist, her hand covering her fish skeleton tattoo. When she saw what he was looking at, she tightened her grasp, white light glowing faintly against the front of her jeans.

Slowly, Roman lifted his eyes to her face.

She flicked her rose-gold brows up, as if to say, *What?*

Dean stepped around them with a knowing smile and pushed the door

open. "I'll be right outside," Dean drawled, leaving Roman alone to stare at
Shay.

She stared back.

"Got something to hide?" Roman asked, indicating to the tattoo she
was still covering up.

"Not at all," she said smoothly, her face perfectly serene. "Shall we get
going?"

Roman gave a stiff nod. "Time to go, Pax."

"One sec, I'm almost done."

Roman watched the screen, Shay doing the same, both of them
refusing to look at each other as Paxton finished his game. The tinny music
drifted through the speakers, declaring his victory.

"Yes!" he hissed, throwing his hands in the air.

"You're really good at that," Shay told him.

"Thanks!" Pax said, beaming. He grabbed his backpack and headed
for the door, Itzel munching away on the ice cubes they'd dumped
inside.

Shay gestured for Roman to lead. "After you."

Roman tried not to frown.

Another motel. Another night under the same roof as this beautiful
thief.

If this kept happening... Fuck, he might break. When it came to Shayla
Cousens, his self-control was already thinner than a soap bubble. And every
night they spent together threatened to pop it for good.

Hopefully tonight would not be that night.

———

ANOTHER NIGHT in the same four walls as Roman Devlin.

Shay tried not to dwell on the horrible toll this was taking on her heart
as she followed him and Paxton into the dark parking lot of Wacky's
Waffles. To where Dean Slade and his Death Dealers stood talking and
laughing by the vehicles.

Dean's uncanny resemblance to Donovan had unsettled her in the
beginning, she couldn't lie. But it hadn't taken long for her to learn that the
two brothers really were nothing alike. While the sight of him may be a
jump scare, Dean was the good apple, just like Roman had claimed. He was
funny, kind, patient. It was hard—impossible, even—not to like him. He
looked a lot like Roman too, but that didn't surprise her. The Slades all

shared such similar features, you'd be stupid *not* to see that they were related.

"Hey, you three," Dean greeted them with an infectious grin as they joined the group. "Ready for some introductions?" The day had been such a whirlwind, Shay hadn't even realized that no one, apart from Dean of course, had had the chance to introduce themselves. The Death Dealers had ridden in separate cars and kept watch out front of the diner while they ate, so this was the first time they were really seeing each other up close.

"Sure—you start," Roman prompted, his husky voice muffled by the cigarette he'd placed between his teeth. He sparked his lighter, the orange glow of the flame kissing his handsome features.

Dean fired off the names of his Death Dealers, indicating to each with an index finger. "This is A.J., Bobby, Nash, and Jacob, my ride-or-dies." Then he pointed at himself, his smile growing. "And I'm Dean." The men were all around the same age—late thirties, early forties. All except Nash, who looked to be in his mid-twenties. And Nash was—

Staring. He was staring. At Shay. He had cropped dark hair, an abundance of tattoos, and pale blue eyes. He was attractive, yeah, definitely—but it was hard to notice when you had competition like the god that was Roman Devlin standing right there, smoke rippling out of his lips.

As Nash kept staring, Roman made a dramatic show of glancing between them, looking pissed.

Wait a minute—did Roman's eyes just darken? She could have sworn the parking lot was growing darker, too.

Holy shit, was he...was he *jealous?*

Shay pressed her lips together to stifle a smile. Oh gods, this was too good!

Roman began their side of the introductions, starting with himself. "I'm Roman Devlin. This is my little brother, Paxton." A pause. He gestured to Shay, and when he spoke next, he pinned his cold stare on Nash, his tone dripping with attitude. "—And this woman here, her name's *Taken.*"

Shay blinked.

She whipped her head around to glare at Roman.

The Death Dealers barked laughs that snapped Nash out of his trance. He ripped his eyes off Shay, an embarrassed chuckle slipping out of him. "Sorry," Nash muttered, scratching at the back of his neck.

Shay's face warmed.

Dean clapped Nash on the back. "My nephew's spoken, Nash—this one's taken." To Roman, whose black stare remained on Nash, smoke from the cigarette in his teeth curling toward the starry sky, Dean winked and said, "Don't mind him. He's like this all the time. Can't resist the ladies."

Shay cleared her throat. "Actually, my name is not *Taken*, and Roman does not speak for me," she said, shooting a firm look at Roman. "My name is Shay. Shay Cousens." She stepped forward, extending a hand to Nash first, then the others. Roman's stare tracked her every move as the men exchanged pleasantries with her, a few snickering in amusement.

Gods, this was beyond awkward. And there was Nash again, trying not to stare—and failing.

"I'm single, by the way," Shay said to Nash, just to irk Roman.

A prickle walked down Shay's spine as something dangerous stirred in the air.

Yep, the parking lot was definitely getting darker.

Served him right. She was tired of Roman's back and forth—telling her that he wanted her gone, insisting that what they'd shared was a meaningless fling, trying to leave her in the middle of the night. Now that they weren't facing the threat of going to jail, and she had time to reflect on everything that'd happened...yep, she was pissed.

"Here." Dean tossed Roman a key.

"What's this?" he asked, squinting at it in the dark.

"Your new whip."

"My new...what? Whip?"

Paxton gasped with excitement and began jumping in place. "A new car?!" he exclaimed, beaming up at Roman.

Dean indicated to the sexy black muscle car nearby. "That one there. That baby's yours."

Roman's brows went up. Paxton jumped faster. "To borrow," Roman clarified.

Dean was shaking his head. "To keep. I know you've always had a thing for Stacey, so. She's all yours."

"Stacey?" Shay asked.

"I name all my cars," Dean explained. "This here is Stacey. And those two there, that's Rose and Iris." He indicated to the other two cars. "Seeing as the cops took your ride," he said to Roman, "she's your new one." He opened his arms in presentation. "Happy Escape from Donovan Day."

A surprised chuckle slipped through Roman's lips. "No way. You're giving me this? You're giving me *Stacey*?" He walked over to the car, Paxton following so closely on his heels he was nearly stepping on them, the backpack that held Itzel swinging from his shoulder. The rest of their group followed. Shay refused to check and see if Nash was still watching her.

Stacey was nice. Really nice. The car was such a perfect fit for Roman, it might as well have been made for him. It was an older model that had been restored to pristine condition, paint sparkling like liquid night, the chrome of the bumpers shiny as mirrors.

"Get in," Dean said, opening the driver's door for him. "Try her out."

Roman promptly put his smoke out and got in the driver's seat. Dean shut the door, window already down.

Roman turned the key in the ignition—

The engine fired up, a deep, sexy growl ripping through the night-cooled parking lot.

Paxton beamed. "Rev it!"

Roman smiled and revved the engine, the candle smoke of the magic that powered the car thickening the air. "Sick," he said, that smile growing so big his dimple showed, his big, scarred hands doing that *thing* with the wheel again.

Shay gulped. He *really* needed to stop doing that. Every time he did it, she had to stop herself from jumping his damn bones.

"What do you think?" Dean asked him, walking up to brace a hand on the roof of the car.

"I think...Stacey's going to blow my fucking mind." The way he said it, in that low, growly tone he usually reserved for the bedroom, made Shay's mind short-circuit, her mouth drying out.

Dean grinned. "Feel like racing to Blue Gables?"

Roman looked up at him, that adorable smile tipping his lips up. It made Shay smile too, despite how frustrated—for multiple reasons, one the sexual kind—she'd felt a moment ago. Gods, she was *so* fucked, wasn't she? "Really?" Roman asked.

"Yeah, why not? Let's have some fun." He pushed off the car and made for his own. "Loser buys everyone breakfast tomorrow."

It was such an odd thing to say, with everything going on—*let's have some fun.* But fun was exactly what these two brothers needed.

Shay let Paxton have the front. She squished into the tiny back seat, where she watched their smiles more than she watched the road as they raced against Dean, the other Death Dealers following behind, down the dark, starlit highway.

84

HEAVEN'S GATE
ANGELTHENE, STATE OF WITHEREDGE

"Darien," said a female voice. Echoey and distant.

He kept his eyes shut, watching with his Sight as neon grid-based street patterns, fluorescently colored buildings, and multi-hued trees zipped through his mind. So many colors, so many shapes and symbols and coordinates, all passing by at a speed so swift it was dizzying.

Behind closed lids, his eyes rapidly flicked about. Sweat beaded on his upper lip and temples, but he hardly noticed. His physical body was miles away, his mind elsewhere. Drifting. Searching.

"Darien," the voice said again. Little louder this time.

Something snapped. Two fingers pressing together, somewhere close by —right in front of his face.

Several male and female voices said his name all at once—

"Darien."

His black eyes flew open. He was sitting on the couch at Heaven's Gate, elbows on his knees. Ivy stood before him, the glowing shades of her multi-colored aura accentuating the frown on her face, fingers poised to snap again if need be.

Now that his eyes were open, she straightened and dropped her hand.

"You say something?" He blinked the Sight away. His eyes were on fire, and his head was *pounding*. How long had he been tracking?

Without the glow of her aura getting in the way, his sister looked even more concerned than she had a moment ago. "Your nose is bleeding," she said.

He tipped his head back and pinched the bridge of his nose. "Ah—fuck. Shit." Blood was rolling down his lips and chin. He was going to get it all over the damn couch.

Ivy frowned.

Where he lay on the smaller sofa, video game console in hand, Eugene gaped.

"What's the matter?" Darien asked him. "Scared of a little blood?"

"You say *fuck* a lot," the kid said, his lisp thick.

"Hey," Kylar protested from the kitchen. He pointed a stern finger at his little brother. "Watch your fucking mouth."

Jack chuckled.

"I'm just saying," Eugene grumbled. He returned to his game. "When's Paxton gonna be here? I'm bored."

"Kids these days," Kylar said, shaking his head. "They've got a million electronics in front of them, and they still complain about being bored."

Eugene glared. "A million? I only have *one!*" He lifted the console.

"Lose the tone, termite."

Lace came around the couch, a box of tissues in hand. "Here." She offered it to him, and he grabbed a fistful from the box.

"Thanks." Head back, he pressed the wad of tissues against his nose.

"I think you should take a break," Ivy said.

"I will." It was a lie. He had no intention of stopping. Not until he found at least *one* of them, for gods' sake. He refused to accept that they were dead. If he kept looking, they had to turn up eventually.

"Any luck?" Kylar asked him.

The others were cleaning up the mess from dinner. Loren was there too, pausing in the midst of stacking dishes to look his way. Her pretty face was lined with worry, her mouth all pouty. Beautiful—she was so beautiful, she took his breath away.

He sighed. "No." He'd sat down by himself in the living room while the others finished making dinner and had stayed there for over an hour, tracking everyone who was still missing. Travis, Max, Dallas, Jewels, Aspen, Dominic, Blue, even *Malakai*, he tried them all.

But to no avail—not even *one* measly thread to follow. And now that he'd been at it for over an hour, according to the clock on the microwave, he knew he was pushing his luck. Even for people who were seasoned in tracking—people like him—holding the Sight for that long wasn't just hard as hell, it was also dangerous. It put a lot of strain on the mind, and if you didn't heed the warning signs from your body, you could risk passing out, being hospitalized for a brain bleed, or, worse case scenario, becoming brain*dead*. His body was already telling him to stop, but—

Travis. Max. He had to find them. Had to at least know that they were okay, for fuck's sake.

He took a look at the tissues in his hand. They were soaked in blood. He grabbed a few fresh ones from the box Lace had left on the coffee table and tipped his head back, putting firm pressure on it. Soon as the bleeding stopped, he'd try again.

But Ivy, as if reading his mind, repeated, "I think you should take a break."

"I said I will. In another hour."

Before Ivy could go off on him, Tanner said, "Telecommunications are down." He was at the dining room table, laptop open before him.

Lace whipped her head his way. "In Yveswich?"

"And beyond. That whole general area—not all of Ker, but all of Yveswich and some of the smaller communities nearby."

"Landlines, too?" Darien asked, his question muffled by his plugged nose.

"All of it."

Arthur said, "Is it due to the power?"

"No," Atlas replied. "Someone cut it on purpose."

"What do you mean *someone*?" Jack said. With disgust he added, "It was obviously the imperator."

"Can you get it back up?" Darien asked.

Tanner sighed again. "That's...a big ask."

"I wouldn't even know where to start," Kylar said as he helped himself to a pinch of leftover shredded cheese. "Do you think it's doable?" He tipped his head back, sprinkling the cheese into his mouth. He was Roman's hacker, and while he was excellent at his job, there was only one Tanner Atlas.

"Yes. But...my main concern is time," Atlas said, cupping his chin with one hand, the other scrolling. "We have less than three days until the military hits Yveswich, and I'm not sure I can get it back up that quickly."

"Try," Darien urged. "Do whatever you can, just— Try," he repeated, breathing deeply as a Surge began to pound its fist on the door of his mind. He was about to pay for all the salt he'd snorted in the past hour. "Please," he added.

"Starting now," Tanner confirmed. He sat up straight, keys clacking.

Darien locked eyes with Loren. She stood by the table, her stack of plates forgotten.

She dropped her gaze and added another dirty plate to her stack.

"How are you feeling?" he asked her. Her tattoo was glowing, but it was a soft blend of blue and red. Red was the danger zone. Blue was relatively safe. And a blend of both was...well, not bad, but not great, either. It was better than solid red, though.

She pursed her beautiful lips in thought. "Worried," she admitted in a quiet voice, her eyes downcast.

His brows pulled together. "Worried? About what, sweetheart?"

She tucked a curl of hair behind her ear. "About you."

"Oh." He checked on the tissues in his hand. The bleeding was slowing down. "This is nothing, baby. I'm fine." Too much salt, that's all it was. Plus some mental strain, but it was nothing he couldn't handle.

"Take a break," Ivy insisted before returning to the kitchen, where Jack was loading the dishwasher. "And eat something, for the gods' sake."

He was about to get up when he spotted Loren heading toward him. In her hands she carried a glass of water and a plate with four soft tacos dressed up all beautifully. The sound of the ice clacking against the glass reminded him of a certain Hob he hadn't stopped thinking about—and still had to figure out how to find.

"I hope you like all the toppings," she said as she carefully set the plate and glass on the coffee table before him. "I tried asking you what you wanted on them, but you didn't hear me."

"I love all of them. Looks perfect, baby. Thank you."

"You're welcome." She bent down to kiss the top of his head.

He got up and went to the kitchen to chuck out the tissues and wash the dried blood off his hands and face before diving into his food, enjoying the tacos more than he would have if he'd made them himself. Everything always tasted better when Loren made it.

"Does anyone have any questions about what we discussed?" he asked the group, twisting around on the couch to see everyone.

"Yeah, I got one," Jack said.

Darien sensed a joke coming, but he decided to humor his goof of a brother-in-law and prompted, "Shoot."

"Why does Atlas always get to stay home while the rest of us bust our asses in the streets?" He kept his head down as he loaded the dishwasher—fighting a smile, no doubt. Darien could hear it in his voice.

Tanner took the bait. "Are you serious?" he asked, glaring over his shoulder.

"It's Jack, he's never serious," Lace said.

"You wouldn't last one day in my position."

"I'm just twisting your nipples, Atlas," Jack said. "Relax."

Darien said, "All right, any *serious* questions?" When Jack raised his hand, a very non-serious smile curving his lips up, Darien said, "No more, Jacky."

"It's a good one, though."

"No."

"But it's about Arthur."

Arthur gave him a look that suggested he'd had enough of Jack's shit. "I think I'll pass, Mister Steele."

Jack lowered his hand and cursed under his breath. "You guys are no fun."

Everyone glanced at each other as they continued on with different tasks, waiting to see if anyone spoke up.

Arthur said, "It's more a request than a question, but I might need the blueprints for those missiles."

"Whatever you need, we'll help you get it," Darien vowed. "Just tell us where and when."

"Lucent Enterprises. But we'll need Roark for that one."

"I'll talk to him when I see him tomorrow." He took another bite and scanned the room as he chewed. Swallowed and said, "Any other questions?"

Nobody said anything. That settled it, then.

He washed his food down with water before facing Tanner. "Do everything you can to get communications back up, or this isn't going to work."

"I'll do my best."

Figuring out where the others were was the first step, and to do that they had to get a hold of them. If they were still trapped in Yveswich...

He hoped his plan to bust them the hell out of there would work.

LATER THAT EVENING, Loren lay awake by herself in her bedroom at Heaven's Gate. Missing Darien, wherever he was. He was probably still busy tracking—which was exactly what she wanted him to take a break from.

About an hour ago, Ivy had left the house with Jack, Lace, and Kylar. They had split into two groups and hit the streets in search of answers regarding Mortifer and the men who'd broken into Hell's Gate—and where they might find some of them. Arthur and Eugene were asleep, and Tanner was working on getting telecommunications up and running in Yveswich. He would likely be at it all night.

Suddenly, her bedroom door opened.

She sat up, squinting to see in the moonlit room. Was it Darien? Her heart started to pound—

But it wasn't Darien. It was Bandit. He stood in the doorway, his eyes glowing like red fireflies. His rubber chicken toy was in his mouth.

"Bandit?" she whispered. "What are you doing in here?"

He took her question for an invitation to come inside, paws padding across the floor. *'I bring a peace offering.'*

Her brows went up. "A peace offering?"

He came closer and opened his mouth. The chicken plopped onto the floor with a squeak.

"You're giving me Cluckles?"

He sat down. *'If I do, will you stop being angry with us?'*

"Oh, Bandit," she said with a soft laugh. Bandit must not have gotten the memo; she wondered what it was like for other people and their Familiars. How the mental bond worked.

Bandit licked his chops. *'Please. Take the chicken.'* He nudged it closer with his nose. *'We cannot handle another day of Darien's sour mood.'*

"We?" she echoed.

'Me and Cluckles, of course.'

She tried her darn best not to laugh, but it was so hard when he was this serious about the chicken. "Oh. You don't have to give me your chicken, though, Bandit. Really."

He tilted his head. *'I don't?'*

"No," she said, unable to stop her laugh this time. "Darien and I already made up."

Bandit blinked his glowing eyes.

Yep, he definitely hadn't gotten the memo.

Boots pounded on the stairs. Down the hallway.

Darien appeared in the doorway. *"Bandit,"* he hissed. "It's late. What the hell are you doing?"

'Nothing.'

To Loren, Darien said, "Is he bothering you?"

'I'm not bothering anyone,' Bandit said. *'I brought her a peace offering. It's a good one, too.'* He puffed his chest out with pride.

Darien came into the room. "A peace offering?"

'I don't want her to be mad anymore,' Bandit said. *'But she said you already made up and rutted, so I get to keep Cluckles.'*

"Rutted?" Darien asked with a snort. "All right, that's enough. Go on —git." He pointed at the door with his good hand. "Unless you'd like to see us *rut* again."

'Eww, eww!' Bandit scampered out, abandoning Cluckles on the floor.

When Darien faced her, he was fighting a smile. "Sorry," he said.

"That's okay. He could have stayed." She tugged the quilts up to her chin, hoping he wouldn't notice that she was wearing one of his shirts—a soft, black one. She'd stolen it from his bag while he was distracted with tracking. She could have worn her pajamas, yes, but they didn't smell like him. "Are you leaving?"

"For a few hours."

She scanned his clothes—the tattered long-sleeve henley, the ripped jeans, the combat boots. "You're having a Surge, aren't you?"

He didn't reply. Instead, he asked her, "Will you be okay while I'm gone?"

"I think so." Her tattoo was glowing steadily with a blend of blue and red light that illuminated the puffy white duvet. Blue—even just partial blue—plus no flashing meant she was in the safe zone. White would be better—but she hadn't seen the ink turn white since she was a child.

"You'll be safe here," Darien said. "More than you would be if we were at Hell's Gate. No one knows about this place but us."

"Have you ever lived here before?" He'd told her about this place a couple of months ago, but they hadn't talked about it much.

"No. We only bought it to use during emergencies." He didn't look impressed that the emergency that had finally prompted them to move here was his uncle. "If you need anything, you text me, okay? I'll only do one round and I'll keep my phone on me the whole time."

"You'll answer mid-swing?"

A smile flirted with his distracting mouth. "Anything for you," he vowed.

She smiled back, but it was fading quickly.

"I don't have to leave," he said gently. "I'll stay if you want me to stay."

"No, it's okay. I know there are things you need to take care of."

"You're one of them," he said. Her heart melted. He gave her a minute to think about it, and then he asked her, "Would you like me to stay?"

She *did* want him to stay. But she had things of her own that she needed to do, so she told him, "You can go. I'll be fine for a bit."

"Are you sure?"

She nodded.

"Okay." His boots thumped as he came a little closer, stealing the last of the oxygen in her lungs, and bent to press a kiss to her forehead. "Love you, sweetheart."

"I love you, too." She tipped her face up, until he gave her what she wanted: a kiss on the mouth.

He straightened and lightly squeezed her foot through the blankets. "Text if you need me, and I'll drop everything and come right back. Sound good?"

She nodded, her ankle warm from his grasp. "Sounds good."

"Have a good sleep, my love." He let go and backed out of the room, watching her as he slipped out the door.

She listened to the familiar pounding of his boots until she couldn't hear them anymore.

And then she grabbed her phone off the nightstand and typed a message to Sabrine.

LOREN

> Have you found anything yet?

SABRINE

> Girl, it hasn't even been 24 hours… Lol. I'm going to need longer than that.

Loren tried not to frown.

A moment later, her phone buzzed with a new message.

SABRINE

> I found a few websites that look promising. If you want to read through a couple of them, I could use the help.

LOREN

> Of course I want to! 🖤 Send them over.

SABRINE

> K! One sec.

Sabrine sent her a short list of website links. Loren flicked the lamp on, sat up, and began to read. With Darien gone, she managed to make a lot of progress without the risk that he might catch her. She started a list of important facts—any detail, no matter how small, that might help, she made note of it.

She stayed awake for as long as she could—until her eyes were too tired to stay open. It was past Witching Hour when she drifted off, hope kindling in her heart.

She might not be able to save herself, but she would save him.

85

BLUE GABLES
BRONTE, STATE OF KER

The interior of the car was so quiet, Shay could hear crickets chirping in the grass by the motel called Blue Gables. She was in the passenger's seat, Paxton having traded spots with her after the adrenaline-hungry males had gotten their fill of drifting, racing, and doing burnouts on the moonlit highway. He was dozing off in the back, Chance and Sayagul already fast asleep.

Stacey had won the race against Dean's slate-gray Iris, so Dean had offered to pay not just for breakfast tomorrow, but for the rooms, too. He was with a couple of his men in the Blue Gables office, hopefully booking several rooms with two beds each. Ideally, it'd be nice if she got her *own* room, but...

She wouldn't get her hopes up. Luck was in short supply these days.

Roman was brooding behind the wheel, his eyes and tousled hair a shade darker than normal. Neither of them had said anything to the other since their more-than-awkward introductions with the Death Dealers out front of Wacky's Waffles. She had a feeling his brooding was the result of what she'd said to Nash—*I'm single, by the way*—but she wasn't quite sure.

What she *did* know was that Shadows hadn't liked that.

Too bad, so sad. He couldn't have it both ways—couldn't tell her that he wanted her gone one minute and then tell complete strangers that she was taken the next. Unless he was going to come forward and express how he *really* felt about her...well, as far as she was concerned, she was very single. And she refused to let some indecisive, brooding asshole of a Shadowmaster with commitment issues lay claim to her. She deserved better than that.

A bell chimed in the night. Boots crunched in dry dirt.

Dean rounded the corner of the motel with Bobby and A.J.

"Any luck?" Roman asked through his open window.

Dean smiled and held up a key. "Four rooms. You guys are in nine." He tossed Roman the key. "Two beds, plus a pull-out. Since you're both very much single." He braced his hands on his knees and bent down to see inside the car, his teasing smile spreading as he glanced between them.

Shay's brows bumped up. Number nine? *Seriously?*

Heads turned toward her, Roman's included.

Oh shit, had she said that out loud?

Dean said, "You superstitious? You can have one of the others, if you want. But they don't have a pull-out couch."

What were the other numbers? Nineteen, ninety, and ninety-nine? Good gods, she wouldn't doubt it.

She cleared her throat. "Nine is fine. It just...reminded me of something."

Dean's smile grew impossibly big. "Another pull-out incident?"

Roman rubbed the stubble on his chin. The corner of his mouth was tipped up, as if he were fighting a smile.

Shay's face warmed.

Dean wheezed a laugh. "I'm just joshing. Anyway, your room is sandwiched between ours. You need anything, you just bang on the wall, okay?"

Roman nodded. "Yeah, alright."

"Don't worry about anything. Living it twice, remember?"

"Yeah, I remember." But he sighed, and he *did* look worried.

"At ease, Rome," Dean insisted. He drummed a hand against the roof of the car in farewell. "Have a nice time with the pull-out."

A.J. and Bobby chuckled.

Shay slithered lower in her seat and cupped a hand against her brow.

"We'll see you in the a.m.," Dean called.

In the a.m. Sure. All she had to do was make it through another night without jumping Roman Devlin's bones.

Pfft. Easier said than done.

SHAY HAD BEEN asleep for barely an hour when she was jolted out of her dreams by a painful Surge.

With a sharp gasp, she sat up, her head spinning as she took in the motel room with eyes that flashed between the Sight and regular vision.

Nugget was partially covered with a blanket that stifled his glow, rendering her surroundings too dark to see. But the room was quiet enough to suggest that Roman and Pax were fast asleep on the other bed and the pull-out couch. Chance was snoring, Sayagul's nose was whistling, and Itzel was slumbering in the mini fridge. Everyone was having a wonderfully deep and peaceful sleep.

Everyone except her. Joy.

Gods, her heart was racing so fast, it was painful. Lightning crackled through her blood, threatening to sear her veins and char her flesh. *Burn her alive—*

With a fearful gasp, she staggered out of bed and tiptoed to where their bags sat. But it wasn't *her* bag she reached for. It was Paxton's.

Stealing from a twelve-year-old boy wasn't her proudest moment, but she was desperate. If she didn't get a suppressant into her system...

Gods, it'd be bad. Really freaking bad. It was either a suppressant or an orgasm, and current sleeping arrangements—plus her shaky relationship with a certain infuriating Shadowmaster—determined that the latter was definitely *not* an option.

Nope. No way. Roman wasn't doing her any more favors.

She eased the prescription pill bottle out of the side pouch in Paxton's backpack. Now, all she needed was water. She could drink from the tap in the bathroom, but she didn't want to wake Paxton up.

Wearing a pair of pajama shorts and Roman's shirt—which she absolutely should *not* be wearing, yet here she was, still wearing it like an idiot—she crept to the door, eased the lock open, and slipped out into the night.

The cool air kissed her skin, making it a little easier to breathe. She took several deep, gulping lungfuls before stepping into the light of the bulb mounted outside the door so she could read the label.

These were the same pills she always took. The only difference was the higher dose.

Perfect. A higher dose was exactly what she needed.

Now for the water.

She stepped out from beneath the overhang, trying to remember where in the hell she'd seen that vending machine—

"Sneaking around, are we?" drawled a husky male voice.

Shay whirled, hand flying to her throat. "What the *hell*, Roman!" she hissed, her heart pounding nauseatingly hard. But—

Wait a minute. Where *was* he?

She spun around, searching for him. "Where are you?" she fumed in a hushed voice.

"Look up."

She tipped her head back—

There he was, lying on his back on the roof, right above their motel room.

"What are you doing up there?" she whispered.

"Watching the stars. I just saw a falling one." He lifted a cigarette to his lips, the end burning a bright orange.

She cleared her throat. "All right, well—you have fun with that."

"Where are you going?"

"Nowhere."

"Doesn't look like nowhere."

"It's none of your business!" she clipped. "Now, if you would excuse me—"

"You're not excused." His statement froze her mid-step. He was still staring up at the starry sky, looking like he didn't have a care in the world.

She scoffed. "What are you, my jailer? I don't need your permission to leave."

"You said it first," he pointed out.

A laugh burst out of her. "You are so annoying!"

He rolled—literally *rolled*—off the roof and landed lithely on his feet like a freaking cat, his knees bending to absorb the impact.

Shay blinked, annoyed with herself that she was turned on by something so simple. Everything this man did lit her up like a light.

"Show me what you got in your hand." He flicked his cigarette butt aside.

She tucked her hands behind her back.

"Shayla," he chastised. The way he purred her name, in that growly, sinful bedroom voice, sent a rush of heat to her pelvis—so strong, she had to cross her ankles and press her thighs together. He held his hand out in request, scarred palm skyward. "Give it here."

"Give what here?" she breathed, nearly tripping over her feet as she uncrossed her ankles and backed away. Her heart pounded harder, the heat in her most intimate areas intensifying—

Gods, she had to get away from this man. Now. Right now.

"I know you pride yourself on your thieving skills," he said, that deep, throaty voice giving her full-body shivers, "but you gotta admit, stealing from a twelve-year-old kid is a new low."

He took a step toward her. She took a step back. Pebbles dug into her bare heels as he backed her into the parking lot.

"Give it here, pup," he said again, beckoning with a gentle curl of those inked fingers. She was pretty sure he'd done that exact movement inside of her at Motel 58—the technique that had made her fracture like a lightning bolt and whimper his name.

Now, she made a small, embarrassing noise in her throat. "No."

"Shayla," he said again, in that same growly tone.

"Stop that." Her voice came out weak. Breathy.

He cocked his head. "Stop what?" Those gold-flecked eyes danced.

"Using that tone."

When he spoke again, he did not stop using that tone. "Why?" He advanced on her, a wolf on the prowl. "Does it turn you on?"

She backed away. "Nothing about you turns me on," she lied.

A smile tugged on the corner of his mouth, his gaze dragging down her body with appreciation. "I'd be offended, if you weren't such a terrible liar."

He lunged—

Shay bounded to the left, back onto the sidewalk—but he was upon her before she could escape. The breath left her lungs in a gasp as he grabbed her around the waist and pulled her against his muscled body, her back colliding with his front so hard she let out an, *"Oof!"*

"Give me the bottle," he growled, his breath warming the shell of her ear as he reached for the bottle with one hand, his other arm ensnaring her waist.

"If you can catch it, I'll let you have it," she said, moving the bottle this way and that. He kept reaching, his hand closing around open air.

"Shayla," he warned.

"Roman," she fired back with the same attitude.

The hard arm around her waist tightened, tugging her so flush against his body that she felt something big and firm digging into the small of her back.

She knew better than to think that was his gun.

"Enjoying yourself, are you?" she said around a wild gasp, keeping the pill bottle forever out of his reach. Gods, she wanted him inside her right now. She had to get away from him, before she did something stupid—

Her eyes blackened as she summoned her illusion magic.

She slipped out of his grasp and skipped away on her tiptoes like a fairy, the band tee she wore swishing against her hips.

He blinked at her, dumbfounded.

"Did you forget who you're dealing with?" she crooned with a triumphant smile. She held up the bottle in victory. "Looks like I win." She turned her back on him. "Better luck next time, Shadows."

Suddenly, the bottle began to tug the other way, as if someone were pulling on it. She whirled, grabbing onto it with both hands, only to discover—

She was playing tug-of-war with a tendril of shadow.

What the hell?

Roman's arms were crossed, his eyes black, shadows stirring around him. A smug little smile ghosted across his lips as Shay tugged as hard as she could, her heels sliding across the pavement. Despite her efforts, the shadow won. The bottle slipped between her fingers, and she watched in disbelief as that wispy vine of darkness carried it over to Roman and offered it to him. He blinked the black away and pocketed the pills, the shadows melting away.

She harrumphed and stamped her foot.

Roman blinked. "Did you just stamp your foot?"

"Fine!" She turned up her nose and pivoted on the heel of that same foot, putting her back to him again. "If you won't share, I guess I'll go knock on Nash's door and see if he can lend me a *hand*—"

She let out a squeak as a big, rough hand closed around the back of her neck. Suddenly she was being spun around, and Roman was gripping her around the throat and pushing her up against the wall of the motel. Her back slammed into it—

And then Roman's lips were crashing against hers, and they were moaning into each other's mouths.

The kiss was hungry. Desperate. He devoured her, his pierced tongue diving into her mouth. His kiss was better than she remembered. He tasted like mint, and tobacco, and Roman, and *gods*—she just couldn't get enough of him.

Too soon, he broke the kiss, his mouth so close to hers she could feel the words he spoke more than she could hear them. "I never want to hear another man's name on your lips again," he said. "Do you understand me?"

"Jealous, Shadows?" she breathed.

"Very." He bunched her shirt up around her waist, his callused hand sliding along the curve of her ass cheek and tugging on her underwear.

"I thought we were just a fling," she said around wild gasps, her head spinning with need. Desire, as that hand dipped below the waistband of her shorts.

"You were never just a fling. You're so much more than that." He dug his fingers into her flesh, fisting her ass, and bent his head, his mouth brushing across hers. "Now say yes. Say yes to me, Shayla. Please." Gods, this man was begging for her, and she knew, in that moment, she was not strong enough to say no.

But she wanted him, too. So she said to hell with it, and gasped, "Yes."

The moment he had her consent, he yanked her shorts and panties down to her ankles, so hard he almost ripped them both.

And then he was pinning her against the wall and hoisting her up, her legs around his hips. She locked her ankles against the small of his back and pulled him closer—as close as she could get him. Desperate for friction—anything to take the edge off the growing ache at the apex of her thighs—she used the wall for leverage—

And rolled her hips, grinding her yearning core against the hard length of him—against his cock that was jutting against his black jeans.

He groaned her name—and she groaned his, her bare clit rubbing against the rough denim. Gods, it already felt so good, but she wanted more. *More.*

"Needy, aren't we, Shayla?" he breathed against her mouth.

"Shut up and fuck me, Shadows." Those words snapped the tether he was keeping on himself.

He thrust his hand between her thighs—

And slid two fingers inside her.

"Oh gods," she cried out. He pushed them in all the way, his predatory focus wholly on her. Watching her unravel and moan as he plunged his fingers in and out. In and out. In and out. "Yes. Yes. *Yes.*"

He captured her moans with a hungry kiss, relentlessly fucking her with that hand.

Her panting breaths were soon edged with whimpers as he picked up speed, pushing her toward that pinnacle—that edge she needed so badly to cross. She dug her fingernails into his arms, feeling the hard muscle flexing beneath her grasp. *Yes, yes, yes.*

"That's it, Shayla," he whispered, his tongue sweeping across the seam of her lips. He caught the plump lower one between his teeth and sucked on it—hard. "That's it." He nipped her lip. "Show me how tight this pussy can get."

She arched her back against the wall, her fingers fisting his windswept hair as he thrust and thrust and *thrust*. Faster and deeper, her ass slapping against the wall with brutal force, her legs squeezing his waist. She was already dissolving, his arms supporting her weight as he pushed her toward the edge of pleasure with every forceful thrust, his callused thumb kneading her clit.

"Gods, Roman—don't stop. Don't stop." She needed him. *More* of him.

She reached down between their bodies and undid his pants, pushing them down just far enough to get his hard cock in her hand.

Roman drew in a hiss of pleasure through his teeth as she tightened her hold on his shaft and started pumping.

"Fuck, Shayla." He was already close, his gaze heated and unhinged. He was utterly consumed by lust—by her. It made her feel powerful, knowing she was the one causing this gorgeous man to unravel like this.

She quickened her speed, and he quickened his own in response, matching her rhythm, his rough fingers curling inside her.

A gasp floated off her lips. She was almost there. She shut her eyes, her toes curling so tightly they cramped as she kept pumping him.

Lightning crackled through the air. Lit up the inside of her eyelids—

Oh shit. *Oh shit, oh shit.* She was burning up— "Roman," she gasped, her eyelids flying open. It was a panicked warning, but he didn't stop, his own eyes feverish with desire, his teeth bared and clenched like a wolf's as he neared his own release.

The storm inside her swelled—

It came to a head at the same time as her pleasure, and she cried out his name, lightning fracturing the sky with a deafening *crack* of thunder as her whole body tensed with a staggering orgasm.

When Roman uttered a curse, she realized some of her power had exited her body through her fingertips. Veins of lightning twined up his arms, his shoulders—

"Oh no—oh, Roman. I'm so—"

"Don't you dare apologize," he growled. "And don't you dare stop."

She didn't. She kept going, and as he got close he withdrew from her hand and pushed himself inside her, thrusting like an animal—

And then he groaned—so low and deep, she felt the outburst skitter across her bones. "Fuck—*Shayla.*" His body jerked against her as he found his release, dragging out his pleasure with several rapid, uneven thrusts.

She came a second time, his name floating off her lips as she tipped her head back against the wall. It was so good, *he* was so good, she was seeing stars.

"You okay?" he asked her, breathless.

"Better than."

He wrapped both hands around her thighs to support her, then hung his head on her shoulder. Shay slipped her arms around the back of his neck, fingers tangling in his thick hair. He smelled delicious. Like sweat, and mint, and Roman, and tobacco, and that *cologne*...

They stayed like that for several minutes. Just breathing together.

And then reality crashed around her, and suddenly she felt...sad. She didn't want this to be over, and a part of her was worried that she had made a mistake.

As if sensing where her mind had drifted, and how her heart was begging for more of him, Roman raised his head, tilted her chin up with one hand, the other arm still holding her up, and slanted his mouth across hers.

This kiss was different than the others. It was softer. Careful.

It felt like a love letter.

His pierced tongue swept across hers in a slow and sensual dance. He savored it, tasting her with slow, methodical strokes.

When he broke the kiss, he rested his forehead against hers. "Truth or lie?" he asked, his breath warming her lips. "We're idiots."

She gave a husky laugh. "Truth."

He nodded. "Truth."

"We really need to stop staying at motels," she breathed.

"Agreed."

"Are we both in agreement that this was just part of the survival code?"

"Survival," he mused. "Yeah, I think we can call it that."

They laughed together, softly, and then he kissed her one more time.

She may regret this tomorrow. But tomorrow wasn't here yet, and in that moment, as Roman held her, she decided it was worth it.

Whatever happened next, this was worth it.

SHAY WAS IN BED, about to drift off when she heard the door to the motel room open. It was Roman, slipping in quietly and turning the deadbolt. She watched his silhouette as he toed off his boots and slipped his shirt over his head.

He'd spent the past hour on the roof by himself. Watching the stars. And thinking, definitely—about what, Shay didn't know. And she wasn't sure she wanted to. He'd once accused her of being hot and cold, when really *he* was the unpredictable one.

As he walked quietly across the dark room, she expected him to return to his own bed—the one closest to the door. Instead, he rounded hers. The covers whispered as he got underneath them—it was the first time she'd ever seen him willingly *restrict himself,* as he'd once said—and snuggled up behind her, wrapping a strong arm around her waist.

Shay laced her fingers with his. Sensing that he had something he wanted to say, she waited patiently for him to speak.

Finally, he said, his voice whisper-soft, "You were right." His words grazed the shell of her ear and raised a shiver along the back of her neck. "That night, when you came and talked to me at my house...and you accused me of being threatened by my dad..." She heard him swallow. "You were right. He did threaten me. It's why I've been running this whole time, why I've been...why I've been so afraid for you. It isn't because I don't want you, Shay—I do. Believe me, I do. But my dad he...he told me..." Roman inhaled sharply, his next words rushing out on an exhale. "Gods, I can't even say it, that's how bad it is."

Shay let go of his hand—of his fingers that were suddenly so tense, she could hardly bend them—and rolled over to face him. "You don't have to say it, Roman," she said softly. Roman had a sound barrier up to keep their conversation from waking Paxton, but they still spoke in whispers. "It doesn't matter what that horrible monster said—"

"He said he'd have his men rape you," Roman blurted. A prickle of dread shook down her spine. "He said they'd string you up and torture you, like they do me. He said they'd..." His throat bobbed. "Kill you. He said they'd kill you."

Shay tried to swallow, but her throat was too tight. And those were tears she was seeing in Roman's eyes—shining in the dark.

"I don't want that to happen, Shay," he whispered. His voice cracked as he added, "Any of it. I won't be able to live with myself if they lay even one single finger on you—"

Shay pressed her fingertips against Roman's lips. Those perfect, kissable lips she had been biting and tasting an hour ago. Too long ago, already. She wanted to taste them again. "Stop," she said gently.

Roman slipped his rough fingers around hers, kissed her fingertips and lowered her hand. He opened his mouth—to argue, she knew.

But she told him, "No buts. We're in this together. Even if I were to run now, you and I both know that it's too late. Your father will not stop. He will not rest until he finds you, he will not rest until he finds Paxton, and he will not rest until he finds me. Whether you like it or not, Roman, we are in this together. It started with us, and it will end with us, too. What we have to decide is whether it ends with us running or fighting."

Roman's swallow was audible. He scrubbed a hand down his face before confessing, "I don't see a way out."

"We'll make one," Shay said.

Someway, somehow, they were both making it out of this alive.

"Whatever lies ahead, I will face it with you," she vowed, and meant it.

She would not abandon Roman. No matter the cost, she would not run, would not leave these two brothers on their own.

They may not be able to see a way out, at least not at this time...but they would damn well make one. Shay had never had the chance to experience a life of freedom with Anna. She had lost her sister, her closest friend in the whole world, and now that she had fallen for Roman and had grown to love his little brother, too, as if he were her own...she refused to lose them.

And so they would not run. When the time came, they would fight.

They would fight their parents, and they would not just break their chains. They would *shatter* them.

Together.

86

MALAKAI WENT AND GOT US LOST, THE IDIOT

YVESWICH, STATE OF KER

"I tried to tell you half an hour ago," Travis fumed, "you went the wrong fucking way!"

Hours had passed since they'd left the hospital, and here they were, wasting yet more precious time coasting down the canals when they could be sleeping peacefully in warm beds. Bunch of bullshit, and it was all the fault of his least favorite person in the group.

"Shut the fuck up, Devlin," Malakai drawled. "I've had enough of your bitching."

Jewels said, "He's right, Malakai. I think we're lost."

"No, we're not. I know exactly where we are."

Blood boiling, Travis hissed, "And where's that?"

He slowed the boat to a jarring stop. "The Black Market." He got out and moored the boat along the quay. Gray fog billowed across the black water, the fog so thick it nearly swallowed the boat.

If only it would swallow this asshole too and spare everyone all this goddamn suffering.

Max shoved to his feet. "Am I missing something here?" When Malakai refused to answer, instead whistling an annoyingly cheery tune, Max snapped, *"Delaney!"*

"What?" Malakai asked, his tone coated with boredom.

"Why the hell are we at the *Black Market?*"

"We need more weapons," he said matter-of-factly. "And what better place to find some than at the Black Market?"

Max ground his teeth. "Okay, and you didn't consult with any of us, *why?*" He threw his arms wide in question.

"Because you never listen to me." He started walking away, sauntering without a care in the world. He looked like a man taking a walk in the park, not a half-destroyed city with a shadow problem. "Be back in a bit."

"Wait—Malakai!" Jewels protested. Aspen shushed her, her eyes flicking about the pressing darkness. It was darker over here than at the hospital, even with the market being closer to the coast.

The portal was spreading. The air was colder too, his fingers and toes numb, and his breath opaque.

Grumbling, Travis thumped across the boat and jumped out. "I'll go with him." *Someone* had to go with, and it might as well be him. If this idiot died, Jewels would probably be sad—Travis couldn't imagine why, though —and after seeing how upset she was at the hospital...

Well, he didn't want to see that again. So, putting up with her idiot brother was a sacrifice he was willing to make.

Dallas said, "What about the rest of us? Shouldn't more of us come with?"

"Guard the boat," Travis said. He was hurrying after Delaney before anyone could argue.

———

MALAKAI DELANEY COULD *REALLY* USE some peace and quiet and a shred of fucking privacy, but noooooooooo, Travis just *had* to tag along, didn't he? He was like a pesky mosquito, buzzing constantly in his ear and sucking the last of the joy out of his gods-forsaken life.

He walked around the empty stands overlooking the deserted fighting ring at the ghost town of a Black Market, searching for the door that chick at the Duchess had told him about. The door with the green light. Of course Devlin trailed behind him like some lost mutt, muttering under his breath about how stupid he was and how he hoped something ate him.

"You're welcome to go back, Devlin," Malakai said as he rounded the back of the stands and walked into the glow of mercury vapor. "You'd be doing us both a favor." He stopped by the door and dug around in his jacket and pants pockets. Now, where was that coin?...

"Wait...," Travis muttered. He squinted in thought, his skin and clothes washed in a garish lime green. "We're not going *Below*...are we?"

Malakai pulled out a handful of coins and sifted through them, searching for the single limen coin among the ordinary ones. "Scared?" he asked flatly.

"How the *fuck* did you even know about this place?" He pointed at the closed door, moths flitting about the fuzz of green light.

"That chick you guys talked to at the hotel," Malakai said. "The one who said we have weird eyes." After they'd told him about her, he'd sought her out in private, slipping away from the group for all of five minutes with the excuse that he had to take a piss, knowing she'd be able to hook him up with some good shit.

He found the limen coin he'd purchased from her and shoved the others into his pocket.

"Hold on just a goddamn minute," Travis growled as Malakai swiped his hand across the dust caked on the worn door, fingertips groping in search of an engraving. Yup, there was definitely one there. Hell *yessssss.* "We're not really here for weapons, are we?"

"It's not too late to go back," Malakai warned, stepping back and rolling his tense shoulders. Just a little longer, and he'd be flying high.

"You're here for drugs," Travis concluded. His tone was saturated with disgust. "Aren't you? You want to get high, you fucking junkie!"

"You got a boss who's a junkie, too. Don't try acting like I'm special."

"At least he's not insufferable like you."

Malakai glared. "Oh, quit sucking his cock already and admit that he's not the saint you pretend he is!"

"I never said he was a saint—I said he wasn't insufferable."

Malakai rolled his eyes and tipped his head back, glaring at the pitch-black sky. "Devlin. Go back." He pointed in the general direction of the boat. "I'll be there in a bit. Soon as I get my fix."

"I'm not letting you do this." He stalked forward.

Malakai pushed him in the chest so hard, he fell, dust billowing around him.

"Leave me alone," Malakai seethed. Before Travis could stand up, he slapped his palm against the door—right above the symbol of a wolf skull with crossbones and three downward-pointing arrows.

The coin vanished beneath his hand. A breeze that tasted of blood and candle smoke blew his hair back as the dimensions warped, the magic of the otherworld granting him entry.

The doorknob twisted on its own, a buzzer sounded, and the door creaked open.

Travis got to his feet. "You're a fucking idiot!" he spat as Malakai pushed open the door, revealing a stairwell that dove deep into the earth. "The dimensions are blending, the waterfalls are becoming portals, and you actually want to go *Below.*"

Inside, the lights buzzed on, one by one, flickering all the way down to the bottom.

"For Venom," Travis pressed. "Right? You want to take the same drug that might be causing people to go crazy? I never thought you could get any more stupid, Delaney, but you keep one-upping yourself."

"Like I said," Malakai drawled, reining in his temper. Soon, he'd be high. Soon, he'd get a break from all these *thoughts* and all these *worries*, and everything that irritated him would shut the hell up for a bit. "You're welcome to go back," he concluded.

He stepped through the doorway and began his trek down, boots pounding on the stairs.

DARKSLAYERS WERE USED to dealing with creepy places and things. They were used to running head-first into danger and getting so close to death that you could practically taste it. As a Darkslayer himself, there really wasn't a lot that unsettled Travis.

Being Below, though? He couldn't lie; it unsettled him.

"How long is this going to take?" he asked as he paced the room, the air heady with hot tar. The stench made his eyes water and his throat burn.

"As long as I need," Alfie replied, his tone so low and grumbly, the words were barely decipherable. The warlock stood with his back facing them as he worked over the assortment of glassware spread across the long table by the wall. Neon potions and chemicals bubbled, hissed, and spat.

When they'd made it down the stairs and turned the corner into a dank hallway lined on either side with closed doors, they had barely taken one step before Alfie tracked them down. He was definitely high on Venom— the drug he was currently cooking up for a very stupid, potentially suicidal Reaper.

"At ease, Devlin," Malakai drawled. "You can't rush perfection."

Travis kept pacing. "Yeah, well, you can't fix stupid, either," he muttered.

They had already been down here for over an hour. The others would be wondering where they were.

A piercing scream filled the air. Metal rattled in the distance.

He paused his pacing. "What the hell was that?" he murmured.

"Oh, don't mind her," Alfie mumbled, completely unbothered as he mixed and poured. "It's just the Harpy."

"Harpy?" Travis echoed. "You got a Harpy down here?" Harpies were monsters with an avian body and the head of a hideous human woman. Their screams, if heard up close, could be fatal.

They were also very difficult to kill. Even for the most seasoned slayers.

Alfie said, "I'm going to need to see payment before I finish."

"Oh—uhh..." Malakai patted his pockets.

Travis snort-laughed. This was going to be good.

"Uh—hmmm." His eyes lit up with an epiphany. "Cassel said he gave you a down payment!" he declared, snapping his fingers.

"For Morsian darts," Alfie clarified in a bored tone. "Not Venom." He glanced at Malakai with watery, red-rimmed eyes as he poured boiling liquid from a flask. "You do business with him?"

"We're friends."

Travis snorted another laugh. "Liar," he muttered.

"Shut up," Malakai mouthed. To Alfie he said, "Didn't he give you—what was it, twenty or something?" He was fishing—it was obvious. He had no clue what Darien had paid.

Loser.

"Fifteen," Alfie corrected.

"Perfect. You give me the Venom, you keep the fifteen, and we'll call it even."

Travis scoffed. "You can't be serious."

Malakai sliced into him with a glare. "You got a problem?"

"Yeah, I do," he snapped. "You can't just piss away Dare's money like that!"

"He's a billionaire. Pretty sure he'll recover."

"You don't need fifteen grande worth of Venom!"

Alfie said, "This won't make fifteen. I can get ya five."

Malakai said, "Perfect. Keep the rest of the money for those darts Darien will *never* get." The look he threw Travis's way seemed to say, *Stupid*.

"You are unbelievable."

"Yeah, well, you're a whiner. FYI, my sister doesn't like whiners. It won't take her long to get bored of your shit."

Travis bristled. "FYI, I've learned a lot about your sister lately, and I can tell you one thing: You do not deserve her."

"Oh yeah?" he growled. He advanced on Travis, his hands curling into fists at his sides. "And what'd you learn? Tell me what it is that you think you've learned about *my* sister." He stabbed himself in the chest with a thumb.

"That she has less than two years left to live. Yet all you care about is yourself and your need to get high."

Malakai held up an index finger in the air between them. "First things first: You don't know anything. About her, or about me. Second things second: So long as we're trapped here, *none* of us have two years." He sliced that hand through the air, silver eyeteeth glinting. "So let me get my fix and leave me the *fuck* alone." He turned—

"How does your sister feel about having a pathetic junkie for a brother? I might as well ask *you,* since you seem to know everything about her."

Malakai whipped back around. "I'm giving you one more chance, Devlin," he threatened, holding his finger up again. Travis fought the urge to snap it off and shove it up Malakai's ass. "You can either leave right now —" He pointed at the door. "—and maybe, just *maybe,* I'll let you continue to be *friends* with my sister. Or: you can keep flapping your gums like the whiner you are and see where it gets you."

"I'm not going anywhere. And I'm not just friends with your sister—I like her. A lot."

Malakai's nostrils flared. He was like a bull puffing hot air. "Oh, you do, do you?"

"Yeah. And she likes me."

He scoffed. "In your dreams."

"The minute we get out of here, I'm taking her on another date," he declared. "And you?" He crossed his arms and leaned in. "You're going to leave. Us. *Alo—*"

Malakai punched him in the mouth.

Travis stumbled backward, grunting in surprise.

"No one," Malakai seethed, "tells me what to do."

Travis brushed his fingers across the blood on his lips.

And with an animalistic roar, he charged Malakai head-on, plowing him into a row of lockers by the wall. They rattled and fell like trees, metal crashing around them.

Travis swung. His knuckles bit into Malakai's brow. Blood sprayed.

The Reaper swung back.

Travis ducked. But when he came back up, Malakai was already moving.

He landed a blow to Travis's temple, sending him crashing into Alfie's work station.

"Hey!" the warlock barked. *"Take this outside!"*

Travis shoved off the table and whirled—

Just in time for Malakai to smash a beaker against his face.

He shouted out in pain. Blinded by glass, he fell back against the table—

It tipped over. Glassware shattered on the floor, chemicals hissing as they ate through the concrete.

"Look what you did to my face!" Travis thundered. He was livid, blood streaming down his forehead, his cheeks. There were bits of glass stuck in his flesh.

Malakai lunged.

Travis ducked to the side, then charged straight for his gut with a furious scream, pushing the Reaper all the way to the farthest wall. They smacked into it with jarring force, Travis's fingers getting pinched between Malakai's back and the wall.

Malakai kicked him in the gut. Still dazed by the beaker incident, Travis staggered backward and nearly fell.

Malakai punched him in the cheek with his right hand. *Thwack.*

The left—the other cheek this time. *Thwack.*

Stars exploded across Travis's vision. He crashed to the floor, landing on shards of glass—

Frost crackled beneath him, spreading over the floor.

Malakai froze, brow creasing. Alfie did the same, the warlock backing up, eyes wide with confusion and fear.

The floor began to shake. The lights began to flicker.

Travis pushed to his feet. He braced a hand against the vibrating wall as the shaking intensified. As more glassware fell off the shelves and shattered.

As the portal spread, more shadows pouring out of it.

The power went out. The room went dark.

Down the hallway, there was a large *crash*.

"Oh my gods," Alfie breathed, his voice choked with fear.

"Wh—" Travis didn't have time to finish his sentence.

Because the Harpy burst through the wall and started attacking them.

"IT'S BEEN AN HOUR," Dallas said. "Where the hell are they?"

Max lay on his back on the boat deck, watching as the shadows of the Void undulated like smoke against the vermilion glow of the forcefield. Those shadows were so thick, he couldn't see the moon or a single star.

Aspen said, "Should one of us go find them and make sure they're okay?"

"We don't even know where they went," Dominic pointed out. "And their auras are hidden, right?"

"Malakai's wearing a talisman, but Travis isn't," Jewels replied.

"Try tracking them if you want," Max chimed in. "But depending on where they went, you might not see them."

A moment passed before Jewels sighed and said, "I'm trying anyway. It's either that or we split up and some of us go looking for them."

"I don't think we should split up," Blue said around clacking teeth.

"Neither do I," Dominic agreed. "And I also don't think you should be the one who tracks them, Jewels."

"I'm already sick, Dom," she said gravely. "Can't get any worse."

"I'd feel better if you'd let me do it."

She sighed and prompted him with a wave of a hand. "Have at her, then."

It was difficult to remotely track someone without the aid of a street drug, but when the distance to your target was short, like it was from this boat to the Black Market, it was doable.

Everyone kept quiet as Dominic shut his eyes and focused.

A moment later, the Angel said, "Wherever they went, it's spell-protected."

Jewels, looking defeated and tired, rubbed her eyes. "Great."

The boat began to shake.

Not just the boat, Max realized. The city was shaking.

He jolted to a sitting position as the rumbling grew.

The portal spread, opening wide like a mouth. More shadows poured out, suffocating the streets several blocks away. People screamed. Max watched in horror as streetlights popped like balloons, the last of the spells on the buildings guttering out.

He thanked the gods when the shaking stopped. When the lights on this street regained a steady glow, the spells on the buildings flickering back to life.

His chest deflated with a relieved sigh. *Close one.*

But his relief was short lived.

Because those were winged demons dive bombing out of the mush-roomed cloud of shadow. And they were heading this way.

IT WAS SO dark in here, Malakai couldn't see shit as the Harpy slammed him against a wall with bruising force.

A talon clamped over his throat. He tried to push the creature off, but it would not let go. Its *strength*—

He couldn't breathe.

Claws pierced the flesh between his neck and shoulder.

He barked a profanity.

The lights buzzed back on and started flashing.

He kicked the Harpy in the stomach.

The force behind the action caused the creature to release him. She staggered backward several paces, wings flapping, her mouth opening with a wide scream—

Malakai barely managed to plug his ears on time. The sound was so fucking loud, it almost made him pass out. Made him scream in return, eyes burning and watering.

Travis was doing the same.

Alfie, however—

That poor bastard wasn't so lucky. The scream had caused him to faint, his head smacking against the floor.

The Harpy lunged for Malakai, and he dipped to the side right on time —so close, her wing swept across his back.

"Come on, man!" Travis shouted. He was at the door, waving an arm. Malakai felt dazed—distant, as if he were dreaming. "Let's go! We have to run!"

Malakai pressed a hand against the blood gushing from his neck—

And as the walls began to shimmer around him, the floor beneath him rotating as if he were trapped inside a kaleidoscope, he realized that those talons—

The Harpy's talons had poisoned him.

"COME ON, MAN!" Travis shouted at Malakai. "Let's go! We have to run!"

Finally, Malakai snapped the hell out of it—what was *wrong* with him? —and moved.

They bolted, Travis twisting mid-run to launch his daggers at the Harpy. One hit the creature in the knee. The other thudded into her chest. But—

Holy shit. She didn't even *flinch*.

Yeah, running was a good plan.

They sprinted down the hallway, their breaths sawing through the air, boots clapping on concrete.

Behind them, the Harpy tore out of the room. With a piercing hunting call, she barreled toward them.

And Travis realized—

They'd gone the wrong way! Shit. This was not the way out!

Together, they screeched to a halt, boots sliding across the floor. There was no way to get back to the exit—not without facing the Harpy.

"Got any bright ideas?" Travis panted.

But Malakai had nothing smart to say. He was pale and sweaty, and he suddenly sagged against the wall.

"Shit," Travis breathed. "Okay—running it is!" He hauled Malakai against his side, draped the Reaper's arm across his shoulders, and started running—into the hallway to his right.

The lights continued to flicker—faster now. As they ran, the hallway changed. Everything modern about it ended, and soon they were not running down a hallway, but a stone tunnel.

Up ahead, waiting to devour them, was a water pipe, the opening taller than both Travis and Malakai put together.

They ran into the pipe, boots clanging against the metal like a struck bell.

Travis looked over his shoulder—

The Harpy was gaining on them.

He whipped back around—

"Oh—whoa. Shit!" He slid to a stop and dug his heels in, his boots nearly going over the edge of the pipe that ended without warning. His arms screamed in protest as he supported Malakai's weight, stopping him from tipping forward. The Reaper looked like he was going to pass out.

This was an abandoned sewer connector. The dried-out pipe they stood in was one of several that had once filtered water into the impossibly deep and dark room looming just beyond the toes of his boots.

He inched closer. Peered down.

Far, far below loomed a pit of black water, the twining bodies of aquatic serpents breaking the scummy surface. Those serpents had to be hundreds of years old—and likely hadn't had a meal in a very long time.

Wings flapped. The Harpy screamed.

She was coming.

Shit, he was going to have to fight this thing on his own, wasn't he?

He leaned Malakai against the curve of the pipe. "Don't move," he said.

Malakai sagged against it with drooping eyelids.

Travis palmed a knife as the Harpy barreled toward him. Chest heaving, heart pounding, he steeled himself, praying that the Harpy would not decide to scream as she closed in on him. The closer she got, the more fatal the scream—which was exactly why they were so hard to kill.

He would have to be very accurate with his throws.

In the corner of his eye, he saw something fall.

Malakai was tipping off the edge.

"Delaney!" Travis reached for him, but he wasn't fast enough, and before he knew it the Reaper was plunging head-first into the serpent-infested water.

87

BELOW
YVESWICH, STATE OF KER

Travis had two options.

1. Fight the Harpy on his own
2. Take his chances with the water serpents

The odds of surviving either were slim to none. But that was Jewels's brother plummeting into the murky depths. And while Travis certainly wouldn't shed a tear if this son of a bitch drowned or got eaten, he cared too much about Jewels to stand by and allow either to happen.

So, he picked option two.

He spun and jumped, the Harpy reaching for him with snapping talons that snagged the back of his jacket.

And then he was in a free fall. Hurtling toward the black water. Wind tore at his clothes and forced tears out of his eyes.

The Harpy unleashed an ear-shattering scream.

Travis cried out in pain. He dropped the knife he was holding, rammed a finger into each ear—

And broke the surface of the water with a stinging *SLAP*.

The velocity behind his descent, combined with the Harpy's dreadful, brain-melting screams, was nearly enough to shove him into oblivion. But the water rushing into his ears was a blessing in disguise. And as gravity sucked him farther down, the distance and the crushing weight of the water rendered her lethal voice powerless.

Safe. He was safe down here.

From the Harpy, anyway. He still had to deal with the serpents. He couldn't decide which was worse.

The water was pitch-black and so cold it shocked his heart into an unsteady rhythm. He gave himself two seconds to gather his bearings, and then he started swimming down.

He made it about six feet when he spotted Delaney. His eyes were shut, body buoyant and drifting.

Travis swam, slicing his arms through the frigid water and rapidly kicking his feet. He had to be quick; he sensed something hunting him.

How the hell he was going to get *out* of here after, he had no clue. That was a problem for near-future Travis.

When he made it to Malakai, he grabbed him around the middle and swam up, using his own air bubbles to guide him toward the surface.

Rows of jagged, arm-length teeth glinted in the murk.

Oh shit.

He paddled backward and ducked his head, narrowly escaping the snapping jaws of a Karkharia, the armor of scales on its impossibly long body passing close enough to touch. He twisted—

Another one was coming.

He dipped left, Malakai a dead weight in his arms.

The Karkharias started swimming laps—walling him in, he realized. In the blink of an eye, there were scales everywhere, the serpents rotating around him in a cyclone. Their bodies were so long and tangled up, to attempt to swim through them would be like fighting through an inescapable maze.

It was terrifying. There was literally nowhere to go.

His lungs began to cramp. Desperate for air, for *life,* he took his chances and swam up.

Up.

Up.

The Karkharias kept spinning, their twining bodies getting closer with each rotation.

He sensed something approaching from behind.

He turned. Saw massive jaws opening.

This was it. This was where he would die—in this watery grave.

He braced himself—

White light drenched the water. So bright, he was forced to shut his eyes.

The serpents screamed and fled, their swift escape generating strong currents that twirled him around and flipped him head over feet. He opened his eyes—

Shit—he could no longer tell where the surface was. And his lungs—

His heart seized, the pain so sharp it was like a knife had been punched into his chest, blade twisting. His vision fuzzed over, the last of the air leaving his lungs in a trickle of bubbles.

Just as he passed out, Malakai drifting out of his hold, he saw a silver-haired woman reaching for him, her body limned with heavenly light.

She had the wings of an angel.

IF MAX MANAGED to survive this, he was going to find Malakai and kill him.

He pulled a knife from its sheath and plunged it into the fleshy throat of the winged demon pinning him to the boat deck. The creature screamed. He wrenched the blade free and stabbed it again. Again. Again. Black blood sprayed and sprayed, until it collapsed on top of him with one last click of its jaws, the sour warmth of its final breath wafting across his face.

With a mighty roar and an upward shove of his legs, he threw the corpse over the side of the boat.

No sooner had it toppled into the canal than another monster just like it was sweeping toward him with open talons, its piercing screech rattling the night.

His sister took that one down with a battle cry and an upward thrust of her hands. Fire blasted steadily out of her red-hot palms, as if her arms were not arms at all, but flamethrowers.

Max flinched away from the sweltering heat, his mind flashing between the present and the horrible past he'd never stopped running from.

Alive, not dead. Alive, not dead. He forced himself to believe it—that his sister really was alive.

Maya had never burned.

She *was* the burning.

As he watched her, with fear and awe, her fire sputtered out. Panting, she sagged forward and braced her hands on her knees.

A monster that looked like a massive bat was swooping toward her.

"*Maya!*" he thundered. "*Look out!*"

She whipped around—

The creature grabbed her under the arms and took off into the air.

Max leapt to his feet and sprinted across the deck, dodging the others who were mid-battle. He grabbed an automated rifle off the bench and started firing. Bullets peppered the creature's wings like a hole puncher. It screamed and plunged into the canal—

With Maya still ensnared in its talons.

"*Max!*" Blue screamed as she drowned another creature with her magic. "Max—*the water!* The water—*she can't be in the water!*"

He dove into the canal and started swimming.

About a dozen meters away, Maya was floundering. Coughing and screaming for help. Screaming Max's name.

Drowning. She was drowning.

How ironic that he would be forced to watch his sister die by water instead. Life was cruel.

"*Maya!*" He swallowed water. Coughed. Swam faster. "Hold on, I'm coming! Hold on—"

Her head went under.

"*MAYA!*"

A current pushed him forward.

It was Blue, standing in the boat hull with outstretched hands, her magic generating a wave in the canal. Max rode that wave straight to where his sister had vanished.

And with a deep breath, he dove.

He found her passed out several feet below the surface, bubbles exiting her slack mouth in a steady stream. He grabbed her around the waist and kicked for the surface.

He broke it with a gasping inhale. "Maya, stay with me!" he shouted, coughing. "Stay with me—I'm going to get you to shore! I'm going to get us to shore!" But as it turned out, getting to shore was the least of his concerns.

Because more monsters were coming. An impossible number of winged nightmares, all heading straight for them.

On the boat, the others were forming a group—guarding each other's backs, weapons raised before them.

Max swam harder. The creatures flew faster.

White, blinding light drenched the block. Blazing brighter than the sun.

He hissed, hand flying over his burning eyes.

The monsters fled, their screams of pain cleaving the air.

As the area fell quiet. The light started to fade.

He tried to open his eyes, but they were burning so badly he had to keep them shut. He kept swimming, groping blindly for the ledge.

A strong hand clasped his. He got out, hauling Maya along with him.

"Thanks," he gasped, not bothering to see who'd helped him out as he lay his sister flat on her back.

"Maya?" he panted.

No reply. He prepared to start chest compressions—

She came to with a burst of phlegmy coughs. He turned her onto her side as she retched up a mouthful of water.

Footsteps clapped down the street. The others were heading this way.

And standing over him with a kind smile, her white wings tucked in tight, was a female hellseher, her hair a hip-length sheet of quicksilver, the ends dripping water onto the cobbles. Her cheekbone was marked with a small tattoo.

The white feather of Vita.

With her were two other winged hellsehers. One male, the other female, both brunette. Their cheekbones were inked with the same tattoo.

"Who are you?" Max rasped. But he no longer cared.

Because Travis was limping this way, his arm wrapped around Malakai's waist. The Reaper looked like he was about to pass out.

Max wasn't sure what surprised him more: the sight of Travis supporting most of Malakai's weight, or the three Sylphen standing before him.

The female with the silver hair spoke, her voice as pleasant as wind chimes. "Your friends here ran into some trouble with a Harpy and a couple of Karkharias in the Below."

Harpy? Karkharias? The *Below*?

What the *hell* had happened?

"You must be Maximus Reacher," she said. She offered him a hand. "My name is Raina Cruso. Head of the House of Violet."

"I CAN'T BELIEVE my brother had the audacity to smash a beaker in your face, and you *still* risked your life to save his stupid ass."

Travis couldn't believe it, either. The prick hadn't even said thank you, but it wasn't like he had expected it. For someone like Malakai, who could hardly make it five minutes without saying something offensive, it was unrealistic to expect things like thank-yous or apologies. The closest he'd come to a thank-you was the night they'd shared a beer on Roman's roof, but it seemed that was a one-off thing.

They were back in the boat. The city was darker now than before he'd gone Below, and there were thin sheets of ice floating in the canal that thunked against the boat as they pushed their way through, the engine working overtime. If the ice got any thicker, they wouldn't be able to travel by canal again.

After Raina had rescued them from the Karkharias and slain the Harpy, then flown them up one by one, she'd introduced herself and explained what she and the two Darkslayers who were with her—Charlotte and Silas were their names—were doing in the Below.

They were looking for a way out. Checking to see if it were possible to slip under the forcefield if they went not just underground, but into a liminal space. Needless to say, their plan had unfortunately confirmed what Travis had already feared.

There was no way out.

They were running out of time—it was clearer now than before he'd gone Below. He swore he could feel Death's cold breath wafting across the back of his neck. All he wanted was to talk to his brothers one more time. Talk to Darien and the other Devils before he died. Was it too much to ask? He knew he'd made a mistake by coming back to Yveswich in the first place, but being stuck here was a cruel punishment.

Max was steering the boat. Raina and the other two Sylphen were flying just ahead—guiding them. If it weren't for Raina and that insane light power she'd used to drive away the monsters, both in the waters Below and at the canals, there was a good chance they'd all be dead right now. Any injuries were minor; even Maya, who'd crashed into the canal, was on her way to recovery, a blanket wrapped around her shoulders. She was cold and wet, yes, but she insisted she'd be okay once she got in front of a fireplace and fully dried off.

"Thank you," Jewels said, her breaths puffing in the air. "For saving him." She slid a hand across Travis's knee and gave it a light squeeze. Her touch warmed his icy blood. "If it weren't for you, he..." She swallowed. Quickly, she took her hand off his knee, as if she hadn't realized she'd put it there, and interlocked her fingers in her lap. "Well, I wouldn't have a brother anymore."

"I did it for you." The confession slipped out before he could stop it.

Her green eyes lit up, and maybe it was the darkness playing tricks on him, but he swore he saw a dusting of blush on her cheeks. "I figured."

The jerk they spoke of was still dazed, his body still in the process of eliminating the poison from the Harpy's talons, but he looked to be improving. Slowly. Aspen was busy stitching up the nasty wound between his neck and shoulder, which she had—wisely—insisted on disinfecting first with the emergency kit she'd found in the boat.

"Hold still," Aspen scolded for the fifth time since leaving the Black Market. She was kneeling beside Malakai on the bench, fighting to keep the needle steady as Malakai fidgeted and swayed and did anything *but* sit still. "I said *hold still,*" she repeated.

"I *am* holding still," Malakai grumbled.

"If you really believe that, I'm concerned," Aspen said. Dominic chuckled.

"It's Reacher's driving," Malakai said. Louder, he said, "He's ass at driving a boat!"

"You're one to talk, Malakai," Max fired over his shoulder. "You drive like you're drunk."

"And you drive like a five-year-old!" Malakai shot back.

Travis snickered and shook his head. "At least he's feeling well enough to argue," he whispered to Jewels.

Jewels gave a soft laugh. "Agreed."

They were heading to the House of Violet—the Darkslayer House that belonged to the Sylphen—to clean up and get some rest. Travis wasn't fully convinced they should be trusting the members of another Darkslaying circle, especially when these people worked for Donovan, but...apparently, they were friends of Malakai's. The same friends he'd mentioned in the recent past, who used to work as Wyverns for Cerise Brinton but had broken away and started their own circle. Malakai claimed they were trustworthy, but... Well, after the events of this evening, Travis had good reason to doubt him.

Regardless, he needed sleep. He was exhausted and soaked to the bone. If the Sylphen killed him in his sleep...well, whatever. It wasn't like he had much longer to live, anyway.

"My brother wasn't really down there for weapons," Jewels whispered, "was he?"

"No," he replied. "He wanted Venom."

She sighed. "Gods, he's an idiot." She could say that again. "Did he end up getting any?"

He shook his head. "Alfie was still cooking it when the Harpy attacked us."

"Good," Jewels said. She looked her brother's way again. "At least he won't be tempted to take any, then."

"Agreed."

As they made their way to the House of Violet, Travis found himself thinking of his family. Darien, Jack, Ivy, Tanner, Lace. Roman and Pax.

Wherever they were, he hoped they were okay.

Wherever they were, he hoped they were safe.

88

THE UMBRA FORUM
ANGELTHENE, STATE OF WITHEREDGE

"What'd you do to your hand?" the Butcher rumbled. He placed a joint between his lips, sparked a lighter, and lit up.

Where he sat across from Casen in his tiny office at the Umbra Forum, Darien settled into a more comfortable position and kicked his booted feet up on the desk, crossing them at the ankles. Even with the door shut, the roar of the audience watching the fights was so loud, the walls and floor quaked, a mug that was stuffed with pens and knives rattling on the desk.

"Got it caught in a car door," Darien replied.

Casen winced. "Ouch." He took a drag so deep his stubbled cheeks hollowed out, then blew three smoke rings at the ceiling, the skunky smell of Boneweed tarnishing the air. His chair creaked as he tipped back, balancing his weight on the back legs. "You want any?" He offered him the joint, the cherry glowing.

"No thanks."

He took another hoot. "All right, what's this favor you mentioned?" he asked, smoke jetting out of his nostrils. "What d'you need?"

"I need you to ask around about any Hobs that have recently been sold through black market avenues," Darien said.

Casen's brow furrowed. "Hobs? Why?" He thumped his chair forward and tapped the end of the joint against the edge of an ashtray. "You missing one?"

"Our house was broken into a little while ago, and my Hob was stolen. I'd like to get him back, but to be honest I don't know where to begin."

"What's he look like?" He twisted to grab a notepad and a pen from the pile of junk scattered across the top of a filing cabinet. "Any identifying features?"

Darien exhaled through his nose. "He's small—only about a foot tall. His eyes are red. He's got webbed feet, and the bottoms are red."

"Webbed?" the Butcher echoed, forehead pinching as he slapped the notepad onto the desk and clicked the pen. "Like a duck?" The pen scratched the page as the Butcher jotted everything down.

"Yeah, sure, like a duck. And he loves ice." His throat tightened, but he cleared it and managed to squeeze out, "Name's Mortifer."

The Butcher's eyes sliced up to meet his, smoke from the joint curling toward the ceiling. "I'll ask around, but I haven't heard anything about any Hobs, least not these last few weeks. Usually, when one's sold through my avenues, I'm the first to know about it."

Darien tried not to frown. "All right," he said with a sigh. "Thanks."

The Butcher was studying his expression. "You look like you could go for a match."

Darien didn't deny it. He was already wearing his fighting clothes, his duffel bag dumped at his feet.

Casen glanced over his shoulder, at the clock that hung on the wall among a collection of crude neon signs. "Next one starts in fifteen, if you're up for a little bloodshed," he said.

"Always." He took his feet off the desk, grabbed his duffel, and stood, slinging the strap over his shoulder. "Any rules I should know about?"

Casen smiled, placed the joint in the ashtray, and got to his feet. "Nah. Just entertain me."

———

THAT WAS EXACTLY what Darien did—and he enjoyed the shit out of it. Too many nights had passed since he'd last had the pleasure of ripping someone apart, and he refused to waste one second of this pure fucking *bliss*.

He set himself loose upon the other fighters in the caged ring. He was an animal—slashing throats, breaking bones, bashing heads against the chain-link.

Four opponents remained. The crowd was losing their minds.

The air whistled as a spiked bat swung for his head.

He ducked and spun, delivering a roundhouse kick to the side of the guy's head. As he went down, Darien took the bat out of his hands—

And whacked it against the man's head so hard the bat broke in half. Wood splintered, red pulp misting the air. The crowd screamed louder—

An attack came from behind him.

He spun, punching his fingers through the vampire's throat—then ripped that throat clean out.

He grabbed another man by the head and twisted. *Crunch,* went his neck.

One fighter remained. He was cowering in the corner of the ring, gripping a crowbar with white-knuckled hands. On shaking legs, he stepped forward and swung—

Darien snatched the crowbar out of his grip and whipped it aside.

The man backed away. "P-please."

He hated when they begged. They were the ones who willingly walked into this ring, for fuck's sake. If you couldn't fight, stay in the audience.

"Hit me," Darien said. He prowled forward, boots thumping as he backed the man into the corner. "If you can hit me," he continued, heart pumping with adrenaline, "I'll let you live." It was an empty promise—this match would crown only one person the victor. And that victor would be him.

Regardless, the warlock took his chances and swung—

Darien evaded his fist with ease, then delivered a few punches of his own, alternating hands. On the third strike, the man crashed against the cage wall and fell. Darien threw himself on top of him and laid into his face with bloody knuckles—

He blacked out. When he came back to himself, it was to the ear-splitting squall of a bullhorn and the wild screaming of a blood-hungry audience.

The ring announcer jumped into the cage. As Darien got to his feet, the announcer grabbed his wrist and thrust his hand skyward, declaring him victor to a crowd that roared and stamped their feet.

Darien ripped his arm free and climbed out of the cage.

ABOUT AN HOUR LATER, Darien wrapped a towel around his waist and pushed the stained shower curtain aside, the metal rings screeching across the rusty pole.

The moment the group of men gossiping in the change room caught sight of him stepping out of the shower stall, they fell silent. One of them coughed. Another cleared his throat.

Darien was well aware that he was the topic of their conversation. He'd heard them yapping while he showered, their voices muffled by the stream of the scalding hot water as he'd scrubbed off all the gore. Apparently, they had not expected him to be in here.

"You got something to say," he began, voice echoing in the sudden quiet as he crossed the drafty room that stank of sweat and mildew, "say it to my face."

No one spoke.

Water rolled down his back and dripped off his hair as he sauntered to where he'd left his duffel bag on the bench and pulled out a set of clean clothes.

The men—all of them—grabbed their shit and left.

He got dressed, stuffed his bloody clothes into a garbage bag, then sat on the bench and pushed his feet into his boots. He'd just finished lacing them up when he heard a sound.

Gunshots—rapid-fire gunshots popping through the building.

Upstairs, people screamed.

Footsteps thundered.

More gunshots.

Muffled shouting. Someone was barking orders, but the voices were too far away to make out what they were saying.

The door banged open. The Butcher rushed in, pale-faced and panting.

Darien shot to his feet. "Hell's going on?"

"Cops," Casen gasped. "They're raiding the place. Hurry—you gotta go before they see you—"

"What about you?" Quickly, he slung the strap of his duffel bag over his shoulder. "You can't stay here, either—they'll arrest you."

"I'm going Below," he panted. "They can't catch me there. Follow me."

He grabbed the rest of his things and left the change room. The Butcher led the way, down blue-lit hallways and around corners, until they reached a row of attached lockers pressed up against the wall.

He grabbed onto an edge and pulled. Metal scraped across the floor as he hauled the lockers away from the wall, exposing a squat doorway that had been cut into the concrete behind it. "Get in."

Darien squished behind the lockers and bent down far enough to see inside.

It was an old sewer tunnel. The waterway was dried up, the smooth stones of the arched walls shining like emeralds in the mercury vapor lantern-light.

He ducked inside.

"This'll take you out by the river overpass," Casen said, his words echoing in the dank space. "Don't come back to the market until you get the okay from me."

Before Darien had a chance to reply, he was pushing the lockers against the wall and sealing him inside the tunnel.

Lace Rivera drummed her spiky black fingernails against the steering wheel of her car—a black model similar to her favorite red one that had been towed to a wrecking yard—watching as the moonlight glinted across the swift currents of the Angelthene River, like swirls of cream in black tea.

She was parked several blocks from the Umbra Forum. Ivy was in the passenger's seat, Jack and Kylar in the back. They had combed the streets in Angelthene's seediest districts for almost four hours, but they had nothing to show for their time. They would have to try this again tomorrow. And the night after that. And the night after that. They wouldn't rest until they found Gaven Payne. Darien wanted every person that had trespassed on their property hunted down and done away with. There were a few he was saving for himself, but Gaven was the one they all wanted.

They would take that son of a bitch out together.

Ivy turned on her phone screen and checked the clock. "He probably blacked out and lost track of time," she said. She shut off the screen.

"Should one of us go in and find him?" Kylar asked.

"Absolutely not," Ivy replied. "That's a strict *no* in our house."

Jack said, "How late is he?"

"About twenty minutes. I'm sure he'll be here soon."

A fist pounded on the window.

Lace jumped. "Gods above," she breathed, her heart skipping like a stone as she beheld the dark, hooded figure standing by her door.

She lowered the glass. "You scared the shit out of me."

Darien was out of breath. "Cops are raiding the Umbra Forum. Arresting a bunch of people—"

Jack said, "What, why?"

Ivy added, "What's going on?"

"I don't know. But I plan on finding out. Ivy, Kylar—I want you to come with me. Lace, Jack—go back to the house. Make sure Loren's fine. And call me if anything's up."

"Copy," Lace said. She started the engine.

Kylar and Ivy left with Darien, and Jack climbed into the front.

"I hate missing out on all the fun," Jack grumbled.

"Yeah, well, the cops are probably looking for you still, so it's better if you lie low."

Just then, multiple police sirens punctured the quiet. Behind them, in front of them, and across the river, red and blue lights flickered.

"What is happening?" Jack breathed.

"I don't know," Lace said. She put the gear in drive. "Let's get out of here."

SEVERAL BLOCKS NORTH of the Umbra Forum, Darien rolled his car to a stop by the Angelthene River and watched the cops and detectives bustling about the crime scene they'd sectioned off with yellow caution tape.

"Looks like a homicide," Kylar murmured as he leaned forward in the passenger's seat with all-black eyes.

"I can't say I'm surprised," Ivy said. Darien wasn't, either. This area suffered from a lot of crime. Homicides were a daily occurrence.

He searched the huddle of cops and MPU agents for any familiar faces. Two in particular. He didn't see that Glen prick, but—

A broad-shouldered male detective was crouching beside the body. When he straightened, his tan hand holding a phone against his ear, Darien caught just enough of his side profile to confirm who it was.

He pulled out his own phone and typed a message.

DARIEN

Turn around.

When Finn ended his call, he checked the screen.

He turned, the silver rings around his pupils reflecting the glow of passing headlights as his eyes found the car. Then he glanced around, checking to make sure no one was watching as he typed a reply—

Darien's phone buzzed in his hand.

FINN

This isn't a good time.

DARIEN

When is?

FINN

An hour from now.

DARIEN

Meet me at the Doghouse. And don't show up looking like that, or you'll get eaten alive.

"What's he saying?" Kylar asked.

"I told him to meet us at the Doghouse."

89

THE DOGHOUSE
ANGELTHENE, STATE OF WITHEREDGE

Darien's head was *pounding*. Harder than the music shaking the floor beneath his combat boots. Harder than the fists of the two men beating the shit out of each other across the room, bouncers in the midst of breaking up the fight.

The subterranean strip club was packed. When they'd first arrived, the bouncers had recognized him and Ivy and hooked them up with a table at the back—farther from the stage, where dolled-up dancers twirled on silver poles beneath strobe lights, and closer to the bar, where a couple of topless witches poured drinks, their silhouettes obscured by a thick screen of Boneweed and cigarette smoke.

Finn was supposed to have been here ten minutes ago.

Usually, he would've had zero problem with all of this—the crowds, the pounding music, the cloying reek of perfume, alcohol, vomit, and body odor. But after fighting at the Chopping Block and sweating out the last of the Venom in his system, his withdrawals were already back.

With a fucking vengeance.

The mishmash of scents nauseated him. The cacophony of music, shouting, laughter, and clinking glasses raked across his skull like nails on a chalkboard. He felt like he was crawling out of his damn skin. He could hardly sit still.

Another five minutes that felt more like twenty dragged by before a man approached their table, his features concealed by a heavy hood and the low brim of a ball cap.

"I was under the impression that we'd be meeting alone," Finn said quietly.

"I gave you no such impression," Darien replied, his own face partially obscured by the shadows beneath the hood of his black sweatshirt. He sipped his beer—lukewarm and watered down—and added, "Anything you have to say, you can say it in front of my sister and my friend, too."

Finn glanced over his shoulder, at the crowds of customers talking and laughing and drinking at the tables surrounding the stage. He relented with a sigh and sat down. "You couldn't have picked somewhere a bit easier to find?" He dragged his chair in.

"You've never been here before?"

"I've heard of it," Finn said. "But I've never *been* here, no. And I expected it to, you know, have a normal door." Right—not the flat cellar-style doors. "I walked by this place three times before I figured it out. I thought it was a door to the Below." He folded his arms on the table. "I'm guessing you asked to meet up because you're curious about the crime scenes."

"Crime scenes?" Ivy repeated, idly swirling the wine in her glass. "Was there more than just the incident at the river?" She sipped.

"There've been over a dozen attacks tonight," Finn said. Ivy raised her brows. "And the only reason I'm telling you this is because I know you're connected in some way to everything that's happening in Yveswich."

"You'd better not be blaming us," Darien warned.

"Not at all. I don't agree with what my colleague put you through, and I have no intention of doing the same. But, if you have any information to share, I could use all the help I can get."

Ivy said, "Tell us about these attacks."

"Every victim so far has been human, half, venefica, werewolf, vampire —you name it. The offenders are...of the hellseher population," he finished, speaking hesitantly. Cautiously. "We've managed to apprehend only two of the offenders and have brought them in for questioning, but that won't be happening until tomorrow morning. We have them in holding cells until then."

Darien said, "What kind of attacks are we talking about here?"

Finn leaned in close. "The victims...," he began with a whisper. His throat bobbed. He began again. "The victims...they were all bitten to death."

"*Bitten* to death?" Ivy and Kylar hissed.

Their conversation stalled as people walked by their table.

As soon as they were gone, Ivy whispered, "And you said these people are *hellsehers?*"

Finn nodded, his face a grave mask. "Earlier this evening, we responded to an emergency call—the first of the night. We managed to get there just in time to see the attack happen. The offender... He had black eyes with dark lines in the surrounding skin." He indicated to his own under-eye with a pinky finger.

"Like Venom users?" Kylar asked, glancing Darien's way.

Finn nodded.

"Is that why the cops raided the Umbra Forum?" Darien asked. "Because they think Venom is the cause?"

"That was Glen's call." Of course it was. "I tried to tell him that we should wait until we get the results from the autopsies, but he insisted on getting a head-start on taking down the drug operations. He accused us of letting it go on for too long." He paused for a moment, his nostrils flaring with irritation. Once he'd composed himself, he continued. "They shut the whole thing down, fighting rings too, and arrested every dealer, vendor, and buyer they could get their hands on."

"Shit," Darien hissed. He scrubbed a hand down his face. He would need to find other avenues for the talismans, then.

And salt. In a city this large, with endless covert operations at his disposal, you'd think it would be a cinch. But securing a new dealer would take up more of his time.

He'd see if he could get in contact with the Butcher, somehow. Tomorrow. The task wouldn't be easy; now that Casen had gone Below, into a liminal space that was guaranteed to be a dead zone...

But he'd rather go through the Butcher than piss his own time away looking for a new dealer. With everything that was going on, he didn't have time for that.

"Why's Glen making the calls?" he demanded. "I thought you were Head Detective."

"Not anymore."

"Did you step down?"

"I was demoted."

"What for?"

Ivy added, "Are they allowed to do that?"

"If there's a good enough reason," Finn replied. "Long story short, they didn't like the questions I was asking." Why did that not surprise him? After everything he'd seen on the news, with the imperator covering up all the shit happening in Yveswich, it made sense that he'd attempt to conceal any other eerie happenings that were linked to the Veil, too. Less eyes on him—less shit for the public to freak out about. "They want someone who takes orders and keeps their mouth shut, and I guess I'm having a hard time being that for them."

"So they took away your position," Ivy concluded, shaking her head in disappointment.

"For now. And gave it to Glen."

"What else do you know about these attacks?" Darien asked. "What makes them think it's the Venom, anyway? Just the eyes? That hardly seems like concrete evidence."

"Personally, I don't think it's the Venom." He tossed a glance over his shoulder to make sure no one was listening, watching. "I think there's a link between these attacks and what's going on in Yveswich," he whispered.

Darien said, "Explain."

"Reports of these attacks started pouring in the night of the explosion, beginning with Yveswich, and since then similar incidents have been popping up in most major cities across the continent."

"Only the major cities?" Darien asked. "Which ones? Be specific."

He sighed and rubbed his chin. "So far? Yveswich, Tyrmouth, Whispervale, Shadowhaven, and now Angelthene."

Ivy and Kylar looked his way. He knew what they were thinking.

Were these all major cities that ran along the seam? The sealing points that Helia had used to erect the Veil, possibly?

"So, if you don't think it's the Venom," Ivy began, "then what *do* you think it is?"

"PCR tests point to the emergence of a lethal, highly pathogenic virus they're calling the *Venenum virus.*"

Darien made a sound of irritation in his throat. "They're really trying to blame the Venom, aren't they?"

"If you ask me, I don't think they're out of line for taking precautions regarding the drug," Finn said. "There's a strong possibility that Venom, due to its supernatural origins and chemical makeup, could be contributing to the spread. Making it more contagious, perhaps—I don't really know."

Darien scowled. *Great.* If only he'd known this before he'd taken a dose at Hell's Gate.

Finn continued, "We still have a ways to go before we have all the answers, but this is the only thing that makes sense right now. The cities are all too spaced out. So, the chances of the virus being airborne..." He sighed through his nose. "Even if Venom's not the cause, we'd be stupid not to look into it."

"How many of the attackers had Venom in their blood?" Darien pressed.

"That's...a difficult question to answer. Once the high wears off, the drug is undetectable in blood tests, so by the time our coroners get around to conducting the autopsies, they can't find any trace of the drug."

Darien scoffed. "So, basically, you don't know jack-shit," he concluded. Judging from Finn's answering frown, he didn't appear to be a fan of that statement.

Kylar chimed in. "You said you managed to arrest a couple of the offenders. Did you run tests on them?"

"We drew blood, yes, but the results aren't in yet. Whether we were fast enough this time remains to be seen."

A hush fell over the table, everyone processing the information.

Finn said, "My question for you guys is this: Can you tell me anything about what's happening in Yveswich?"

Ivy and Kylar shared a glance. Looked at Darien.

"I'm not saying you're responsible for any of it," Finn said. "But photographs don't lie. Street cameras caught you going into Caliginous on Silverway the night of the explosion." When they still didn't say anything, Finn pressed, "Look, this is serious. If we don't get to the bottom of this, it could have a detrimental effect on the hellseher population. It's happening already—fear mongering is causing hellsehers in positions of authority to temporarily be demoted or laid off. A few of my buddies in the hellseher division are currently on paid leave—and these are people who don't even take Venom. This could cause a rift in society, and I would like to avoid it if we can."

Darien thought it through. It was horseshit that they were singling out hellsehers so quickly into their investigation. And while he knew he and his Devils could wind up in the line of fire if this continued to escalate, being as they were not only hellsehers but *Darkslayers*, people who were already under the radar for their unconventional way of living...

He couldn't risk it. He didn't trust Finn enough to let him in.

Finn waited, looking desperate, hands open in silent request.

"I'm sorry," Darien said. But he didn't sound sorry at all.

Finn's shoulders sank, the hope fading out of his eyes.

Darien finished off the last of his beer and added, "We don't know anything."

As they drove back to Heaven's Gate, they discussed everything they'd learned from Finn.

Kylar said, "You think those cities all run along the seam?"

"They could," Darien said. "There are only three people who would know for sure: Erasmus, Cyra, and Tamika." He ticked them off on his fingers. They couldn't ask the latter, since she was still in an induced coma —Sabrine had called Loren to update her after going by herself to the hospital to bring flowers to Tamika. But as for Erasmus and Cyra...

He and Loren would be paying those two a visit tomorrow. With Roark.

"You haven't been taking any Venom," Ivy asked, eyeing him, "have you?"

They were in the North End now, fancy-as-fuck houses flitting by. The expensive protection spells covering the spotless streets rippled across the corners of his vision, like light filtering through a prism in multi-colored streams.

"No," he replied. "I *have* Venom, but I won't take it. I promise."

She accepted with a shallow nod. "Okay." But she didn't sound convinced.

"Loren's going to get me on a tonic," he added.

"A tonic?" Kylar echoed.

"Yeah, she works at an apothecary—she's good with plants. She said it'll help push the Venom out of my system faster. It would usually take a week, maybe ten days to get over the worst of the symptoms, but she said this tonic will halve the time." Every time he thought he couldn't possibly love her more, she did something else that proved him wrong.

"Good," Ivy said. This time, her smile was real. Possibly the first real smile she'd given him since all the shit that went down in Yveswich. He'd been wanting to talk to her for a while—since the night she'd stormed out on him back at Roman's—but no words felt good enough. "Good, Darien," she said again. "I'm proud of you."

"Thanks." He gave her a half-smile.

She returned it, but hers didn't touch her eyes.

He hated hurting his sister. But he didn't know how to fix this, how to tell her that he was sorry.

When they made it back to Heaven's Gate, Darien checked on Loren while Kylar and Ivy filled in the others—those who were awake, anyway—

on everything they'd learned from Finn about the attacks and the Venenum virus. Tanner was right where they'd left him at the dining room table, still hard at work restoring communications in Ker, a fresh pot of coffee brewing in the kitchen.

As for Loren, she was fast asleep. Darien had asked her to sleep without a talisman on, for two reasons. One was to preserve the magic of the talismans, since they were getting hard to find and she was safe and completely hidden inside these walls. The second reason was so he could check on her aura.

Blue was still the most vibrant shade, thanks to her swim at the recreational center. The others, though, were dim. *All* of them were dim, including white, which was usually her brightest. But her tattoos hadn't changed since he'd left the house, so he took it as a sign that she'd be okay for the night. He'd be up here soon, and he couldn't wait for that. To sleep in the same bed as her. Hold her and listen to her precious heartbeat.

He grabbed a change of clothes and went to another room to put them on, so he wouldn't wake her up. Then he went downstairs, where he grabbed a plastic zip-lock bag of Stygian salts from the kitchen drawer.

He stayed there on that couch for the next few hours. Searching for the missing members of his family. Travis—who he felt like he'd failed. And Max—who he owed an apology over that stupid-as-fuck argument that never should have happened. His best friends. His brothers.

But no dice. The more time that passed without at least *one* of them showing up, the more worried he got. The more salt he snorted. The more time he spent attempting to track them in the abyss of his mind.

He had to find them.

He *had* to find them.

90

HEAVEN'S GATE
ANGELTHENE, STATE OF WITHEREDGE

It was just after dawn when Loren awoke the following day to the cooing of mourning doves. She yawned and stretched, reaching for Darien—

But his side of the bed was empty, the sheets cold.

She blinked her tired eyes. Half-asleep and confused, she sat up, scanning the space, looking for any sign of Darien.

She frowned. Had he gotten up already?

The hardwood floor threatened to freeze her toes off as she got out of bed and crossed the room, stepping over Bandit's rubber chicken that had been chewed within an inch of its life. She eased the door open and quietly made her way downstairs.

The house was bathed in the silvery light of a rainy spring dawn. The blinds on the windows that overlooked the backyard were open; she could see Jack tending to the in-ground swimming pool, his jacket sparkling with drops of rain. He appeared to be scolding his Familiar, Twitch, but to no avail. The jaguar was a menace—running laps around the pool, knocking over flower pots, and simply being a rambunctious pain in Jack's butt. Bandit was out there, too; it looked like he and Twitch were teaming up to wreck Jack's morning.

She slowed when she spotted Tanner at the kitchen table. He was asleep in front of his laptop, his head resting on his folded arms. Curled up by his feet was Silver the wolf, his guttural snores sawing through the air.

Maybe I should go back upstairs, she thought. She didn't want to wake them—

She was about to turn around when she spotted Darien—fast asleep on the couch in the living room. He was lying on his stomach, his head turned to the side, one arm curled around a throw pillow.

Gods, was he beautiful. She loved him so much, it hurt. Seeing someone as dangerous as him in rare, vulnerable moments like this, when the lethal edges of his face were softened with sleep...it never got old. Ever.

As she stood there, admiring him, fighting the urge to go over to him and kiss him awake, something caught her attention.

Bloody tissues and zip-lock bags of Stygian salts were scattered across the coffee table, most of the salt used.

The breath left her lungs in a quiet, disappointed sigh.

How long had he been tracking? Judging from the alarming number of blood-soaked tissues, the answer was *too long*.

She tiptoed across the rug to get a closer look at him—

Oh gods.

She crept even closer, her stomach tightening into knots.

Oh gods, was he not breathing?

Her heart started to race. She flattened a hand against his back—

And felt it rise with a slow inhale.

She let out her own breath.

Breathing. He was breathing.

The stick of bare feet on the floor pulled her focus to the hallway.

A yawning Ivy was coming this way with bedhead. Soot, her blue-eyed dog Familiar, mirrored the yawn with one of her own. Following a short distance behind them was Lace and her purring cat Familiar.

When Ivy spotted Loren standing there, with her hand flattened upon Darien's rising and falling back, she froze, her eyes flaring with alarm. "Is he okay?" she mouthed.

Loren nodded and straightened, her hand slipping off Darien's warm, muscular back. He was sleeping so deeply, he didn't even stir.

Lace came over to stand beside Ivy, the two female slayers taking note of the salt and the tissues. They shared a look and a frown. And then Lace walked to where Tanner was asleep at the table and woke him up by gently squeezing his shoulders.

He mumbled sleepily. "What's going on?" he slurred. He lifted his head, his cheek indented with the shape of the watch on his wrist—

Ivy pressed a finger against her lips. "Shh," she whispered. She pointed that finger at where Darien lay on the couch.

Tanner got up, craning his neck to see Darien. When he spotted him, he frowned, too.

"Can I talk to you?" Loren whispered. "All of you." She beckoned for them to follow.

They did. Loren led the way, looking for a good place to talk. She settled with the sitting room at the front of the house. They were far enough away that Darien shouldn't be able to hear them, but Loren still opted to whisper.

"How long was he tracking?" she asked. Her question was for Tanner, who was rubbing his right eye, still half-asleep.

He checked his watch. "Two or three hours, maybe? He was still at it when I passed out, and that was around four."

"He can't keep doing this," Loren hissed. "He's going to hurt himself."

"Agreed," Lace said.

"I think we all agree, but how can we convince him to stop?" Tanner asked.

Lace said, "We can offer to take turns. Today, I'll do the tracking, and Ivy—you can take over for the evening. That'll give him a full day of rest."

But Ivy was already shaking her head. "He'll never agree to it. He *knows* we aren't as good at tracking as he is."

"What do you mean?" Loren whispered. "I thought you guys were all good at tracking."

"We are, when the targets are close by," Lace said. "That's why Dark-slayers have designated cities or zones. It's not just a territory thing—tracking is a lot harder when a target is far away. And with Ker being as far as it is..." She trailed off, her mouth shifting into a frown.

Loren nibbled on her bottom lip, thinking. "I want you to try anyway."

"He won't listen," Ivy said.

"Make him. *Please.* I don't want him to hurt himself—"

"Talking about me?" said a deep, attractive voice.

Loren whirled.

Darien stood in the doorway, his dark hair all messy, a handsome little smile on his sleepy face.

"No," she blurted.

He leaned against the wall, sliding his hands into the pockets of his black sweatpants. That smile grew, his dimple almost—*almost*—making an appearance. It was still a real smile, though, even without that adorable dimple. And it was all for her. "You're such a little liar." That voice, so low and growly, sent a rush of heat to her face.

And lower, too. Even while in the process of waking up, her head groggy, her body was already begging to feel him inside her again. The fun she'd had with him yesterday was so good, she'd fallen asleep dreaming of how it had felt. She'd hoped he would come to bed when he got back last night and wake her by stripping off her clothes, as he so often did, but...

Well, she hadn't been that lucky.

Lace cleared her throat. "I'll put the coffee on." She took her leave.

"I'll, umm..." Tanner scratched the back of his neck. "I'll give Lacey a hand." And then he was gone too, and it was just Ivy and Loren left.

And the blue-eyed Darkslayer in the doorway, who was still staring at her.

"I guess making coffee is now a two-person job," he said, those eyes dancing.

"I actually want to talk to Loren for a second, please, brother," Ivy piped up. When he didn't move, she added, "Alone."

But he didn't get the memo. His eyes were fastened on Loren, the intensity in his stare making her blush.

Ivy waved her hands in a *shoo* motion. "Go on. Go. Give us some privacy."

He shrugged away from the wall and backed into the foyer.

"Farther!" Ivy called.

He took one step back—just one. "This is far enough."

Loren had to press her lips together to stop a laugh from bubbling out. Darien must have noticed, because next thing she knew, he was cracking a grin so bright, it almost knocked her right off her feet.

"No, it's not!" Ivy argued. "You can still hear us from there!"

"I'll put a sound barrier up."

"No!" Ivy's response was practically a growl, and she looked like she was strongly debating ripping her hair out. "No more magic for you! I'll do it." She sighed. "Stubborn ass."

He really was stubborn. *Darien 'Stubborn' Cassel,* was right. How were they supposed to convince him to take breaks from tracking when he refused to even do *this?*

One firm blink turned Ivy's eyes black. Loren felt her magic form a bubble around them, the black curve sparkling with faint colors in the morning light streaming in through the blinds.

Then she blinked the black away and took a moment to consider what she wanted to say.

"I want to apologize," she began in a soft voice.

"For what?" Loren asked. But she had a feeling she already knew.

"I haven't been nice to you lately, and...well, to be honest, I'm ashamed of myself. The bargain was my brother's decision, and I shouldn't have treated you as if you encouraged him to do it. I just..." She crossed her arms and stared at a corner of the room, her eyes glassy. "I love my brother. He's been there for me for literally ever. And I don't want to lose him," she admitted, her voice cracking with emotion. She slid her teary eyes to Loren and whispered, "But I love you too, Loren. You're like a sister to me."

Loren's eyes stung, her throat so tight she couldn't swallow.

"I don't want to lose you, either," Ivy continued. "This whole situation is just..." She sighed deeply. "Fucked up," she concluded with a hard, forced laugh. "You're a part of our family now, and the thought of losing either of you..." Her eyes flicked to her brother—her amazing brother, who, Loren knew, even without looking, was watching them. Watching *her*. Quieter, Ivy said, "You've changed him. And I mean that as the highest compliment. Before you came along, he wasn't...he just wasn't happy," she confessed with a sigh. "He always had more lows than he did highs. And I know he isn't perfect, I know he still has a lot of demons he's fighting, but...you've really brought him to life, Loren. You made someone who always wanted to die want to start living instead. You saved him. And I can't thank you enough for that."

Loren swallowed the lump in her throat. "You don't have to thank me, Ivy," she whispered. This was so unexpected, she had to try not to burst into tears. "I should be the one thanking you—for everything you guys have done for me..." She would never be able to repay them. Everything they'd done, everything they'd sacrificed... It was too much.

"You're a part of our family," Ivy repeated. "No matter what happens, that will always be true. From now on, I promise to manage my emotions better and not take them out on you. Okay?"

"I'm not angry with you for being upset," Loren insisted. "I hope you know that. And..." She glanced over her shoulder. Darien was leaning against the front door, pretending to be interested in the chandelier. He sure was adorable for someone so dangerous. "I'm just as upset as you," she continued. "I was just taking my emotions out on him instead." She tried to smile, but she was too emotional.

"Will you forgive me?"

"Of course I forgive you."

Ivy opened her arms to her.

Loren stepped forward, and they embraced.

"Love you," Ivy said again, squeezing her tight.

"I love you, too," Loren breathed, squeezing her back.

"Okay, Darien!" Ivy called, dropping her magic as they broke apart. "You can have her back now!"

By the time Loren turned to look at him, he was already in the room, as if he couldn't wait to get in here.

"I hope you guys are hungry," Ivy said as she tightened the string of her black robe and walked into the kitchen. "I'm making pancakes."

Loren barely heard her. Because Darien was in front of her then, stepping so close, he snatched the air out of her lungs.

"Good morning," he said, that bass tone making her heart skip, her body turning all warm and fuzzy.

She interlocked her fingers before her. "Good morning."

His eyes dipped to her lips, then dragged down her body...slowly... The longer he looked at her, the hotter his stare got. She loved when he looked at her this. "How'd you sleep?"

"Fine."

His brow scrunched with curiosity, a crooked little smile pulling on his mouth. "Is that my shirt?" He tipped his head to one side.

She crossed her arms. "No."

"Did you take it out of my bag?"

She had to bite the inside of her cheek to keep from laughing. "Maybe."

That smile grew, his dimple making an appearance. "You little thief."

"You didn't come to bed last night," she said.

His smile vanished. "No, I...passed out." He scratched at the back of his neck she was absolutely certain didn't itch. "Must have been really tired," he added.

"Darien," she reproached. "You were tracking for way too long." He opened his mouth, but before he could argue, she said, "Please don't lie. Tanner said you were tracking for two or three hours."

He shut his mouth. Set his jaw.

"I'd like for you to stop pushing yourself so hard," she said. "Please."

A tense beat of silence followed her request.

Slowly, his features sank into a very deep frown.

Her heart started to pound, but she stayed the course, well aware that his family was listening. They were pretending they weren't, but she had lived with them all long enough that she could tell. "I already talked to the others," she said. "They're going to take turns looking for Max and Travis so you can have breaks."

He shut his eyes. "Baby...," he began with a hoarse whisper. "You're asking me to stop looking for my family?" When he opened his eyes, he looked tortured, his pupils flaring so big they almost swallowed the blue.

"No. I'm asking you to let the rest of your family help."

"They can't hold the Sight for as long as I can."

"We knew you were going to say that," Ivy said in a singsong voice as she grabbed a mixing bowl out of the cupboard.

Tanner drawled, "Aaaaaand here comes the argument..."

Darien turned his head toward the kitchen. "What is this, an intervention?" he called.

"Yes," Loren said. To her surprise, her reply was echoed by Ivy, Tanner, *and* Lace, everyone's voices melding into one.

Darien blinked. But his surprise was quickly fading, his focus returning to Loren. "Sweetheart, if they're in Yveswich, it's going to be really hard to find their auras from here," he explained, his tone gentle. "I'm the only one who's found targets from this many miles away."

"Darien—" She tightened her crossed arms, fingers grasping the soft fabric of his shirt that fell past her thighs. "You said you want me to start taking better care of myself—right?"

A muscle feathered in his jaw, but he said, "Right."

"Well, it goes both ways." She fiddled with the shirt. "I would like you to take it easy, please."

The back door opened, and Jack walked in, shaking his hood off. "Sup, fam?" He whipped the door shut.

"Shh!" Ivy hissed.

Jack's brow creased. "What?" he mouthed.

"We're going to find them," Tanner called from the kitchen. He came to stand in the doorway to the sitting room, a mug of steaming coffee in hand. He took a sip. "I'm going to get communications back up, Darien, I promise. And then we're going to get them the hell out of there."

Darien's brows rose, but he kept his eyes on Loren. "This really is an intervention," he said, almost to himself.

Footsteps sounded on the stairs. A moment later, Kylar and Eugene appeared, walking toward the kitchen.

When Kylar spotted them—spotted Ivy, Lace, and Jack coming to stand with Tanner in a small army—he said, "Just wait a sec, Gene." He yanked on the back of his brother's shirt, pulling him up short. "They're having a family meeting or something."

"But I'm hungry," the kid whined.

Loren looked at Darien with expectance.

He looked back at her. And then he sighed and said, "All right, baby. Okay."

"Okay, what?" she pressed. She wanted him to promise.

"I won't push myself so hard with the tracking," he said.

She tried not to look surprised, but she was. She hadn't expected this to go so smoothly. "Do you promise?"

"I promise."

The others dispersed, returning to their cups of coffee, Ivy opening the fridge door to grab the rest of the ingredients for pancakes.

And then Darien was sweeping Loren off her feet, making her shriek in surprise, and carrying her bride-style into the kitchen.

"When are you guys meeting Roark?" Ivy asked as Darien navigated everyone in the kitchen. Loren tucked her legs in so she wouldn't kick Lace, who was stirring cream and sugar into her coffee.

"Ten," Darien replied, checking the time on the clock as he kicked out a chair at the table. He lowered Loren to her feet, and she practically fell into the seat, her head still spinning. Darien held onto her, not letting go until he was certain she wouldn't faint.

"What kind of tea would you like?" he asked her.

"Green, please."

Jack said, "Make sure to videotape Erasmus's reaction." He set a bottle of syrup on the table. "He's going to shit his pants the minute he sees you *and* Roark on his doorstep."

The thought of facing both of her fathers at the same time made her feel entirely different butterflies—the bad kind, not the kind still swarming in her stomach from Darien. She was nervous, but—

She wanted answers. And it was high time she got them.

———

"ALL RIGHT THEN, what can I do for you, kid?" The Butcher's voice was so low and grumbly, it vibrated the phone speakers.

Darien sat on the edge of the fountain out front of Heaven's Gate. Loren was inside, putting on her shoes and jacket.

He checked his watch. It was almost time to meet Roark at Erasmus's townhouse in Oceana. Time to finally get some answers to all these questions brewing up a storm in everyone's heads.

Just him and Loren were going. The others were staying here. Kylar, Lace, Ivy, and Jack would be taking turns tracking while Tanner kept up with his efforts to restore communication channels in Ker. Darien knew it was unlikely that the others would be able to pick up on auras from this far away—they didn't have enough experience tracking beyond the boundaries of Angelthene for that—but he'd made a promise to Loren. And he didn't break promises—not when he made them to her.

He only hoped Atlas would win the fight—and quickly. If they didn't find out where Travis and Max were—and kickstart their plan to break them the hell out of Yveswich, if they really were trapped in there—he just might lose his grip on sanity.

"I need you to hook me up with as many Avertera talismans as you can get your hands on," Darien replied.

The Butcher grunted. "That might be tough."

"How tough?"

"They're getting hard to find, and the price has spiked like you wouldn't believe."

"Oh, I believe," Darien said. He blamed himself for the lack of inventory and the spike in cost. He'd bought so many of them since meeting Loren, it was only realistic to expect this would happen eventually.

"It'll take me some time, but I can probably bring a few in for you from Tyrmouth."

"How long do you think it'll take?"

His thoughtful exhale rattled the phone. "Few days. How urgent is it?"

"Urgent," he stressed.

"I'll do my best."

The front door opened, and Loren walked out, her rain jacket draped over her arm.

"That your girl?" the Butcher asked.

"Yeah, I gotta go."

"I'll call you as soon as I get my hands on some."

"Thanks." He hung up and met Loren halfway down the driveway. She wore her hair down today, the soft waves and loose ringlets bouncing with every step. As they drew closer to each other, a little smile tugged up the corners of her full lips. And that splash of freckles on her nose...

Fuck, was she beautiful, or what? He was the luckiest man in the world.

All he needed now was to get Travis, Max, and Mortifer back home, and everything would be right in his world.

"Ready, gorgeous?"

She drew a deep breath, then blew it out slowly. "I'm nervous," she confessed.

He took her hand into his and laced their fingers. "I'll be right there with you for all of it," he vowed. He lifted her hand to his mouth, kissed the back of it, and added, "Forever."

She smiled, those stunning, ocean-blue eyes twinkling. Rain began to fall as she surged up onto her toes, tipping her face skyward. Darien bent down, their mouths brushing as she whispered, "Forever," and kissed him.

91

THE EARLY BIRD
BRONTE, STATE OF KER

"Pass the syrup, please?" Paxton asked.

Shay lifted her eyes from her plate and clashed gazes with Roman. He was staring at her from across the table, the arousal in his eyes—no gold this morning—suggesting he found her far more mouth-watering than he did the food on his plate.

"Pass. The. *Syrup?*" Paxton repeated.

Roman snapped out of his trance with a blink, his abrupt change in expression so comical, his brother might as well have dumped a bucket of ice-cold water over his head.

Shay clamped her lips together to fight a smile.

"Sorry," Roman said, clearing his throat. "Here." He passed the syrup to Paxton.

"Thanks," Pax muttered.

Shay tore her eyes off the Wolf of the Hollow, who was unabashedly staring at her again, and scooped the last of her hash browns onto her fork. She had to put a stop to these dirty thoughts that were spinning through her *own* head, most of them memories of their fun against the wall of the Blue Gables motel last night, or someone at this table was going to call her out.

It would probably be Dean, who hadn't stopped smiling since the moment they'd sat down, as if he were indulging in some inside joke they weren't aware of.

The Early Bird was swarming with the breakfast rush. There were so many people, both inside and outside the restaurant, that they'd decided to dine in two separate groups, so whoever wasn't eating could stand watch. Bobby, Nash, A.J., and Jacob had already had their turn and were currently outside, talking and laughing and smoking by the collection of muscle cars glittering in the sunlight. Once they were done here, the Death Dealers would be heading back to Tyrmouth, while Dean accompanied his nephews all the way to Angelthene. Roman had tried to tell his uncle that he didn't need to trouble himself with driving that far, but Dean had merely told him he hadn't come all this way for nothing—and that he was not a fan of wasting his own time.

Shay really liked him. Him and his inappropriate jokes were exactly what they'd all needed.

"So," Dean said as he spread a thick layer of strawberry jam across his toast. "How was the pullout?" His wink was for both of them.

The small scar by Roman's mouth indented as he fought a smile.

Shay's face warmed. As much as she liked Dean and his sense of humor, it was far too early for this.

Pax said, "I slept on it. Roman doesn't pull out."

Roman choked on his toast. He coughed and banged a fist against his chest, his other hand reaching for his water. He took a sip, eyes watering, and squeezed out, "Excuse me?"

"You don't pull out," Paxton repeated, looking thoroughly confused by his brother's reaction. "You've never heard that joke before?"

"Uhh..." Roman took another swig, his eyes meeting Shay's over the rim of his glass. He swallowed and said, "I'm a little concerned where you heard this...*joke*...and what you *think* it means."

"I heard it from Darien," Paxton replied.

Shay's brows bumped up, Roman's doing the same as they shared a look.

Dean was quietly laughing and shaking his head as he devoured his food, enjoying this way too much.

"He said it means a person prefers beds," Paxton said with a shrug. "I don't really get it. Kylar laughed pretty hard at it, though." He took a bite out of his last strip of bacon—the one he was clearly saving for the end of his meal.

"I bet he did," Roman said around a startled chuckle. When he looked Shay's way, they were both fighting the urge to laugh.

Dean leaned toward Roman and hissed in his ear, "You're going to have to ask Darien about that one."

"Oh, I will," Roman said, his brows still high. "I definitely will."

They finished their breakfast and left the diner. It was a beautifully sunny morning, the air so warm Shay was able to strip off her jacket. Perks to being closer to Witheredge. Closer to Angelthene's semi-arid climate, and farther from Yveswich's heavy veil of fog and drizzle. The farther she got from her hometown, the easier she could breathe, think. Another six to eight hours, and they'd be passing the sign welcoming them to Angelthene.

Another six to eight hours, and they'd be starting over somewhere new.

She couldn't wait. Anna would be so proud.

"Hold up just a sec, Pax," she said, hurrying to catch up to the kid as he practically raced after his brother. They were heading across the lot—to where the Death Dealers stood with Dean by the cars, everyone saying their goodbyes. "Let's give Itzel her breakfast."

Pax held still so Shay could unzip the main compartment of his backpack.

"Please don't bite me," she said to the Hob, carefully lowering the plastic cup of ice cubes into the backpack. The Hob peered up at her with hot pink eyes, but, to Shay's surprise, she didn't bite. Roman hadn't been so lucky that morning, and he had a new scar on his hand to show for it.

The moment the cup was in, Itzel started munching.

Dean slid his sunglasses on. "So, which one of you wants to ride with me?" he asked as Shay zipped up the backpack.

"Why don't you ride with Dean, and Pax and I will take Stacey?" Shay suggested to Roman.

"Fine by me, as long as Paxton's okay with it," he said. He mussed up Pax's mop of hair.

Paxton shrugged. "Fine by me," he said, echoing his brother.

"Wait a minute," Roman drawled, squinting at her with suspicion.

She drew back her head. "What?" As Roman continued to eye her, she demanded, "Why are you looking at me like that?"

"You just want to have a turn with Stacey," he accused, the gold flecks in his irises glinting in the sunlight. "Don't you?"

Shay couldn't help it—she grinned. "So what if I do?" She'd been itching to get behind that wheel since the moment she'd seen Roman's hands caressing it.

"I fucking knew it."

"What's the matter, Shadows?" she purred. "Don't like sharing your women?"

"Absolutely the fuck not," he said, those eyes darkening. But he reached into the pockets of his black jeans, searching for the car key.

Shay pressed her lips together to fight a smile as he kept patting his pockets, looking more confused by the second.

"You lose the keys?" Dean asked him.

"I just had them—"

"Looking for something?" Shay drawled. She dangled the key before her, the metal winking in the bright light.

Dean's men chuckled.

A slow smile spread across Roman's face. "You little thief." His combat boots crunched in the dry earth as he stepped right up to her, his nearness causing her to gulp, and closed his hand over hers, trapping the key in her fist. In that low, husky voice that made her shiver, he told her, "I expect to see a burnout."

THEY MADE it into the state of Witheredge in the late morning.

Roman couldn't tear his eyes off the side mirror—off Shay, who'd lit him up like a light when she'd done a burnout on the highway out front of The Early Bird. She and Paxton were laughing and smiling and belting out the lyrics to a song, the volume so loud the bass was shaking the car.

As he watched Shay dancing in her seat, Roman couldn't help but smirk, shaking his head. Yup, she'd definitely wanted a turn behind that wheel.

"So," Dean began with a clearing of his throat that yanked Roman's eyes off the side mirror. Off Shay. "I'm happy to hear you didn't waste any time taking my advice."

Roman glanced sidelong at his uncle. "What?"

"About not letting *The One* get away," Dean said with a wolfish smile.

Roman blinked.

"Oh, come on," Dean drawled. "You can't hide anything from your old uncle." He leaned across the car to whisper, "I heard you." He sat straight again and waggled his brows. "You were right outside my room, and you were both being very loud. Especially for two people who are definitely *not* into each other." He smiled at the road.

Roman stared out the windshield. "I don't know what to do," he confessed. He knew what he *wanted*—and that was a life with Shay. A new future for both of them. But that didn't mean that what he wanted was the right answer here.

Dean dropped his smile and sighed. "Remember what I said. About your dad and his stupid rules. You want this girl, you go after her. End of story."

"What would *you* do?" Roman asked him. "If it were you? If *The One* you speak of was being targeted by someone like Don?"

A haunted look entered Dean's eyes. He stared out at the road, the apple of his throat bobbing. "I would've wanted to protect her," he admitted. "Same as you."

"So, you *wouldn't* have said screw it and just did what you wanted, then."

"Our stories are different. It may not feel like it, but you and that Selkie have the upper hand right now. Getting out of Yveswich was step number one. If you think about it, that whole security breach situation is a bit of a blessing in disguise for you two. Your dad has no home to go back to at this time, and neither does her mom, for that matter. You guys managed to get away, against all odds. You can go anywhere—anywhere you want. The world's yours."

Roman sighed. "Then why doesn't it feel like it?"

"Just keep your chin up."

"I'm trying." Silence prevailed for a few minutes before Roman remembered something he'd been meaning to talk to Dean about. "Pax had a couple of weird episodes after we left Yveswich. I was hoping to get your opinion."

Dean frowned. "What do you mean by *episodes?*"

"We were evacuating, I was driving, he was fine, and suddenly, out of nowhere, he started screaming and covering his ears. *Make it stop, make it stop,* he was saying. His eyes turned black, a bunch of dark lines appeared in the skin around them, some of his blood vessels popped... Scared the shit out of me. I thought he was dying or something."

"Surge?" Dean guessed.

"He's had them before, but never anything like that. It was super weird —my windshield shattered and the brakes failed... We went off the road, the car was smoking. Then the same thing happened again, a couple of days later. We were staying at a motel in Arbor—that was the day before you showed up. Long story short, a group of Don's men found us and attacked, and Pax, he..." He trailed off, his mouth suddenly so dry he could hardly swallow.

The memory of those men, popping like balloons, their blood spraying the motel, the ground... His breakfast threatened to come back up.

"Pax what?" Dean prompted.

"I don't know, he..." Roman drew a shaky breath. "He snapped."

"Snapped," Dean repeated, his brow scrunching.

"Yeah, something in him just...I don't know, *snapped,*" he said again, throwing a hand up in an *I-don't-know* gesture. "That's the best way to describe it. This...*power,* unlike anything I've ever seen or felt, just blasted out of him. He killed them," Roman concluded, the confession raspy. "Don's men—Paxton killed them. Every last one of them. Almost killed me and Shay, too. It was like they vaporized. There was hardly anything left of them but some blood." The closest comparison Roman could think of was when Darien had exploded the head of that demon at the harbor. But that was *just* the head. The level of magic it would have taken Paxton to make those men disintegrate like that...

Roman swallowed another surge of nausea.

For a moment, Dean just drove, deep in thought. Then he said, "You still have him on suppressants?"

"Double now."

"He's going to have to learn how to control it."

"How are you supposed to control something like that, though? It was complete insanity. I've never seen anything like it."

"You figured out how. To control yours. You had a similar...*episode.* " He curled his fingers into air quotes. "You were only ten when it happened." Dean spoke of it so casually, as if Roman should already know what he was talking about, but—

Roman was clueless. "When *what* happened?"

"Your first Surge. I wasn't there—I only heard about it secondhand from your mom."

"Okay, and what happened?" Roman pressed.

Dean's brow furrowed, but he explained, "Apparently, you started screaming out of nowhere, your eyes were black, your ears were bleeding. You killed five of your father's men that day, and it was completely an accident. He put you on suppressants for a few years, and by the time he took you off them... It never happened again. Least not that I've heard of."

Roman's head spun as he thought it through. Tried to remember what Dean was telling him. But—

"Why don't I remember that?" he asked.

Dean shrugged.

'*Do* you *remember?*' Roman asked Sayagul in private.

Sayagul was listening intently, the dragon just as confused as Roman. '*No,*' she said.

"I don't remember taking any suppressants, either."

"Sometimes the mind will bury things," Dean said. "To protect you. It's a defense mechanism. That might be why you can't remember."

Roman glanced in the side mirror. At Paxton's silhouette in the car behind them, the kid grinning from ear to ear.

Would Paxton's mind bury the events of the past few days? To protect him, the way Roman's had? Or would he be haunted by what he'd done for the rest of his life?

"Don't worry," Dean said, reaching up to adjust the rear-view, his own attention shifting to Pax in the reflection. "He has a far better support network than you did at his age."

Roman chewed his lip, wracking his brain for these buried memories Dean had referred to, but he came up empty.

"Anyway," Dean began a moment later. "Do you think it's safe enough to tell me now? What really went on in Yveswich?"

Roman had already thought about it last night when he'd drifted off— about telling Dean. He knew they could trust him, but it was more the idea of telling a story that wasn't his—Darien's and Loren's—that made him hesitant.

But he sighed and said, "It's a good thing we've got a long drive ahead of us." He grabbed his water bottle from the cupholder, twisted the cap off, and took a swig. He swiped a drop of water off his chin and added, "This is going to take a while."

92

THE HOUSE OF VIOLET
YVESWICH, STATE OF KER

I t was mid-morning when Max rolled out of bed at the House of Violet, but you'd think it was midnight from how black the sky was. He'd slept for only about seven hours, but in that short amount of time the darkness had not just spread, but deepened, too.

Dallas was still sawing logs, her cheek covered in drool. Knowing Dal and her absurd sleep schedule, she'd be out for at least another hour. As for Max, he needed coffee, stat. And if his nose wasn't lying, he'd find a fresh pot brewing in the kitchen. He opened the bedroom door and lumbered out.

Raina and Silas were making breakfast. All of the lights in the area were on, and yet it still felt too dark. Eerie, as if the Void were creeping in through every crack it could find to gobble up the last of the city's light.

When they'd arrived last night, the Sylphen had given them a quick tour of the house before finding guest rooms for everyone to sleep in. While the house was huge, a few people in their group had needed to crash on couches in dens or sitting rooms. Raina and her family were very accommodating, and it was all thanks to their friendship with a certain Reaper who'd almost gotten them all killed last night with his sheer idiocy at the Black Market.

Being here, though…somewhere that still had electricity and a working spell system…somewhere *safe*… Max supposed he could forgive Malakai for his screw-ups, just this one time.

"Morning," Max said as he slid onto a stool at the marble-top island.

The kitchen was big, beautiful, and bright, just like the rest of the house. Max could only imagine what it would look like on a normal day, with daylight streaming in through the windows that covered almost every wall. The sun was starting to feel like some figment of his imagination.

Raina flashed him a smile. "Morning. Did you have a good sleep?"

"Fantastic." He hadn't even dreamt—that's how tired he was. But when he'd opened his eyes, it had taken him a long time to remember where he was and how they'd ended up here. While half-asleep, being stuck in Yveswich had felt like some horrible nightmare his mind had dreamt up, but when he'd fully woken up and realized it was, in fact, *not* a nightmare... but was very, very real...

Well, he hadn't wanted to get out of bed. That was for certain.

Silas said, "Can I get you some coffee?" He was Raina's brother, his short hair the same rare shade of silver. They were both in their late twenties, Max would estimate. Same with Charlotte, Raina's Third. The Sylphen were a small circle; there were only three of them.

"Yeah, please," Max said.

"Cream and sugar?" He grabbed a mug from the cupboard by the fridge.

"Yeah, please," he said again.

Footsteps on the hardwood floor pulled Max's attention toward the hallway. Jewels and Travis were heading this way, both groggy, the former lifting a hand to her mouth to stifle a yawn. Critter, her white bat Familiar, was sitting on her shoulder.

Max scanned the cuts all over Travis's face—and grimaced.

Travis frowned. "Is it that bad?" He slid onto the chair beside Max, Jewels claiming the one on Travis's other side.

"You said Delaney smashed *one* beaker in your face or ten?"

Jewels snickered. Critter hopped off her shoulder and walked to the fruit bowl—to the bananas inside. When the bat pointed with a wing, Jewels grabbed a banana and peeled it. "It's really not *that* bad, Max." She paused in the midst of peeling and brushed her fingertips across a gash in Travis's forehead—the deepest one. Travis blushed. Wow—he really liked this one, didn't he? That was a first. "He'll be healed within a few days," she added. She broke off a chunk of banana and fed it to Critter.

"Speaking of a few days," Max began with a sigh. He mumbled a thank-you to Silas as he placed a mug of hot coffee in front of him. "That light power of yours," he said, addressing Raina, who looked over her shoulder at him as she portioned the food across the plates on the counter. "Is it powerful enough to see inside that darkness?" He gestured outside—to the supernatural black shroud steadily swallowing the city—and took a sip of coffee. The warmth spread through him, thawing the ice in his veins. It was cold as hell now, even with the furnace on full-blast.

Raina shook her head. "No, unfortunately not. That was the first thing we tried. We had some friends we were looking for during the evacuation, so we tried going into the South Financial District to look for them, but—" Her eyes—silver, just like her hair—grew heavy with emotion. "No luck," she concluded with a sad smile.

"Even if it did work," Silas added, "her light doesn't last that long. She gets drained pretty quickly."

"Do you have it, too?" Max asked him. "The light thing?"

"No, that's all Raina. She's the special one," he said with a wink. His sister gave a soft, half-hearted laugh. "Coffee?" he asked Travis and Jewels.

"Please," they said.

Max tried not to let on that he was disappointed. If Raina's light had given them a way to see in the darkness seeping out of the Void, they might've stood a chance at surviving longer. But—

That was probably wishful thinking, actually. Once the darkness took over, it wouldn't be long before all the oxygen was sucked out of Yveswich. So, either way...

They were dead meat.

The rest of their group joined them not long after Silas finished pouring Travis and Jewels some coffee—including Dallas, to Max's surprise, who staggered down the hallway in a pair of Raina's pajamas, her copper hair a rat's nest. Malakai and Aspen were the last to join, the former looking miserable, but better health-wise. With all his shit currently in the laundry, he wore a borrowed shirt and a pair of sweats, the former too small for him.

"Hey—hey, dickhead," Travis said as Malakai made a beeline to the coffee pot. Travis cupped his hands over his mouth and repeated, "Hey, dickhead!"

Malakai grunted over his shoulder, Creature—who was perched there—doing the same.

Travis said, "Your nipples are showing. Just thought you should know."

The Reaper merely gave him the middle finger.

Everyone sat down at the island and the kitchen table to eat. Scarlet was wrapped up in a blanket, still shaking from head to toes from being dropped in the canal last night. She looked pale. Even her hair, the strands usually so warm, seemed cooler. Ashen, almost. Magenta was fine, but still quiet as ever. She kept close to Scarlet, always shy around anyone else.

"So," Travis began, the word muffled as he chewed a bite of toast. "You guys said you went Below to look for a way out. Did you try the Necropolis, too?" The Necropolis was an ancient, crumbling city below the streets of Yveswich, otherwise known as *The City of the Dead*. Max recalled Kylar telling him that. An old tourist attraction that was now overrun with monsters.

Raina nodded. "We tried, but two of the entrances are swathed in shadow, and the only entrance we did find was caved in."

"What about trying the waterfalls?" Travis's question was for Max and Dominic, his steel-blue eyes leaping between them.

But the Angel's brow furrowed; he had not been present for that conversation. "What do you mean?"

Jewels chimed in. "Travis and I were talking about them last night. He said Roman mentioned that the Veil is thinner by places of constant movement, like waterfalls. Apparently, the blending of the dimensions is turning them into portals."

"Veil?" Charlotte and Silas echoed.

Max stiffened. So did Dallas.

As for Travis, his face smoothed with an epiphany. "Oh gods," he breathed. "You don't know."

"Know what?" Silas asked.

Max spoke up. "It's a portal," he said. "The shadow is coming from an inter-dimensional portal to Spirit Terra." Screw it—they were all going to die anyway. These people deserved to at least know and understand what was about to take them out.

"Spirit Terra?" Raina repeated. "I thought that was—"

"A myth?" Max asked. "A bedtime story? So did we."

"So the Veil is real?" Charlotte asked.

Max nodded. "The Veil is real." He could feel his sister watching him. Magenta, too.

Magenta whispered something to Maya in Ilevyn.

Raina said, "How do you guys know this?"

Max made eye contact with Travis. Then Jewels, Aspen. Malakai was so busy stuffing his face, he didn't seem to be hearing one word of the conversation, Creature smacking loudly on the banana he was stealing from Critter.

Travis said, "We have a friend who—"

"Whose dad works for the Fleet," Max interrupted. Dallas shot him a grateful look. "We heard it from him. The imperator is trying to avoid public outrage and panic, so he's chosen to only keep the Fleet informed. From our understanding, that's why they cut communications."

"So...," Travis said, circling back to their former topic. "Waterfalls." He took a sip of coffee. "Thoughts?"

Max was already shaking his head. "Won't work. We have no idea where they lead—it would be a gamble. And if we end up in Spirit Terra, we won't be able to breathe."

The conversation didn't go on for much longer after that, nobody wanting to slip up and say something they shouldn't say. About Loren and Darien. About the Well. Any further questions that came up, Max answered, and he kept his answers short. Straightforward.

When everyone was done eating and started helping Raina, Charlotte, and Silas clean up the mess, Dallas wandered into the living room to take a look at the glass display cases hanging on the wall. Pressed behind the glass were pairs of impressive wings, some with silver feathers, others white or gold.

"What are these?" Dallas asked. She looked over her shoulder at Raina, who was loading up the dishwasher with Charlotte. "Fleet wings?"

Raina nodded. "Yes. I used to work for the Fleet."

Dominic said, "As a solider?"

"No. As a designer."

Dallas's brows went up. "Wait—you *built* their wings?"

Raina smiled proudly. "Built *and* installed. Not all of them, of course, but I was one of their head designers." Glass clinked as she slid in the drawers on the dishwasher and turned it on.

Dallas slid her gaze back to the wings. "Does that mean you know how to remove them, too?" she asked quietly. When her throat bobbed, Max found his own shifting in answer.

She was really doing this, wasn't she?

Raina studied the destroyed wings that were fastened to Dallas's back. There was empathy in her gaze. "Yes. I can attach and remove them."

For a moment, Dallas got really quiet. Contemplative. Then she drew a deep breath and turned to face Raina. "I would like you to remove mine."

THE COUCH CUSHIONS SANK, snapping Max out of his thoughts, as Travis threw himself down beside him.

"You gotta relax, man," Travis said as he slung an arm across the back of the couch.

Max tried, but his knee was bouncing, and he couldn't stop listening to every little sound that came from the room Raina and Charlotte had brought Dallas into. Until Travis showed up, he was the only one in here, the others having left to other rooms, leaving Max alone to brood.

Travis continued, "They're not even doing anything invasive. It's nowhere near what her surgery was like."

Max sighed. "I know, I just...can't help it." All Raina was doing was removing the wings from the outside—nothing invasive, like Travis had said. Nothing like Dal's surgery, which the doctors and Healers had put her under for. A few painkillers were all she'd need to get through this.

Quick, simple, and easy.

Still, Max couldn't stop fidgeting.

Despite his concerns, he was proud of Dallas for doing this. Those wings were nothing to her now but a burden. They were too destroyed to get her airborne. And, even if they'd made it back to Angelthene, she would've had to get them removed—or fixed—there.

He lifted his head to see Maya shuffling into the room, that blanket still wrapped tightly around her shoulders.

"Can I talk to you?" she said quietly. Her question was for Max.

He felt a little bitter still, but he told her, "Sure."

Travis got up and left, leaving the two of them alone. Once brother and sister, now strangers.

Max waited for Maya to speak.

"I wanted to thank you," she began.

His bouncing knee stilled. "For what?"

"For diving into the canal to save me."

"You're my sister," Max said. At that, her eyes softened. "I already lived through your death once." He cleared his throat and choked out, "I didn't want to lose you again."

An awkward silence descended. They stared at each other from opposite sides of the room, neither of them talking.

Max broke that silence by gesturing to the other sofa across from the one he sat on. "Why don't you have a seat?"

For a long moment, she looked at the couch, as if her decision was life or death.

"It won't bite," he said.

She smiled a little, then sat down, tucking the blanket around her legs. "I owe you an apology," she began. "I know I haven't been the sister you remember, but...being in that facility...it changed me. I never thought I was getting out of there, Max." She lowered her gaze. "And, when I finally did... well, the last thing I expected was to live long enough to see you again."

Max had to take a moment to process her words.

Maya was apologizing. She was *actually* apologizing.

Maybe...maybe things could finally be better between them. Go back to how life used to be. Well, for the last two days they had to live, anyway.

"What did you think?" he asked her. "When you saw me, I mean."

"I was...surprised. And happy."

"You were happy?"

"Of course," she said, as if it should be obvious. "You're my brother, Max. Of course I would be happy to see you."

He swallowed. "Well, thank you," he said. "For the apology. And for taking the time to talk to me."

She picked at a thread on the blanket. "Do you think we can start fresh?" she whispered.

A smile pulled at his mouth, and she answered it with one of her own. The kind of smile that reminded him that this really was his sister. This really was Maya 'MJ' Reacher. "Yeah," he said, "I think we can start fresh. You ready to be Maya again?"

She nodded. "Yeah. I think I'm ready to be Maya again."

His smile broadened. "Welcome back, sis."

She snickered. "Thanks." She buried her hands in the blanket to warm them. "Do you ever see Dad anymore?"

His smile faded. "Never."

"And...Mom?"

He thought about what he should say, and settled with, "She hasn't changed."

The half-smile that ghosted across MJ's mouth was filled with sadness. "I didn't think so."

They'd always hoped she would—secretly and quietly hoped their mother would turn things around one day. Get clean. Improve her life and relationship with her children. He'd lost all hope of that the day he'd walked into her pig-stye of a home in that trailer park and found out, from his mother's own mouth, that she'd sold Maya in exchange for money. Money that she'd spent on booze and drugs.

He wouldn't tell his sister that, though. Not now. Not today.

The click of a door opening had him sitting up straight and looking toward the hallway. Toward the room Dallas was in.

Slow footsteps on the floor.

And then Dallas appeared, Raina and Charlotte flanking her. The minute Dallas's amber eyes met Max's, she smiled and spun around carefully, showing him her wingless back.

When she stopped spinning, her smile faltered. "How do I look?" She was back to her old self, and yet better, somehow. She looked lighter, and Max knew it had nothing to do with the weight of her wings and everything to do with her controlling parents.

Today, she had shed herself of more than just her wings.

Max smiled. "Like you," he told her.

Dallas smiled back.

93

OCEANA
ANGELTHENE, STATE OF WITHEREDGE

The heavy rainfall turned the world beyond the windows of Darien's car into a blurry watercolor painting.

In the district of Oceana, where they were parked out front of the townhouse that belonged to Erasmus and Helia Sophronia, Loren tried her best to sit still. But Roark was late. And as far as her other parents went, there was no sign of them, either.

She didn't realize how cold she was until Darien cranked the heat and angled the vents so they were facing her. "Thank you," she said, pressing her stiff, shaking fingers against the vents. They felt like icicles.

"Do you want my jacket?" He was already reaching for the zipper, ready to strip it off for her. All he had on underneath was a black t-shirt.

He'd get soaked as soon as they stepped outside, so she told him, "I'm fine."

But Darien looked concerned. "If you decide you want it, don't hesitate to tell me. And don't worry about me being cold. Deal?"

She nodded. "Deal."

Another fifteen minutes went by, and there was still no sign of Roark. She was growing increasingly anxious. Was he not coming?

Darien opened his door, a rush of fresh, rainy air sweeping through the car and teasing the dark locks of his hair. "Let's go try the door, baby," he said.

She followed him out, up the wet and puddled front steps, the rain dampening her hair. She stood right beside Darien beneath the shelter of the overhang, remembering back to the last time they were here together, as he rapped a tattooed fist against the front door. Once. Twice. Three times.

No answer.

Tires splashed through puddles on the road. Loren squinted over her shoulder and saw a white sports car pulling up behind Darien's.

It was Roark.

The driver's door swung open. He stepped out, popping an umbrella.

Loren pulled up her hood and walked carefully down the slick steps to meet him on the sidewalk, Darien shadowing her every step of the way.

"Sorry I'm late," Roark said, his amber eyes flicking between them. "I had a bit of trouble finding the place."

"That's okay," Loren replied at the same time that Darien said, "Don't worry about it."

Roark tipped back his umbrella and squinted through the sheet of rain, at the townhouse where his old friends lived. "Are they home?"

"Doesn't look like it," Darien said. He blinked the Sight into his eyes and scanned the front entrance. "Their auras are cold. Doesn't look like anyone's been here in days."

Loren suppressed a sigh. So much for getting answers.

Suddenly, the world starting turning like a rain-drenched carousel, and she practically fell against Darien, her fingers latching onto the sleeves of his jacket for balance.

"Whoa—baby, what's going on?" He wrapped a strong arm around her waist and blinked away the black. "You all right?" He tipped her chin up, his eyes—brimming with concern—roving over her face.

"Yeah, just—" She blinked rapidly, but the world wouldn't hold still, and she was seeing three of Darien instead of one. "A head rush, or something."

Darien wasn't convinced. Angling his body in such a way that it would be easy for him to catch her should she fall, he took her hand into his and tugged up both of the sleeves on her left arm—the rain jacket and the baby-blue long-sleeve she wore underneath.

The moment he saw the bead of white light pulsing through the Caliginous on Silverway tattoo on the inside of her wrist, he ground his teeth and muttered, "Fuck."

"Maybe the rain will help if I take off my hood?" Loren suggested, breathless.

"It won't be good enough, baby," he said, a muscle in his jaw ticking as he clenched it. "And besides, you're freezing." He unzipped his jacket and pulled her into a hug. She slipped her arms around him—underneath the shelter of his jacket—and rested her cheek against his warm, solid chest. She shut her eyes and concentrated on the feel of his heart beating steadily against her as the world continued to spin. It was so much stronger than her own, that heartbeat.

She'd missed this more than she'd realized. Being close to him was almost enough to make her forget all about her gyrating head and her weak, fluttering heart.

Please don't stop beating, she begged her heart. *I still have to save him.*

"I don't know if you recall," Roark began, "but the last time we spoke before you left for Yveswich, I mentioned there was a chamber being built at Lucent Enterprises."

"Yeah, I remember," Darien said, a note of hope in his voice as his hands rubbed her back in comforting circles. "Is it ready?"

"They just finished the final touches. If you'll allow me to glamor you, I can get you in so she can have a treatment."

"How risky is it?" Darien's deep, inviting voice rumbled from his chest into hers, making her shiver for a reason unrelated to the cold and the rain.

"The wing it's in is newly renovated and isn't open for use yet. There aren't any cameras, but the others in the building will need to be masked, and I'm afraid that's beyond my capabilities."

"That won't be a problem," Darien said as he got out his phone, typing with one hand while he kept his other arm wrapped snug around Loren's waist.

As he made a call, the ringing line barely audible over the drumming of the rain on her hood, Loren made eye contact with Roark. He was usually so impossible to read, but right now she swore he looked...concerned. A father who genuinely cared about the wellbeing of his daughter.

"Kylar," Darien said as his friend picked up. "I'm going to need you to do us a favor."

DARIEN KEPT his arms wrapped around Loren from behind, doing everything in his power to keep her warm, as Roark pressed buttons on the touchscreen by the door to the reverse chamber at Lucent Enterprises.

The hallway they stood in was painted a blinding shade of white, the air so cold they might as well be standing inside a refrigerator. Even to Darien and his stupidly high body temperature, it was freezing.

True to Roark's word, no one was around but them, no cameras mounted on the walls. Kylar had kept up with them as they'd made their way through the massive building, masking the security tapes as they went from hallway to hallway and stairwell to stairwell. Glamors didn't work on cameras, so masking the feeds was their only option.

Despite how hard she tried to hide it from him, Loren was still shivering so violently, he could hear her teeth chattering. The shaking hadn't stopped since she'd nearly fainted out front of Erasmus's townhouse. And now that she was barefoot and wearing nothing but the white two-piece bathing suit Roark had grabbed from a room across the hallway, it was only getting worse. Darien was so damn worried about her, he felt like *he* was going to faint.

Roark said, "Do you remember which colors you used the last time she was in one of these?" Buttons beeped as he pressed the screen.

"All except black and gray," he replied, rubbing his hands up and down Loren's arms to warm them. Her skin was icy and pebbled with chills.

Roark pulled up a color wheel on the screen and activated every color, apart from black and gray, which had its own wheel that was separate from the rainbow option. That particular wheel consisted of a gradient that started with a light shade of gray and ended with the deepest black. Darien could only imagine how many of those shades made up his aura. A dark and ugly mess was probably what he'd see, if he ever had the chance to look at his inner self.

"Who uses the black and gray wheel?" Loren asked, her teeth clacking so hard, he could barely understand her. Desperate to help her, he tightened his arms around her, holding her close. She leaned back against him, hanging onto his sleeves.

"People with shadow and death magic," Roark replied.

"People like me," Darien said with a smirk as he rested his chin on the top of Loren's head. "Right?"

"Do you have black magic?" Roark asked him.

"Sure do."

"Is it possible to activate both wheels at the same time?" Loren asked her dad.

"It is," Roark said, sounding curious as to why she was asking. "You don't want black or gray, though, Loren. That's the opposite of what you have. Your aura is light and healing. If we were to activate the black, chances are..." His eyes darted Darien's way, and he hesitated a moment before settling with, "Well, let's just say I don't think it would be good." He pressed one more button, and the chamber whirred to life.

Inside, the lights flicked on, and tiny spheres of magic every shade of the rainbow winked into existence, flitting about like fireflies. Droplets of water began to vibrate through the air, running from ceiling to floor and floor to ceiling.

"All jewelry off," Roark instructed.

Darien shifted Loren's hair to one shoulder and unclasped her necklaces—the talisman and the solar amulet. He slid them inside his jacket pocket for safekeeping. She took off her charm bracelet herself, and he tucked that away, too.

"You got any gloves?" he asked Roark.

"Gloves? What for?"

"She has conduit tattoos."

Loren held out her hands, showing Roark the sun and moon inked on her palms. He made no comment, showed zero surprise.

"One minute." He left, heading to the same room where he'd found the bathing suit, and returned a moment later with a pair of wrist-length white satin gloves. He gave them to Loren, and she put them on.

Darien pushed the door open and held it for her as she walked in, her bare feet splashing in two inches of bath-warm water scented with citrus oil. The chamber looked the same as the one in Yveswich, complete with a floating glass tabletop in the center.

"Do you need me to lift you up there?" he called as she judged the height of the tabletop.

"No, I think I'm good," she said. She planted her hands on the glass and pulled herself up.

As soon as she was on and lying flat on her back, her hair tumbling over the edge of the thick glass, Darien shut the door.

He watched her through the window the whole time she received her treatment. Seeing his girl lying there like that, her eyes shut and her body still, brought back so many bad fucking memories. His throat tightened as if a hand were squeezing it, and his heart started to pound as he recalled one of the last times he was with her, in a chamber just like this one—banging a fist on the table and screaming for her to come back to him.

'Go, Bandit—please!' he'd bellowed as his heart cracked in his chest. *'Bring her home!'*

'WAKE. THE. FUCK. UUUUUPPPPPPPPP!'

His eyes shuttered. He drew a deep, calming inhale.

"You warm?" Roark asked.

Darien tore his eyes off Loren to find Roark observing him. "Venom withdrawals, actually," he said. It probably wasn't the right thing to admit to your girlfriend's father, especially when you wanted to one day marry said girlfriend, but it sort of just slipped out.

"Does Loren know?" Roark asked, his gaze lifting to the beads of sweat Darien could feel prickling across his forehead. He couldn't wait until these symptoms were behind him and he felt like himself again.

"I talked to her yesterday. We stopped by her workplace and she picked up a tonic that's supposed to help people like...me." They'd had barely enough time to swing by Mordred and Penelope's before heading to Erasmus's townhouse, but she'd insisted on making the stop. He'd already taken a dose, but Loren said it would be about three days before he was back to new.

"She's excellent with natural healing," Roark said. "She'll have you back to new quicker than if you were fighting it on your own, with less chance of relapse, too."

Darien didn't reply. He just kept watching Loren, his breaths thinning out as those bad memories once again resurfaced—

"What day are you on?"

"Sorry?" Darien asked. It took every ounce of his willpower to tear his attention off Loren.

"How many days have you been off the Venom?"

"Umm..." He gave a soft, humorless laugh and admitted, "One. I caved yesterday afternoon and took a hit. That was before I talked to her."

A few minutes of silence passed.

"The cops think Venom is to blame for a handful of homicides that have occurred in the last few days," Darien ventured.

Roark's brow creased. "You know about those?"

"I spoke to Detective Finn Solace last night. He tried asking me if I know anything about what's happening in Yveswich. His personal opinion is that this new virus—the *Venenum virus,* they're calling it—isn't connected to Venom, but to the falling of the Veil." He studied Roark's expression, searching for any tells.

Finally, Roark said, "He's not way off."

Darien stood up straighter. "You know what's causing it?"

"It's the Tricking."

His face smoothed with shock. "The Tricking?"

"It's mutating," Roark began. "The disease started mutating the minute the Veil was blown open in Yveswich. Remember when we spoke on the phone, when I told you that I'd run into a few complications that'd led to a change in orders?"

Darien nodded.

"The Tricking patients at Yveswich General Hospital—those with Stage Three—randomly started attacking staff, visitors, other patients. It's similar to what happened with the first Well replica—when the missing women were later discovered to be the new breed of monster."

"Can the virus be healed the same way, then?" Darien asked. "With the same antidote?"

Roark shook his head. "They've already tried—it didn't work."

He cursed.

Roark continued, "There are ancient wellsprings of magic in every section in Spirit Terra, and it's the shadow magic in the Void that is activating the spread of the Venenum virus and triggering those who are infected with it to randomly attack—maul, basically, like a wild animal, biting, clawing, you name it—whoever is closest to them at the time. The first victim was Tamika Isley—she was attacked by her mother, who was sick with Stage Three Tricking."

"Tamika? We know her." Shit—*that* was the reason she was in the hospital? "She wasn't bitten, though—she was stabbed."

Roark nodded. "Right. Because she was the first victim, right at the time the Veil fell, the virus reacted with Charlene differently. It still caused her to act out of violence, but with a weapon instead of teeth."

Holy shit. "Why aren't you working with the MPU on this? They have no clue what's going on—Finn's desperate for answers. If the virus is that deadly, why isn't anyone working together?"

"It's the imperator's orders." Of course it was. "He's trying so hard to cover this up and keep his reputation clean, that he is willing to risk the spread of this virus and the lives of potentially millions of people." Roark briefly lowered his gaze, his throat bobbing. Darien could feel—sense—his stress levels through his aura. "If it gets out of hand, millions *will* die. The infection is spread through a person's saliva—if bitten by an infected person, the virus can turn them within hours. In the short time since the first attack, those who are infected have begun to rapidly mutate physically. If it goes on for much longer, they will hardly be recognizable to anyone who knows them."

Shit. It *was* just like what happened with the missing women. The Loren lookalikes the imperator had shoved into the first Well replica.

"We have to tell them," Darien said, heart pounding. "Finn—someone has to tell him so he can work on quarantine."

"I plan on it. I have a feeling Glen already knows the truth, since he seems to be answering directly to the imperator, so I plan on going straight to Finn. How we stop the virus, however...*cure* it...that is something we will have to figure out, as quickly as we can. And I believe it all ties back to simply re-sealing the Veil. If we shut the Veil, we stop the virus."

Made sense.

"And it's not just hellsehers, then?" Darien pressed. "The cops and the MPU are only targeting hellsehers. Charlene was a witch, no?"

"Correct. Hellsehers simply use their magic more than the rest of the population, so they are more likely to have Stage Three Tricking and come down with the virus. And the eyes—the black eyes with the lines around them—" He indicated to his own under-eye. "It's just a physical symptom that only hellsehers get. So their argument about Venom..." He shook his head. "There is no argument. It's not the Venom at all—it's the Tricking."

Darien should feel relieved, but—

There was nothing about this that relieved him. No—it stressed him the hell out.

All this talk of black eyes with lines around them reminded him of Paxton—the episode Roman had told him about.

"I have a twelve-year-old cousin who had an intense Surge a couple of days ago—his eyes turned black, and his brother said there were lines around them, too. He's only twelve, though, and he never uses his magic— there's no way he has the Tricking. Any thoughts on that?"

"Your cousin," Roark mused. "Same magic as you?"

"Same magic as me," he confirmed. Roark waited to see if he'd piece it together himself, and he did. "The wellsprings of magic," he breathed.

Roark nodded. "All these years, the Veil has been acting as a barrier—a buffer. So more sensitive individuals with magic—especially shadow magic —are now susceptible to worse Surges. I suggest this cousin of yours gets on a high dose of suppressants to help keep his magic levels normal until the Veil is re-sealed. He won't be able to control his power at his young age, so getting him on suppressants would be wise."

"Yeah, I think his brother already has him on some." Roman was supposed to get to town tonight; he'd talk to him then.

Darien looked in through the window at Loren, thinking back to when Jewels had suffered a seizure and gone into cardiac arrest when the portal was opening wider. She was only Stage Two, but her body must have been reacting to the portal poorly, the same way as Loren.

"Do you think this is the reason Erasmus and Helia are gone?" he asked Roark, tearing his focus off Loren. "If I estimated correctly, they left town around the same time the explosion happened." The traces of color left behind by their auras backed up his suspicions.

"I think it's very possible. They would know more than I do about the Veil and how to close it, and with them suddenly up and disappearing like this...well, I believe you could be right. They might have left if they know of something that could give us the upper hand here. Something that might have required they leave town in order to get."

"Or they're running," Darien said with disgust. They'd run before. Why not run again?

Roark seemed to be weighing his response. "Something tells me they aren't running. Not this time."

They stood there in silence for several minutes, watching Loren through the window.

Darien's thoughts drifted to Travis and Max. If they were stuck in Yveswich... If there were Tricking patients in there that were mutating and going on killing sprees... People who would soon mutate into monsters, the way the victims of the first Well replica had mutated...

As if reading his mind, Roark said, "Have you heard from those friends of yours?"

He shook his head. "Not yet. Which reminds me—Arthur told me to ask you for the blueprints for those missiles."

"Oh yes, that's right." He unzipped his jacket and reached into the inside pocket. "I have them right here." He passed him two rolls of shiny paper. "If you're planning on instructing your friends on how to make one of those, I must advise you that building one from scratch takes a long time."

"How long are we talking?"

"Weeks."

Darien cursed.

"But," Roark began. "If they didn't need to build one from scratch, and instead only had to charge a new warhead..."

"It's doable?"

Roark nodded. "It's doable. But charging the warhead would require raw magic from the anima mundi, and with the Control Tower currently stuck in a Battleshort..." He frowned. "I've been trying to think of a way around it, but in order to get magic from the anima mundi, it needs to be channeled by something like the Control Tower. Something designed to draw magic *up* from the earth."

Darien leaned against the door and thought it through. "Magic from the anima mundi is just raw, unfiltered magic, right? In all different colors?"

Roark's brow creased, but he confirmed, "Right."

"Would you need every color, or would a few do?"

"Not every color, but most."

Darien's mind spun with ideas.

Solutions.

"I think I have an idea," he breathed.

"How are you feeling?" Darien's deep, rich voice echoed down the hallway as Loren stepped out of the chamber, her damp feet dripping water all over the floor. He reached for her hand, and she slid it into his, the feel of his warm, callused palm awakening the butterflies in her stomach.

Her treatment had lasted just twenty minutes, but she already felt a whole lot better. Not perfect, no—never as healthy as before she'd fallen into a coma. She didn't imagine she'd get back to her old self any time soon, but she'd gladly take how she currently felt over the intense, debilitating fatigue that had overcome her outside of Erasmus and Helia's townhouse. The chills had subsided, and she felt stronger than before, her skin no longer sallow, but glowing.

"Better," she told him. Judging from the look on his face as he scanned her with onyx eyes, the treatment had worked.

Roark reached behind her to shut the door to the chamber, and then he pressed a few buttons on the screen. The chamber shut down with a whir that juddered the floor beneath her bare feet.

She was about to head into the change room that was still under construction when Roark spoke.

"If you have questions about anything we discussed, don't hesitate to call," he said to Darien. "Arthur shouldn't have a problem with the warhead, but...well, you never know."

Warhead? She'd noticed them talking intently while she was in the chamber. She would ask Darien to fill her in during the drive back to Heaven's Gate. Later, after dinner, she would be going with Darien to meet Roman in the North Financial District.

"Thanks," Darien said with a nod. "I'll give you a shout if we need anything."

"Did you hear anything about the helicopter?" Loren asked.

Her question had Roark dropping his gaze to the shiny floor. He took a moment to compose himself, and by the time he answered her, he did so in the voice of a commander. A man giving a battle brief—not a father whose daughter might be dead.

"The helicopter went down just off the coast of Yveswich a few minutes before the forcefield went up."

Her stomach dropped.

Dallas. Max. That must mean...

They were either trapped in Yveswich or—

She could not stomach the other option.

Roark added, "The report came from one of my officers, who's since pulled out of Yveswich. It's all the information I have, I'm afraid."

The feel of Darien's warm, sturdy fingers gently squeezing hers popped the bubble of panic that had closed over her head. "We're going to get them out," he said. "We're going to bring them home."

Loren hoped he was right.

94

FINANCIAL DISTRICT
ANGELTHENE, STATE OF WITHEREDGE

Roman geared down as he approached Angelthene's North Financial District. Shay was in the passenger's seat, one arm extended out her open window, her hair swirling in gusts of fresh evening air. Following closely behind them were Dean and Paxton. They'd raced down the last stretch of the highway I-5 into Angelthene, everyone flying high on the reality that they'd made it.

They'd *finally* made it.

It was probably just an illusion, that high—one that would soon wear off, like an adrenaline rush. For all Roman knew, Don could be here right now, in this very city, waiting to wreck his life all over again.

Right now, though, he would grant himself the space to relax. Even for just *one* night. He had to breathe—and so he would let himself breathe.

As he pulled into the parking lot of a strip mall, most of the businesses shut for the evening, Dean followed, Iris's headlights bleaching the pavement. They parked out front of a blood donor clinic, the red neon sign that was shaped like a droplet of blood flashing in the night.

Roman got out, Shay doing the same on her side, and drew a deep, deep breath, soaking in the scents of Angelthene.

Of *freedom*.

A breeze that smelled of magic—sugar and smoke—and creosote stirred through the lot and sent Shay's strawberry blonde hair into a dance. She shut her eyes, tipped her head back, and inhaled deeply. Basking in her newfound freedom, just like Roman.

He couldn't stop staring—*admiring* her. The city lights cast a silvery glow on her skin, bringing out the smattering of freckles on her nose and cheeks. And that rose-gold hair of hers...

Yup, he was fucked.

'*I think* in love *is the more appropriate term,*' Sayagul said with a snicker.

In love? Yeah, maybe.

Maybe.

"Welcome to Angelthene, small fry," he said.

Shay opened those pretty green eyes—and grinned. "Welcome to Angelthene, Shadows."

He sucked in another breath through his nose. "Smell that?" he said on the exhale.

"Trash?" she teased, her eyes dancing. "Puke? Blood?" Yeah, maybe a little, but—

"Freedom," he said. Her grin broadened.

"Well, what'd I tell ya?" Dean said with a smile as he and Paxton stepped out of Iris, their doors thumping shut. Dean opened his arms in presentation and declared, "You made it."

"I was starting to think we never would," Roman confessed, taking in the canvas of stars winking softly above their heads. He took out a cigarette, placed it between his teeth, and lit up.

Paxton was gazing out at Angelthene's skyline with awe while snacking on the last of his fries, his hand buried in the brown paper bag. They'd stopped at a fast food joint at the Miracle Plaza before heading here, everyone too starving to wait any longer to eat.

"So, what do you think, Pax?" Roman asked him as he slid his lighter into his pocket, smoke rippling out of his lips.

"I think it's cool," Paxton said, still marveling at the sight of a brand-new city. He'd rarely ever left Yveswich, and when he did it was either with Donovan or his school. Pax had been a prisoner to Ker's capital just as much as Roman was prisoner to it.

To their father. This change was good for the both of them.

And the Selkie who'd come with, her face alight with excitement as she, too, scanned the tall buildings scraping Angelthene's twilit sky. They were all starting over tonight. Sprinting toward a new beginning.

"Think we should do some sight-seeing tomorrow?" Roman said.

Paxton beamed. *"Really?"* he exclaimed.

"Yeah, really." He took a drag and blew the smoke away from Pax. "We'll get Darien to be our tour guide."

A laugh bubbled out of Paxton; the sound made Roman smile. Despite all the shit they'd lived through these past few days, his brother was happy. It made *him* happy. "Darien the Tour Guide," Paxton said, still chuckling. He stuffed another fry into his mouth.

"When was the last time you were here?" Dean asked.

"Fuck, *years*. I haven't been here since before Travis moved." His mention of his other brother had him looking north—toward Yveswich.

He took his phone out and checked for any new messages.

Still nothing. It had been...how many days now?

Too long. Travis should have contacted him by now.

Shay was studying him. The look on her face told Roman she knew exactly what he was thinking. She didn't ask him anything about Travis, though—for Paxton's benefit, Roman knew. The last thing the kid needed right now was to worry about anything else. His life was difficult enough.

Roman would handle the situation with Travis. Would protect Paxton from unnecessary stress—just like always.

A pair of headlights swept across the parking lot, drawing Roman's attention to a sleek black sports-car.

"Is that Darien?" Shay asked, squinting as those headlights lit up her face.

"Looks like it."

The engine growled as Darien parked two stalls down. He shut off the car and got out, Loren swinging open the door on the passenger's side. Darien waited for her to round the car, his lethal gaze picking apart the night for any threats. He took her hand, and as they began heading toward them, Darien finally tore his attention off Loren. Looked their way—

And bristled at the sight of Dean, his free hand drifting toward the gun that was strapped into his front waistband.

Dean noticed—and barked a husky laugh. "Got you," he drawled.

Darien visibly relaxed, Loren peering up at him in question as they joined their group. "You scared the shit out of me," he breathed. "I almost had a heart attack."

Dean wheezed another chuckle.

"He scared you?" Loren asked. "Why?"

"He looks just like Donovan." To Dean, he said, "Where the hell did you come from, anyway? What happened?"

Paxton said, "He rescued us. We got arrested—"

"Well, *Paxton* didn't get arrested," Shay said with a snicker. "Roman and I did."

"It was like something out of an action movie!" Paxton gushed. "You should've seen it. Dean came out of nowhere and saved our asses!"

"Butts," Roman corrected.

"Butts—sorry," Paxton said. He ate another fry.

Dean said, "You must be Loren." He stepped forward and offered her a hand. "I'm Dean Slade—the Cool Uncle."

"Dean the Mean," Darien said. "That's what we all call him."

"Nice to meet you." She shook his hand.

Darien gestured to Dean with a tip of his head. "What'd you tell him?" he asked Roman.

"Everything."

Darien's brows went up. "Everything?"

Roman shrugged, took one last drag on his cigarette, and added, "Sorry."

"I won't tell anyone," Dean vowed—entirely serious.

Darien sighed. Then nodded and said, "I know."

It had taken Roman a long time to explain everything to Dean—and then it had taken even longer to convince him that he wasn't pulling his leg. Even now, his uncle looked like he couldn't figure out if he was awake or dreaming as he glanced between Darien and the blonde mortal tucked against his side, her hair swirling in a breeze.

Roman was afraid to ask, but he took a deep breath and said, "You hear from Travis?" He tossed the cigarette butt to the pavement and flattened it beneath his boot.

Darien shook his head. "Tanner's been working on getting cell service back up in Ker."

"It's out?"

"The imperator cut it."

"Shit." Travis had to be trapped in there, then—there was no other explanation for why he hadn't called. "What about Max?"

"I haven't heard from him, either." Darien was studying him with empathy. Paxton had grown quiet, his fries forgotten. "You guys are probably tired. Why don't you follow us to Heaven's Gate—you can get comfortable there. It's not far from here—about twenty minutes."

Roman squashed the emotions that were threatening to drown him— forced himself to be strong for Pax—and said, "Sounds good to me. Lead the way."

95

HEAVEN'S GATE
ANGELTHENE, STATE OF WITHEREDGE

While everyone was beyond happy to have Roman and the others sharing their home here at Heaven's Gate, there was one member of their group who was not thrilled, and that was Bandit.

The dog stood in front of the fridge, glaring up at the female Hob, who'd scampered up to hide behind the cereal boxes the minute Roman had carried Paxton's backpack into the house and unzipped it. Unleashing the noisy, pink-eyed terror upon Heaven's Gate and everyone living peacefully within its walls.

'*This is unacceptable!*' Bandit was saying. '*Outrageous, is what it is! All this darn monkey is going to do is steal Cluckles again! I will NOT stand for it!*' BARK. BARK.

Loren tried not to laugh, but she had to admit it was hard. Especially when she made eye contact with Ivy first, followed by Lace, both women having equally as hard a time as Loren with containing their laughter.

Where she stood beside the kitchen counter, Loren took the dropper out of Darien's tonic and dripped twenty drops into a mug. She was mixing it into tea this time, so it would taste a little better. The herbs were earthy and bitter, and she'd noticed him fighting not to gag and grimace when he'd taken his first dose earlier that afternoon. He'd made no complaints, and had tossed it back in one swallow like a champ, but if she could make it taste even a *little* bit better for him by adding it to tea and sweetening it with honey, she would gladly take the time to do it.

Everyone else—the Devils, Arthur, Kylar, Dean—was scattered throughout the kitchen and living room, still in the process of filling each other in on everything that had happened while they were apart. No detail, no matter how small, was left out.

Where he sat at the kitchen table, Darien opened a bag of Stygian salts and shook his head in annoyance as Bandit continued to kick up a noisy fuss about Itzel. Bandit's barking pierced the air, interrupting multiple conversations and causing people to talk louder than they should have to.

"Bandit," Darien warned, cutting off the dog that was standing on his hind legs, his front paws scrabbling against the fridge door. "Enough already."

Bandit placed all four feet on the floor and let out a low growl.

"I said *enough,*" Darien repeated as he zipped the plastic bag shut.

Bandit relented with a brazen snort and went to the sofa. He plopped himself down beside Arthur and shut his eyes, pretending to sleep. After only a moment, he opened one eye and *kept* it open—fixed on Itzel.

"Morty is *not* going to be happy when he gets home," Jack said with a chuckle. He was curled up on the couch with his wife, the two sharing a blanket and watching a comedy movie with the volume on low. Lace and Arthur were in there, too, the latter looking like he could doze off at any minute. "It'll be a battle of the Hobs."

"We'll buy a second fridge if we have to," Darien said.

Loren carried the mug of steaming tea across the kitchen and carefully set it down in front of Darien. "Here you go," she said. "I mixed it into some tea and added honey. It should taste a bit better now."

He gave her a soft smile. "Thank you, baby. You spoil me."

"You're welcome."

She went back to the counter to grab her own cup of tea—chamomile—and sat down beside him as he used the edge of a credit card to drag some Stygian salts into a line.

"Who are you tracking?" Roman asked. He stood behind Shay's chair as she devoured a slice of leftover pizza. Pax and Eugene were currently in the basement—in a room with reclining seats and a television so big, it could pass for a movie theater. There was even a popcorn machine and a candy stand Kylar had stocked with chocolate bars and sour candies.

Darien said, "Travis and Max."

"You can locate targets from this far away?" Roman asked his cousin. "If they're in Ker, I mean?" He did a good job of hiding how worried he was about Travis, but Loren could see it in his eyes.

Darien said, "It's difficult, but yeah, I can."

"Impressive," Shay said. She licked tomato sauce off her thumb. "Did anyone teach you how to do that, or did you learn it yourself?"

"Myself." Darien shut one nostril with a finger and inhaled the line of black salts through a cut plastic straw.

"Can *you* do that?" Roman's question was for Dean, who had his feet kicked up on the coffee table in the living room.

"Not a whole state over," Dean said around a yawn, his eyes watering with fatigue. "But I've found a few targets in cities that are about...I don't know...five, six hours away from where I was at the time."

Roman's brows went up.

Dean added, "That was in my younger days, though. Your old uncle's getting tired." As if to prove a point, he shut his eyes and laced his fingers across his chest. Loren thought it was funny how he referred to himself as old when he had to be in his late thirties.

"We had to have an intervention this morning," Tanner said as he rapidly clicked his mouse. "He was giving himself nosebleeds."

Shay huffed a laugh. "I bet your girlfriend loves that."

Darien gave Shay a heavy look.

She ignored him and said, "Don't you, Loren?" She finished off her slice of pizza and dusted the crumbs off her hands.

Loren merely glanced sidelong at Darien, who returned the look but didn't say anything. She'd already given him enough hell for pushing himself so hard, but she couldn't say she was upset with Shay for driving the nail home.

"I'm tracking them once, and then I'm done for the evening," Darien said to Shay. "I already had one intervention, I don't need another."

Shay snickered. She gave Loren a wink and mouthed, "I got you."

"Thanks," she mouthed back.

Darien was about to shut his eyes and start tracking when Paxton and Eugene walked into the room. "Hey, you two, don't touch these," he told them, indicating to the bag of black salt on the table.

"We just wanted some cereal," Paxton said as he and Eugene headed to the fridge.

Eugene muttered, "Can't do anything around here."

"Gene," Kylar rebuked. "We heard that."

Darien said, "That's fine, but I'm telling you now, don't touch these. They're not for kids—they'll hurt you."

"He knows," Roman drawled. But even *he* gave his brother—*and* Eugene—a stern look.

Paxton peered at the stimulants on the table. "I've seen that salt stuff a bunch of times," he said to Darien. "I'm a Slade, remember? My dad doesn't exactly run a kid-friendly household." At that, Jack snorted.

"I'm just saying, don't touch them," Darien concluded.

"Heard you the first time," Paxton said. "Where are the spoons? Am I allowed to touch those?"

Shay snickered. "Lippy little shit, hey?" she whispered to Roman, tipping her head back to smile at him.

"In the drawer by the stove, smart-ass," Darien said.

Bowls and cutlery clinked as Paxton and Eugene helped themselves to some cereal. The kind that was loaded with sugar.

Darien shut his eyes.

The room got very quiet. Ivy muted the volume on the TV. For several minutes, the only sounds in the house were the munching of ice chips and cereal. The kids had claimed a couple of seats at the table, both gaping at Darien as they chowed down.

Eugene opened his mouth to say something—

Kylar shook his head, his gray eyes flaring with a warning.

Eugene snapped his mouth shut.

Loren counted every minute that ticked by—she couldn't help it—as Darien held the Sight, his eyes moving behind closed lids. Tanner clicked away on his mouse and typed on his keyboard. In the reflection of the glasses he didn't need, Loren saw columns of computer code and colored runes that belonged to various spell systems.

And then Darien opened his black eyes. Everyone turned his way.

The look on his face...

Loren had seen that look before. She sat up straighter, her heart pounding.

Darien blinked away the black and said, "They're in Yveswich." His tone was hollowed out with dread.

Shock silenced the room for about a minute. Even though they'd all feared—and assumed—as much, Darien looked like he could hardly believe his own words.

And then the murmuring began.

"Where are they?" Roman asked above the din. "Who'd you see?"

"Travis."

Roman paled. He grabbed the back of Shay's chair, holding onto it so tightly, his knuckles showed white through his skin. Shay reached over her shoulder to grasp one of his hands. Steadying him.

"He's in the South Coastal District," Darien added. "He's the only one I can see, but I'd bet you anything he's got Max and the others with him."

"My dad found out the helicopter that picked up Max and Dallas crashed in the ocean before the forcefield went up," Loren said. Her words were for the benefit of everyone but Darien, who already knew.

Roman took his tense hands off the back of Shay's chair and started to pace, running his fingers through his hair repeatedly. Shay looked like she was about to say something to him, when suddenly, Tanner spoke.

"Oh, holy shit."

Darien sat up straighter. "Atlas—"

"I got it!" Tanner exclaimed, a surprised smile ghosting across his lips.

Those who were in the living room—even Arthur—stood up.

"You got it?" Ivy and Lace asked at the same time.

Tanner's smile spread into a proud grin, his eyes alight with hope. "I fucking *got it.*"

96

THE EYRIE
YVESWICH, STATE OF KER

"What are you doing out here?" came a pleasant, female voice.

Travis looked over his shoulder.

Jewels was walking through the open gates of the House of Violet. Her hands were bundled in her coat pockets, her moon-pale hair blown back by gusts of frost-kissed wind.

"Just wanted some air," he said, his breaths puffing out in the shape of small clouds. His answer wasn't exactly a lie; he was starting to feel stuffy from being trapped in that house all day while the world around him slowly darkened and died.

She came to stand beside him, and sighed. "Yeah, I think we're running out of that, hey?" She splayed her fingers across her chest, idly rubbing the skin right above her heart.

The city had grown quiet. The bomb blasts and gunshots that had shaken the streets every hour since the Well replica exploded had died off, leaving behind no sound but the roaring of monsters and the spine-chilling screams of the people who had fallen prey to them. Even the civil defense sirens had been shut off.

Surrendering. Yveswich was surrendering. Falling to the Void. Travis wouldn't be surprised if he and the others were some of the last survivors. In the short time they'd spent at the House of Violet, more districts had succumbed to the shadow, leaving less than a quarter of the city untouched by blinding, supernatural darkness. Most of those districts were located near the coast.

The ones that were deeper inland, however...those were mostly dark. And quiet.

Travis had almost forgotten Jewels was there, when suddenly she whispered, "I'm sorry, Travis." Her green eyes were fixed on the billowing mass of darkness. She was trying not to look at him—trying to keep him from noticing the shine in her eyes.

His brow furrowed. "You're sorry? Why are you sorry?"

"I feel" —she swallowed— "partly responsible for you being stuck here. If I hadn't..." She dropped her gaze to the frozen ground and toed at a rock.

"If you hadn't what? Gone into cardiac arrest?" Travis said with an upward flick of his brows. "It's not your fault, Jewels. It was my decision to stay, remember? Don't blame yourself for something you didn't do."

She sighed. A tear slipped down her cheek, sparkling in the muddy glow of one of the only streetlights on this block that was still working. Soon, all the power would go out. Soon, they'd freeze or suffocate. He couldn't decide which was worse.

"Hey," he said softly, turning fully to face her. "Not your fault." When she still didn't respond, he pressed, "I mean it. 'Kay?"

It took her a moment, but finally, she nodded. "'Kay."

And then Travis did something he'd never done before—not for any girl.

He brushed the tear off her cheek with his thumb. The physical contact caused her heart to accelerate, and his was soon doing the same when she leaned into his touch instead of pulling away, his palm forming to the supple curve of her cheek. Her skin was soft and warm, despite the raw night.

"I'm not ready," Jewels said, her voice breaking.

Travis's chest tightened. He knew she wasn't just referring to *this* end— the one they were facing now.

She was not ready to die at all, whether it was from the collision of two warring dimensions or a disease that had no cure.

Fleeting and fragile—that was what life was. Not just for mortals, but for everyone. And he had taken it for granted. All of it. His health, his freedom, his immortality, his *life*. He longed for another chance—just one more. For himself, and for Jewels. Max. The others.

Why had it had taken something like this for him to realize it? To appreciate all that he had? This wasn't the first time he'd faced the prospect of death, but for some reason this was hitting him harder than the others. Maybe it was because of his brothers. Maybe it was because the only other

Devil who was here with him was Max. Maybe it was because he'd had longer to think about it this time around, to realize, *Oh shit, I'm actually going to die.*

Maybe it was that. Maybe it was all of those things.

"Come here," he said quietly. He wrapped an arm around Jewels, pulled her against his side, and rested his cheek on the top of her head. It took her a moment, but eventually she wrapped both arms around his waist and leaned her head against his shoulder.

They stood there awhile, gazing out at the ruins of Yveswich. Just breathing together, for what might be their very last night.

"Just for the record," Jewels began, sniffling in the cold, "if I could spend my last minutes with anyone...anyone in the world..." She tilted her head to peek up at him. "I would choose to spend them with you, Travis."

The confession struck him dumb.

He was about to stutter through some lame-ass reply he'd jumbled up in his head when the front door of the house swung open behind them. Footsteps thundered down the steps.

Travis turned—

Dallas and Max were sprinting across the yard, their shoes crunching in the frosted grass.

Max cupped his hands over his mouth and shouted, "Get the hell in here!"

"What's going on?" Travis called.

"Phones are working again!" Dallas exclaimed. She was beaming.

Travis's jaw dropped, and he glanced at Jewels. "Holy shit," he breathed.

She let out a startled laugh, her face alight with hope. "Well, would you look at that?"

Travis knew exactly who they had to thank for this...miracle. That's what it was—what *Atlas* was. A miracle.

He took Jewels by the hand, and together they ran into the house.

97

HEAVEN'S GATE
ANGELTHENE, STATE OF WITHEREDGE

Roman paced across the kitchen. The others—everyone, including the kids—were crowded around the table. Most were gathered around Tanner, who sat before his laptop. The hacker was wholly focused on his screen, ensuring communications stayed up.

If they were cut again... If Travis didn't have a chance to call...

Roman stiffened as he felt a gentle hand glide down his forearm, fingers circling his wrist.

It was Shay.

"He'll call," she said softly. Her touch freed the breath in his lungs and melted the tension right out of him. "Give him a chance."

He forced himself to stand in one spot. Forced himself to breathe. He slipped his wrist out of Shay's grasp, but instead of pulling away like she expected him to—he could see it in her face, no matter how hard she tried to hide it—he laced his fingers with hers. Her aura warmed in response, and he felt her studying him out of the corner of her eye before she cleared her throat and turned her attention to Atlas.

Tanner said, "It's probably unrealistic to think they'll call right away. Give them a minute—"

Someone's phone started buzzing. It was Darien's.

The room got quiet enough that Roman swore no one was even breathing.

Darien took his phone out of his back pocket and checked the caller identification.

"Who is it?" Roman gritted out.

Darien merely answered the call with a swipe of his thumb, placed the device flat on the table on speakerphone, and said, "Cassel."

A burst of static rattled the speakers. And then: "Darien, it's Travis."

Fuck.

Roman's throat clamped shut. Hearing his brother's voice again—hearing how upset he was—was a kick to the fucking nuts.

Darien's eyes shuttered—the only sign of the storm of stress Roman could sense stirring inside him.

When Paxton's gaze found Roman's in the room full of people, and he saw the concern shining in the boy's eyes, Roman forced himself to snap the hell out of it. To put on a brave face for his brother and mouth, "It's okay."

But Pax was pale, and his heart was racing so fast, Roman could hear it from over here.

When Darien opened his eyes, every last trace of defeat was gone. What took its place was determination—fierce and unwavering. "Travis, where are you?" he demanded.

This time, it was Travis's ragged inhale, not the static, that scraped down the line. "I'm in Yveswich. I didn't make it out on time."

Guilt slammed into Roman with the force of a semi. He'd failed to help Travis when he'd had the chance, and now...

Dean must have sensed how he was feeling, because he looked his way, his gaze heavy with empathy.

Travis continued, "We tried, but we were too late and the boat tipped over. We wrecked our phones in the ocean." A heavy pause. A splintered inhale. And then: "I'm so fucking sorry, Darien—"

"Who's with you?" Darien asked.

Travis took a moment to compose himself before replying. "Max, Jewels, Dallas, Aspen, Malakai, Dominic, Blue. We've also got Maya and Magenta with us." Roman noticed when Loren stiffened at Travis's mention of Dallas.

Dallas was alive—they had confirmation of that now. Alive...but not safe.

They all stood to lose someone. Someone important.

Ivy stepped between Jack and Kylar, getting as close to the phone as she could, and said, "Travis, where, *exactly*, are you?"

"The House of Violet." At that, Tanner started typing on his laptop, keys clacking.

With his hand still clasping Shay's, Roman quietly walked over to stand behind Atlas, Dean stepping aside to give him room. On Tanner's browser was a map of Yveswich.

"We were at the Black Market last night and almost got killed," Travis went on. "Long story short, Raina and Silas Cruso and Charlotte Demeure found us and basically saved our asses. This is Raina's phone I'm calling you on."

Darien said, "All right, how's it looking there? What's the visibility like?"

"It's getting worse," Travis admitted, his voice husky. "It's easier to see closer to the coast, but the shadow is spreading farther inland."

"Can you still see the Control Tower?" Tanner asked. His eyes were fixed on his screen—on the navigation arrow he was dragging across the map. To the Control Tower.

Roman shared a glance with Shay.

Voices murmured in the background.

And then Travis said, "Yeah, kind of, why do you ask?"

"Because we have a plan," Darien said. "But you'll need to act quickly. We spoke with Roark—he said the tower's stuck in a Battleshort, which means the forcefield can't be shut off, and the military plans on blasting the city with missiles at Witching Hour in two days."

Oh shit.

Travis cursed. More voices murmured in the background.

Roman released Shay's hand and started to pace again—he couldn't help it. He felt like he was going to puke. He could feel multiple people—Shay, Paxton, Dean, Kylar—tracking his movements. Sayagul was, too, the dragon watching him silently from his shadow that moved across the kitchen floor.

"Why the missiles?" This question came from Max. "What's the point of that? They just decided they want to kill the last of the survivors, or what?"

"It's a long story," Darien said. "But listen—I've got Arthur here with me, and we believe our plan is doable. Hold on—I'm going to let him talk to you, all right? Here he is."

Darien stepped aside and went to stand by Loren's chair as Arthur shuffled closer to the table. "Hello—Travis?" Arthur called.

A brief delay, and then Travis said, "Hey, Art."

A few other people voiced their own greetings in the background. Roman recognized Malakai, Aspen, Dominic, Blue...

"Travis—listen closely," Arthur began. "Roark tells me there's a military base not far from the coast. Is that correct?"

"Yeah, we were there yesterday," Travis said, his tone coated with curiosity.

"What I would like you to do, Travis," Arthur said, "is break into the military base. Tanner will be able to get you in, and from there I am going to help you grab what you'll need from the armory."

A pause. Roman listened intently, hearing this news for the first time himself. While everyone had filled each other in on the shit that'd happened while they were apart, Roman, until now, hadn't heard anything about this plan. About the missiles, and how the hell they were going to get Travis and the others un-stuck.

"And what are we looking for?" This question came from Jewels.

"A missile with a chargeable warhead," Arthur replied.

The pause that followed was heavy. Roman could practically *feel* the doubt and confusion filtering down the line, and he couldn't help but feel some of that doubt—and confusion—himself.

If Darien felt any, he didn't show it. "This is your ticket out, Trav," he said. He had taken up position behind Loren like a bodyguard, arms crossed over his chest. "You're going to have to trust us and just *do it.*"

The speakers crackled. Everyone in the room shared glances.

Tanner's attention went to his computer—checking to make sure the connection wasn't lost.

"Travis?" Darien called. "You there?"

But it wasn't Travis on the other line anymore—it was Malakai.

"Hey, fuckface," the Reaper said by way of greeting. "Guess who?"

Darien tipped his head back, his eyes rolling skyward.

"Thanks for the boat idea," Malakai continued, his tone saturated with sarcasm. "It worked great—I've always wanted to die in Yveswich."

Jack and Kylar chuckled.

Malakai said, "What, exactly, do you want us to do with a *missile?*"

Darien said, "I want you to take out the Control Tower with it."

———

"Okay, and how are we supposed to charge this warhead?" Jewels asked.

Travis sat beside her on the couch in Raina's living room. Everyone was gathered around the coffee table—around the phone Travis had set down in the center of it—as they talked through the details of this plan with Arthur and Darien.

It was Darien who said, "With the magic of everyone in your group."

A beat of silence. And then Raina said, her tone doubtful, "And this will work?"

"Yes," Arthur replied, "it will work, but everyone will have to pitch in. It will require a high output of magic, so you are going to feel drained afterward and likely won't be able to use your magic for at least a few days."

Travis scanned the group, silently creating a mental list of the types of magic—the colors—of everyone in the room. Red, white, black, blue, and pink. Was it enough?

"We only have five types of magic, though," he said to Arthur.

Charlotte whispered, "I have storm magic. Will that help?"

"Charlotte says she has storm magic," Travis said. "So, six."

"It'll be enough," Arthur said.

Darien had just started talking again, when Malakai interrupted. "Have you *seen* the fucking tower?" the Reaper demanded. "It's practically alive—nothing can go near it. The energy that's coming off of it is insane."

Arthur tried to reply—

But Malakai wasn't done. "I'm supposed to believe this missile, that we're going to spend only two days charging, is going to take it down?"

"You're talking to a *weapons technician,*" Darien retorted. "Pretty sure he knows better than you."

Malakai merely grumbled. He slumped against the back of the couch and crossed his arms, looking pissed.

A quiet voice—young and male—drifted through the background. "Can I say something?" The sound of that voice was enough to nearly push Travis into an emotional spiral. He was barely hanging on by a damn thread, and now—

A beat of silence, a murmur of a male voice that sounded like Darien, or maybe Roman, and then Paxton was on the other line.

"Hi, Travis, it's Paxton. It's your brother."

Travis's eyes started to burn. "Hey, Pax. Nice to hear your voice."

"Yeah, you too. I just wanted to say that I love you. And you're going to be okay."

"Thanks, bud. I love you, too. Is Roman...?"

"He's here, too." A pause, and then: "He says hi."

Travis highly doubted that. Especially when several seconds passed, and Roman said nothing.

Absolutely. Fucking. *Nothing.*

The reality of that stung. Badly.

"All right, well—" Travis rubbed his brow with his thumb and forefinger. "Thanks, Paxton."

"We'll see you soon, 'kay?"

"Yeah," Travis said. "Yeah, damn right you will."

"Okay, bye," Paxton said. At that, Dallas shared a small smile with Aspen and Jewels, the latter mouthing, "Awe."

"Bye, Pax," Travis said.

Darien was back on the line right away. "Any other questions?"

Malakai leaned forward. "Yeah, when's this break-in happening?"

Darien said, "Tonight."

THE ROOM WAS quiet for several minutes. Now that Travis was no longer on the line, this new silence was deep and haunting.

Loren slid her gaze to Darien, who hadn't stopped staring at his phone since the minute the screen went black. Since he and Travis had said goodbye to each other—for what might, but hopefully wouldn't, be the last time.

Paxton looked so sad. He was staring at his hands that were folded in his lap, his eyes hidden by his mop of hair. Loren's heart hurt for him.

And Roman... She didn't know the Shadowmaster very well, but she did know that he was the kind of man who hid his emotions with skill. And right now...

Right now, nothing was hidden. The bleak look on his face... Gods, it was unbearable.

Ivy was the first to break the quiet. "Okay, so I hate to be the bearer of bad news, especially when your plan sounds like it's going to work, but there's a big problem we need to address. As soon as that tower comes down, we have no idea how far that darkness is going to spread."

"She's right," Lace said. "For all we know, it could cover all of Ker."

Kylar added, "Which leaves us with two problems." He ticked them off on his fingers, his spider- and phantom-shaped rings flashing in the mellow kitchen light. "Problem one: Travis and the others won't be able to see. Problem two—"

Roman finished his sentence. "They won't be able to breathe."

"There's a Lucent Enterprises location in Yveswich," Arthur said. "Roark would know if they have syringes there. We can speak with him tomorrow and figure out where they keep them."

Tanner said, "Okay, so they'll have to steal and charge the missile, get it someplace high up—somewhere they can easily hit the tower—and they'll also have to get the syringes?" His brows jumped up.

Darien said, "It's a lot to ask, but they have enough time."

"Yeah, barely," Roman said bitterly.

"Okay, but what about what I mentioned?" Ivy asked. "If they can't see anything the minute the tower comes down, they might as well be trapped under a forcefield still."

"I can guide them out," Darien said.

The room got quiet. Very, very quiet. As everyone shared glances, it became obvious that they were all thinking the same thing. And Loren—

She felt sick to her stomach. The nightmares just kept coming, didn't they?

"Darien...," she whispered.

Ivy was shaking her head. "The risks—"

"Losing Max and Travis is a bigger risk," he said firmly. "I can do it, and I'll be fine." When he noticed Loren staring up at him with concern, he smoothed the hair at the top of her head. She reached for his hand, and he took it into his, his fingers warming hers. "I'll be fine," he said again. But her heart only beat harder.

Keys clacked as Tanner typed on his laptop. "I was able to get into the Fleet system earlier, and I found a live feed of the shadow in Yveswich." He pulled it up on the screen, and everyone gathered around to have a look.

Loren got up and walked with Darien to the other end of the table, her hand clasped in his. Sensing that she was looking at him, he lifted her hand to his mouth and kissed the back of it, his breath warming her skin.

"Look." Tanner shoved his glasses onto his head, briefly rubbed his eyes, then jabbed the screen with his index finger. "Lucent Enterprises is here."

Loren's stomach pitched downward.

It was engulfed in shadow.

"Which means," Tanner said, "if they need to go in there for the syringes—"

"I'll get them in," Darien said. That meant he'd have to track for even longer. Gods... She was going to throw up.

Roman said, "You seem pretty damn sure that you can do this, but that's literally *hours* of tracking, Darien. That's fucking insane, and you know it."

"I'll be fine," Darien said again. Not firmly, not rudely—calmly.

But Roman persisted, "And what if you're not? I think we need to have a backup plan, just in case. Do you still have those swords?"

"I have one," Darien replied.

Ivy said, "I have the other."

"Where's the third?" Darien asked the group. "Does Max have it?"

"Hold on—I'll text him," Ivy said. She got her phone out. "What's Raina's number?"

Darien pulled out his phone and gave it to her.

As she typed up a message, Darien said to Roman, "You're going back, aren't you?"

"You bet I am." His golden-brown eyes shone with determination. "I'm going to be there for Travis when that forcefield comes down. If worse comes to worst, I'll be able to see if I have one of those swords."

Kylar concluded, "And get in there if something happens and Darien can't hold the Sight for that long."

Darien threw a glance over his shoulder—at the clock on the stove. "You think you can make it back by the time the forcefield comes down?"

Dean said, "He drives like a lunatic. He'll make it. And I'm going with him."

Roman started. "What?"

"What?" Dean challenged. "I didn't come all this way, get you settled in Angelthene, only to let you fuck back off to Yveswich."

Roman was shaking his head. "You don't—"

"Your dad's still out there, kid," Dean interrupted. "He's still hunting you. You're not safe."

"I'll go with them," Shay said. Roman opened his mouth to reply, but Shay cut him off, raising a stern finger. "Don't you dare try to argue with me."

Roman shut his mouth, looking conflicted.

It was Lace who said, "You guys will have to take some of that serum with you. There's no point in going if you can't get into the shadow without suffocating."

Ivy shut off her phone screen. "Max said he lost the sword."

"Shit," Darien muttered.

Roman said, "So this is happening, then. I'll leave for Yveswich tonight with Dean and Shay, we'll be ready to go in when the forcefield comes down, and in the meantime you—" He gestured to Darien with a nod. "—will plan to guide them out as far as you can until we get there."

"I don't want you going in there unless I absolutely have to take a break," Darien said. "Understand?"

"What are these swords you speak of, anyway?" Dean asked. To Roman, he added, "You didn't mention any swords."

"They're blades of black adamant," Ivy replied. "They turn into mirrors in the Void, and for whatever reason, they're visible in the dark. Only the swords—nothing else."

"And what's this *Void* again?" Dean asked. "I feel like my mind's spinning." He gestured to his temple with a rotating finger. "I can't keep up."

Kylar said, "It's one of the dimensions in Spirit Terra."

"The worst dimension imaginable," Jack added with a small chuckle.

"And that's where the shadow's coming from?" Dean asked.

Darien nodded. "That's where the shadow's coming from."

"And you can't breathe in the shadow?"

"You can't breathe in Spirit Terra, no matter which dimension you're in."

Ivy added, "The Control Tower has essentially been keeping the portal at bay, patching it shut in a sense, which is why the people who are still there can still breathe, and why not all of the streets have been blinded by the Void."

"And we're about to take it down," Dean mused, looking equal parts overwhelmed and fatigued. He turned to Darien and said, "Once we're close enough, I can always take over with the tracking if you need a break. You just let me know, and I'll be ready to jump in."

Darien accepted the offer with a dip of his chin.

And it was that quiet acceptance that lifted some of the weight that was squashing Loren's lungs. Once Dean was close enough, he could handle some of the tracking so Darien didn't have to do it all.

As long as he'd be willing to accept the help. Admit when he needed it.

She scanned Darien's face now, watching as his inky hair gleamed in the light. He was studying Roman.

The Shadowmaster said, "So, we all know our next moves."

"You get back to Yveswich," Darien began, "you make sure you're there for when the tower comes down, and if that darkness spreads, and tracking fails for whatever reason, you use the swords and you find Travis and the others and you get the hell out. Good?"

Roman nodded. "Good."

Darien scanned the room. "Any other questions?"

No one spoke. No one argued.

"All right," Darien said. "Then it sounds like we've got ourselves a plan."

98

HEAVEN'S GATE
ANGELTHENE, STATE OF WITHEREDGE

Darien's boots pounded as he walked, sword in hand, down the hallway on the third floor. Toward the guest room where Roman had placed his belongings only a few hours ago.

He was in there now, grabbing everything he hadn't even had the chance to unpack. He had more than enough time to get back to Yveswich before the forcefield came down, but he'd be taking a longer route as a precaution. Avoiding the places where Don's men were more likely to be lying in wait. On top of that, they'd need to stop at a motel. It was late, and he and the others were beat from the long drive here. The drive they were going to have to make all over again.

Darien was almost at the door when he heard footsteps behind him. He turned—

And paused when he saw Ivy walking this way, the other sword in hand.

He and his sister had barely talked since she'd learned about the years he'd traded to the Widow. He'd wanted to talk to her—wanted to apologize —this whole time, but no words would ever be good enough. What the hell was he supposed to say, *Yeah, sorry that I'll be dying soon, I know it hurts your feelings, but there's nothing I can do about it?*

He hated disappointing people. Ivy, especially, but—his whole damn family. He'd disappointed—upset—all of them.

Ivy slowed as she drew near. For a moment, they faced each other, with nothing to break the silence but voices from other areas in the house.

"Here." She offered him the sword.

Darien closed his fingers around the hilt. "Listen, Ivy—"

"It's okay, Darien." Her voice held none of the edge it'd had these last few days. She sucked in a breath. "I mean—it's not actually okay. It'll never be okay, but— I'm done fighting. We can agree to disagree and just...carry on." She crossed her arms. "You're my brother, I love you, and I...I don't want to waste any more of the time we have left fighting with each other."

He swallowed. "Ivy—"

"It's okay," she said again. But her eyes were shining, and there was a wobble to her chin that she was trying desperately to hide. "Don't ruin it with an apology that doesn't solve anything." She gestured to the open doorway to Roman's room. "Now get going."

Darien stood there for a moment. Looking at his sister and wondering how he deserved her. Deserved any of the Devils.

And then they parted ways, Ivy heading downstairs while Darien walked down the hallway and into Roman's room.

He was pretty much ready. All his bags were zipped up, his backpack already slung over his shoulder. Paxton's bags were there, too.

"You're taking Paxton?" Darien asked as he added the swords to Roman's pile.

"I'm taking Paxton," Roman confirmed as he put on his jacket. "He told me he wanted to come with, and I'm not going to tell him no."

"I'd go with you, but I need to be here for Loren," Darien said. "If something happens to her..." He sucked in a sharp breath, then blew it out in a heavy sigh. "Well, we're all fucked. And I lose the woman I love."

"You forgot the part where you die, too," Roman said with dark humor.

The corner of Darien's mouth twitched.

It had never been about him, though. The fact that his life was tied to Loren's changed nothing. Even if he hadn't made that deal with the Widow, he would still protect her just as hard. And every time her life was threatened, it was not his own he was worried about. It was only hers.

It had only ever been about her.

"The first thing I'm going to do when I see Travis," Roman began, staring blankly at the wall, "is tell him how sorry I am. I made him feel like shit when he decided to stay behind with Jewels, and I feel...I feel like it was my fault. Maybe, if I hadn't hit him so hard with my words, this wouldn't have happened. Maybe, if I had taken a moment to actually think through what was happening on a larger scale, I could have gotten him out on time."

"Don't beat yourself up too much. I've felt the same as you ever since I had that stupid argument with Max. And I didn't even apologize to him on the phone." Darien had regretted it since the minute he'd ended the call. Max had been right fucking *there,* and Darien hadn't taken the opportunity to say something kind to him.

"You'll get another chance," Roman said.

"So will you."

Roman sighed. "Hope so."

Darien said, "Keep looking up."

"Yeah," Roman said on a heavy exhale. "Keep looking up."

CRICKETS SANG in the dark yard as Roman walked to his car. Shay and Paxton were with him. The fact that Pax was wide awake was surprising, given the late hour.

The front door swung open behind him. Roman didn't turn to see who it was as he began loading his and Paxton's belongings—the bags they hadn't even had the chance to unpack—into the back seat. Judging from the gait, it was Dean.

He was proven correct when his uncle's gravelly voice floated through the night-chilled yard. "Rome?" he called. "Can I talk to you for a sec?"

"Make it quick—we gotta head out," Roman said as he crammed more shit into the car. Time was tight. Now that Paxton was coming, they would have to stop at a motel at some point and get some rest, which was something he likely would've avoided doing if Paxton had stayed behind. And then there was the longer route they'd have to take, which would add about six, maybe seven hours to their drive.

He stepped aside so Shay could place her bags inside, and then she wove past Dean and got into the passenger's seat.

Roman faced his uncle, noting the concern on his face. "What's the matter?" Roman asked him.

Dean lowered his voice. "Do you really think this is a good idea?"

"Do I think what's a good idea?"

"Taking Paxton."

"Yes," Roman said, his tone firm and resolute. "I do." To his little brother, he said, "Get in the car, Pax." He beckoned.

Paxton squished in—climbing between the front seats and into the back.

Dean stepped forward. "Roman—hear me out. I'm begging you."

Roman faced his uncle with reluctance. "What?"

"Just because you made it to Angelthene doesn't mean your dad's not looking for you anymore. You have to think of Paxton—"

"I *am* thinking of Paxton," Roman growled. "I'm *always* thinking of Paxton, and don't you dare to try to tell me that I'm not." He got the car keys out of his pocket.

Dean was staring at him with a look of apprehension. Fear.

"Look," Roman began with a sigh. "I split up from him before the explosion happened in Yveswich. Shit went sideways while we were apart, and he could have been killed. I'm not about to have a repeat of that shit and risk losing him again. Now are you coming or not?" He grabbed his last bag—the one that was too big to fit in the back seat—and walked around to the back of the car.

Dean followed. "I get where you're coming from, Roman—I understand."

Roman popped the trunk. The space was small—barely big enough for this one bag. That was the downside to sports cars. It was either no trunk, or one too small to really fit anything into.

Dean continued, "But your dad doesn't even know about this place." He gestured to Heaven's Gate, golden light spilling out of windows onto the dark lawn. "This is the safest place for him."

"The safest place for him is with me," Roman countered. He dumped the bag into the trunk and slammed it shut.

"Can we just hit pause for a second and talk this through—"

Roman rounded on his uncle. "You are *not* going to try to tell me what to do," he hissed.

"I'm not—"

"No offense, Dean, but you haven't even been a part of our lives in fucking *years. Years.*" Dean winced, but Roman didn't let up. "I'm not about to just let you, someone who couldn't even be bothered with us up until—what, two days ago?—step in and make decisions for me as if you know anything about *my* life." He jabbed himself in the chest.

"Roman, come on—please—"

"I've heard enough. If you want to come help, come help. If not, stay out of my way."

He got into the car without another word. He fired up the engine and left, not waiting for Dean to get into his own car. Not looking in the rear-view mirror—at the sight of his uncle standing in the yard, staring after him in defeat.

"Everything okay?" Shay asked.

"Yeah, everything's fine," he said. But his blood was hot, and his heart was pounding.

The gates swung open, and he drove through them, the security spells washing across the car.

He knew Dean made sense, knew he was only trying to help, but—

Roman refused to separate from Pax. They'd had too many close calls lately, too many times where he thought he'd lost his brother—for good.

It wouldn't happen again.

Maybe he was making a mistake, but—

He glanced at Paxton in the back seat. He already had his video game console out, the screen suffusing his freckled face with light.

Pax had wanted to come with. Had told Roman that he wanted to be there for Travis, too. The kid had been denied so many choices in life, stripped of so much happiness, that Roman did not have the heart to tell him that he had to stay behind.

Headlights approached in the rear-view.

It was Dean.

Roman drew a deep, steadying breath.

He'd apologize to Dean later.

Right now, he was going to get Travis. He was going to get his other brother—the one he'd lost—and bring him the hell home.

99

THE MILITARY BASE
YVESWICH, STATE OF KER

"Isn't it past your bedtime, old man?" Malakai hissed into his headset. He stood with Aspen down the block from the military base, watching for the guards who were doing their rounds.

They'd all left the House of Violet shortly after talking to the others who were in Angelthene. It was almost Witching Hour, but being trapped in a city of perpetual darkness rendered time meaningless. Malakai didn't even have a sleep schedule anymore.

Not that he'd ever really had one to begin with.

Arthur, however, did. And Malakai was having a fantastic time pestering the old guy.

The speaker crackled. "You'd be lost without me, Mister Delaney," Arthur said, "so I figured I could sacrifice a few hours of sleep."

"Awwww, you shouldn't have."

Another crackle, and then Atlas hissed, "Can you guys focus? If you mess this up—"

"At ease, Atlas," Malakai drawled. "Don't be a bitcher like Devlin."

A burst of static. And then: "Hey, I heard that," Travis protested, his fierce whisper causing the speakers to crackle.

Malakai wheezed a laugh.

As much as he hated that scrawny fucker for trying to date his sister, he had a hell of a good time picking fights with him. Maybe it wouldn't be so bad having him around a bit more.

He flicked off the mic on his headset and whispered exactly that to Asp.

She snickered, her catlike eyes shining all pretty in the muddy glow of a streetlight. "I told you he'd grow on you."

He flicked his mic back on and said, "Hurry it up, Atlas. It's cold as balls out here."

"I'm trying to time it right, you ignoramus!" Tanner said. Malakai chuckled. "Trav, you ready?"

"Yup," Devlin replied.

"The guards are passing in thirty seconds," Malakai said, watching the guards from where he and Aspen were hidden.

Atlas said, "Spells will come down then, and that's your shot. Don't be seen."

Devlin said, "I'll do my best."

"Why do they get the fun job?" Malakai hissed to Aspen.

"I'd rather be out here," she said, her teeth chattering. "We have the easy job—they're the ones doing all the heavy lifting."

"We can literally hear you," Jewels groused. "Maybe turn off your mic before talking shit—"

"Now," Atlas said. "Get in there now—go."

Malakai kept an eye on the guards as his sister and Devlin darted over the chainlink fences and into the military base.

"Fuck me," Malakai said with a smile as they landed lightly on their feet inside the base. "It worked."

TRAVIS STUCK CLOSE to Jewels as they crept through the military base on cat-soft feet.

According to Roark, there were no anima mundi missiles on site, which would've made their lives a whole hell of a lot easier. But there were missiles with the same framework, so all they had to do was steal one of those and bring it back to the House of Violet to charge it.

While Tanner was able to guide them through the building using the video feeds on the security cameras, it was Arthur who they had to call on video when they made it to the armory.

The place was *loaded*. It was a good thing Jack wasn't here, or he'd likely set off some bomb out of pure, unbridled curiosity. He'd had a dangerous fascination with fireworks a few years ago, and had nearly scorched Travis's hair off in the back yard at Hell's Gate. He had a battle scar to show for that.

Where he and Jewels were crouched behind an armored vehicle, Travis whispered, "For someone so good at technology, you suck at holding a phone still, Arthur." He chuckled as he watched the old man practically fight for his life to hold the phone straight. He was in the kitchen at Heaven's Gate; Travis recognized it in the background.

The fact that the others had been forced to vacate Hell's Gate because of Don was...well, it made Travis uneasy. But it was the right choice. Better to be safe than sorry, no matter how much they hated to be pushed to this point.

Arthur righted the camera. "Move the camera back to the left, Travis," he said, his voice coming through the headset instead of the phone. "It's that one," he declared.

Travis crept forward and tried to grab the missile—

"Holy hell, this thing's heavy," he breathed.

"I tried to warn you," Arthur said.

"Hold on," Travis grunted. He was already sweating. "Stay on the line —I need to use both hands for this." He slipped the phone into his back pocket, then lifted one end of the missile while Jewels went to the other. "Ready?" he asked her as she curled her fingers under the base.

She nodded. "Ready."

They hefted the missile up and carried it through the building. It was hella awkward, but it worked. Tanner stayed on the headset, watching on the cameras and directing them to either hide or go a different route if he spotted military personnel moving about. Eventually, they made it outside.

As they waited in the shadows of the building for Tanner to lower the spells for a second time, Travis leaned against the icy-cold wall and took a moment to catch his breath. Jewels was doing the same, the missile lying on the pavement between them. That thing was stupidly heavy. Way heavier than it looked. Once it was charged and they were ready to move forward with the last step of their plan, they'd have to move it with vehicle transportation, then take turns getting it up onto the roof of the tallest building that aligned with the Control Tower.

"So," Travis began, panting. "When we get back to Angelthene...you want to go out again?"

The speakers on his headset crackled, then Malakai said, "Heard that."

Jewels beamed, but she did not turn off her mic as she said to Travis, "I would love to go out with you again, Travis."

Travis smiled. "Cool."

Malakai grumbled on the other end. But he did not object.

Travis took it as a win.

Tanner came through on the headset. "Spells are coming down in five seconds."

Travis counted. One, two, three, four, five...

The minute he felt the spells fall in a downward ripple that made his blood purl in his veins, he and Jewels were moving. They had to go through the gate this time, the missile way too heavy to get over the fence, and from there they crossed the dark, deserted road and disappeared into an alley between two buildings, narrowly avoiding an armored vehicle that was coming around the corner.

"Shit—hurry," Travis breathed. He was at the end of the missile, walking forward while Jewels walked backward.

Loose gravel crunched under tires. Whoever was driving that thing was getting closer, and they were way too exposed in this alley.

But there was a dumpster up ahead, and that was where they hid.

"I feel like a goose," Jewels hissed as she waddled backward, steering the long, heavy missile to the shadows behind the dumpster.

Travis's chuckle sounded more like a grunt, the veins in his neck straining beneath his flushed skin.

He ducked behind that dumpster—right on time. As the armored vehicle passed by the mouth of the alley, he and Jewels set down the missile and took a breather. Sweat gleamed on her forehead, and she wiped at it with the gloves she'd borrowed from Raina.

By the time they made it to where the Reapers were hiding, they found Malakai pacing, and Aspen rubbing her arms to warm them, her teeth chattering.

"Now what?" Malakai said as Travis grunted, carefully lowering his end of the missile as Jewels lowered hers.

"Now we have to charge the warhead," Aspen said. She waved Travis and Jewels aside and said, "You guys take a break, we'll carry it from here."

They'd come here in a truck that belonged to the Sylphen. That truck was parked about a block over—far enough away not to raise suspicion, if any soldiers were to spot it.

When they got back to the House of Violet, the charging began.

Pulling raw magic up from the anima mundi, in the amount of power they would need for a missile of this size, was not possible without something like the Control Tower. Not even cristala charging stations would work, as those used filtered magic, not raw.

But, with everyone in their group taking turns powering the warhead, it would become a weapon strong enough to take down the Control Tower.

Blue had blue magic.

Raina had white magic.

Malakai and Travis had black magic.

Charlotte had purple magic.

Magenta had pink magic.

And Maya...she had red.

It wasn't every color. But it was enough.

Maya's turn would have to wait until the end, though. She had still not fully recovered from falling into the canal, so everyone else would take turns charging first. The amount of magic it would take would require recovery periods for each person, but as long as they took turns, the warhead should be fully charged by the second day.

Just in time to get the Control Tower down and get the hell out of here.

100

HEAVEN'S GATE
ANGELTHENE, STATE OF WITHEREDGE

The next day passed too quickly, each tick of the clock a sword hanging above their heads. Arthur spent most of that time on the phone, instructing those who were trapped in Yveswich on how to go about dismantling the missile and charging the warhead.

By the time evening rolled around, a deeper sense of foreboding had settled over Heaven's Gate. Loren stood in the dark foyer, unable to tear her eyes off Darien as he tightened the straps on her bulletproof vest. Of course, she was the only person wearing body armor. The others didn't have to.

A lock of jet black hair hung in Darien's eyes, the end fluttering with every calm exhalation. She fought the urge to reach up and smooth it back. Run her fingers through his hair. Pull him down to her level and kiss him.

Jack, Ivy, Lace, and Tanner were in here too, lacing up their boots and strapping guns and knives onto their bodies. Preparing for a very personal vendetta. Their Familiars—Bandit, too—stood by the door in a small army of their own, their eyes glowing in the dark like varicolored fireflies. Moonlight trickled in through the big windows, causing the ornate chandelier to glimmer like an ice sculpture.

Calm. Everybody was calm, focused. Even Twitch, who was usually too rambunctious to sit still, was silent and observant. Though there was a nervous tic around the jaguar's left eye, one that never fully went away.

As Darien tightened the last strap on the vest, those striking eyes of his flicked up to meet hers. "How does that feel?" he asked her, his bass voice echoing in the large, open area.

She rolled her shoulders and rotated her arms. "It's a little snug, but I think it's good."

He gripped two of the straps and pulled her toward him, so quickly she bumped into his chest with a muffled squeak of alarm. "I wish I was taking this off of you instead," he breathed against her mouth. Her body warmed as he nipped at her bottom lip.

Jack said, "I feel like I just walked onto the set of some squirrelly porno."

Tanner stifled a laugh.

Loren fought a smile as well—one that Darien was soon mirroring. She felt the shape of that smile against her lips as he bent to kiss her, his hands still wrapped possessively around the straps of her vest. That vest was a precaution he'd insisted on taking, and one she'd agreed to without argument. The last thing she wanted was for Darien to use his magic any more than he needed to, especially with how many hours he'd have to spend tracking tomorrow.

She tried not to think about that—about the missiles that were scheduled to strike Yveswich in less than thirty hours—and instead focused on the feel of Darien's mouth on hers.

When he broke the kiss—too soon, as always—she was out of breath.

He let go of the straps and skimmed the edge of her jaw with a scarred knuckle affectionately.

Then he turned his focus on his family. "Everyone ready?"

"Ready," they murmured.

He inclined his head toward the door.

The Devils filed out into the dark front yard, the Familiar Spirits leading the way. Darien took Loren by the hand, and together they walked out of Heaven's Gate.

They were heading to the Hunting Grounds to pay a visit to Lionel Savage—another name on their list of people they were crossing out one by one. Another person involved in the break-in and the disappearance of little Mortifer.

Hopefully, by the end of the night, the score would be settled, and Mortifer would be back home.

IN THE STUDY at the Hunting Grounds—the house where the

Huntsmen lived—Loren sat by herself on the couch as five of the Seven Devils did what they did best: They killed. Brutally.

Her lungs were too small, the smell of blood turning her stomach like a washing machine. Each breath she drew sliced through her teeth in audible gasps.

She was going to throw up the lasagna she'd had for dinner, wasn't she? She was going to throw up the food Ivy had spent hours making—

But then Darien was crouching before her, that cold, hateful mask on his face slipping—just for her. The edge in his eyes softened, the reaction so at odds with the massacre going on behind him.

"Close your eyes, baby," he whispered.

She obeyed. He gently grasped her wrists, lifting her shaking hands until they were resting over her ears. The air shifted as he stood, and she felt his absence as if she were missing a limb as he walked away, returning to finish the job he had come here to do.

After tonight, there would be no Huntsmen left, save for one. Harley Savage, Lionel's son and Lace's cousin. Harley was about Travis's age. The Devils had explained to her that his father treated him cruelly—as cruelly as Randal had treated Darien and Ivy when he was alive.

After tonight, Harley, who'd been forced to step outside and keep quiet, would be Head of the Hunting Grounds.

In Angelthene, killing the members of another Darkslaying House was forbidden. But Lionel had broken another, equally strict rule when he'd made the mistake of trespassing not just on the property of another House...but the *Head* of Angelthene's Houses.

This was payback.

It was also a message. A very clear and ruthless message: *Don't fuck with us.*

For several minutes, Loren kept her eyes closed and her ears plugged.

And then she took a deep breath, lowered her hands, and opened her eyes.

Darien noticed immediately, his eyes—so full of rage and self-loathing —snapping to her face.

She held his lethal stare. *I'm not afraid of you,* she thought. *I see you, Darien, and you do not scare me.*

He seemed to understand. Understand and accept what she was giving him.

Because he lowered the sound barrier he'd put up to protect her.

The screams of the Huntsmen pierced the air. Awful—those screams were awful. Spine-chilling.

But she did not cover her ears. She did not close her eyes. She watched, and she was not afraid.

BACK AT HEAVEN'S GATE, Loren found Darien waiting for her by the swimming pool behind the house.

Standing in her swimsuit in the empty, lamplit kitchen, she peeked out at him through the blinds. He was sitting on one of the pool chairs, wearing only a pair of black shorts. It was Witching Hour, and the yard was dark, save for the soft glow of string lights and garden lanterns.

As she watched him, he bowed his head, the locks of his hair sliding forward as he cupped his brow. In his other hand, he held a pendant, his fist swallowing it up. Only the silver chain was visible, and it was the gentle swaying of that chain that alerted her to the fact that his hands were shaking.

She opened the door and slipped outside, the ground beneath her bare feet cooled by the breath of night.

Darien made no indication that he was aware of her presence as she crossed the yard, her feet making sticking sounds on the flagstone path. The shadows of the night drew attention to every impressive muscle in his back, every bit of ink that made up his tattoo. Every scar as well. As she drew near, she slid her hands across his broad shoulders, feeling the ridges of all those scars beneath her palms.

He loosed a long breath, his rigid muscles relaxing beneath her touch.

"Are you okay?" she asked him.

"I'm fine," he said quietly. But he wasn't fine—she knew that.

So she asked him again, "How are you, really?"

He hesitated, just for a moment, rubbing his brow with his thumb and forefinger. "I'm tired, baby," he confessed, his voice husky. "I'm very tired."

A weight tugged on her heart. He looked exhausted, but when he'd said he was tired, she knew he hadn't meant the physical kind.

He lowered his hand with a barely audible sigh, and opened his eyes.

Black—his eyes were black. He never got a night off, did he? Even after everything that'd happened with the Huntsmen, all the blood he'd spilt, his demons would not let him rest.

He opened his fist and studied the pendant in the palm of his hand. It was the locket—the one shaped like a pair of overlapping angel wings. "I was hoping we would've found him by now," he said.

Mortifer. He was talking about Mortifer.

Before Lace had delivered the final blow to the uncle who'd emotionally scarred her, Lionel had snitched on Gaven Payne in an attempt to save his own life, revealing that it was the weapons dealer who'd taken Mortifer into his possession the night of the break-in. But Gaven's aura was being masked, and every time the Devils tried to track him, they were met with a dead end.

Loren could only imagine the defeat they must be feeling. So much bloodshed...for nothing.

Gazing blankly at the moonlight glinting off the turquoise water in the pool, Darien whispered, "I've watched the security footage from that night more times than I can count. And every time I watch it, I ask myself why he didn't run. He can teleport, for fuck's sake. He could have just—*poof*—disappeared. But he didn't. He stayed right where he was, on that fucking fridge. And I remembered...before I left to bring you to Yveswich, I asked him to take care of the house. I asked him to watch the house and look after the others. I told him it was an important job and that I trusted him to do it for me." His throat bobbed. "That's why he didn't run. Because of me." His eyelids fell shut. "He didn't run because of me."

She wordlessly slid her arms around his shoulders, holding him closer. "It wasn't your fault—"

"I want him back." Darien's confession was a cracked whisper.

A minute of silence passed, and then he drew a breath, opened his eyes that were still a charred black, and said, "I'm worried about Travis and Max, too. I feel like I failed them." He cupped his mouth with one hand and stared out at the yard, his other hand forming a new fist around the locket.

She crouched beside him and laid a hand across his thigh. "Darien, look at me," she said gently.

He didn't; he just kept staring blankly at the pool. His expression was so filled with torture, it made the space behind her eyes ache.

She slipped her hand across his chin and turned his head so he was looking her in the eye. As she held his stare, the black of the Sight went away after two blinks.

"They're going to be okay," she told him. "I promise."

He took her hand that was still grasping his chin into his and kissed her fingertips.

"Is there a picture?" she asked him. She got up and sat down beside him on the chair, his thigh warming hers. When his brow flickered with question, she gestured to the locket in his hand.

"Oh—yeah, do you want to see?" Carefully, he opened the locket and passed it to her.

The woman in the picture was his mother. Elsie Cassel.

"She's beautiful," Loren said.

"Thank you." His voice was gruff.

"She has your smile," she told him, glancing between him and the photograph. She had his dimple, too, in the same cheek. "Did she give you this necklace?"

He nodded. "I put the picture in there myself. After she..." He didn't finish his sentence.

Gently, she snapped the locket shut and flipped it over. Engraved on the back of it in admirable calligraphy was the phrase, *Love Must Always Win.*

"What does it mean?" she asked him.

"It's a reminder. To choose love, kindness. To never lose sight of the things that matter. And that love is a powerful force that always triumphs, no matter how dark the road."

She turned the locket from side to side, watching as the limited light in the area glinted off the finely carved letters. "Beautiful," she said. She handed it back to him.

For a few minutes, they sat there together beneath the stars, Darien marveling at the sky while she marveled at him. It was one of those very rare moments when she could get away with watching him without those unnervingly gorgeous eyes catching her. She knew he was fully aware that she was staring; there was nothing that slipped by him. But in that moment, she felt like she could *really* look at him. Take in all his perfections—yes, perfections, she didn't believe he had a single *imperfection*—at her leisure.

As he put his necklace back on, he said, "Want to go for a swim?"

"I'd love to go for a swim."

He got up, and she was about to follow when he suddenly scooped her off the chair and threw her over his shoulder.

She squealed, her hair tumbling down his back. "Darien!" she protested. But he was already walking, holding her in place with a large hand on her ass cheek.

Wait.

Oh gods.

"Wait—" Oh gods, he was heading for the pool! "Darien, do NOT throw me in the water!—"

He did exactly that.

She screeched as she broke the surface, water blasting around her.

By the time she came back up with a gasp, he was in the pool, too—swimming toward her.

"How *dare* you!" She splashed him in the face.

He shielded with a hand and let out a low chuckle.

"No sex for you tonight," she said as he smoothed his drenched hair back.

He arched a brow. "Oh, really?"

No. Not really. Even just looking at him, his muscled arms parting the water as he swam toward her like a shark, had her body warming by several degrees.

She backed up. Up—until her back hit the pool wall.

And then Darien was there, caging her in place with a hand braced on the ledge on either side of her. He pressed a hard kiss to her mouth, then gathered her into his arms, their damp bodies sticking together as he slowly spun her through the water, his hands gripping her by the waist.

"I love you, Loren Calla." The way he said it—as if they didn't have much time left—sent a tremor of fear from the crown of her head to the balls of her feet.

She knew why he said it that way, though. So she didn't question him.

Time was running out for those who were trapped in Yveswich, yes, but it was running out for her, too. *Just* her—not Darien. She'd see to that. Was working on saving him in every spare second she had.

She draped her arms around his neck and slipped her fingers through the damp strands of his hair, pushing it back from his face in the way she knew he liked. "I love you, Darien Cassel," she said.

Then she pulled him down to her level and kissed him.

DARIEN HAD trouble sleeping that night. He was simply too worried. About Max and Travis. About Mortifer. He couldn't relax.

He felt like an asshole as he kept waking Loren up with his tossing and turning. Eventually, he rolled onto his side and studied her beautiful, sleeping face, watching as the candlelight played with her golden hair and her soft features. As the minutes wore on, his eyelids gradually grew heavy, and he slipped into a light sleep.

When he woke up, no more than one hour later, he'd somehow ended up with his head resting on her stomach, an arm wrapped around her waist.

She was fast asleep, one arm draped across his shoulders, her other hand resting on the back of his neck, her fingers faintly twitching as she dreamed.

It was funny—he was the one who protected her physically, but she was the one who protected him mentally, emotionally. She took care of him in the areas where he struggled to take care of himself. He felt at peace when he was with her, and each day he was blessed to spend with her was a gift.

When he drifted off again a few minutes later, it was to the sound of her precious heartbeat.

He didn't wake up again after that, and the dreams he had were good dreams, all thanks to the angel who held him through the night. When he was with her, everything felt like it was going to be okay. Maybe not right now...but one day.

The world may be loud, and the future uncertain, but this...this was what heaven felt like.

This woman and her beautiful soul were his heaven.

101

THE HOUSE OF VIOLET
YVESWICH, STATE OF KER

Cans clunked together as Travis rummaged around in the fridge at the House of Violet, grabbing as many beers as he could carry. Tonight could very well be his last night alive, and he didn't plan on wasting it. No—he planned on getting rip-roaring drunk.

With Jewels.

A shadow darkened the kitchen floor.

Travis looked up from where he was crouching in front of the fridge—

And rolled his eyes into the back of his head when he beheld the male Reaper standing above him.

"What do you want?" Travis demanded as he added another beer to the pile of cans and bottles in his arms.

"A beer," Malakai said.

Travis scowled. "Is this a habit of yours or something? Show up when someone has beer, like some kind of fucking beer fairy?" He stood and kicked the door shut. With the glow of the fridge gone, the kitchen was so dark, he could hardly see anything.

"You don't need twelve beers," Malakai griped.

Is that how many he had? "They're not all for me. Some are for your sister."

He grunted. "I think you can spare one."

"There's more in the fridge. You don't need to steal mine." He didn't bother pointing out that the reason there were any left was because he was carrying the maximum.

Malakai opened the fridge and dug one out of the back. "So, you and my sister throwing an end of the world party or something?" He kicked the door shut.

"Yup, and you're not invited." He was about to walk away when Malakai spoke.

"I'm sorry."

Travis paused. Slowly, he turned around, blinking dramatically. "Come again?" If he'd had a free hand, he would have cupped it over his ear.

Malakai sucked in a sharp breath and mumbled, "I'm sorry."

And then the Reaper gagged so hard, his eyes watered. He turned in a circle, shaking his arms as if to rid himself of chills, the unopened beer in his hand sloshing. "I think I just threw up a little."

"Wow," Travis said flatly. "I never thought I'd hear those words. Jewels convince you to say that?"

"Aspen, actually. She said I'm a dick for putting everyone in danger, and I kinda like her, so. You get what you want. But don't expect it again." He pointed a finger in warning. "Got it?"

Travis couldn't help but smile. He shook his head and turned—

"Don't think this means we're friends now!" Malakai called after him.

"Whatever you say. See you tomorrow, asshole."

Malakai cracked open his beer. "See you tomorrow, dickhead."

The last sound Travis heard as he walked down the hallway, toward Jewels's room, was the gulping of Malakai's throat as he guzzled that beer.

TRAVIS COULDN'T STOP GRINNING as Jewels belted out the lyrics to the song blasting through the stereo speakers, her fingers wrapped around the neck of a beer bottle.

They were sitting across from each other on the floor in his bedroom, completely shit-faced and snort-laughing like idiots.

She tossed her head to the beat, her pale hair swirling about her rosy-cheeked face. Then she passed him the pretend microphone, thrusting the bottle at him. He took it and sang, well aware that he was way off tune and probably sounded like a dying bird.

Who cared, though? Not him. For all he knew, he was dying tomorrow, and he refused to waste one second on something as trivial as embarrassment.

By the time the song ended, they were breathless and grinning.

Jewels reached over and turned down the volume. "So," she said, brushing strands of hair out of her face, her chest rising and falling with her panting breaths.

"So," Travis repeated. He drummed his fingers against his beer can and took a swig. He was so drunk, the floor was tilting and the walls were spinning.

"What's the first thing you're going to say to Roman when you see him?"

The question was nearly enough to sober him. "I'm going to tell him... that I'm a fucking idiot."

"Good start," Jewels praised. She took a sip of beer. "That's a good start."

"And I'm going to tell him that I'm *never*"—he sliced a hand through the air—"coming back to Yveswich—for real this time." At that, Jewels trilled a laugh. Travis smiled back, but it was soon fading as he said, quieter now, "And that I'm sorry. I'm going to tell him I'm sorry."

"Good plan," Jewels said, nodding. She swirled the last of the beer in her bottle. "All good plans." She downed the last sip, her mouth shaping so perfectly over the lip of the bottle.

"And...," Travis said, a new smile pulling on his mouth. He couldn't stop staring at her—at that pretty face, those big, green eyes, the generous curve of her lips.

She squinted one eye at him. "And what?" she prompted. She licked her lips, sucking briefly on the lower one.

"And I'm going to tell him about this girl I like," he said, fuelled by liquid courage and the invisible sword hanging above his head. "Like, *really* like, not just a little." He held up his thumb and forefinger. "A lot," he said, about an inch of space between his fingertips.

Jewels gasped. "Wow!" she pretend-gushed, her eyes flaring. "That's a lot! Like, a lot a lot!"

He chuckled and lowered his hand. "Not sure if she feels the same way about me, though," he said with a noisy clearing of his throat.

"Oh, Travis," she purred. The way she said his name had him imagining how it might sound if he had her in the bed, her legs around his waist, their bodies moving as one. "Of course I do." That little bit of humor on her expression faded as she added, "I just..." She sighed. "I was scared."

"Two years or two days—it doesn't matter to me, Jewels," he said, his voice gruff. "It doesn't change that fact that I really...really...really...*really*... like you." He cleared his throat again.

She held up her thumb and forefinger. "This much?"

"More."

She widened the gap.

"More," he said again.

She raised her brows. "You sure about that?"

He smiled. "Really sure." But that smile was soon fading, his nerves getting the better of him, as he said, "You know, I've been thinking... In case we don't make it out of here tomorrow...it would probably be a good idea if I kissed you now."

"Mmm," she hummed, her lips twitching with amusement. "Just in case?"

He shrugged. "Better to be safe. No regrets, right?"

She set down her bottle and crawled across the floor toward him. "No regrets," she whispered, desire burning in her stare.

And then she closed her eyes and planted her mouth on his.

Soon, they were stripping off each other's clothes, and Travis was gathering her into his lap and picking her up, wrapping her legs around his waist as he stood. He carried her to the bed, kissing her the whole way there.

Tomorrow would still come. But tonight, Travis would enjoy himself. He'd wanted to get laid one last time, and he truly felt glad that it was with a girl he really...

Really...

Really...

Really liked.

"Okay," Maya began. "Okay, Max, you can do this."

Max sat across from his sister at the table in the kitchen, a room he and the others had turned into a workstation. A place to charge the warhead that would get them the hell out of Yveswich.

It was his turn now. The others had taken turns these last two days, pouring their magic into the warhead with short intervals of rest. All different colors of magic swirled inside the cloudy, bullet-shaped warhead— all except red.

Fire magic.

Max drew a deep breath and lay his hand upon the warhead, feeling the powerful magic humming within. It made his teeth sing.

"I don't know if I can do this," he said with a sigh.

Maya placed her hand on top of his and bent her head so they were at eye level with each other. "You can," she said softly. She was still wrapped up in that blanket, her power levels too low for her to do this herself.

It would have to be Max.

Maya added, "I believe in you, Max."

He inhaled again, feeling his lungs stretch. As he exhaled, he shut his eyes.

"You have to call upon your magic," Maya said. "And you can't be afraid of it. It doesn't control you, Max—*you* control *it.*"

As he focused, he felt it stirring within him. A flame kindling in his chest.

He began to sweat. His breaths thinned out—

"Breathe," Maya said. She kept her hand on his. Her touch was grounding. Calming. "Don't be afraid of it."

He focused harder, concentrating on bringing that magic up from the depths of his soul...all the way to the surface.

One breath in... One breath out...

One breath in... One breath out...

His palm began to heat up. Sweat prickled down his spine and across his brow, but he kept his focus on his magic, on the fire he refused to be afraid of.

No more. *No more.*

His sister was alive and here—sitting right across from him.

She was alive. She had never burned.

His mother had told him a lie—a terrible lie that had scarred him deeply. It would be a while yet before he could say he was fully healed from the emotional and mental damage. But the journey toward healing started now.

His palm grew hotter. But it didn't burn, didn't hurt. It felt...

Like the sun. The sun on a summer's day. Warm, but gentle.

"That's it, Max," Maya whispered. "You're doing it—it's working."

A startled laugh slipped out of him as he felt his magic trickle out of his body and into the warhead. It glowed in response, but he kept his eyes shut, refusing to open them until this was done. If he let himself look at the fire...

"Just a little more," Maya whispered.

The heat in his palm deepened. Spread up his arm. His heart began to pound—

"Just breathe," Maya whispered.

Max breathed.

A few minutes later, she patted the back of his hand and said, "Let go. You can let go now, Max."

He let go. Opened his eyes.

The warhead was glowing brighter. Swirling with all different colors of magic. White, blue, magenta, black, violet—

And red. The magic of the Inferno.

Max smiled at his sister. "It worked," he said, his voice hoarse and coated with surprise.

Maya smiled back, tears sparkling in eyes that glowed with warmth. "You did it, Max."

WHEN TOMORROW ARRIVED, and they finished charging the warhead—right on time—Travis and the others fastened their weapons belts in the foyer of the House of Violet and finished programming their headsets.

In exactly twelve hours, the military would be hitting Yveswich with missiles of their own, the magic of the anima mundi having the ability to pass right through the destructive forcefield and obliterate what was left of Ker's capital—and all the people in it.

According to Roark and the intel he was receiving in secret while on a leave of absence, the Fleet would be aiming strategically, avoiding the Control Tower. They wanted to keep the forcefield up—

While destroying everything else. Just in case their plan didn't work.

Assholes.

Travis flicked on his mic. "Hey, Atlas," he said. "You there?"

A crackle. And then: "I'm here."

"Perfect. We're just about to head out."

"All right. I'll be here if you need me."

He flicked off the headset.

"All you dipshits ready?" Malakai asked as he tied his hair back.

"Ready," Travis said. The others echoed him.

Malakai inclined his head toward the door. "Let's move."

Max opened the door, and together they walked out into the brisk, dark city, the air pierced by the guttural snarls and howls of thousands of monsters—

And prepared to enter the abyss.

102

HEAVEN'S GATE
ANGELTHENE, STATE OF WITHEREDGE

"And then I found this passage here," Sabrine said. "Listen."

Propped up on pillows in bed at Heaven's Gate, Loren watched Sabrine on the video call on her laptop that was open on her thighs. The wolf cracked open a big, leather-bound book that was so old it was crumbling.

Sabrine had just started to read the passage when Loren heard Darien's voice floating up from the stairs. It sounded like he was halfway up them.

"Hold on," Loren hissed. "I think Darien's coming." She listened—

Yup, he definitely was.

"I'll call you back," Loren said. She snapped her laptop shut just as Darien walked into the room.

"Hey, beautiful," he said. "Who were you talking to?"

"Singer," she fibbed.

The dog was curled up on his favorite cushion by the big windows. The sound of his name had him blinking his eyes open and lifting his head.

"Is it time?" she asked Darien as he paused beside the bed.

"Just about."

"You're going to my parents' house now?" He had to get something from Roark—something he needed for tracking.

"After I meet with the Butcher," he replied. "I need more salt."

"Where's he been staying, anyway?"

"Somewhere Below. But I'm not going there" —*thank gods*, she thought— "I'll be meeting him in Black Alder." He scanned her arms—the tattoos that were glowing against the front of her shirt. "You'll be okay for a bit?"

"Don't worry about me today—I'm fine. You've got a lot on your plate."

"I'll always worry about you." He came closer and kissed the top of her head. "I should be back within the hour, but I'll check in once I'm done in Black Alder."

"Okay."

He slipped her hand that was resting on her laptop into his and gave it a light squeeze. "Doing some online shopping?" he asked, his eyes flicking to the computer.

"Of course—with your credit card."

He snickered and stepped back, his fingers trailing off hers as he headed toward the door. "Call me if you need anything, okay?"

"I will."

"See you in a bit."

She listened to his footfall, and once he reached the foyer, she opened her laptop and called Sabrine back.

"Hey," Sabrine said as the video call connected.

"Hey," Loren whispered, sitting up straighter. "What did you find?"

EXACTLY NINE HOURS remained when Darien pulled his car to a stop in front of the apartment building where the Brights lived.

Nine hours until Witching Hour. Nine hours until Yveswich and the last of the survivors who were still trapped beneath the forcefield would be blasted apart with anima mundi missiles.

Nine hours until Darien's life would change. Whether it would change for the worse or the better remained to be seen.

Roman, Shay, Dean, and Pax were keeping in touch as they traveled back to Yveswich. Last Darien heard, as long as they encountered no delays, they should arrive at the outskirts of Ker's capital just as the forcefield came down. As for Travis and Max, their group had managed to fully charge the warhead—right on time.

Their plan had worked. Against all odds, it had worked.

He grabbed his phone from where he'd tossed it onto the dash and found Loren in his contacts. He'd left Heaven's Gate less than an hour ago, and while he could claim that his reason for texting her was simply to see if she was safe, he had another reason.

He missed her.

> **DARIEN**
>
> Hey pretty girl. Everything ok?

> **LOREN**
>
> Ivy's favorite frying pan went missing and she has a feeling Itzel stole it.

Darien fought a smile. A warm spring rain began to fall upon the car in a fine mist as he typed up a response.

> **DARIEN**
>
> Case of the Missing Frying Pan—I'll get on it right away.
>
> I was talking about you though.

> **LOREN**
>
> I'm fine, but I miss you :(

> **DARIEN**
>
> I miss you too, sweetheart

> **LOREN**
>
> Hurry home?

> **DARIEN**
>
> Anything for you

> **LOREN**
>
> ♥

> **DARIEN**
>
>

Damn rights he would hurry home. He couldn't wait to be back with his beautiful girl again—as soon as he was done here. As soon as he had the last thing he needed to get Travis and Max the hell out of Yveswich.

He opened his door and stepped out beneath an overcast sky. As he crossed the rain-speckled road, heading for the entrance to the apartment building, he called Tanner.

The hacker picked up on the second ring. "You ready?"

"I'm ready." He was at the front doors now. The same doors he'd walked through with Loren last fall—back when he was nothing to her but a stranger. A threat. So much had changed since that day—since they'd sat down across from each other at Rook and Redding's—that these past few months sometimes felt like a dream.

Except, she was better—far better than any dream he could have ever dreamt up.

Keys clacked in the background. And then Tanner said, "Spells are coming down in three...two..."

"One," they said in unison.

Darien's blood thrummed as the intricate spells of the expensive-as-hell security system came down—dropping like a heavy curtain.

He whipped the door open and walked in, his boots pounding as he crossed the foyer.

"Elevator's ready and waiting," Tanner said. "I made it easy on you and programmed in the penthouse suite."

"Couldn't have opened the doors, too?" Darien teased. "You're slacking, Atlas." He pressed the button to the lift, and the doors hissed open.

As Darien got on, Tanner said, "If you'd like to give me a raise, I'll consider opening the doors for you next time, too."

Darien chuckled.

Sure enough, just as Tanner had promised, the button for the penthouse was already activated. The doors slid shut, and the elevator lurched upward.

"You in?" Tanner asked.

"I'm in."

"All right. Call me if you need anything, but if not, I'll see you in a bit."

"See you in a bit," Darien echoed. He hung up.

The lift opened onto a short hallway that led to the private entrance to the Bright Penthouse. He ate up the length of that hallway with several swift strides and rapped his fist against the door. Waited a few seconds before knocking a second time.

The lock clicked, and the door swung open.

The minute Roark took in the Darkslayer standing on his doorstep, his face smoothed with a level of shock that was almost comical. He glanced behind Darien—at the empty hallway. Clearly wondering how in the hell he had made it past all the security features.

And how he could ensure it wouldn't happen again.

"We could have done without the theatrics and simply arranged to meet downstairs," Roark said. He offered Darien a tiny plastic pouch. Inside was a small amount of bone dust. "Is this enough?"

"It'll have to be." He took it and tucked it away in the inside pocket of his jacket. Mixing the dust with the Stygian salts would allow him to see the auras of the monsters in Lucent Enterprises and beyond—and give him the ability to guide Travis and the others *around* the monsters to avoid being attacked. In the time that had passed since the Blood Moon, Lucent Enterprises had begun tests and experiments on the creatures; Taega had managed to take some of the bone dust from the lab without being seen.

"Are they finished with the warhead?" Roark asked.

Darien nodded.

The glint that entered Roark's eyes suggested he was impressed. "Right on time."

"Right on time."

Roark sucked in a deep breath and said, "And Dallas?"

"She's alive. She's with them."

Roark nodded. He tried to hide the concern in his eyes, but Darien could see it. "Good."

Darien offered Roark his hand.

For a moment, Roark just looked at it, surprise etched into his face.

And then he clasped it.

"Thank you," Darien said.

Roark merely nodded. "If you need anything else, don't hesitate to ask. Taega and I are both willing to help."

"Will do." He was about leave, but decided to ask Roark the question that had been eating at him ever since he'd left Yveswich. "If you don't mind my asking, why the sudden change of heart? Why all of...*this?*" He gestured between them, and to the bone dust in his pocket.

Roark took a moment to consider his response. "Let's just say I...woke up." The corners of his mouth lifted slightly.

He had changed. And Darien was willing to bet that seeing one of his daughters lying in a comatose state in a hospital bed had been the trigger.

Darien wouldn't judge. Not anymore. Not when he himself wanted to change, one day. Not when he wanted to do better, too.

So he merely said, "Thanks," one more time.

Roark nodded.

Darien turned and walked down the hallway. To the elevator. It wasn't until he was inside the lift that Roark shut the door to the penthouse.

As the elevator slid into a smooth descent, Darien breathed deeply, preparing himself for what he was about to do. It would be challenging—he wouldn't deny that. It also came with risks—lots of them. But he'd meant what he'd said to Ivy.

Losing Max and Travis was a far greater risk. That was part of his family that was trapped in Yveswich, and he would gladly face any threat that came his way head-on if it meant he could bring them home.

ROARK BRIGHT HAD JUST FINISHED SHUTTING and locking the door, his chest sinking beneath the weight of what was happening in Yveswich—with his eldest daughter who was trapped there—when Taega called his name from the study.

"Roark!" Her voice was panicky and breathless. "Roark—get in here! Hurry."

Quickly, he walked into the study and found her standing in front of the computer. On the monitor were dozens of different video feeds. Live footage from the security cameras that were interspersed throughout the building.

"Taega, what is it?"

"Look." She gestured to camera five—the one that faced the front entrance to the apartment building.

When Roark beheld the figures on the screen, stark as silhouettes as the sun began to sink below the horizon, the blood drained from his head. "Oh my gods."

WHEN DARIEN EXITED the elevator on the ground floor of the apartment building, he felt lighter—happier—than he had in days. On the ride down, he'd taken some of the Stygian salts mixed with the bone powder, so they'd have a chance to take effect by the time he would need to start tracking.

He checked his watch. In about an hour, Travis and the others would arrive at Lucent Enterprises. The timing couldn't be more perfect.

With a deep breath, he walked through the front door—

Pain like a lightning strike slammed into the back of his neck, causing his mind to short-circuit. Raw magic wove between his teeth and ripped through his muscles, his nerves.

His knees slammed into the ground.

Out of nowhere, he was being surrounded by cops, all shouting and pointing guns at his head.

And stepping out of a cop car—one of many that were parked along the curb, blue-and-red lights flashing—was Detective Glen, a pissed-off look on his face. The cops—there were *dozens* of them, all armed to the teeth.

Darien's stomach and heart fell out of his body.

No.

Two cops came up behind him. Demanding he put his hands in the air.

Without thinking, he whirled, raw magic from the taser still ripping through him like electricity, and threw both officers through the front doors. The men screamed, glass smashing.

Another two came forward, guns raised. Darien kicked their feet out from under them. They crashed to the pavement—

Warning shots were fired. He ducked as more glass shattered, a bullet zipping through the air, so close to his head it almost grazed him.

There were too many. Too many guns, too many officers, he hardly knew where to look—

And there was a prisoner transport van parked by the curb. The words painted on the sides and back doors churned his stomach and pushed his heart into an unsteady rhythm.

BLACKWATER PENITENTIARY

"Darien Cassel," barked Detective Glen. *"You're under arrest!"*

Darien couldn't breathe. Barely managed to squeeze out, "I don't understand." He could hardly speak, the raw magic in the taser muddying his mind and rendering his limbs practically useless—

"Cuff him," Glen said.

Cops swarmed him. A few were hellsehers—brought here today to match the strength of the person they were apprehending.

Darien fought like hell. He roared and thrashed and tried everything he could to get away, but—

For the first time in his life, he was overpowered. Outnumbered. And before he had a prayer of stopping them, handcuffs—brimstone—bit into his wrists. Clicked shut.

His magic died out as the brimstone smothered every last spark of his power. He felt weak. Sick.

Three cops took his weapons, his phone. Then forced him to his feet.

Behind him, there was shouting. Footsteps. Glass crunching.

"What the hell is going on here?" said a male voice. It was Roark. With him was Taega. Their faces were twisted with shock, rage.

"Ah, Mister Bright," Glen said with a cruel, mocking smile. "Fancy meeting you here."

"Where are you taking him?" Roark demanded.

"To Blackwater."

"Now wait just a minute, you can't do this—"

"Actually, I can. And you, Commander—oops, I mean...*Mister Bright* —have no say here."

Taega hissed, "What the hell are you talking about?"

Glen handed Roark a sheet of paper. "You've officially been demoted by word of the imperator, which means *exactly* what I just said: You no longer have any authority."

Roark scanned the papers, his face going bone-pale.

"Enjoy your early retirement, former commander," Glen drawled.

And then Darien was being hauled away. Toward the open back doors of the prisoner transport van.

Roark rushed after them. He was shouting, but Darien could hardly hear him over the roaring of the blood in his head, the pounding of his heart that felt too weak.

His magic was threatening to burst out of his skin, but he *had* to control it. If he failed... If a Surge happened—

It would kill him. The brimstone would cause his power to backfire, and it would injure no one but himself.

"I'd behave yourself if I were you, Mister Bright," Glen was saying as two officers shoved Darien into the back of the van. "You don't want to end up like him, do you? You're better than that."

In the back of the van, the officers forced him down—forced him to sit on the hard bench that was bolted to one wall. Metal clinked as they fastened his cuffs to the chains that were attached to the bench.

His world shrunk and spun, his breaths thinning out—

As the officers stepped out, he managed to find his voice.

"You're not going to fucking get away with this!" he spat, chest heaving.

Glen sauntered over to stand in the open doors. He put his hands on his hips, his lips tipping up with a cruel smirk. "Look at you—right where you belong, I'd say."

Darien lunged, but the chains snapped taut, yanking him back against the bench. "Fuck. *You,*" he seethed.

Glen's smirk sank into an icy frown. "You're going to Blackwater, Cassel," he declared. "And if I have it my way, the only way you'll be getting out is in a body bag!"

PART FIVE

THE ABYSS

103

ANGELTHENE
STATE OF WITHEREDGE

In the back of the prisoner transport van, the brimstone cuffs robbing him of every last drop of magic, Darien fought.

He threw all his weight against the doors, but they didn't budge, didn't dent. The chains confining him to the bench snapped taut with every lunge, his cuffs cutting into the skin of his wrists.

Bleeding—his wrists were raw and bleeding.

He was running out of time. *They* were running out of time. Travis and Max—

He couldn't breathe. Chest heaving, heart pounding so hard he was damn near passing out, he threw himself against the doors, bruising his body to the bone.

Again.

Again.

Again.

Through the gaps in the window guards, he watched as Angelthene's urban sprawl faded with distance.

Sometime later, the van turned a corner. Kept driving and driving and just fucking *driving*. All signs of city life faded, not one person or vehicle to be seen for miles. Nothing but barren hills and chainlink security fences, loops of barbed wire at the top. The green bubble of Angelthene's force-field was hardly visible from here.

Too far. He was too fucking far.

The van came to a brief halt at the controlled entry point to Blackwater

Penitentiary. He could hardly hear the muffled voices of the guards over the pounding of his heart, the roaring of blood in his throbbing head. Boots crunched in the dirt as the guards performed their security checks. Eyes peered in at him. Flashlights shone.

A few more minutes went by, and then the van rolled forward.

The thick spells covering the maximum security prison washed across the vehicle like a crushing tide, so strong, they made him dizzy. Lightheaded.

He shook his head to clear it and threw all his weight against the doors —*bang*. Again—*bang*. Again—*BANG*. "Come on," he panted. He kept trying, refusing to give up. He almost knocked himself out, his chains yanking him backward with each lunge.

BANG. CLANG.

BANG. CLANG.

"Come on—please. *Please. Please. PLEASE!*"

But it was no use. He was trapped, and because of him, because he hadn't been more careful, Travis and Max were going to die.

As the van drove up to the entrance to Blackwater, he crashed to his knees, the chains of his cuffs clanging as he bowed his face to the floor—

And screamed.

"Do you think I was too hard on him?" Roman's eyes flicked to Dean's reflection in the rear-view.

The long drive had given Roman plenty of time to think. To calm down and realize that his reaction back at Heaven's Gate was completely uncalled for. His uncle had done nothing but help him. He didn't deserve to be yelled at like that.

They were back in Ker. They'd gone a different route and had made it across the state-line without incident—likely because the last place Donovan would expect to find his sons was in Ker. If anything, Yveswich was—oddly—the safest place for them right now.

"He'll forgive you," was all Shay said. She was getting nervous—Roman could tell. Going back to Yveswich...fuck, he didn't like it, either.

"Hey," he said softly. Slowly, she raised her eyes to his face. "It's going to be okay."

She merely nodded, her hands clenched and white-knuckled in her lap.

Donovan wasn't the only threat scouring the states of Ker and Witheredge in search of them.

Athene was, too. The Selkies of the Riptide.

And Shay had *still* chosen to come with. Risk her life to be there for him and Paxton.

He felt a sharp pinch in his heart. He glanced sidelong at Shay, studying the worry on her face...the tense fingers that were interlocked in her lap.

His phone started buzzing on the dash. He grabbed it and checked the caller I.D.

It was a number that wasn't in his contacts.

"Who is it?" Shay asked.

His first thought was that it was his dad. Or maybe a different Shadowmaster—someone calling on behalf of Donovan. But with all this shit going on, he didn't want to *not* pick up.

"I don't know," he replied. He swiped to answer and lifted the phone to his ear. "Yeah?"

"I need to speak with Shay," came a panicked, female voice.

Roman's stomach flipped over. "Loren?" he bit out. Shay was listening intently. In the back seat, Paxton paused his game and sat up as Roman said, "What's going on? Is everything okay?"

"Darien's been arrested." Her sobs rattled the phone. "I need to speak to Shay right now, please." Shay was already reaching for the phone as Loren screamed, *"Right now!"*

IO4

LUCENT ENTERPRISES
ANGELTHENE, STATE OF WITHEREDGE

Blackwater Penitentiary, the others had told Loren, was one of the most dangerous maximum security prisons in the world. Most prisoners were killed within forty-eight hours of setting foot inside the spell-protected walls—either by guards, other inmates, or the monsters that were rumored to be kept inside cages of their own, unleashed by the warden and the guards upon chosen prisoners in fighting rings inside the building.

The prison ran off its own source of magic that was completely separate from the rest of the city. No power outage had ever succeeded at stripping off its magic. No hacker had ever managed to break in.

Loren would've much preferred not knowing any of this.

She tried not to consider the odds of not just breaking in, but getting *out* too as she stood with Roark by the door to the Caliginous Chamber at Lucent Enterprises. The others—Jack, Ivy, Lace, and Kylar—were keeping watch at opposite ends of the hallway, guns raised, while Tanner, who was at Heaven's Gate, masked the security feeds and finished gathering everything they'd need for their plan to break Darien out of Blackwater.

Roark keyed in the security code and selected every color on the screen —all except black and gray. The chamber whirred as it came on, white light bathing the pearly interior.

"Try to relax," he said as Loren reached for the door handle. She *was* trying, but she was impatient. She wanted to get to Darien. Inside the chamber, balls of multicolored light winked awake and floated about the space like fireflies. "The magic will enter your system quicker if you're calm."

She nodded once, drew a deep, steadying breath, then opened the door and stepped inside. Warm, orange-scented water splashed under her bare feet as she crossed the room. She hopped up onto the floating tabletop and lay down on her back. Only when Roark shut the door, did Loren shut her eyes.

Staying calm was next to impossible when she knew Darien was being taken to Blackwater. Taken to the worst prison on the continent. Her heart was racing, her body temperature so warm she felt like she was burning.

This had to work. Their plan *had* to work.

Minutes ticked by; she counted each and every second. She had her arms crossed tightly over her chest, her fingers tapping out an anxious beat. She was so stressed out, she felt like she couldn't breathe—

"Loren," Roark said through the intercom.

She turned her head to look at him. He was staring in at her through the window in the door, his brow scrunched with concern.

Roark was the one who'd called her. He'd been there when Darien was arrested. Out front of the apartment building where Loren grew up.

"You need to relax," Roark said again. His tone was gentle. "Trust that this is going to work."

It took all her strength just to nod. "Okay," she whispered. She returned to her former position and stared up at the water spouts on the ceiling, just for a few seconds, before shutting her eyes again.

To calm her nerves, she decided to relive the happy memory of when Darien had walked into the reverse chamber in Yveswich to join her for her treatment. He was wearing those white Caliginous on Silverway shorts that made his summer tan stand out. While the others had whistled and howled upon seeing him dressed in something he wouldn't usually wear, Loren had blushed. He'd looked so good in them.

As the minutes ticked by, she lost herself in the happy memory, wandering so deeply she began to relive it, remembering bits of the conversation she'd had with the man she loved with her whole freaking heart. The man who did not deserve all this pain, all this suffering.

"Do you think Tanya's right?" she asked him. Now that she was lying down, Darien only looked taller and more intimidating.

Blood rushed to her face as she imagined what he would look like directly on top of her, instead of beside her like this.

Darien said, "About what?"

KAYLA EDWARDS

"That this could hurt me? Or you?"

"It won't hurt me," he said with resolution. *"And I've already been in here with you twice. I don't know if it's related, but you didn't wake up until I was in the chamber with you."*

She hadn't woken up until he was in the chamber with her.

She hadn't woken up until he was in the chamber with her.

Loren bolted up, so quickly her head spun. "Dad?" Her shout echoed.

Roark peered through the window at her, his eyes brimming with worry. He flicked on the intercom. "Loren? Is everything—"

"Turn black on," she said.

Confusion flickered across his features. "I beg your pardon?"

"Turn black on. Keep every color on, but add black. *Only* black." Not gray—just black. The color of Darien's magic.

"Loren, I don't think we—"

"Dad, *please,*" she said, a sob rising in her throat. She swallowed it down and whispered, "Just trust me. Just this once."

For a long moment, Roark stared at her, conflicted.

"Please," she mouthed.

His nostrils flared as he drew a sharp breath, then he turned his focus to the screen and activated black.

The balls of color floating through the room were soon joined by a new shade: pitch black. Shadow magic, death magic—call it what you wanted, but Loren was not afraid of it. This was the type of magic Darien had, and while it could indeed be used to destroy, kill, and blind, she knew it would not hurt her.

She had not woken up out of her coma until Darien had come into the chamber with her. No matter what excuses anyone tried to hurl at her, no matter what facts they had in their arsenal of knowledge to back them up, that spoke volumes. Black magic—shadow magic—was what she was missing.

She was sure of it.

With a deep breath, she lay back on the table, shut her eyes, and finished her treatment. This time, as those fuzzy spheres of shadow magic bobbed around her, she felt calm. She breathed deeply, focusing on relaxing every tense muscle, one at a time. Letting as much magic in as her body would allow.

Fifteen minutes passed quickly—and by the time she got out, the tattoo on her forearm was not blue, not red.

It was white. A solid, softly glowing white.

She had not seen this shade since she was small. Since the day she'd lain upon an examination table in Angelthene General Hospital while a nurse carefully drew the medical symbol on her arm. She could still remember the sour taste of the lemon-flavored lollipop the nurse had given her to help distract her from the pain.

It wasn't just the serpent tattoo that'd changed, either; the bead of light that had been pulsing through the Caliginous on Silverway tattoo for days on end had also been absorbed into her skin, leaving the ink black and ordinary. She felt energized. Brand new.

Whole.

Her father's jaw fell slack as he beheld the tattoo of the serpent-entwined rod. The tattoo he'd brought her to the hospital to receive when she was only a child.

"My gods," he breathed. "It worked."

105

FINANCIAL DISTRICT
YVESWICH, STATE OF KER

Travis and the others made it to the street where they'd find Lucent Enterprises right on time.

"I think we might actually be early," he said as he checked the time on his phone. "Yup—early."

The city was so cold, he could hardly feel his toes, could hardly move his fingers that were wrapped around an automatic rifle. Up ahead, stretching all the way up to the forcefield, was a massive wall of black shadow. The whole of the Lucent Enterprises building was engulfed in that darkness. Utterly blinding, it was the perfect habitat for monsters.

Literally. Travis could hear them roaring up a storm in there. The only consolation in this mess was knowing the monsters wouldn't be able to see them once they went inside—as long as they kept their shields of magic up to mask their scents and sounds. They were all pretty drained from taking turns charging the warhead, so relying on their magic was...well, risky. They would have to take turns. Make sure no one was using their magic for too long.

The rest of their group—Dominic, Blue, Maya, Magenta, and the Sylphen—were currently heading to the roof of the tallest skyscraper in the South Coastal District, one that aligned perfectly with the Control Tower. As long as Dominic managed to aim true, that tower would be coming down in no time. The Angel was the best person for the job; Travis had zero doubts that he could hit any target.

Including one that was barely visible. Like the tower.

Now that they were really doing this, Travis realized how lucky they were that the Control Tower was so tall. About half of it—the bottom half—had been completely devoured by shadow. It was at the top half where Dominic would have to aim. It didn't really matter *where* the missile hit, though, just as long as it hit. The raw magic would be powerful enough to collapse it.

As Travis waited for Darien to call, he rolled his shoulders and recited the plan in his head. Using it to fuel him.

1. Get the syringes so we don't stop breathing when the tower comes down.
2. Meet up with the others in the South Coastal District.
3. Take down that fucking tower.

He hadn't felt this hopeful in days. The moment he saw Roman, he'd give him the biggest hug and smooch on the cheek. He could already picture him growling and wiping the spit off his face. He couldn't wait.

"When's that asshole supposed to call you?" Malakai asked as he paced across the sidewalk.

"Darien," Travis corrected, "is supposed to call me—" He checked his phone. Frowned. "—three minutes ago."

The rest of the group—Malakai, Aspen, Jewels, Dallas, and Max—shared glances. Sure, Darien wasn't the most punctual person in the world, but it wasn't like him to be late for something like this. Something that was literally life or death.

"I'm sure he's just getting ready," he assured them.

Jewels rubbed her chest.

Aspen whispered something to Malakai and cupped her throat.

Yeah, it was getting hard to breathe. Especially now that they were over here, where the shadow was thicker. Suffocating. The minute that tower came down, there was no question they'd all drop dead if they didn't have the life serum in their bloodstreams.

Malakai said, "I hate to be the bearer of bad news, but if we don't do this right the fuck now, we're going to run out of time."

"He'll *call,"* Travis snapped. "Just give him a second."

Malakai muttered under his breath, but didn't argue.

Travis turned his back on the group and took out his phone, triple checking to make sure he still had bars of service. All looked fine, but—

Darien was now eight minutes late.

"Come on, Darien," he mouthed as his heart started to race. "Come on."

106

ANGELTHENE
STATE OF WITHEREDGE

L oren could scarcely breathe. She couldn't stop staring at the clock, her heart and stomach pitching downward in tandem with every minute that ticked by, as Ivy sped through the streets of Angelthene, pushing the jeep as fast as it could go.

She had to trust that this would work. That she'd be able to follow the instructions Shay had given her and make a miracle happen. Asking Tanner to break into a maximum security prison, with time in such short supply...

It simply wasn't possible.

It was up to her. She would have to trust—*believe* in herself. She only hoped she would succeed at holding the illusion long enough to get not just herself through the entry point, but the others as well.

They would not be able to use it to get back out afterward. She wouldn't have enough power to cast another illusion for that. So she would have to hope that they'd be able to navigate the prison, make it to Darien, and get back out on their own, without the aid of a new illusion.

By the time they made it onto the quiet road that led to only one destination—the prison—night had fallen, heavy and quiet. She had the sense that everyone was holding their breath as Ivy rolled the jeep down the road.

A police SUV was parked just ahead.

"Is that Finn?" Lace asked, tightening her grip on her gun.

As if he'd heard them, Detective Finn Solace stepped out of the SUV and waved them down. They'd asked for his help with this, since he'd been to the prison before and knew his way around. Loren hoped they could trust him.

Ivy pulled over on the side of the road, and everyone got out.

"Finn," Ivy said by way of greeting, her tone taut with stress. "Thank you for doing this."

He acknowledged her with a dip of his chin. "The guards do their perimeter checks every hour. They went by here just a few minutes ago, so we'll have to be quick."

Jack said, "We've got a Hob who can camouflage the jeep. It should hold for double that time." Itzel may be young, but Kylar had assured them that she had a lot of practice with vehicles.

"Good," Finn said, breathless with adrenaline. "Everyone, get in."

They moved—piling into the five-seater SUV. There weren't enough seats, so Jack opened the liftgate and climbed into the back. Kylar was on the phone with Tanner, letting him know it was time for Itzel to take control of the jeep. It was a tight fit in here, but, according to everything Loren had learned from Shay, having everyone so close together like this should help her cast and hold the illusion. Less space to have to cover—to stretch her magic across.

"Say a prayer, everyone," Finn said as he buckled up. "If this doesn't work, none of us will be coming out of these walls."

He started driving.

IN A CELL ON DEATH ROW, Darien paced across the tiny space that had nothing in it but a steel bed, a steel toilet, a sink, and a writing desk. They'd unlocked the chains of his cuffs but left the cuff part on just long enough for him to change into an orange jumpsuit before reattaching the chains. They were taking no precautions, giving him zero chances.

With the brimstone on, he might as well be mortal. The longer he had them on, the weaker he felt. And it wasn't just his power. He *physically* felt weaker, too. Even the thought of throwing a punch while wearing these fucking things fatigued him.

Being in here reminded him of his father's time in these walls. Never had he imagined he'd be the one in a cell, wearing these clothes and these cuffs. Randal had been let out before his execution, slipping through one of many cracks in the corrupt justice system, as so many pieces of shit like him often did. But Darien knew he wouldn't be that lucky. Not when the MPU had already bypassed all the legal steps that technically should have been taken to get him in here. Not when it was the imperator himself who'd ordered him arrested. The man whose word was above all.

He would die in here. Would rot in these fucking walls. A part of him had already withered and died. The part that knew, in a matter of hours, Max and Travis would be blasted apart by missiles. The part that knew Loren only had until her twenty-first birthday to live, and there was nothing he could do now to change it.

He'd failed. Protecting her had become his calling. Loving her had become his purpose. She was his future, his everything, and now...

He'd fucked up. He'd fucked *everything* up.

He paced faster. Breathed harder. His magic was rising up inside him, but he couldn't let it bite. If he did, if he let it get out of control, he'd pay for it. It would backfire, and he'd be the one—the *only* one—getting bitten.

There were no bars on this cell. No windows. It was a simple box with a steel door, a narrow opening in the steel. It could only be opened from the outside, its sole purpose for the guards to slide trays of food through, then promptly close it again. He couldn't see anything beyond these walls, not even with his Sight, the spells far too thick.

So he didn't know anyone was there until he heard the clanging of keys outside the door.

Until the door creaked open, and four prison guards, all armed to the teeth, appeared. With them was Detective Glen.

The prick gave him a cruel smile. "This place suits you," he said, his weasel-like eyes scanning the disgusting quarters. "Even more than the van."

"What do you want?" Darien growled.

Glen gave a cocky little smirk and said, "Follow me."

107

ANGELTHENE VALLEY

ANGELTHENE, STATE OF WITHEREDGE

"This is it," Ivy said from the passenger's seat, her breaths quickening as the perimeter walls surrounding Blackwater Penitentiary loomed out of the darkness. She reached behind her and clasped Loren's hand. Looked her in the eyes and said, "You can do this. I believe in you."

Loren drew a deep, deep breath as Finn steered the SUV toward the controlled entry point.

"We all do," Lace chimed in. "We all believe in you." Jack and Kylar murmured their own agreements.

Loren took out her phone and pulled up the photographs of the Blackwater staff members Tanner had sent her. He, too, had included his own words of encouragement.

TANNER

You're not alone in this. We believe in you.

You can do this.

Loren took one more steadying breath and focused on summoning her white magic—*just* the white—directing it toward the conduit tattoos on her palms the way Shay had taught her. If she failed to guide the magic through the buffer...

She could stop her own heart. And then Darien's would stop, too.

"We're almost there," Finn said, his words tight with stress. "There's no going back now—they've seen us."

"I've got this," Loren said, inhaling. Exhaling. The metallic sun and moon on her palms began to glow.

Part of their agreement with Finn was that he would tell no one and ask no questions. Not until after—for the questions, that is.

Not until this horrible night was behind them.

Not until Darien was back home and safe.

Another inhale, another exhale—

"Now," Ivy whispered.

She released her magic in a wave that rippled through the interior of the SUV like a breeze.

The illusion accomplished three things.

One: It changed Ivy, Finn, and herself into night-staff prison guards.

Two: It rendered Lace, Jack, and Kylar completely invisible. The latter was much harder to do; changing an appearance versus making it disappear entirely required a higher output of magic. She could already feel her conduit tattoos burning, her magic trembling at the edges.

Three: It transformed the vehicle into one owned and registered under the name of one of the staff members. The one who Finn was disguised as.

She was so focused on holding the illusion, she didn't hear a word Finn said as he spoke in a casual, friendly tone to the guards at the gates.

But then the man was asking for his I.D., and another was coming around to the passenger's-side door and shining a flashlight in Ivy's face.

"Name," the guard snapped.

Ivy gave the name of the woman she was disguised as.

"I.D.," he demanded.

She handed over the fake I.D. Tanner had given her.

Loren's heart was pounding, but she held firm to her illusions and kept her expression calm and unbothered as the guard shone a light on her next.

"Name," he demanded.

She gave it.

"I.D."

Her hand didn't tremble as she took out the I.D. card and gave it to the guard. He looked it over with his flashlight, then handed it back.

"They're good," he declared, lowering the light. "Let them through."

Loren loosed the breath in her lungs.

A buzzer sounded, and the gates swung open. Finn drove through—

Her magic fooled the spells, too. The thick, impenetrable spells of

Blackwater Penitentiary...the spells that had never once been tricked, breached...

She had fooled them.

And they were in. Holy gods, they were in.

They did it. She *did it*.

As the gates swung shut behind them, Loren dropped the illusions with a pained gasp. She curled over herself, her knee bouncing, arms clutching her chest. Her racing heart.

Lace rubbed her back.

Finn glanced at her in the rear-view, looking as concerned as he was stunned.

"Are you okay?" Ivy asked, twisting in her seat.

"Yeah," Loren gritted out. But she was fatigued. Her white magic was fully drained, and she knew she would not be able to use it again. Not tonight.

They were on their own.

Blackwater Penitentiary loomed like a leviathan, the building so tall it seemed to blend in with the sky. Finn drove the SUV to the staff parking lot, where they all prepared to face the horrors that lay within.

THE RATTLING of chains and the pounding of boots were the only sounds slicing through the quiet as Darien followed Glen through the prison. There were two guards in front of him and two behind, the latter nudging him in the back with their guns as cells upon cells upon cells passed by.

They led him out of death row—into a different wing of the prison, where the cells had bars he could see through. Prisoners paced in the cramped spaces, others shouting and swearing as they passed.

Darien slowed as he caught sight of a male hellseher twitching and pacing, his eyes black. There were dark lines in the surrounding skin.

Stage Three Tricking. Not even the prison was safe from the Venenum virus that was coming to devour their world.

A gun jabbed him in the back. "Keep walking."

They passed a room labeled CONTROL ROOM 8B. Through the open door, Darien spotted two guards sitting in front of a collection of screens, all with live security footage. They turned to look at him as he passed. They were wearing headsets.

About another ten minutes went by before they pushed through a door and down a hallway lined with swampy green lights.

Glen stopped at a door on the left and gestured for Darien to enter. "After you," he said with a bow and a flourish of his hand.

Darien gave him a heavy, hateful look as he passed, not liking this one fucking bit. He walked into the room—

And froze when he beheld who sat behind the table, an ankle crossed over a knee.

Gaven Payne's lips curved upward with a cold smile. "Hello, Darien."

There was a small cage on the table. Inside was a Hob, his tiny fingers wrapped around the spell-protected bars. When he saw Darien, his red eyes —brimming with fear—widened, and he let out a little, lamb-like bleating noise of recognition.

Darien was so distracted by Mortifer, he didn't see Glen as he came up behind him and punched a knife into his side.

108

FINANCIAL DISTRICT
YVESWICH, STATE OF KER

The ground beneath Travis's boots quaked. Stones clacked. Buildings vibrated. His teeth rattled in his skull.

He shared a look with Jewels. Max.

Deeper in the city, closer to where the portal was located, monsters roared and screeched.

The darkness began to spread like spilled ink.

"Holy shit," Dallas breathed. The shadow—

It was moving this way.

"Back up," Malakai commanded. He grabbed Aspen by the arm. *"Back up, back up."*

Together, they backed up. Backed away as the darkness crawled toward them, engulfing so much of the street it pushed them away from Lucent Enterprises by one whole block.

"Shit," Jewels said as they kept walking backward. "Should we run?"

"No," Aspen gritted out. "No, it's slowing down—see?"

Indeed, it was. The rumbling stopped, and so did the spreading of that pitch-black wall. They stopped walking, tipping their heads all the way back as they stared up at the towering mass of blackness. It was so high, it scraped the forcefield. Magic sparked and sputtered as the forcefield fought to contain it.

Travis turned, his breaths thinning out as he looked for the Control Tower.

Still visible. Barely.

His phone buzzed with an incoming call. He loosed the breath in his lungs and picked up. "Atlas?" he gritted out.

"We have a problem," Tanner said.

"Yeah, you're telling me. Where the hell's Darien, man? We're freaking out over here—"

"I'm going to try to guide you through."

"How?" Travis asked, panting, heart pounding. "You can't even see us—"

"I managed to get the spell feeds for Lucent Enterprises up on my computer. They're hella glitchy—they look like they might go out at any second, but we can't wait any longer. We need to do this now, or you're going to run out of time."

"Fuck." Travis pushed a hand through his hair, squeezing a fistful of it so hard his knuckles cracked. The others were watching him, eavesdropping, casting apprehensive glances at each other. "Atlas, once we're in there, if the spell feeds go out—"

"This is the *only* option," Tanner said. His tone was strained.

"But Darien—"

"Darien's in Blackwater, Travis."

A collective gasp rippled among the group. All the blood left Travis's head, so swiftly he swayed on his feet.

"Blackwater?" he whispered. He raised a hand to his mouth. What the *hell* had happened—

"We have to try this on our own, Trav," Tanner urged. "Do you at least know where the front doors are? If you can get in, I can do my best to guide you from there, but you'll all have to take off your talismans. The spell feeds don't extend beyond the building, so I can't see you on the street. You'll need to find the doors on your own."

Travis cursed under his breath.

"The front entrance faces south," Atlas said. "Put me through to your headsets and stick together as a group."

"Okay."

"Hold hands if you have to. Just please don't get separated, whatever you do."

"Okay," Travis said. "Okay—hold on."

It took him two tries, but he managed to put Atlas on speakerphone, his hands trembling as he pulled up the hands-free call settings on the device. The darkness was so thick, his phone screen seemed dim.

"What about the monsters?" Max asked as the call connected through everyone's headsets with a sharp burst of static.

Travis slid his phone into his pocket.

"I can see them," Tanner responded.

"How many are there?" Aspen squeezed out.

A beat of silence. And then Atlas said, "Lots."

109

BLACKWATER PENITENTIARY
ANGELTHENE, STATE OF WITHEREDGE

Darien whirled. He grabbed Glen by the wrist, twisting it back so far he shouted out in pain and dropped the knife.

As it clattered to the ground, Darien's heart stalled at the sight of the black blade. At the red-hot, glowing lines forking through the glasslike material like molten lava.

Brimstone. The prick had stabbed him with a fucking brimstone blade.

The guards were shouting.

"Freeze!"

"Don't move!"

"Get back against the wall!"

"Hands where we can see them!"

Darien spun, kicking the gun out of the hands of the closest guard. Lightning-fast, he punched the butt of that gun into the guard's mouth, cracking teeth. He yowled in pain, blood gushing down his chin.

The trigger snapped under Darien's finger as he pulled it, blasting another guard's brains out. He wasted no time before shooting the first guard—the one whose mouth he'd smashed open.

The third guard started firing.

Darien ducked as bullets peppered the walls. Stone and dust sprayed. With a battle cry, he ran straight at the guard and pushed him against the wall. His bones barked with the impact. Just as the guard squeezed the trigger, Darien thrust his elbow up, redirecting the bullet—

BANG. Into the skull of the fourth and final guard, it went.

Dead. All four were dead. Only Gaven and Glen remained.

It was Glen who was attempting to pick up the knife.

Darien lunged. Consumed with blind, lethal rage, he grabbed onto the back of Glen's neck and smashed his face against the corner of the doorframe.

Once.

Twice.

Three times.

Four.

He didn't stop until he was dead, his face hardly more than red goo.

Darien let go. Glen's body crumpled to the floor.

A hand clamped onto his nape. All at once, his muscles seized up as pain sawed through his body in white-hot bolts. He couldn't think, couldn't breathe, but he knew it was Gaven, the lazy fucker finally getting up from the table to join in on the fight. His Aether powers flowed through Darien like a taser. His mind was short-circuiting. His heart jolted, threatening to give out, flatline—

He flattened his boot against the wall and pushed, shoving Gaven back—

They crashed into the table, tipping it over. Mortifer's cage clanged to the floor. The shock of the attack was enough to put a pause in Gaven's magic.

Darien seized his opportunity and moved. He wrapped the chains of his cuffs around Gavens' throat and pulled—as hard as he could.

Gaven whipped forward and then threw his head back, smashing the back of his skull against Darien's nose.

He shouted out and crashed backward onto the floor. Blood gushed from his nose. He twisted onto his stomach, reaching for the brimstone blade that was dripping his blood onto the floor.

"Going somewhere, Cassel?" Gaven panted as he climbed onto his back, his weight pushing the last of the breath out of his lungs. Gaven wrapped an arm around his throat and squeezed, cutting off his airflow. He winced and twitched as lightning crackled and wove between his teeth, frying his fucking nerves.

He kept reaching. Even as the edges of his vision began to go gray.

He did it for Loren. For Travis. For Max. For Ivy.

For Mortifer, who was screaming in that cage, his tiny hands pulling like hell on the bars.

The tip of his finger grazed the knife handle, turning it just enough—

He grabbed it and punched it over his shoulder.

Right into Gaven's eye.

A scream. A squirt of blood.

He stabbed again.

Again.

Again.

Again.

Until the arm around his throat loosened and Gaven's body went slack on top of him.

His vision shimmered. His ears rang. "Fuck." With a guttural cry of pain, he dragged himself out from under Gaven, took the keys out of the asshole's pocket, and crawled across the floor, blood streaming out of his mouth. He reached for Morty's cage, missing twice. Somewhere, deep in the back of his blurry mind, he became aware of a sharp, rhythmic beeping.

Sirens. Someone had sounded the emergency alarm. Red lights were flashing, bathing every room and corridor in the color of fresh blood.

"Mortifer," he choked out. His fingers were shaking so hard, he could barely slide the key into the lock. It was only the sight of Mortifer's frightened face, the anguish in his eyes, that gave him the strength to turn that key and open the door.

Mortifer backed up and covered his face with trembling hands.

"Morty," Darien rasped. He blinked away the fog. Swallowed blood. "It's okay. You're safe now. You're safe. It's me—it's Darien."

Mortifer, still quivering with fear, peeked between his fingers.

"Don't be afraid." He dropped the keys and opened his arms. "It's just me. It's just Darien. You *know* me—I won't hurt you, I swear."

Finally, Mortifer lowered his hands. His eyes were sad.

Darien broke. "I'm sorry," he choked out. A wobbling sob ripped out of him. "I'm so sorry, buddy." Blood dribbled down his chin and dripped onto the knees of his jumpsuit. "Come on." He beckoned with fingers he could hardly control. "I'm going to get you home."

Mortifer scampered out of the cage. Hesitated by his knee.

"There you go," Darien encouraged as Mortifer ventured closer, his webbed feet making sticking sounds on the concrete floor. "There you go— I got you. I got you. Get on." He lowered his shaking hand, and Mortifer got on, climbing up the length of his arm. "Max and Travis need our help. We're gonna help them, okay? We'll do it together."

He pushed to his feet and crossed the room. Stepped over dead bodies and splashed through puddles of blood. He braced his hands against the walls, leaving bloody fingerprints everywhere he went. With Mortifer on his shoulder, hanging onto the back of his neckline, he staggered down the hallway.

Toward the control room.

110

LUCENT ENTERPRISES
YVESWICH, STATE OF KER

It was by sheer, dumb luck that Max and the others made it through the black shroud that had swallowed Lucent Enterprises and up the steps to the front entrance.

Everyone was holding hands. Max had taken the lead and was blindly feeling around for the doors.

In the days since the explosion, the darkness had grown thicker. For what good their Sight was doing them, they might as well be blind. The spells Tanner could see on his computer were completely invisible to them. The darkness was so suffocating, it made Max feel claustrophobic.

Someway, somehow, they made it into the building and up to the nineteenth floor. After crawling blindly up the stairwell and into the wing where Roark—who was now at the house with Tanner—claimed the staff kept a small store of the syringes. The stairwell they'd taken to get here had no monsters, but this nineteenth floor—

It was crawling with them.

Sweat trickled down Max's back as he led the way, one careful step at a time, through the pressing darkness. Malakai was using his magic to mask any sounds they made, talking included, while Aspen used hers to disguise their scents. Everyone would have to pitch in. Take turns. It was the only way to survive this—to stop one person from burning out more than the others.

As they followed Tanner's instructions, Max concentrated as best as he could on the here and now. But knowing Darien had been arrested and locked up in Blackwater, on death fucking row...

How they were ever going to get out of this... Fix everything that was broken...

It was endless. All this shit was endless, and he couldn't see a way out.

"The door you're looking for is coming up on your left," Tanner said, his words punctuated by bursts of static. Max hoped—prayed, for possibly the first time in his life—communications would hold. "Keep going," Tanner murmured as they moved forward. "Keep going... There—left. Go left."

Max turned, and everyone followed into the laboratory.

"There are three monsters in there," Tanner said. Great. "Just stick to the path you're on and head straight for the far wall."

Clicking in the dark. Hissing.

An ear-splitting roar and a *crash* as two of the creatures broke out into a fight, knocking over something that shattered. Max felt an object roll into his boot. Dallas hung onto the back of his jacket. Together, everyone clinging to each other, they made it to the back wall.

"Hold on," Tanner said. "I'm going to pass you to Roark."

The line crackled. Nobody made a sound as the monsters screamed and bit each other, not five feet behind them.

"Max?" Roark said. "Roark here. Can you hear me?"

"Loud and clear," Max said. Sweat trickled down his spine.

"There are two cupboards in front of you. I'm going to need you to feel around and open the doors of the one farthest to your left."

Max followed Roark's instructions. The others stayed close as he let go of their hands and felt around, locating the cupboard that was farthest to his left. Then he opened the doors and rummaged around in the cupboard, praying he was grabbing the right thing. If they got all the way out of here, only to discover he didn't have the right syringes...

Roark said, "It should feel like a small black travel case with a zip closure."

"I think I got it."

"Open it. There should be twelve syringes in each. You'll need two cases."

Max ran his fingertips across the syringes, counting twelve in each travel case. "I count twelve in each," he said.

"Good. They're the only item in Lucent Enterprises that is stored in such a way. I don't believe it's possible to mess this up."

"All right," Max said. "Thanks."

"I'll hand you back to Tanner."

"Dad," Dallas gasped.

A pause.

"I just want to say—if we don't make it out of here... I just..." An audible swallow. Her hand tightened around Max's, and he squeezed it in encouragement. "I want you to know—"

"Dallas, you *will*," Roark said. Fiercer, he repeated, "You *will* make it out of there. Say it with me."

Another swallow, and then Dallas said on a shaky whisper, "I will. I will make it out of here."

"I'll see you at home in a couple of days," Roark said, in a tone far softer than Max had ever heard him use. "Okay?"

Dallas inhaled, the sound smoother now than before. Max could sense that her aura had calmed. "Okay."

"See you soon," he said again.

A crackle, and then Tanner got back on. "All right—turn around. Let's get you out of there."

Max was sweating so badly, the cold air made him feel wet.

They were almost out of the room when the building began to shake. It grew to an unholy magnitude. Glass shattered down the hallway.

It stopped as abruptly as it started.

"Atlas?" Max gritted out.

"No." Atlas's whisper was barely audible. *"No, no, no."*

Max's heart started to race. "Atlas? What's going on?"

"The spells," he choked out. "The spells are out, Max. They're out—*I can't see you!"*

III

BLACKWATER PENITENTIARY
ANGELTHENE, STATE OF WITHEREDGE

No sooner had Loren and the others made it into the prison than the guards sounded the emergency alarm.

A loud, warbling sound pulsed through the building. Flashing lights came on, bathing the concrete walls and floor in blood red.

Where she walked with the others in a tight group, down a narrow, drafty corridor that would take them to death row, Loren froze, the others doing the same. Heads swiveled. Hands tightened on guns.

At first, Loren believed the alarm had been sounded because someone had spotted them.

But then the prison filled with guttural roars and piercing, hair-raising screams, and she realized it was something worse.

Far worse.

The screaming, the roaring—she couldn't pinpoint its origin.

It was coming from all over.

Kylar, chest heaving, said, "Have we been spotted?"

Finn shook his head. "No. No—something else is going on," he panted, the sweat on his face glistening in the flashing lights. "Something else is happening."

And then the building began to shake. The tremors increased in magnitude. Everyone grabbed onto each other as they tried not to fall.

Loren had the feeling this was not an ordinary earthquake. It was the portal—even from one state over, it was beginning to cause earthquakes in other areas.

And possibly even disrupt the security system of one of the most heavily fortified prisons in the world.

"What the hell's going on?" Ivy breathed as the shaking subsided, strands of her dark hair sticking to the sweat on her temples.

"It's the portal," Loren choked out. Dread prickled down her spine. "It's spreading."

The roaring increased in volume. Whatever was making that sound...

It was hungry.

And it was getting closer.

"Move," Lace said, waving her gun in a forward motion. "Everyone, move—now. Now!"

They started running.

DARIEN WAS SO DIZZY, he felt like he was running on ocean waves.

He staggered down the hallway as if he were drunk, leaving bloody handprints all over the walls, and stumbled through a doorway marked with a sign that read Control Room 8B.

The room was empty. Abandoned. Blood and claw marks marked every surface, a few of the screens smashed.

He practically fell into one of the swivel chairs and picked up a telephone with blood-slick, shaking fingers. Mortifer was holding onto the back of his neckline; Darien could sense him watching with concern as his fingers that were dripping blood hovered over the buttons.

On a wobbling breath, he gritted out, "Fuck. *Fuck*—I don't know what number to call Travis on!"

Through the haze of his brimstone-addled mind, it took him a minute to realize that he could call Atlas instead. Atlas could help.

That was exactly what Darien did. As the line rang, he clutched the stab wound in his side, his head spinning so rapidly it felt like he was stuck in a hurricane.

"Come on, Tanner," Darien whispered. A wave of nausea threatened to engulf him. He swallowed bile. "Pick up, pick up, pick up."

Was the building shaking, or was it just him? Everything was vibrating, and he swore he heard the sound of distant screaming—

Tanner picked up on the fourth ring. "Who is this?"

"Tanner, it's me."

A loaded pause. And then: "Holy shit—Darien? Are you okay?"

"No," he admitted around a blood-thickened sob. "I need you to get me through to Travis."

Tanner swore. Keys clacked in the background.

Darien lifted his hand off the stab wound. Looked down—

The bleeding was getting worse.

Another sob rose in his throat. He swallowed it down and said, "Hurry, Tanner. *Hurry.*"

112

LUCENT ENTERPRISES
YVESWICH, STATE OF KER

Deep in Lucent Enterprises, Travis hung on tight to Jewels's hand, his other wrapped firmly around Dallas's, as they picked their way blindly through the dark.

It was suffocating, this blackness. Travis could honestly say he had never been more afraid in all his life. A few minutes ago, Tanner had hung up to take another call. He hadn't called back yet.

They'd tried tracking on their own to navigate the darkness, but there were two problems with that. One: Whoever was tracking was not able to multi-task; holding the Sight required too much focus, so it was impossible to do something like walk while tracking. So every time they tracked for a short distance, they had to pause, then pick up walking again once they navigated one hallway. Two: After taking turns charging the warhead, they were drained.

Travis had tried getting a hold of the others, but they hadn't answered —still in the process of moving that heavy missile, probably.

They would just have to keep moving. Keep moving—and try to find their way out of here on their own.

He could smell the monsters moving about. Had he been able to see, he knew the sight of this place would have shocked him. More than once, he'd nearly tripped over the telltale lump of a corpse, his boots sticky. His throat hadn't stopped burning with bile since the minute they'd left the lab.

Jewels's hand was trembling in his. He gave that hand a soft, comforting squeeze. She squeezed back.

His headset beeped with an incoming call.

Everyone paused. Travis let go of Dallas's hand, just for two seconds—just long enough to flick the button that would answer the call.

"Hello?" he whispered.

"Travis, it's Darien."

Murmurs rippled through the group.

"Darien, holy shit, are you okay?"

"Never mind that right now—I'm going to get you out of there." He was talking the same way he always did: firmly and confidently, as if nothing was wrong.

Travis knew that was far from true.

Darien said, "You passed the stairwell. Turn around."

Everyone turned as a group, swapping hands. Travis took the lead, switching places with Malakai. Darien was able to track only one person at a time, and right now he was tracking Travis.

"Can you see okay?" Travis asked as they started walking, back the way they'd come. Toward the door to the stairwell that they'd passed without even realizing it.

"I can see fine. In about twelve yards, you're going to hang a right." A beat of tense quiet as they all walked the distance, then Darien said, "Right—now. Turn right."

Travis fumbled for the handle and opened it.

It was hell navigating the stairs when they couldn't see, but they did it —all nineteen floors. When they came out on the ground level, Travis exhaled in relief. They weren't in the clear, though—not yet. The building was huge; even just the ground floor would take a while to navigate.

The door to the stairwell had just clicked shut behind them when Darien said, "Travis—Travis *stop.* "

Everyone froze.

Darien whispered, "Don't fucking move."

A guttural growl ripped through the dark. Closer than Travis cared to admit. He held still—

The reek of an exhaled breath wafted across his face, the smell so sour it made him gag.

"IT CAN FUCKING SEE YOU!" Darien's warning shredded the speakers.

Something sharp punched into Travis's gut, and he was thrown into a wall.

IN THE CONTROL room at Blackwater Penitentiary, Darien hung his head in his hands, knee bouncing as he listened to the screaming, the roaring, the shouts of pain.

"Come on," he muttered, fisting his hair. "Come on, guys—come *on.*"

Jewels screamed Travis's name.

Bodies hit the walls and floor.

Max shouted in pain. Bellowed for Dallas— "Where's Dallas? *Dallas, where are you?*"

The only sound missing was gunshots. They couldn't fire in the dark, not when they were blind and just as likely to shoot each other as they were the monster. And, even if they *could* shoot it, this particular monster had been birthed from the Void. A creature with a black stone in its head. The same breed they'd fought at the carnival, the same breed Darien had killed at the harbor.

More shouting, more screaming, more roaring, coming not just from the phone speaker, but deep in the prison, too.

On the security cameras, Darien saw that the cell doors were open on several floors. The prisoners had escaped and were running rampant in the hallways. Slaughtering the guards, each other.

He clutched his stab wound, applying firm pressure. His vision went out of focus, and he fought the urge to faint.

Stay alive. He had to stay alive.

Just a little while longer.

MALAKAI COULDN'T GET a read on this bitch. And he had been thrown into the walls so many times, he could scarcely breathe.

He slammed into the floor, landing on his fucking face. The impact nearly sent him spiraling into oblivion.

The air peeled apart as claws swiped for him—

He rolled.

The creature's claws punched into the floor—right where his head had been, Malakai would bet.

He pushed to his feet, rallying his magic—and with a mighty roar that rivaled the monster's, he blasted this bitch's head into a pulp that misted his face. The floor trembled as its body collapsed.

He took a second to breathe. Check himself for injury. And then he gritted out, "Everyone alive?"

"Alive," Aspen confirmed.

"Same," Jewels panted, Dallas's voice melding with hers.

Boots scraped as the others pushed to their feet.

Travis said, "I got a claw in the gut, but I think I'll live."

"Reacher?" Malakai inquired.

"Fine," Max bit out.

Malakai flicked the button on his headset and said, "Guess what, asshole? You're not the only one who can take down those sons of bitches."

A chair creaked, and then Darien said hoarsely, "Everyone alive?"

Malakai spat out a mouthful of blood. "For now. Get us out of here."

"All right, I'm tracking *you* now," Darien said. He sounded spaced out. Everyone felt for each other's hands as Darien added, "Be fast."

113

SOUTH COASTAL DISTRICT
YVESWICH, STATE OF KER

The portal was spreading. The ground was shaking so violently, Travis had already fallen on his ass several times as he ran. The others kept pace beside him. Pushing themselves faster than they had ever moved before.

With Darien's help, they'd made it out of Lucent Enterprises, across the canal that was now frozen solid, and into the South Coastal District. It was light enough over here that they were able to see on their own, giving Darien a break from tracking until after they got the tower down.

On the other line, Darien was quiet. *Too* quiet. Occasionally, Travis's sharp hearing picked up on a ragged inhale or a softly uttered swear word, but other than that, Darien stayed silent.

Nobody dared ask him what'd happened. Where he was. Why he was breathing so heavily.

Why he sounded like he was in excruciating pain.

On, they sprinted beneath a charcoal sky, through the wreckage of the South Coastal District. That's what all of Yveswich was now: wreckage. Every time the portal spread, resulting in more earthquakes, more darkness, and more monsters, what remained of Yveswich fell to the might of the Void.

They were almost there. Travis could see the apartment building where the others were waiting for them.

A burst of static spat through the speakers of his headset. "We can see you," Dominic said.

Hope kindled in Travis's heart. "Get ready," he panted.

"Whatever you do, Feathers," Malakai added, "try not to miss."

They made it to the fire escape and started climbing.

ROMAN WAS DRIVING SO FAST, Dean could barely keep up. For the past hour, his boot had been glued to the accelerator as he flew through red lights and stop signs, engine whirring as he pushed it to its limit.

They were almost there. He could see Yveswich from here. The crimson half-sphere of runes shining above the ruins of his old home.

Movement from above drew Roman's attention to the dark sky.

Combat planes.

Shit.

The planes were early, and the tower still wasn't down.

Beside him, in the passenger's seat, Shay's breathing thinned out.

She'd spotted the planes, too.

"Come on, Travis," Roman murmured. "Come on, come on, come *on.*"

He had to make it.

Travis *had* to make it. Had to survive.

If he didn't, if Roman lost his brother once and for all, he would never forgive himself.

"EVERYONE READY?" Dominic asked as they threw their needles aside, the injection sites in their necks glowing with faint teal light.

Everyone answered the Angel with nods and murmured confirmations.

Where he'd set up the missile by the edge of the roof, Dominic took aim.

Travis and the others lay down flat on their stomachs in a row just behind Dominic.

"Three," the Angel began. He squinted one eye shut, his focus fixed on the Control Tower—on the top half that was barely visible through the otherworldly murk. Had they taken any longer to get here, they would not have been able to see it.

Had they taken any longer, this would not have worked.

A loud whir drew Travis's attention west. To the starless sky above the dark and stormy ocean. Those red lights that were barely pinpricks from here...

Those were navigation lights.

The planes were already here.

Travis's heart started to pound.

Jewels reached over and clasped his hand, squeezing his fingers hard enough to bruise. He could hear her heart pounding, too.

"Two," Dominic said. "One."

Travis whispered, "Boom."

SHAY SAT FORWARD in her seat. "Roman?" she whispered.

Roman glanced her way as he prepared to reduce speed behind the lines of traffic on highway I-5.

In the time since Tanner had restored communications, it seemed word had gotten out about the bullshit that was happening in Yveswich. News reporters were here. And so were the family and friends of the people who were still trapped beneath the forcefield. People were protesting. Enraged.

"Pup?" he asked.

"It might be a good idea to stay back—"

It all happened so quickly.

The Control Tower came down with a BANG that lanced through the air.

The forcefield rushed outward like a popped balloon.

Seismic waves buckled the pavement. Hot light and a grit-choked gust that stank of saltpeter swallowed the road, and before Roman could so much as blink, the car was flipping. Shay and Paxton were screaming. And then—

He smacked his head against a hard surface, and everything went black.

WHEN ROMAN CAME TO, it was to the sound of distant screaming and crying.

The highway had been completely destroyed. Ripped apart, as if by the claws of some ancient leviathan. Cars lay in burning skeletons. And the bodies—

There were bodies everywhere. *Everywhere.* And Roman—

He wasn't even in the car anymore. No—the collision had launched him out of it. The car had been crushed. Shredded to ribbons. Somehow, he'd ended up on the road, the raw and bloody flesh of his cheek sticking to the pavement.

With a growl of pain, he pushed up onto his hands and knees. "Pax?" His ears were ringing, so loudly he could scarcely hear his own voice. The world shimmered. Went in and out of focus. "Shay?"

No answer.

"Dean?" he called. The shout echoed far and wide.

Still—nothing.

His vision tunneled as he caught sight of his uncle sprawled across the road, next to what was left of Iris. Dean, he—

He wasn't breathing.

"Dean?" Roman gritted out. *"Dean!"* He tried to stand, but fell. Started to crawl toward him—

In the corner of his vision, Roman saw a flash of rose gold hair.

Shay lay nearby. She was limp, and there was blood all over her face. So much blood, it was as if she were painted with it. Her chest was still, her eyes stuck open and blank.

Something in Roman broke.

Snapped.

"Shay?" Her name burst out of him on a splintered, tear-choked sob.

Behind her, trapped partially underneath the twisted wreckage of the car, was Paxton. He wasn't moving, either.

Roman swayed. "Pax?" he whispered. He crawled over to him. Gently pulled him out from beneath the car and gathered him into his arms. Brushed the mop of hair off his forehead. He lowered his head to Pax's chest, listening for a heartbeat.

But his chest was still. Quiet. As still and quiet as Shay's.

"No," Roman choked out.

Sayagul started crying. Screaming for her boy.

With Paxton still cradled in his arms, he reached for Shay, feeling for a pulse.

There was none.

A sob ripped out of him. Followed by a guttural scream that sliced his throat apart as he hugged Paxton's limp body, bowing over him to cry into the boy's shirt.

Shay.

Pax.
Dean.
They were dead.
They were all fucking *dead.*

114

1-5

STATE OF KER

Shay wrenched open the passenger's-side door and practically fell into the street. Bloody and battered, she crawled across the cracked pavement, twisting around so she could get her hands on the destroyed passenger's seat.

"Paxton," she gasped. She tried to slide the seat forward, but it was jammed. She lowered her head to see inside the crumpled car—

Paxton was passed out in the back seat. He croaked as he came to, slowly blinking his heavy eyelids. "Wh-what?" he slurred. He had a cut on his brow, but apart from that, he was okay, thank gods. "What happened?"

"Come here, Pax," she urged softly. She brushed shards of glass off the seat, then opened her aching and trembling arms to him. "Come on—let's get you out of there."

He climbed out of the car with care, tucking his hands into his sleeves to shield his fingers from the shattered glass and bits of sharp metal.

"Come on—you're almost there," Shay encouraged, shifting forward on her knees. As soon as he was close enough for her to reach him, she took him by the hands and helped him out, then gathered him into an embrace.

He threw his arms around her, burying his filthy face against the side of her neck. She could feel his heart racing.

"Are you okay?" she asked, holding him tight.

He sniffled. "Yeah. Think so." He kept holding onto her, his arms trembling as hard as hers. She heard his breath hitch—

"It's okay—shh, it's okay." As she held him, murmuring words of comfort, she scanned her surroundings, processing the damage.

There had to be over a dozen casualties. People were crying, others groaning in pain, a few screaming for help.

Behind what was left of Roman's car lay a body.

It was Dean.

Shay paled. *Gods above.*

"Pax." Gently, she disentangled herself from his grasp and pushed to her feet. "Stay here, okay? Stay *right there*—don't move. I'll be right back."

She could feel Paxton watching her as she sprinted over to Dean. Past crying and injured people and burning vehicles. In the distance, there were sirens. She crouched down beside Dean and checked his pulse.

It was faint. A barely-there flutter.

"Shit," Shay hissed.

She got to her feet and pivoted on a heel. Searching for help. For—

Wait.

Wait.

"Where's Roman?" she squeezed out.

Paxton staggered to his feet and craned his neck, scanning the road in search of Roman. His brown eyes—shining with fear—snapped to her face.

Shay's heart seized. "Where is your brother?" She hardly recognized the sound of her own voice, could hardly feel her body as terror overcame her, threatening to lock up her muscles, stop her heart.

She started running up and down the highway. "Roman?" she called. Faster, her heart pounded. Faster, she ran, her head swiveling about.

There was no sign of him.

She sucked in a breath and screamed, *"Roman! ROMAN!"* Where the *hell* was he? *"ROMAN! ROOOOOOOMAAAAAAAN!"*

She couldn't breathe. Couldn't *think*—

A gasp came from behind her.

Shay whirled—

"Shay," Paxton whimpered.

It took her a moment to make sense of what she was looking at.

Who was standing just behind Paxton, an arm locked around the boy's neck. Just below the woman's eye was a tattoo of a water droplet.

The water droplet of the Riptide.

"Pia," Shay whispered.

Pia lifted the gun in her hand—

And pointed it at Shay's head. The hollow *click* of the safety being disengaged spurred Shay's heart into a faster sprint.

"Don't move." Pia's whisper was hollow—as dead as her stare.

"Pia," Shay said again. She took one step—

"I said don't move!"

Shay raised her hands above her head. "Okay," she said calmly. "Okay."

She chanced a look around. There were no other Selkies here. Just Pia.

Good. That was good. It meant she had a chance at a fair fight.

So she raised her hands higher. Focused on calming her pulse and discreetly rallying her magic as she whispered, "Where are the others?"

Stalling—she was stalling. Giving herself time to think of a plan.

The sirens were getting closer. If the cops arrived, if she could create enough of a scene—

"Not here," Pia bit out. "We've been looking for you for days." She shook her head, her upper lip curling back over her teeth as she hissed, "You shouldn't have done it, Shay."

"Done what?" Shay asked.

"Ran!" Pia spat. "Taken that psycho's kid!" She bumped her gun into Paxton's chin.

A small noise of fear escaped Paxton's throat.

"Pia," Shay whispered. "Please, Pia. Put the gun down."

But she was already shaking her head. "I can't."

"You can. You don't have to do this."

"Yes, I do!" she exclaimed, a loud sob shattering the icy night. "I *have* to kill you." Her lips wobbled as she added, "Or he's going to kill me."

ROMAN'S WORLD was crashing around him.

Kneeling on the ground, he sobbed uncontrollably over his brother's body, his tears soaking his face and Paxton's shirt. His chest was still, his skin pale and icy.

Dead. His brother was dead, and he was never going to be able to move on from this, would never forgive himself—

Suddenly, the air shifted. Peeled back, as if a door had whipped open with enough force to cause a sharp breeze.

The screaming, the crying, the sirens, the chopping of rotary blades...all of it faded away. Leaving behind nothing but cold and hollow silence, interrupted only by the thumping of his pulse in his ears.

And then an echoey male voice said, "Hello, Roman."

Roman opened his damp eyes. Raised his weary head.

Standing there, among the wreckage of the I-5, was Donovan Slade, his two-headed wolf Familiar stalking out of his shadow to stand beside him. All the other people, the commotion that had been going on all around him...all of it was gone. It was just the two of them.

Roman's mind spun as he glanced between the lifeless boy he was cradling in his lap and his father.

His hand flew to his neck—to the missing talisman.

'Something isn't right,' Sayagul had said, the day Darien had sprinted into the purple house.

Back then, something wasn't right. And now...

Something wasn't right here, either.

Roman's mind spun as he remembered everything Roark had told Darien—about the falling of the Veil. The wellsprings of magic that had been tucked away behind the curtain for so long. Don had always had the magical ability to create hallucinations, use his shadows to force a person to see things that weren't there—only, it was stronger now that the Veil was falling.

He was stronger now.

As if he wasn't strong enough already.

"This isn't real," Roman whispered.

Donovan smiled. His eyes were as black as pitch as he said, "You're catching on quickly for once."

Roman laid Paxton—the *hallucination* of Pax, not the real thing, thank gods—down carefully on the pavement. Slowly, he got to his feet. "What the hell do you want?" he whispered.

"I want my kid back," Don replied.

Roman shook his head. "You can't have him," he choked out, nausea swirling in his gut. "I won't let you have him."

Donovan gave a cold smirk. "I find it so funny how someone like you—someone so weak and pathetic—actually believes you stand a chance against someone like me. After *everything*. Have you not learned your lesson, Roman?"

Roman kept his mouth shut.

Don slid his black stare to Dean. To the illusion of his eldest brother's dead body. There was zero remorse in that stare. Zero feeling. Roman knew it was only an illusion, but...

The man standing before him was empty. A diabolical shell.

"Nice little family reunion you've got going on here," said Donovan.

"I want you," Roman began, chest heaving, "to leave us the hell alone."

"Oh, I'm sure you do. You'd all be one big, happy family then, wouldn't you? Father and son, together at last."

Roman turned very still. For a moment, time felt like it stopped, and so did his heart. "What the hell are you talking about?" he demanded.

A cold chuckle. And then: "You really don't know, do you?"

Roman waited. The longer he stood there, his attention flicking between his father and his uncle, the thinner his breaths became. The harder his heart pounded. The faster his stomach churned.

Donovan began to pace. Circling him like a hungry lion. "Haven't you ever wondered, Roman...why Travis has a dog for a Familiar? Why Paxton has a dog for a Familiar? Why your mother had a dog for a Familiar?" A loaded pause. And then: "Why I...have a wolf?"

Roman was no longer breathing.

And he swore his heart outright *stopped* as Donovan continued, "And why you...have a dragon?" Don flicked his brows up in question.

Roman's focus jumped to the wolf Familiar lurking at Don's side, eyes glowing in the dark.

"Ever wondered...," Don continued, his upper lip curling back over his teeth. "Why my brother has the same Familiar as you?"

Roman shook his head—not in answer, but denial. "You're full of shit," he hissed.

"Am I? Look at the facts, Roman," he challenged. "Or shall I spell it out for you?"

Roman kept shaking his head—it was all he could manage.

Don continued, "Brutus is a dragon. Black body, green eyes... Looks a lot like Sayagul. Wouldn't you agree?"

Roman opened his mouth. Shut it. Squeezed out, "Dean's my..."

"Dad—yeah. Your whore of a mother fucked around with him—back before you were born."

'It was before your time,' Dean had said to Roman that night at Wacky's Waffles, when Roman had asked him who *she* was—*The One* that had gotten away.

It was *literally* before his time.

Had Dean known? Did Dean *know* Roman was his son?

Don continued. "It took me a while before I found out. Before I...clued in. It was their naughty little secret. One that only the two of them shared." A cruel smile that was more a baring of teeth slashed across his face. "No reason to tell me, right? I mean, *I* was the one who was marrying her. *I* was the one who gave her everything she wanted. And yet, somehow, it wasn't good enough for her. *I* wasn't good enough for her." He poked himself hard in the chest. Smirked. "No—it was my *brother* she wanted," he said through clenched teeth.

'Your fault'—that was what Don always said. *'She died because of you.'*

'He's lying,' Sayagul had cried, countless times in that dungeon in the House of Black, while Roman hung there from chains.

But he hadn't lied. Don hadn't lied, at least not about that.

Helen Devlin had died because of *him*. Because of Roman. And Donovan—

Donovan had murdered her in cold blood.

Because he'd found out that Roman was not his child.

And Sayagul—

'The suppressants,' the dragon whispered now, her voice small and hollowed out with shock. *'Dean mentioned suppressants—'*

"You drugged me," Roman whispered.

"Found out about the suppressants, did you?" Don said. "Took you long enough."

Donovan had drugged him—must have slipped a banned suppressant into his food during his teenaged years, when his magic was still maturing. Which would explain why Sayagul was so small—something Roman had not thought twice about...until now.

Until he'd found out that Dean was his father, and Dean had a dragon who was ten times the size of Sayagul. The size Sayagul *should* be at Roman's age.

Donovan had intentionally weakened him. *Wrecked* him.

Roman felt like he was floating. Disconnected. "You ruined my life," he whispered. When he spoke again, his voice was no longer a whisper. It was a deafening scream that ripped his throat to shreds. *"You ruined my FUCKING LIFE!"*

Donovan was unfazed. He stood there, his lips tipping up with a cruel smile as he watched. Watched as Roman unraveled.

He had been waiting a very long time for this.

Roman's head spun with questions. Epiphanies.

Cold, hard facts.

"Pax—" he gasped.

"Is not your brother, no," Donovan said, his black eyes shining with triumph. "Pity no one told you sooner. Could have saved yourself all this heartache and pain."

Paxton was not even his brother. They weren't brothers at all.

They were cousins. *Half*-cousins.

Everything Roman had sacrificed. All those years at the House of the Black—

Roman forced himself to breathe. Calm down. Think rationally.

He got his emotions under control. Raised his chin. "I see what you're doing," he said in a level voice. It didn't shake, that voice. It was sturdy, just like the rest of him.

No more. No more running, no more cowering.

No fucking more. It was *over*.

"You're trying to drive me away from him," Roman continued. "You're trying to push us apart." He shook his head mechanically. "But it's not going to work."

The look on Don's face was telling.

That was exactly what he was doing. Why he'd chosen to reveal this information right here, right now, after all these years. While his son and his nephew—*nephew*, not son—were on the run. This moment had been carefully designed to wreck Roman's life, setting fire to everything he'd believed in for twenty-seven years, everything he'd stood for. At exactly the moment Donovan needed it most.

And right now, what he needed was for Roman to surrender Paxton.

Too bad for him. Roman loved Paxton. Brother or no, he *loved* him, with his whole damn heart. With every shred of his being. There was no force in this world or the next that could drive them apart.

Don drew a sharp breath. "We can do this the easy way or the hard way, Roman. The decision is yours. Either you can give me Paxton...or I come after you. It's that simple. But, should you choose the hard way, know that I will hunt you down. Every day for the rest of your gods-forsaken life, I will hunt you...until I find you. And when I find you, I will kill you, slowly and painfully."

The threat didn't scare Roman—it fueled him. "I'll never let you have him," he snarled.

Don's expression sank into something dangerous. "Is that your decision?" It was a warning. A threat.

But Roman wasn't afraid—not anymore.

His eyes turned black. The thick shadows on either side of the road began to move—two big masses racing toward each other. They collided with a *bang* and rose at his back, unfurling like a pair of great wings.

"This ends," Roman snarled. He lowered his chin, tendrils of shadow weaving between his fingers. "Right. *Now.*"

With an outward thrust of his hands, those shadows blasted forward in a lethal black wave—

They crashed into Donovan.

He disappeared. Right in front of Roman's eyes.

And so did the illusion he was trapped in.

———

"Pia," Shay whispered. "Put the gun down. Please."

Trembling, Pia shook her head.

Shay shut her eyes, feigning defeat. When really, she was summoning her magic.

The illusion powers that blackened her eyes.

The moment her lids flew open, she moved.

Oblivious to her powers, Pia kept her gun trained on the spot where Shay had been standing a moment ago—the illusion that was still standing there now—while the real Shay lunged across the pavement, reaching for that gun.

But Shay was tired, and her illusion wore off sooner than she had planned.

Pia spotted her and spun.

Paxton ducked, screaming out a warning just as Pia's finger snapped down on the trigger—

A searing pain exploded through Shay's stomach.

She crumpled forward, taking Pia down with her as she crashed to the pavement. As they fell, Shay slapped her lightning-charged palm onto Pia's neck—

And roasted her alive.

Shay's old friend screamed and convulsed beneath her. The smell of burning flesh singed her nostrils and turned her stomach. But she did not remove her hand—not until Pia was dead.

That was when the cops and ambulances arrived. But Shay could barely see or hear as she keeled over on the ground, her blood soaking through her shirt.

Paxton was screaming. Screaming and hugging her. Calling for help.

The last thing Shay saw before her world began to fade was Paxton's crying face.

She would remember that face forever.

ROMAN WATCHED in disbelief as the destroyed road and the bodies of all those people—of Pax, Shay, Dean—eddied and melted away like smoke, leaving true reality behind.

He turned in a circle, taking in his surroundings in pieces.

The road was still destroyed, yes. But there was life here. Among the wreckage of vehicles, there were ambulances and cop cars and fire trucks and helicopters. Paramedics and Healers rushed about, loading people onto stretchers to be taken away in ambulances or airlifted to hospitals.

Pax. Shay.

Where were they?

A familiar face caught Roman's eye.

It was Paxton, rushing alongside two paramedics wheeling a stretcher toward a helicopter.

Roman lurched into a jog. That jog broke into a run.

"Pax!" he called. *"Pax!"*

When Paxton spotted him, he sprinted over, sobbing uncontrollably as he crashed into Roman and wrapped his arms around his waist.

"Paxton, what's going—"

"It's Shay!" Paxton cried. His sobs ripped apart Roman's heart. "It's Shay—she's hurt! There was a lady, and she hurt her!"

Roman's soul left his body. He grabbed Paxton by the hand and ran to the stretcher, skidding to a stop beside it.

When he beheld who lay upon it, her eyes shut, her face sickly pale, his knees wobbled and he nearly fainted.

"Shay?" he choked out. "What the hell happened?" he asked the paramedics. *"What happened?"*

"She's been shot. We're airlifting her to a hospital."

He froze—briefly. And then he hurried forward, following them. "Wait. Wait, wait—please. At least tell me where you're taking her—please, I have to know where you're taking her!" He grabbed onto the side of the stretcher, refusing to let go.

"Angelthene General Hospital," the man said. "We're going to need you to stay back."

He did—just for a second.

And then Roman barged through, ignoring their shouts of protest as he took Shay by the hand. Her skin was icy cold, her fingers limp. "Shayla," he breathed. "Shay, can you hear me?"

Slowly, her eyelids opened. "Roman?" she rasped.

"Shayla, I'm here. I'm here. I got you."

"What's going on?"

"They're taking you to Angelthene. I'm going to find you there as soon as I get back, okay?"

"Okay," she croaked.

"I'll find you." He lifted her hand to kiss the back of it. "I promise." He forced himself to let go, even as his heart begged him not to, even as his feet continued to shuffle forward as Shay was lifted into the helicopter.

Dean was being airlifted out, too. Roman spotted him on another stretcher. He was unconscious.

The world spun beneath Roman's feet. Just when he'd thought his life was being pieced back together, it was being shattered again.

"Roman?"

Shay's small voice had him hurrying forward, keeping one hand wrapped around Paxton's. "Yeah, Shayla, I'm here," he panted. "I'm here."

"I love you," she whispered.

The confession pierced his heart. Rendered him speechless.

Before he had a chance to reply, her eyelids slid shut, and he was forced to step back, clearing the way for the helicopter to take flight. It took all his self-control not to throw himself in there. Not to force those paramedics to take him with.

As he watched the helicopter take off, wind from the rotary blades slashing across his face, he realized—

He loved her, too. He'd loved her before—had whispered the confession into the darkness at Motel 58, when he feared he may never see her again. But he loved her even more now than he had back then. The thought of losing her again was enough to nearly bring him to his knees. A life without Shay wasn't a life he wanted to live. A life without Shay was like the world without rain. And Roman loved the rain.

With his hand wrapped around Paxton's, Roman watched, his heart crumbling into dust, as the beautiful thief who'd stolen his heart and the father he never knew he had were taken away from him.

115

THE HARBOR
YVESWICH, STATE OF KER

They'd made it to the harbor. Against all odds, they'd made it to the harbor.

When the tower had collapsed, the mass of shadow had blasted outward, moving past the coast. Rushing out toward the ocean. And because it had blinded them, there was no telling how far it had spread, but—

They were in the boat now. All of them were crowded in a group, holding onto each other. The fact that they all fit—*barely*—was a miracle in itself.

Malakai was driving. Max listened in on his own headset as the Reaper conversed with Darien, whose voice was getting fainter by the minute.

He'd guided them out. As soon as the tower came down, Darien had guided them, all the way from the South Coastal District to the harbor. And now, he was staying on the line to ensure they found their way out of the darkness.

Max's heart hadn't stopped pounding since they'd set foot in Lucent Enterprises. He held on tightly to Dallas's hand as the boat dipped and splashed over the waves, icy water he couldn't see misting his face. It was impossible to tell where they were going, but—

Getting out of the shadow was their one and only goal right now. And it was easier in the boat than it was to attempt to run blindly through the destruction of the city. This was quicker.

Minutes passed, and Max began to fear the shadow had spread too far to get out. That perhaps the life serum coursing through their bloodstreams would be absorbed by the time they got out of here. But then—

Slowly, Max rose to his feet, a few of the others doing the same.

Blinked in disbelief.

He could see.

They could *see*.

There was the ocean—a vast expanse of black water stretching all around them, the foamy waves capped with pearly moonlight.

And there was the coast. He spotted the I-5, at the top of that craggy hill, the blue and red lights of cop cars, ambulances, and fire trucks flashing in the gloom.

The others threw their hands up and cheered. Max was too shocked to join in.

Dallas grabbed him by the arm, and she was grinning up at him as she exclaimed, "We did it, Max!" Tears sparkled in her eyes. A little sob came out of her as she said, "We made it!"

He merely gathered her into his arms, kissed the top of her head, and hugged her. Hard.

Travis flicked on his headset. "Darien," he said, panting. "We made it. We made it, Dare. We're safe."

It took Darien a moment to reply. Everyone fell quiet, their short-lived joy fading as they waited. Travis pressed his earpiece in farther, straining to hear over the boat's engine and the splashing of the waves, the whirring of flying helicopters.

Finally, Darien spoke, his voice small—so small, it almost didn't sound like him. "Safe," he repeated, breathless. "You're sure?"

"Yeah," Travis said, his brow creasing with worry. "Yeah, we're safe. Promise."

"Good."

Max thought that was the end of it, when suddenly—

"Max?" Darien's voice was hoarse and so quiet, Max could hardly hear him.

He pressed his earpiece in further and said, "Yeah, Dare?"

A pause. And then, "I'm sorry."

Max's chest tightened. "Me too, Darien," he said, his throat so thick, he couldn't swallow. "Me too."

"I'll see you at home, okay?"

Home. His eyes welled with tears.

"Yeah," he said. "I'll see you at home."

"I love you," Darien said. "Both of you."

Max shared a glance with Travis. Together, they said, "We love you, too, Darien."

Darien cut the line.

Nobody spoke again as Malakai steered the boat toward the coast.

Toward life.

———

THEY FOUND Darien in Control Room 8B.

The minute Loren caught sight of him, where he had collapsed on the floor in a pool of blood, she almost collapsed, too.

A small, broken sound burst out of her. The others called Darien's name.

Mortifer was there with him. Standing beside Darien's head, his tiny hand flattened against the Darkslayer's cheek. The minute the Hob caught sight of them, he started bleating—calling for help.

Silence—there was only silence in her head as she lurched forward and crashed to her knees beside the man she loved.

"Darien?" She was so far away, so detached from her body, that she did not recognize her own voice or her own hands as she started screaming his name and shaking him. "*Darien? Darien! DARIEN!*"

No response.

Someone had stabbed him. The amount of blood—

There was too much.

And he was hardly breathing.

Loren screamed and screamed and screamed—

And then Ivy was there beside her, stopping her from doing it—from healing him.

The female Devil grabbed onto both of Loren's hands. "Loren, you can't," she said. She was crying, too.

"I *have* to save him!" Loren sobbed. *"I have to!"*

Behind her, Jack swayed and grabbed onto the desk. Lace and Kylar and Finn were saying things, but she couldn't hear them over the silence in her head and the sound of her own screaming—

"We will," Ivy was saying. She tightened her hold on Loren's blood-slick hands, forcing her to look her in the eyes. "Loren, listen to me—we will. We need to get him out of here. He's going to live, okay? He's going to live, but we need to get him out of here. *Now.*"

The alarms in the prison were still going off. Those red lights continued to flash.

Loren didn't know how they made it out—she was too focused on Darien to pay attention to anything else. Somehow, though, they did it. They made it out of Blackwater Penitentiary and the utter pandemonium that had broken out within its walls and yard.

She didn't really become aware of anything else until she was back in Ivy's jeep, Darien's head cradled in her lap. A few of the people in their group had caught a ride with Finn; there wasn't enough room for everyone to fit in one vehicle, not with Darien sprawled out and bleeding on the seat.

It was silent in here. Too silent. Loren ran her fingers through Darien's soft hair, his blood soaking her pants. Mortifer was in her lap, hugging her waist while she held on tightly to Darien.

As they drove back to Heaven's Gate, her eyelids slid shut, and the tears began to fall.

116

‪⅂-5‬

STATE OF KER

"Come on, Travis," Roman murmured. "Come on, Travis. Come on, Travis. Come on, Travis."

He stood behind Paxton in the middle of the highway, his hands resting upon his brother's shoulders. Together, they watched with bruised hearts as hundreds of people, stumbling and weeping with relief, emerged from the ruins of Yveswich.

Taking down the Control Tower had unleashed what could only be described as a storm of absolute, impenetrable darkness—one that had swallowed the entirety of Ker's capital in one fell swoop. Already, it had spread beyond city limits, slicing the I-5 and the surrounding land in half with a massive black wall. The temperature had plummeted below freezing, turning his toes and fingers numb and his breaths into small ghosts.

Yveswich had once been a great city, its population standing proudly in the millions. Many citizens had already evacuated, sure—but Roman knew, just from watching as this small trickle of people staggered into the arms of family and friends, healthcare workers, and military personnel, that far more lives had been lost than saved. Those who were alive had, without a doubt, been closer to the outskirts—closer to where the shadow was thinnest and the oxygen had not run out.

As Roman waited, he scanned the faces of everyone who passed. Looking for anyone he recognized.

Looking for Travis.

Minutes ticked by, and there was still no sign of him.

Roman felt like he was going to throw up. He slid his phone out of the back pocket of his jeans—ripped and bloodied from the crash—and checked the screen for messages, calls—any indication that he might need to grab the swords and head in there.

But there was nothing. And so he was forced to wait. To wonder. Worry.

Around his neck, he wore a new Avertera talisman—his very last one. He had no idea where the fuck Donovan was, but—

Keeping his aura exposed was a bad idea. Don already knew where he was, yes—he'd made that clear with that absurdly realistic illusion he'd cast. But the last thing Roman needed was for that psycho to still be tracking him and decide to show up before they had a chance to get away from here.

Paxton pushed up onto his tiptoes, craning his neck to see through the crowds.

And then—

He gasped and stumbled forward, the action causing Roman's hands to slip off his shoulders.

Roman followed Paxton's line of sight.

His breath caught as he saw him. Saw Travis—limping up the hill that sloped down to the rugged coastline, his hand clasping Jewels Delaney's.

'Oh, thank gods,' Sayagul breathed, the dragon's words weak with relief.

As weak as Roman's knees that were threatening to buckle.

Following closely behind Travis and Jewels was Maximus Reacher, his arm looped through Dallas Bright's.

And there were Malakai Delaney and Aspen Van Halen.

Dominic Valencia and Blue.

That wasn't all—no. Five other people were with them—three with wings of white feathers. Raina and Silas Cruso and Charlotte Demeure. The two that didn't have wings were young, both female, one with hair a startling shade of pink, the other reddish brown. Several were limping, Travis included, others supporting each other with arms slung around shoulders.

Roman lurched forward. "Travis?" he croaked. The wind howled, snatching his voice.

Travis slid his gaze their way, searching. As soon as he saw them—saw his brothers—he froze.

"Travis!" Paxton called. "Look, Roman—it's Travis!" He pointed.

Silent in shock, Travis stumbled forward—one step. Two. His hand slipped out of Jewels's grasp.

Paxton was smiling. "Travis!" He waved one arm above his head, then added the other and started hopping in place. "Travis, over here!"

Travis paused again. Blinked several times, as if he couldn't believe what he was seeing. He glanced over his shoulder at Jewels, as if to ask her, *Are you seeing this, too?*

The female Reaper smiled, tears sparkling in her eyes. "Go," she told him.

And just like that, Travis was running.

Roman broke into a sprint of his own, his mind blank with shock and relief, both so intense they were almost debilitating. Paxton kept pace beside him, the kid smiling big as he called Travis's name—*Travis! Travis! Travis!*

They ran. Past ambulances and fire trucks. Paramedics and Fleet soldiers.

Roman collided with Travis hard enough to bruise, Pax latching onto them, too. Their arms were around each other, and Travis was speed-talking, but Roman didn't hear any words. All he cared about was that his brother was alive, and he was.

Travis was *alive.*

"I'm sorry," Travis was saying. Roman could smell the salt of the tears coursing down his cheeks. "I'm so sorry, Rome! I'm a fucking *idiot—*"

"Travis—," Roman tried.

But Travis just kept apologizing—for staying behind, for not being quick enough to evacuate, for getting himself stuck, for being an idiot.

Roman grabbed Travis by the shoulders and pulled back—out of his grip that was firm enough to bruise. "Trav—"

"I'm never coming back to Yveswich! Fuck this place, it can rot in hell—"

"Travis," Roman repeated.

Travis blinked, as if finally realizing where he was and who he was with. *'He's in shock,'* Sayagul said. *'You're in shock, my dear Travis.'*

"It's okay." Roman's voice was a hoarse whisper. "It's okay."

"I'm an idiot," he said again, his words thick with emotion.

"Yeah, okay—fine, you're an idiot," Roman said around a laugh, his own eyes damp. Travis chuckled, too.

And then they embraced—one more time. All three brothers, holding onto each other.

Brothers, yes—all of them. That shit Donovan said didn't matter. None of it mattered.

This, though? *This* mattered.

This was his family.

As Roman clung to Travis and Pax, he vowed, right then and there, in the red and blue glow of the emergency lights sweeping across the highway, not far from that sinister black wall, that he would never let anyone—not even Donovan Slade—drive them apart.

Ever.

The ground began to vibrate. All along the highway, people cried out, a few losing their balance from the might of the tremors.

The pavement cracked apart beneath their feet. Roman backed up, pulling Travis and Paxton along with him, all murmuring in alarm at the sight of the fissures glowing red-hot.

After a few minutes that felt like years, the shaking subsided. The heat glowing in the cracked ground cooled.

Together, they turned—staring out at the unseeable ruins of Yveswich.

The blackness of the Void was spreading—billowing up toward the sky like thick smoke from a wildfire. It moved swiftly, blotting out the stars.

In that darkness, there were monsters—roaring and screeching and snapping their teeth. Droves of winged nightmares flew out over the ocean, swooping toward white-capped waves in search of prey.

Roman's mouth dried out. "Holy gods."

Aspen reached for Malakai's hand, and he gave it to her, his face pale as he laced his fingers with hers.

Max's throat bobbed. "What have we done?" he whispered.

There was nothing to stop it now. No forcefield confining the spread to one area. There was no telling how much time their world had left, but...

It was coming.

The end was coming.

And when it arrived, they had to be ready to meet it.

———

"ALL RIGHT, DEVLIN," Malakai said to Roman as the world went to shit behind them.

Travis barely heard him—he was too busy staring at the mass of shadow ballooning toward the sky. It was so thick, it looked like the world was being swallowed by ink.

Malakai continued, "You came all this way to rescue our sorry asses, and I got one thing to say about it: Where the hell's your car?"

Travis forced himself to tear his focus off the Void.

Malakai said, "Is that it there?" The Reaper pointed with a scarred finger at the highway—and the wreckage of the vehicles spread across it. They were little more than scrap metal now.

The look on Roman's face was telling.

Travis didn't give a shit about a ride, though. He was *free*. He was out of that hellhole, and as far as he was concerned, life was good.

Well...apart from the Void devouring everything. That was a problem for future Travis.

Roman winced. "Yeah, it's...it's one of those," he admitted.

Malakai lowered his hand. "Wow," he said in a deadpan tone. "Some rescue plan."

"We got into a *car accident*, asshole!" Roman snapped. "It's not like I planned for this!" He waved a furious, tattooed hand at the mayhem breaking out as far as the eye could see.

Travis fought the urge to point out that there wouldn't have been enough room for everyone in Roman's car, anyway. He didn't feel like arguing right now.

Malakai sighed. "Well, we're all stranded now. Guess we'll have to thumb it." He pushed his way through the group, knocking his shoulder into Dominic's, and started walking.

The Angel scowled over a shoulder and flicked his wings out with attitude.

"Delaney!" Reacher called after him through bared teeth. To the others in the group, he growled, "I'm about to kill him."

"What?" Malakai didn't even bother turning around. He was already so far away, they could hardly hear him. "What do you want?"

Jewels cupped her hands over her mouth and shouted, *"Where are you going?"* An icy wind gusted down the road, sending her pale lilac hair dancing about her face.

"Crazy!"

She rolled her eyes. "Where are you *really* going?"

"Home," Malakai replied. "I've had enough of this shit. Catch you dirt-brains later."

Raina gave a soft laugh. "Typical Malakai."

"What did he just call us?" Dallas hissed.

Dominic said, "I think he said *dirtbrains.*"

"Dirtbrains?" Blue whispered, her cobalt brows inching together.

Dallas clucked her tongue and shook her head. Several people called after Malakai, but he ignored them—no surprise there.

Soon, they were following. Everyone was following.

Turned out, they didn't have to thumb it, because the military brought transportation. They all piled into the first ride that came available, and then they were on their way back to Angelthene.

Back home. Only once he was settled into a seat in a crowded bus did the reality of that sink in.

They were going home.

The world was literally falling apart, and for all Travis knew, he could be dead tomorrow, but right now?

Right now, he was going *home*.

117

LOCATION UNDISCLOSED

Athene Cousens held her head high, refusing to balk as two Shadowmasters led the way through the big, dark house. To the dining room facing the back.

Donovan Slade sat by himself at the head of the table. His eyes were shut, his hands resting palms-up on the wood.

The Shadowmasters gestured for them to stop. She and Balthazar, who walked at her left, immediately froze. Everyone waited in complete and utter silence as Donovan focused, his eyes rolling and flickering behind closed lids. The longer he sat there, not moving, not speaking, the quicker Athene's breaths came, her pulse a rapid drumbeat in her neck.

Finally, Donovan opened his black eyes. "Athene," he said with a dip of his chin. Balthazar, he ignored. Did not even look his way. He banished the black with one firm blink and reached for the bottle of tequila on the table. He poured himself a glass and tossed it back.

"You wanted to speak with me?" Athene asked. By the grace of the gods, her question came out steady, even while her legs threatened to collapse beneath her.

"I did, yes," Donovan said, his tone polite.

Too polite.

He set down the glass and got to his feet. "I'm sure you've heard by now," he began as he rounded the table, "what went on outside of Yveswich. With one of your...Selkies." His boots pounded as he strode across the room.

Along the perimeter of that room, the shadows began to stir. They crawled up the walls like smoke, a few tendrils snaking around the fingers of Donovan's hands that hung loosely at his sides.

More darkness spread behind him, a great mass unfurling like the wings of a fallen angel, as Donovan came to stand directly in front of her, his shadows hissing as they followed.

"You disappoint me, Athene," he said, his voice lethally quiet. He raised a finger between them, the simple, unthreatening action causing her to flinch. A quiet noise of alarm rose in her throat, and she barely managed to swallow it down. "One job," he whispered. His shadows echoed him. *'One job,'* they said. "All I asked...was for you to bring me Paxton, Roman...and your daughter. And you couldn't even give me *one,"* he snarled through bared teeth. His breath that reeked of tequila and tobacco wafted across her cheek.

Athene's lips trembled, and she clamped them shut. She stared straight ahead as Donovan came closer. So close, she could see her reflection in the shining black orbs of his eyes. So close, she could feel his every breath puffing against her cheek.

Those eyes were cold. Hideously empty.

"Every mistake, from now on," Donovan hissed, his shadows once again echoing him, "will have consequences."

Where he stood at her side, Balthazar gurgled, his hands flying to his throat.

Slit. His throat had been slit. By what knife, what hand, Athene did not dare look to find out.

His knees crashed to the floor.

Athene did not dare move. Didn't dare breathe too loudly. Her vision blurred with tears as Balthazar keeled over, his blood puddling across the floor as he fell still.

Donovan came in close, so close they were practically touching, and whispered, "You will not disappoint me again. Do you understand me?"

"Y-yes, Donovan."

He pulled back. Studied her face, one corner of his mouth curving upward with a cruel, mocking smile. "See yourself out."

It cost her all her strength just to turn. To walk out of that house, Donovan's shadows whispering as they nipped at her heels.

She did not have the courage to look back.

118

HEAVEN'S GATE
ANGELTHENE, STATE OF WITHEREDGE

In their room at Heaven's Gate, Loren sat beside Darien on the bed and ran her fingers through his silken hair.

He was fast asleep on his stomach. His head was turned toward her, his face smooth and expressionless.

Nearly two days had passed, and he was still trapped in a deep sleep, his body flipping between sweating and shivering—or both. Nearly two days, and during that whole time Loren had hardly left this room. Ivy and the others brought her breakfast, lunch, dinner, tea—delivered straight to the door Loren kept partially open.

The house, although filled with family and friends, was quiet.

So, *so* quiet.

Roman and the others were not back yet, but according to Kylar, who was staying in touch with them while they traveled back, they should arrive sometime today.

After the crash outside of Yveswich that had claimed many lives, Shay and Dean had been airlifted to Angelthene General Hospital. But while Dean had been placed on life support, Shay had since been transferred to home care. The demand had come from Roman; it wasn't safe for Shay to be by herself at a public health facility. Not while Donovan and Athene were still actively looking for her. And so she was here now, at Heaven's Gate—unconscious, but recovering. Just like Darien. Dean's Death Dealers were in town and keeping watch over him at the hospital. Whether he stayed here or was transferred to the hospital in Tyrmouth remained to be seen.

One more time, Loren ran a gentle hand through Darien's hair, pushing the coal-black strands away from his beautiful face. She rested that hand against the back of his neck, his skin hot with a fever, and whispered, "I love you."

He didn't respond. Didn't so much as stir.

With a shaky inhale, she scrubbed the tears off her cheeks. She had not even realized she was crying.

Movement in her periphery drew her attention over her shoulder.

It was Mortifer—hopping onto the bed.

"Hi, Morty," she whispered.

The Hob merely went and sat by Darien's pillow. It had become his spot; he, too, hardly ever left.

"Is Itzel hogging the fridge again?" she asked him.

He nodded, the red-tipped black flames on his head flickering.

"She's not sharing the ice either, is she?"

He frowned. Shook his head.

"Well," she said with a heavy sigh. "You're welcome in here any time."

He merely scootched closer to Darien and gave the back of his neck a comforting pat with his tiny, shadowy hand.

A fight had broken out the minute Mortifer came home—carried inside by Jack—and spotted the pink-eyed Hob on the fridge, peering out from where she hid in the dark, narrow space below the cupboards. The two critters had started hissing like cats and slapping each other. Jack and Kylar had barely managed to pry them apart and had placed them both in time-out.

It might take a while, but Loren had a feeling the Hobs would come around. Learn to share their precious ice and the prized spot on top of the fridge. Learn to like each other, even. Eventually.

Someone knocked. Loren turned—

Standing in the doorway was Roark.

She was so surprised to see him, it took her a moment to move. To get up and follow him into the hallway. As she walked across the room, she threw a backward glance at Darien—making sure he was okay. That his back was still rising and falling with steady breaths.

"What are you doing here?" she whispered. She shut the door—only halfway.

Roark scanned her puffy-eyed, tear-streaked face. "I thought I would check up on you," he said. "See how you're faring."

She crossed her arms and slumped against the wall, staring at the floor with vision that blurred with a flood of fresh tears. "Not good," she admitted. Her voice cracked.

"The others said it was brimstone." An inquiry.

She nodded. "I'm worried that it's something worse," she rasped. "He was holding the Sight for so long..."

She drew a slow, steadying breath.

Her heart was breaking. And it would continue to break into even smaller pieces until Darien opened his eyes. Until she knew he was okay. That he would live.

They stood there for awhile in silence. Loren stared at the floor with tear-blurred vision, her father observing her with a level of empathy she had never seen or felt before.

Eventually, Roark said, "He'll be okay."

When she lifted her gaze to his face, the tears slipped free, one down each cheek. "Do you really believe that?" The question was hoarse and wobbly.

There was no way of knowing for sure—she knew that. But sometimes, it helped to hear it from another person's mouth. Confidence. Reassurance.

"Yes," Roark said—confident and reassuring.

Before she could think it through, before she could stop herself, she was stepping forward and throwing her arms around him.

Roark stiffened. He lifted his arms—holding them out at his sides, as if he didn't know what to do with them.

And then those arms closed around her, and she was sobbing uncontrollably into his jacket.

Her father simply held her.

She could not remember the last time he had done such a thing. Never, maybe. But in that moment, it was exactly what she needed. It didn't fix anything that'd happened, no—but it made her heavy, broken heart feel just a little bit lighter. A little less broken.

Made her believe—hope—that maybe Roark was right. Maybe Darien really would be okay. He *had* to be.

He had to be.

WHEN SHAY CRACKED open her eyes, she did not recognize the bedroom, nor did she remember how she'd ended up here.

What she *did* recognize, however, was the man sitting in a chair beside the bed. Watching over her. His elbows were resting on his knees, his scarred and tattooed hands clasped before him. Dark, windswept hair dusted a pair of bold brows, the soft strands partially obscuring eyes that were a remarkable shade of golden brown.

"Hiya, pup," said Roman 'Shadows' Devlin. That voice, so low and husky, made every instinct in Shay sit up straight.

"Roman?" She was so exhausted, she could hardly speak, her question no more than a crackle. She tried to scoot up—

He stopped her with a gentle hand wrapping around her forearm. The physical contact—and the feel of those warm, callused fingers gripping her —made Shay's heart bounce out of her chest.

It kept bouncing as Roman left his hand there, his thumb brushing across her wrist.

"What happened?" she asked him.

"You got shot." Rage simmered in his stare.

Oh. Right. She remembered now. Remembered Pia, holding a gun to Paxton's head. Remembered the car flipping down the highway as the magic of the forcefield buckled the pavement. Remembered running up and down that highway, shouting for Roman, who'd disappeared.

"Is Travis—"

"He's fine. He made it out."

"And Darien?"

Roman hesitated. "He's...recovering." That meant he'd made it back home, then. Loren had succeeded at getting them into Blackwater Penitentiary.

"How long have I been out?"

"Two days."

Two days. It hadn't felt that long.

"You terrified me, pup." His swallow was audible. "I thought I lost you."

Her snicker was forced. "Pfft—keep dreaming, Shadows. I'm not that easy to get rid of."

She thought he might smile, but all she got in response was the barest twitch of the left side of his mouth. That stupidly attractive mouth she couldn't look away from, not even now.

Roman let go of her arm and sat back in his chair, the movement causing the muscles in his thighs to flex. Even in her current state, with her mind all groggy from painkillers, she couldn't help but stare as he clasped those big hands of his between his thighs.

"I want to talk about what you said," he began. "When you were being loaded into the helicopter."

Oh shit. Shay's heart started to pound. Had she said what she thought she'd said?

Roman's eyes softened like sun-warmed honey as he finished, his voice low and gentle, "You said you love me."

Shay's pounding heart stumbled two beats.

Yup, she'd really said it.

Well, there was no going back now. And she'd might as well find out, once and for all, how this ridiculously attractive, insanely wonderful Shadowmaster *really* felt about her.

No more lies. No more bullshit.

Roman was watching her intently. "Is it true?"

She tried to swallow, but her mouth was too dry.

Here goes nothing, she thought.

She sucked in a deep breath and said, "What would you say if I said yes?"

Silence stretched between them. Shay's heart was beating so hard, she knew Roman could hear it. Knew he could sense through her aura that she was thoroughly and quietly freaking out

Finally, he said, "I'd say you're a fucking idiot."

She couldn't help it—she flinched. "Ouch." She looked away from him, her throat threatening to shut.

But then Roman continued, "And I'd say you're too good for me."

Slowly, reluctantly, she slid her eyes back to his.

"I'd say I'm a wreck and I have nothing good to offer you," he added.

A pause.

And then Roman said, "And I'd say that I love you, too."

She drew her head back. "What?" Had she heard him correctly? Or was she so doped up that she was inventing things in her head? Maybe she'd died and gone to the Fifth Dimension to live out some pathetic fantasy—

But Roman's throat bobbed, and he said again, "I love you, too, Shayla Cousens. I'm so. Fucking. In love with you that I—" He looked away for a moment, and then finished, "—I can't ignore it anymore. I am thoroughly and hopelessly in love with you."

She blinked. "I must be dead," she blurted.

He got up, towering over her like a dark angel. "Not dead," he said, his eyes tender. "And I thank the gods for that."

She held her breath as he bent down and kissed her on the mouth.

Softly. Intimately.

When he broke the kiss, he pulled back a bit, looking her right in the eyes as he smoothed an unruly strand of her hair back from her face.

Then he sat down beside her on the bed and carefully brushed something off her cheek. "What's this?" he asked. He showed her what he was referring to—the tear sparkling on the pad of his thumb. "I thought you said you never cry, and yet, I *swear* I've seen you cry at *least* four times, pup." He gave her a crooked smile. "Maybe even five."

"Pfft—I don't cry," she sniffled. But even as she spoke, another tear slipped free, and she wiped it away. "My eyes are just...leaking."

Roman gave a quiet laugh, then kissed her again and rested his forehead against hers. "Paxton and I were lost before you came along," he whispered, his words coasting across her mouth. "When we look at you...we both feel like we're home. Like we finally have a home." He lifted his head and flattened his hand over her heart. "You stole my heart, Shay."

"Well, in my defense, I am a thief," she said.

Roman smiled.

Shay grinned back.

Their world may be falling apart, but this right here...

No one could touch this. No one could take away what they had.

They would rebuild. Someway. Somehow.

Together, the Shadowmaster and the Selkie would rebuild.

***

ROMAN STOOD with the others around the table in the kitchen. There were so many people here now—Devils, Angels, Reapers, Elementals—and yet it had never felt so quiet. So empty.

The only people who were not down here were Darien, Loren, Shay—who was still bedridden, but healing—and the kids.

It was day three, and Darien had still not woken up. Slowly, he was recovering from the effects of the brimstone, his immune system fighting it off as if he were battling poison. Rest was the only remedy. He would have to overcome it on his own.

The clock ticked. For a long while, no one spoke.

And then Lace whispered, "What do we do now?"

Weary glances were her only response.

Everyone was tired. Defeated.

Lost.

Against all odds, they had managed to survive. But they were far from safe.

A war was coming. And if they had a prayer of stopping it, they would have to act.

They would have to fight. Together.

"We figure out how to get the Veil back up," Roman said.

Heads turned his way.

"We take down the imperator," he said, "and anyone else who's ever made the mistake of fucking with us." His heart pounded with determination, adrenaline, as he concluded, "And we finish this."

EPILOGUE
ANGELTHENE, STATE OF WITHEREDGE

"You're sure you want to do this?" Lace asked.

Loren breathed in deeply, filling her lungs with the scent of sun-baked wildflowers and dusty earth. "I've never been more sure of anything in my entire life," she said.

No truer words had ever been spoken. Saving the man she loved had become her one and only goal. Ever since the night she learned of Darien's trade, all she cared about was finding a way to reverse it. To give him back the years he never should have lost. And now that she knew *how* to save him, she was hurtling straight toward that goal.

She would not rest until she achieved it.

As she walked toward the crumbling stone fountain, she trailed her fingertips through the sea of coarse, waist-high grass, the ground crunching beneath her sneakers. The sunset cast a warm glow across the land, causing the field to shimmer like spun gold.

Once upon a long-forgotten time, this land might have been considered beautiful. Peaceful, even. Now, it was a place of bargains and beasts. Hidden costs and dark consequences.

The wind picked up to a howl, the temperature plunging so swiftly it sent a cold prickle up her back. As she paused beside the old structure, a palpable, supernatural silence swept through the area, dampening the sounds of city life. The honk of car horns, the steady trickle of music leaking out of restaurants and storefronts, the chatter of pedestrians—all were rendered mute.

Her fingers did not tremble as she drew a small knife from the pocket of her jeans and unfolded it, the tip flashing in the sunlight. Beside her, Lace did the same with her own blade. Neither of them spoke as they cut open their palms, slicing from the base of the index finger to the heel of the hand.

Warm blood trickled down the inside of Loren's wrist as she stepped up to the fountain. She held her hand over the bucket and squeezed her fingers into a fist, bright red droplets plinking like rain. As soon as she was finished, she stepped back to allow Lace to do the same, human and hellseher blood blending together.

With her good hand, Loren grabbed a small roll of bandages from her other pocket. She unwound the length of it, then wrapped it tightly around her throbbing hand and tied it, blood seeping through white gauze.

Lace dropped four limen coins—two per visitor—into the pail. The *clang* of metal against metal rang like a bell across the otherwise silent field.

"Ready?" Lace asked her as she grabbed the handle of the bucket. While the wound in Lace's hand was already healing, Loren's continued to burn and bleed.

Loren drew a deep, deep breath...and nodded. "I'm ready."

Lace tossed the bucket into the depths of the fountain, and together they stepped up onto the edge.

The field darkened as the sun slipped below Angelthene's skyline.

Another day had passed, and Darien had not woken up, had not fully recovered from the effects of the brimstone. Joyce was making regular visits to the house to tend to him, using her doctor's knowledge and Healer's potions to help him recover while in the safety of his own home. Every hour since that horrible night at Blackwater Penitentiary, Loren spent in bed with him, murmuring words of comfort. She hoped he could hear her through the fevered haze of his mind and would soon come back to her.

Darien had not left her—abandoned her—while she was in a coma, not even for one night. She would not abandon him, either. No matter how long it took, she would be there for him when he opened his eyes.

A soft, damp cloud of fog that smelled of sugar and must folded over them. Swiftly, the magic of the Crossroads carried them away. To the In-Between.

To the bottom of the Wishing Fountain—a dark, liminal space between realms, where the walls had no windows, and the flickering cobalt light had no source.

It took a moment for Loren's eyes to adjust to the thick darkness, and when they finally did she saw the Widow watching her, the spider's eyes shining like black eggs.

"How lovely it is to see you again, Liliana Sophronia," said the spider. She turned toward the platinum-blonde Devil and said, "You as well, Miss Lace Rivera. Charmed." She bowed in greeting, her sticky hammock of webs flexing beneath her weight.

Loren dipped her chin in response, Lace doing the same.

They stepped off the fountain, oily water splashing under their shoes.

Loren was about to speak, but the spider beat her to it.

"It has all come true," she whispered, her focus fastened upon Loren. "It should not surprise me, and yet you and that Devil shock me to my core."

Loren lifted her chin. "What, exactly, are you referring to?"

"Everything," the Widow answered.

She could not help but shiver. "The Devil you speak of came to you not long ago for a trade."

"The one involving your pet."

Loren swallowed. "Yes. When he came that day to speak with you, you...told him something. Something about...about me. You told him that I'm not going to live past the age of twenty-one." Her eyes burned, and her throat threatened to shut, but she managed to squeeze out, "Is it true?"

A beat of silence. And then: "Yes. It is true."

The floor tilted beneath her feet. "It isn't fair." The statement came out on a shallow, pained breath.

"It's life." The Widow's tone was gentle. Compassionate. "Nothing is ever fair."

"I love him so much." Tears slid down her face.

"I know, my dear," said the Widow. "I know."

It was true: It wasn't fair. It was bad enough that she was mortal, and Darien immortal, doomed to go their separate ways eventually, but now... now, she would have even less time with the man she loved. Now, she would have to say goodbye to him sooner.

Once upon a time, she'd told Darien that she would love him forever. But she had not expected her forever to end so soon.

Loren wiped her face dry with the back of her hand, gauze scraping her cheeks. "Is there a way around it?"

The Widow hesitated. And then: "The future is never set in stone."

That was good enough for her.

She stamped out the fear and sadness that threatened to envelop her and said, "You took more years from him than necessary when he came to you to bargain for the life of my dog."

"More than necessary, yes, but only because he was willing to give them."

"Why did he do it?" she choked out.

"My dear, I believe you already know why."

She did. But that didn't mean she was happy about it.

"That man loves you very much," the Widow said. "His sacrifice should come as no surprise to you." It didn't surprise her—not at all. From the moment she'd met Darien, all he'd done was give. He had given her everything.

Now, it was her turn to give back to him.

"I want them back," she bit out. "The years he gave you—every extra year, I want them back." She sucked a shaky breath in through her teeth and added, "Please."

The Widow took a moment to consider what she was asking for. And then she said, her voice hardly more than a whisper, "What are you willing to give me in return?" Something about the creature's tone told Loren she already knew what she was about to offer—and had perhaps been waiting a very long time for this day to arrive.

It was all the reassurance Loren needed. That what she planned on offering would be enough,

So she told the spider, "I offer you your freedom."

A pause—heavy and peculiar.

"And what makes you think freedom is something I lack?" It was not a real question, Loren knew. The Widow was testing her. Feeling her out to see how much she knew.

Loren had learned plenty. With Sabrine's help, she had unveiled a great deal of mysteries surrounding the Nameless beings. She was all but armored with knowledge, and she would damn well use it to her advantage.

Spirit beings like the Widow had been trapped in the In-Between for hundreds of thousands of years, since the day Helia split the world into two realms—the realm of the living and the realm of the dead. The split had resulted in a gap—in the trapping of creatures like the Widow within a strip that would eventually be referred to only as the *In-Between*. The unintentional imprisonment of creatures that had once been free, and were now forced to live out their eternal years in solitude, their only company the daring visitors who sought them out in hopes of striking a bargain.

Freedom was something they very much lacked.

"When was the last time you left this room?" Loren challenged.

Her question seemed to stump the spider. The area descended into a thoughtful silence, interrupted only by the dripping of moisture from the ceiling and the crackle of a cold, blue flame no one could see.

"I cannot remember," the Widow said, "what it looks like." She tipped back, peering skyward.

Loren shared a glance with Lace.

The world. She could not remember what the world beyond these walls looked like.

Loren waited as the Widow thought it through.

"I will accept your offer, Liliana Sophronia," she said, lowering her gaze from the unseeable sky. "I will give Darien Cassel back his years, in exchange for freedom."

The fact that she was accepting the offer meant Loren had a way of following through—of giving the Widow her freedom. Maybe not now, but eventually. Had such an offer been beyond her capabilities, the Widow would have never agreed.

Loren took out her pocketknife—

She paused, the edge of the blade glinting with bluish light as she tipped it from side to side, thinking. "I have one more request, before we seal the deal," she declared, staring at her reflection in the knife. "I want you to show me what happened—the day Darien came to see you. The day he bargained for the life of my dog." She lowered the knife and lifted her head. "Will you show me?"

After a brief pause, the spider said, "Look into the fountain."

Loren braced herself with a deep breath.

She stepped forward, gripped the rough stone edge of the fountain, and peered into the water.

Into the past.

"WHAT ARE you willing to trade for the dog's life, Darien Cassel?"

Deep in the Crossroads below the Wishing Fountain, Darien Cassel crouched on the edge of the basin, the cut in his palm burning. The spider, ancient and hungry, was smothered in supernatural darkness, her eight eyes peering at him through the gloom.

"What's your price?" he countered.

"When trading for a life, the price is always the same."

"Time," he concluded. It didn't surprise him. He'd visited enough Cross-

roads to know what to expect. A person's life was made up of precisely what the spider was asking for: time. Everything a person did, every accomplishment, every failure, every experience, no matter how small, was only made possible because they had time. Tonight, Darien was bargaining for a life—a dog's life, yes. But it made no difference. It was still a life, and therefore it would still cost him time.

"Time, yes," the spider mused. She dragged out the word, as if savoring it. Tasting it like fine wine. "Such a fickle beast, time. Uncontrollable. Unreliable. Cruel, yet kind. Constantly changing, forever moving forward. Difficult to predict. Mortals mourn its swift passing and long for more. Lamiae and lycanthropes have fought wars and sold their souls to attain it. Even your kind, the one they call hellseher, stems from greed. Time is what everyone covets most, and yet you...you, Darien Cassel, do not balk at the idea of parting with yours. I find that curious. Might it have something to do with the mortal woman on whose behalf you bargain?"

"It has everything to do with her. But you already knew that," he accused, narrowing his eyes. "Does toying with your visitors amuse you?"

"It intrigues more than it amuses. And you do intrigue me, slayer. I've met many an immortal being, but none quite like you..."

A hush fell over the Crossroads. Darien could feel the creature studying him like a specimen in the dark.

"I will trade you the dog in the form of a spirit, and what I ask for in return is a portion of your time. The dog will live the remainder of his days in the girl's shadow, and he shall only pass when she does. A fair trade, wouldn't you agree?"

"Depends," he countered. He knew better than to agree before hearing the full terms of the bargain. "How many years am I paying you?"

"Ten should suffice."

"To be taken at the end of my life, when death arrives by natural cause, and no sooner," he clarified.

"To be taken at the end of your life, when death arrives by natural cause, and no sooner," she vowed.

"So it shall occur to no one that the years are gone," he added.

"So it shall occur to no one that the years are gone," the spider repeated. "The decade will leave you peacefully, the day Obitus comes to lead you home. And you shall know no different."

The thought of this—not just death, but meeting it ten years sooner—should frighten him, he knew. But it didn't scare him at all. There was little that did.

He took the knife out of his pocket—

"You have fallen for her," the spider observed.

Darien froze.

"If you hadn't, you would not be here."

Darien kept his mouth shut. He owed this gluttonous creature nothing more than what he was offering.

But the Widow wasn't finished. "I wonder...," she began, leaning forward in her webs, her front legs clicking together, "what you might say...if I were to tell you when Death shall come knocking at her door."

A wave of cold dread coursed through Darien. "You know?" He squeezed the knife handle. "You know when she's going to die?"

Nameless creatures had an uncanny ability to predict the future, but not all of them chose to dabble in that area. The Pale Man was one of the few who specialized in predictions; foresight was his strength that had driven thousands of morbidly curious visitors to his chalk door. Countless souls had walked willingly into his den to learn the hour of their death, and few had come back out, meeting that hour far sooner than they'd planned.

But the Widow hadn't lied when she'd said that time was difficult to predict. A person's life was made up of nothing more than a series of decisions; one event led to another, followed by another...and so on and so forth. The Widow may claim to know the hour of Loren's death, but until it found her, nothing was set in stone.

"Her days are numbered," the spider said. "Perhaps more than you realize."

"Explain," he barked.

"Lily is one of a kind. There is no one like her. It is true what the one named Calanthe tells you: She possesses a very special magic you will learn more of soon. But I must stress...and I told Lily the same: If she uses her magic, she will die."

If she uses her magic... Darien's head spun. There were always loopholes.

"You just said you know when Death will come knocking at her door," he began. "Will this happen only if she uses her magic? If she resists, will she live a full life?"

"If she uses her magic, it will merely happen sooner. But I regret to inform you that a full life is not in the cards for Lily. Due to mistakes made by others, she is doomed to die by the age of twenty-one."

Darien almost lost his balance and fell into the fountain. He barely righted himself in time. "She's what—? Doomed? By mistakes made by others? What does that mean?"

"It means that no matter what you do, no matter how hard you try to save her, she will leave this life by her twenty-first birthday, and not a day later."

Darien couldn't breathe. His surroundings spun—

"This upsets you," the Widow remarked.

"Of course it upsets me," he gritted out. "I love her." The truth rang through the fountain—clear as the toll of a silver bell. Quieter, he repeated, as if convincing himself, "I love her."

He did, didn't he? He was in love with Loren Calla. He had been lying to himself for some time, trying desperately to wedge distance between them, if only to protect her from his life, his mistakes, his enemies, just him in general—

Because she deserved better. Better than him. The best life she could get, whatever and whoever that involved, she deserved it.

But he loved her. He was in love with her.

And it was this truth that had him blurting, "What if I traded my life for hers?"

His question seemed to stun them both. The Widow took so long to respond, Darien was beginning to think she wouldn't.

But then she said, "I'm afraid it can't be done."

"My life is worth more than hers, though," he argued. "And I say that with the utmost respect for her. Take me, and let her live." The last word came out broken. Splintered. It took him longer than it should have to realize why.

He was crying. He never cried, and yet here he was, sobbing to an immortal creature over a woman he couldn't have.

"I'm very sorry, but I cannot accept," the spider said softly.

"This is bullshit," he spat. "Take me too, then. If she dies, I'm going, too." He pointed at the spider with his knife. "Because fuck all of you, that's why."

The spider wasn't fazed by his tone, the insult. "You wish to die at the same time as the girl?"

Darien's heart was pounding so hard, he thought he might throw up. All these months he'd spent protecting her, getting to know her, loving every part of her—and he'd have to say goodbye to her anyway.

He wasn't sure why he'd expected any different. His whole life was made up of nothing but tragedies. What was one more?

Despite the whirlwind of emotions he was trapped in, he managed to grit out, "Yes."

"And you will give to me the rest of your immortal life the minute her

heart ceases to beat and she is considered medically dead? Past the point of resuscitation?"

"Yes."

"Death will find you both in less than thirteen months' time. Where and when will be left up to circumstance. This is your final chance to turn back."

"I'm not turning back," he declared.

"Then draw your blood, Darien Cassel, and I shall see it done."

He did not hesitate as he raised the knife to his palm and slashed the blade across his skin.

CAST OF
CHARACTERS

THE SEVEN DEVILS

DARIEN CASSEL — Head of Hell's Gate and lead Darkslayer in Angelthene. Formed the Seven Devils when he was nineteen. He is Randal Slade and Elsie Cassel's son, and Ivyana Cassel's twin brother. He has extremely powerful magic from the Void that allows him to kill sentient beings with his mind.

MAXIMUS REACHER — Darien Cassel's best friend and second-in-command. He has a younger sister named Maya. He and his sister both possess fire magic from the Inferno, though Max, due to his fear of fire, has never attempted to use his.

TRAVIS DEVLIN — Darien Cassel's cousin. Also known as *The Devlin Devil*. He has two brothers: Roman Devlin and Paxton Slade. He was born in Yveswich but moved to Angelthene at the age of seventeen. His magic comes from the Void.

JACK STEELE — Ivyana Cassel's husband. Jack is the newest member of the Seven Devils and the family jokester. Before he joined the Devils, he made a lot of enemies as a compulsive gambler and swindler. Any magic abilities are unknown.

IVYANA 'IVY' CASSEL — Darien Cassel's twin sister, born seven minutes after Darien. She is the daughter of Randal Slade and Elsie Cassel. She's been married to Jack Steele for two years. As Darien's twin, it can be presumed that Ivy also possesses magic from the Void.

TANNER ATLAS — Hacker for the Seven Devils. He is Doctor Joyce Atlas's son. He and Darien became friends after Darien stood up for him against school bullies. Any magic abilities are unknown.

LACE RIVERA — Niece to Lionel Savage. Former member of the Huntsmen, though it was never made official. She was Darien Cassel's first serious girlfriend. Any magic abilities are unknown.

THE REAPERS

MALAKAI DELANEY — Head of the House of Souls and Right Hand of Darien Cassel. He is Jewels Delaney's older brother. Possesses magic from the Void that allows him to kill sentient beings with his mind.

VALEN HAYES — Malakai Delaney's Second.

SYLVAN WOLFE — Malakai Delaney's Third. Named after Sylvan the god.

ASPEN VAN HALEN — Best friend to Lace Rivera, and twin sister of Clover Van Halen. Assists Clover with hacking spell systems, databases, etc.

~~BRODIE VERLICE~~ — Twin brother of Macen Verlice. Former Reaper. Died during the events of *City of Souls and Sinners*.

~~MACEN VERLICE~~ — Twin brother of Brodie Verlice. Former Reaper. Died during the events of *City of Souls and Sinners*.

JEWELS DELANEY — Malakai Delaney's younger sister. She is sick with the Tricking.

CLOVER VAN HALEN — Aspen Van Halen's twin sister. Hacker for the Reapers.

THE HUNTSMEN

LIONEL SAVAGE — Head of the Hunting Grounds and former Right Hand of Randal Slade. He is Lace's uncle and Harley's father.

HARLEY SAVAGE — Lionel Savage's son, and Lace Rivera's cousin.

SETH MARKSMAN — Second to Lionel Savage.

COLTON ADLER — Third to Lionel Savage.

ARCHER SAVAGE — Nephew of Lionel Savage. Lace and Harley's cousin.

SHEPLEY MARKSMAN — Hacker for the Huntsmen.

XANDER PRICE — Assistant hacker to Shepley Marksman.

NATHAN RHODES — Newest member of the Huntsmen.

THE ANGELS OF DEATH

DOMINIC VALENCIA — Head of Death's Landing and former member of Angelthene's Aerial Fleet. Conrad Valencia's brother.

CONRAD VALENCIA — Dominic Valencia's brother and second-in-command. Former member of Angelthene's Aerial Fleet.

HANLI SHADID — Third to Dominic Valencia and former member of Angelthene's Aerial Fleet. Aided the Devils during the Well explosion at the end of *City of Gods and Monsters*.

DYLAN REED — Hacker for the Angels of Death. Former member of Angelthene's Aerial Fleet.

GWEN REED — Assistant hacker to Dylan Reed, who is also her brother. Former member of Angelthene's Aerial Fleet.

THE WARGS

CHANNARY GRAVES — Head of the House on the Pier. The Wargs have an assortment of rare magical pelts that are enchanted with shifter magic.

LUMEN GRAVES — Channary's daughter and Second.

UMBRIELLE GRAVES — Channary's daughter and Third.

~~VALARY STERNBERG~~ — Darien's former friend with benefits. After threatening Loren in *City of Souls and Sinners,* Darien had her excommunicated by Channary. Presumed dead after the events of *City of Souls and Sinners.*

CHRISTA COPENSPIRE — Recently moved back to Angelthene from the city of Skylen. Her relationship with Darien Cassel was long-distance and solely physical. It nearly progressed into a serious relationship, but things ended badly between them before this could happen.

JACINTHA COPENSPIRE — Christa Copenspire's sister, and assistant hacker to Isabella Moss.

ISABELLA MOSS — Hacker for the Wargs.

RYLEIGH WITT — Sister to Vanessa Witt.

VANESSA WITT — Sister to Ryleigh Witt.

THE VIPERS

JUDE MONSON — Head of the Den of Vipers. Former friend of the Devils. He had a fall-out with Darien Cassel in *City of Souls and Sinners* when Darien promoted Malakai Delaney to Right Hand.

NADIA MONSON — Jude Monson's wife.

JESSA GILCHRIST — Darien Cassel's former friend with benefits. Aided the Devils at the end of *City of Gods and Monsters*.

SAGE MONSON — Hacker for the Vipers. She is Jude Monson's sister.

CARTER MCKENZIE — Jude Monson's cousin and Second.

IVAN GILCHRIST — Jessa Gilchrist's cousin.

RACE HUNTER — Jude Monson's Third.

JASMINE ROSE — Member of the Vipers. Assistant hacker to Sage Monson.

DARKSLAYERS OF YVESWICH

ROMAN 'SHADOWS' DEVLIN — Shadowmaster and Head of the House of Black. Known as *The Wolf of the Hollow.* He is Darien's cousin and Travis and Paxton's older brother. His ability to control shadows comes from the Void. Any additional powers are unknown.

SHAYLA 'SHAY' COUSENS — Member of the Riptide. She is Athene's daughter and Anna's younger sister. Her illusion magic is from the Eye, and her storm powers are from the Aether.

KYLAR 'KY' LAVIN — Second and hacker to Roman Devlin. He has a little brother named Eugene. Possesses magic from the Void.

DONOVAN SLADE — Head of all Darkslaying circles in Yveswich. He is Randal and Dean Slade's brother, and the youngest of the three. He has three kids: Roman, Travis, and Paxton. His powers come from the Void.

ATHENE COUSENS — Head of the Riptide. She has two daughters: Shay and Anna Cousens. Gifted with illusion magic from the Eye.

~~ANNA COUSENS~~ — Second to Athene Cousens. She is Athene's daughter and Shay's older sister. Presumed dead after the events of *City of Lies and Legends.* She had storm magic from the Aether.

PIA — Third to Athene Cousens. Anna's friend.

LARINA BARLOWE — A Shadowmaster who answers to Donovan. She is Blaine's sister.

BLAINE BARLOWE — A Shadowmaster who answers to Donovan. He is Larina's sister.

BEATRICE — A Selkie who works for the Riptide.

KAILANI — A Selkie who works for the Riptide.

WILLOW ADAMS — Third to Roman Devlin.

ADHAM— A Shadowmaster who works for Donovan.

SYBIL BRINTON — Second to Cerise Brinton.

EILIDH BRINTON — Third to Cerise Brinton.

AUSTIN PRESCOTT — A Wyvern who works for the House of Red.

BROCK PIERSON — A Wyvern who works for the House of Red.

RAINA CRUSO — Head of the House of Violet.

SILAS CRUSO — Second to Raina Cruso. He is also her brother.

CHARLOTTE DEMEURE — Third and hacker to Raina Cruso.

HELLSEHERS

THE TERRAN IMPERATOR — The most powerful person in all of Terra. His real name is Quinton Lucent.

KLAY LUCENT — Quinton Lucent's son. He was instructed to watch Loren in *City of Souls and Sinners*.

~~RANDAL SLADE~~ — Former Head of all Darkslaying circles in Angelthene. He is Darien and Ivyana's father and Elsie Cassel's husband. Died during the events of *City of Gods and Monsters*.

GAVEN PAYNE — A weapons dealer and one of Randal's former business partners. He is under the imperator's employ. Possesses magic from the Aether.

JOHNATHON KYLE — CEO of Lucent Enterprises.

HELIA, AKA CYRA SOPHRONIA — Loren's mother and Erasmus Sophronia's wife. Operating under the alias of a rabbit messenger, she hired Darien Cassel to find Loren in *City of Gods and Monsters*.

BLUE — An Elemental with water magic from the Mist.

JOYCE ATLAS — Tanner's mother. She is a doctor at Angelthene General.

MAYA 'MJ' REACHER — Max's younger sister. At the end of *City of Souls and Sinners,* Blue revealed that Maya is still alive and goes by the name 'Scarlet'. She has fire magic from the Inferno.

PAXTON SLADE — Roman and Travis's little brother.

EUGENE LAVIN — Half-human hellseher. Kylar's little brother and Paxton's best friend.

BLAZE — An Elemental with the magic of the Inferno.

GOLD — An Elemental with the magic of the Aether.

SAGE — An Elemental with the magic of Terra Firma.

VIOLET — An Elemental with the magic of the Aether.

MAGENTA — An Elemental with a unique blend of white and red magic.

AURORA — An Elemental with a rainbow aura. Powers: unknown.

ONYX— An Elemental with the magic of the Void.

~~TYSON GELLER~~ — Former Reaper. Killed by Darien in *City of Gods and Monsters*.

~~HELEN DEVLIN~~ — Roman and Travis's mother. Deceased before the events of *City of Gods and Monsters*.

CLARE SLADE — Paxton's mother. She is married to Donovan Slade.

KYLE — Tattoo artist and owner of Diablo.

~~KORAY AND XANDER~~ — Rogue hellsehers. Killed by the Seven Devils in *City of Gods and Monsters*.

~~LIAM~~ — Former Reaper. Killed by Darien in *City of Gods and Monsters*.

IAN GRAY — A Reaper who was excommunicated by Malakai in *City of Gods and Monsters*.

GIOVANNI — Tattoo artist and owner of Giovanni's Tattoo.

DEAN SLADE — Randal and Donovan's brother. The eldest of the three.

HUMANS

LOREN CALLA/LILIANA SOPHRONIA — Daughter of Erasmus and Helia Sophronia. After her father created her with the Arcanum Well, she was gifted with its magic and became the only person capable of locating the Well. When she was a baby, her parents left her on the steps of the Temple of the Scarlet Star, where she was soon adopted by Roark Bright. It was Taega's choice to give her the last name 'Calla', so she would have some connection to her real name. As of the beginning of *City of Smoke and Brimstone,* her known powers involve healing, time manipulation, opening and closing portals to Spirit Terra, turning her aura into a shield of protection, and understanding and speaking the spirit language.

ARTHUR J. KIND — Former doctor and weapons technician for Lucent Enterprises. When Elsie Cassel first moved to Angelthene to be with Randal, Arthur became her doctor and very close friend.

ERASMUS SOPHRONIA — Creator of the Arcanum Well and Loren Calla's father. Founder of the Phoenix Head Society.

~~ELSIE CASSEL/EMBERLEY SLADE~~ — Darien and Ivy's mother and Randal Slade's wife. When she moved away from home to be with Randal, she changed her name from Elsie to Emberley. Died before the events of *City of Gods and Monsters.* Although her death was declared a suicide, Darien and Ivy suspect she was killed.

WITCHES AND WARLOCKS
(VENEFICAE)

DALLAS BRIGHT — Roark and Taega's daughter. She is a student at Angelthene Academy and a trainee in Angelthene's Aerial Fleet. She is Loren's best friend and adoptive sister.

CASEN MARTEL/THE BUTCHER — The lead Blood Potions dealer in the state of Witheredge. Runs the Umbra Forum in Angelthene. Has a daughter named Chloe.

TAEGA BRIGHT, NEE TINE — Roark's wife and Dallas's mother. Former member of the Phoenix Head Society.

ROARK BRIGHT — The Red Baron and General of Terra's Aerial Fleets. He is Taega's husband and Dallas's father. His real name is Elix Danik, and he was an original member of the Phoenix Head Society. He was born mortal.

FINN SOLACE — Head Detective for Angelthene's Magical Protections Unit.

TAMIKA ISLEY — An optometrist at Angelthene Optometry.

~~TANYA~~ — Receptionist for Caliginous on Silverway. Died during the events of *City of Lies and Legends*.

MORDRED AND PENELOPE — Owners of Mordred and Penelope's Mortar and Pestle.

ALFIE — A drug and weapons dealer who works at Yveswich's Black Market.

BENJAMIN — A grave robber who lives in Dusk Hollow cemetery.

CAIN NASH — A criminal who was after the Well in *City of Gods and Monsters*. Darien helped Finn put him behind bars.

IVADOR LANGDON — Former Headmaster of Angelthene Academy. Died during the events of *City of Gods and Monsters*.

DENNIS BOYD — Owner of Puerta de la Muerta and Chrysantha Sands's former employer.

MILES OSBORN — Headmaster at Angelthene Academy.

AGATHA — Hedgewitch and owner of Agatha's Post-Secondary Education for Botany.

ETHAN, CHAD, AND GARRETT — Students at Angelthene Academy.

ANTONIO PEREZ — A mob boss who owns the Pit.

GRAYSON PHIPPS — A teacher at Angelthene Academy.

CHLOE MARTEL — The Butcher's daughter.

CLAUDE VAN ARSDELL — Sabrine's father.

GLEN — A detective working for the Yveswich Magical Protections Unit.

WEREWOLVES
(LYCANTHROPES)

LOGAN SANDS — Head of the Silverwood District and alpha of all werewolf packs in Angelthene. Also known as Shadowback.

SABRINE VAN ARSDELL — Best friends with Loren and Dallas. Logan turned her into a werewolf in *City of Gods and Monsters*. Because of her witch blood, she is still capable of using magic, even as a wolf.

SEBASTIAN — Second to Logan Sands. Also known as Cryo. Member of the Guardian Pack.

CHRYSANTHA SANDS — Logan's sister. Also known as Tundra. Member of the Guardian Pack.

CASH — Third to Logan Sands. Also known as Silverrain. Member of the Guardian Pack.

~~BLEDDYN SANDS~~ — Logan's father. Died before the events of *City of Gods and Monsters*.

Big — Head Chef for Silver Claw.

VAMPIRES
(LAMIAE)

~~CALANTHE CROFT~~ — Head Vampire of the district of Drakon and former Head of the House of the Blood Rose. Died during the events of *City of Souls and Sinners.* In *City of Lies and Legends,* it was revealed that she was killed by her son Jaden Croft.

EMILIE CROFT — Calanthe's daughter and heir to the House of the Blood Rose.

JADEN CROFT — Emilie's half-brother.

BAYLOR — Former manager of the Devil's Advocate.

VIKTOR — Member of the House of the Blood Rose.

LENORA ALDONOLD — Member of the House of the Blood Rose and Calanthe Croft's Second.

DESIREE DENALDI — Heir to the House of the Silver Torch. She has a twin sister who is also an heir.

COVENS, PACKS, AND HOUSES OF ANGELTHENE

VENEFICAE COVENS OF ANGELTHENE

UPPER WEST
LOWER WEST
NORTHWOOD
FARHALLOWS

WEREWOLF PACKS OF ANGELTHENE

GUARDIANS
QUEENSWATER
EASTSIDE
BLACK MIRROR

VAMPIRE HOUSES OF ANGELTHENE

BLOOD ROSE
SILVER TORCH
CORPSE FLOWER
HAMMER ORCHID
BLUE LILY

FAMILIAR SPIRITS

BANDIT — Darien Cassel's Familiar. Short-haired dog with cropped ears and a cropped tail.

SINGER — Loren Calla's shepherd dog Familiar. Brought back from the dead by the Widow, a deal made by Darien Cassel, who paid for the dog's return with years off his immortal lifespan. The number of years and the conditions surrounding the agreement are unknown.

MORTIFER — House Hob of Hell's Gate. Formerly owned by a mob boss before he was rescued by Darien Cassel.

CREATURE — Malakai Delaney's Familiar. Bat with an arrowhead tail. Favorite food is bananas.

TWITCH — Jack Steele's Familiar. Jaguar with facial tics.

SOOT — Ivy Cassel's canine Familiar. Nearly identical in appearance to Bandit.

GRIM — Maximus Reacher's Familiar. Mountain lion.

GHOST — Dallas Bright's Familiar. Winged tiger.

SILVER — Tanner Atlas's Familiar. Wolf with a sweet tooth.

NOBLE — Travis Devlin's Familiar. Mastiff dog.

CINDER — Lace Rivera's Familiar. House cat with sapphire eyes.

PEBBLE — Sabrine Van Arsdell's Familiar. Crow.

ITZEL — House Hob. Belongs to Roman Devlin.

SAYAGUL — Roman Devlin's Familiar. Small dragon. Loves gummy bears.

NUGGET — Shay Cousens's Familiar. White seal pup.

CHANCE — Paxton Slade's Familiar. Puppy.

CRITTER — Jewels Delaney's Familiar. Bat.

SIROCCO — Dominic Valencia's Familiar. Hawk.

BRUTUS — Dean Slade's Familiar.

THE NAMELESS

THE WIDOW — A giant spider. She built her home in the Crossroads known as the Wishing Fountain. Her real name is Araneae.

THE PALE MAN — A humanoid creature who lives in a gilded den beyond the Chalk Door. He is fond of riddles and has the ability to predict the future.

THE FAUN — A horned creature who walks on cloven feet and lives beneath an old fig tree in Angelthene National Forest. Darien paid a visit to this creature when he was fifteen to see if he could make a trade to have his mother back.

~~THE SOUL-EATER~~ — A creature who guarded the Crossroads under the Strangler Fig in the community of Whitebridge. Killed by a creature of the Veil in *City of Souls and Sinners*.

~~THE BASILISK~~ — A giant serpent that lived in the tunnels below the city of Yveswich. Slain by Darien Cassel during the events of *City of Lies and Legends*.

MISCELLANEOUS

MR. CRISPY — A plant that lives on the windowsill at Mordred and Penelope's Mortar and Pestle. Mr. Crispy helped discover the antidote for the curse in *City of Gods and Monsters*.

MISS PRICKLES — A plant that lives at Mordred and Penelope's Mortar and Pestle. She developed a crush on Darien Cassel after hearing his voice in *City of Gods and Monsters*.

CLUCKLES — Bandit's rubber chicken and the bane of Darien's existence. Darien purchased the toy from Whisker's Pets and Things on the Avenue of the Scarlet Star.

ACKNOWLEDGMENTS

First off, I want to thank my husband, for always making me smile and laugh, for being the best brainstorming buddy, and for being such an incredible partner. Thank you for handling everything in the real world while I ignored you for this fictional one (you can have your wife back now! lol). I love you more than words can convey.

To my family, for always believing in me, even—*especially*—when I don't believe in myself. I love you guys.

To Sarah Hansen at Okay Creations, for another absolutely stunning cover. Your talent never fails to leave me speechless. I already can't wait to see the covers for the rest of the series (plus any others you create for me in the future)! You're the best—seriously.

To my agent, Kimberly Whalen, for your unconditional support and dedication, and for helping this series grow in such huge ways. Signing with you was a dream come true. Thank you for everything you do for me and my books!

To Virginia Allyn, for creating the maps of my dreams. You are so talented, and I am beyond grateful that I had the opportunity to work with you. Thank you for capturing the spirit of Angelthene and Yveswich so perfectly.

To Christina Routhier, for all the time you spent proofreading this beast of a book, and for always being so flexible with my timeline and delivery schedules. Your support and friendship mean the world to me!

To Christan Acree, for the friendship, the laughs, the memes, the inside jokes, and, of course, for all the beautiful character art! Working with you has been such a joy, and I will never stop being grateful for all the art you've done for me. Thank you for being such a bright light and great friend.

To my ARC team, for loving these books and for screaming about them from the rooftops. You are all amazing!

Last but not least, I want to thank *you*, the reader. None of this would be possible without you. Every post, every video, every recommendation, every piece of fanart, every cosplay, every comment telling me how much you love the Darkslayers and their dark and gritty world... Just know that I appreciate everything, and I am so grateful for each and every one of you. Your love for this series makes the hard days worth it. I hope to see you again in the next installment for another crazy adventure in Angelthene!

On a station platform, with nothing to read,
and a four-hour train journey stretching ahead of him...

That's where the story began for Penguin founder Allen Lane.
With only 'shabby reprints of shoddy novels' on offer,
he resolved to make better books for readers everywhere.

By the time his train pulled into London, the idea was formed.
He would bring the best writing, in stylish and affordable
formats, to everyone. His books would be sold in bookstores,
stationers and tobacconists, for no more than the price
of a ten-pack of cigarettes.

And on every book would be a Penguin, a bird with a certain
'dignified flippancy', and a friendly invitation to anyone who
wished to spend their time reading.

In 1935, the first ten Penguin paperbacks were published.
Just a year later, three million Penguins had made their
way onto our shelves.

Reading was changed forever.

—

A lot has changed since 1935, including Penguin, but in the
most important ways we're still the same. We still believe that
books and reading are for everyone. And we still believe that
whether you're seeking an afternoon's escape, a vigorous debate
or a soothing bedtime story, all possibilities open with a book.

Whoever you are, whatever you're looking for,
you can find it with Penguin.